Praise for:
THE GOLDEN KEY

"This three-way collaboration is original in concept and superior in execution. Characterizations and world-building are finely realized; Rawn and company have done their homework on art, and overall, the romance justifies every one of its nearly 900 pages and demands its place in most fantasy collections." —*Booklist*

"Using prose, the authors gloriously illustrate this concept—that pictures are more valuable than words. The world the authors create is entertaining . . . . what makes this massive tome interesting are its detailed descriptions of the making, and uses of, painting, and the creative way the authors play with the magic." —*Locus*

"To define (**The Golden Key**) within one genre is impossible. Suffice it to say this nominee for the World Fantasy Award is a remarkable book . . . . one of the most absorbing books I've read in some time. I give it my highest recommendation."
—Catherine Asaro for the *SF Site*

"Another fabulous fantasy collaboration . . . an impressive bit of world-building. As one would expect, the fascinating background is meticulously brought to life . . . we are held spellbound by this dark fantasy all the way through its mesmerizing conclusion." —*Romantic Times*

The GOLDEN KEY

MELANIE RAWN

JENNIFER ROBERSON

KATE ELLIOTT

DAW BOOKS, INC.
DONALD A. WOLLHEIM, FOUNDER
375 Hudson Street, New York, NY 10014
ELIZABETH R. WOLLHEIM
SHEILA E. GILBERT
PUBLISHERS

In Memory of
Elsie Balter Wollheim
June 26, 1910–February 9, 1996

Since the 18th century, many painters have been obsessed with the idea of a Golden Key—that is, a piece of knowledge, a formula or technical trick that would unravel the mysteries of the art of painting . . . . The answer is, of course, that there is no such thing.

—JONATHAN STEPHENSON,
The Materials and Techniques of Painting

CONTENTS

GALERRIA

The
GOLDEN
KEY

PEINTRADDOS HISTORRICOS

(from History in Art *by Fernandal Grijalva, privately printed, 940)*

Death of the Tza'ab, 716 by Grimaldo Serrano, 916. Oil on wood. Serrano Family Collection.

This is a typical Serrano painting: a scene from history—romanticized, politicized, and lacking all symbolism—commemorating the death in battle of the Tza'ab "Diviner of the Golden Wind." Yet the placement of his figure, far to the left of the action, indicates that he is anything but the central focus of the piece. Serrano is more interested in painting the fierce expressions on Tza'ab faces even as they flee the battlefield, foreshadowing the coming century of vengeful raids by the Riders on the Golden Wind.

Two other faces are of note. The Shagarra captain who slew the "Diviner" bears a striking resemblance to Serrano's Duke Alessio II, an obvious flattery; the dying Tza'ab himself is strongly reminiscent of the self-portrait of Bartollin Grijalva, Serrano's bitter rival.

Battle of Rio Sanguo, 818 by Bartollin Grijalva, 918. Oil on wood. Galerria Verrada.

Another commemorative painting, this one carefully researched for accuracy of position, clothing, and detail. Alesso do'Verrada's likeness was taken from contemporary drawings; eyewitness accounts were consulted for placement of armies as well as individual figures. The angle of sunlight is precisely what it was at the season, day, and hour of the battle.

For all its exactitude, this painting is steeped in symbolism. Alesso's military genius is evident in the arrayment of his troops but also in the designs embroidered on his cloak (leaves of oak and mint for Bravery and Virtue, lupine flowers for Imagination, and so on). The wealth he gained by marriage to an Anthalussan heiress is plainly displayed in the gold of his sword and spurs, and more subtly in the patterns of corn and wheat in the tooling of his saddle. His nommo do'guererro, "Shadow on the Golden Wind," is shown in the darkness falling on the barbarian about to die beneath his sword—yet his eyes are not on his victim but on the Rider nearby, who will be the one to kill him. The malevolent spirit of the Empress of Tza'ab Rih, instigator of the war, is seen in the fallen larch tree nearby (Arrogance) and the flowers trampled beneath the hooves of Alesso's horse: columbine for Folly.

The river where Alesso won his great triumph was renamed Rio Sanguo for the blood that flowed that day. His son Renayo consolidated the victory by establishing Tira Virte's southern borders; the contemporary Serrano painting commemorating Renayo's acclamation as Duke and the founding of Tira Virte as a nation has been lost, but a partial sketch of it exists in the Galerria Verrada Archives.

Death of Verro Grijalva
by Caballo Grijalva,
892.

Oil on wood.
Galerria Verrada.

In 823, Duke Renayo chose as his bride Jesminia, sole heiress to Shagarra after her brother's death at Rio Sanguo. After their marriage at her father's castello, they journeyed home to Meya Suerta—where a small caza was slowly becoming Palasso Verrada—but along the way disaster struck. The company was attacked by a band of renegade Tza'ab, and though the Duke and Duchess escaped harm, many courtiers were killed—including Renayo's dearest friend and cleverest captain, Verro Grijalva.

This is the scene depicted here: violent in composition and color, vibrant with motion. Duke Renayo cradles his dying friend's head in one arm while the other hand gestures frantically for a physician; the Duchess kneels nearby, her hands covering her face, her jewels rendered so blurrily that one can almost see her trembling as she weeps. In the background, soldiers ride in pursuit of the Tza'ab, who carried off Verro's twin sisters and a dozen other ladies-in-waiting. The wind whips tree branches, cloaks, and the Duchess' unbound hair. Only Verro Grijalva is still; though his gaze is cloudy with death, his fingers are locked on the sword lying beside him, as if he tries to will himself back to strength in order to rescue his sisters.

Compare this rendering with the smaller *Death of Verro Grijalva* in the family's Galerria, painted in the year 832 by Piedro Grijalva.

Rescue of the Captives, by Miquellan Serrano, 828. Oil on wood. Serrano Family Collection.

The high degree of artistic competence of this most talented of the Serranos is evident in this painting, his technical brilliance used to vicious effect. Commissioned by Duke Renayo as a companion painting to the above, this piece was rejected for its insulting portrayal of the unfortunate women captured and raped by the Tza'ab.

All fourteen ladies are in various stages of undress, their expressions as they emerge from the tents ranging from the startled to the horrified—except for the Grijalvas (identified by the azulejo rosette pattern of the shawls clutched around them). Larissa and Margatta are portrayed as angry and annoyed, as if the rescue party interrupted them in the midst of willing bedsport.

Duke Renayo and all his soldiers show nothing of their weariness at having chased down the renegades for twenty long days; all appear as fresh as if they had just emerged from their own chambers at home. But the Tza'ab are shown half-clothed (and filthy besides), and in their faces is craven terror. The twenty small children fleeing into the hills are naked, dirty, wild-eyed; close examination reveals they have not the features of children but of grown men and women, darkly and ominously Tza'ab.

As for the history behind the painting—all fourteen ladies were recovered, all the bandits were killed, and all the treasure (piled in a tent to the right) taken back to Meya Suerta. Duchess Jesminia ordered this wealth divided amongst the women to provide for their support, for all had been unwed virgins and no man would marry them now—especially after each bore a child within the year. These chi'patros ("Who is the father?") were, like their mothers, shunned and despised—as were the half-breeds also rescued from the Tza'ab camp. In fact, several of the women took their own lives shortly after giving birth.

It was surmised that women had been abducted before to bear Tza'ab's bastards, only to be killed once the children were weaned; one of the rescued boys innocently stated that his mama had been sent away because his patro wanted him to grow up Tza'ab. Possibly the renegades planned to father and raise a band of half-breed children to infiltrate Tira Virteian towns and cities.

But none of the children grew up Tza'ab. They grew up as Grijalvas, for that family adopted them all. In 859, Meya Suerta was scandalized when Duke Renayo's will deeded a palasso and its surrounding city block to the Grijalvas in thanks for their generosity. But all the chi'patros remained a despised reminder of Tza'ab outrages, and the Grijalvas were thereafter painted with the same brush.

Allegory of Maternal Love, attributed to Natan Grijalva, 834. Watercolor on paper. Galerria Grijalva.

This charming portrait of two women and their ten-year-old sons—one handing her child a basket of symbolic flowers, the other teaching her offspring to read from a devotional—is said to be of Larissa and Margatta Grijalva and their chi'patro sons. Few artists of any period work in miniature—this oval painting is only three inches long—and of the eight examples in the Grijalva collection, six are by this artist, youngest brother of Larissa, Margatta, and Verro Grijalva. So it is mostly likely his work, depicting his twin sisters and his nephews.

There is defiance in this picture, for all its tranquil domesticity. The boys' Tza'ab features and coloring are deliberately contrasted with the gray eyes and lighter skins of the women. For their Tza'ab blood the chi'patros were shunned, despised, and suspected of every evil; Ecclesial arguments raged over whether they even possessed souls. By showing the mothers giving their sons religious faith, literacy, sincerity, honesty, generosity, loyalty, and industry, the artist lays claim for the chi'patros to personal and societal virtues that few were willing to grant them.

*Duchess Jesminia at
the Ressolvo,*
by Liranzo Grijalva,
881.
Oil on canvas;
unfinished.
Galerria Verrada.

This painting, a straightforward documentary rendering of an event witnessed by
the artist, records the last official act of
Duchess Jesminia's life. Though already
ill from Nerro Lingua and only three days
from death, no trace of disease is evident
in her radiant face, which the artist has
delicately haloed with sunlight through
the windows behind her. She watches with
a gentle smile as the chi'patros are reconfirmed in the Faith. The
expressions of the Premia Sancta and Premio Sancto are not so be-
nign, even as they give their blessing. The religious leaders of Tira
Virte felt as the rest of the city did, that even though the Grijalvas
suffered more deaths than any other family, the chi'patros were to
blame for Nerro Lingua ("Black Tongue," named for its most ominous symptom), from which one in four persons died. It was whispered that this was retribution from the Mother and Son for having
taken in the chi'patros.

The day after his mother's death, Alessio I issued an Edict pro-
claiming all Grijalvas to be under perpetual protection of the Dukes
of Tira Virte. But this law did not defend them against the hysterical
mob—originally assembled to mourn their beloved Duchess—that
attacked Palasso Grijalva. Many, including Margatta Grijalva, died
before the Shagarra Regiment restored order. It is said that Liranzo
was interrupted in the middle of this painting that night, and injuries
taken in the fighting prevented him from finishing it.

The artist was the chi'patro son of Larissa Grijalva, the same child
probably portrayed in the miniature above. He is seen in the shadows
of the Cathedral Imagos Brilliantos, identifiable by the paintbrush
half-tucked into his pocket and the Chieva do'Orro around his neck.

*Self-Portrait of
Garza Serrano,
Lord Limner, 906.*
Oil on wood.
Galerria Verrada.

The intensifying rivalry between the
Serranos and the Grijalvas is the motiva-
tion behind this arrogant self-portrait:
the artist shows himself in the full ceremonial regalia of Lord Limner, but with
robes of Serrano brown embroidered in
the family's feather sigil and boots
planted firmly on broken tiles bearing the Grijalva azulejo
rosette.

Skeptics assert that talent cannot manifest in successive generations, that simple proximity to great genius produces pallid copies in progeny. Evidence to the contrary is found in music (the Bacas, to whom brilliant musicians were born for two centuries), medicine (the do'Maio line), and literature (the Doumas—father, two sons, and five granddaughters). The Serrano artistic tradition has lasted for over a hundred years. Yet the Grijalvas are unique, for few are their males who evidence no talent for art.

Intermarriage between Grijalvas and chi'patros—for no others would consider the girls as brides or the men as husbands—produced another curious result: by the second generation, approximately half the males were discovered to be sterile. This has been attributed to inbreeding and some strange lingering effect of Nerro Lingua, but no one knows for certain.

*Marriage of
Alessio II and
Elseva do'Elleon,*
by Saabasto Grijalva,
894.
Oil on wood.
Galerria Verrada.

*Betrothal of Joao and
Miari do'Varriyva,*
by Yberro Grijalva,
921.
Oil on wood.
Galerria Verrada.

Death of Joao,
by Yberro Grijalva,
924.
Oil on canvas.
Galerria Grijalva.

Until 875, it was traditional to gift a bride with a painting of her marriage. This custom was the foundation of the Serrano reputation and fortune. It was Liranzo Grijalva who first suggested that paintings also act as legal certification. Combined with universally understood iconography, a picture would be a certificate of public record.

In these three paintings, separated by a mere thirty years, can be seen the evolution of documentary painting and the rich symbolism it demands. Though the *Marriage* is delightful in its simplicity, only the bride's flowers show the traditional good wishes (roses for Love, ivy for Fidelity, thistles for Sons). The union of Elleon to Tira Virte is sealed by the union of these two handsome people, documented in the painting only by the straw motif delicately embroidered in gold on the curtain behind the couple.

Contrast this lack of embellishment with the *Betrothal* of their son Joao. The bride's family sigil, the white chrysanthemum (a pun on *verro*, "truth," and Varriyva), figures prominently in the em-

broidery of her gown; she approaches Joao across a vast lawn of
green grass that signifies Submission; golden roses symbolizing
Perfection bloom near lemon blossoms for Fidelity in Love. Joao,
standing on the Palasso Verrada garden steps, holds out a nosegay
of both as he smiles at his betrothed. But this painting also records
a trade treaty—thus the distant background of Castello Varriyva
with a merchant's caravan traveling the road below amid a field of
corn that signals Riches.

Joao and Miari enjoyed only a few years of wedded happiness.
It is said that Yberro Grijalva, who painted the *Betrothal* and, only
a few years later, Joao's *Death,* mixed his paints with his own tears
for joy at the first and grief at the second, for the young Duke had
been his cherished friend. The abundance of floral and herbal symbolism in the latter painting shows the maturation of Grijalva art
and insight, and the use of iconography to make a visually powerful painting even more effective, both emotionally and as legal
documentation.

Thus have painted documents become more binding than anything written on paper. Variations of dialect can accidentally—or
deliberately—confuse, but a picture of an event on wood, paper, or
canvas transcends language. Not only betrothals, marriages, births,
and deaths are so recorded, but also treaties, wills, and deeds of
ownership. And only Tira Virte, with its astonishingly vital tradition of art, can supply enough limners to paint copies for all parties
concerned. During the last fifty years, the work of Serrano and
Grijalva Masters has become not only legendary but essential to
the conduct of personal, mercantile, and state business.

GALERRIA 943

Sario Grijalva saw at once what had become of her; where she had *gone,* despite her physical presence. He knew that look, that blind glaze in eyes, the stillness of features, the fixed feyness of expression. He even knew how it felt: he, too, was what some might call victim. He himself named it potential. Promise. Power. And his definitions were unlike those of others, including the moualimos, the teachers who for now defined his days in the workshops of the students.

Petty men, all of them, even those who were Gifted. They spoke of such things as potential, as promise; even, quietly, of power, and knew nothing of any of them.

He knew. And *would* know; it was in him to know.

" 'Vedra," he said.

Bound by her inner eye, she neither answered him nor moved.

" 'Vedra," he said more clearly.

Nothing.

"Saavedra."

She twitched. Her eyes were very black; then slowly the blackness shrank, leaving another color behind. Clear, unmuddied gray, unsullied by underpainting, by impure pigments. It was one of the things about her unlike so many others: Grijalva gray eyes, unusual eyes, the markers of their mutual Tza'ab ancestry, though his was cloaked in far more ordinary clothing: brown eyes, brown hair, desert-dark skin. Nothing in the least remarkable about Sario Grijalva.

Not outside, where men could see. Inside, where no one could see but he, because the only light available was the kindling of ambition, the naphtha of his vision.

He looked upon her. She was older than he, and taller, but now she huddled upon the colonnade bench like a supplicant, a servant, leaving him to accept or deny preeminence. She turned her face up to him, into a shaft of midday sunlight that illuminated expression in quiet chiaroscuro as it illuminated the wood-speckled paper attached to a board, the agile, beautiful hands. With a quick, unthinking motion she tossed unkempt black hair out of her eyes; saw him then, registered his presence, marked identity—and answered, dredging awareness back from the vast geography of her other world, confined by the bindings of her inner eye.

"Wait—" Clipped, impatient, imperative, as if *he* were the servant now.

They were all of them servants, Grijalvas: gifted and Gifted alike.

"—wait—" she repeated—softer now, pleading, asking understanding, forgiveness, all underscored by impatience—and sketched frantically upon the paper.

He understood. There was compassion in him for her, unalloyed comprehension. But impatience also, his own for other reasons, and more than a little resentment that she should expect him to wait; she was not and could not be Gifted, not as *he* was Gifted.

Therefore he could answer: "There is no time, 'Vedra. Not if we are to see it."

Silence, save for the scratching of her charcoal upon the inferior paper.

" 'Vedra—"

"I must get this down . . ." And unspoken: —*while it is alive, while it is fresh, while I see it*—

He understood, but could not coddle it. "We must go."

"A moment, just a moment longer—momentita, grazzo—" She worked quickly, with an unadorned economy of movement he admired. Many of the young girls labored over their work, as did many boys, digging and digging for small truths that would strengthen their work, but Saavedra understood better what she wanted to do. Her truths, as his, were immense, if unacknowledged by either of them as anything other than ordinary, because to each of them such truths were. They breathed them every moment.

As did he, she saw those truths, that light, the images completed by her mind in all the complexities, exploring none so much as freeing them with a minimum of strokes, a swift stooping of her gift.

Luza do'Orro, the Golden Light, the true-talent of the mind.

He watched. For once he felt like moualimo to student, teacher to estuda. It was not he laboring beneath the unrelenting eye of another, but she beneath *his* eye, doing nothing for him but for herself instead, only for herself; she understood that freedom, that desire for expression apart from the requisites of their family, the demands of the moualimos.

"No," he said suddenly, and swooped down upon her. His own vision, his own Luza do'Orro, could not be denied. Even for such dictates as courtesy. *Even for her.* "No, not like that . . . here—do you see?" They none of them were without pockets or charcoal; he took a burned stick from his tunic and sat down beside her, pulling the board and paper away into his own lap. "Look you—see?"

A moment only, a single corrected line: Baltran do'Verrada, Tira Virte's Duke, whom they had seen only today in the Galerria.

Saavedra sat back, staring at the image.

"Do you see?" Urgency drove him; he must explain before the light of his vision died. Quickly he scrubbed away what he could of the offending line, blew it free of residue. The portrait now, though still rough and over-hasty, was indeed more accurate. He displayed it. "The addition here gives life to the left side of his face . . . he is crooked, you know. No face is pure in balance." He filled in a shadow. "And there is his cheekbone—like *so* . . . do you see?"

Saavedra was silent.

It struck him like a wave: he had erred. He had hurt her. " 'Vedra, forgive me—" Matra ei Filho, when someone did that to *him*— "Oh, 'Vedra, I'm sorry! I am!" He was. "But I couldn't help myself."

She put her charcoal into her tunic pocket. "I know."

" 'Vedra—"

"I *know,* Sario. You never can help yourself." She got up from the bench and shook out her tunic. Charcoal dust clouded. Her tunic was, as his, stained by powdered pigments, dyestuffs, binder, melted resins, oil, all the workings of their world. "It is better, what you have done."

He was anxious now, thrusting the board and pinned paper back into her hands as he rose hastily. "It was only—" He gestured helplessly. "It was only that I *saw*—"

"I know," she said again, accepting the board but not looking at the sketch. "You saw what I didn't see; what I *should* have seen." Saavedra shrugged, a small, self-conscious lifting of her shoulders. "I should have seen it also."

It lay between them now. They were alike in many ways, unalike in others. She could not be Gifted, but she was gifted, and more so than most.

He saw again in his inner eye the image. No one would mistake it. No one could have mistaken it for anyone other than Baltran do'Verrada *before* he had altered the sketch, but he had altered it nonetheless.

He was sorry to hurt her. But there was exactitude in his Gift, a punishing rectitude: there was no room in his world for than anything less than perfection.

"Regretto," he said in a small, pinched voice. Inside his head: *Nazha irrada;* don't be angry. *Nazha irrada, 'Vedra.* But he could not speak it aloud; there was too much of begging in it, too much humility. Even to her, even *for* her, he could not bare so much of himself. "I'm sorry . . ."

She was in that moment far older than he. "You always are, Sario."

It was punishment, though for her it was merely truth, a bastard form of luza do'orro. He valued that in her. Truth was important. But truth could also punish; his own personal truth had transformed the rough sketch from good to brilliant, with merely an added line, a touch of shadow—he understood it all so well, it burned in him so brightly that it was beyond his comprehension how another might not know it.

His truth was not hers. She was good, but he was better.

Because of it, he had hurt her.

" 'Vedra—"

"It's all right," she said, tucking hair behind her ears. A bloody speck glinted there: garnet stone in the lobe. "Do'nado. You can't help it."

Indeed, he never could. It was why they hated him.

Even the moualimos, who knew what he could be.

"Where are we going?" she asked. "You said it was important."

Sario nodded. "Very important."

"Well?" She repositioned the board, but did not so much as glance at the image on the paper.

He swallowed tautly. "Chieva do'Sangua."

It shocked her as much as he expected. "Sario, we *can't*!"

"I know a place," he told her. "They will never see us."

"We *can't*!"

"No one will see us, 'Vedra. No one will know. I've been there many times."

"You've seen a Chieva do'Sangua?"

"No. Other things; there hasn't been a Chieva do'Sangua for longer than we've been alive."

She was taken aback. "How do you *know* these things?"

"I have open eyes, unplugged ears—" Sario grinned briefly. "And I know how to read the *Folio,* 'Vedra; I am permitted, being male."

"To *look,* eiha, yes; but it's too soon for you to read so much. Do the moualimos know?"

He shrugged.

"Of course not! Oh, Sario, you've read too far ahead! You must be properly examined before permission to read the *Folio* is granted—"

He was impatient now. "They won't know we're there, 'Vedra. I promise."

Beneath charcoal smudges, her face was leached of color. "It's forbidden—it's *forbidden,* Sario! We are not Master Limners to see the Chieva do'Sangua, any more than you are permitted to study the *Folio*—"

Again, he could not help it. "I will be. *I* will be." *And Lord Limner also!*

Color flared briefly in pale cheeks; she, being female, would never be permitted to study the *Folio,* or to be admitted to the ranks of Master Limners, the Viehos Fratos. Her purpose was to conceive and bear them, not to be one. "You aren't one yet, are you?"

"No, but—"

"And *until* you are, you are not permitted to see such things." She glared at him, clearly still stung by his reminder that gender as much as blood precluded her from rising as he would. "And it's still true: we are not Master Limners to see the ritual. Do you know what would happen to us if we were caught?"

Abruptly he grinned. "Nothing so bad as Chieva do'Sangua."

She ignored the sally and shook her head definitively. "No."

He smiled. "Yes."

Now she looked again at the sketch. *Her* image, that he had made come truly to life with the single quick stroke of his charcoal here, and a bit of shadow there.

Neosso Irrado they called him; Angry Youth—and with reason. He tried them all. Tested them all. But they knew it even as he did: the Grijalva family had never, since the Gift had come upon them, known anyone with his talent.

He was surely Gifted. Unacknowledged, undefined, as yet unconfirmed. But they knew it as surely as he did. As surely as Saavedra, who had told him so once, long before he saw it in his teachers' eyes, because the moualimos would not speak of it.

Yet.

He would be a Master Limner, one of the Viehos Fratos . . . how could he not? The Gift surged within him despite his youth, despite the fact no one would yet consider admitting it.

Lord Limner, too. He thrust his chin into the air proudly. *I know what I am. I know what I will be.*

Saavedra's mouth twisted. She looked away from the sketched face because his living one demanded it. "Very well," she said.

He had won. He always won. He would go on winning.

No one, not even the moualimos, knew yet how he might be beaten. Or even if he could be.

⊶━━⊷

The man hastily reached for and caught the boy's hand. "This way, Alejandro . . . through here, do you see? No, let the candlerack be—this way, if you please . . . No, no guide sheet; and no, the curatorrio is not necessary. We shall do well enough on our own, we two . . . here, Alejandro, this way. Do you see? You are related to every do'Verrada hanging here on these very walls. In fact, you may well see your own face peering back at you from innumerable frames. Look you—here . . . do you see?"

He waited; was ignored.

"Alejandro."

Had the boy somehow become deaf between the night and the morn?

"*Alejandro Baltran Edoard Alessio do'Verrada,* if you please: attend me!"

Belatedly, "Patro?"

Not deaf, then, obviously; merely—*always!*—distracted. It was age—or, more appropriately, youth—as well as the wholly anticipated trait of distractability; was the boy not his son?

His son. Matra Dolcha, yes!—and with duties to tend despite his youth; or perhaps it was better to say duties to *be* tended, one day. For now Alejandro was clearly too distracted—and distract*able;* for now there were but quiet truths to be told, though as yet only small and supposedly inconsequential, vast histories unveiled, infamous battles refought, endless genealogies unfolded . . . .

The father, caught in reverie, sighed. Such knowledge was vital to the training, if subtle and as yet unmarked, of a son who was also Heir.

"These are the *Marriages*—Alejandro!" Eiha, he was never still, this boy, *never* still . . . was much more taken up with, he supposed, the altogether natural pursuits of his age: food, and the obsessive need to be constantly active—with little attention left over for such tedious things as leisurely educational strolls through Meya Suerta's renowned Galerria.

He grinned in wry self-deprecation. *Especially with his father!*

At the moment the busy boy's fancy was struck by a group of children his age gathering like hungry hound pups in the high-vaulted foyer of the gallery; none of the litter would be permitted to enter, of course, while the Duke and his son were present. The Duke saw the middle-aged, slight man whose linen-clothed throat glinted gold quietly deny entry to his charges—but all of them spent the unexpected delay staring hard at those who took precedence over them. And Alejandro stared back.

Matra Dolcha, but this boy has the attention span of a gnat. Smiling wryly, he clamped a broad, ring-weighted hand over the curl-capped dome of the skull, threading strong callused fingers through disarrayed dark hair, and physically swiveled the head on its slender neck so that the boy had no choice but to look in the direction his father meant him to. "Alejandro."

"Patro?"

"They are Grijalva children, no more. Did you see the necklace and device that man wears at his collar?"

Alejandro shrugged; he was infinitely bored by talk of unknown men and equally unimportant devices.

"Chieva do'Orro, little gnat: the Golden Key. It betokens a Master Limner, and the others with him, who are not yet masters of anything, are here to study the works painted by their ancestors . . ." He paused. "Alejandro, can you at least give the same grace to those they painted, who are *your* ancestors?"

The boy squirmed. "Are they to be limners, too?"

"Indeed, it is likely. They are Grijalvas."

Bright eyes slewed in the direction of the foyer where the litter stood as one. "Do all Grijalvas paint, Patro?"

The Duke cast a glance at the adult with the children—their teacher, most likely, a quiet elder entrusted to guide and ward the wisdom and artistry of the next generation. "They paint as they have always painted, but also they are responsible for the wherewithal to do it. It is the Grijalva family which makes the materials used in art. It is their purpose, Alejandro. Their gift, if you will." The hand lifted from the skull and gestured toward the wall. "Now, look upon this—this one here, before us . . . *Alejandro!* What do you see?"

Looking upon the *boy,* one saw an expression of manifest impatience. And, of course, distraction. He twitched, fidgeted, cast another quick glance across his shoulder at the children clustered at the entrance. "A painting, Patro."

Indulgence was the luxury of nobility. The father smiled and did not reprimand. "A painting, yes. Does it speak to you, this painting?"

The boy's smile was fleeting, a youthful echo of the father's, but it lent an impudent glint to lively hazel eyes. "It does, Patro. It tells me I should return to the Palasso and practice my bladework."

"Bladework, eh? Instead of hanging about the Galerria surrounded by tedious paintings documenting even more tedious marriages?"

The response was quick. "I will not be a limner, Patro. I am not a Grijalva, but a do'Verrada whose face hangs on these very walls."

Eiha, a clever gnat—though many of the faces had been painted by Grijalvas. "A swordsman, then, eh, little do'Verrada?"

"I would rather, Patro."

"Eiha, so would I." The father's eyes glinted now in older echo of the son's. "But you will rule Tira Virte one day, Alejandro, and a wise ruler realizes it need not be always by the sword."

"But paintings, Patro?" The boy had not yet learned the subtleties of Court; he was honest in disbelief, in fleeting indifference, as yet knowing nothing of derision or condescension. "How may a man rule through a painting?"

All innocence—the boy, the question—as it should be. But it minded the father, abruptly, unpleasantly, of the latest story making the rounds, initially quiet but now blatant as a knife in the belly. There were rumors at Palasso Verrada of magics, of a dark power manifesting itself within the city, aiming for the Court, for the ducal family itself.

The father's smile died away. The hand, stroking the importunate curls of his duchy's Heir, stilled abruptly as he looked back at the Grijalva children still clustered in the foyer. *Innocent, at this age? Or is it fed them in the womb, this dark magic Zaragosa speaks of?*

In wan and ocherous sunlight—the Galerria was kept dim so as not to ruin the paintings with exposure to sun, to oil lamps, to candle flame—the ducal ring glinted dully: blood-black, and its cradle of gold in the tangle of dark hair. It was only with great effort that he resumed his affectionate display; and greater effort expended in adopting a tranquil smile. "A man rules using the tools that are given him, Alejandro. A wise man learns never to discard—or to overlook—any of them, lest there be danger in it. Now, or later."

"But, Patro—"

"Look at this painting, Alejandro. Look, now, Neosso do'Orro, and tell me what you see."

The boy made a great work of expressing elaborate acquiescence: thin shoulders heaved under an overdone sigh of such duration the father marveled that his son had any breath left to speak. "A painting," the boy said, "of your marriage to Matra."

"So simple a thing, Alejandro?"

"There is you. There is Matra. There are the Courtfolk."

"Name them, if you would please me."

The boy did, quickly, impatiently, slurring together all of the names of those he knew into one unbroken string: those who inhabited Court, and therefore his world. Innumerable relatives, multitudinous dignitaries, countless hangers-on who believed themselves of such import that no Lord Limner *dared* to leave them out of the celebratory painting.

"Now may we go, Patro? I'm hungry."

Always hungry, this ever-empty belly— "Is there nothing else, Alejandro? Does this painting say nothing to you?"

The boy hitched his shoulders. "It says you married Matra. But everybody knows that." The grin was quick-striking as summer lightning. "Am I not here? Is there not another baby in Matra's belly? Of *course* you married Matra."

The father sighed. His sigh was not of either the duration or the ostentatious impatience embodied by his son's. "So you are, little gnat . . . but does it say anything else to you?"

The boy fidgeted. "Is it supposed to?"

Again the small unpleasantness insinuated itself into an ordinarily imperturbable calm. *By a Grijalva, it might say far more than we imagine—or so Zaragosa would swear.*

But the marriage portrait of Baltran Alejandro Rafeyo Riobaro do'Verrada and Lissabetta Teressa Luissa Benecitta do'Najerra had not been painted by a Grijalva; rather, by a Serrano, Zaragosa's late father, formally installed as Lord Limner and therefore whose commission it was to document such things as treaties, betrothals, marriages, births. Anything of great or passing import to the grand folk of Tira Virte was documented, from the most mundane of a favorite court bitch whelping puppies, to a dramatic ducal death scene. But now the Serrano son acceded to the father's place—as Alejandro himself would one day accede to his father's place—and spoke of unpleasantries, of magics and dark power . . . whispered comments that had a Grijalva painted it, the Holy Mother Herself only knew what might have become of Tira Virte and her Duke.

"Patro?"

The hand closed again over the cap of dark curls. "Never mind, Alejandro. The time will come when you understand."

It would, of course. It had to come. Alejandro was his Heir; as future Duke of Tira Virte, he would be taught the truths of his place.

And the truths, if there were such as Zaragosa Serrano claimed, of the Grijalva magics?

The Duke rejected it. *No. There can be no such thing. They have served us too well, the Grijalvas. There can be no truth in it.*

It nagged: But if there *were?*

He turned to face the foyer, to face the children squarely. He saw vivid, eager expressions, large eyes of every color, hair of every hue, and quick, agile hands clutching charcoal, chalks, and paper. Grijalva-made chalks and paper, Grijalva-made faces and hands, and the brilliance of a Grijalva gift Zaragosa Serrano was too blind, too selfish, too afraid to see. To admit.

There was none so different to set any apart from his own son: clever, quick, bright-burning Alejandro, his Gilded Youth, his Neosso do'Orro.

Baltran do'Verrada made a brief sound of impatience as he turned away again to look at the painting documenting his marriage to the Duchess Lissabetta. The Duke humbly touched his lips and his heart with fingertips, murmuring the ritual words: *"Matra ei Filho protect her"*—for the Duchess was recently confined for her latest lying-in.

The painting was, of itself, merely a routine masterwork, if such could be claimed of any painting created by a ducal appointee. It was, in fact, one of Guilbarro Serrano's, the current Lord Limner's late father, but there was more to the painting than color, form, brushwork. There was a world within the massive gilded frame: story, symbology, promises made and unmade, political refinements done and undone, even prophecy.

Lost to the undiscerning eye amidst the elaborate trellises and flowered fretwork were faint traceries of faces reflected in the long jewel-toned windows of the Audience Hall in which the marriage took place: four round, smiling, young faces, mostly transparent; future children promised to the Duke and his new Duchess.

As yet there were but three young faces in residence at Palasso Verrada—and two of them were cold marble effigies deep in the undercroft.

Matra ei Filho, I beg you, be so gracious as to permit me a second son, a brother for Alejandro; and two sweet daughters who will make worthy brides. . . . Prophecy, eh? So far there was nothing of two of the faces in the glazing but grief. *Zaragosa would have me believe there is a Grijalva to blame for it, no doubt!*

It was overwrought imagination and blatant selfishness, no more; limners were an arrogant lot, all of them, routinely convinced one's talent might be overtaken by another. The world they inhabited was no less convoluted of politics and personal ambitions than the Court itself.

"A fool," the Duke muttered. "Moronno. And his artistry pleases me less and less."

"Patro?"

Do'Verrada was wrenched out of his pettish reverie. "Nothing, Alejandro. Do'nado." He sighed again. "So, shall we tend your appetite, little gnat?"

In answer, Alejandro darted down the gallery toward the foyer, where all of the Grijalva children were made to draw back at once and permit the Duke's Heir to pass unmolested by even so much as a breath.

Also waiting was the liveried ducal escort, a detachment of the Shagarra Regiment, which closed in about the boy immediately. Alejandro, oblivious to such things as he took for granted, turned back impatiently. "Coming, Patro?"

"Coming, filho meyo. I am old, do you see, and cannot skip so blithely as you."

"Very old," Alejandro agreed gravely, and then burst into laughter that was mimicked by the clustered Grijalvas, though they were hushed at once by their teacher.

"Very old," do'Verrada echoed as he moved into the foyer to join his son. *But not these children . . . they die so young, so many Grijalvas.* He met the eyes of the man wearing the Chieva do'Orro, and saw the calm acknowledgment of time's too-hasty departure in them; would he live to see any of his students gain a full complement of skills? *Not a gift I would request, were it in me to do so— nor would Zaragosa request it either, had he the wit to consider it! The Nerro Lingua robbed them of hardihood; there is little enough time for any of them to plot such nonsense as harming anyone with nonexistent magics.*

Aloud he muttered, "Mennino moronno," and decided to request the Lord Limner to attend him upon his return to the Palasso. It was time they had this out, lest it poison the entire Court.

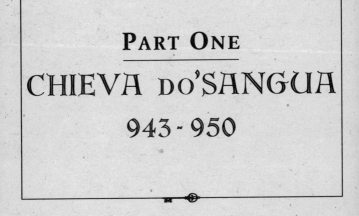

PART ONE
CHIEVA DO'SANGUA
943 - 950

◆→ ONE ←◆

Saavedra followed out of habit; if Sario did not overcome her objections with his clever, twisted logic coupled with incandescent excitement—though it was rare when he couldn't—he appealed to her sense of loyalty and a perverse desire to protect him. If she did not see to his welfare, did not personally try to guide him when she could, surely he would be punished yet again for yet another perceived transgression when he was but merely curious. His inquisitive nature simply could not bear to be held ignorant, and—despite his always frustrating inclination toward disobediences large and small—he was, after all, her closest companion, her *only* true companion.

He understood her. Completely, utterly, unquestionably. They spoke the same language, an inner silent language of the limner's art and heart; recognized identical truths and power in the ambitions of their talent, the constant yearning for more, for better, for *best* in every undertaking, even in crude sketches. Luza do'Orro incarnate, mutually evidenced and mutually comprehended.

No one else knows what is in me. No one else frees me to be as I wish to be. And yet . . . "Matra ei Filho!" she cried as he caught her hand and dragged her to a narrow coiled stairway. "We can't, Sario. We shouldn't be doing this!"

"Of course we shouldn't, cabessa bisila; if we should be doing it, there wouldn't be any risk."

"You *want* risk!" It was accusation, not question. "And my brain is larger than a pea!"

He grinned slyly. "Not when you protest so much about something that interests you as much as it interests me."

Yes, it interested her. Eiha, it interested her! Sario spoke of hidden, forbidden things, a ritual to which women were never admitted, and only those males found worthy of admission. She had no doubts Sario's day would come—how could it not, with the burgeoning talent she knew as Gift?—but he was as yet too young for consideration. He was eleven, not thirteen; the moualimos ignored his blatant attempts to impress them, to seduce them through elaborate sketches and graceful paintings into admitting his talent, and the Viehos Fratos—eiha, she doubted they even knew he existed! Any more than they knew *she* did.

I know . . . She had always known. He burned with a concentrated flame far brighter than any she had yet seen in Palasso Grijalva, even in the sprawling niche-tangled maze of the family premises, and she had met everyone. There were not so many of them now as the genealogies once boasted. The Nerro Lingua had killed so very many.

The plague had engulfed Meya Suerta, a selfish, unrelenting conflagration of infection that presented itself as high fever and swollen, blackened tongue. It killed nobility and commoners alike throughout the city, then cruelly invaded the rest of the duchy. All in Tira Virte lost loved ones, providers, servants, masters. But no family suffered as much as the Grijalvas.

We still suffer. And so they did. In addition to killing nearly two-thirds of the family, the Nerro Lingua had also rendered much of the male seed infertile. Even now, sixty years later, the Grijalva family suffered depredations of the loins as well as of ducal favor; far too many males died before age fifty, and they had not placed one of their own at Court since the Nerro Lingua. The last Grijalva Lord Limner died in the plague, as so many Grijalvas died, and was replaced by, of all things, a Serrano.

The Grijalvas quite naturally expected it to be an interim appointment only—had they not sent a limner to Court for the thirty-five years prior?—but such confidence proved misplaced. Except for their successful production of materials used by limners, they were overlooked. Too many of them had died, too many important, talented, established Grijalvas; in the aftermath of plague, as they struggled to recover, other families less stricken overtook their places.

The rival Serranos, of course, jealous of their recovered ducal favor, argued that the Protection issued by Alessio I was wholly enough, better, in fact, than Grijalvas deserved. In return Sario called them such epithets as she would not herself speak, and was quite rightly beaten for it; such blatant criticism, precociously clever-tongued or no, was not permitted on the family premises. But Saavedra knew it was true, what Sario said; Zaragosa Serrano, Duke Baltran's Lord Limner, was naught but a passable hand, a man with neither heart nor inspiration.

A graffiti-crafter, no more! . . . and why the Duke had seen fit to appoint *Zaragosa* in his late father's place was beyond Saavedra's comprehension. They all of them, every Grijalva, knew he was worthy merely of the common art of the road. Either copyist or

Itinerarrio, certainly no better, and yet his was the vital task, through his paintings, to document in detail the business of the duchy.

"Here—'Vedra, *here!*" Sario snatched at her hand again and dragged her into a tiny closet large enough for only a chamber pot, or perhaps a cluster of brooms; but there was a heavy canvas curtain—exquisitely painted, of course—instead of a wall, and even as she framed a question, Sario jerked fabric aside. "Through here—beware the steps."

Indeed, there were steps. He was not large enough to truly drag her, but his weight tugged unceasingly at her shoulder. He was as intensely passionate about secrets as about his art; eiha, but she did not blame him. He was Gifted, she was convinced, and such true artists as Sario, so talented, so brilliant in their burning, countenanced no interference by any individual, even a moualimo.

Surely they see it in him. Surely they know what he is. . . .

Surely they did. And perhaps it was why they were so harsh with him, to cap the naphtha flame that would not burn out, but could, in its power, consume even its source.

I have nothing of that gift. No, of course not; she was a woman, and the Gifted were only male. But she was gifted to some degree, surely. Sario even said so. When he knew she doubted her talent.

So much between them, so many bindings on them. Even now. Even this.

"'Vedra, here—" He darted around a corner, down another set of shallow steps, loosed her hand long enough to unlatch and pulled open a narrow, lath-and-plaster door, then nodded at her. "Go up! Go up quickly, and I'll latch the door from inside!"

She reluctantly moved into the opening. "Sario, there is no candle!"

"Fourteen steps, twice over. Count, 'Vedra. Or you will have me believing you *are* a cabessa bisila!"

She counted. Her steps lagged, but she counted. He came up behind her, as promised; she could hear his eager breathing in the confines of the narrow staircase. "Where are we going?"

He hissed her into silence. "*Bassda!* They'll hear!" Up and up, fourteen steps twice, and a low-roofed storage chamber. Hastily Sario ducked in the darkness, then flattened himself against the door. "Down here."

She could sense the wall before them. Carefully she felt about, located the stone brickwork, then knelt. "I can't see any—"

He caught and yanked on her hand, whispering frantically. "Down here, moronna! Bassda!"

Saavedra flattened on her belly, even as he did on his own. It was a supremely undignified posture in such a small, crowded space, and the stone beneath her body was cool through the thin weave of her linen tunic and baggy trousers. Summer sandals scraped toe-leather into brickwork. "Sario," this time very softly, "what do you—"

"Here." He clasped her hand, carried it against the wall, to a separation between it and stone floor. A seam, a crack between wall and flooring. It ran nearly the width of the tiny closet. "Come close, 'Vedra—you can see into the Crechetta."

For the moment she cared less about the chamber below than the one they inhabited. She could think of no good use for a storage niche so difficult to reach, coiled away like a serpent in the belly of Palasso Grijalva. "Why is this chamber here?"

"Ask questions later, 'Vedra. For now—" his voice tightened, "*look upon the Chieva do'Sangua.*"

Zaragosa Serrano waited in perfect silence until he had the attention of his Duke. "You know it is true, Your Grace. Have I not said it was true?"

Baltran do'Verrada lingered at the window. The thick glazing was wavy and warped, distorting the view beyond: the meticulously-groomed courtyard and gardens outside the ducal apartments of the Palasso Verrada. In high summer the grass was verdant, the lush vegetation in full bloom, the citrus trees weighted with rich, succulent bounty that graced his table each morning; but his spirits were not so moved as to be seduced away from a more serious concern.

Matra ei Filho, grant that the child be born safely, and my Duchess recover swiftly. Fingertips to mouth, to heart. It was good he had summoned Zaragosa; he needed the distraction.

The Duke swallowed wine from the gem-studded silver cup—chilled by snow brought down from the Montes Astrappas, the mountain border between beloved Tira Virte and haughty Ghillas—and turned slightly to admit the slender limner into his awareness. A quiet glance over a shoulder earned him the full panoply: riotous color of every fabric and texture, and—Matra Dolcha!—a *thing* perched on young Serrano's head.

He did not look directly at Zaragosa Serrano—he would not favor him so highly, not immediately—lest the man gain even more arrogance. "Is that a new hat?"

Thus reminded of his neglect, Serrano snatched the feather-be-

decked scrap of crimson velvet from his head. "Your Grace, a trifle, no more."

Do'Verrada grunted. "An expensive trifle, no?" *And ostentatious, as always.* He sipped more wine: pale spring-hued vinho
bianco, Lacta do'Matra, of course; his favorite summer vintage,
and the most favored of all Tira Virteian wine exports. *I must have
the Master Vintner in to see how the season fares.*

"Your Grace, I am honored by your generous reception of my
talent. And, Your Grace, speaking of talent—"

Do'Verrada cut across the circuitous circumnavigation of the
topic; he spent entirely too many hours of his life listening to the
like from Courtfolk. "You believe I should revoke the Ducal
Protection of the Grijalva family."

Serrano spoke with an impassioned zeal that betrayed his inse-
curity. "Oh, Your Grace, I do believe it justified, Your Grace! . . . in
view of what they are."

"Mere copyists? You would not give them the benefit of true
artistic talent, I know, but they have served Tira Virte and her
Dukes very well for many years, Zaragosa, which is precisely why
my great-grandfather issued the Protection. And even the Serranos
should be grateful; without the Grijalva paper, canvas, and materials such as paints, where would your folk be? Still scrawling graffiti frescoes on new walls wet with peasant urine?" He permitted
himself a smile as Zaragosa went white as the Matra's Blessed
Milk; the current Lord Limner's talent had indeed first been discovered in the back alleys of Meya Suerta. "They have served art
equally as well as the duchy, Zaragosa. They have—and know—
their place."

"They wish to climb too high, Your Grace—and they will use
dark magics to do so."

Do'Verrada turned now to face him fully. "I have spoken with
several of the Courtfolk—it need not be said who they are, of
course, so do not ask me with those eloquent eyes!—in order to
learn more of this power you speak of. There are those who speak
instead of your jealousy, Zaragosa, those who say you bear the
Grijalvas ill will for no sound reason beyond fear you will lose
your place."

Zaragosa Serrano colored. The splotchy flush clashed horren-
dously with his red-and-purple doublet and particolored hosen.
"Your grace, the Serrano family has held the confidence of the
do'Verradas for decades—"

"Yes, of course, but do you fear you will be dismissed as Lord
Limner? You personally, Zaragosa?"

"Your Grace, I—"

"Do you fear your talent is threatened by that of the Grijalvas?" *Or perhaps your color choice? Perhaps I should look again at your most recent paintings, yes?*

"Your Grace, they are the next thing to half-breeds, barbarian Tza'ab bandits—do they not acknowledge this themselves, Your Grace, with reference to chi'patros?" Serrano was in full spate now, like a cataract unhappily squeezed by too many fallen boulders. "'Who is the father?'—they admit it, Your Grace! They are riddled with Tza'ab blood. And they are as nothing compared to the Serranos, who are pure in blood to the days of the great Duke Alessio I. We do not name bandits and bastards in our ancestry!"

Quietly do'Verrada asked, "Then why do you fear them, Zaragosa?"

"I have *told* you, Your Grace—"

"That they have some unknown and unnameable power." Do'Verrada sighed. "Do you know, I was at the Galerria today. I took my son, that he might be acquainted with such things as he must know. There was a clutch of Grijalva children there." He paused. "They appeared nothing worse to me than children, Zaragosa—perhaps even Serrano children."

"They are not!"

Do'Verrada lifted an eloquent eyebrow; Serrano had forgotten the honorific. "No, indeed; as you say, some of them are descendants of those first bandit-bred Tza'ab chi'patros. But a man, looking on them, sees nothing but what he sees when he looks on any family. Children, Zaragosa."

"Your Grace, I have told you what they are!"

"You have told me what you *believe* they are—and, do you know, I very nearly succumbed? I believed, Zaragosa. For a moment, one moment, standing there before my *Marriage,* I believed . . ."

"Your Grace, you *should* believe—"

". . . and then I recalled that if it were true, what you tell me, how could it not also be said of Serranos?"

"Your Grace!"

The Duke smiled. "Oh, admittedly you are pure in blood to the time of my ancestor, the great Duke Alessio I. But it might yet be argued that this is nothing more than Court politics, Zaragosa, and that you, seeing fresh talent in the Grijalvas growing beyond the execution of common and fair copies made of your paintings—and wishing to vehemently deny such self-described blasphemy!—

seek to damage them so there is no chance any of that family might be appointed to the position you yourself hold."

"Your Grace! My family has held this position for nearly sixty years!"

"And before that, Grijalvas did."

"Three of them only." Immense derision. "And very briefly."

"Three. Caught between Serrano and Serrano." Do'Verrada smiled. "It might be argued that you wish to discredit those who may be worthy of the position you yourself hold. Well, I say let there be proof."

"Proof! But, Your Grace, we *know* it to be true!"

"Who does, Zaragosa?"

"The Serrano family, Your Grace! We know it."

"Then provide me with proof."

"Grijalvas were not always painters, Your Grace. They were common craftsmen, no more, manufacturing such things as true limners require."

"That is your proof? The development of artistic talent? But, Zaragosa, it might then be argued that you yourself—and your father before you, and his father's brother before *him*—claim a share of these magics, this dark power. Three Grijalvas served as Lord Limners prior to your great-uncle's and father's appointments to the post—and then were replaced. By a Serrano."

"They grew frightened, Your Grace, and returned to the common crafts so as to avoid exposure."

"Leaving the appointment as Lord Limner to your grandfather's brother? Come, Zaragosa, why would a family of such power as you describe willingly step away from Court? It makes no sense."

"Has anyone ever accused the Grijalvas of having sense, Your Grace?"

It was a small-spirited, mean-minded insult. But it angered the Duke. "Despite their lack of nobility, the Grijalvas have been closely allied with Tira Virte and the do'Verradas for more than one hundred years, Zaragosa. Are you forgetting Verro Grijalva? Despite his common birth, he was perhaps the greatest captain the armies of Tira Virte have ever known. There is no doubt he would have been named Marchallo Grando over all the armies one day— had he not perished defending my grandfather, Duke Renayo." More tellingly, so Zaragosa would not miss it: "Had he not died in Renayo's arms."

Serrano wisely was silent.

Do'Verrada signed. "Surely you understand I cannot have it said I would countenance revocation of the Protection without proof,

Zaragosa. The Court is riddled with political dissension; only a fool would give this rumor credence without proof."

Grudgingly: "Indeed, Your Grace."

"Then provide it, Zaragosa. Show me proof that the Grijalvas have this dark power you speak of, and—if indeed there *be* sustainable proof—then I will revoke what my grandfather instituted. They will have to leave Meya Suerta and become no more than Itinerarrios, all of them, making their way as they can on the roads of the duchy. And no hope of ever rising once again in the armies, in trade, or of sending one of their own to Palasso Verrada as Lord Limner."

Serrano's face was still; he spoke stiffly through a compressed mouth. "Proof, Your Grace, is often difficult to obtain."

"But necessary." Do'Verrada smiled, though there was nothing of humor in it. "Eiha! But I may have a new son or daughter before the day is out, and I weary of this topic. Put on your new hat with its elegant purple feather—*so* elegant, Zaragosa!—and find me this proof. Only then shall we speak of this again."

"Your Grace." White-faced, Zaragosa Serrano turned smartly and strode from the chamber. Wisely, very wisely, he did not put on his new hat with its elegant purple feather until he was out of the ducal presence.

"Moronno," Do'Verrada murmured. "If a Grijalva *should* replace you as Lord Limner, at the very least, half of it shall be of your own doing!"

Saavedra's belly clenched. This was wrong, *wrong,* to witness the Chieva do'Sangua. It was denied to all but Limners, the Gifted males, for a reason; and even though she had no doubt Sario would one day be admitted to the ranks, he was yet a boy and *not* admitted—and she only a female. If discovered, they would be severely punished.

"What if they find us?" she whispered. "Me they will beat, but you—eiha, Sario, would they deny your Gift?"

"They can't do that," he whispered back. "The Gift is too important, too powerful. They need me."

So secure in his talent . . . but she was not. She knew no security save that which was offered any Grijalva woman: the chance to bear children, to increase their numbers again and to provide hope that any male-child born might be Gifted as Sario was.

Saavedra shivered. The saliva dried in her mouth. Though

cramped, she touched her lips, her heart. "Eiha, Matra ei Filho, protect us both—"

"Bassda!" Sario whispered vehemently. "If you are such a moronna, *go.* I will not miss seeing this because of you—"

She could leave . . . she *could,* but she knew she wouldn't. He would make her suffer for it; and, for all that, a perverse curiosity, dreadful in its birth, undeniable in its growth, transfixed her to the stone.

She put her cheek against the brick floor. Through the crack she could see the central portion of a large chamber—the Crechetta, Sario called it—though its sides were cut off by the abbreviated width of the seam. It was a completely enclosed room, a whitewashed interior chamber within Palasso Grijalva, with neither casements nor lamps to light it. Only a single fat candle on a tall twisted-iron stand set against the wall, and also an easel, a shrouded painting upon it, and a sturdy wooden chair.

"*Peintraddo Chieva* . . ." Sario whispered, his head pressed against hers.

"What? What is that?"

"A masterwork. A self-portrait. I will be required to paint one as well, to be approved as a Limner. All Gifted are." His breath gusted against the floor. "It *must* be a *Peintraddo Chieva!*"

Men's business, and boys'; Saavedra felt lost in Sario's murmurings. She wondered uncharitably if he shrouded so much in secrecy and half-spoken comments merely to tease her cruelly, to remind her that what he could know, she could not. He had done it to others. He had never done it to her.

A windowless chamber, a single candle set on iron, a covered painting on an easel, one lone chair. Stark, minimalist, empty; oddly naked.

And then men came into the room.

She knew them all. Gifted, each one; Master Limners—Viehos Fratos, in the private tongue of Grijalvas—wearing the Chieva do'Orro on chains at their throats, or dangling nearly to hips after the fashion of sanctas and sanctos who wore on cords the sacred keys and locks of their respective orders. It signified their piety and devotion to, like gender with like gender, the Mother and Son.

The keys of the Grijalvas meant something else altogether.

Thin of breath, she again touched fingertips to lips, to heart.

Those in the chamber mimicked her.

For a moment Saavedra knew sheer panic; had they seen her? Did they mock her?—and then realized no, of course not, they merely prepared to undertake a ceremony that naturally would be done in the names of the Mother and Son, for all things done in Tira Virte were in Their Blessed Names.

Even blasphemy?

"Matra Dolcha," she murmured breathlessly. *Where did such a thought come from?* "Sweet Mother, protect me—"

"Bassda, 'Vedra!"

"Bassda yourself, cabessa merditta!" Much stronger insult, that; head of excrement instead of brain of pea. "Do you know what they are going to do?"

Sario smiled. "I think so."

Matra Dolcha—blessed Matra ei Filho—

Sario's exhalation hissed in the darkness. "Yes . . . eiha!— *yes*—"

Saavedra shut her eyes.

"They have brought someone in . . . *filho do'canna*—it's Tomaz!"

"Tomaz?" Saavedra's eyes sprang open; she ignored the vulgar alley-argot. "What are they doing with Tomaz?"

"Not 'with' . . . *to*."

" 'To'? " She shifted closer to the crack, scraping her nose against the wall. "What do they mean to do?"

Sario's voice was thinned by fascination. "Chieva do'Sangua."

The Bloody Key. It made no sense. The only Key she knew was golden, the Chieva do'Orro of the Grijalvas; and the keys and locks, separated by gender, by order and service, of the sanctos and sanctas. She had heard Chieva do'Sangua referred to only once prior to Sario's mention earlier, in furtive whisperings between boys—punishment, they had said, happily horrified, sacred discipline of the damned. "What is that—eiha, Sario!—*what*—"

Below, one of the Master Limners stepped quietly forward and stripped away the brocaded cloth covering the easel; and indeed, as Sario had said, the painting displayed was of Tomaz Grijalva, was truly a masterwork—she could judge its quality if not its detail even from her hidden place high over the chamber—but not as Tomaz was now: as he had been five years before at age fifteen. Two years after he had undergone Confirmattio and was declared Gifted.

Sario had said he, too, would be required to paint a self-portrait. A *Peintraddo Chieva.* "Sario—"

"Neosso Irrado," he whispered. "Angry Youth—just like me."

"Tomaz has always been a braggart, Sario, full of loud and empty talk of such things as he knows nothing—no one thinks anything of it."

"Neosso Irrado."

"Then this is punishment for that?" *Sacred discipline of the damned,* those boys had said. "Why? What has he done? What will they do to him?"

Sario scraped impatiently at a dusty lock of unruly brown hair that threatened his vision. "Bassda, 'Vedra. Wait, watch, and you will see."

She waited. She watched. She saw.

And vomited onto the floor.

— ◆ TWO ◆ —

Sario, recoiling so quickly he smacked his head against the slanted ceiling, had never been so disgusted in his life. "Matra Dolcha, 'Vedra—"

But she was beyond hearing, beyond marking his appalled disgust, beyond anything but shock so deep as to paralyze her. She crouched awkwardly, limbs trembling as she gasped and gulped in the aftermath of her belly's rebellion. Tangled hair straggled into her face, obscuring her expression.

They dared not linger; he dared not shout or otherwise show his extreme displeasure lest those in the Crechetta hear them, find them, punish them . . . and he, as she, had just witnessed a punishment he would never banish from memory, even if he lived forever.

Therefore Sario clamped his mouth shut on further elaborate complaints and instead grabbed a handful of her linen tunic. He tugged. " 'Vedra, get up! Get *up*—we have to go—"

And they did go, immediately; she managed awkwardly to find her feet at last with his urging, to flail upward, gagging still. She clamped hands against her mouth so as to seal in any further calamities.

The tiny chamber stank. Sario tugged again on her tunic and headed down the steps; he knew the staircase well, better than she. It took effort to get her down without losing her to a tumble.

"Out," he hissed. "We have to go out, outside. If they heard you—" It was possible, though perhaps not, but they dared not risk discovery. What they had witnessed . . .

Down and down, fourteen steps counted twice; at the bottom he unlatched the lath-and-plaster door, stuck his head out warily, then plucked at her tunic. "Come on, 'Vedra, we have to go outside."

"Stop pulling, Sario!" She yanked the tunic away, then dragged it upward to scrub her mouth and face violently, as much to rid her memory of truth, he knew, as to clean away the proof of her weakness.

Such actions guaranteed he would not now catch any part of the fabric to pull her onward. " 'Vedra, hurry!"

Out through the painted curtain, into the corridor, winding through the mazelike coils and angles away from the central rooms, where people gathered—they avoided people, now—and to a door that he unlatched hastily, nimble fingers working, and shoved open on a gusty breath of relief.

Sunlight flooded in; they tumbled outside, squinting, like a brace of awkward puppies into an alley near the side of the compound: cobbled alley, narrow, and slanted from either side toward the center, where it met in a shallow gutter to carry rain and refuse away. But there was no rain now, not today, only bright and blinding sunlight leaching into the cracks in their souls and illuminating unrepentantly, reminding them of what Chieva do'Sangua was, what it meant, what it did, how it was accomplished. . . .

—*bells*—

Meya Suerta throbbed with bells.

In the pure light of the summer sun, Saavedra's face was white as a corpse-candle. Even her lips, so tightly compressed, were pale, as if she feared to be ill again.

Sario's disgust was not lessened, but in view of her obvious discomfort he was moved to suggest a solution. "The fountain," he said briskly. "Come on, 'Vedra—you need cleaning."

He took her there to the fountain nearest Palasso Grijalva, to the primary fountain in the zocalo, the square of the artisan's quarter, where they and everyone else involved with the trade and craft lived. In the heat of the day most people lingered indoors, partaking of cool fruit drinks or relaxing drowses, though now the bells began to draw them out of doors again.

Saavedra leaned over the stone ledge and scooped up handfuls of water, sluicing her face. The front of her tunic was soon sodden, but Sario thought a water-wet tunic far more bearable than one exhibiting the proof of her weak belly.

Distracted, he frowned. *So many bells*— From the cathedral, every Ecclesia and Sanctia in the city, but rung in celebration, not tolled in memorial.

Saavedra hooked her elbows atop the lowest basin and leaned there, staring down into the water. Tangled, sweat-dried curls cascaded over her shoulders, floated atop the surface of the water. Spray like a cataract from the finial of the fountain—the Matra Herself with arms outstretched—set a net of mist in the coiled strands of black hair.

Something pinched inside of Sario. They were so alike, yet so unalike. Tza'ab blood ran in both of them. Her skin was not so dusky as his, but her eyes were a clear, unsullied Tza'ab gray, clean as fountain water. He was dark as a desert bandit, though of a different hue than the olive-skinned Tira Virteians.

He saw the rigidity of her shoulders, the pallor of knuckles locked over the lip of the ledge, clinging as if she dared not let go for fear of drowning, or falling.

"Matra ei Filho," she murmured, "In Their Blessed Names, grant him release from his torment—"

" 'Vedra—"

"—let him not suffer what they have done to him—"

" 'Vedra—"

"—Blessed Mother, Holy Son, let him know peace and no pain—"

"Oh, 'Vedra stop it! You sound like a sancta, speaking no word but that it has to do with the Matra ei Filho!"

She unclamped one hand, lifted trembling fingertips to lips, to heart. "—grant him release—"

"I'm going to leave you here!"

Saavedra looked at him. He had never seen such an expression in her eyes: she was sickened, frightened, confused, but also angry. "Go, then," she said thickly. "Go, Neosso Irrado, and look again inside your head to see what they did to Tomaz. Is it so easy a thing to wipe out of your mind?"

It was not. But he did not have her softness, her weakness; he was male. He could bear it. He had seen what any male would see, were he Gifted; when the time came—*if* the time came—for another Chieva do'Sangua, he well could be one of the Viehos Fratos in the Crechetta instead of an outsider hiding in a closet.

I don't want to wipe it out of my mind. I want to see it again. It was, after all, the only way he could understand it, could study what was done, so he would know how. It was a hunger, knowing how. "Magic," Sario murmured. "That was *magic,* 'Vedra!"

With a muffled sound of disgust, Saavedra turned away. She tossed wet hair back from her face, tugged her tunic back into some semblance of proper shape, and looked around the zocalo. "Bells," she murmured, brightening. "Birthing bells . . . the Duchess has had her baby!"

It mattered not at all to Sario, who cared little about such things as ducal babies. Except— "*Merditto!* The Duke will have that filho do'canna Zaragosa Serrano paint the *Birth* . . . Matra Dolcha, but that graffiti-crafter will inflict yet *another* mediocre painting upon the Galerria, and Grijalvas far more gifted than he will have to paint all the copies!"

Color flared in her cheeks. "Well, when *you* are Lord Limner, you can make certain the Galerria boasts only your masterworks, eh?"

She meant it as derision, as repayment for his impatience; he had annoyed her yet again. But he did not take it as such. "I *will* be Lord Limner. And I *will* paint masterworks. And the Serranos will be reduced to copying *my* work."

"Oh, Sario—"

"I will." The bells, pealing again, nearly drowned out his words. "Zaragosa Serrano had best count his days, Saavedra. They will be mine soon enough."

Alejandro Baltran Edoard Alessio do'Verrada, in the transitory and negligent space of time between the dawn and noon, was transmogrified from only child to older brother. This time he was old enough to comprehend the change and what it wrought; before, twice before, he had been too young to know anything but that his mother shut herself away and cried, and his father, who ordinarily spent much time with his son, went away from both son and wife, away from the city entirely, to Caza Varra, a private ducal retreat.

It could yet happen again, of course; no newborn was assured of life except he or she be properly blessed by the Matra ei Filho. If found lacking in grace, the blessing was denied and the child died. It was after all not fit to be a citizen of Tira Virte if the Matra ei Filho denied that blessing, so the death therefore was a gift.

Or so the sanctos and sanctas claimed, echoing the words of their superiors. The Premia Sancta and Premio Sancto did not always agree—or so snippets of gossip said—but in this they were united: stillborn children or infants who died were not worth mourning.

So his mother the Duchess had locked herself away so no one but her ladies might know she cried, and his father departed the city. And he was left to fend for himself in Palasso Verrada.

Today he fended for himself not because of a baby's death, but because of its birth; today he was superfluous. And so he occupied himself by contemplation of his state in the world, and curiosity about such things as what *exactly* happened when a baby died. Two younger sisters had died; were entombed in the undercroft with other do'Verradas . . . and yet supposedly they had been denied the blessing of the Matra ei Filho because they *did* die; so it did not follow that children denied the blessing should be put into family tombs with carved marble effigies marking their brief presences in the world.

It made no sense to Alejandro. What happened when adults died? Surely they had been blessed throughout their lives, or they would have died as children; and when they died as adults they were mourned, sometimes extravagantly so. But had the Matra ei Filho, for some unknown but naturally exalted reason, withdrawn the blessing bestowed at birth? Was that why adults died?

No one in the Palasso seemed moved to explain it to him. The servants grew flustered, red of face, and fled. Those of higher rank, whom he accosted as he found them, even departing the garde-robes, were no more able to explain it; or were unwilling to, because many of them told him—politely, of course—that perhaps he might take his questions to his nurse.

But his nurse was with the new baby, and he was denied entry into the private quarters where his mother and new sister resided. And so eventually he wandered into the kitchens, where the cooks were preparing a First-Day Feast—*Premia Dia,* as she was a girl-baby—in honor of the new ducal daughter. He was given a bowl and spoon to lick, then banished, kindly, to a corner, where he would be allowed to play duke in the cooks' duchy—but only from a distance.

And so it was that the boy who would one day rule them all was told for the first time in his life that he was different; that life was divided; that some in the world were more favored than others; that he and those of his house were better than everyone else in the entire duchy.

Because, they explained, that was the way the world *was.*

The cooks, turnspits, and potboys seemed only too willing to discuss with him what death was, and what life was, and how the Matra ei Filho, blessed be Their Holy Names, differentiated between children born to do' Verradas and peasants, the campones-sos; between the nobility and the merchants; certainly between pure-born Tira Virteians and half-breed Tza'ab chi'patros; between the holy sanctas and sanctos and the Premia Sancta and Premio Sancto, and even the lowliest initiatas and initiatos, but newly admitted to orders, who were nonetheless, because they served the Matra ei Filho, better than everyone else.

Except for the do' Verradas, naturally, who were more blessed than anyone . . . although that summing up spawned a heated discussion between meat-cook and baker over who was truly more important in the eyes of the Matra ei Filho: His Grace the

Duke, who gave order to the duchy, or their Honored Eminences
the Premia Sancta and Premio Sancto, who gave order to the
Holy Ecclesia, which claimed primacy over all the myriad
smaller Sanctias and shrines scattered throughout the city and
the duchy.

Bored by philosophical semantics, however badly phrased in
vulgar gutter slang, Alejandro climbed off his stool, gravely set the
licked bowl and spoon on the seat, then went out of the kitchens altogether.

This day had brought two births, then: his sister's, as yet unnamed; and his understanding that power accompanied his family's name. *His* name.

He was Alejandro Baltran Edoard Alessio do'Verrada. One day
everyone in Tira Virte, possibly even the Premio Sancto and
Premia Sancta, would do what he asked—or told—them to do. He
would have as his responsibility, by the grace of his birth and the
blessings of the Mother and Son, the shaping of the world.

Alejandro giggled. One day he could cause to have changed
anything he wished—even a thing so inconsequential as the color
and flavor of his favorite candy.

Which today was chocolate so dark as to be very nearly black.

Outside, Ecclesia and Sanctia bells pealed a welcome to the new
little do'Verrada. Inside, the ten-year-old Heir grappled with the
newfound realization that he was not and never could be like anyone else.

⟍—⟋

In the netherworld between dark and dawn, Saavedra did not sleep.
She lay awake from the moment she went to bed in her tiny student's cell, knotted of limbs and belly as she coiled upon herself in
an attempt to ward her body against fear, against comprehension,
against the lurid colors of what she had seen slashed like smeared
paint across the paletto of her inner eye.

Tomaz.

Chieva do'Sangua.

And Sario, blissfully fascinated.

Neosso Irrado, Sario had called Tomaz. Had called himself. And
it was true; she had known Tomaz as an angry young man, too old
to be called boy, too young to be called master. Gifted, and thus
gifted beyond many, even other Grijalvas, Tomaz was frequently
given to dramatic displays of artistic temperament, to complaining
unceasingly about certain traditions of the family. And to a vast and

abiding impatience to share his Luza do'Orro with the world inside the Palasso Grijalva so that one day he might step outside of it into the light of Tira Virteian approbation for a talent far surpassing that of jumped-up Serranos, or of any others who called themselves painters.

Just like Sario.

Given to so much, Tomaz Grijalva. And now—given to Chieva do'Sangua.

She was at that moment—had been since witnessing the truth of rumor, the sacred discipline of the damned—sickened by what she was: Grijalva. Subject to its joys, its truths, its talents, its gifts—and its Gifteds. And now undone by the same truths, the deeper, hidden truths of what power of talent was, and the Gift.

No woman bore it. No woman was permitted certain knowledge. No woman was admitted to the private dealings of Gifted males, the Viehos Fratos. She had resented it; now she blessed it. They were blind, all the other Grijalva women, asked only to bear children. Denied the Gift, they wielded no power beyond that of the household. Claimed no magic. Knew no truth.

Innocence, she had felt prior to this day, was a quality much exaggerated, robbing women of equality. And yet now, this moment, *because* of this day, she would never be innocent again.

Saavedra twisted in summer bed linens. They were soaked beneath her, as was her nightshirt. Her eyes were gritty with exhaustion, but she could not sleep. And so she got up and went to the window overlooking one of the small starlit inner courtyards of the Palasso Grijalva, to the table before it, hosting ewer and basin. It was meant for washing; Saavedra poured water into the basin, cupped it in both hands, lifted, and drank. Then poured the remaining water over her chin and neck and down the front of her nightshirt, so that it stuck to budding breasts, the slight curve of her belly, the indentation where Matra, in the womb, had set holy lips to unborn flesh; to the tops of her thighs.

She was twelve years old. In a handful of years she would be married, bearing children. Until then, she would not sleep again without seeing what was done to Tomaz Grijalva, Neosso Irrado.

"Blessed Mother and Son," she murmured, "let Sario be not so angry as Tomaz."

Let him be not so foolish.

Sario put on dark tunic and baggy trousers, soft felted slippers, and went out from his tiny estudo's cell into the corridors. He took with him candle, flint, and striker, but did not light it; he tucked all into his voluminous tunic pocket—accustomed to chalks, bits of dried resin, pigment powders—and made his way all the way back to the narrow corridor so close to the Crechetta. He slipped behind the painted curtain, into the chamber beyond; climbed and descended stairs, reached at last the narrow lath-and-plaster door. There he paused, lighted the candle, and put his hand upon the latch.

It was in him to know if they knew, any of them, that he and Saavedra had discovered the odd little closet. If the residue of her sickness remained, noisome as it might be, they were safe; if someone had cleaned it away, they were discovered. And no doubt a search would be instituted, no matter how subtle, to discover who had been in the hidden closet over the Crechetta during Chieva do'Sangua.

He was himself prepared to clean up Saavedra's mess, though he ought to make her do it. But he would not; he took responsibility for urging her to accompany him, though he had not expected such a weak stomach. It was a task he set himself, to learn if they knew, and if they did not he would make certain they never did.

Sario lifted the latch and opened the door. The candlelight, even from a poor stub of lumpy, pungent wax and smoking wick, filled the entrance and fled like vermin up the twenty-eight stairs, pausing only at the edge of the slant-ceilinged closet itself.

Movement. Sario froze. *They know—they've found out—*

Again movement, coupled with a voice made raw by screaming, thickened by crying. "Who is that? Is someone there?" A scrabbling from above. "I beg you, aid me . . . O Blessed Mother, *aid me—*"

Sario gulped breath. *Matra Dolcha, are we found out?* No, surely not; would he be asked for aid if so? *Unless it be a trap—* His hand trembled, and the flame nearly went out. He steadied it with effort, groping one-handed for the latch. *If we are found out . . .* And then into attenuated illumination at the top of the stairs scrabbled a body, which huddled itself precariously on the sharp-angled cusp of the tiny closet floor and the narrow staircase.

Sario, startled for the first time in his life into abject and utter silence, stared gape-mouthed at the man.

"Have you come to help me?" The man braced himself against the walls with racked, bone-fevered hands, knuckles swelling flesh obscenely, lumps and calluses disfiguring what had been agile fingers, disciplined fingers, now wrenched awry until what the man used to steady himself was little more than warped, misshapen claws. Gold glinted briefly in the rich folds of costly fabric; he had been a vain man, once, who catered to self-adornment. "Are you there?"

The candle spilled light into all but the most distant of the corners. And yet the man asked if Sario were there.

I am . . . but he said nothing, could say nothing at all, not yet; merely swallowed heavily, painfully, and gazed in sickened fascination upon the opaque milky substance that filled the man's eyes.

The body was young, the flesh, the bones, the hair, the features. He was in all ways, in all things, Tomaz Grijalva, fine-boned and blazingly talented, Gifted and gifted. But Neosso Irrado.

And duly disciplined.

Realization was absolute: *This is what it was for.* The direst punishment that could be visited upon a Gifted Grijalva: discipline of the damned. As indeed this man was damned.

Sario's voice echoed softly in the confines of flame-washed imprisonment. "You will never paint again."

Tomaz spasmed. "Who is that? Who is there? What do you want? Have you come to gloat? Is this a part of the punishment?" Startled from balance, he scrabbled for purchase with ruined hands. "Who are you, cabessa merditto?"

Sario laughed. He could not help himself. "Neosso Irrado, Tomaz . . . just like you." And then an irrational comprehension crashed into his mind and bounded unchecked onto his tongue like an untrained, ill-mannered hound. "But *wiser* than you . . ." He hiccuped with brief laughter. ". . . because me they will never catch!"

"Filho do'canna—who *is* that?"

Fascination overrode shocked horror now. They had denied him so much, the moualimos who saw youth in place of talent; who recognized the talent and tried to contain it, to turn it, to make him distrust it in the name of their traditions, their control. What crouched before him now, begging help for blinded eyes and ruined hands, was the fault of his teachers, of the Master Limners, of the Viehos Fratos who ruled without imagination, without the wit to acknowledge his gifts.

They are afraid of me . . . they will do to me what they have done to Tomaz. Fear. Why else was there justification to destroy another's talent? Tomaz's Luza do'Orro remained in his brilliant if undisciplined mind, but the means to share it with the world was forever denied.

Discipline of the damned. Profanation incarnate of what the

Grijalvas worshiped, a far more exacting deity than the Blessed Mother and Her Son.

The Gift. The Golden Key—Chieva do'Orro. And its use.

Sario drew in a careful breath. A cruel, unrelenting focus replaced shock with an unnamed lust far more powerful than that of his youthfully pretentious loins. "How was it done, Tomaz? Yes, I saw them do it—I saw them paint the afflictions into the *Peintraddo Chieva,* and thus they were visited upon you!—but *how* was it made to affect you? How was the magic worked?"

The body collapsed upon itself. "Filho do'canna," Tomaz sobbed brokenly. "They have sent you to bait me!"

"Oh, no . . ." Sario closed and latched the door behind him. "En verro—it is truth, I promise: no one has sent me. I came to learn a thing, and I have learned more." The candle flame guttered, but Tomaz did not, could not, mark it. "I am Gifted, Tomaz, as are— *were*—you, but I want to know how such things are done. I *need* to know—they will claim me too young, a mennino moronno, but I have a hunger in me!" Matra Dolcha, the hunger! "I need to know *now,* so I may be prepared." *So what has happened to you will not happen to me.*

Silence. Then Tomaz blurted, "Do'nado. I can tell you nothing."

No, *not* nothing, *not* denial—not from one who knew the secrets, the truths. "Why not? Do you bear them loyalty, after what the Viehos Fratos have done to you?"

Tomaz's unsteady breathing was loud in the staircase. "You are not to know until you have achieved Confirmattio."

"It begins with the *Peintraddo Chieva,*" Sario said intently. "Doesn't it? A self-portrait, perfect in every way . . . and it was *their* Gifts which brought these afflictions upon you, Tomaz! What loyalty is owed?"

Silence, save for breathing. And then, hollowly, "They will not grant me release. Much as I have no wish to live as this, they will not release me."

"Neosso Irrado," Sario said very softly, "share with me your truths."

Tomaz laughed wildly. "You see what truths can gain you!"

Sario chewed his lip, then revealed his personal truth that only Saavedra knew. "I have read in the *Folio.*"

"So? We all read in the *Folio!*"

"I have read *ahead.*"

"How?" Tomaz accused now. "It isn't permitted."

"What you did was not permitted. You did it anyway. That's why you're here."

It startled Tomaz into a nearly coherent shout. "When they come, I will tell them you were here!"

Sario wished to hiss him into silence as he had with Saavedra. Instead, he relied on a truth even Tomaz could not deny. "We live so short a time, we Grijalvas . . . our days are as weeks to others. Yesterday, you had fifteen or twenty years left before the bone-fever twisted your hands, before the milk-blindness robbed you of vision . . . but now you have none. No years at all." He paused. "Tell me, Tomaz, and I will do whatever you ask."

"Mercy. That is what I ask. That you would release me from this horror to the Matra's sweet mercy." Tomaz's face, painted into a chiaroscuro of light and shadow by Sario's candle flame, was overpainted now by a torturous knowledge and helpless grief into grotesque *caricaturro* of the handsome young man he had been but hours before. "Yes, I will tell you—and then you must kill me!"

Sario's need for a comprehension of his own talent and gifts did not lead him to a knowledge of how to undertake such a thing as that. The thought and its conception stunned him. "You said—you said '*release*' . . . not '*kill*'!"

Tomaz's desperate laughter cracked. "Are you so young, then? So very young, that death is unknown to you?"

Stung, Sario retorted swiftly. "I know death! The Summer Fever took both my mother and my father three seasons ago!"

"And so they have had you since, the moualimos? Eiha, then I cry your pardon." Tomaz sighed. "It begins as it always begins, for Gifted Grijalvas, even for *you,* one day: with the *Peintraddo Chieva.* And so it ends as well. Destroy it, mennino moronno, my fellow Neosso Irrado, and you grant me my release."

"En verro?"

Tomaz barked a brief, bitter laugh. "En verro. By my very soul."

Matra Dolcha!—here, then, was the first of the real truths, the incandescent Luza do'Orro of the Grijalva Gift.

Sario's hungry inhalation hissed. "Tell me!"

⊶ THREE ⊷

"So," the woman said, "will you leave me now? Set me aside?"

The man smiled. "Never."

"You have a son. You have a daughter."

"Having legitimate children does not predispose me to set aside a woman who brings me contentment, even if the relationship is not properly sanctioned by the Ecclesia." Beside her, in the massive, draperied bed—her bed, his bed; one and the same for two years—he stretched prodigiously. "Matra Dolcha!—but this pleases me! She is healthy, they say, and like to thrive; *this* time the Matra ei Filho have blessed us."

" 'Us?' "

His spine felt younger already, though it cracked alarmingly. "Tira Virte. Me. The Duchess. And you, viva meya; if I am blessed, you are blessed."

Silence. She lay curled beside him, feet intertwined with his own, but she was not much given to silence; if she held it, she was not pleased.

He levered himself up on one elbow. Her back was to him; he could see the long curve of her delicate spine lying so shallowly beneath smooth young flesh. *So young—so much younger than I.* With gentle fingers he traced the line of the spine from neck to waist, counting idly: *—premo—duo—treo—* "What is it? Have I not put your fears to rest?"

An elegant shrug of a single pearlescent shoulder, once dusted with costly scented Ghillasian powder, now drying after their exertions. The bed linens drooped; she was modest only in a curtain of rich brown hair, and the fall of silk across her hips.

"Viva meya, what is it? Do you require further proof of my affection? My devotion?" He sighed, letting his hand fall away. "Have I not presented you with the deed to this manor? You are a wealthy woman, suitably honored . . . and your future is secured. What more could you want?"

She shifted now, turning to face him. Tendrils of hair, seduced by the dampness of recent lovemaking, coiled against her hairline. "Security for my family."

He laughed, then silenced his mirth as he saw she was serious.

"Your brother is Lord Limner at Palasso Verrada. Others of your family inhabit Court. You inhabit my bed more often than the Duchess. What more security is there, Gitanna?"

Her lush mouth, blushed by his attentions, was eloquent, though what it issued was not—quite—a plea. "There is one small thing, Baltran . . ."

He could not help but touch her again, to claim the flesh of her breast as his and only his, cradled against his palm. "Name it, then."

"Revoke the Ducal Protection of the Grijalvas."

He stilled.

"Is it so much, Baltran? They traffic in dark magic . . . they plot to replace my family in all things of importance—"

"Gitanna—"

"—and no doubt they would as soon replace *me* with one of their chi'patro women—"

"Gitanna."

"—and if they are not stopped, they will destroy you, Baltran, you and your family—and claim the duchy for themselves!"

He withdrew from her warmth, her wheedling, her woman's warfare. Without assistance he could not dress completely—and the servants were under strict orders not to enter the bedchamber— so he donned his clothing unassisted: hosen; loose summer-weight lawn shirt, crimped cuffs and collar untied; soft, thin-soled leather shoes, studded with polished brass at toes and heels. He did not attempt the doublet with its formal and convoluted intricacies.

"Baltran!"

He turned to her, clasping the massive, ornate bedpost with a long-fingered hand as he leaned forward. On the forefinger glinted the ducal ring, bloody red in a shaft of midday sunlight slanting through shutters left ajar.

"For this, I will not blame you, Gitanna . . . not entirely. They seek to use you in this, when I refuse to listen to their pleas otherwise; eiha, I suppose I cannot blame them for that—they believe what they believe—but I will not lie abed with the same political pettiness that chokes the Court. Recall what is between us, viva meya, and that it has nothing to do with politics or Grijalvas."

She was very pale, luminously so. "But it was politics that brought us together! There, at Court—my brother brought me there for you, Baltran—"

"Or for any wealthy, influential man who might be seduced by your redoubtable charms; it happened to be his Duke." The hand, partially obscured by pleated cuff, tightened upon the bedpost. "You know nothing of what you request, Gitanna. You know nothing of Grijalvas."

"I know they are riddled with baseborn bastards, Baltran! And can even you name how many of them now have Tza'ab blood in their veins? Can even you swear they do not answer that blood, and plot revenge upon Tira Virte for their defeat at Rio Sanguo?"

"They are Grijalvas," he said steadily, "all of them. Their unfortunate ancestors—who, I remind you, had no choice in their circumstances!—were accepted as such by the Duchess Jesminia herself, may the Matra ei Filho bless her gracious name—" fingertips to lips, to heart, "—and no one in the do'Verrada family shall ever neglect to serve her wishes in this."

"That was more than one hundred years ago!" Gitanna cried. "She is long dead, Baltran—and surely she would admit that the blood of her own family is more important than the blood of either Grijalvas *or* Tza'ab bandits!"

"Grijalva blood, spilled in that battle—that is why it became known as the River of Blood, Gitanna, there was so much!—is one of the reasons the do'Verradas rule today," he said quietly. "You forget yourself, Gitanna. You forget your history."

"I know my history, Baltran!" She sat upright now, bed linens wrenched up to modestly cover what a scant hour before had given him so much pleasure. "Oh, yes, bless the name of the gracious Duchess Jesminia who took in those defiled Grijalva women and welcomed their half-breed bastards—but look also at what it has brought us! They live now as serpents in the very bosom of Tira Virte, in Meya Suerta itself. If the Tza'ab chose to attack, they would have confederates right here, Baltran!"

"The Tza'ab as a unified enemy were destroyed utterly at Rio Sanguo," he said patiently; it was not a new argument, though never had it issued from her lips. "Additionally, without a holy man to lead them—what *remains* of them—they will never again attempt to take back the lands that now are ours."

"But they *did* lay waste to the borderlands, Baltran, for nearly one hundred years! The Diviner's death did not break their hearts; it made them desperate to redeem that death. That's why the Empress fielded so many against us decades later. And there could be yet another Tza'ab chieftain who styles himself a second Diviner."

"Skirmishes, Gitanna; and when there are rich lands to be won there will always be skirmishes, even as Pracanza attempts to carve away our lands. But those of Tza'ab Rih will never be the threat they once were. There is no heart, despite the mouth that wails so eloquently of loss and endless demands for reparation."

"But—"

"Trust me in this, Gitanna . . . Verro Grijalva himself destroyed the *Kita'ab* before he died. Without the Diviner *and* their holy book, there is no guidance, no unifying plan. And even a pretender who claims the Diviner's name cannot hope to reassemble the Riders of the Golden Wind and lead a Tza'ab army without the *Kita'ab.*" He shook his head. "They are broken as a force, I promise you . . . those born of Tza'ab Rih are fallen, the Diviner killed, his Riders shattered. They are all of them merely bandits again—an occasional nuisance, no more. They are no threat to Tira Virte."

"But the Grijalvas *know* things!"

He laughed, in good humor again despite her desperation. "So do you, viva meya. So do you! And so long as you do—and how to *use* those 'things'—you shall please me well!" He held up his doublet. "Now, come dress me as hastily as you *un*dressed me; it is time I returned to the Palasso."

Her mouth formed a mutinous line even as she climbed out of bed to help him into his doublet. "You are wrong, Baltran. You dismiss our concerns too lightly."

"As I have told your brother, given proof of your beliefs I will indeed move to prevent what you fear. But the Grijalvas themselves were broken by the Nerro Lingua, Gitanna, even as the Tza'ab were broken by battle . . . too few are born now, and too many die before their time. Their blood—their bandit-bred Tza'ab blood, Gitanna!—is too weak. So is their seed."

She tended his doublet with experienced, efficient fingers, tucking here, straightening there, braiding and lacing and knotting and looping. "It requires only one, Baltran. One man of magic, bent on destroying you."

He smiled as she tied the collar of his billowy lawn shirt, his cuffs, then smoothed the doublet over it. "And who would that be, Gitanna? Have you a candidate?"

She shook her head. "You make too light of it, Baltran."

"Because they have neither the grounds nor the means to do what you fear. They have their own code of honor, Gitanna—and that is precisely why Verro Grijalva gave his life to save my great-grandfather Renayo. They serve. They do not rule. Had they wanted to, they might have won Tira Virte by acclamation after Verro's actions against the Tza'ab, but it was *us* they acclaimed· Do'Verrada. Not Grijalva."

Her mouth was a thin line, flattening the lush curves that so attracted him. "He *died,* Baltran. Who can say what might have become of him?"

"He was hailed a hero, never a Duke. Even while he lived."

She looked him square in the eye. "Once you do'Verradas were no better than Grijalvas. Warlords, Baltran, no more—though clever enough and strong enough to take *and* keep. But look at you now. You rule absolutely. All of Tira Virte worships the do'Verradas—after the Matra ei Filho, of course, and the Ecclesia—but who is to say the Grijalvas do not long for the same thing?"

"Eiha, woman, you weary me with this! I will tell you again: they are a small family severely weakened by the plague. Many of their women cannot conceive children, many of their men cannot sire any. They may never regain their numbers, nor even their physical strength. And they are, as you say, riddled with Tza'ab blood, which is considered a taint by the Ecclesia and many of the citizens—the Tza'ab are infidels, after all, condemned in the eyes of the Mother and Her Son." He shook his head. "Do you really believe Tira Virte would accept a Grijalva as Duke?"

The exasperated protest did not even slow her. "It is fortunate for you Verro Grijalva *did* die, Baltran. You do not know what he might have planned had he survived."

Patiently he said, "It was in Alesso's name our people fought, and then in Renayo's when we consolidated the duchy. Never in Verro Grijalva's." More pointedly, he added, "And never in the name of any Serrano."

She had the grace to color. "No," she murmured, "we inspire nothing, we Serranos—"

"Except do'Verrada lust." He smiled, forgiving her. "Viva meya, I thank you for your concern, but you would do better to trust in me than in your ambitious family."

"If we are ambitious, it is to retain our place—not to throw down the do'Verradas from theirs and fill it with Grijalvas."

"Matra Dolcha, Gitanna, I cry you let it be done, this argument. Bassda! I weary of it."

Though naked, she was clad in certainty. "Let none of them come to Court, Baltran. Ever."

He sighed deeply, not troubling to hide exasperation. "As long as I live, your brother is Lord Limner. Other than art, the Grijalvas have no avenue by which to join the Court. And when I die, it shall be my son's decree who succeeds to the position."

"He is a boy, Baltran."

"Just so, Gitanna . . . and unless I expire of overindulgence in your bed—far better that way, I think, than of a poisoned Tza'ab dart as Verro Grijalva did!—Alejandro will not be making any appointments until well after his majority." He tugged at the crimson-embroidered cuffs of his shirt beneath stiff doublet sleeves. "And now it is time I paid my respects to the Duchess. Today we formally name our daughter before the Ecclesia." He bent slightly, planted a kiss on her brow, and was gone.

Saavedra, much exercised and out of sorts, found Sario at last in the family galerria within Palasso Grijalva. In the ten days since they had witnessed Chieva do'Sangua each had avoided the other, as if afraid to be reminded of what they witnessed. But now she sought him out; they had been too close for too long to remain apart, and the secret too great to keep to oneself alone. It must be shared with him—*had* to be shared with him—who knew what she had seen.

The Galerria Grijalva was not as the Galerria Verrada. It was much smaller, less grand, and distinctly private; no one entered without permission, and permission was never granted save to Grijalvas, who had no need of it.

"Sario—" He was a slender nonentity in the distant dimness at the far end of the chamber, standing very still before one of the older paintings in the galerria. The long whitewashed chamber was empty save for themselves—and countless paintings of long-dead people—but she lowered her voice nonetheless. The determined whisper carried straight to him. It was an innocuous question; let them hear, if there were any near enough. "Sario, why were you not in drawing class this morning?"

He turned his head away from the painting then and looked at her. Shocked, she saw that he had lost significant weight; his face was very thin, and the shadows of the chamber, lit by its whitewash and little else, created angled contours she had never seen before. He was of the age when boys grew overnight, all awkward of limbs and voice and movements, but this was not growth. This was something far more serious.

"Sario!" She hastened the length of the gallery to his side. "Are you ill?"

He turned back to the painting, hitching a thin shoulder. "No!" A long pause; the set of his mouth was bitter, too bitter for a boy. "Why do we have nothing but copies here?"

"Copies?" Full of other thoughts, the question at first meant nothing. But the answer took no effort. "The originals are in the Galerria Verrada, of course. Or in private palassos."

What filled the galerria were carefully cataloged copies, placed in meticulous arrangement intended to best flatter the paintings, their colors, their composition. Gilt frames, wooden frames, canvas and wood and paper, patinaed and illuminated by natural light permitted entrance by strategically-placed windows and the angle of intricate shutters, as well as precisely-plotted placements of iron candle-stands, closely attended by quiet-colored clay jugs of water and sand, in case of fire.

"But we painted them," Sario said. "*We* did. Grijalvas." He looked at her again. "They rob us of our heritage."

He leaves me behind so often. . . . "Who does?"

"The do'Verradas. Serranos. The rich folk of the city." The hollows beneath the angle of his cheekbones were dark as a dusting of soot, limning brittle bones as sharp as his tone. "They commission the great works from graffiti-crafters like Zaragosa Serrano, strip us of what we once were—and ask us to paint *copies* of our own works!"

Saavedra followed his line of vision and looked at the painting. It was a huge canvas, framed in a heavy, ornately-carved wooden frame: *Death of Verro Grijalva.* He was depicted as a miraculously attractive and unbloodied hero dying in the arms of his beloved Duke Renayo—blessed be his memory—with whom, the stories claimed, Verro Grijalva had been friends since childhood. The slackness in Verro's handsome face confirmed his death, but it was not that which transfixed the eyes. It was the grief in Renayo's face, the expression of deep sorrow, of a great and terrible anger—and of fear.

"A copy," Sario declared bitterly. "The original hangs in Palasso Verrada."

Saavedra studied the painting. The play of light and shadow intrigued her; chiaroscuro was difficult to paint properly, but this artist had been a master. Piedro Grijalva; only a Grijalva, grieving as much for his kinsman Verro as for Renayo do'Verrada, could properly capture the intense emotions of the moment.

"Tza'ab," she murmured, for in the background, in the upper right corner, was a lone man, dusky-faced as if burned permanently dark by the desert sun, yet remarkably pale of eye. Magnificently mounted upon a gape-mouthed black horse, he wore dramatic robes of brilliant green, all aglitter with brass and glass, and in one hand clutched a brass-bound carved wooden tube through which had flown the poisoned dart that took Verro's life.

Saavedra doubted the Tza'ab warrior had been so close as was depicted, or surely he would have been killed by do'Verrada forces. But such was the way of art: one re-created truth, remade history, in honor of the subject.

At the behest of the patron who ordered it painted?

"Tza'ab," Sario said, looking at the green-clad warrior. "Perhaps a kinsman of ours. As Verro was." He turned directly to her. "Tomaz is dead."

The shift in topic, the baldness of the statement, shook her. "Dead? But—"

"They destroyed his talent, his Gift, by painting him blind, by painting him crippled in the *Peintraddo* . . . Chieva do'Sangua, the 'discipline of the damned'—but now he is dead."

"Matra ei Filho! Sario—"

"Dead," he repeated. "Now he need not suffer."

It had been ghastly, what they had seen, but Tomaz had not at any time appeared in danger of dying. Only of suffering. *As they intended him to suffer.* And he *had* suffered, she was certain, though she had sickened so soon thereafter that she had seen little beyond the physical results, and then only in a combination of shocked observation and a flash of insight, of too-vivid—and too accurate—imagination.

"If they intended him to die, why not kill him immediately?" she asked.

Perspiration gathered at his temples, across his upper lip. "They didn't intend him to die."

"Sario—"

His face lost the last remnants of color. He was white, so white he aspired to the starkness of Renayo do'Verrada's face in the painting, the bloodlessness of shock and stark realization that nothing could be changed; that all was altered forever. " 'Vedra—*I* did it!"

It confounded her; he had gone ahead somewhere without her. "Did what?"

It hissed in the galerria. "Killed him!"

"Tomaz?"

" 'Vedra—oh, 'Vedra—"

"But—how?"

He trembled. She had never seen him so frightened. Even in the closet, in the secret chamber above the Crechetta, where terrible things were done. "You saw how they painted his eyes white in the *Peintraddo*—" he said, "—how they painted his hands all twisted—"

"Bone-fever," she murmured. "Yes. They painted out his eyes and made his hands over into those of an old man."

"It *happened,* Saavedra! You saw it! You saw what became of him!"

She had. Oh, Matra, she had. And so quickly, so very quickly: one moment whole, vital; exuberantly, defiantly Tomaz, and the next . . . "But they didn't paint him *dead.*"

"*I* killed him."

"Oh, Matra—oh, *Sario*—"

"I did it, 'Vedra." His dark eyes had gone black, utterly black, so that he was, in his own way, blind as Tomaz had been, though with horror rather than with the milk-blindness that affected so many old ones. Black eyes, white face, and a tensile trembling that threatened, she feared, to shatter his very bones. "I made him die."

"How do you know?" It was all she could think to ask. She knew him, comprehended the terrible talent that drove him in his dreams, equally awake as asleep. "Sario—how *can* you know?"

"I thought to burn the painting, but I had seen how what was painted was inflicted upon the body, and I didn't want to *hurt* him—"

"Sario—"

"—so I didn't burn it after all . . . I just put a knife in the canvas where I thought his heart would be." His eyes were black, so black, infinitely black, like a fire burned out and doused with too much water. "But—I missed. I went to him, to see . . . and he was still alive. Wounded, but alive, because I was not precise enough . . . and so, and so—" He swallowed so heavily she saw his throat convulse. "I burned it after all. He told me that would work."

All she could say was his name. No question, no statement; only his name, in horror and disbelief. Of him. For him.

"They don't know yet. They haven't found it yet. But they will."

She put her hands over her face, rubbing, scrubbing, stretching it this way and that, hiding from the world, the truth, his matter-of-fact retelling, even as she hid her own response from him. Fear for him. Of him.

" 'Vedra—what do I do?"

It was appeal. From him. He was infinitely young again, a boy of eleven years, prodigiously talented, demonstrably Gifted, but a boy. Who had done a terrible thing.

And now he pleaded with her to tell him what to do.

She took her hands away at last. "No one knows."

"They haven't found the painting yet—or what remains of it."

"And Tomaz?"

Even his lips were white. "I haven't looked."

"Looked where?"

"Where he was. In the secret chamber. Where we were."

"He was *there?*"

"They put him there."

"Are you certain he's dead?"

"He told me . . . he told me to destroy the painting. And he would—be released." He bit deeply into his bottom lip. Beneath the surface, blood fled. "I'm afraid to look."

"Then you don't *know*—"

"He said it would kill him! He said he *wanted* it!"

Her chest hurt. Her belly and head felt all hollow, insubstantial, emptied of contentment with all but the small complaints of insignificant lives. "Then—we have to find out. We have to know for certain."

"They'll find out. They'll find *out*—and do the same to me!"

Saavedra stared at him. She had never before seen Sario afraid of anything. "If he is dead—*if* he's dead, they will find out. And the painting . . ." She swallowed back the knot in her throat. Only one answer existed. She doubted Sario, so clever-witted, was unaware of it. He simply could not speak it aloud. The task was left to her. "Then we'll have to make sure what they find is what we *want* them to find."

He looked drugged on poppy-juice: blackened eyes, whitened face, words slow to form. " 'Vedra?"

She drew in a breath. *Matra, I beg your aid in this—grazzo, please, I beg you—* "Where is the painting, Sario?"

"In the Crechetta."

"Then we have to go there."

"And do what?"

She looked at the painting before them. A copy of one of their family's greatest works. "Burn it," she said flatly. "Burn it down, all of it. Everything in the Crechetta."

"But—"

"And then we must be found, so they know how it occurred—not why, but *how*—so that they may punish us for it, but never know—*never know, Sario*—why we did it."

" 'Vedra—"

"It's the only way."

It was. She knew it. He knew it.

They had been bound for so long, by so many intangibles. And now by this.

"It's the only way, Sario."

He touched trembling fingers to his lips, then to his heart beneath the shabby, stained summer tunic. "Matra ei Filho, aid us in this . . . oh, Blessed Matra, give us strength . . ."

Saavedra wanted to laugh; at last he mouthed devotions, craved divine blessing, required intercession from someone other than his evanescent self-will—and her.

But she didn't laugh. She couldn't. She could only stare blindeyed at the painting and think of Tomaz Grijalva, his Gift destroyed by the desecration of his self-portrait, his life destroyed by Sario's actions.

And us? she wondered. *What of ourselves do we destroy with this?*

The answer was implicit: innocence.

So much destroyed in the space of ten days. Even as Nerro Lingua had destroyed most of a family; as a Tza'ab dart had destroyed Verro Grijalva.

She looked at the painting. Sario had summed it up, the vast and naked truth of their ancestry. Grijalva. And Tza'ab.

They were direct descendants of Verro Grijalva, as the genealogies proved. And, for all they knew, equally directly descended from the *Kita'ab*-quoting Rider of the Golden Wind depicted in the painting, servant of a dead man.

As they now served Tomaz.

⊶ FOUR ⊶

They did not see him, all the women. They were too taken up with his mother, the Duchess; too concerned with fitting the ceremonial robes properly, with tying up the laces of the loose gown beneath, with the drape of costly fabric, with the arrangement of her hair, with the coloring of her face.

She was beautiful, her son supposed. They all said she was.

But as for this, this *thing,* lying in the lace-swathed ducal cradle, he supposed nothing at all save that it—they called it a *"she,"* but he saw no evidence of humanity, let alone of gender—was little better than a lump of silk and lace and cloth-of-gold, aglitter with seed pearls and gemstones crusted on the array of ribbons sprouting like the waters of the fountain before the Cathedral Imagos Brilliantos.

Usually she spouted complaints as unceasingly, though he admitted she was at this moment silent; asleep, she was unquestionably more tolerable than awake.

He was hidden behind the massive cowled cradle, lost in an excess of sheer panoply. No one saw him. No one shooed him out.

So many women clustered around his mother. "Your Grace, a moment longer—" one of them said; from long familiarity, her tone chided gently.

"A moment longer, and I shall expire from the sheer *weight* of this nonsense. Alizia, take care! If you stab another pin in like that, you will surely break open my skull!"

Alizia murmured apology, tending the hair more carefully, and the skull beneath.

"Better—eiha, I would sooner avoid this altogether . . . I would sooner spend my time with little Cossimia at my breast instead of witnessing her held aloft like sweetmeats from the beast most recently killed—Teressita, what did I say of those laces? I am no longer so young as I once was, and my waist will not *go* so small . . ." And then the tone changed from fretful exasperation to grim recrimination. "What would he think of *her* if she bore four children? Would he find *her* so attractive when she is like to burst with the fruit of his seed? Would he praise her extravagantly for the narrowness of her waist after bearing four children?" And then the tone altered again. "Eiha, what does it matter? Men are men. Let him keep his Serrano delicacy . . . let him feast on her until his teeth rot! It is I who have given him a son, and it is *I* who shall be painted as the woman at his side—although I should insist that someone other than Zaragosa Serrano do it! Matra Dolcha, but men are blind. Does he not see that Serrano will paint me plain?"

Alizia spoke first. "You are not plain, Your Grace!"

"Nor am I the Lord Limner's sister," the Duchess snapped. "It serves him better to spend his meager talents on his sister's image than on mine."

Teressita was matter-of-fact. "He will cast her off, Your Grace. You, he will never renounce."

"Not so long as I bear him children—*Alejandro!* Matra ei Filho!"

He was seen. She had turned to look at the cradle, at the daughter who was to be formally named within the hour, and he was seen.

"Alejandro—" She was there in a rustle of cloth, trailing streamers of ribbons and unpinned tendrils of hair. "Oh, Alejandro . . ." She smelled of powder and scent. He did not know what beauty was, but he could not conceive that any woman might be considered more beautiful than his mother. She was—his *mother.* "I am sorry you heard that. But you will know it yourself, one day, when you are Duke." Her eyes, so large and dark, were sad. "Shall I tell you the truth, then? Shall you know it so soon?"

Alizia said, "Your Grace, there is little time."

His mother did not even so much as glance back at them. "There is always time for my son. As for this—eiha, but he must know it one day." She sighed, managing a smile for him as she knelt down amidst fantastical robes, fine linens, gem-crusted, gold-tipped ribbons; the murmured regret of all her women. "It comes with our state, you see. A man marries a woman not for love, but for the agreements of the families, for the politics of the times . . ." Her hands were on his shoulders, gripping firmly. "But no matter what else may happen—no *matter* what else!—he will always be your father, and I will always be your mother."

In a tight little voice he asked, "Always?"

"Always," she declared. "Marria do'Fantome, the 'shadow marriage,' is undertaken in most unions, Alejandro, when practicality and politics guide the match instead of love."

It was the first time she had ever spoken to him as an adult. It made him proud. It made him stand up a little taller. "Why?" he asked. "Why must it be so?"

"Because the Matra ei Filho blessed us in the womb, Alejandro, and conceived that we would be of the highest born. Your Patro rules, and one day *you* shall rule. We are not given the freedom of choice."

"But if we rule—?"

Her smile matched her eyes: infinitely sad. "One must make sacrifices for family, for country. So will you, one day."

"You don't love Patro?"

The Duchess sighed. For a moment he thought she might cry, but instead she firmed her lips. "As much," she said, "as I am permitted."

It made no sense. He was a child again, unschooled in the language, the emotions, of adulthood. "Patro doesn't love you?"

Her hands stilled upon his shoulders. "As much as he permits himself." She touched his hair then, stroking untamed curls, gentling them with fingers. "But never, ever question if we love you. Of course we do. I swear that to you by the Matra ei Filho." She kissed fingertips, then pressed them to her heart.

He looked at the silk-and-lace bundle in the cradle. "And—her? Even so small and smelly?"

His mother laughed. He rejoiced to see and hear it, though there was no explanation; his question was not, he considered, meant to amuse. "As she is small and smelly, so were you once. And yes, we love her also."

Alejandro looked away from his sister to the woman who had borne them both. "When I marry, I will marry whom I wish."

Amusement fled. The spark of her smile, the warmth of her eyes, faded. "So you may believe."

"I *will.*"

Her fingers, cradling his face, were cool. She bent, pressed soft lips against his brow. "I hope it may be so."

How could it not? He would be Duke. *The* Duke of Tira Virte.

"Pray for it," his mother murmured, then rose, rustling, and turned to her women, pressing the flat of her hand against her belly. "Tighten the laces," she said. "He must see me as I was, not as I am . . . and so must all the Courtfolk. So must the Lord Limner. I will not have them say of the *Peintraddo Natalia* done for my lovely little Doña that her mother the Duchess is *fat!*"

Sario watched, mute, as Saavedra made the world right again; as right as it ever could be, for those who had witnessed atrocity.

In the Crechetta there was little light save what they brought to it in a single clay candle-cup. It was an interior chamber, washed with an ocherous finish as opposed to white paint as was the Galerria, so that in the light Saavedra carried, small, insignificant cup of wax and flame, the room glowed amber and ivory, with the faintest sheen of tarnished gilt. Wavering shadows made the chamber stark, shaped of few appointments: the iron candle-stand, the plain wooden chair, the cloth-draped easel.

And the self-portrait, the *Peintraddo Chieva,* of Tomaz Grijalva.

It yet stood upon the easel. Saavedra drew in an audible breath and pulled the cloth back, freeing the image from its brocade shielding.

Sario indeed had burned the painting, but poorly: a charred hole marred the center of the canvas, encompassing Tomaz's breast, but no more. He had not destroyed the entire painting.

"Matra Dolcha," Saavedra murmured. "Oh, Sweet Mother—" Her fingers, holding cloth, trembled.

"I couldn't," he said. "I thought someone might smell it . . . might come. I grew frightened, and put it out."

She moved, releasing brocade. Now she stood before the easel, studying the painting. He saw the tautness of the flesh stretched over the bones of her face, the pallor, the stillness in her features, the bloodlessness of her lips as she pressed them together. A tangled mass of black curls fell behind her shoulders, though strands persistently escaped to shadow temples and brow. The quiet light was kind to her; he saw in that moment a promised purity of feature that men would long to paint.

I will paint her—I . . . Of course he would. Who else? Who better?

She murmured beneath her breath, touching fingers to lips, then to heart. Sario looked again at the painting to see as she saw: the masterwork of an artist both gifted and Gifted, the subtleties of brushwork, the expert blending of the colors, the smoothness of the paints so carefully tempered by hand—by *his* hand; the creation of the face, the torso, from nothing but sheer talent, from eye, from Luza do'Orro—and the ability to transform what was seen in a mirror to what bloomed upon the canvas.

Tomaz Grijalva. The likeness was perfect.

As was the ragged hole burned into the torso where a man's heart lived.

Another, looking upon it, cried out aloud of loss, of destruction, innocent of truth. Sario, looking upon it, would cry out silently of nothing but that they might be caught.

"Sario . . ." Saavedra turned great and glittering eyes upon him. "This is the truth, what you have said—"

He inhaled noisily. "Do you think I would *lie?*"

"You have."

"Never to you!"

No. Never to her. She shut her eyes a moment, wet dry lips, murmured again as if seeking strength.

"You saw him," he said. "You saw what became of him. He sat there, *right there,* in that chair—and they painted him crippled! They painted him blind! You saw it, 'Vedra! For yourself; do your own eyes lie?"

She clamped both hands over her mouth.

"Yes," he said, "it made you ill, what you saw. And you question me now?"

"I have to." It came out muffled, until she took her hands away. "I have to, Sario . . . because—because what we saw—"

"—was magic," he finished.

"And what *you* did, burning the hole in the heart—"

"—was also magic."

"Then you . . . then *you*—oh, Matra ei Filho, then you are Gifted as was Tomaz, as all the Viehos Fratos—"

Now he could smile, though it was merely a ghastly stretching of his lips. "Did you ever doubt it?"

"But that means every Gifted male . . ." She turned to the ruined portrait again, whispering prayers repeatedly as she kissed fingertips and pressed them against her heart.

"He told me the truth," Sario said. "And then begged me for release."

"But you don't *know* he's dead!"

He looked at the painting. At his own handiwork. "He said burning would work. That I had no access to the proper paints—but destroying the canvas would work. I think he must be dead."

She drew in a breath. Released it. Drew another, and let it go as well. Then turned to him abruptly. "They must know," she said. "You must go and fetch them."

"Fetch—?" It sent a shiver down his spine. "Who?"

"The Viehos Fratos."

" 'Vedra—"

"They must know. They must come and see." Quietly she set down the cup of flame upon the floor. Then she lifted the portrait from the easel and placed it meticulously upon the candle-cup, so that fire crisped and caught the charred edge of the hole Sario had already burned. "Go," she said.

He stared at her. He watched openmouthed as she struck down

the easel so that it fell across the burning painting. Now the brocade cloth burned as well.

She turned upon him a fierce, singularly fixed glare. Then she opened her mouth and shouted, "Sario! It's *burning*—go and fetch aid!"

He stared at her; at the blazing painting.

"Go," she hissed. And then shouted again, begging aid and forgiveness, and he saw what she meant to do.

Blame herself. For tripping. For knocking the easel over. For burning up the painting in a terrible accident.

Tomaz Grijalva: dead. And now his painting as well.

⸺⊷ FIVE ⊷⸺

Saavedra was given no time, no time at all, not to change clothing to something more appropriate, not to catch her breath, not even to relieve herself. They simply escorted her without deliberation into the private quarters of Raimon Grijalva, one of the Viehos Fratos. And left her there. Alone. Meant to face a man she had never spoken to, nor had been addressed by, ever; his task was the ordering of vital family business, and she was wholly inconsequential.

Or *had* been.

Saavedra, in her contrived rush to put out the flames in the Crechetta, had—in full view of those Sario had summoned—scorched much of her tunic and trousers, and very nearly caught her hair on fire. All in all it had been an immensely successful undertaking: Tomaz's portrait was almost entirely destroyed, with more than enough damage done to account for a death she and Sario were to know nothing of—and she had risked herself in attempting to douse the flames. Surely they would see that, the Viehos Fratos. Surely Aguo Raimon would.

Meanwhile, he was not present. She was left to wait, quite unattended, upon his pleasure—or, perhaps, his *dis*pleasure—and she found the task excruciatingly difficult. Anticipating his words, his disapproval, his punishment, knotted her belly so tightly she feared she might never be able to eat again.

Which might please Sario, because then I would have nothing in my belly to lose!

It was a small room, a solar, built of arched embrasures in one wall so that sunlight was given leave to enter in full measure. The bricks of the wall were handmade, hand-smoothed, chinked together with mortar, then smoothed again by hand, so that one brick was indiscernible from another. And over it all was layered thin clay, the warm sunbright clay that made her spirit soar, that freed it to fly. Colors and textures did that to her, giving release to her mind so she might imagine anything, and, in the imagining, transfer it to hands, to paper, to canvas; even perhaps to a wall still damp with new paint, a fresco of the landscape that lived within her head.

But that landscape now, despite the warmth of the sun-bright clay, was not at ease; was freed only to imagine the worst of possible punishments.

It was a room for relaxation, filled with soothing patterns and colors: a high-backed wooden chair, cushioned in rich sienna-hued velurro; a stool for Aguo Raimon's feet; a table with books upon it, and a pot holding summer blooms; fine-loomed rugs upon the floor and intricate tapestries on the walls, depending from iron rods and ornate brackets.

A room for the taking of one's ease, not for punishment—and yet she could not divorce her mind from that despite the soothing surroundings. Beauty could calm, but also kill, as was proved by the destruction of Tomaz's self-portrait.

Saavedra fidgeted. *He will have been told how I tried to put out the fire. Surely he will see what I risked to repair my transgression.*

But Aguo Raimon, stepping into the small solar from a chamber beyond, did not in any way suggest by expression or posture that he saw anything of what she had risked. And she recalled that to them, to the Viehos Fratos, the destruction of the painting destroyed also a life. A punished Grijalva, a disciplined man, but now a dead man.

She shivered. *I wish Sario were here.* With him present, she would think to protect him, and it was far easier to answer in defense of another than to defend herself.

But he was not present. They had taken him elsewhere, and now it was her task to explain without hesitation—or with only the proper hesitation—how she had come to burn a painting that was to have been unknown to her. Despite the chamber's name, women were not permitted in the Crechetta.

Show him no fear. Let him suspect nothing beyond the obvious: you went where you were not meant to go, and you caused an accident. Accordingly she raised her chin and let the man look at her, even as she looked at him.

Aguo Raimon wore black velurro, wholly unadorned save for the slender chain of gold around his collar. Saavedra followed the line of the fragile links and sought its ornament at mid-chest: the Golden Key of his family, and hers. A small Chieva, withal, though intricately made; on her it would be too large, but Raimon Grijalva was not a small man. The leonine mane of dark hair that flowed back against his shoulders sprang vigorously from his scalp; he was a young, vital, active man, renowned for quiet fairness as well as talent.

And abruptly she knew this man was due honesty, insofar as she dared it. "Forgive me!" she cried, falling to her knees. "In Their Blessed Names, I beg your forgiveness!" The floor was carpeted, but the stone beneath was hard on the bones of her knees. Saavedra clasped her hands against her breast and bowed her head. "Matra ei Filho, I never meant it to happen . . . I only went—I only went because—because—" She drew in a noisy breath. "—beçause it was forbidden. I admit it." She did not permit herself to raise her eyes, to see the man's expression. "Aguo, I beg you—I *swear* to you—it was not intended!"

"You have done a great wrong, Saavedra," he said very quietly.

"Yes—eiha, *yes,* I know—oh, Aguo, I swear I never meant for the painting to be endangered—"

"Far more than the painting was endangered, Saavedra. Far more than the painting was destroyed."

She clamped her mouth tight on further pleas. Did he know what they knew, she and Sario? Did he know the truth of what they had intended?

"Discipline," he said.

Her mind turned inside out, frantic with implications. Did he mean the Chieva do'Sangua? Surely not. He would not admit it to her. He would never say that her actions had also killed a man as well as his *Peintraddo Chieva.*

"Discipline," he repeated. "The erosion of which could destroy our family as the Nerro Lingua so nearly did." His tone softened. "Rise, Saavedra. I am not Premio Sancto to hear your confession and absolve you of this. I am merely a Grijalva."

"And Il Aguo," she murmured.

"I have that honor, yes . . . Saavedra, rise. I would have you look at me."

Trembling, she rose. She met his eyes—gray, like her own—and nearly quailed. His features were severe for his age, but his eyes were not. She saw something in them very like compassion.

"I was your age once," he said. "I went where I was not to go, as you did. No one knew it, and thus I was not punished; but neither did I destroy a painting out of sheer clumsiness."

"I tried to stop it," she murmured. "I did—but I was too late."

"Paintings burn too quickly to save, once touched by flame," he said. "It's one of the reasons we take such care of our work, Saavedra . . . you are fortunate you did not burn yourself as well."

"That wouldn't matter," she said, and then blurted out a purposeful falsehood. "Tomaz may paint another, may he not? I mean—I know it won't be the same, not exactly the same, but he is a very gifted painter, Tomaz is—could he not paint another?"

Severity and humor, so at odds with one another, were instantly banished. She saw in his eyes an acknowledgment he could not make to her: what was destroyed was far more than a painting, and could never be replaced.

"Indeed," he said with an undertone of dryness, "it could never be the same."

"Does he know?" she asked quickly. "Has anyone told Tomaz? Eiha, he will hate me for this . . ." Saavedra scrambled to summon the proper tone, to obfuscate what she knew with what she might otherwise believe. "And he has the right! It was a beautiful painting!"

"A masterwork," Raimon Grijalva confirmed. "A self-portrait is required of all young men who would be acknowledged as Gifted."

"Does he know yet?" she asked.

Il Aguo's expression was stark. "I think there is no way Tomaz could *not* know," he answered precisely. "But—you need have no fear of repercussion. There will be no punishment by Tomaz."

"But he would have the right!"

"He would, yes. But—" He made a brief gesture. "Saavedra, it is of no consequence."

"No consequence!" She was appalled; she had to be, did she not? She knew the truth of the *Peintraddo Chieva,* but he did not know that. *I must pretend I am thinking only of Tomaz, and what he would think of me for having destroyed his painting. . . .* "Of course there is consequence! Look what I have done!"

"Look what you have done," Il Aguo said. "Indeed. And I think you know."

It took effort to keep from blurting out the wrong thing, to concentrate so tightly on what she *should* know, not what she did. "You will punish me," she said hollowly.

"Of course," he answered. "You abrogated proper compordotta." Exacting and perfect behavior, as defined by the Viehos Fratos for the family.

Her mouth was dry. "What am I to do?"

"Not what you are to do, Saavedra . . . what you are *not* to do."

"Not—?"

"You are forbidden Sario's company for one year."

It shocked her. "A *year?*"

"One whole year."

"But—" This was wholly unexpected, and as painful. "Aguo," she said faintly, admitting to him what she would not admit to others, not even to Sario, who probably knew, "he is my only friend."

"I know that. As the painting was Tomaz's only self-portrait of any consequence."

Even in the midst of anguish, she grasped at subterfuge. "He can paint another, Aguo!"

"No," he said. "He cannot."

Of course he could not. Dead men painted nothing. But she clung to dissimulation. "Not another just like it, perhaps, but another to take its place."

"No, Saavedra. Such things are painted only once. That is what gives them consequence."

That, and whatever magic was in them. Saavedra bit into her lip. "Then I am to be exiled in my own home?"

"You are forbidden only Sario's company. You will see him, of course—that can hardly be avoided within Palasso Grijalva—but you will not be permitted to speak to one another, or spend time together other than in the classes you take together. And, as to that—" He smiled briefly, "—it has been brought to my attention that you have much skill for a young woman, Saavedra. And you are of an age when those of us responsible for such things begin to consider which young men and women shall be matched according to talent."

A wave of heat coursed through her flesh. Saavedra said nothing.

"He has led you astray, our little Neosso Irrado . . . do you believe we are blind? You are a good girl, Saavedra, but too trusting of Sario's intentions. You permit him to lead you into improper compordotta, when he would do better to follow *your* example. Do not think we have no understanding that it was he who led you into the Crechetta—it is not in you to do that which is forbidden."

This left her speechless, though her mind worked frantically.

"Poor company," Raimon Grijalva said, "may mislead even the elect."

She no longer thought of herself, of what she had done, only of what Sario might be. "But—he's not truly bad, Aguo! He is Gifted, I know it!"

"Your loyalty does you credit, Saavedra."

"It's more than that, Aguo." She surprised herself with her certainty, but it was so powerful she could not suppress it. "He's different, Aguo Raimon. He's *more* than everyone else."

His expression now was curiously blank. "How do you know this?"

"I feel it," she answered. "I just know it, Aguo. It's here in my heart." Saavedra touched her breast. "He never was like anyone else, right from the beginning. And they know it. It's why they treat him so badly, why they taunt him, mock him, try to make him feel small . . . because they sense it in him, too, Aguo. He can be everything they long to be, but know in their souls they can't be. It's the true-talent, Aguo, but also the spirit." She looked for understanding in the quiet eyes. "There are those of us who dream, who long to be the best ever; and those of us to whom it *isn't* a dream, but something that will be attained. Something that must be." Saavedra sighed a little. "They are jealous of him, Aguo. Even the moualimos, who know what he can be. You see—"

A lifted hand silenced her. "Indeed, we do know who is most likely to embody the talent we cherish. But discipline is vital, as is compordotta . . . a gift can only be honestly and effectively wielded for the good of the family when one understands that misuse of it can cause adverse consequences."

Mutely, she nodded; Tomaz had certainly suffered such consequences.

"There are so few of us now, you see—we must safeguard those of us who are left. We dare not permit an angry young man to harm the ordering of the family."

Now she shook her head.

"You will do better apart from him, Saavedra. Let your own talent blossom; rely not so much upon his Luza do'Orro when you claim your own."

It shocked her; he knew of such things?

Raimon Grijalva smiled. "The moualimos are exacting and sometimes impossible to please, but they are also keen observers of talent, Saavedra. You have more than your share of it."

"Not as much as *he* has."

"Sario? Well—perhaps not . . . but without discipline, talent is nothing. If it cannot be controlled, of what use is it?"

They moved away from dangerous topics now and into the philosophy of art itself. She came alive beneath his gaze. "But there is honesty in wildness, Aguo—a painter must also be permitted to let himself run free, to see how far he may allow his talent to carry him."

"Within reason, of course. But without rules, without discipline, all would be wasted."

"But, Aguo, are we not Grijalvas? Are we not free to express ourselves as no other family may?"

"As we do." He smiled. "Do not attempt to divert me, Saavedra . . . I grant you he has talent, and likely is Gifted, as we shall discover soon, but untrained talent may lead one astray from family needs and goals."

"He wants to be Lord Limner," she blurted. "And he *could*. He is good enough! Would you deny the Grijalvas the opportunity to replace a Serrano with one of us, merely because he is occasionally wild?"

" 'Occasionally,' Saavedra?"

"He chafes, Aguo, as surely you must have chafed! You said you were young once, and went where you were forbidden . . . do you see where it has led you? You are a Grand Master, one of the most renowned limners of the family—it should have been *you* named to Guilbarro Serrano's place instead of his modestly-talented graffiti-crafter of a son!"

He was very quiet for a long moment as she recollected who she was, and who he was. "You truly believe Sario is that talented?"

"I think he is capable of painting anything! Of *becoming* anything!"

He nodded, eyes hooded obliquely. "Yes, it may be so." One hand clasped the Golden Key depending from its chain. "It may indeed be so. Well, we are finished, you and I—you have been given your punishment. Now go and wash and change your clothes—be certain you have not burned yourself, Saavedra—and remember that this 'exile,' as you call it, is to last a year. There will be no mitigation of my decision."

"No, Aguo."

He kissed his fingers, which contained the key, then pressed them against his heart. "In Their Blessed Names, I declare you dismissed."

Though she wore no key, Saavedra mimicked his motion. In silence—he would tolerate no more protestations—she turned and left the solar. *I need to tell Sario*— And then she comprehended the full magnitude and exquisite appropriateness of her punishment.

"Matra Dolcha," she murmured, full of painful tears, "if you can hasten time, I beg you do it now!"

Raimon Grijalva turned as the man entered the solar. He immediately gestured to the high-backed, cushioned chair, but the other shook his head slightly and instead moved to one of the deep-cut windows. His back was to Raimon.

"Yes," the other said thoughtfully, "I do see it now. You were correct to have me come."

"Premio Frato," Raimon acknowledged.

"She could become as important to our plans as the boy himself." He turned then and faced Raimon. "I think there is no doubt now that it is the Tza'ab blood. There was always talent in our family, but this is different. This is—more. There have been changes in our talent, in our blood."

"The genealogies suggest the Tza'ab blood is a factor, but nothing was noted until after the Nerro Lingua," Raimon said.

The other gestured. "It is possible, of course, but we must also remember that the Nerro Lingua itself played havoc with our record keeping. I will not discount it, but it may simply be that the changes were not recorded in the aftermath of the plague. There was so much to do."

"Of course." Raimon tended the chain against his doublet. "Will you have wine, Premio Frato?"

"Perhaps later." The older man, the First Brother among the Viehos Fratos, was craggy of feature, bold of bone. He turned again so that the light from the window painted half his face. "I have studied the girl's portfolio. She shows astonishing promise. And you say she is thirteen?"

"Twelve, Premio Arturro."

"Twelve. Well, we have time, but not so much that we must dawdle." Arturro Grijalva smiled. "And as clever with her tongue as with her hands."

Raimon's mouth hooked briefly in an ironic slant. "As clever in her own way as the boy."

Arturro sighed. "Our little Neosso Irrado . . . well, we shall have to take him in hand. Tomaz was unfortunate—particularly in what happened with the *Peintraddo Chieva!*—but Sario may well offer more trouble than even Tomaz. He is Gifted as the girl believes, as well as insatiably ambitious far beyond his age. He is not truly a boy, but a mixture of boy and man—and is therefore dangerous."

"Why is it," Raimon began, "that the ones with the most talent lack self-discipline?"

"As well you should ask, Raimon!" But Arturro softened it with a fond smile. "I begin to think it is a requirement, an aspect of the Gift itself . . . those boys who are *too* dedicated to following every rule exhibit nothing more than adequate ability. They question nothing, and therefore never challenge themselves, never challenge their talent."

"And the Gift?"

The Premio Frato's expression tautened. "That, too. And that is why this boy may well be dangerous. It is a fine line, Raimon, the Gift and self-control . . . he must be let off the lead to develop the talent, to challenge and thus extend it, but he must not be loosed so long that he does not come back to the hand."

"As I came back," Raimon said ironically.

Arturro's smile was sweet. "Eiha, you came back!—and were justly rewarded for it."

"And Sario?"

The older man touched his Chieva. "He must be watched, Raimon. He must be closely watched. One can see the hunger in his eyes, the transcendence of his Light—and also a little fear." He sighed. "There is so much at stake now . . . we have labored so long to restore the family, and now that we have the Gift. . ." Arturro's face was troubled. "It is such a slow process, this reestablishment of the family, but we dare not hasten it. We dare not let the do'Verradas suspect what the true nature of the Gift is."

"There are whispers already," Raimon said quietly. "The Serranos suspect."

"Let them. They are . . . 'modestly-talented graffiti-crafters.' " Arturro's amused expression acknowledged Saavedra's accuracy. "We have the protection of the do'Verradas, and that is no small thing . . . so long as the ducal family suspects nothing of the Gift, we shall be safe."

"Zaragosa Serrano has the Duke's ear."

"And the sister, Gitanna, has more than the Duke's *ear.*" Despite the statement's questionable taste, it was fact; Arturro did not shirk the unmitigated baldness of his observation. "But Baltran do'Verrada values her for something other than cleverness, even if such were said of her; and Zaragosa is a fool, a witless moronno who takes more pleasure in his fundamentally tasteless addiction to lurid color than in the intricacies true art requires . . . no, he is no threat. I think the boy poses more threat than any Serrano."

"And he a Grijalva," Raimon murmured.

"But that is how it must be. Now. We are—not what we once were." Arturro closed one hand around the Golden Key depending from his collar. "We must be very careful with Sario. Eiha, but he is a prodigy, yes?—and although we require that hunger in order to bring the Gift to life, it must be carefully controlled. As he must be."

" 'The seed of our destruction lies within our own loins,' " Raimon quoted.

The Premio Frato sighed. "And in our prodigious talent. Well— let it be so. We were not made to rule, we Grijalvas; too much has befallen us even if we were in a position to take Tira Virte for our own. There is the Tza'ab 'taint' the Ecclesia has called damnation, the brevity of our life span, the weakness of our seed. No, it shall never be our task to take Tira Virte, to rule it, but to enlighten, to educate, to entertain . . . and certainly to guide the *prospects* of our country. Quietly. Subtly. Wisely."

"Matra ei Filho willing."

"Indeed," Arturro said, fingertips to lips, to heart. "As I think They must be, to let us come so far."

SIX

Gitanna Serrano, lingering contentedly at midday in the central zocalo with tumbling fountain spray lightly bathing her upturned face, was startled out of her reverie as her elbow was roughly grasped. She fired up to shout her outrage—how dare anyone lay hands on the Duke's mistress?—but caught it back unspoken as she recognized her brother. "Zaragosa! What?"

With much haste and far less gentleness, he pulled her away from the fountain. "We have to talk."

"Must you *drag* me?" She righted herself on uneven cobbles. "Matra Dolcha, 'Gosa, people are beginning to stare!"

"Let them." He ushered her briskly across the cobbled zocalo into one of Meya Suerta's innumerable shrines. "What we have to discuss cannot be heard by others."

She hissed as the carved and studded wooden door banged into a shoulder; he had misjudged its weight. "Well, you have certainly ensured they will *try*—Zaragosa! What is so important that you must be so rough?"

The door dismissed, he pushed her around the corner into one of the tiny niches containing an icon. Gilt paint glowed in muted sunlight let in through shuttered windows and the thin illumination of fat, scented candles set out in clay cups, upon wood and iron racks. "Bassda, Gitanna!" He glanced around quickly. There was no one in earshot. "Listen to me!"

There was little else she could do; accordingly, she listened. At first she was hard-pressed to give him the attention he so blatantly craved—she was angered by his rude handling of her—but she let the resentment go as she heard him out.

When at last he finished, she sighed prodigiously. "Eiha, I have tried," she told him, letting the wall prop up her spine. "I have, 'Gosa, but the Duke can be stubborn. You know that."

"He dismisses me too easily," Zaragosa said. "He sends me off to paint yet another family portrait, complaining that I meddle in what does not concern me."

"You!" She rearranged the pearl-freighted silken scarf draped around her shoulders. "At least you he sends to paint! Me he sends off to bed, telling me not to worry my pretty little head about such things as politics." She glared at the icon; the serene expression of the painted Matra was an offense to their very real concerns. "I have tried to cajole him, to tease him, to make him swear in the midst of bedplay, but he refuses. He claims the Ducal Protection is inviolable."

"It is not," Zaragosa retorted. "But one needs *proof* to make him understand what we're facing."

Gitanna pulled away from him and walked to the small table on which the icon stood. Dried flowers bedecked the embroidered cloth, faded blooms left by someone asking intercession of the Mother; this was Her little shrine, not Her Son's. "How are we to find proof?" Gitanna demanded, swinging back. "We are not Grijalvas to walk unmolested into their Palasso. They are insular, secretive—they take great pains to keep themselves private from others, so no one realizes the scope of what they intend."

"Infamy," he said. "They will bring down to the do'Verradas so *they* may claim the duchy."

"Well," she said grimly, "so long as we Serranos retain our places at Court, they will not gain a foothold. You must paint whatever he wishes you to paint, 'Gosa . . . you must keep his favor."

That sat ill with him. "And you as well, Gitanna!"

"Yes," she agreed calmly, "I as well. But you as Court Limner know more security than a Duke's mistress; me he may replace at any time, on any whim, but unless illness carries you off, he cannot replace you. Only Alejandro may appoint another Court Limner, when he becomes Duke in his father's place."

"An odd boy," Zaragosa said, chewing idly on a thumbnail as he leaned a padded shoulder against the hand-smoothed wall.

"Odd or not, you should befriend him," Gitanna suggested. "I can do nothing—my only power is in Baltran's bed, but you have the freedom of the Palasso. You hold the Duke's favor."

"But not the Duchess's" he said grimly, words distorted by the thumb still at his teeth.

"Does that matter? You were Baltran's appointee, not hers. She has no power."

"Beyond bearing heirs."

Gitanna grimaced. "Well, I was never promised anything more than what I have. If I bear him children, they will be bastards. He has his heir in Alejandro—"

"—who will decide if a Serrano shall replace me, or someone of another family."

"Then make certain *only* a Serrano may replace you," she said. "We cannot let those cursed chi'patro Grijalvas steal our place

from us. Befriend Alejandro, 'Gosa. Prove to him we are his allies
in all things."

"He is but a boy, Gitanna! Would you have me waste my days on
a feckless child?"

"Eiha, you are a fool sometimes, 'Gosa! Don't you understand?
It is an investment, this 'wasting' of days! He will be Duke one day
. . . and if you are his friend, he will naturally look to someone else
of our family when the time comes that a new Court Limner is appointed."

Color flared in his thin face. "You mean when I am dead!"

"Well," she said matter-of-factly, "you *will* die, one day, or become disabled by age. Why deny it? Find a solution, 'Gosa. Do you
think my time as the ducal mistress will last forever? Matra
Dolcha, no! My time is limited, and I accept it . . . he will not keep
me as long as he keeps you."

He had stripped one thumb of nail; now he proceeded to the
other. "I don't know, Gitanna . . ."

Frustration clamped her teeth shut tightly. He was too shortsighted to fully understand the ramifications of what they needed to
do, lest they suffer for its lack of success. "Coddle the boy," she
said. "Earn his trust, his affection. Make yourself indispensable to
him."

"What could I be to a ten-year-old child?"

" 'Gosa," she declared without leavening her disdain, "for a man
who paints for a living you have an astonishing lack of imagination."

It stung, as she intended. "Matra Dolcha, Gitanna—"

"Think," she said plainly. "Think it through. Paint yourself a
portrait, 'Gosa. Surely you can do that."

He glared at her, mutilated thumbs forgotten. "If this is how you
speak to the Duke, it is no wonder he believes you fit only for bedplay!"

"Bassda," she said wearily. "Go back to the Palasso and think on
what I have said. We have presented it to Baltran in a straightforward manner, and we have failed. It is time for us to try another
way."

"He wants *proof.*"

"Then we shall have to find it," Gitanna said calmly. "Or manu-
facture it."

Saavedra stopped in the corridor before the narrow door of her tiny
estuda's cell. Beyond it lay her private world where she called her

own such things as a bed, a chest containing clothing, a table and stool before the deep-cut window. Little more, save for the necessities: a basin and ewer, a night pot behind a screen. And imagination.

The family believed that privation fed inspiration, that absolute privacy was necessary so that solitude encouraged exploration among the tools at her beck, such things as an understanding of proportion, the way the body fit together in the bending of a wrist, the way a corridor appeared broad at the near end but small at the far. There were classes to teach such things, but solitude refined it; a person left alone often created a world within the mind, and the artist put it to paper, to canvas, brought to life what was not real with such power as paint and chalk.

There were, of course, Grijalvas who did not exhibit the true-talent, who were no more than adequate; even those who lacked all artistic talent. Such persons were not condemned for this lack—the Matra did not bless everyone—but neither were they trained the way those who exhibited talent were. Saavedra was.

She had told Aguo Raimon the truth: Sario was her only friend. He had done her the courtesy of not telling her to find another, and for that she was grateful. Perhaps it was because he understood. He was after all a Grijalva, talented, Gifted—and he knew how the family was run. It was a city within the city, a smaller Meya Suerta that did not claim a Duke save for those men who by consensus had the ordering of the family "city." Palasso Grijalva, the sprawling cluster of conjoined buildings fed by the blood of its people moving through corridors and courtyards, was a duchy in and of itself. The Grijalvas honored the do'Verradas in all ways—many of them had died for the do'Verradas—but they conducted family business independently, in perfect privacy.

And now in the midst of that privacy, that solitude, she would be punished for a transgression the depths of which even the Viehos Fratos did not know. Yes, she had burned the painting; that of itself was worthy of punishment. But she had also aided Sario, who had committed murder.

The latch rattled as she put her hand on it. She was free this hour, free the rest of the day. She supposed she could go to one of the family galerrias and study the works of her ancestors, supposed she could go out of doors into one of the courtyards, or even into the cobbled zocalo that bound all the guild quarters together, but she did not wish it. She would instead go into her tiny room and think over what had occurred, and what it meant for the future.

And so she went in, aware of a painful loneliness, and found Sario there.

"Matra Dolcha!" She slammed the door shut at once and leaned against it, as if to keep out anyone who might discover them together. "What are you doing here?"

He stood in the corner near the hinges—a slight, thin-faced boy—so the open door would hide him should anyone else inhabit the corridor. But the door was closed now, and Sario safe; he left the corner and came out into the cell, fidgeting, pulling threads from the hemming of the pocket of his tunic. "What did they say?" he asked.

She was shocked to see him, but shock wore off and was replaced by relief; she could share with him now what was required of her. "We are denied one another's company for a year."

Color faded. "They can't *do* that!"

"Oh, Sario, of course they can." Depressed, Saavedra sat down on her narrow cot. "They have the ordering of our lives from birth to death—they can do whatever they wish. And *will* do it, if they find you here." She eyed his nervousness; it was unlike him to seem so tentative. "Did they speak to you?"

"Not yet." A lock of hair obscured his eyes; he shook it back impatiently. "They will, but they don't know where I am. They can't come get me if they don't know where I am."

"But they will," she countered reasonably; he never saw beyond what he so badly wanted to see. "If you are nowhere else, they will look for you here."

He swore beneath his breath. "Then I will say what I've come to say." He reached into his pocket and tugged forth a folded paper. "I've written it down. Here."

She took the proffered paper, unfolded it, flattened it, examined it. "What is it?"

"A recipe," he said tautly.

"A *recipe?*" Had he gone entirely mad?

"Tomaz told it to me."

She frowned. "But—for what? These ingredients make no sense. They are not for cooking, nor are they for paints."

"They do make sense," he said steadily, "if you have read far enough in the *Folio*."

She nearly crumpled the paper. "Sario, I'm not permitted to read the *Folio*."

"But I have. Some of it." He sat down next to her on the edge of the cot, leaning close to indicate the words scribbled hastily on the tattered paper. "These are nonsense words meant to mislead anyone who should come across them. But I know the secret to them. Tomaz told me how it was done, and this is the recipe."

She was still at a loss. "I don't understand, Sario. Why are you showing this to me?"

He inhaled quickly, noisily, then let the words come too rapidly for sense. "Because—because I want someone to know. I *need* you to know, 'Vedra, before I begin."

"Begin?" she asked suspiciously. "Sario, what are you up to now?"

His face was drawn, tense. Even though he clasped his hands tightly, she saw the minute trembling. "I must do something, 'Vedra. I have to. Tomaz was made to be a victim because he never understood what the *Peintraddo Chieva* was—until it was too late."

Neither did she. "But you do."

"I do. Now. And so I must do this—"

"Sario—"

"—to keep them from killing me."

"*Killing* you! Sario—are you mad? Who would wish to kill you? Why?"

"Neosso Irrado," he whispered.

"Oh, no . . . this is mad, Sario—"

"That is what they call me. Neosso Irrado."

Saavedra managed a laugh, albeit weakly framed. "Because you are frustrating, Sario. You break rules, talk back, question everything, refuse to do what you are asked—"

"Just like Tomaz:"

It drove her into silence. Saavedra stared at the paper, at the list of nonsense words, trying to understand the cause of Sario's fear. And fear it was; but augmented by a peculiar determination. He would do it. Whatever it was, he would do it. She knew of no one as willing as he to risk a very real danger.

"What is it?" she asked sharply. "What is the *Peintraddo Chieva* but a self-portrait?"

Sario's mouth jerked briefly. "A means of control," he answered. "A *secret* means. What we saw, you and I, above the Crechetta."

Saavedra remembered all too vividly what they had seen above the Crechetta.

"Punishment," he said tautly, "for troubling them. For improper compordotta. For being—Neosso Irrado."

"Oh, no—"

"Tomaz was Neosso Irrado."

It seemed an obvious answer. "Then don't *you* be!" she cried.

His face was pinched. "I can't stop, 'Vedra. I can't help myself."

"You can! Just *stop.* Don't talk back, don't question everything, don't break rules, accept the compordotta—"

"Don't you see? When it doesn't make sense, what they ask; or when I see another way, a *better* way, I have to tell them! I can't ignore what is obvious to me, even if no one else sees it . . . it would be dishonest. It would dishonor my talent. You know that! You *know* that!"

She knew that. She had felt it herself.

"They will blind me," he said, "as they blinded Tomaz. They will cripple my talent as they crippled his hands."

She had seen it done. "Sario—"

"I have to do this, don't you see?—so I may prevent them. Tomaz told me the way, though he couldn't realize it." He hitched a thin shoulder. "He told me how he painted his self-portrait, the ingredients he used . . . but he painted in ignorance. I will not."

Her mouth was dry. "How, Sario? How can you prevent the Viehos Fratos from doing whatever they wish to do?"

"By outwitting them," he said. "I am young yet, too young, but surely they will test me soon. Surely they will discover that my seed is infertile, and then they will know; it is only the final proof, 'Vedra . . . everything else is known. It lives here, in my soul." He touched his breast. "You know I am Gifted."

"Yes," she said rustily. "I have always known."

"And thus I am at risk. I must be what I am meant to be, because it lives inside me—but they wish to control it. And that is how they used the *Peintraddo Chieva.*"

Her breath ran shallow. "What is altered in the self-portrait is visited on the body."

"Yes."

She had seen it. Had watched them do it, the Viehos Fratos in the private Crechetta: carefully, meticulously, with surpassing skill they had painted the portrait blind, crippled—and so did Tomaz become. Sario had injured the painting—and so had Tomaz become.

"Matra," she whispered, pressing a trembling hand against her lips. "Matra ei Filho . . ."

"I will paint them their painting," he told her. "I will do as they tell me to do. I will give them a *Peintraddo Chieva*—but it will not be the first one. It will not be the only one. It will not be the *real* one. That, I will keep. That, I will lock away. And only you, and only I, shall know the truth of it."

SEVEN

Meya Suerta was a city of many faces, of many hearts. Which face one saw, which heart one touched, was determined by such predictable things as birth, as craft, as gift, as beauty—and certainly as wealth. But the true soul of the city lay in its *un*predictability, and the turgid flow of lifeblood within its people; even within those born elsewhere, strangers to Tira Virte, save they lived in her now, died, and were buried in her soil, blessed in their passing by the Matra ei Filho.

The old man did not wish to die in Tira Virte; did not wish to be buried in her soil; did not wish to be blessed by the Mother or Her Son. His own God was male, whose seed was plentiful, and whose sons were many. And the grace of whom the old man knew he claimed; his God was not so fickle as to deny blessings to the unborn or the newly born, the children who were taken before adulthood. He understood much about Tira Virte, and little. For all he had lived in her lands, in her cities—and now in the city itself—for half of his long life, Meya Suerta was a stranger to him in all the ways that counted.

Not cruel, save in that she could not understand what he was. Not angry, in that she punished him. And neither was she indifferent; he earned a decent wage. But she was not Tza'ab Rih.

But in truth, what was? Tza'ab Rih as he had known it was fallen, brought down by a series of calamitous events engendered, he supposed, by what some undoubtedly termed the follies of a religious madman; but to this man here, this aged man, such opinions were the follies, and nothing short of blasphemy.

How could no one see it? These lands had belonged to Tza'ab Rih. No one of any wit at all could fault a realm for wishing to keep what it once had, nor for trying to recover what had been lost over time, when incursions from others—from those who began to call themselves Tira Virteians for the bounty of their green land—were subtle, when incursions were viewed as nothing more than a family wishing to make a living, to shape a life.

But too many had come. Too many had settled. Too many lives were not of Tza'ab Rih. They spoke of the Mother and the Son in place of Acuyib, and so the Diviner, the Most Holy, the Lord of the

Golden Wind, had sought wisdom from the *Kita'ab,* in whose pages the words of the God Acuyib—the only God who mattered—were written.

The old man had seen it. The *Kita'ab*—or its remains. His eyes had been blessed to witness what was revered within his land: the pages of carefully-scribed text bordered and illuminated most extravagantly, with stunning skill, by those who served the Diviner, who in turn served Acuyib.

And Acuyib had said, within the pages of sacred text, that Tza'ab Rih was most blessed of all lands within his dominion, and that it was for his chosen to safeguard its bounties, its peoples, its vast array of the faithful contained within its borders.

Its *borders.*

Thus did the Diviner of the Golden Wind assemble his most select, and train them, and sanctify them in Acuyib's Holy Name, and title them Riders of the Golden Wind, and send them out to reclaim the old borders that others had encroached.

Thus did war begin.

Thus did the *end* begin.

The old man sighed. So many years ago. So many prayers ago. So many deaths ago. And so his Tza'ab Rih was fallen, and now he made his home in the capital city of the victor-by-proxy, many years removed: Baltran do'Verrada, whose ancestors had broken the Diviner's Riders, his city, his heart; and, by employing such devoted and devastatingly effective warriors as Verro Grijalva, destroyed the *Kita'ab.*

He refused to live as Tira Virteians lived. Once, yes, he had; in Tza'ab Rih many of the folk built homes of brick and lived within them, but when the Riders were assembled, luxuries were forbidden until such a time as lost lands were recovered. And so the warriors had caused tents to be made, and learned to live without such roots as others knew: it was wiser, the Diviner said, to ride the Golden Wind than to anchor oneself forever on one small patch of land while others, lacking theirs, left what had been home to live within the cities.

And so they rode the Golden Wind. Horseback, always moving; sleeping in the saddle or in wind-billowed tents.

He had no horse now, and no saddle. But he did own a tent. And he made one small patch of the land now called Tira Virte his own Tza'ab Rih.

Within the tent, the small tent, an old warrior smiled. Then slowly, creakily, abased himself and prayed.

Though others, in the aftermath of calamity—requiring explanation for what was inexplicable—claimed Acuyib a weak God for permitting so much death, and the Diviner a madman, the old Tza'ab was serene. There was reason in all things; one could not question Acuyib and remain faithful. One simply believed, and served.

He believed. One day the prayer would be answered. One day another would come. One day Tza'ab Rih would be born in the breast of a man, even if he be a stranger. Even if he be born in what was now Tira Virte, that once was Tza'ab Rih. From the heart of the enemy would come Acuyib's savior, a second Diviner. So he had seen in the magic, and had come to live among the enemy if not *of* him.

Death might be cleaner than living so, but Acuyib had not decreed it. And so the old man lived as he had lived for decades, secure beyond supposition in the certainty of his faith.

Alejandro scowled. Behind him stood the backdrop: A monstrous drape of purple velurro hemmed with braided gold cord, bedecked with massive tassels. Beyond *that,* albeit muffled, sounded the cacophony of the summer day: the drone of bees tending the scarlet vine blossoms spilling onto the sill of the unshuttered window; the staccato whirring of hummingbirds in competition with bees for nectar; the dueling songs of mockingbirds in complex conversation; the occasional outbreaks of laughter from the gardeners tending the courtyard below.

But where he was, the noise was far more prosaic and therefore wholly tedious: the tuneless humming of Zaragosa Serrano, intermixed with self-satisfied comments to the easel he faced; the scratch of chalk on pebbled, wood-speckled paper; the annoying half-whistle of breath sucked in and blown out between pursed lips.

Behind him, beyond him, the world beckoned. Alejandro fidgeted. He chafed. He felt the burgeoning of impatience that threatened to prove painful unless he found release. He could not be still much longer. He was made to move, not to stand stiffly, unnaturally, so a thin-faced, crimson-clad peacock could make annoying noises.

Alejandro, discommoded, scowled more blackly yet.

This time Serrano, looking up from his sketch, protested, albeit politely. "No—eiha, no, Don Alejandro . . . could you lift your chin again, grazzo?—only a moment longer, en verro . . ."

Alejandro did not lift his chin again. He continued to scowl.

"Grazzo, Don Alejandro—"

But Don Alejandro rejected the plea. "No more," he declared, relaxing from the stiff pose into a natural posture. "You are too slow."

"True art requires time, Don Alejandro—"

"Other artists don't take so long." The boy left the backdrop entirely and arrived to inspect the board on which the Lord Limner sketched his image. He scowled more deeply. "That isn't me."

Zaragosa's chuckle was forced. "Subjects rarely recognize themselves . . . but of course it is you, Don Alejandro. This is but a rough sketch, the merest beginning—"

"It doesn't look anything *like* me."

"Perhaps not precisely, not just yet, but it shall, Don Alejandro—when I begin painting—"

With the definitiveness of youth, Alejandro shook his head. "I've seen Itinerarrios and street artists do better than that."

That stung. Deeply. Zaragosa Serrano colored a deep and most unflattering shade of red much at odds with the crimson of his summer doublet.

Alejandro took careful note of it. "It is *my* face," he pointed out reasonably. "I want it to be correct."

Serrano, outraged, glared. "It *is* correct—have I not said it takes time? Have I not said that this is but the roughest of beginnings? Have I not said that once I begin laying on paint—"

"Yes, yes," Alejandro interrupted, employing his father's ducal impatience—it always got results. "But if it isn't to look like me, why must I stand here for most of the day when I would rather be out there?"

Out there was indicated by a wave of one arm, encompassing the unshuttered window. Summer sunlight poured in, as did temperate air and the sounds of the world beyond. But Zaragosa Serrano had struck Alejandro on many occasions as deaf to all but what he heard inside his head; it was a great jest among the Courtfolk that one could call him every epithet known to the language when he was caught up in his work, and he would merely grunt detached acceptance.

"This is to be your *Peintraddo Natalio*—"

"It won't be my birthday for two months yet."

"Of course, but a great work of art requires *time*—"

Alejandro stared penetratingly at the preliminary sketch a long moment, then shifted his unwavering hazel-eyed stare to the artist. "Even the Courtfolk say you are slow."

Zaragosa Serrano, already red with barely contained frustration, now turned corpse-candle white. Alejandro found it fascinating that mere words could hold such power over a man's skin color.

"They say that?" Serrano's chalk broke in his hand. "They say that?" He tossed down the pieces. "They say that, do they?" Now he snatched up a cloth and threw it haphazardly over the sketch. "Do they say that?"

Alejandro nodded gravely.

"*Filho do'canna!*" The Lord Limner forgot entirely he was not to swear before his Duke's son—who of course knew all the words anyway, having spent time in the kitchens, in the stables, even in the guardroom, where every male born appeared to have intimate knowledge of a wide array of wondrously dramatic invective. "All of them, the pigs and sows . . . they know nothing of greatness, nothing—they spend their hours painting their pox-plagued faces, when they would do better to allow me to paint them on canvas the way they *wish* their flesh to look, each and every one of them—chiros all of them, rooting in filth for the single delicacy of gossip, of intrigue, of political expediency!—while I spend every hour of my day laboring to serve as the Duke wills it . . . what then, are they lacking the stench of human wastes? *Merdittas albas*, are they?" His foot crushed the discarded chalk into the stone floor, grinding it into powder. "What am I but Lord Limner, after all?—*Lord Limner,* appointed by the Duke himself to document the lives of the do'Verradas, the business of the city, the duchy—even of such chiros as those who inhabit the Court . . ." His face now was empurpled. "Do you think it is easy for me? Do you think I find it effortless to spend my days begging and pleading for a nobleborn to 'turn this way, lift your chin, hold the smile just so—ah, no, *this* way, if you please—oh, a moment longer' . . . *bassda!* I am ill-used indeed for my time, my talent. I should paint them all as what they are, and call it *Il Chiros do'Tira Virte* . . . and it should be a masterwork to reflect the truth of this Court!"

Alejandro blinked. "I should like to paint you the way you are this moment. And call it *Il Borrazca.*"

But the storm that inspired Alejandro's title had blown itself out. Now, in its aftermath, a trembling and fearful Lord Limner gathered his inconsequential dignity and took it—and himself—out of the atelierro.

The campaign thus was won, and with little effort expended. Alejandro, grinning, made his escape into the day.

Claiming illness, Sario fasted for two days. He drank nothing but water. On the morning of the third day he rose, collected his urine in a clean receptacle, filled a single glass vial with a portion of the contents, sealed it, set it aside.

The night before, though it was summer, he had lit his brazier. Into an iron pot he had placed small chunks of amber, the resin of trees; now it was melted, ready for use.

He washed his hair in clean rainwater and, while it was still wet, took up a knife and cut a hank from the back of his neck. With infinite care he trimmed the hair so that its shape, density and texture mimicked that of a brush; he then carefully married the trimmed hair to the slender stick of unpolished wood, tied it on with thread, then sealed it with melted resin.

Next he drank an infusion that, within five minutes, drove up his body's temperature alarmingly. Feverish, racked with shudders and tears, he clung stubbornly to two vials and murmured prayers that he had not miscalculated; when within moments he broke out in a rolling sweat, he thanked the Mother and Her Blessed Son and collected both tears and perspiration in the bottles, sealed them, set them aside.

He spat prodigiously into a fourth tiny vial, sealed it as well, put it with the others.

He opened a finger with a heated lancet, counted the dollops of blood as they fell into a tiny bottle, sealed it also.

Urine. Tears. Sweat. Saliva. Blood.

One more fluid to be harvested before he could make the magic work.

His breathing quickened. Quietly he rose and slipped out of his sleeping smock. He looked down at his body: still boyishly slender, lacking the flesh, the muscle, the power of an adult male. But he was a male withal, though young yet, and all of him knew it. Most mornings proved it.

This morning he had not spilled his seed. He found it somewhat annoying; he had been prepared. But now it would require something more than dreams, than imaginings, than unknown instinct crying out for release though he knew little of what it was.

He was virgin still, and would be until sent to the fertile women for Confirmattio. Not for tumbles in dark corners was he; not for secret assignations in the midst of night. Nor were any of them, who might be Gifted. A boy's awakening was very nearly a sacred thing in the Grijalva family, because so much of their livelihood, their survival, depended on it.

If he were fertile, he was not Gifted. If he sired a child, he was nothing but a man. And for such as he, in whose brain and body burgeoned such talent and ambitions, fertile seed would prove his undoing.

What he had done this morning was forbidden; he had not yet undergone Confirmattio, was not yet admitted, not yet permitted such knowledge, such power as what he undertook. But time ran on swiftly, too swiftly; he dared not let it go without accelerating his own grasp upon it, to control it before it controlled him.

Before it controlled him.

For a moment his spirit quailed. What he undertook now was a watershed in his life. If he turned his back on it, rejected it, life went on as it had. If he grasped it, if he accepted the responsibility, life was forever changed.

I'm just a boy, his inner self said.

In boyhood was safety. In mediocrity also. In lack of ambition. In the serene acceptance of one's limitations.

I could be just like everyone else. I could paint, and teach, and maybe sire children, live out my life in peace.

But the Light in his heart, his soul, flared up in conflagration and burned to ash the trepidations. All that remained was the talent, the Light, the hunger.

He stared fixedly at random motes caught upon pale sunlight slanting through warped shutters. "I am Sario Grijalva. I *will* be Lord Limner—because now I know how."

One more fluid to be collected. He was young, but he knew how. His body had taught him.

He need only think of *her.*

◆ EIGHT ◆

Nothing remained in the Grijalva Crechetta to mark what had occurred there five years before, when a young woman's curiosity and clumsiness had killed a man. Much time had passed, and such things were set aside in the daily concerns of the family. What concerned the Viehos Fratos now was also the future of their family, but with controversy attached.

Sario Grijalva, Confirmed, Gifted, one among them now—save for this moment, this meeting—had unexpectedly, inexplicably, established himself as the Limner among them who most promised to become the one they had planned for. And it did not please them.

The Viehos Fratos had divided themselves even before the gathering within the Crechetta. They had in the two years since his Confirmattio come to know Sario as a truly talented as well as remarkably Gifted painter; that was unquestioned. But aside from the talent there was the matter of compordotta: he was not and had never been amenable to control.

Some felt that could be overcome. Some were convinced it provided a pivot point for defiance, for a rebellion that might prove disastrous.

They had argued for hours now, gathered around a linen-bedecked table laden with fruit, comfits, wine, water, crockery bowls of flowers that scented the close air, unleavened by window, in concert with honey-tinged beeswax candles. And yet no conclusion had been reached.

Frato Otavio, sour of expression as well as manner, shook his graying head vigorously. "We dare not," he said; yet again he said it. "There are others."

"Students," Aguo Raimon said very quietly. "Sario is Confirmed . . ."

"Then let it be one of *us,*" Otavio insisted. "I grant you, I am too old, but there are others among us younger—even *you,* Raimon!"

Raimon, seated across from the older man, smiled diffidently. "For that I thank you, Frato Otavio—but I think we have little choice."

"How is that?" interjected black-haired Frato Ferico, at Otavio's left. "There are twenty-one of us here—"

"And there should be a twenty-*second*," Frato Davo interrupted from his place beside Raimon, slapping the flat of his slender hand against the table's surface. "Sario was Confirmed two years ago and accepted into our number. He should be here. Is it fair we decide his future without his presence?"

Otavio muttered beneath his breath, then heaved himself upright in his carved, velurro-cushioned chair. "We aren't deciding his future, Davo. We are *discussing* it—"

Ferico overrode once more. "It still remains there are twenty-one of us, does it not? Eiha, surely we can select one from among those of us present here and now."

"Sario is our youngest," Otavio declared, making it an insult.

Raimon tilted his head in graceful acknowledgment. "Youngest, yes—and perhaps the most Gifted."

Thunderous silence. Then the argument broke out anew.

Raimon sighed. He caught the eye of the Premio Frato and smiled faintly, wryly; Arturro did not smile back, but a glint in his eyes suggested he was not entirely unappreciative of what Raimon had wrought. And then he knocked once upon the table with a knuckle.

The others silenced themselves. Even the most fulsome of them.

Arturro lifted the knuckle, lifted the hand from the table and set it back into his lap. It had hurt to knock the wood, but he did not let it show. It was a necessary discipline he asked of himself, to let no sign betray his increasing infirmity. At nearly fifty he was, by Limner terms, a very old man.

"Who among us has not ever questioned the Viehos Fratos?" he asked. "Who among us has not chafed beneath the demands of such rigid compordotta as we must cleave to? Who among us has not suggested alternatives to what already exists?" He nodded. "We know what we are, and we know what we must do. But in Limners the task is made far more difficult by our greatest handicap: a stunted life span."

There was not an expression among them now that was not wholly still.

Arturro nodded. "Thus, youth should not be decried as disadvantage." That was for Otavio, whose disagreeable face reddened in response. "Our Dukes, the do'Verradas, do not experience the same handicap as we Limners . . . they are long-lived during peacetime, during years without plague, and thus it does not occur to them that the most gifted, those whose talent burns the most brightly, may burn themselves to death—*and that we would willingly do so in service to the duchy.*"

He had them now, even Otavio, Ferico, and Davo, traditionally the most mettlesome of them all. "Baltran do'Verrada is in excellent health. To us, at forty-three, he walks the cusp of death, but to those who are not Limners such age is not so great. We cannot expect Don Alejandro to succeed to the Dukedom any time soon, perhaps not for two decades or more, and thus the one among us who meets our requirements for a candidate *must* be young." He smiled slightly. "I will be dead, of course. So will some of you, certainly Otavio, nearly as old as I, and likely Ferico and Davo as well. Certainly half of our present number, perhaps nearly all . . . perhaps even Raimon, albeit unlikely as he is the youngest save for Sario; nonetheless, even alive, Raimon would be of an age—*for a Limner*—that renders him unlikely to be selected by the new Duke. There is no one in the city who is not aware of our handicap." Indeed, no one in the duchy; it gave their enemies, such as the Serranos, much fuel: weak seed, weak blood, without worth. "Thus our task is to find a younger man whose talent, whose Gift, makes him ideal to succeed Zaragosa Serrano as Lord Limner."

"He is *sixteen*," Otavio objected.

"And in ten years he will not be," Davo countered quickly.

Arturro smiled. "Precisely. And how many of us would not wish ourselves back to that age, that *youth*—that we might know there were twenty years left to us, instead of the one, or three, or five?" He looked at each of them, seeing the agreement in quiet eyes, stilled expressions: there was no man among them save Raimon and Sario who had a decade left, and likely but half the years at most. "We must not look at the here and now, but borrow the future and bring it to us, so we may shape it."

Ferico shook his head. "Sario is not our future."

"Ungovernable," Otavio muttered.

"No man is ungovernable who lives among the Viehos Fratos," Raimon said clearly. "Or have you forgotten Tomaz?"

They none of them had forgotten Tomaz.

"Nor, I think, has Sario forgotten Tomaz. And a reminder is not impossible." Arturro smiled faintly and adroitly altered the topic. "I would like to nominate Aguo Raimon for advancement to the position of Il Seminno. He has served me well these past six years, as he has served *us,* and if we are to look to the future of the family, we must look to its present as well. Many of us will not be alive when Don Alejandro succeeds his father, and if we are to train Sario for the position of Lord Limner, we must have in place a man who has earned our trust. He will be Sanguo one day, I have no doubt, but for now he must be more than Aguo."

"Grazzo, Premio," Raimon said huskily. "But—I fear I am not worthy."

"You are." Arturro raised a hand against further protest. "Is there a man among us who disagrees?"

Davo said dryly, "Should we not have Sario in to at least vote on *this?*"

Ferico snorted. "What man would vote *for* his keeper?"

"Ah, but are we not all his keepers?" Arturro asked. "Are we not also the keepers of one another, and thus of our family?"

"So long as we hold any man's *Peintraddo Chieva,* there is no threat," Davo declared. "From any of us."

"Only *to* us," Raimon said, "if we prove ungovernable. And who among us can claim no one ever despaired of each and every one of us when we were young?"

"Personal ambition must be subjugated," Arturro said quietly. "It is *family* ambition that takes precedence, so we may recover what was lost to the Nerro Lingua. Strength. Position. Respect."

"Numbers," Raimon said quietly. "But that, too, is lost to us now. We have only the Gift to aid us, and we must use it wisely."

"Wisely?" Otavio shook his head definitively. "Sario cares little enough for the restoration of our family. He thinks only of himself."

Ferico nodded, plucking cloves from a pierced orange left in a crockery bowl to serve as scenting against the closeness. "He is too consumed with questioning our precepts."

"So was I," Arturro said. "Once."

Even Raimon was startled. "Premio? You?"

"Of course." Arturro laughed easily. "I think it is a requirement."

Indignant, Otavio protested at once. "*I* never questioned—"

"Eiha, 'Tavi, of course you did," Davo said wearily. "Will you have me recite the times? I can do it word for word; you never hid your frustrations when the moualimos insisted you practice tedious perspective when you wanted to work instead with the sweet curves of a woman's breasts and buttocks."

It stirred laughter from them all, a grudging grimace from Otavio.

"We have his *Peintraddo Chieva,*" Davo said briskly. "And it was Sario, after all, who was found with the girl who destroyed Tomaz's self-portrait; do you think he of all people doesn't know what would become of him if we determined disciplining was needed?"

"Sario is not a fool," Raimon said. "Merely the one among us whose talent most likely will place a Grijalva at Court again. And that, we should recall, is the true point of this discussion."

"Indeed," Arturro agreed, "as I believe some of us may have forgotten." Quietly he looked over them all: Otavio, Davo, Ferico, Joao, Mequel, Timirrin, the others. All talented. All Gifted. All wholly dedicated to the recovery, preservation, and enhancement of an old family so very nearly destroyed. "It is our task to set aside petty arguments, personal ambitions, and sublimate our wills to the greater good of the family."

Otavio grunted. "Will Sario?"

"He must," Raimon murmured.

"And if he refuses?" Ferico threw out a handful of discarded cloves onto the linen cloth in fretful annoyance, as if he would as forcefully scatter arguments. "He is an unsteady foundation, yet you propose to build our entire city upon him."

"We have time," Arturro said. "Time to prepare him. But we can only do it properly if we are agreed."

Otavio's expression hardened. "Too young."

Ferico nodded. "And too angry."

"Neosso Irrado," Arturro agreed, "but a young man who will be older, and perhaps far less angry, when the do'Verradas are in need of another Lord Limner." He looked directly at Otavio. "I understand your concerns, old friend, and I will not so glibly dismiss them as you might fear. Sario *must* be ours, and we must be certain of it. We cannot afford to question our decision, nor to distrust the Grijalva who may restore our place at Court."

Raimon's expression was startled. "Premio—"

Arturro ignored him. "The Chieva do'Sangua was developed expressly to punish any Gifted who sought to use his talent for himself rather than for his family . . . though he has done nothing more as yet than annoy a number of us, perhaps there is cause for a reminder." He nodded at Otavio. "If you wish, Otavio—and if the others are in agreement—you may invoke the Lesser Discipline."

Otavio's thin-lipped mouth sprang open at once, but he clamped it shut again before he spoke. After a moment of turbulent silence, he glanced at the others. "Is there agreement?"

"He has done nothing," Raimon protested.

"Yet," Ferico snapped.

"He questions us," Otavio said austerely.

"One *learns* by questioning," Raimon countered.

"Within reason," Ferico clarified.

Raimon looked for support from the Premio Frato, but the old man remained silent. "I say again: he has done nothing. We cannot punish a man for what he has not done."

Otavio echoed Arturro. "Let it be a reminder."

"Had we done the same with Tomaz, perhaps he would not have faced the Chieva do'Sangua," Ferico put in pointedly. "Have we learned nothing from that?"

Davo sighed, pushing his shoulders into the carved chairback. The key at his collar glinted. "There is merit in both arguments. Sario tests us for reasons known to some of us as wholly natural in one so Gifted—and also for reasons known only to himself. But if there are no clearly defined boundaries, he may breach them through ignorance."

"Or spite," Otavio said sourly. "I put nothing beyond that boy."

"Nor I," Raimon said quickly, "if we speak of talent."

"Let it be done." Ferico again took up the orange plucked nearly naked of its cloves. "As a hound must be leashed, let us leash Sario. Let him feel the collar."

Otavio nodded approval, then looked directly at Raimon. "We do not propose to choke him on it. But if you fear for the boy, administer the Lesser Discipline yourself."

Raimon's expression was stark. "As Il Aguo, it lies beyond the bounds of compordotta."

"But you are Il Seminno now," Otavio said, smiling, "as we have approved you." He took into his hand the Chieva do'Orro, kissed it, then pressed it against his heart. Gold links, sparking in candlelight, spilled through his fingertips. "In Their Blessed Names, let this be your first act, Raimon . . . if for nothing more than to prove you are worthy."

Saavedra sat upright on the stone bench in the central courtyard of Palasso Grijalva, where the scent of citrus perfumed warm air: lemon, orange, grapefruit, and others, their deep emerald-hued leaves intermixed in subtle harmony with the smudgy silver-green of olive trees laden with bunched streamers of fruit. One pale, paint-stained hand clutched the drawing board on which the paper was fastened, braced against her thigh, as the other moved fluidly, easily, sketching in with sharpened charcoal the details of a face.

So much with so little effort, the gift of true and inescapable talent that burned within her, scorching her spirit until she let it go in sheer conflagration of creativity. The line bisecting the features was quickly but effectively rendered: the merest shadow here suggested the clean bridge of a nose, there the deeper shadow carried the bridge into the smooth upper curve of the socket, and below it the high arch of a cheekbone in three-quarter profile. Clear, well-made contours, though young yet, soft-fleshed, not fully formed; it promised to be a handsome man, what now was pretty youth.

In the warmth of the day she wore little beyond what she must: a loose sleeveless linen tunic, dyed madder yellow once but now faded to wan saffron, bleached summer-weight skirts in place of childhood trousers, and sandals that offered little more than thin sole and strategically placed straps to ward flesh against sun-heated brick. The mass of black hair was bound back in a straggling scarlet ribbon, though shorter, finer ringlets tangled in disarray around her face. Heedless, she shoved wisps aside with the back of her wrist, then bent again to her board.

The sketch commanded all her attention. The mouth, smiling— she had never seen any other expression on his face—the slight amused upturn of the corners of his eyes; the fine lift of expressive eyebrows; the curve of a rebellious lock of dark hair that disdained the company of others pomaded into acquiescence beneath a gold-trimmed hat of blue velurro, bedecked with a curve of chevron-stippled feather that swept down across one shoulder.

More shadowing here, and there; the maturing chin that portended eventual adult stubbornness—she smiled at the knowledge—and beneath it the high, intricately embroidered and pleated collar of his fine-worked lawn shirt, laced in gold-tipped blue silk cord; the merest suggestion of shirred brocade summer-silk doublet with hasty shading here and there, the slight and subtle patterning within the wave of the fabric itself . . . quickly now, before the image left; and later the detail, the patience.

Shadow fell across her. Frowning, Saavedra shifted enough to put the board back into full sunlight.

"He has a crooked tooth," Sario declared definitively.

Saavedra gritted her own. "I'm not doing teeth. His lips are closed."

"You should do his teeth. A flaw should not be hidden."

"No?" She lifted her face into his shadow and arched brows elaborately. "I thought the task of a limner was to *find* favor with his subject, lest he lose the commission."

His mouth twisted in scornful disgust. "You are infatuated with him, like half the girls in Meya Suerta."

"He has a crooked tooth," she agreed serenely. And so he did. "But it does not detract." And so it didn't.

"Because he shows his blinding grin so frequently no one *sees* it. No woman, that is."

Saavedra grinned. "Jealous of Don Alejandro? Eiha, Sario—if

you hope to be named Lord Limner, you had best find favor with the man who must appoint you!"

He scoffed with elaborate succinctness. "I think he will not turn his back on me because I admit freely he has a crooked *tooth*."

"It's only a little crooked," she pointed out, "and how do you know? You have never met him. It might matter very greatly to him what ducal 'flaws' you care to depict."

"Teeth are difficult," Sario said. "Closed lips are easier. I only meant that if you wish to grow in your art, you should challenge yourself."

She was not subtle in her laughter, nor in her mockery. "No, you didn't! Eiha, Sario—you meant to remind me that Don Alejandro is not perfect. That he has a crooked tooth. That *your* teeth are infinitely and perfectly straight."

Sario bared them in a wolfish grin. "They are."

Saavedra hitched a shoulder in eloquent nonchalance. "Teeth are important," she admitted equably, "but they are hardly the only thing an artist looks at."

His voice, newly-broken, scraped. "Or a woman?"

She sighed, muttering dire comments within the confines of her skull. She had no compunction about saying them aloud, save he usually out-argued her merely by dint of tenacity, and she was not in the mood. Clearly he would not permit her to go back to her sketching. "Do I think he is handsome? Yes. Am I infatuated with him? Perhaps . . . though I am not certain a *man* truly knows what that means to accuse one of it, as his pride does not permit him to ever admit to such girlish folly as that—" She flashed him an arch smile. "—and certainly *you* would never allow yourself to lose so much control of your emotions!"

Stung, he scowled. "How do you know?"

Blithely she answered, "A woman would interfere with your ambitions, Sario. You would never permit that."

Ruddy color bloomed in cheeks like a mottled sunburn, though he was too dark to burn; and in summer, his desert-bred flesh merely deepened and did not blister. "How do you *know?*"

She grinned. "I know you."

One hand twitched, reached, then was pulled back to his side. Tautly he said, "But not everything, 'Vedra."

Abruptly troubled, she looked away hastily from the intensity of his fixed and eloquent gaze. "No," she confessed, "not everything. You are a man, and Gifted—and one of the Viehos Fratos. I can never know everything."

His tone was odd. "Do you want to?"

She looked back at him sharply. He was in that instant open to her, unshielded behind the arrogance that annoyed so many, behind the impatient ambition and cynicism that annoyed even *her*. He was in that instant the boy of five years before, eleven in place of sixteen, helpless to engineer what would save him from the discovery that he had killed a man, that he had known ahead of time how the Chieva do'Sangua worked, and its magic—and that he had used it unaided to destroy a masterwork and thus a Grijalva life, when there were so few to risk.

His voice was stripped of all save bitter honesty, and in it, this moment, resided a stark vulnerability he hid from everyone else. "I would tell you anything you asked."

And in that instant she understood completely what she had not, until moments before, so much as imagined. They were no longer children, certainly not within a plague-racked and artificially insular society whose survival depended solely on the ability to produce more Grijalvas. Sixteen was young, but not too young; there were fathers not long out of boyhood. In no wise was he a child—he was sterile, not impotent—nor, since her courses had come, was she a girl considered too young for motherhood.

She looked again to her drawing board, gazing blindly at the image of Alejandro do'Verrada. And it struck her, in odd juxtaposition with her fragmenting thoughts, that her nails were rimed with bits of charcoal like blackened frost.

Why am I thinking of that at this moment?

To avoid Sario's intensity, the intent of his confession.

Matra Dolcha, aid me. Carefully she said, "You are Gifted, Sario."

The fine straight teeth flashed briefly in quick gritting. "And thus I am sterile," he said clearly, "but not in the least unable."

Hot-cheeked, she stared even more fixedly at the half-completed sketch of Tira Virte's glorious young Heir. "I am meant to bear children."

To most men, men who were not Limners, it would be taken as insult, an implication that he could not do the one thing that proved a man's potency. But here it was the truest of all honors: a Grijalva who sired children did not bear the Gift.

"A waste," he said in disgust; then, as she gasped in shock, "eiha, 'Vedra—not a waste to bear them, but to be *limited* to that when you could offer so much more!" Vulnerability was vanquished by a habitual impatience; he suffered no one who could not share his vision. "Do you think I am blind? You have your own Gift, 'Vedra—"

"No!" She stood up so quickly the drawing board nearly tumbled from her hands. Charcoal snapped; she tossed its fragments onto the bench. "Matra Dolcha, Sario—don't you see? I am not Gifted. I can't be. No matter how much you may wish it. No matter—" She gestured futility, then blurted bald conviction. "—no matter *how* much you wish to turn my attention from another."

"You believe . . ." Like a hound, he hackled. Even his lips went white. "It isn't that, 'Vedra—"

"It is." She smiled sadly. "We aren't children any longer. You are one of the Viehos Fratos, and I am to bear children when it is decided who best I should suit. And so our childhood is left behind . . ." Very softly, she said, "And you resent what is lost with it."

He shook his head. "I regret nothing. A child has no power."

"No. No more than a woman." Saavedra sighed. This was a conversation—an inept and cross-purposed conversation—she had never imagined having. "You—*want* me, perhaps, because—because you are of an age to fasten upon the woman who is closest to you." She looked away quickly from his taut face and finished in a rush, "But it is no more than that. I promise you."

"Do you?" His eyes glittered beneath uncut, untamed dark hair that shielded the fine, smooth brow. "How can you promise anything? You say you know me, but—" He broke off a moment, wincing, and lifted a hand to his left collarbone. "You may *believe* you know me, but—" Fingers pressed fine cloth against his flesh. The topic was altered abruptly by irritated surprise. "Am I *bitten?*"

And so the awkwardness was banished. Relieved, Saavedra set down the drawing board and began to untie the lacings of his crimped collar; one of the Viehos Fratos put aside the tunics and trousers of childhood to wear the clothing of a man, though Sario, as was habitual, had left off his doublet and wore only high-waisted hosen and creased lawn shirt. "Here, let me see—no, move your fingers."

Affronted protest: "It *stings.*"

"Let me look, Sario." She loosened the laces, pulled the collar apart so that a strip of hairless, dusky chest lay bare, and the gold chain across it that dipped lower into shirt folds. "Here—you see?" She turned back the crumpled shirt. "What is this? I've seen no bite like this! Not three bumps all in a perfect row."

"Let me—" Fingertips explored the flesh, sliding beneath the chain. "Like a burn—" And then he froze into absolute stillness. Color drained from his face, and the rage that engulfed his dark eyes startled her by its magnitude. " 'Vedra—you have the painting. The self-portrait."

"Of course, but—"

"Safe?"

"Where we left it, in my cell." She frowned. "What is it?"

"Filho do'canna," he hissed. "How *dare* they?"

"Sario—"

"Don't you see?" He caught one of her arms, clamping down. "They fear me. And so they seek to *control* me, to remind me they hold my *Peintraddo Chieva*."

"But they don't," she said. "*I* have it."

"The real one, yes. But the one I gave them, the one I painted and presented as my masterwork . . ." Muscles rolled in a taut jaw; his would not boast the square, clean lines of Alejandro do'Verrada's, but there was nothing girlish about him as he matured out of boyhood. "It is not truly a *Peintraddo Chieva*, but there is enough of me in it—there had to be!—that I would know if they sought to use it against me." Dark eyes were dilated black despite the blaze of the day. " 'Vedra—come with me. There is a thing you must do."

"Sario—"

"Come with me . . . we must go to your cell."

"But—"

He caught her hand and pulled her. "Adezo! They will expect me to come to them, to ask why—I must show them what they believe will be there."

She went with him because she had no choice; and harkened back five years to the closet above the Crechetta, and the Chieva do'Sangua. Then he had pulled her, urgent and determined, and she had no more choice now.

Then, he was shorter than I, and slight. He was taller now, though his was not the frame that would carry excess flesh or a warrior's hard muscling. His bones and muscles were long, his expressive hands large; by the time he finished growing, he would claim an elegance lacking in the shorter, squarer Tira Virteians. *Tza'ab blood, they say*— And also, uneasily, *What will it do to me?*

Inside the corridor leading to her tiny quarters . . . There were no locks. He unlatched and flung open the narrow door to her small estuda's cell, pushing her inside. "Candle," he said curtly, shutting the door behind.

"I have one, of course. Sario—"

"Lighted?"

"Yes, but—"

"Bring it here." Without leave he threw himself down on her narrow cot, stretching flat. One hand tore aside the collar of his shirt, baring the faintly curved line of bone beneath taut flesh and the furtive glitter of gold chain. "The marks are not enough, not as they are. You must do more."

Saavedra fetched the burning candle to the bed. "What are you asking, Sario?"

"Hot wax," he said briefly. "Three drops: here—here—and here." Fingertips indicated the faintly reddened spots already present. "Now, 'Vedra."

"*Burn* you? Sario, for the love of the Mother—"

"Yes," he hissed. "And for my survival. If they learn I am not burned, not as I should be, they will know the truth about the *Peintraddo* in their keeping. 'Vedra—*now.*"

"Matra Dolcha," she whispered. "You are mad."

"But alive," he said harshly, "and whole, which is what I will *not* be if they learn the truth."

She clamped her jaws shut. She would do as he asked, but not without argument. "Why would they do such a thing? What have you done to provoke it?"

"Such trust . . ." He grimaced. "Nothing. Do'nado." He craned his head, trying to peer down at the precise trio of blemishes along his collarbone. "Will you do it?"

"Patience," she chided, giving in, "or I will spill it all, and they will know from that."

"They will expect me to come at once. I can't tarry."

"A spoon," she said absently.

It astonished him. "Spoon?"

"Momentita . . ." To her table by the window, all of five steps away, then back, and she sat down carefully on the edge of her cot. "You must be very still, Sario."

Stretched flat on her bed, he stared intently a moment, fresh color moving in his face as he studied hers. He stirred oddly—and then his gaze altered even as his color faded. He watched narrow-eyed as she spooned up a measure of liquefied wax from the clay candle-cup. She was aware of the pallor of his face, the faint sheen of perspiration, the abject determination and simmering anger.

"Be still," she said again, pulling aside the chain with its weight of Golden Key, and with great concentration positioned the spoon so the wax droplets would land precisely atop the faint blemishes.

Premo. Duo. Treo. She heard the hiss of his indrawn breath, smelled the sweet tang of citrus-scented wax. Carefully she inspected her handiwork, then returned the candle-cup and spoon to the table.

"Done?" He sat up, fingering the wax. Chain links chimed faintly, slithering across flesh to snag on rumpled lawn.

"Let it harden. Then peel it off."

He did so, eventually flaking away the dried wax droplets. "Well?"

She inspected what lay beneath, sliding a finger under the chain to gently touch the flesh beside the wax burns. She heard the quick intake of his breath; pain? Or something else. "It may scar," she said evenly. "The skin is tender here, not like callused fingers." And she took her hand away.

"All the better." Loosened lacings and the Chieva dangled as he stood up. "And now I will see *why* they felt it necessary to remind me of my fragility!"

He was gone before she could speak again, leaving the door open in his haste. Saavedra sighed, then smiled wryly. "Fragile? You? *Never.*"

⚮━━◈ NINE ◈━━⚮

With grim, crisp efficiency—and no little anger—Sario yanked open the unlatched inner door leading into the Crechetta. As expected, his eyes immediately confirmed the presence of his *Peintraddo Chieva* upon an easel, naked of embroidered cloth, which had been peeled back and left drooping behind like a cloak half-slipped from a shoulder. But then he stopped registering anything beyond the man who waited beside it.

"You!" Sario blurted.

The slender, dark-clad Grijalva waited in silence. Wan candle-light glinted laggardly off the intricate small-linked chain that circled his neck, then spilled down the front of his summer-silk black doublet. From it depended the symbol of his Gift: Chieva do'Orro.

Him I can deal with— Sario hesitated a moment, then loosed a quiet sigh. He was able now to release some of the tension in his stiffened shoulders; this man of them all had never decried his habitual hasty temper or impatient skills. But his expression was nonetheless unwontedly severe for the good bones of his face. "Aguo Raimon—"

A quiet, singularly brief interruption: "Seminno."

Sario froze. Tension renewed, rushed back. *One word, one correction . . .* it indicated much. Anger reaffirmed itself, if icy in place of scorching. "So. My congratulations, *Seminno* Raimon . . . but it explains nothing."

"Should it?"

To give himself time to master himself—this was not the man he expected to confront, and thus his stride was broken—Sario turned to the door and closed it with explicit care, making no sound even as he set the loose latch. He summoned extreme if alien patience; when he turned back, he saw the same implacable expression on the new-made Seminno's face.

It encouraged nothing so much as wariness. Aside from himself, Raimon was the youngest, albeit more than a decade older than Sario—and by far the most bearable of them all.

Or had been. Sario drew a steadying breath, then in slow understatement pulled aside the folds of his shirt to display blemished flesh in mute question and challenge.

Raimon said nothing, made no movement; if he marked the blemishes, he made no indication it mattered. *Then why inflict them upon me?*

Gritting teeth, Sario released the fabric and looked at the *Peintraddo*. He saw what was expected: three small, evenly-spaced holes carefully burned through paint to expose stained canvas beneath.

"I have done nothing," he said in a low tone that was no less telling in its suppressed anger. "Nothing but what I am required to do."

Raimon's gaze was level and infinitely clear-eyed. "You frighten them."

It was not in the least what Sario anticipated. He stared.

Raimon sighed and smiled faintly, a familiar brief crooked hooking of his mouth. "We are all of us tested thus, Sario. I no less than you."

Irony was marked, but Sario was still too upset to pay it tribute—or to heed the opening offered by the only member of the Viehos Fratos he considered a friend, if such could be suggested of any of them who plagued him. "But—that?" A sharp gesture indicated the painting. "I was given to understand the only time Chieva do'Sangua was employed was in the rare case when a Gifted overstepped his bounds enough to threaten the family. Have I done so? Ever?"

"This was not—and is not intended to be—Chieva do'Sangua," Raimon said plainly. "This is a warning. And you are expected to heed it."

It was incredibly and exquisitely unfair all at once. "Heed that I am punished for their *fear?*" Sario shook his head; hair in need of cutting tugged against loosened collar. "If this is done, then surely they should look to themselves. I have been Confirmed according to the rites, my masterwork properly painted, and I was accepted two years ago into the ranks of the Viehos Fratos. Nothing was out of order, or surely I would have been denied. If they fear me so much, why should I be given such honor?"

"Do you view it as honor, Sario? Or the means to an end?"

He hesitated, righteous rage forestalled; renewed respect for Raimon's customary shrewdness reminded him to take care. "But the end desired by all is that one of us *should* become Lord Limner again, so we may guide the Dukes in the ordering of the duchy—"

"And some men would fear that," Raimon said. "Serranos. Others."

Self-control fled. Passion replaced care. "But not Limners! Should we not honor the man among us who regains what was lost?"

"And you intend to be that man."

"Should I not?" Sario spread his hands. "Have you never wished it could be you?"

The clean features softened slightly. "I *expected* it."

Relieved laughter bubbled up from Sario's chest and broke free. *Perhaps he* can *understand*. "There! Eiha, do you see? We are not so unalike after all."

"But it will not be my task," Raimon interjected softly, irony banished a second time. "Should Baltran do'Verrada die tomorrow, perhaps it would . . . but he will not, short of being assassinated, and he is too beloved for that. Thus it shall fall to his son to appoint a new Lord Limner, and I will be too old."

Saavedra claimed he lost his temper too often, that others heard the anger and not the words. With effort Sario tamed his tongue, locked away the impatience, attempted reason. "We are raised to believe in our hearts we are better suited for the role than any other family in Tira Virte," he appealed, "and yet when one of us aspires too openly to that role, he is punished."

"Not for aspiration," Raimon said. "For willfulness. For discourtesy. For questioning too broadly—too *disruptively*—the precepts of the family. For improper compordotta. For taking into his own hands the ordering of his Gift."

"But it is *my* Gift—"

"*Our* Gift, Sario," Raimon's tone was abruptly cold; he was wholly Il Seminno, wholly of the Viehos Fratos. "And by that you merit such punishment as this. It is not *your* Gift, *your* goal, *your* appointment, but *ours!* Grijalva. We do this for the family, not for the ambitions of a single man. Gifted or no, Sario, it is your responsibility to work with the family toward restoration of what once was ours."

"And I will gain it!" Sario cried. "Leave me be, Raimon. Leave me *free* to do what I must, and I will be the first Grijalva at the right hand of a do'Verrada Duke since before the Nerro Lingua!"

"Free to wrest the duchy away from the anointed Duke?"

Sario stilled. Raimon was a fair man, a pleasant man, the one among the Viehos Fratos he felt he could speak with openly, but now, in this astonishing moment, he saw a different man. One capable of visiting harm upon the flesh by harm done to a painting. *He is as they all are, bound by his own weakness to outdated beliefs and rituals, not knowing the truth of power. . . .*

Quietly he asked, "Is that what you fear? That I want the duchy for myself?"

Raimon's expression was stark. "There was a time when it might have been ours," he said softly. "When others were poised to hail a Grijalva as savior, and thus our present—and our future—would have been significantly different. But Verro Grijalva died, Sario. He took a Tza'ab dart meant for Renayo do'Verrada, and died in his Duke's arms."

"And thus sealed our role as servants forever," Sario said bitterly.

After a moment, Raimon shook his head. "You are the most gifted—and Gifted—Grijalva I have ever known. And the most dangerous."

It stung. Far more deeply and painfully than expected. "You fear me, too?"

"The very thing that drives you to such ambitions in your work, that is your personal Luza do'Orro, could overtake and transform you, Sario. Ambition, to be effective, to be *useful,* must be controlled and directed. Or it is nothing more than base, selfish lust."

"Power," Sario answered baldly, stripping away from it the civilized speech and cutting to the bone.

Raimon met the challenge without prevarication. "Yes. Naked, infinite power, as you would have it be. But that day on the battlefield a Grijalva's death determined the role Grijalvas would play in life, in the ordering of a new realm—*and it is not as rulers.*"

Sario laughed softly, though it was lacking in humor. "Had Verro let Renayo do'Verrada die, we would be Dukes instead of limners!"

"Perhaps. Perhaps not. But he made that choice."

"Not for me."

"But it was, Sario. He made it for us all—and then the Tza'ab made it certain."

Sario knew; they all knew. "By stealing Grijalva women and getting bastards upon them."

"Chi'patros," Raimon said quietly. "Our ancestors."

"Despised and hated by the others, especially the Ecclesia!"

"It was basest infamy, what the Tza'ab did to those women, but it became our infamy as well. The Tza'ab were the enemy, Unbelievers—and they dishonored our family, bred a taint into our blood . . . which in turn was reviled by others who were untainted." Raimon adroitly redraped the *Peintraddo* with its brocade cloth, hiding the blemished image of a young boy whose talent was manifest, if not the blazing of ambition. "The Ecclesia has made it clear they consider us unclean because of the infidel taint. It is one of the reasons they hate us. But there is more, you see. We are *different* from them, and difference is feared."

"They are sanctified fools!"

"Some of them, yes. Others believe sincerely. But so long as the Ecclesia claims us tainted, the people will believe it as well." He paused a moment, as if seeking self-control, then continued. "But there is something else, Sario. The strength of a ruling family lies in its potency, in its life span. We are weak in both."

"Once we were *strong* in both."

"And the Matra ei Filho spurned that strength." Raimon shook his head. "The Nerro Lingua was punishment, Sario . . . we overstepped. Grew too bold. And thus we were humbled."

"Tell me," Sario said acidly, unable to stop himself, "did the Mother and Her infant Son actually *say* so?"

Raimon did not answer with anger or equal hostility, but with a serenity Sario found infinitely galling. "A true Limner understands and embraces divine metaphor, even as it is visited upon him."

"But—"

"Bassda!" Curtly banishing equanimity, Raimon stepped forward smoothly until he stood very close to Sario. "Do you count me a fool? A cabessa bisila? It is your freedom to do so, of course—I will not stay you from the privacy of your thoughts . . . but do not believe for one instant that you are alone in ambition, in the Luza do'Orro that demands release."

"Then why—"

Raimon abruptly and without habitual decorum tore back from his left wrist the doublet sleeve and cuff of his shirt. "I have worn your shoes, Sario! I have even worn your name: Neosso Irrado!"

As he was meant to, Sario looked upon the bared forearm. Across the inside of the wrist where the flesh was most tender, an age-silvered weal was deeply scored.

"The Lesser Discipline," Raimon said curtly. "The men who

ordered it done are dead, of course; they were on the cusp at the time. I can tell you only what they told me: that divisiveness and disruption does not serve the family and shall not be tolerated."

Sario wet dry lips. "And so they quenched the fire in you."

"Did they? Have you studied my paintings of late?" Raimon's features were stark as bleached canvas. "Not 'quenched,' Sario—redirected. And I have come to believe that if I can be of some small service to my family—my poor, denuded family—that it is in all ways enough for me."

"I don't want 'enough,' " Sario said. "I want *more*."

Raimon's smile was bittersweet. "Then I don't fear you, Sario . . . I fear *for* you." He cut off an answer with an inclination of the head. "Your pardon, grazzo—but I have other duties." And abruptly he was gone, opening and closing the door in equal silence.

Stiff as a spitting cat, Sario waited, trembling, letting the tension and anger bleed off. And then he walked to the draped easel and flung back the cloth, baring the self-portrait that bore traces of his essence, but not all that was required of a Gifted male Grijalva granted membership among the elite.

Power. But not enough.

Sario nodded at the self-portrait. He was safe. He would always be safe. No matter what they demanded of him. No matter how frightened they were.

He smiled at his image. "Verro Grijalva was a fool."

<hr/>

Gitanna Serrano stared fixedly into the priceless mirror, a gift of the Duke after their first Astraventa, the Tira Virteian celebration of the month called the "starry wind" when the stars fell out of the sky and were trapped within mirrors carried by celebrants. This was not the actual mirror used in the ritual—it was too large, too elaborate, and much too costly—but a remembrance gift, something to mark the first night they shared a bed.

But that was so many nights ago, so many Astraventas. Gitanna inspected every inch of her face with a hard, relentless scrutiny equal to a man weighing his enemy. And in a way it *was* her enemy, that which looked out of the painted glass, for it reflected time.

The delightfully fresh, vibrant young woman who had come to Court, who was seduced during Astraventa, was indisputably gone, vanquished by the battles no less dangerous for all the weapons were words, the campaigns political intrigue. Winter, summer; supply trains were not an issue, nor the harvest, nor the location of water and grazing, suitable terrain. Only advancing age, and retreating beauty.

The battle, she feared, was lost, the war nearly ended. Seven years he had come to her, seven years since that first night when he had given her signal honor by keeping her as his mistress, but seven years tacked on to a woman's youth made the woman old.

Gitanna grimaced. A man merely grew old*er*. A woman grew old.

There was no gray in her hair. Pomades and lotions kept her skin soft, denied Tira Virte's summer sun, despite humidity, the power to ravage her. She had taken pains to bear no children, and so her waist remained slender and supple, her hips unsprung, her breasts firm. But there was no denying that she was not as she had been.

She closed her eyes a moment. Quietude took her; she heard the faint drone of bees near her unlatched shutters, the distant barking of a dog, and, rising from the courtyard, the muted laughter of a woman. She sat utterly still, moving only to breathe—and felt the faint trembling of her eyelids, defiant to her intent.

The latch rattled.

Gitanna smiled her relief. *He has not dismissed me yet.*

The door opened, and again the latch rattled as the bolt was shot, sealing the chamber against intrusion. Eyes yet closed, she gave herself over to smell, to sound: the rustle of fine clothing as he moved, the faint acrid tang of physical exertion mixed with the scent of horse. And the sound of awed exhalation as he saw her bared breasts reflected in the mirror.

"Matra Dolcha," he whispered, as if in supplication.

Her eyes sprang open. It took all of her strength not to swing around, not to twist her body, not to stare in bitter astonishment.

So. It had come. *No time, after all.*

Alejandro smiled. It was his father's smile, though its undeniable charm was without intent, without calculation. He had learned neither yet, and simply was—himself.

A nervous himself. No more the boy, but not quite a man. Tall, and daily growing taller; broadening through the shoulders, though they lacked the mass of maturity; wide-palmed hands skilled at such things as the sword, the knife, the reins—but unskilled in this.

He drew in an unsteady breath. "He said—it is for you to do."

After a moment she rose. Exquisite lace dripped from powdered, scented shoulders. She slid it off with an imperceptible shrug, let it drift like weightless snow to the carpet-strewn floor, where his clothes would soon lie also.

"Yes," she said.

The father had made her a woman. Let her make the son a man.

TEN

Saavedra asked four people before she received the answer to her question: *in the Galerria.* And so she went there and found him utterly lost to reality, intently studying a cluster of paintings hanging in a shadowed corner.

He was rapt within his own mind, arms folded hard against his chest as if he held in his heart or held out fear. The angles of his face were sharp as glass, underpainted by an edge of bone that threatened to burst taut flesh; his black scowl was augmented by the forbidding tension in his mouth.

"So," she said, "I came to see if you would partner me to the festival. But if you are in *that* mood . . ."

She waited. Nothing. He did not rise to her gibe.

"Sario." She looked at the cluster of paintings: none of them large, none of them older than perhaps a month or two. She could smell the resin, the binders, the astringency of the ingredients. "Not yours," she said.

"Raimon's."

"Raimon's?" Saavedra looked more intently at the paintings. "But—why?"

"I was invited to," he said icily. "He had a point to make."

After a moment she ventured it. "And did he?"

He glanced at her briefly, annoyed, still scowling. "Did he what?"

"Make his point."

Something blazed up in dark eyes, engulfing them; was extinguished with effort. "He did."

"And?"

His tone blistered her. "You wouldn't understand."

It shocked her. Then her anger, slow to kindle but every bit as warm as his, flared. "Oh, *I* see—we are merditto alba today, are we? Too grand for a mere woman? One of the Viehos Fratos, Gifted, Confirmed, so much better than I! Regretto—forgive my intrusion . . . I will purify your air by taking myself from it!"

"Wait!" He caught her arm as she swung to stalk away. "Saavedra—wait! I'm sorry—nazha irrada, 'Vedra."

"I *am* angry," she answered, "and I will be if I wish to be; you are not the only one with claim to the emotion." She glared and snatched her arm away. "Matra Dolcha, Sario, I am not to be treated that way, not as you treat the others. We know too much of one another, share too many secrets. Take out your frustration and impatience on someone else!"

"But you were here," he said logically. "And—you asked."

"Eiha, I asked! It was a natural thing to do." She glanced again at the paintings. "What is so important about Aguo Raimon's most recent paintings?"

"*Seminno;* he has been elevated. And I accused him of losing his Luza do'Orro," Sario said. "I was angry—"

"You are always angry, Sario."

"—and said some things I shouldn't."

"If you told *him* he had lost his Light, yes!" She gestured. "You have only to look at these paintings to see he has not."

"You can see it. His fire. His—Light."

"Of course I can." She could see everybody's Light.

"Then what do you see?"

"In *his* paintings?" She considered, examining them briefly. "It would require study."

"No, no . . ." Urgency broke through. " 'Vedra, what do you see just—just looking at them? Talent? His Gift?"

"*A* gift," she clarified promptly, certain of her knowledge. "He is not as good as you."

Sario colored deeply. "As—*Raimon?*"

"Sario, I have told you. You are the best. Of all."

" 'Of all,' " he echoed blankly.

"All," she repeated. "You deserve what you most desire: to be Lord Limner at Palasso Verrada."

The flush faded. He was white, chalky white, his eyes huge and black. "Why do you believe in me so? What have I done to deserve such loyalty?"

"You haven't *done* anything. You're just—you." Saavedra shrugged. "I don't know, Sario. But there's a fire in you. Or perhaps it's that your Luza do'Orro is too bright to ignore." She smiled self-consciously. "You are everything they say of you, you know, Neosso Irrado . . . but it doesn't matter to me. I see what also is there. What is underneath."

"Underneath?"

"The paint," she elaborated. "The layer upon layer of carefully tempered paint, made to be thick, and heavy, and impatiently slopped on with a paletto knife, so all the delicacy and detail is lost and only the dullness remains." She shrugged. "A mask, like fresco plaster, behind which you hide."

He was perversely fascinated by what she had begun. "But if I am hiding behind it, if I have layered on the paint like fresco plaster, how can you see what lies beneath?"

She found herself answering plainly, without prevarication or hesitation. "Surely a moth must feel the heat, yet still flies to the flame."

Sario whispered it: "And is burned to death."

"Sometimes," she agreed readily. "But all of them know the Light."

He blinked. He was lost within his mind, wholly apart from her. And then came plunging back. "Would you?" he asked.

"Would I what?"

"Burn to death in the flame?"

"Never," Saavedra answered, quick and hard and certain, and saw the flare of recognition and comprehension in his eyes.

"You have helped me before," he said.

"Helped you, yes. Before—and again, no doubt!"

He did not acknowledge her attempt at irony. "You burned Tomaz's *Peintraddo*."

No humor in him at all. He seemed to want something of her, a promise made, an oath sworn, some sign of commitment greater than she had offered before, or believed was necessary.

Abruptly she said, "You ask too much."

He recoiled. She had shocked him deeply.

I didn't mean it like that. "I can't know what I would do," she explained, trying to soften the blatancy of her declaration. "Until the time, until the moment . . ." Saavedra looked at Seminno Raimon's paintings, automatically marking color, technique, composition; he was a master, of course. "We put ourselves into our work, Sario, a little piece of ourselves each time. You can see Raimon in there, if you look for it." She gestured, indicating with a sweep of her hand the shadowed collection. "But I wonder, is there enough? Do we use too much of ourselves—" Saavedra stopped short. She had spoken figuratively, not literally, the way an artist uses imagery, but now a door unlocked itself and opened before her, swinging wide from out of the darkness. "Is that—is *that* why we die?"

Sario understood instantly. His mouth opened, worked, shaped words, but no sound issued forth.

"No one knows," Saavedra said intently, picking her way carefully as what had been idly said blossomed into speculation, into extrapolation. "They blame the Nerro Lingua . . . but what if it's more? What if it's something else?" She looked again at Raimon's work, feeling hollow and light inside—and close, all of a sudden, far too close to a flame whose heat she could not feel. "Sario, what if a man paints too *much* . . . and uses himself up?"

"Then—then—" His voice was hoarse. He saw it as she did, acknowledged the brutal suspicion no matter how preposterous the theory sounded, and did not insult her by refuting the possibility. "If that is true, and we *didn't* paint . . ."

"Would we live a normal life?" A chill walked her spine, slowly and deliberately, setting the hairs on her flesh to rising. "We all of us paint, Sario—every Grijalva born. But only the Gifted die so very young."

He was frightened. *She* had frightened him. "All Grijalvas die young!"

"Not all of us. Not women. Not men who lack the Gift." She turned to stare at him, at the golden key hanging from its chain. "None die so soon as the Viehos Fratos, who bind their images with—themselves."

With spittle, she knew; and sweat. She recalled how damage done to his *Peintraddo* manifested in his flesh, but only to a minor degree, as if what was damaged was not fully empowered. He had implied it, had begged her to burn him with candlewax so the manifested damage would look legitimate. So there must be other things, ingredients he undoubtedly had not told her. She knew more than most, too much; he had shared with her what his world was like, now that he had left behind the trappings of their mutual childhood.

But he knew more. Unequivocally. "Matra—" he whispered, "—Nommo Matra ei Filho . . ."

Now she was frightened. "If you stopped—"

"I can't!"

"If you were to *stop* painting—"

"I *can't!*"

"If you were never to paint again—"

"I would sooner die than never paint again!"

Saavedra shivered. He knew more than she, but he did not deny what she feared was true.

"I will stop," she said hollowly. "Women do—we learn, we paint, and we stop. We bear children. I am not meant to paint—and I will stop, and I will live longer . . ."

" 'Vedra, *bassda!*"

It was not enough. She had to speak it all, to bring it into the light where they could both see it. "But you will not, and your Luza do'Orro will blaze more brightly than most, and you will die."

Blindly she gazed at the paintings. "Raimon will die too soon. *All* of you die too soon, every Gifted Grijalva."

A shudder convulsed his slender body. "I won't stop. I can't. Stop painting? I would *die*—"

It escaped before she could stop it. "And so you will. Die."

He pushed past her then, bumping her shoulder. It was not rudeness, nor insult; she had shaken him so badly he could barely walk. She watched him go, watched the hunched line of his shoulders, watched the wavering steps. Then she turned back again to Seminno Raimon's paintings.

"If," she said, trembling, "if I destroyed them all as I destroyed Tomaz's *Peintraddo*—would he live longer? Would Raimon not die?"

And Sario, whom she would outlive, because Grijalva women, who did not paint, lived substantially longer than Gifted males.

She could not imagine the world without Sario in it. And nor, she knew, could he.

Fuega Vesperra. A heathen month, a heathen festival to celebrate heathen rites . . . the old man took solace in his own rites and rituals celebrated for the true god, Acuyib, Father of Heaven, Lord of the Golden Wind, whom he was quite certain found such apostasy affront and abomination. But then *he* knew it as well, and also found it so, and therefore did what he could to mitigate it by performing his own private prayers frequently so as to soften the slight to Acuyib.

In his paneled Tza'ab tent, girdled about by the stone palassos, plasterwork Sanctias, the brick and tile zocalos of Meya Suerta— hard, everything hard, subjugating sun, and soil, and wind!—the old man worked the latch on a casket of waxed and polished thornwood, bound and tacked by brass. Swollen fingers were not so adroit as they once were—cursed be the humidity, so different from his beloved desert!—and so it took longer than anticipated, but at last the latch was released and he lifted the lid.

Green silk lay beneath, its edges freighted with glass and gold, beneath a scattered mantle of protective elements. Tza'ab magic incarnate: dried stalks of desert broom, for Purity and Protection; a fragile netting of cress, for Stability and Power; leaves of lemon, holly, and hearts-of-palm, for Fidelity and Health, Foresight, Victory. He gently folded aside the silk, taking care not to crush the scraps of plants, and took from beneath the shielding a tube of finest, thinnest ivory-hued leather.

Other tubes remained undisturbed as he loosened the gold wires stitching the cap to the tube and slipped it, allowing it to dangle from one glinting wire, then with careful fingertips drew the rolled parchment from its protective insulation. A faint whiff of carnation, cedar, and honeysuckle accompanied it, denoting several of the scents symbolically linked to Acuyib: Magical Energy; Strength and Spirituality; Devoted Affection.

In Tza'ab Rih, the holy texts had not been stored so. But that was in the days of the Diviner himself, when the world had been at peace and such things as a collection of illuminated pages could be safely bound inside a book . . . but times changed, and war decreed differently; the *Kita'ab* now, that which remained of it, was in his keeping, one old man in the lap of the enemy. No true book remained, no flat illuminated pages bound by leather and gold and gemstones, merely a few sheets, some torn, some scorched, some stained—blessed!—by Tza'ab blood, carefully rolled and stored in spell-stitched leather tubes, and hoarded in a thornwood casket bound by brass and belief.

He did not know what had become of the leather book covers. He was certain the gold inlay had been scraped away, the gemstones pried out of their settings. Probably the leather had been burned altogether; so much had burned that day, including human flesh, when the Grijalva Apostate had surprised the caravan and stolen from it, from Tza'ab Rih, from every man, woman, and child of the desert, the most sacred of texts, the most holy, the wise teachings of divine Acuyib set down in inks, in images, in words of such power only the select were permitted to read them.

Others, of course, were *told* them, through the offices of the Diviner.

So many pages lost, so much text, so much of Acuyib. So much of the magic. But the power remained, as did one member of the Order permitted to read the words: *Al-Fansihirro*.

The old man smiled tremulously with relief and gratitude. One alive, only one—but one was enough, because one could teach another. It mattered no longer that he had been driven out by the defeated of his own people who cursed him for worshiping a powerless god, for serving a holy man weak enough to die. That he was exile, outcast, *estranjiero* within his own borders. The task remained, and he carried it out.

He brought the rolled parchment to his lips, briefly touched them to the tubed page, barely a breath of a touch—he smelled old smoke, and death—then cradled the page gently in gnarled hands against the paucity of his chest, swathed in Tza'ab robes.

Green, of course. Rich, brilliant green. The color of Al-Fansihirro.

The lush vegetation of Tira Virte—literally "green country"—was of a different hue, and a far different spirit. Its people were barren of belief, empty of Acuyib's blessings, and did not know it. They prated of their Mother and Her Son, of their sacred dual deity, and did not realize what fools they were, what ignoble children, to ignore the God who had made the world.

Sometimes it was easy to forget why he had come, why he remained. His heart yearned for the sere heat of the desert, for its spare, desolate beauty that shaped and made a man. But his duty lay here, here where he disdained the enemy even as he called them friends in their own language. Because among them were his own, albeit they were tainted with the enemy's heathen rites, the enemy's blood, and were thus blinded.

Those of his people, *his* blood, were born here, lived here, died here. And in between remained ignorant of their God, their heart, their heritage.

But mostly of their power.

She had ridden him hard, cajoled him, roused him, *used* him, proving the stallion had more miles in him than he suspected, albeit the labors were of an impatient and wild young animal, wholly unschooled. He scented the mare, wanted the mare; knew what he was to do, but not how to do it properly. The first lesson therefore had been hers to teach, and so she had taught him.

He slept now, sated, sprawled across two-thirds of her bed in unthinking, selfish abandon, cutting her off with a diagonal slant that offered no room for her feet. But she had no mind to sleep and sat up instead, leaning into silken cushions stacked against the ornate headboard shrouded in gauzy draperies, festooned with tasseled cords. The day began to die; they had been hours abed.

She wondered which of his country manors the Duke would deed to her, added to the townhome he had already bestowed. She wondered how much of an annual allowance he would settle upon her. She wondered of what quality—and quantity—the jewelry would be.

She wondered who shared his bed now, while his son shared hers.

"Pluvio en laggo," she murmured, as tears started up in her eyes. She dashed them away bitterly; no, no protests for her: that rain was in the lake. Baltran would offer her a sturdy boat with good shelter against the storm, but he would never now grace the decks with his ducal presence.

"I told him," she murmured tersely. "I *told* 'Gosa it would be this way . . . a Lord Limner he will keep, but a mistress he will not!"

Alejandro stirred. Gitanna sealed her mouth against further complaint; let her say such things in her head, where the Heir could not hear them.

But even as she made the decision, he opened his eyes. Pale brown, flecked with green; fine counterpoint, when coupled with dark brown hair and lashes, to the olive complexion of their shared Tira Virteian ancestry.

He came awake smiling, briefly displaying teeth in a sweetly boyish smile. One was slightly crooked, she noted now with eyes instead of with her tongue, turned a little on edge so that the squared tip was layered somewhat aslant atop its neighbor. She wondered if any of the official portraits showed the imperfection, or if her brother had avoided portraying such things as physical flaws in his duties as Lord Limner. She had never paid any attention to Alejandro beyond what was required for courtesy's sake; Baltran was her world.

Damn Zaragosa; he would keep his place while she was sent from hers!

Alejandro stretched languorously, laughing deep in his throat. His voice had broken two years before into a fine baritone, very different, thank the Mother, from his father's bass, or this would be more difficult than it already had been.

"What happens now?" he asked, loose of limb and lazy.

"Now? More, if you wish." She hoped not. But she would not forbid him.

"More?" He grinned again, blindingly; he would win them all with that smile, and no effort expended. "You know better than I: have I any left to offer?"

Gitanna bared her teeth, though he saw it as a smile. "The do'Verrada bloodline runs to stamina."

"So." He was young, so young—a decade her junior—but not precisely a boy; and he had grown up in the house of a ruler. "And potency?"

He would speak of horses, then; eiha, and why not? There was truth in it enough. "The Duchess conceived four children. I would presume so."

"Yet only two survived." He hitched himself up on an elbow and propped his head against the heel of a broad palm.

"Potency has nothing to do with survival," she countered, "unless one argues that without the potency there can be no seed to survive."

"*Shall* we argue it, then?"

"If you wish, Don Alejandro."

He grimaced. "I wish to be Alejandro, not the Duke's Heir."

"But you are."

"In this?"

"In all things. Alejandro."

The quick, flashing smile lit humor-crinkled eyes. "What becomes of me now?"

"Whatever you desire."

"And if I desire you?"

"Then I am here."

"For as long as I wish?"

Did he probe to learn, or because he knew? "I think you are to do whatever you wish to do. I am—yours." For this day at least, and possibly the night, before she was sent away. Matra, but it stabbed deeply, so painfully. *I am no longer your father's.*

He stretched again, working kinks from a shoulder. "What becomes of you?"

Bitterness lashed out. "You ask too many questions!"

Into the startled silence that followed she heard his breathing cease, then begin again. She muttered a prayer in her head—how could she have been so foolish as to use that tone with *him*?—and prepared herself to endure the anger, the curses, the scorn.

"Eiha," he said eventually, "it is the best way to learn answers."

She stared at him, shocked speechless, and saw he was serious.

"Is it not?" The grin—and crooked tooth—flashed again. "But then that is another question, and I have offended once more."

Sixteen, just. Sixteen, and no longer a virgin, and more cheerful of temperament, less sparing of his laughter, than one might expect in a ducal Heir whose behavior, so very often, was rigidly circumscribed by inflexible tradition.

Was this what Baltran was like when he was a boy?

"Your brother," he said, "is not a particularly gifted painter."

"Matra ei Filho, he is *too* a gifted painter—" And then she broke off, because he was laughing at her. "Why?" she asked sharply. *Why provoke me?*

"To see if what I expected came to pass." He levered himself off his arm and sat up, mindful of his nudity as he pulled a linen sheet across his depleted lap and settled against the headboard. The side of his knee brushed her lower leg, was drawn away, then crept back again; he was not yet accustomed to the ordering of bodies after intimacy. "I am told everyone will tailor answers in accordance to what they believe I wish to hear."

"And did you expect what came to pass?"

He had no nervous habits. He was settled now, at ease, and focused on what was said; unusual for Courtfolk, who sought truth in what *wasn't* said. "If you had intended to tailor your words, you would not have answered as you did. But I had honesty of you, not Court speech."

Gitanna shook her head. "Not in bed." *Your father never wished it.*

"Then perhaps I should spend more time in bed."

"I have no doubt," she said dryly, "that indeed you will."

"Do'Verrada potency?"

"Stamina," she retorted. *And unflagging interest!*

Alejandro looked thoughtful. "I was told you had no wit."

"No wit! *Who* told you that?"

"My mother."

Gitanna sat immobile, tailoring her answer into noisy silence.

"So," Alejandro remarked. "She lied."

"Duchesses never lie."

"Mothers do," he said. "*My* mother does. She says she hates my father." He let the back of his skull rest against the carved headboard. "And that, you see, is very definitively a lie."

She had not expected, ever, to discuss the Duchess with her son, least of all after she of all women had bedded that son. "In her place," Gitanna said, "to my son, I would lie also."

"Because you are my father's mistress."

"Because she loves him."

"As he loves you."

Her response was immediate. "Baltran does not love me! Trust me, Alejandro—there may be bindings upon us, a thing of men and women, but there is no love in this. En verro."

"Because you cannot wed?"

Now he was young after all, to ask such a thing when he meant no harm by it, only desired to learn. "Noblemen do not wed their mistresses."

"If they loved them?"

"Politics," she said crisply. "Surely, in this Court, you have heard of such."

"Merditto!" he said vulgarly. "How could I not?"

"Eiha, how could you not?" Gitanna sighed and slid down against the headboard, snagging gauze on the scrollwork. "How could anyone in Palasso Verrada not be steeped in it?"

"Will he have you back?" he asked baldly.

Tears brimmed. "No."

"Gitanna—"

So, he knew her name. "No," she said again, turning her head away.

"Why not?"

Because this is his way of telling me it is ended. "Because—because . . . no man cleaves to a single woman."

"No man?"

Viciously, she said, "No man that I have heard of!"

"And if that man should wish to?"

Gitanna Serrano laughed. It was a brittle, desperate sound, and it caused him to stare, eyes wide and astonished. "What—will you keep yourself to *me* now that we have shared a bed?" She saw the startlement in his eyes. "There," she said, "you see? En verro."

After all his questions, his smiles, his laughter, the Heir to the duchy had no answer to offer.

ELEVEN

Sario stood utterly still, rooted into cobbles like a grandfather olive tree, splayed and ancient trunks split into ornate candelabra. He had arrived, seemingly all at once and without any physical effort, in the midst of the Zocalo Grando in the center of the city—or what had been the center before vital growth spilled into sprawl. Overshadowed by the many-tiered marble fountain and the massive twin-towered Cathedral Imagos Brilliantos, he was buffeted by the press of the crowd on festival day—Fuega Vesperra, to celebrate conception (and, no doubt, to *cause* it)—deaf to the noise as he was blind to the light, wholly alone amidst the tight-packed throng milling like a frightened flock of sheep with no dog in attendance.

He supposed he had walked. Perhaps he had run. But he stood here now, very still, very stiff, very cold despite the day, and found the key on its chain clasped so tightly in the fist of one slender hand that the gold bit into his flesh.

Chieva do'Orro. What all Grijalvas longed for, were they born male: to be more than merely gifted but Gifted as well, and blessed, honored among the family to ascend to a higher level of talent, technique, training, and the blazing light of sheer genius.

"For what?" he murmured bitterly. "To burn more brightly than another, only to be blown out an hour later?"

If it were true . . . *if* it were as Saavedra suggested. As she stumbled, all unwittingly, upon a hideous possibility even he, of the Viehos Fratos, had never heard in whispers, had never thought to ask. Had never so much as *imagined,* even to paint it.

He gripped the Chieva more tightly. "What if they don't know? What if *none* of them knows?"

They spoke of the Nerro Lingua, the deadly plague that racked the city, the duchy, but had so diminished the Grijalvas that even now, over sixty years later, they struggled to survive. Meya Suerta, for all the city's bounty, was not kind to the weak; a man needed size, as a family required numbers, to make a safe way in the world.

But they believe otherwise . . . Sario could not discount the plague, for the records, though incomplete, provided documentation that prior to the Nerro Lingua *all* Grijalva males lived longer. One need only go into the Galerria Grijalva and look upon the paintings to see the truth: the family had been vital, the family had been numerous, the family had been ranked among the highest, the strongest, the most richly favored in the ordering of the duchy.

"But now we die," he murmured. "What Duke would appoint a Grijalva to a lifetime post if that lifetime as an adult spans but thirty years, and within *twenty* of them the body and skills diminish?"

Someone jostled him from behind, jarring his shoulder: a squat Meya Suertan clutching an oil-soaked cloth sleeve of festival food. One city-bred cheek bulged greasily. Sario caught the pungent aroma of garlic, olives, onions, simmered overnight in rosemary and oregano, washed down now with spring wine; heard the muffled imprecation—his stillness caused a hardship for others who preferred to move—but did not respond. Only when a second voice grumbled more pointedly another vulgar comment did he rouse, and then it was to anger.

Chi'patro, the man had called him.

Sario could not argue, would not fight. In point of fact, it was truth: his parents had not been married. But that truth did not sting. That truth was not what the man referred to.

Being a bastard was one thing, and infinitely bearable within a family where such was not a stigma. But chi'patro was a wholly derogatory term applied only to Grijalvas, to insult Grijalvas *specifically,* whose once-honorable ancestry was widely and luridly known to be permanently tainted, as the sanctos and sanctas took care to remind everyone.

Tza'ab revenge. "Who is the father?"

Sario clamped his mouth shut on a stinging rebuke. There were no grounds for it, not now, with what he acknowledged; had he and Saavedra not stood before Piedro's *Death of Verro Grijalva* and looked upon both halves of their whole? Grijalva, and Tza'ab. Verro, dying in do'Verrada arms—and on the hilltop behind him a green-clad Tza'ab warrior, an Unbeliever, who had killed the greatest hero Tira Virte had ever known.

"He might have been Duke," Sario muttered, watching the city man stride away. "*He* might have been Duke—and I might have been also."

But he was not. He was Grijalva, and chi'patro. He was Tza'ab, and enemy.

And had, if he were *very* lucky, thirty more years to live.

Sario Grijalva lifted stinging eyes to gaze upon the bell towers of the great Cathedral. His fist yet was closed around his Chieva do'Orro. "Grazzo do'Matra," he began, deliberately ironic, "I thank you so very deeply for such blessings as you offer to an impure chi'patro moronno."

Seminno Raimon, rigid spine pressed against the doorjamb, clasped Sanguo Otavio's shoulder as the older man came in. "Rapidia, grazzo—he weakens quickly . . ." And to Davo, behind Otavio: "It comes now. Adezo. There is no time at all. . . ."

"Are we all here?" Davo asked, pausing before the door.

"No—no . . ." Raimon cast a quick, assessive glance over the others gathering like crows—and so they were, he realized with a start: crows at the death site, waiting for the living body to become dead. "We are missing Sario—and Ferico—"

"No." Ferico came up and put a hand on Davo's sleeve to ask mutely for passage. "*I* am here, but Sario . . . eiha!—have you ever known Sario to be where he is expected?"

"—no time . . ." Raimon murmured distractedly.

Davo moved aside, but Ferico did not enter at once. "Have you summoned sancta and sancto?"

Raimon hesitated minutely. "I sent for the Premias, yes, but—"

"Premias! Are you mad?" Ferico exploded. "They won't concern themselves with the passing of a Grijalva!"

Otavio joined them, expression severe. "And should we wish it? This is a private matter—"

"And we have not been of any import to the Ecclesia since before the Nerro Lingua," Ferico declared. "We Grijalvas do not count—"

"Chi'patros," Davo said plainly. Even in succinctness it was eloquent explanation, and a damning one.

"Bassda!" Raimon hissed. "Will you have us argue even at Arturro's deathbed?"

"And why not?" Ferico murmured dryly. "He would wish us to be as we are."

Tension lessened; Raimon could not suppress a brief smile—and then reflected that both the irony and the smile would be welcome to Arturro.

Despair abruptly engulfed him; what would the new order bring? "Matra Dolcha," he said fervently, "I wish this had not come!"

"It comes to us all," Otavio said repressively.

Davo clasped and lifted his Chieva do'Orro, pressing it against his lips. "Nommo Matra ei Filho," he whispered. "In Their Blessed Names, offer this man peaceful passage, good light along the way—"

Otavio made a rude sound. "This man may well have passed already during all this lengthy chatter—we had best attend him. Adezo!"

Raimon lingered even as the others turned toward the bedchamber adjoining the solar. "Sario—"

"He is not here!" Ferico snapped. "Would you have us request Arturro politely delay his death long enough to find him? Bassda!—let him be where he is, Raimon. He has never been one of us; why should he be so now?"

"He *is* one of us—"

"Bassda," Ferico repeated. "There is no time."

Otavio smiled with poisonous insincerity. "If you value the boy so much, why not have him paint Arturro's *Peintraddo Memorrio?*"

"*If* you can ever find him." Davo clapped a hand on Raimon's stiff shoulder. "Come. We can bicker later. Amaniaja."

Amaniaja. Tomorrow. Always, with so many: amaniaja.

But Arturro would never see it. This day was his last.

Saavedra accepted her task without question, without comment, without protest. She would do anything for Seminno Raimon, who had always been kind—and who just this moment looked tense and distraught—and obligingly went out into the streets in search of Sario. It was, she knew, an unlikely hope; and why Raimon expected *her* to be able to find him when two others sent out had not . . . eiha, but perhaps Seminno Raimon knew her better than she thought. As she knew Sario better than any other.

But still . . . in the midst of a festival day? She doubted she could find her shoes, albeit she wore them; Meya Suerta today would be impossible.

Zenita: noon, and noisy with it. Sanctia bells throughout the city tolled the hour, the celebration. Today, as every year, the Mother conceived the Son, and ten months later, at daybreak of Nov'viva Premia, the Son was born.

Just now she wished it *were* Nov'viva; though spring, the day was warm, made sticky with early humidity and the press of too many people. Nov'viva could be cold, but there were never so many visitors—raw provinciales—as there were during Fuega Vesperra.

Already the mass of hair pinned up but hours before came loose of its crimped copper tethers. Weight clogged her neck, straggled laggardly down her spine. She shielded her eyes from the glare of the sun with a hand against her brow, and saw in silhouette, looming above the rooftops one street over, the massive bell towers and tiled roofline of the Cathedral Imagos Brilliantos.

If I could climb into one of the towers . . . Surely from there she would find Sario even in the crush in the Zocalo Grando—but it would not be permitted. She was not a sancta, not even a noviciata; worse, she was chi'patro. There was not a sancta or sancto within the entire city who would let her ascend the tower to look for another chi'patro. And though she could in poor light be mistaken for a full-blooded Tira Virteian, they would know better: by the paint stains upon her clothing, by the chalk dust beneath her nails, by the clinging scent of solvents. Members of the Ecclesia searched avidly for such signs.

Saavedra's mouth hooked tautly. Under her breath she murmured, "I wonder how they justify their devotion to the Duchess Jesminia? It was *she* who gave us welcome!"

Of course, the Duchess Jesminia had been a do'Shagarra, wed to a do'Verrada.Do'Shagarra and do'Verrada did precisely whatever they chose to do.

But Saavedra supposed the tower was not so vital after all. Surely she would be deafened by the pealing of the bells, and not even for Sario would she sacrifice her hearing.

"Hot . . ." She lifted the fallen hair from her neck—and then knew what she would do. "The fountain!" It was tall enough, and cool enough—and infinitely more quiet than the belltower—and no one would disapprove no matter what her blood; if anything, there would be difficulty in finding space on a basin tier that was not already taken.

One street away, little more than a stone's throw, but it took time and effort to make her way through the crowd. In the end she shut her ears to the curses, the strident comments, and simply thrust herself through the throng, ignoring bruised toes, snagged clothing, tumbling hair. By the time she reached the Zocalo Grando she was sheened in sweat, and battered by careless feet and elbows. Her shoes, sandals only, provided little protection; she swore to herself she would seek a cool bath as soon as she found Sario and they returned to Palasso Grijalva.

If she found Sario.

"Merditto alba," she muttered. "Such a fortunate man, to be so gifted, so blessed, so *certain* . . . you walk through the city as if you were Duke yourself!"

Or the Duke's Lord Limner.

"Matra," Saavedra breathed, "you believe it is only time . . . you believe yourself it already."

But Zaragosa Serrano was Lord Limner, and Duke Baltran yet lived. It would be Don Alejandro's duty, when he was Duke in his father's place, to appoint the new Lord Limner.

"Bassda . . ." She worked again through the crowd, made her way to the fountain. As expected, there were wreaths of children festooned on the carved tiers, luxuriating in spray or even standing in the basins with water up to their knees. "Seminno Raimon has given you a task, 'Vedra—" She hiked the loose folds of crumpled linen skirts. "—and this task you shall perform—*Matra*, no, don't push!" She glared at the boy who competed for her place upon the marble edge. "There is room for us both, meninno." Saavedra clutched wet stone, soaking hem and sandals. The cool water, slopping over, turned worn leather soles slick beneath her feet. "I may look like a moronna, but this is the only way—and besides, I am cool . . . *nommo do'Matra!*" She wavered, astounded, as a hand touched her foot.

"Forgive me," a man said diffidently, "but you did not hear me over the noise of the water."

Nor over her mutterings as well. Saavedra, taken aback, stared down at the man. He was not what one might expect to find in the midst of Meya Suerta on festival day, braving the crush; he was old, very old, far beyond fifty, perhaps even beyond *sixty*. "Nommo Matra ei Filho," she murmured. "Why are you not dead?"

"Because," he said simply, "I am not a Grijalva."

He knew. Looking at her, he knew. *But—I am not a Gifted, to wear the chain and key* . . . And he was not a sancto to know her by her paint and chalk. She was merely a woman, no different from any other. Tira Virteian, Pracanzan, Ghillasian—it simply did not matter. No one, looking at her, knew what she was.

"Chi'patro," he said gently, and her conviction was shattered. "Ai, no," he said as she wavered, clutched again at marble, "please—grazzo . . . will you take my hand? Will you come down?"

It was an ancient hand, thin, spotted, palsied, tendons standing up in wiry relief beneath parchment flesh, but extended without hesitation to steady her. Saavedra considered the hand, considered coming down, considered what he knew and how he had come to know it, and what had brought him to her.

Beneath the crisp, precise folds of a bleached linen turban, the face was no less aged than the hand. But it smiled, it crinkled a multiplicity of creases into warmth and kindness, and clear gray eyes promised equal comfort.

"Honor an old man," he suggested, "and share some sweet juice with him. You need not fear, *al-adib zev'reina,* we shall not be alone. You will have familiar company."

The term he used was foreign, inflected with a rhythm she had never heard. "*What* familiar company?"

"Another Grijalva," he answered. "Another chi'patro."

"But who—?" And then she knew. "Sario."

"Ai, Sario. . ." Withered lips trembled in compressed smile. "If you know how I have prayed, *al-adib zev'reina!*"

"What is that?" she asked, clinging yet to marble. "What is that you call me? In what language?"

"Ai, forgive an old man, grazzo . . . it is strange to you, I know, the lingua oscurra. To Sario also."

" 'Dark tongue?' " Saavedra frowned. "*Nerro* Lingua was a plague."

"Ai, no, forgive me." He placed the hand against his heart. "I am estranjiero, a stranger to your land. I speak your language—I have lived here many years—but there are times my own tongue is simpler, times it sings a richer song." Once again the palsied, blemished hand was extended. "It means the 'Hidden Language.' "

"Lingua oscurra." She considered it. "And why should I accompany a man who must hide his language?"

"Chi'patro," he said deliberately, neither taking nor offering offense, "how is it that you can ask me such a thing?"

It silenced her. The spray now was chill, setting her to shivering. "He is with you? Sario?"

"He gave me to say, should you question the truth: 'Nommo Chieva do'Orro.' "

In the Name of the Golden Key. Tantamount to an order. But from Sario, no matter the circumstance, not entirely unexpected.

And proof that it was he: no one but a Gifted Grijalva knew the phrase, save for her, with whom he shared so much.

And now this. An estranjiero who speaks a hidden language. " 'Cordo," she said. "I'll come." And bent to put her hand into his surprisingly firm grasp.

TWELVE

The crows took their leave of the chamber housing the dead. Candles were extinguished one by one as each Gifted departed until only a single flame remained, as the man remained whose breath was to damp its light; but he could not bear it yet. Let it bloom a little longer as a lone candleflower, so he could offer a final companionship to a man who had been his father in all ways but one.

It hurt. Eiha, but it hurt— "Oh, Matra," Raimon murmured, locking rigid fingers into thick hair as he bowed his head. "Oh, Matra Dolcha—has his soul reached You yet?"

Perhaps not. Perhaps not while the flame yet blossomed on the wick.

Surely, in this, a chair was improper. Raimon slipped out of it awkwardly, graceless in grief, and lowered himself to rest, knees against the floor. He felt the roughness of uneven tile underneath the thin rug. "Nommo Matra ei Filho . . ." The prayer came easily, with utter sincerity; this man of them all deserved swift passage and certain welcome. "If You will but accept this man's soul, I would gladly surrender my place with You—"

"And are you so certain you shall have a place?"

Startled, Raimon twitched; he had heard nothing, no sound of admittance, no quiet voice announcing entry. She was simply *here*.

And he knew her. *Blessed Mother*— He pressed a hand against the bedframe to steady himself briefly as he rose. He swallowed before he could speak. "Premia . . . Premia Sancta—"

"I asked you a question, Grijalva. Are you so certain *you* shall have a place?"

The emphasis was slight, but he understood it. He was meant to understand it.

Despite his intentions, outrage kindled. It took every effort not to offer discourtesy, but humility in its place. *Give her no reason to say ill of me beyond what she manufactures.* "Premia." He bowed elegantly, submissively, one hand against his heart.

The door stood open behind her. She was a blaze of white in wan shadows, unleavened by light. White robe, white coif; a trickle of silver hanging to her waist. The bones of her face were severe, but not so severe as her eyes. Malice inhabited them.

He flicked a glance at the open door, and understood again. *She does not care who sees, or what is heard.* And it would be unkind.

He began once more, in perfect courtesy. "Premia Sancta, regretto . . . forgive me for my presumption."

"All you Grijalvas presume." A thin, spare voice, her diction precise so he would mishear nothing. "You presume your minor talent worthy of recognition. You presume your limners worthy of elevation. You presume your souls equal to those of others. You presume to regain a place you lost through the divine punishment of the Mother and Her Son."

Raimon's mouth dried even as his flesh sheened itself with nervous perspiration. Malice now was banished. She was all the more frightening because there was no passion. She declared it: it was so.

He swallowed tightly. "Premia, grazzo—I sent for you—"

"So you did." No passion at all. The dark eyes were flat and hard, framed by the simplicity of a plain linen coif drawn tight beneath her chin. "You presumed, and you sent."

Humility waned abruptly. Grief stripped him of self-control. "What have we done?" he cried. "What sin have we committed? We serve the Blessed Mother, we worship Her Holy Son, we tithe to the Ecclesia, we glorify Their Exaltedness with our art—"

One upraised slender hand silenced him. "You soil us," she answered. A simple declaration.

It was astounding, even from her. "*Soil* you!"

The hand disappeared within a fold of pristine robe. "I have spoken with the Duke many times, as has the Premio Sancto. We believe the blessings of the Ecclesia should be denied you Grijalvas."

"*Why?*"

Abruptly dispassion was vanquished, malice reclaimed. Livid color rushed into her thin, sallow face, flushing it a most unbecoming hue. "Because you are abomination!" she hissed. "Because you *remind* us of the dishonor!"

Raimon pressed crossed hands against his chest. "It was more than one hundred years ago!" he cried. "Oh, Matra, how many centuries must we endure this? We have done nothing! Do you believe we *invited* the dishonor?"

"Your women were there," she said curtly, "among the others. They were there, and they were carried away—without much protest, if one looks at Miquellan Serrano's brilliant peintraddo historrico for the truth!—and Tza'ab estranjieros got half-breed children upon them. Worse, they *lived to bear them.*"

Miquellan Serrano's so-called peintraddo historrico, *Rescue of the Captives,* was a masterpiece of bigotry and cruel imagination, no more. "The Duchess also was there," Raimon reminded her.

"Bassda!" White as her linen robe, the Premia Sancta kissed her fingertips, then pressed them to her heart in token tribute to the blessed Duchess Jesminia. Between her fingers glinted a chain not unlike his own. All sanctas wore the symbol of their office: tiny silver locks. The sanctos wore the keys. Each order, divided by gender if not by determination and exactitude, was half of a whole in Ecclesial service. "You profane the city," she said. "You profane the Ecclesia. You profane the air we breathe."

"Your Eminence—"

"Bassda!" She silenced him again, viciously, merely with her tone. "The Premio Sancto refused to come, as he should have. He recommended to me that I also refuse, but I sought the opportunity to look upon the man, the dying Grijalva chi'patro, and to tell him to keep his curs chained within their own kennel. Do not presume again to summon any sancta, Grijalva. Our eyes are closed to you."

He could barely force breath through his constricted chest. "He is dead," Raimon managed. "It doesn't matter any more if you have come."

The woman disagreed. "Of course it does. The message is given, no? And must be obeyed."

To bear enmity for years long past, such hostility for an ancient dishonor . . . He struggled not to shout condemnation. "We were not at fault. *Not* Grijalvas."

"Of course you were. Why else did the Matra permit those women to be dishonored? Why else were the children permitted to be conceived? Why else were so many born? And *why else* was the Nerro Lingua so particular in its punishment of your family? You have been marked out by our Most Holy Mother as abomination. In her wisdom she has punished you for the dishonor, the taint, by visiting upon you the Nerro Lingua, and the Ecclesia follows Her guidance." One thin hand clasped the silver lock into a knob-knuckled fist. "Pray within your walls as much as you wish, chi'patro, but the Mother and Her Son have no mercy for Grijalvas."

Raimon cast off discretion. "Then you have perverted Them," he accused. "You have polluted Their hearts with your selfish, misguided fanaticism—"

"Bassda!"

"—and one day we Grijalvas *shall* regain what we had, including the Holy Blessings of the Mother and Her Son, and they shall know the truth of how They are served by such as you and yours, and those of the Premio Sancto!" He was trembling with outrage. "—Nommo Chieva do'Orro!"

Her face now was pinched and white, ageless in asceticism. "Oh, yes," she said acidly, "your sacred Golden Key. One would believe you worship *that* above the Matra ei Filho!"

"Not above the Mother and Her Blessed Son. Above the Ecclesia and its unholy politics."

"The Ecclesia *is*—" And she broke it off.

"Oh, yes?" It was his turn to spill the acid. "Were you intending to say the Ecclesia *is* the Mother and Son? Oh, but to do so is basest blasphemy, heresy, no?—and what, do you think, would be adequate punishment for it? A plague? Another Nerro Lingua?"

"Nommo Matra ei Filho," she murmured, as if in supplication. "I pray You give me strength—"

"To circumvent a family you believe tainted, when we were merely victims!"

"Whores," she said icily. "Every one of them. The *Rescue of the Captives* proves it."

Illumination kindled. "What is your family name?"

"The Ecclesia is my family. My name is Premia Sancta."

"Before," he said steadily. And then laughed bitterly. "But no, do not trouble yourself to dissemble. I believe I know the answer." Raimon paused. "And is the Premio Sancto *also* a Serrano, as was the artist?" He paused, timing it. "As is the Premia Sancta?"

Dark eyes flashed. "Bassda," she hissed. "I will hear no more from you!"

Raimon extended a hand. "The door is there," he said plainly. "I suggest you use it. Adezo."

When the woman was gone, when the room was empty of vilification and bitter family rivalry, Raimon Grijalva turned again to the man in the bed. Very carefully he knelt once more upon the frayed, thin rug, bowed his head, and began the simple prayer the Ecclesia would never offer. "Matra ei Filho . . . accept this man's soul, who labored so long and well to serve You, his Duke, and his family."

Long indeed, for a Limner. From birth through depletion to death, Arturro Grijalva had survived fifty-one years.

The tent was little more than a framework of willow withies, bound and braided with reeds in intricate knotwork patterns, overdraped with doubled panels, a flutter of pennons stitched with green into complex designs. The inner layer was a gauzy, loose-woven fabric of time-suppled flax; the outer, though rolled up and tied neatly into a perimeter hemming the top, was a heavier, close-loomed canvas, oiled against the rains of autumn and winter. The tent was neither round nor square but an odd marriage of both, a series of flexible, slightly curved panels fastened into a whole, seamless and apparently impervious to the vagaries of weather. And yet it was a *tent*.

In the center of Meya Suerta.

He had not been to this street before, because the Grijalvas kept to their Palasso and the artisans quarter. Today, during Fuega Vesperra, he had wandered purposely, rejecting the habits of his family, the cowardice that kept them sequestered. And he had discovered the tent. A tent wholly alien within the city, and yet ignored as if no one else saw it.

Sario, in its center, could not see how anyone might miss it. He had marked it instantly upon turning the corner. It had drawn him, brought him to its entrance with the colors, the patterns, the knotwork. It intrigued him to learn how it was attached to the ground, how it rooted into packed dirt and cobbles. Surely it was staked somehow; great winds occasionally howled down through the corridors of city dwellings, ripping away awnings, market stalls, cart shrouds. A tent could not withstand such.

Nor, he thought, should it withstand a festival day, or the city at all; and yet despite the throngs outside, fuzzily visible through the gauze, there was little sound. It was as if wax were stuffed into his ears, diminishing nearly all of the world's song save for an understated hum, like the drone of distant bees. And despite the unruly crowd, its fabric and frame remained whole.

He knelt. Beneath his doubled knees lay a rug of intricate design, of strange ornate devices and stylized plant renderings at odds with Tira Virteian tastes. And the colors—*eiha, the colors!* He had known they existed, but never used them in his own work, which leaned more toward vivid hues as opposed to muted tones. He saw beneath him, despite the loomed fabric, the colors of another land: the rich rust of iron oxide; the pinker tones of rose-blushed sandstone; sparing but deep bloodied raisin verging on purple; seams of blue and green, though soft and barely visible. Unseen when examined but undeniably *felt*.

Like art . . . like passion . . . Accustomed to the warm subtle tones of Meya Suerta's brickwork, its clay and cobbles and plaster sun-bleached ocher, oyster, and ivory, Sario's eyes were drawn again and again to the rug, examining color, composition, theme but he could not identify the theme. That one existed he knew; the repetition of certain patterns made it obvious, the arched, knotted interlocking series of plant stems, leaves, petals, the meticulously clean-lined and oddly familiar borders. He *should* see the theme, should identify it. He had trained his eye for years to see the whole even in a vast array of infinitely intricate parts.

The response was instinctive, abrupt, characteristic. "I should use this . . ." Of a sudden, illumination: subtlety contained power as much as bold color.

Already his mind busied itself sketching the beginnings of a new work, a landscape of sere and sparing color, of brittle but binding tints unlike those he now employed. Even the tones of the flesh could be altered, when painting a portrait. "Sweet Mother . . ." He traced the stem of a woven plant "growing" from beneath a knee. "What I could do with this—"

Sound. He broke off thought, glancing up quickly to the flap that served as a door into the tent. He saw through gauze to the world beyond: the old man, and Saavedra.

Artistic absorption shattered. He felt again the confusion, the unease, the vague fear, though all was coupled with a perversely burgeoning fascination. *What he said . . . what he told me . . .* But questions he'd left unasked because he was made mute, too astonished by conception of new thoughts, strange thoughts, as yet fragmented and tentative. *What the moualimo said to me—*

Moualimo? No—*estranjiero,* an old foreign man wandering in wits the way it sometimes took them.

Moualimo. Yes—but what was there the old man could teach him? Color? Pattern? Sario glanced briefly at the loomwork beneath his knees. *He has this to teach me.*

The tent itself and the artistry of its appearance had been enough to bring him here; the invitation extended by the old man initially startled when Sario discovered him, whose expression then altered into delight and gratitude had been enough to *leave* him here. And then he had seen Saavedra in the crowd, had spoken of her—and the stranger had gone to fetch her.

Now Saavedra was here, and he felt safe. *She will understand.* She hesitated even as the old man pulled aside the drapery to ad-

mit her. Sario rose, blinking in the shaft of pure sunlight unadulterated now by the sheer netting of gauze, and waited.

'Vedra always understands.

Gauze-defined, day-diffused sunlight was gentle and immensely flattering. He saw the delicate mixture of expressions in
her face: in the fine, clear gray eyes; the high, oblique cheekbones; the clean contours of jaw. The set of eloquent black
brows divulged her concern, and the line of her mouth, pulled
straight, compressed flat into unfamiliar severity. He wanted
abruptly to soothe those concerns, to soften that mouth . . . "Luza
do'Orro," he murmured beneath his breath. "Oh, but I had forgotten." And had become too consumed, too ambitious, too
wholly Gifted to note more than with the artist's eye instead of
with the man's.

He had known. His body had known. He was no child, no innocent, awkward mennino to remain ignorant of such things. He had
been Confirmed years before according to the rites of the family:
four women in his bed, four fertile women for several nights each,
and none of them got with child. And neither were any of them, beyond the first, unsatisfied with his efforts.

He was infertile, not unable. As he had told her once. As was
proved time and again when he desired a bedding, though all too
often the fire of his loins sublimated itself in art.

Only she understood him. Only she ever had.

Sario opened his mouth to speak, to explain what had happened,
what the stranger had told him, to share with her as always what
was in his heart, but Saavedra herself forestalled him. She slid a
quick, wary sidelong glance at the old man as he came in beside
her, then looked only at Sario. He could see she was frightened.
And also rigorous in duty. "You are summoned." She clipped her
words. "Seminno Raimon."

He could not help himself. "Let him wait."

It shocked her. "Sario—"

"Let him *wait,* 'Vedra." It was not what he had intended, this
whip-quick, decisive tone. But urgency fed him now; he sensed a
completeness and purpose, as if a pattern never known broken was
abruptly mended. And the old man's expression, oddly, was
serenely satisfied. "What he has told me—"

"What?—in his 'hidden language?' In his hidden tent?"

"The tent isn't hidden, 'Vedra—"

"I didn't see anything until he brought me inside!"

"*I* did. I saw from the end of the street!"

"So you did," the old man said complacently. "Acuyib has blessed you with the inner vision."

Saavedra did not lack for decisiveness. "You have been summoned," she repeated. "Matra Dolcha, Sario, have you forgotten what you are?" She indicated with a subtle movement of her head the chain and key against his breast, tangled in creases of wilted, soiled lawn. "We are not to refuse the responsibilities of our family."

"What does Raimon want?"

A second quick, slicing glance at the old man. "I don't *know*," she said tersely. "But—he was not himself."

Sario grimaced. "He is of the Viehos Fratos. No one may be himself, once he is of their number."

"*Sario!*" Color stained the delicate tones of her face, so that the bone of her jawline stood out pale in taut relief. "This man is estranjiero!"

"Not here." The old man's rebuke was gentle but crisply definitive. "Not within my home. And no more estranjiero than either of you, who share my blood."

"Your blood!" Shocked. Angry. Uncertain of all but confusion. "I am a Grijalva—"

"And chi'patro," the old man reminded her. "Both of you. I myself am not. I can count back all of my generations to Acuyib's Great Tent itself, but you are more than what you believe."

"Tza'ab," Saavedra breathed. "*That's* what you are. I recognize the turban from the painting . . . from Piedro's *Death of Verro Grijalva*. It is a different color, but it is the same."

"Ai, I am found out!" The old man, unexpectedly, retained most of his teeth, though they were stained yellow; now he flashed them briefly. "*Zev'reina,* I beg you—give me time—"

"I have none!" She was, Sario noted with an artist's detached eye, white and black at once: white of face, of lips; black of eye as pupils dilated. "And neither does he have time." She turned sharply to Sario. "You are summoned to Seminno Raimon."

"Let him wait." The Tza'ab quietly echoed Sario's words of a moment before. "Truly, you will see the sense in it. I promise."

"And what is it worth, your promise?" Sario had never seen Saavedra so rude before, or so frightened. "What are you to us? Estranjiero—foreigner and enemy—"

"Not to you. None of those things. One is not estranjiero or enemy within these walls, beneath my roof, breathing the very air exhaled by Acuyib." The ancient face reflected no hurt, no offense, that she should be so discourteous in a place he had welcomed her. "You have come home, Children of the Golden Wind. And at least one of you will never stray again."

⊷ THIRTEEN ⊷

Forty-three years had not yet robbed Duke Baltran of a power-ful, easy grace. Smoothly he hooked his right leg forward across the pommel, then simultaneously turned in the saddle and kicked free of the left stirrup to jump down all of a piece, landing lightly and balanced as a fencer. The informal dismount had not been taught by the Premio Chevallo charged with instructing him in equine mastery as a boy, but adopted as a time-saver by a vigorous, active young man. It made him feel young to employ it even now, despite the occasional twinges in his knees. It was easier—and po-litically sound—to let the others see him so vigorous than to admit to the first depredations of bone-fever, a common complaint of folk living in a city built so near marshland. The Grijalvas were riddled with it.

Far better to be of another family entirely than that sadly weak-ened bloodline! One silver-banded rein was draped across the stal-lion's massive neck; the other the Duke tossed at the young groom come out at a run from the stable block to tend his master's mount.

Baltran did not hesitate as his companion, clattering up to join him, also dismounted—as quickly, though with markedly less grace as he briefly caught spur in stirrup—but strode across the flagged courtyard even as he stripped leather gloves from his hands. Nor did he hesitate as that companion hastily threw reins at the horse-boy and scrambled to catch up; both men were tall, but the Duke had had more years to accustom himself to the length of his stride.

"Patro—"

"I have told you, no?" Baltran deposited the dusty gloves into the waiting hands of a servant come out to aid him even as he walked toward the Palasso. "It simply is not done."

"But—"

"There are *reasons* for it, Alejandro. Can you imagine what your mother might say?"

Alejandro matched him now stride for stride, moving with loose-limbed ease that promised to echo his father's grace if he ever finished growing. "Why would she have to know?"

"She wouldn't *have* to know, Alejandro, but she *would*. Women do. The servants attending you and your mistress would know, and they would whisper of it to their friends, who would then know, and the friends would tell *their* friends, and soon enough the women attending the Duchess would know—and there you have it. The Duchess herself would know, and she would have plenty to say."

"I could keep her elsewhere."

"Your mother?" Baltran grinned at his son's horrified expression. "No, no—eiha, have you no sense of humor?" Still walking, he began to unlace the cords of his leather hunting doublet. "Ah, but no, there is no humor in this—I should recall it myself. It is never amusing when a boy wishes to take his first mistress." More laces undone, the chest-flap pulled wide, the garment divested and shed into the deft hands of his body-servant. "I have no objection if you wish to keep a mistress, Alejandro, but I would suggest you select another."

"But I want *her,* Patro—"

"Why? Because she took you to a place you had never before experienced? Because she made you feel things you had not expected to feel?" Baltran, taking pity—his son's face was white and tense—halted and swung to face his Heir. "Matra, I know—I do know, Alejandro . . . but it cannot be done. It *should* not be done."

"But I am the Heir . . . and if I desire it—"

"Alejandro." Baltran summoned patience. "Alejandro, you are indeed the Heir, and you will be able to do many things in life when and as you wish them. But they should only be done after much thought."

"I *have* thought, Patro."

The Duke waved the body-servant away despite the sweat-soiled folds of shirt clinging to his torso; he would not strip here in the courtyard, and neither would he make his son trail him into the Palasso like a submissive puppy begging for attention. "You have thought, Alejandro, yes. I have no doubt. But there are details perhaps you have not considered."

"Details?" Given ground to stand, courage kindled: Alejandro was less rushed now and coolly insistent. "I want her. You don't. What more is there than that?"

"Political concerns."

"She's a *mistress,* not a princess . . . what value does she have in politics?"

Baltran untied soiled cuffs and began to roll back full sleeves, displaying thick, tanned forearms. "She was *my* mistress, Alejandro—and she is a Serrano. While she may well seek an alliance—perhaps even a marriage—with a wealthy nobleman, it would not serve for her to leave my bed for yours."

The son was annoyed. "You have another woman in yours, Patro."

The father grinned easily. "So I do. And for all you know, it may even be your mother . . . but that is not your concern. You must think again, Alejandro, and see what lies ahead. Gitanna Serrano, cast off from the Duke but given to the Heir . . . aside from the problem of your mother's reaction, there would be the reaction of the Court."

"What does it matter *which* woman I take to bed?"

"Because it does. It always does. It must—unless she be a comely maidservant pitifully grateful for the attention . . . but such a woman would not be a part of the politics, merely a convenience. That is of no moment. If you wish to tumble such, you have my blessings—but if you wish to install a woman in the Palasso you must take greater care."

"Patro—"

"Bassda, Alejandro . . . I weary of this subject. You have my word on it: Gitanna Serrano is not to be your mistress. She served to make you a man and so you are, but you would be better served to look elsewhere for a bedpartner. Perhaps to the do'Brendizia, or the do'Casteya—the Serranos have been elevated quite enough, grazzo, with Zaragosa as Lord Limner, Caterin as Premia Sancta, and Gitanna in my bed!" He shrugged broad shoulders. "It was unwise of me, but I was smitten by the mennina. It lasted longer than expected . . . eiha, it happened; what more can I say? As for now, I cannot dismiss either Zaragosa or the Premia Sancta—"

"—so you dismiss Gitanna."

The Duke laughed, amused. "It is somewhat easier to replace a mistress than Lord Limner or Premia Sancta, yes? In the former case, I should have to die; and in the latter, *she* would."

"And that is why? You cast her off because of *politics?*"

Baltran's grin faded. "I cast her off because I wearied of her constant prating against the Grijalvas, her repeated demands that I revoke the Ducal Protection—Matra Dolcha, I hear enough of that from the Premia Sancta!—and because I prefer another." He shrugged dismissively. "You will see, Alejandro . . . when a man is offered the choicest of innumerable wines, he often prefers to sample the grapes before selecting the variety he wishes to drink after dinner." He softened his tone, curbed the irony; he remembered his own impetuous youth and how detached condescension infuriated him. "Alejandro, I assure you of this: you are not in love with her.

She is your first woman, and you are quite understandably infatuated with her. Eiha, aren't we all infatuated with our first?" He
grinned reminiscently; Trinia had been exquisite to look at and
generous in bed. "But there will come a woman, and there will
come a time, when you recognize the difference."

"*One* woman, Patro?"

"One," Baltran answered soberly. "I knew, once. I knew it instantly."

"But—it was not my mother."

"Eiha, no . . . I care deeply for your mother, Alejandro—I respect and admire her, and there is no question of my affection for
her—but no, she was not the one. That one died."

It shook the Heir visibly. "Died?"

"Bearing the son who would have been your half brother." The
Duke glanced away, staring briefly at the sun. That time was
passed, and more passed now. "Regretto, filho meyo—but I must
go in and refresh myself. There is an embassy due from Pracanza
later today, and I must prepare for it."

"Pracanza? Do you think they are seeking terms?"

"Demands," Baltran answered crisply, turning toward the
Palasso. "That's all they ever make, the Pracanzans. Demands."

"What kind of demands, Patro?"

Baltran paused, then clapped his tall son on the shoulder. "No
need for you to concern yourself just yet! Enjoy your newfound
manhood, Alejandro, and know in good time I will introduce you
to the intricacies of diplomacy—*and* Pracanzan demands!"

In the private, sunny solar that had housed so many stimulating and
pleasant discussions with Arturro Grijalva, Raimon leaned against
a pillar in false nonchalance and contemplated the man who sat in
the chair, one hand filled with a goblet of wine and the other with
his key and chain, chiming them absently in his cupped palm as if
he tested the weight of coin.

Raimon crossed arms across his chest, shoulder blades set firmly
against masonry. He was not at ease, but the posture allowed him
to seem as if he were. "It will be Otavio."

The other twisted his mouth thoughtfully, considered it, then
sighed and nodded. "I see no other possibility."

"He is not an Arturro."

"No man is an Arturro." The other shook his head. "I approve no
more than you, Raimon, but I think 'Tavi will not prove a disastrous Premio Frato. He is not a stupid man."

"Only shortsighted. Arrogant. Unwilling to consider how things change—how things *must* change, to affect greater change."

"Eiha, it is difficult for an older man, Raimon." Davo, eight years senior, grinned. "You may feel the same when you are 'Tavi's age."

Raimon was not amused. "I doubt it."

Davo's smile faded. "So. What do you propose, then?"

Raimon lingered a moment, then scraped himself off the pillar and moved to the high, arched window. The scent of vine blossoms was heavy as a cheap perfume sold to the peasant women, the camponessas, on festival day, underscored by the thick humid weight of freshly trimmed grass below in the courtyard, where gardeners labored. In summer everything grew profusely, warmed by heat, nursed by moist air . . . others departed the city at the worst of the season, but Grijalvas never did. There was work within the Palasso. Always work.

Raimon sighed quietly but did not turn. He spoke to the air framed by the hand-smoothed embrasure. "I think we must undertake to serve our own designs."

"Raimon! Matra Dolcha, it is well you say this to *me*. Do you know what would happen if another heard you say so?"

"Most probably Chieva do'Sangua."

Davo now was alarmed. "And do you not care? Does it not distress you—"

Raimon turned sharply. "What distresses me is that we have our first and best opportunity to place a Grijalva at Court in several generations, and it will be thrown away by a moronno who detests a boy more gifted—and Gifted!—than he."

Davo gestured. " 'Tavi has always been difficult—"

"Otavio is impossible, and you know it!" Raimon caught and held his breath, reestablishing self-control, then blew it out in a noisy exhalation. "I know. I do know. And perhaps it is only my fear speaking, Davo—but I do fear. You know as well as I that Sario is our best hope."

"Only if he is controllable," Davo reminded. "Nommo Matra ei Filho, Raimon—I have never known a Grijalva so difficult to deal with!"

Raimon smiled faintly. "Not even me?"

Davo laughed indulgently. "Eiha, you had your moments . . . but you also displayed sense, Raimon. Eventually."

Beneath his cuff, the flesh of his wrist sent a ghostly reminder of the pain of the Lesser Discipline. "Eventually," Raimon echoed. "But have you another course to suggest?"

Davo did not hesitate. "There is no other."

"Then what—"

"Because we cannot take it into our hands! That is not how we conduct ourselves." Davo shook his head. "Compordotta, Raimon—*always,* the behavior must be correct."

"Even if it is wrong?"

"You know why," Davo said quietly. "Without the controls of compordotta, without the promise of the invocation of such things as the Lesser Discipline and the Chieva do'Sangua, we could become monsters."

"Otavio might argue Sario *is* a monster."

"And he may. But only if the boy is given leave to act improperly. And without the guidance of the Viehos Fratos, without the proper preparations, he will. Sario is—Sario."

"And if we do not see Sario named as Lord Limner?"

Davo shrugged. "Then we wait."

"For how long? Fifty years? Five hundred?" Raimon shook his head. "We have been resoundingly fortunate the do'Verradas have thus far sired clever, astute Dukes, but that could change . . . the incursions and depredations of Pracanza and other countries could well rob us of our strength and make it a simple matter for war to come upon us. A war that might destroy us."

Davo's expression stilled as if he had heard words beneath the words. Slowly he said, "You mean the Tza'ab. It isn't Pracanza or Ghillas or any of the other countries that concern you, it's the *Tza'ab.*"

Raimon sighed and collapsed against the wall beside the window, letting stone uphold his spine as he shut his eyes wearily. "En verro. I do fear them."

"They were *destroyed,* Raimon! The Diviner was killed, the Riders of the Golden Wind defeated, the *Kita'ab* itself burned. By our own kinsman! The tribes were left in such disarray they will likely never again serve a woman even if she calls herself their Empress—and no male has been born to the Diviner's line in nearly a century. They are no danger to us. They have lost their heart, their soul."

Raimon lifted the back of his skull from the wall and looked hard at Davo. "How do we know?"

Davo blinked. "How do we know?"

"How do we know there are no Riders left, no fragments of the *Kita'ab,* no man willing to rouse Tza'ab Rih once more?"

"Because—" Davo stopped, then began again. "Because it has been too long."

"Too long?" Raimon twisted his mouth. "How long is *too* long, Davo, to attempt to reclaim what was precious?"

"But—"

"Do we not do the same, Davo? Each boy born, Confirmed, trained, we pray will be the one to recapture what was lost . . . do we not do the same? What is to say the Tza'ab do not wait, as we wait, and train, as we train, the one candidate most likely to reclaim the position? For them, the Diviner; for us, Lord Limner. One and the same, Davo—except they want to destroy Tira Virte, while we wish to preserve it."

Davo clearly struggled with the concept. "But we do not *know,* Raimon! There may be no truth in it. No truth at all."

"Of course," Raimon agreed quietly. "En verro, I could be wrong. Of course."

"Oh, Matra," Davo whispered. "Oh, Matra Dolcha."

Raimon gathered his Chieva and lifted it to his lips, then pressed it to his heart. "Nommo Matra ei Filho, may there be no truth in any of it."

But he feared very much there was. And with the Ecclesia as an enemy, Duke Baltran surrounded by Serranos, Grijalvas denied entry to the Palasso Verrada and Court—eiha, what was left? Compordotta? But circumscribed behavior was wholly ineffective and definitively deplorable when it enabled enemies to use it to their advantage.

I require a key. Raimon closed a hand around his Chieva. *A living key.*

⸺⬥ FOURTEEN ⬥⸺

Alejandro was, he deduced, formally dismissed, and probably forgotten. His father had spoken; life thus remained as it was. Gitanna was, or would be, gone. But Alejandro's world, despite his father, was changed. Life did *not* remain as it was, because life for him was altered. The yearnings he had felt now were answered, and he was more than content to let the question be asked as many times as it could be, so long as the answer was always the same.

But the woman would be different. *Patro has proclaimed it.*

Bemused, Alejandro watched the powerful figure of that father stride away across the courtyard, bound for the Palasso and ducal duties. There was no hesitation in the effort, no lessening of vigor, no tenderness evident in limbs or joints. Alejandro had seen nothing, ever, that could dim the fire of his father.

Have I any? He spread his hands and examined them, turning them this way and that. *Have I any of his fire, or am I merely a spark?* And one so often doused in his father's impressive presence.

"Merditto," the Heir murmured, scrubbing thick hair into a spiky tangle. He scowled as the Duke climbed the steps and disappeared into the shadowed recess framing the low door; he used a side entrance, not the Portalla Granda. "No. He will save that for the Pracanzans."

Alejandro sighed. He was at loose ends now, denied Gitanna's bed as well as participation in the politics of Court. It was not that he wanted so desperately to be a part of politics—no one living in Palasso Verrada could avoid them altogether—but that he was so easily dismissed, as if he played no part in Tira Virte's welfare.

Hands settled now on hips, Alejandro hooked a booted toe beneath a loose cobble and pried it up from its bed. One sharp kick sent it tumbling across its neighbors. And then he turned on his heel and marched toward the gate, politely refusing the groom who came running up with an offer to fetch him a fresh mount. "No, grazzo—walking will settle my temper!"

And if his father in one breath denied him Gitanna while also offering ducal blessing for his son to seek other women, that is precisely what the son would do.

Alejandro smiled as his disposition recovered itself. It was Fuega Vesperra, after all, and most of the female populace would be out in the city's streets. Perhaps the day was not quite doomed after all.

The old Tza'ab lightly placed a hand on Sario's elbow as he stepped toward the tent entrance in pursuit of Saavedra. "No—let her go. It is new to her, this truth. Give her time."

Sario wrenched away, though little effort was required to free himself of the unobtrusive touch. "New to *me,* also!"

"But you have a greater curiosity, no? And the inner vision." The old man smiled, spreading palsied hands in an oddly youthful gesture of innocence. "Is it a sin to be curious? No; even I do not suspect your beloved Mother and Son of renouncing curiosity . ... from it comes your talent, your technique, your hunger for improvement, coupled with the vision, all so you can exalt Their Blessed Names."

Sario regarded him with some suspicion. Saavedra was gone now, lost within the crowd—and it was true, what the old man said: he *was* curious. "You don't worship the Mother and the Son." It was accusation, challenge.

The old man tucked his hands inside the sleeves of his loose saffron-dyed over-robe. "Don't I?"

Sario evaluated the serene expression. "No," he said finally. "You are too much Tza'ab."

"I *am* Tza'ab . . . could I be more? Could I be less? Could I be anything else?"

It was succinct. "Enemy."

"Not to you."

"Why not to me? I am Tira Virteian, and Grijalva—it was both halves of me that caused the downfall of Tza'ab Rih." Sario offered a superior smile. "His name was Verro Grijalva."

"Halves of a half," the old man corrected, indifferent to condescension. "The other half is wholly Tza'ab, and blessed with Tza'ab talent."

Sario felt his face warm. "Will you insult me with that?"

"Insult you? Claiming you half Tza'ab?" Yellowed teeth were displayed, albeit briefly. "Ai, no—to do so would insult more of me than it insults you!"

Sario shook his head. "But you cannot know if I am half Tza'ab. No one does. No one *can.* We have all married one another so many times, we Grijalvas, or gotten children within the family, that I may only have but a drop of Tza'ab blood."

"Look at me," the old man said. "You came to my tent. You *saw* my tent. You could not read the patterns, but you knew they were for you."

"Read the patterns?"

"I knew you at once, as you stood before my tent; and how do you *think* I knew you? You saw my tent—and my face is your face."

Horrified, Sario denied it. "Your face is *old*."

"My face is ancient," the Tza'ab agreed calmly, unoffended, "but the bones beneath the flesh do not change." He tapped his nose with a hooked finger. "Look again, Child of the Golden Wind, and see with an artist's eyes."

Thus challenged, Sario accepted. It took no time at all, and less imagination. No wonder at all that the old man, even in the midst of a festival day, knew him. And spoke to him in the name of Verro Grijalva, which was all that was necessary.

That, and the fascination for the makings of his tent.

Frustrated, Sario muttered a street epithet, then turned away from the entrance flap to face the man squarely. "So, I am more Tza'ab than others—I am dark enough for it!—but what is that to me? I am no less tainted, no less accursed by the Ecclesia. It makes no difference at all."

"It makes every difference. It provides you with the vision."

"*What* vision? What is this 'vision'?"

The old man smiled. "The eye of the artist. The eye of Al-Fansihirro." He went on before Sario could interrupt him. "As for those of the Ecclesia who believe you tainted, they are fools. But not ignorant."

It astonished Sario. "How can they *not* be ignorant? They claim we use dark magic to fashion life as we wish it . . . if that were true—Matra! If that were true!—do you think we would permit them to revile us? Do you believe we would remain a lesser family? Do you think we would not *use* the magic to alter our state?"

"You would," the Tza'ab said, then quietly shifted emphasis. "*You* would."

"*I* would—I?" Sario laughed sharply. "I am trusted by no man among us, and they are all Grijalvas!"

"Because there is truth in the rumors."

"What truth? We have no power!"

"You have *some* power." The Tza'ab turned away, moved to a plump cushion, then carefully lowered himself to sit upon it. "Or you would have been blind to my tent." A gesture indicated Sario should seat himself upon the rug again. "There is more to learn. And so we begin."

"Estranjiero," Sario breathed, "why should I listen to you?"

"Because you are like me," the old man said simply. "Loyal to what lies here—and here." He touched his heart, his brow, then smiled oddly. "Perhaps you *are* me—though I am still alive, and it could be argued that it cannot be so with both of us yet living."

After a rigid moment of bewildered incomprehension, Sario shook his head. "You are moronno luna. A fool who believes he can touch the moon itself and drag it out of the sky."

The old man laughed soundlessly. "Will you have it so, then? Only the moon, when you might have the Desert?"

"What do you mean?"

"With Al-Fansihirro, all is possible."

"With—what? What is that? *Al-Fan*—what did you say?"

"Al-Fansihirro. In the lingua oscurra it means 'Art and Magic'—and there is the first lesson." The old man's gray eyes glinted private amusement. "It is a Tza'ab Order, a holy caste, much as your sanctas and sanctos."

"What kind of order? If it is like sanctas and sanctos, I want no part of it!"

"Like them in loyalty, devotion, lifelong service. Unlike them in deity, means, and methods." The Tza'ab turned to a casket beside his cushion and sprang the latch. "You see, Sario, there are many things in this world a man may be, regardless of his age, regardless of his birth. I am old, yes—to a Limner I must look like a corpse dug up from the soil!—but I am far from useless. What I know, I can teach . . ." He lifted the lid. Sario caught a whiff of aged fragrances, saw a scrap of brilliant green silk. "Ai, but *you* will come to understand."

The old man drew from the casket a slender leather tube. Despite the trembling in his hands, he deftly untied knots, loosened wire, slipped the cap from the end of the tube, then with extreme care drew a rolled parchment from it. Sario, still standing at the entrance poised to flee even as Saavedra, watched in unflagging fascination as the Tza'ab unrolled the sheet. He placed it with care upon the rug, set carved gold weights upon each corner, then gestured invitation.

Sario looked. And was stunned. "Matra . . . *Matra ei Filho!*" Without volition he fell to his knees. "How did you—how *can* you . . . Matra Dolcha, how is this possible?"

"With Al-Fansihirro, all is possible."

"But—but this . . ." And at last he saw the theme he could not grasp before. The pattern now was whole. "—Nommo Matra ei Filho . . ."

"Ai, no," the old man demurred. "In Acuyib's name!"

Sario had no time for strange names and stranger deities. Chilled bone-deep, soul-deep, a shudder racked him. Trembling did not cease as he stared at the weighted parchment. "Do you know what this is?"

"A page from the *Kita'ab*," the Tza'ab answered quietly. "Your kinsman, Verro Grijalva, did not destroy it completely."

Sario stared hungrily, studying the text, the way the letters were formed, the familiar, decipherable hand he had seen and read before, though this particular page was alien. *No—not all was destroyed . . . some he brought back. . . .*

Some Verro brought back, some Verro gave to his family. For what the old man displayed with such infinite pride and reverence was a page of the *Folio* only Limners ever saw.

The Tza'ab *Kita'ab*, their most holy text.

What was worshiped by Tza'ab as the key to their God was studied by Grijalvas as the key to their Gift.

Inane, inexplicable laughter bubbled up inside Sario's chest, trying to burst free. *And again I am reading ahead!*

Saavedra fought her way back through the festival crowd as far as the Zocalo Grando, then to the fountain before the huge cathedral. Children still clung to marble finials and basins, but she pressed them aside and stepped up on the pediment, leaning forward to plunge hands deeply into the cool water. Unmindful of the spillage, of spray, of the soaking of her clothing, she sluiced water noisily to bathe her face.

Relief from heat, from humidity; a cooling of the flesh, but the warmth of anger remained. And she did not know why. He was an old man, Tza'ab or no; what could he do? Did it matter that he knew what blood was in their veins? Everyone knew, when the surname was declared. Even if a single Grijalva were free of Tza'ab blood, the taint adhered regardless. All because a party of women, in service to the Duchess Jesminia, were kidnapped by Tza'ab warriors.

No. That was wrong. It wasn't the kidnapping itself that tainted the women, but the subsequent rapes and the bearing of bastards sired by the enemy. And that *of* all the women thus treated, only the two Grijalvas had not killed themselves from shame or retired from society into various Sanctias. The Grijalva women bore their half-breed children, kept them, and adopted the shunned infants of the other women. And in Palasso Grijalva all the children of rape were also allowed to conceive and bear children.

The Ecclesia would prefer that all of the women died or retired, and that all of the infants had been exposed. Droplets chased down her face. Saavedra clung to the basin, hair completely undone now and dangling into the fountain. Her knuckles were pale beneath taut flesh. *And then there would be no chi'patros, and perhaps no Nerro Lingua, and the Ecclesia would not have to trouble themselves with us.*

And no Saavedra Grijalva. No Sario.

Saavedra closed her eyes. Damp lashes met wet cheeks. *What will the old man do?*

"Belissimia," said a voice, "are you here unattended?"

She started, clutching again at the basin as she opened her eyes to look at the speaker. The sun glazed her vision, but she saw the silhouette: tall, male, informally clad in shirtsleeves and breeches.

"I am free to be," she answered.

"And all to the better."

"Why?" she asked suspiciously. "Is there something you want of me?"

There was laughter in his tone. "What is there a man *should* want of a woman?"

She flung back soaked curls and was pleased to see him shy from a spray of water. Hastily she scrubbed dampness from her brows, blotted dripping chin. "There are many things a man *may* want," she said, "but only one a man like you might consider, asking a young woman if she is unattended."

He laughed softly. "Fuega Vesperra," he said. "Am I wrong to think of conception?"

"But it isn't *conception* you care to pursue," she countered. "Only the preliminaries, the danza before the fact."

"So, you have me . . . and shall we celebrate the festival in the only appropriate way?"

"The only way *I* intend to celebrate it is alone," she declared, "and—appropriately—at home."

"Your unkindness leaves me desoladio!"

"As it leaves me desola*dia*." Saavedra smiled brightly. "Why not cool it in the fountain?" She scooped up a handful of water and splashed it at his face.

"Canna!" he cried furiously, and clamped a broad hand around her wrist. "I should drown you for that!"

"No," another voice said. "I think not. Nommo do'Verrada."

"Do'Verad—" The first man broke off hastily and released Saavedra's wrist. "It's done. Do you see? Done!"

"I see," the other said gravely, "and now you may go. Adezo, if you please—though the latter is merely a courtesy; it pleases *me* that you go, and I am the one who matters."

"Adezo," the other blurted, and made his way off at once.

Saavedra offered the newest arrival a broad grin. "You have a fine gift for command!"

"Do I?" He shrugged. "It was the name, no more. It carries some small weight."

"The Duke's name?—I should think so!"

"Not the Duke's. Mine. He knew me, that chiros."

"Yours? But—wait . . ." Saavedra moved so that the sun no longer shone in her eyes. She saw him clearly now, as she had seen him before, if from a greater distance, and knew him by the sketch Sario had disdained. And it was Sario's oath that came up to fill her mouth. "Merditto!"

"Yours, or mine?" Don Alejandro grinned crookedly. "His, most probably; he was a crude chiros."

"Oh," she said in dismay, staring into his face. "Oh, I did not get it right. Your nose!"

"My—nose?" He touched the indicated feature. "What—what is not right about my nose?"

"No, no—not *your* nose—mine!" Aggravated, she sighed and muttered self-abuse. "The shadow is wrong . . . the line here—do you see?" She touched the bridge of her own nose. "It is off—I made it off."

"Off?" He was clearly still bewildered. "Regretto—but I have no idea what you are talking about."

"No, no—you wouldn't." She scowled blackly. "I shall have to begin again."

"Begin *what?*"

"You."

"Me?" He blinked in astonishment. "But—how is this done? That you can—*begin* me . . . again?"

"With chalk," she explained crisply. "Or pencils. Perhaps watered color, one day . . . I have not advanced to oils."

His face cleared. "Arrtia!"

"Arrtia," she agreed, "though a poor one—or so the teachers tell me, because I am a woman and whatever talent I have is not necessary, save to make talented children." She did not know why she was speaking to him so—babbling, more like!—but she could not stop. It was easier simply to plunge ahead and give him no time to speak, because then she would have to remember again who he was. "I do what I can, learn what I can, and hope when I have borne my children, I can return to my art once more."

"Why not?" He shrugged. "I admit I have never known an arrtia before—always arrtios—but I see no reason you should not be one if you wish."

A Duke's son indeed, to be so sublimely ignorant of the way the world worked beyond do'Verrada doors. "I do wish," she said, "but there will be little time . . . it is expected I will bear children, and children require much attention. Although if it is a son, and the son proves Gifted, I will have no time with him anyway." Saavedra hitched her shoulder and looked away from his fascinated face to the fountain. "I'm sorry—I should not say such things to you." She drew in a deep, hasty breath. "Grazzo, Don Alejandro. I doubt he would have harmed me beyond a dunking—and I am already soaked!—but you have done me a kindness. I will say your name in my prayers tonight."

"Momentita—" He stretched out a delaying hand. "Will you walk with me? The crowd is no place to talk . . . I know! I shall buy you a lemonada and find you a seat in the shade." His smile was dazzling. "And I assure you I will not dunk you in the fountain, or beg improprieties of you, not even in the name of Fuega Vesperra."

As he grinned, Saavedra saw the faint overlap of the tooth Sario had decried. Heat rushed into her face. "Matra Dolcha, no! Eiha, I could not, *should* not—oh, Don Alejandro . . ." A wild glance gave her explanation: the looming Cathedral Imago Brilliantos. "The Ecclesia would never permit it!"

The grin died. "The Ecclesia? Why? What should it matter to them if I buy you a lemonada and sit with you in the shade?"

For the first time in her life she dreaded saying her surname. "I am—Grijalva."

"Are you?" He was neither dismayed nor insulted. "Then it is no wonder you spoke of art—your family are fine painters!"

This was not what she expected. Only trained courtesy allowed her to stammer out a response. "Grazzo, Don Alejandro—you are too kind."

"I am not," he disagreed promptly. "I am truthful. I have been in the Galerria Verrada many times, and there are Grijalva masterworks hanging in the Palasso. I see them every day."

Including Piedro's original *Death of Verro Grijalva*. Saavedra smiled weakly. "Of course."

"So. You are a Grijalva, and I am a do'Verrada. Bassda. Shall we fetch our lemonada and find our shade?"

" 'Cordo," she managed, and was treated again to his brilliant grin. But this time it was neither grin nor tooth she noticed. *No,* she reflected absently, *I did not get the nose right at all.*

◈ FIFTEEN ◈

The boy now was gone, excused, given leave—though he believed it *taken*—to go out into the celebration, but the old Taza'ab believed he would instead proceed straight to Palasso Grijalva to contemplate and hotly reject all he had been told. Such truths as these took time.

Begun at last, the beginning, and an ending reached as well. No more waiting, no more clinging to hope that one would come out of the womb of the enemy, albeit sired by Tza'ab; one *had* come, and now Il-Adib could look to the present and the future instead of to the past.

The old man smiled. His name was spoken again by a Tza'ab in concert with Acuyib's. True enough the accent was imperfect, the tone one of youthful and wary skepticism, but the name was known again, spoken again, by one who bore the blood. No more estranjiero, or Tza'ab filho do'canna as all the cityfolk called him . . . he was once again Il-Adib of the Al-Fansihirro, born to the Desert, to Tza'ab Rih, to Acuyib's service.

One among many; now two. The boy would learn. He had appetite, ambition, a quick and devious mind searching always for challenge, *to* challenge, though refuting those thrown at him with an eloquent grasp of irony that far surpassed his age. It would not be a simple task nor a comfortable journey, but the ending justified all.

And he has the vision.

There had been many Grijalva boys he had watched, even those who walked down this very street, but none had watched his tent because none of them had *seen* it. It was true the Grijalvas were bred out of the Tza'ab blood of their ancestors, but none had been blessed with the inner vision. None but this boy.

Acuyib promised me there would come another.

Il-Adib placed one withered hand atop the polished thornwood casket bound and tacked with brass. Wrinkled, plum-tinted lips stretched into a ghastly smile. "We begin again," he murmured. "I shall make another Diviner, and we of Acuyib's Great Tent shall have back what was stolen from us."

Raimon counted the years as he counted steps. Fourteen of them, twice; and then he stood at the top beneath the low, looming ceiling, and recalled the last time he had been present in the closet over the Crechetta.

Not for unfortunate Tomaz. That had been another's task, another's burden when the Disciplined Limner was discovered unexpectedly dead. Before Tomaz, well before Tomaz, when it was *his* time, and *his* turn, at age twenty-eight—as there were twenty-eight steps—to be Disciplined and to think on it locked away inside the heart of the Palasso, albeit his punishment was not so severe or significant as the Chieva do'Sangua.

His wrist throbbed. Raimon bent and set down the lamp, then clamped a hand over the ache. Beneath the cloth of silk doublet, the fine lawn cuffs of shirt, the scar burned again.

"Suggestion," Raimon murmured. "The magic is dead . . . it has been too long, and I learned what I was to learn."

Indeed. He had set aside such questions as had gained him the Lesser Discipline, or learned to frame them differently. And the meticulous compordotta had served him well. No more doubts from others, no more distrust, no more punishments, no more arrested progression through the ranks of the Viehos Fratos. He was Il Seminno now, one of the loudest voices, though not to offer defiance but alternate opinion.

Eiha, he had *gathered* another opinion, an alternate opinion: Davo's. And it gave him no peace.

They listen to my voice, yet it is not heard. But he had not come here for that, nor even to recall his own punishment. He had come to wait, to meet, to discuss—and to offer a suggestion no other in the family would ever contemplate.

Raimon laughed softly; what it lacked in humor was replaced by bitter triumph. "This one will contemplate it!"

Indeed, this one would, and as the sound of ascending footsteps scraped through the narrow lamp-lighted stairway to the stuffy closet above, Raimon knew what he sought was the best, the only way, and that Sario Grijalva was solely the one who would not only accept the task but perform it perfectly.

Perspiration gathered beneath a fallen forelock. Raimon wiped it away impatiently with a sleeved forearm, then shut his eyes briefly to compose himself. By the time Sario climbed into sight, he was calm. He was prepared. And committed himself to damnation.

Alejandro was shocked as he heard himself tell the Grijalva girl all about Gitanna, his father, his intentions to come and find a woman to prove he could. Would she believe he meant her? Would she fire up the way she had at the city chiros?

They were no longer at the fountain but sat in the shade, as promised, against a cool wall dappled by shadows from a looming olive tree, content to sit atop packed soil brushed hastily clear of deadfall fruit despite what it did to their garments. And he spoke about finding *women;* would she therefore hurl the contents of her crockery cup into his face in lieu of fountain water?

He hoped not. Lemonada was sticky, and it burned when in the eyes.

But all was admitted. It could not be unadmitted. He steeled himself for her withdrawal, for her coldness, for the intemperance of her anger. Yet none of it came.

"Eiha," she said equably. "I do not blame you for that."

"For—wanting a woman? Another woman? Even after declaring I wanted Gitanna?"

She sat mostly in profile, its purity uninhibited by the wilderness of her hair, dried into long curls. He could see the wry downward hooking of her mouth. "It isn't that you want a woman so much, but that you wish to prove to your father that you are a man who does as he chooses."

He considered it. Possibly. "How can you know that?"

She hitched a shoulder. "I have known other men to do the same."

Man. Not boy. It comforted him. But also provoked curiosity. "Have you known many?"

"Men? Eiha, yes—but not I myself, not as you mean." She laughed softly. "I live with men, Don Alejandro, and I am an arrtia. We are trained, you see, to watch the behavior and manners of others."

"Compordotta."

He saw a quick glint in her eye. "To gain the true spirit of a subject, to put into the portrait a portion of that fire, one must observe keenly. One must train the eye. One must understand compordotta."

"All of it?"

Her grin was brilliant, displaying white teeth. Hers were straight. Hers were perfect. Hers were better than his, with the lone crooked tooth Zaragosa Serrano refused to paint into his portraits.

"*Some* of it," she answered. "I am not able to see into minds, only into faces."

"Mine?"

She grimaced. "Enough to realize I made the nose wrong."

He laughed. She had an exquisite way with wry self-deprecation and dry irony, subtle but unhesitating even in his presence. It was not the way most people spoke to him, especially women.

He sobered. "My father explained I don't love her, not truly—but that I am infatuated with her."

"It is likely," she agreed, unperturbed. "Sario believed he was in love with his first woman, but he wasn't. He only thought so, because it was new. Because it made him a man, and proved he was—Gifted."

The momentary hesitation was odd. "He bedded a woman to prove he had artistic talent?"

Now she withdrew, though she remained still against the wall. It was a subtle shift, but he felt it. Especially as she changed the subject. "Will she be sent away now? Gitanna?"

"It is likely . . . he will give her a country estate, some money, some jewelry." Alejandro sighed. "It seems so little after so many years."

"Surely a mistress cannot hope for more."

"I suppose not. And she will be comforted, I have no doubt, that at least her brother remains at Court. Her family will retain some power with Zaragosa there."

"Zaragosa—Zaragosa *Serrano?*"

"Of course. He is Lord Limner."

"I know who he is." She sat rigidly now, clutching crockery. "She is his sister? Gitanna *Serrano?*"

"Yes. Why?"

Her laughter now held a tight, ugly sound. "You are well rid of her."

It shocked him. "Why? What is she to you? What right have you to speak of her so?"

Her face was very white. "Yes—you are correct. My compordotta requires improvement." She rose stiffly, all the relaxed and bantering friendliness banished from her expression. "Grazzo, Don Alejandro, for the rescue, the lemonada—but I must go now."

Matra Dolcha. Why did he feel as if *he* had overstepped when it was she who transgressed? Scowling, he pushed himself to his feet. "Wait. You are not to go until I say so."

Her face colored. Gray eyes glittered. "You order the chiros away, but you order the canna to stay. Quite the man with the animals, no?"

She was *angry* . . . at him? But it was *she* who insulted Gitanna. And yet the words he meant to speak altered themselves into something else entirely, something bled free of affront. "You did say I had a fine way with command."

Anger evaporated. Startled, she stared, and then began to laugh.

She is nothing like Gitanna. No, she was not. And there was no other woman in his life he could compare her to, which he supposed might amuse other men—and perhaps other women, perhaps even Gitanna—but not, he suspected, her.

He took her cup from her hand. "More lemonada," he said. "Momentita, grazzo." If he could not order her to stay, not even with his fine grasp of command, he would at least rely on her good compordotta.

Sario climbed the final steps just short of twenty-eight. He halted at twenty-six, two below the man who waited for him. A lamp stood at the top, washing the chamber with illumination redoubled by the closeness of walls and ceiling. From below, it lent Seminno Raimon's expression an intense expectancy, an odd chiaroscuro of the bones of his face washed white in light while the hollows were stained by shadow.

I should paint him so. But he let it go. There was more to the moment than this. "Seminno," he said respectfully, with genuine regret. "They told me when I returned of Arturro's death."

"I sent for you, Sario."

It pinioned him into stillness. *He has never sounded so cold before, so distant.* "Yes, Seminno."

"Two men were sent, and Saavedra. Did all of them fail?"

This was not the subject of the discussion, but Sario forbore to avoid the preliminaries. He was uncertain of his ground in such surroundings, before a man whom he knew and did not know, all at once. "Saavedra did not fail. But I—I delayed." Hastily he said, "She didn't tell me the Premio Frato had died, or I would have come at once!"

"Saavedra was not given to know. It is a thing of the Viehos Fratos."

"But—the others will know . . . the family. How could they not know?"

"I suspect all of them know by now. But there is a ritual given at the deathbed—you were not here, Sario, and you could not be found, and so you were not present. Your candle was unlighted. Arturro's Paraddio Illuminaddio was not as it should have been."

The Lighted Walk. Sario did not know it. But then, no one of the Viehos Fratos had died since he was Confirmed, and there were rituals and traditions as yet unfamiliar. "Is there nothing I may do?"

"For Arturro? Nothing. He is dead, he has passed, the Paraddio Illuminaddio, though lacking the youngest candle, is completed." Raimon's tone was oddly inflected. "But there is much you may do for your family . . . provided you are willing to contravene every precept. All compordotta."

Another pattern made whole. Outrage kindled to flame. "This is a *test!*"

"No."

He would not accept the denial. "You test me *again*, Raimon! Was not burning my *Peintraddo* enough?" Sario clapped fingers to the place where he had ordered Saavedra to drip hot wax. "What more must I do to convince you? Have I not done all I have been required to do? Have I not completed the tests? Have I not been properly Confirmed and accepted?"

"You have."

"Then why?"

"It is not a test, Sario. It is the means to an end."

Sario shook his head. "I don't trust you."

Raimon's face was bleached linen stretched right to tearing over a framework of brittle bone. "Eiha, I do not blame you. Here, then—let me show you . . ." Deftly he stripped the chain over his head and held it outstretched, golden key dangling. "Come, Sario. Take this. Hold this."

It baffled. It stunned. "Your Chieva?"

Urgently now, "*Take* it, Sario! You must know this is no test, no discipline. It is desperation, no more, *my* desperaddio, and the only way to be certain Otavio cannot thwart what is meant to be."

Warily—it *must* be some form of test—he prevaricated. "If it's meant to be, how can Otavio—"

"Nommo Chieva do'Orro, Sario! Bassda! Do as I say!"

Sario sealed his mouth, stopped his questions, put out his hand. Raimon poured key and chain into it. The metal was warm from contact with living flesh; Sario swallowed hard and shut his fingers over the weight of gold that had not, to his knowledge, ever left the man's neck since he had first been made a Limner.

Raimon's face was stark, stripped of color and character. He was estranjiero, and wholly alien. "Arturro is dead. There will be a new

Premio Frato, and I fear it will be Otavio. I am certain it shall be
he."

"You don't expect *me*—"

"I expect you to hold your tongue and permit me to finish."

Sario clamped his jaws shut. The chain and key seemed to grow
heavier in his clasp.

"You must understand," Raimon went on, "if I believed it possible, I would do this myself. But it is not. There is only you."

Questions burgeoned. Sario asked none of them.

"I need you. I need what you have, what you are. *We* need you,
though no other will admit it. Certainly not Otavio. I am alone in
this . . . save for you."

Sario waited. He could not leave now if the world itself exploded.

"Neosso Irrado," Raimon said. "For that, and for your fire. For
your Luza do'Orro. For your tenacity, your insatiable ambition—
and your ruthlessness." He was so tightly strung his body trembled
with it. "I might have been you—once. I might have taken this on
myself. But they—quenched me, as you once accused."

"No," Sario managed. "I have looked on your paintings."

The faintest glint of comprehension, of gratitude, flashed
through Raimon's eyes, was gone. "Break them," he said. "Break
all of our precepts, our fine compordotta . . . but you must become
Lord Limner."

"Indeed, I *hope* to—"

Raimon's voice was sharp. "No 'hope,' Sario. It must be."

Sario groped for the new pattern, seeking to find the pieces so
they might be properly joined. "If it is possible—"

"Not 'possible,' Sario. For once, for *once,* speak your mind.
Your truth. Don't rely on compordotta." The smile was a grimace.
"Nor will I. And therefore I will say it as a man, as a Grijalva, as a
Gifted: you must use any recourse to make yourself Lord Limner.
Any recourse at all." In lamplight, the dark, fierce eyes were hid-
den behind a glaze of fire. "You hold my Chieva. I am not in this
moment one of the Viehos Fratos. And what you choose to do, *how*
you choose to do it, is not of my concern."

He breathed with effort. "Matra ei Filho," Sario said, "you are
truly afraid of me."

"Only a man who has been near enough to fire to hear his own
flesh sear knows what and how to fear." Raimon stepped down a
single stone riser. He closed his hand over the fist that held his
golden key. "If you are found out, it will mean Chieva do'Sangua."

Sario thought of the old Tza'ab in the tent, and the page of the

Kita'ab that was also the *Folio,* and the power that was promised. Tza'ab magic. Grijalva magic. Born of the same source, hidden by blood, by fire, by old hatred and ancient rivalry.

Lord Limner.

Another watershed. All the parts and pieces of power.

He was older now, but not immune to fear. Not immune to comprehension that each step he took led him closer to something other than what he had been.

But how do I know this was not intended when my father lay down with my mother and she bore me nine months later? Maybe all of this was to happen, even the old man.

And the parts and pieces of power made over into a whole.

Sario placed his other hand atop Raimon's and gripped it. "Nommo Chieva do'Orro, Nommo Matra ei Filho, Nommo Familia Grijalva, I swear I will not fail."

⋙─◉ SIXTEEN ◉─⋘

The door stood ajar, permitting entry. It was a private atelierro within the confines of Palasso Grijalva, set apart in a wing off the central building, the heart of the compound, but Saavedra had never been denied permission to enter. She and Sario shared too much.

She set palm to door and slipped into the atelierro. Summer sunlight flooded the studio: with northern exposure and several tall windows, shutters folded back, the atelierro was ideal for an artist. She was not permitted the same luxury—she was not male, not Gifted, not of the Viehos Fratos—and thus basked in his, soaking up atmosphere. It was a peaceful place, a place of contentment, lending itself to creation.

A narrow door in the northern wall led out onto a small tiled balcony overlooking the central courtyard with its many-tiered fountain. Often she found him there, sketching furiously before the light died; or within the room itself, oblivious to time, to food, to the bells of the Sanctia pealing prayers across the city, and utterly to company, even her own, as he applied paint to canvas.

Saavedra smiled. He was endlessly patient with his own work, and wholly *im*patient with hers. It was a simple matter for Sario to find her, to claim her, to pull her away on one errand or another—often to critique his work-in-progress—and utterly impossible to convince him to let her be even the merest moment so she might find a place in her own work that was appropriate to stop.

But that is Sario. And she forgave it, because no one else would. *I might refuse him . . . I might insist that he leave me to work just once.* But she would not. She understood the insatiable need that ravaged him: to free the fire of his inner vision before it burned him up.

Empty of his presence, his intensity, the room was oddly diminished despite its clutter: raw, primed, and cloth-draped canvases, oiled wooden panels propped against the walls; shelves and tables packed with chipped, wax-plugged crockery pots containing solvents, oils; bowls of dried beeswax, chunky amber and gum acacia that would eventually be melted down to resin; sealed bottles of ground pigment powders; sheaves of tattered paper and vellum bearing bold or intricate scrawls; clouded vials of unidentified substances; brushes, handles, and paletto knives scattered like corn for chickens; and rags festooning the room like the bloodflower wreaths of the Mirraflores festivities.

Saavedra thought to return later when he was present, but an unfinished painting caught her eye. Propped yet on an easel near the balcony door, it glistened wetly, smelled of resin and oil, of a faint coppery tang oddly akin to blood; even, strangely, of the sweet-sour, acrid pungency of old urine—or perhaps it was just that Sario, consumed by inspiration, hadn't bothered to empty the nightpot shoved behind a battered screen!

She wandered to the painting, curious; she had not seen it before, but he showed her everything. The work was far from completion. A portion of the meticulously primed canvas was as yet naked of paint, bearing only the detailed sketches of what he would do, the first thin layers of ground and body color. But most of it was well underway, and she saw the scheme of the thing, the scope—and a very bizarre border, almost like a frame itself though painted onto canvas.

"Matra," she murmured, frowning, "what are you doing, Sario?"

"What I am doing is wholly my business, no?"

Saavedra jumped and swung awkwardly, startled so badly she nearly knocked over the easel. She grasped it hastily, steadied the painting, then turned to face him squarely. "This is not you, Sario .... this is not your style at all."

"What I do *becomes* my style." He wore a tattered cambric shirt liberally daubed and stained by the substances of his talent and something that looked like blood, sleeves rolled back from sun-darkened forearms. Dark hair in need of cutting was tied loosely with a length of leather thong, though one heavy lock swung forward along the line of his jaw. A smear of paint altered the shape of his nose from blade-straight into something less stringent, a smudge of charcoal dust hollowed the steep angle of a cheekbone.

He looks so much like the old man now, that old Tza'ab fool—it's in the bones, the flesh—

Beneath the soiled collar—the shirt was left carelessly untied to fall open nearly to the high waistband of his tight, paint-stained hosen—the chain of Sario's rank glinted against a smooth, dark chest. "I refuse to lock myself into a box, Saavedra. I must be free to paint as I will." He went to one of the worktables, took vials out of a pocket, tucked them away into a box.

"Of course," she replied mechanically; they had discussed this before. "But this border is new, and—"

"Odd?" He smiled, tangibly smug. In two years he had matured completely in body, as Grijalva Limners did; there was little time for awkward adolescence. He was eighteen now, not tall but well-made, slender but inherently graceful, with striking Desert-bred features that would do as well as subject as the artist. In all ways a man, Sario Grijalva, albeit more than most: supremely talented, unarguably Gifted, content within himself as he had never been as a boy. "Yes, odd," he agreed in his light baritone. "It is a Tza'ab convention, the border. The Al-Fansihirro always employed it in their work."

Saavedra bristled to hear him so condescending. "*You* never have!"

"No. But I do now. Here—would you see? Surely you came to see."

Uneasy, Saavedra watched him move around the room crisply, throwing cloths back from canvas. He was often curt with others, but never with her . . . and yet now he treated her as one of *them*.

"Look upon them." He stripped concealing fabric away. "Borders on all of them, yes?"

She looked from canvas to canvas, trained eye naturally noting the composition, balance, use of color—but what she most noted were the indicated borders. Each was different. Some were wide, some narrow, a few ornate, others spare and clean. He had painted interlocking ribbons, braided tree branches, ornate vines; odd, stylized patterns endlessly repeating. Fruits, branches, flowers, herbs, and leaves all played an integral part.

Saavedra stared. "This changes everything . . ."

"Yes," he agreed. "I meant to."

"This is like nothing done before!"

"Not here, no. But it's traditional in Tza'ab Rih."

She looked at *him* now, sharply. "It's that old Tza'ab . . . you spend so much time with him—*too* much time!—and now it's invading even your work!"

"Invading?" he asked mildly. "As the Tira Virteians invaded Tza'ab Rih? Eiha!—but I'm forgetting . . . it wasn't Tira Virte then. Just the do'Verrada and their supporters, even a few Grijalvas." He shrugged elaborately. "But what does it matter, names?—the end was the same. Tza'ab Rih destroyed, the Diviner killed, the *Kita'ab* lost, and lands stolen by those who were then acclaimed Dukes in perpetuity."

"Sario!"

He pressed a flattened hand against his breast. "What,

Saavedra—shocked? But why? It is the truth. *Our* truth. There is no Grijalva living who does not bear Tza'ab blood."

"There may be Tza'ab blood *in* us, but we aren't Tza'ab, Sario! We're Tira Virteian."

"And they hate us for it."

It stopped her utterly. For the first time in months she looked at him to judge, to weigh, to consider who and what he was beyond what she knew, and realized he had at some point become estranjiero.

"That man," she declared virulently. "*He* has done this to you. He's perverted you, polluted you, told you lies. Next you will be wearing a Tza'ab turban!"

"No, no turban," Sario said, laughing, "nor any lies either. What Il-Adib has given me are such truths as you could not imagine, first because you lack the vision of Al-Fansihirro, but also you would never permit yourself the freedom of thought required. You are a good little Grijalva, yes?"

Defying purposeful provocation, she shook her head firmly. "Sario, this is lunacy. He's trying to turn you against your own people."

"The Tza'ab *are* my people."

"But not to the exclusion of others," she shot back. "Matra Dolcha, Sario, have you gone moronno luna? Look around you! You are a Grijalva, born and bred of Tira Virte—"

"*And* Tza'ab Rih."

"They were bandits who stole away those women and *raped* them, Sario! There is no glory in that."

"And thus nothing to revere? Nothing to learn from them?" He flung out a hand. "*Look* at the paintings, Saavedra! Different, yes . . . unlike anything anyone else is doing, yes—but poor? No. Unschooled? No. Worthless? No." His eyes shone. "*Different,* 'Vedra. Just as I am."

"Merditto! You are no different than I, Sario."

Teeth flashed briefly against his sun-darkened face. "Then perhaps you would do well to come to Il-Adib for instruction. He has much to teach."

He was wholly infuriating. "You *are* moronno luna! Do you think I wish to waste my time listening to that old fool? Nommo do'Matra, Sario—"

"Or Acuyib."

It slowed her only fractionally. "Acuyib! Acuyib? Have you renounced the Ecclesia, then? Have you turned your back on the Mother and Her Son?"

Unperturbed, Sario laughed indulgently. "I only meant that there are other names to swear by. And perhaps we *should* renounce the Ecclesia; the sanctas and sanctos have renounced us!"

"Not 'renounced'—"

"Then what else should you call being ordered to worship within your own walls, eh?" He indicated the atelierro. "The Premia Sancta herself ordered us not to pollute the shrines and Sanctias, Saavedra. So much for mercy!"

"She is wrong," Saavedra said tightly, "but it has nothing to do with the Ecclesia. She is a Serrano, after all."

"And so is the Lord Limner. Thus we are powerless to change anything."

Saavedra opened her mouth to contest that, then clamped it shut so hastily she nearly clicked her teeth together. *Lord Limner—* She turned her attention back to the first painting she had observed, still propped upon its easel. Before she had not marked the identity of the unfinished face, merely that it was begun. The border had drawn her attention. Now it was the face. "Holy Mother, Sario. What are you doing painting *Zaragosa Serrano?*"

Something glittered in his eyes, was banished even as he glanced at the box into which he had put the vials. "A jest," he answered blandly. "I thought I would paint his portrait and have it delivered to him—anonymously, of course—so he might know what *true* talent is, albeit he must see it in his own face!"

It made no sense. "But why waste your time on him? On *that?* He is nothing to us, Sario."

"He is a heresy to us. He pollutes what once was an honorable office. When Grijalvas held the appointment."

"Eiha, but I thought you renounced the Grijalva in you and looked now to the Tza'ab!" Saavedra bestowed a mocking smile upon him. "Are you one only when and as it serves, the other as *it* serves?"

"As you are," he answered.

It startled her. "*I* am! I have no part in this."

"But you do, Saavedra. You were a painter, once. Now you are a woman, someone meant to make babies. As it serves the family."

"Filho do'canna," she blurted. "Oh, Matra, what that old man has done to your tongue!"

"My tongue was always my own, as you well know. And as for that, look to your own. Street speech, from you?"

"From you!" she shot back. "It was you who taught me it."

"Well, then." He grinned spectacularly. "We are even, no? And very much alike." He gestured to the painting. "You might try borders, Saavedra. They lend themselves quite well to the composition."

She clamped teeth together. "Affectation."

"Look again. See how the patterns repeat themselves throughout?" He moved quickly to the easel, indicating the sketched portion of the border as yet unpainted. "Do you see? The branch of an almond tree, so; a spray of lavender, here; a cluster of meadowsweet, thusly. And roses, here; do you see? They shall be yellow, I think." He smiled briefly, privately, as he moved his finger. "And all repeating itself *here,* do you see, within the context of the portrait itself . . . do you see what he will be holding?"

An almond branch, a spray of lavender, a cluster of meadowsweet, and a single rose. To be painted yellow, no doubt.

Saavedra shrugged. "You can include those elements without the border."

"But the border draws it all together. It becomes a part of the painting, a frame within the frame."

She shrugged again, elaborately. "I suppose . . ."

He laughed softly. "Innovations in style always meet first with resistance."

That struck home. Saavedra scowled. "The old man taught you this?"

"The Al-Fansihirro always painted such borders into their work. Even into the *Kita'ab.* It's a Tza'ab tradition."

"And I suppose you believe you're one of *them* now, too?— these Al-Fansihirro, whatever they may be!"

"The Order of Art and Magic." He grinned. "En verro, why not? One of the Viehos Fratos, one of the Al-Fansihirro. Only a fool ignores what may aid him in attaining what he wants."

And that, Saavedra reflected, sounded exactly like Sario. Perhaps the old man had not perverted him after all.

Mollified, she nodded. "But I still don't see why you're painting Zaragosa Serrano."

Sario smiled serenely. "As I said, it's a jest—even if he won't ever comprehend it."

"Then why do it?"

"Because it pleases me."

Eiha, but he was the same, and he was not. What was tolerable in the boy because of youth was less attractive in the man. "No importada." Saavedra turned toward the door. "I shouldn't have come."

"Why *did* you come?"

She stopped. Considered. Turned to confront him. "To ask for your opinion of my work."

He arched unsubtle brows. "You know my opinion. I have declared it many times. Your work is far better than any woman's, and even that of many men. But why does it matter? You will waste it, waste yourself—"

"I have no choice, Sario! There are so few of us compared to what we were. Would you suggest that I refuse to bear children merely because of talent?"

He shrugged, turning away to restore the cloth shrouding over various canvases and panels. "Talent is as worthy of birth as a child, 'Vedra . . . but you will set your art aside in the name of that child."

She stood, stiff with anger, and watched him. Curtly she said, "You have no idea what it is to be a woman."

"No," he agreed coolly, "only what it is to be driven so fiercely to paint—just as *you* know that drive, that fierceness, but will reject it out of hand." He looked at her now, no longer tending shrouds. "You are Gifted, Saavedra. I cannot explain how it came to be, but it has. The fire recognizes itself when it burns equally in another." He stepped closer, eager now. "You know how it is done—I have explained it all . . . and if you would allow me to guide you—"

"No!"

He spread his hands. "No Confirmattio, 'Vedra, only the painting."

"So you can harm it in some way to see if it harms me?" She shook her head vehemently. "Even if I *were* Gifted, there is no future in it. The only future for me lies in bearing children."

The mask of his face slipped. But then he gestured sharply before she could respond. "Bassda! Go, then . . . I have work to do." He turned back to the canvases.

Saavedra stood her ground. "It was not the *body* of my work I sought you for, but my work-in-progress. You have in the past had such definitive opinions about the subject matter."

He swung back sharply. He knew. She saw he knew. Color suffused his face, then drained away. "*Him* again?"

"Why not?" she asked lightly. "You have never once felt I got him right."

"You aren't painting Alejandro do'Verrada for *me*, Saavedra—"

"How do you know?"

"Because you are and always have been infatuated with him! Merditto, 'Vedra, do you think I am blind?"

Success: he was angry, shaken out of habitual arrogance into honesty of emotion. "I speak as an arrtia," she said serenely, "as one who wishes to improve her work, no more. What more is there? What more could there be?" She gestured at the painting upon the easel. "You paint Zaragosa Serrano as a jest . . . I paint Alejandro do'Verrada because I have been commissioned."

"Only because he can see you that way, 'Vedra! No vulgar, hateful comments made by others about a do'Verrada keeping company with a Grijalva chi'patro when that chi'patro paints him . . . eiha, 'Vedra, he uses the portrait as an excuse to be near you, no more!"

Ingenuously she inquired, "Then I am not gifted enough to paint him?"

He glowered at her. "You are teasing me."

Saavedra grinned. "Yes. And—no. I *am* painting his portrait. I *do* enjoy his company. There would be talk—there probably *is* talk . . . but none of it matters, Sario."

It astounded him. "None of it matters?"

She smiled crookedly. "As I paint, he tells me all about the different women he is bedding . . . what man who desires a woman speaks to her of such things? Would you?"

"Then he is a moronno," Sario stated baldly. "Matra, *what* a moronno!"

"Friend," she said. "No more. As it should be."

But she was very glad to see even Sario, who knew her so well, could not look beyond *her* mask to know how the truth eviscerated.

~~●~~ SEVENTEEN ~~●~~

The young bravos with him styled themselves dangerous men. They wore swords and two knives apiece: a meat-knife, plus the longer blade that balanced the swords at their hips and lent them an elegant symmetry. They were not dangerous men, however, in anything but profligacy with coin; he was himself far more careful, though of them all he had less need, but saw no sense in ringing down gold so that everyone in the tavern noticed. Of course, that was precisely what they wanted, the would-be bravos, but he forgave them. It was all part of the role they played, stepping outside the truth of their lives into amusing fantasy and a freedom they craved.

His own freedom was two-faced. Far wealthier than they, better served than they, his future infinitely more promising than any they might devise for themselves, and yet he was constrained by the very aspects that gifted him above others.

It chafed, such freedom, when he yearned for something else, though at other times he valued it for its immeasurable wealth. Ironically, freedom wasn't free but infinitely costly.

They clustered, five of them, at a broad, cloth-decked, pitcher-weighted table in one of the city's finest taverns. Four of them were scions of the principal families of Meya Suerta and thus of the duchy itself: a do'Brendizia, a do'Alva, a do'Esquita, and a Serrano, one of Zaragosa's countless cousins.

Alejandro closed his hand upon a pewter tankard of ale, but its journey to his mouth was dramatically interrupted by a woman's lush body landing with definitive demand upon his lap. He caught her easily enough, though not without some wreckage; the tankard, knocked free, spun away, spewing contents, and landed with a dull metallic clank against the hardwood floor. The cloth upon the table, caught along with her skirts, was pulled askew, thus risking the pitcher and assorted tankards. His companions, seeing the risk, shouted various curses and reprimands as they hastily steadied the pitcher and rescued threatened tankards, though ale slopped over rims to stain the cloth.

Alejandro had no breath to reply to their vulgar comments and sallies. The woman's weight was not precisely negligible, and it took some effort to keep her upright before they both overbalanced and joined the tankard on the floor. He grasped her more roughly than intended and resettled her hastily, but that effort, he learned with chagrin, was precisely what she desired. She screamed with delighted laughter, locked firm arms around his neck, wriggled suggestively against his loins.

He winced. His loins, he had discovered some years before, did not always respond quite the way he intended. Predictably, at this moment, his loins welcomed the woman. The rest of him did not. "Momentita, amica meya—"

She wriggled closer, leaning her head against his own so that warm, wine-scented breath gusted in his ear. "Friend?" she asked. "No more than that, am I? But I can *be* more, amoro meyo—"

As she desired. As she intended. Alejandro grimaced, then managed a weak version of the smile his friends claimed—crudely!—could spread a woman's legs with no other effort expended. "Eiha, of that I have no doubt—but you see, my mind is on other things—" Which caused his friends to laugh uproariously; the woman immediately applied a skilled hand to his betraying loins. "—*wait*—" He squirmed uncomfortably. "Matra Dolcha, woman, have you no shame? This is not a common tavern where the women are harlots—" Eiha, it never *had* been! "—and I will be the one who determines how I spend my time . . ."

"And your ducal seed?" Ermaldo do'Brendizia, the most crude of them all. "By the Mother, Alejandro, surely you have enough to spare for the carrida . . . or does the Duke have attached certain devices that render you unable to sow the fertile fields?"

Ysidro do'Alva laughed. "Or do you fear to mingle it with our seed, therefore leaving the child's paternity in doubt?" He slanted a sharp glance at the woman. "But surely she would prefer that? Then she could lay claim to support from *each* of us!"

Tazio do'Esquita grinned. "And would you pay it, 'Sidro? You are notoriously tight with the contents of your purse."

Do'Alva produced the elaborately eloquent shrug they all of them emulated. "So long as other parts of me remain tight, my purse is of no concern."

The woman laughed. "Hah! What do I care about the contents of your purses, menninos? It is the contents of the flesh that interests me most—" Whereupon the hand grew more insistent.

"Filho do'Matra!" Alejandro abruptly shifted his weight to his thighs. With effort he rose, thrusting to his feet, and forcibly set the woman upright. There was no gentleness in it, no attempt at courtesy; he wanted to rid himself of her, of them, of the tavern. He wanted suddenly to be rid altogether of the drinking, the whoring, the griping belly and aching skull that by morning attended such evenings. He felt old and used up, disgusted by the part of himself that had once found this amusing.

He reached into his purse and fished out a coin. Spun it down onto the table, where it chimed faintly against cloth stained wet by spilled ale. "There is your evening," he said. "In my name, drink as you will—but I excuse myself of it."

The others made noises of denial, of protest, extended fresh invitation to sit down once again. But Alejandro shook his head, taking care to untangle swordhilt from tablecloth, ensnared by his efforts to empty his lap of the woman.

It was Lionello Serrano who made no attempt to stay him, but slanted him instead a dark, oblique glance out of curiously malicious eyes. "That girl," he said disdainfully. "That Grijalva chi'patro."

Alejandro froze. His voice sounded rusty. "The painter? But she is *painting* me—that is why I hired her."

"You know what she is," Lionello said. "More than merely chi'-patro, Alejandro. She dabbles in dark magics."

"Filho do'canna," Alejandro said tightly. "If I believed *that,* I would not commission a painting—"

"Or more than a painting?" Lionello shook his head. "We know what they are, Alejandro. We know the truth of them."

"Do you, then? Eiha, I think you are infinitely Serrano in this, Lio, fearful of losing your place. Or fearful of losing your blessing from the Ecclesia. I don't know which your family values more." Alejandro shot the others a hard glance; they were nonplussed, clearly taken aback by the turn of the topic. At least Lionello had not spread the poison. "Well, you may well look to your cousin's work, Lio . . . it decays, and he will not be *my* Lord Limner." It was cruel, mean-spirited, but Lionello touched a nerve Alejandro had not known existed. "Drink," he said curtly. "Drown yourself in the bitter dregs of sour vinho, Lio, as you will have it—but say no more to me of chi'patros and dark magics."

"Or painters?" Do'Brendizia grinned, as if to diffuse the unexpected tension. "Go, then. Visit her if you will, Alejandro . . . have your *portrait* painted. We are infinitely fascinated to learn what talent she has." It was, from him, replete with innuendo, but it was enough to dismiss Lionello's accusations. Ermaldo do'Brendizia, for all his notorious crudeness, was not a stupid man.

Alejandro cast a glance at the woman who had begun it all. Nor was she stupid, though ignorant of the currents of the moment. She looked away from him at once, as if embarrassed she had instigated such tension.

He shook his head. *I have been a fool, to find amusement in this.* "Dolcho nocto," he offered briefly, and departed the tavern.

***

The slender branch of an apple tree, leaves as yet plump, undried, for Temptation, Dreams, and Fame to Speak Him Great.

Bay laurel, for Glory and Prophecy.

Cedar, for Strength and Spirituality.

Myrtle wand, so he might Speak With the Dead.

Palm, for Victory; pine, for Protection and Purification; plum for Fidelity.

Lastly, walnut, for Intellect and Strategem.

All of these things Il-Adib took from the market basket and placed with meticulous care on a square of green silk, just so, infinitely precise; magic was demanding of such things as perfection, lest there be tragedy of it.

Leaves and limbs were layered one atop another in careful intercourse, the veins of each touching the veins of others so that the strength of their power might mingle, enriching the whole. The pattern was made complete. Perfect.

The old man felt a flutter deep in his belly. Anticipation. Exultation. The warm kindling of vindication.

So long to wait, but what is time in Acuyib's Great Tent? Patience is rewarded.

No one that he knew had been so patient. Nor was so old, of the blood of the Desert.

New blood, now. Not pure in content, mingled with that of the enemy, but better that than utter absence. And he knew, as Al-Fansihirro, that one pigment mixed with another often produced a different and richer color. And an entirely new magic.

We need that now, in this new world. The old ways were defeated. The new shall bring us strength. New blood, new magic, a new Diviner.

The scent of tightly compressed and freshly crushed wild geranium commingled with rosemary and sage drifted from the copper bowl set beside the silk, weighting the air inside the tent. Steadfast Piety; Remembrance, Love, and Memory; Wisdom. To lend him the strength to do what he did in service to Acuyib. To Tza'ab Rih.

From one of the leather tubes he drew a parchment, a page of holy text extravagantly illuminated by a hand of great skill equally devout in service to Acuyib. So many brilliant colors, so many infinitely perfect mergings, the precise lines of black, the filigree of gold and silver, the bloom of Art, and Magic. The patterns of his world, that was becoming the boy's as well.

Il-Adib smiled. *Not a boy. No more.* But no less Acuyib's servant, now that he knew.

The old man unrolled and spread the page, weighted it gently with carved gold figurines representative of his Order. So many colors: the rich green sheen of the silk, the sacred color of Al-Fansihirro; the ornate and brilliant haze of transcendent illumination set in a border around the text which, in and of itself, barely breathed the truth of Power, of Acuyib's might. Magic lay in lingua oscurra, the patterns of the borders, not in the common text itself.

So much to teach the boy who was not a boy, but who would become something infinitely greater than even Sario believed.

So much he has learned, but so much yet to learn. Il-Adib took in the sacred scents, read familiar cipher in complex illumination, hidden in plain sight from those without the vision; gazed upon the assembled pattern of magic and knew he had succeeded.

New pigments had been tempered out of new materials. Tza'ab blood crossed with that of Tira Virte, with that of the plague-racked Grijalvas, with the inner vision of the Al-Fansihirro, created a wholly new power.

"For You," he said quietly in his true-tongue, the language of Al-Fansihirro, lingua oscurra. "In Your Name, Great Acuyib, so You might live again in the heart of the Desert, in the souls of her people. I have shaped You another Diviner. May he heed Your Voice; may he heed the needs of his people; may he prove the most powerful of Al-Fansihirro."

Scent drifted. He closed tear-filled, aged eyes, then opened them as something, an insect, bit his chest. Frowning, he unfastened and pulled aside his robes, baring a chest thin but lapped with sagging flesh.

There was no insect, yet a pinprick of blood had appeared beside his concave breastbone.

The aged Tza'ab caught his breath. "Not *yet*—"

Blood welled, spilled, splashed. The brittle rib cage caved in and shattered beneath the blow of the knife that did not in any wise exist in Il-Adib's tent, but elsewhere entirely.

The ancient Al-Fansihirro released his final breath. "—too soon . . ."

And too late.

Saavedra, when summoned to the entry courtyard, was astonished and appalled by her visitor. "What are *you* doing here?"

Alejandro blinked at her in surprise. He had been given entry through the massive wrought-iron gate. One ornate filigreed gate-leaf yet stood ajar beneath the clay-daubed brick archway, as if he thought to flee. On either side of him torches blustered in early evening breeze; it cast light and shadow upon him, limned contours and angles, set gold laces and gemstones to sparking.

Saavedra was disgusted by the blurted question with which she had greeted him. *Holy Mother*— "I mean, why have you come?" She modulated her tone as best she could, still flustered. "I mean . . ." And then, lamely, giving up on all but the truth, "I wasn't expecting you."

"*I* wasn't expecting me." He grinned shamefacedly, fingering the high embroidered lawn collar extending above the doublet. "I mean, I hadn't planned to come. I just—came."

Saavedra was acutely aware of the silent Grijalva cousin who waited behind her, politely distancing himself without deserting her entirely. It was most unusual for anyone to come to Palasso Grijalva at night, and utterly impossible that it might be the Duke's son.

Except he was here.

Courtesy reasserted itself; there were rituals upon which she might depend, if not her own initiative. "Would you have refreshment? Will you come into the solar?"

He hitched a broad shoulder briefly, a curiously defensive motion. Belatedly he pulled off the feather-spiked, blue velvet hat that adorned thick dark hair. "I thought perhaps you would walk out with me."

"Walk out . . . with you? Now?" She was completely flustered. *Matra Dolcha, what is the matter with you? Do you believe he wishes to propose?* Furious with herself, Saavedra managed a tight smile. "I had planned to go to bed . . ." And then wished she'd said nothing of that, because bed was not a place she should—or wished—to speak of before this man. "Cabessa bisila," she muttered.

Alejandro, who heard it, grinned. "Me as well," he said. "I am delighted to see you as uncertain of this as I."

She doubted he was uncertain. Alejandro was never uncertain. "Then why are you here?" And could not help herself: "Is it woman trouble again?"

The deep flush was slow, but unmistakable.

Holy Mother, would she never learn? "Eiha, forgive me, grazzo."

"No," he said with some difficulty. "I mean, yes, it's woman trouble, but not that kind. And perhaps I should not be here at all . . . perhaps I am merely a fool; I hired you to *paint* me after all, not listen to my troubles, or—or . . ." He flushed again, deeply, crushed the velvet hat in powerful hands. "I should have stayed at the tavern." He scrubbed a forearm against unruly hair. "Sweet Mother, this is not coming out right." He offered a sickly grin. "Will your watchdog permit me to explain myself in privacy, or am I to be embarrassed before *two* Grijalvas?"

"My watchdog—" And then she swung sharply. "Benedizo, surely you don't believe harm will come to me from Don Alejandro!"

Benedizo smiled faintly. "Perhaps not," he murmured, and went inside.

Saavedra turned back. "There. Banished. No need for embarrassment."

Alejandro sighed. "That depends on your perspective."

"What perspective do you mean?"

"Yours," he said, "or mine, depending on yours. But I can't wait any longer. I've waited too long."

"Too long for what?" Her spirit quailed. "To tell me you don't like my work after all?" *Oh Mother, of course he doesn't.* She gulped and ventured it. "That you don't wish the painting?" And it so nearly completed.

He was astounded. "Eiha! No! Your work is superb. The *painting* is superb; you have made me far too handsome for a crooked-toothed cabessa bisila!" The infamous grin flashed, displayed notorious tooth, then hid itself behind self-mocking bemusement. "This has to do with your work only in that the subject of it wishes you to grant him a favor."

Relieved, disarmed, Saavedra smiled. "You know I would do anything for you."

Hazel eyes took fire. "Nommo do'Matra ei Filho," he blurted, "I hoped you would say that." And bent to embrace, to fit body to body, to kiss the breath from her lungs.

Saavedra discovered embarrassment had nothing whatsoever to do with the moment. Only shock for an instant. And then merely honesty.

Deep in Palasso Grijalva, tucked away in the closet above the Crechetta where the business of the family was conducted, Sario conducted his own. One lamp, one lamp only, placed upon the step as once Seminno Raimon had placed a lamp, so that it set the world afire. Sario then took from beneath his arm a small framed portrait swathed in burlap, swathed again in fine silk—rich, brilliant green silk—and dropped both lengths of fabric to the floor. He smelled poppy, grass, cypress issuing from the cloth.

He knelt, set the portrait against the wall, studied the work.

Infinitely lifelike. An exquisite rendering. No one looking on it who had seen the subject would not know his name.

Sario spoke that name, then smiled faintly. "I was given leave to do as I must," he explained, "by a man I trust. You, I dare not trust; we share a different vision."

Quietly he lifted into the light the thin-bladed knife. It sparked briefly. Coldly.

"I am not what you would have me be. But there is much use in what you have told me, great power in what you have taught me, and in me they will live on. Your ending is my beginning."

Blood had been the most difficult to obtain. But he had contrived to fall into the old man, scratching him with a fingernail left uncut—the residue caught beneath the nail had been enough.

Sario set one hand onto the frame to steady the portrait; the other carried the knife to the canvas. It had taken time and ingenuity to gather all the necessary fluids, but it had been done. He was prepared.

It began now, the second portion of his life. The first, a mere eighteen years, had been as nothing to someone as old as Il-Adib of the Al-Fansihirro, the sole surviving member of the most holy caste of warrior magicians. All of them killed in the wars with Tira Virte, stolen from Acuyib's Great Tent, until Il-Adib, the youngest of the god's servants, exiled from those so badly defeated, set out to discover what remained of the *Kita'ab,* to found the rebirth of his Order. Both he sought in the heart of the enemy, for it was there, the old man said, Acuyib sent him. To find another with the inner vision.

Sario smiled. Inner vision. Luza do'Orro. He was doubly blessed.

And Raimon had given him leave to do what he must.

Sario hesitated. His mouth was unaccountably dry. *With this all is changed.* All he had ever known.

But vision existed to be served, and light made it possible for a man to see his way.

Sario wet his lips, chanted several fluent phrases in the tongue of Al-Fansihirro, in the lingua oscurra, then pierced the painted heart that lay beneath painted robes.

"I am not your Diviner." He drove the blade through canvas to the hilt. "I am only and always Grijalva. And I *shall* be Lord Limner."

Scents lingered: poppy, for Sleep; grass, for Submission; cypress for Death.

·─ EIGHTEEN ·─

The chamber was in disarray. It was not the Duke's task to be there for the arrangements—he had a multiplicity of servants to select his clothing, to pack them, to be certain of his dignity in every stage of his apparel while out of the duchy—but Baltran do'Verrada was never predictable. In the midst of the maelstrom he shed garments soiled from hunting even as clean ones were packed, snapped out orders to his personal secretary.

The journey was vital to the prosperity and peace of Tira Virte, to the future of the duchy as embodied by its Heir, Alejandro, and the heirs to come of *his* body, and embajadorros, ambassadors, could not be relied upon to always address the vital issues in precisely the way Baltran himself might. They tried, blessed be the Mother's Name, but they could be put definitively out of time by the semanticists the Pracanzan king employed. So Tira Virte paid high honor to Pracanza to prove the suit was desired by Baltran's decision to go himself—but he also was hungry for what was reputed to be prime hunting along the border of Tza'ab Rih, and he always satisfied his hunger. It was one of the advantages of his rank. Besides, the days of the Desert warriors were ended; he would be in no danger. Therefore he would pleasure himself before riding on to the business of Pracanza.

Meanwhile, there was a certain issue to be settled before he departed. The Duke discussed the work of his Lord Limner *with* his Lord Limner.

"Let me not put too fine a point on it, Zaragosa—your skills are diminishing." Baltran do'Verrada eyed Serrano with fleeting compassion a moment later overruled by impatience; there was much for him to do. "It grieves me to be so blunt, but I have no time for anything save truth. I commanded a portrait of my son so that I might take it with me to Pracanza . . . yet what you have offered up is the merest daub, not a true rendering. You know how vital this portrait is, Zaragosa. It opens negotiations for a betrothal!"

The miserable wretch of a limner nodded. Thin shoulders collapsed beneath gaudy clothing grown too large, hands clasped themselves like claws, dismay tempered by pain etched dry arroyos into the flesh of his face. "Your Grace—"

"I simply cannot permit it, Zaragosa." He snapped fingers at a servant, "*Here,* no, not that shirt; I have wearied of it." The Duke turned again to his limner. "You know full well how important such paintings are to the art of diplomacy and negotiation. The entire history of our duchy is documented through these works—*Births, Deaths, Marriages, Deeds, Treaties,* and much more—and they *must* be superb. They *must* be perfect. I cannot have any of them be less than as they should be."

"No," Serrano murmured, "no, Your Grace, of course not—"

"It is not a good likeness of my son, Zaragosa."

He flinched. "No, Your Grace, as you say—"

"And if I am to present it to the King of Pracanza to open betrothal discussions, it *must* be a good likeness." He permitted his hands to be stripped of blood- and sweat-soiled rings so the flesh might be properly washed. "My son is a man much praised for his face, his form, his personal charm. Would you have Pracanza and his daughter take him for less than he is?"

"No, Your Grace, no, of course not—"

"Then what are we to do, Zaragosa?"

The man seemed to wither further: an aged raisin born of once-plump grape. "Your Grace, if I might be permitted to speak—"

"Speak, then! Would I prevent you?"

Serrano offered a sickly smile. "I have been ill, Your Grace. I improve, of course," he added hastily, "but—I have been ill."

"The matters of state do not wait on illness, Zaragosa."

"No, Your Grace, of course not—but I could begin anew—"

"There is no time, Zaragosa; I depart tomorrow for Pracanza. And so I have decided that another painting shall go in place of yours."

Breath rattled in Serrano's throat. "*Another* painting? But— Your Grace . . . Nommo do'Matra, *I* am Lord Limner! I!"

"I cannot present your painting to Pracanza. Therefore I shall present another." The Duke turned aside, studied a letter drawn up and presented by his secretary, nodded and dismissed him. "We are fortunate that my son commissioned another artist to paint him, thank the Mother, and it shall have to do."

Serrano was deathly white. "Who?" he rasped. "Who is the artist?"

Baltran waved a hand. "I don't know his name, Zaragosa. This was a private agreement made between my son and the artist, but I have seen it—it was delivered two days ago—and it is superb. A perfect likeness, full of spirit and honesty. Precisely what I need."

He paused. "Alejandro does not yet *know* I need it, but he will not protest. It feeds a man's vanity to know his potential bride shall see him at his best." The Duke flashed a brief grin. "In my progeny the best is attained; his sister, once grown, shall marry into Diettro Mareia, and the Pracanzan girl for Alejandro will settle this dispute over borders at last."

Gray as a plague-riddled corpse, Serrano barely nodded. "But surely Your Grace knows the artist's *family*."

Baltran do'Verrada laughed. "What, Zaragosa—do you fear I will replace you with a lowly Grijalva?" He shook his head, grinning. "Your place is secured as long as I live, Zaragosa. But this does not mean I must accept inferior work."

"No, Your Grace—"

"Therefore I suggest you regain your health, so you may also regain your skill." He gestured crisp dismissal. "You may go, Zaragosa. Dolcha mattena."

But for Zaragosa Serrano, creeping out of the chamber, the morning was far from sweet.

Sario hesitated only a moment before the tent, then caught a handful of fabric and pulled the door flap aside. He knew what he would find—knew what he *should* find—and was therefore not shocked but relieved, even secretly pleased, by what he saw in the dusky interior: one old Tza'ab man slumped in death beside the rug of now-familiar, now-decipherable patterns.

He knelt beside the corpse, pulled aside the disarrayed robe. Looked upon his handiwork, for which he had not been present.

"Sweet Mother . . ." Exultation abruptly filled his heart.

It was not pleasure in the man's death, but triumph, immense satisfaction that he himself had wrought it. And not that he had intentionally killed, but that he had succeeded. It was necessary to succeed. It was necessary to know that he could do what he intended, what he *needed* to do, to become what he must.

"I know," he said. "I know it, now." So much power, so much magic, so many ancient skills possessed by no one else in Tira Virte, not even the Viehos Fratos, who did not know they themselves and their vaunted Gifts were no more than leavings on the platter presented by Al-Fansihirro.

Sario, privy to private humor, smiled in perverse appreciation. *In the Blessed Name of the Mother and Her Most Holy Son, we serve Acuyib of Tza'ab Rih.*

Irony of the purest sort. Certainly heresy.

He was meant to go to Tza'ab Rih. Meant to seek out and rouse in the name of Acuyib the Riders on the Golden Wind, to give life and breath and heart to a people left too long without it. But he would not. Such was not his goal.

"I want to paint," he told the old man. "I want to paint what has never been painted. I want to be what we have not been for three generations, broken by Nerro Lingua. I want to be best of them all, my argumentative Viehos Fratos, best of every Grijalva, every Limner, best of every *Lord* Limner since the very first was appointed." He paused. Waited. Was not answered. "You see, there is much for me to do. There is no time for me to be and do what you desire, and Tza'ab Rih is not my home. Its people are not my people. You are not my father."

Silence. Quietly he let slip the drapery behind him and knelt on the rug beside the dead Al-Fansihirro, the last of his Order save the man who had murdered him.

I am no longer the same. I am more than I was, more even than I believed I could be, than I told Saavedra. This old man has given me a key even as the Viehos Fratos have. He shut his hand over the device dangling against his breast. *I can't be afraid. I can't permit it. I am what I am, what I've always wanted to be . . . but there is more yet. And Raimon has given me leave.*

He would have done it anyway. But Raimon had given him leave.

Sario studied the silk, the pattern, the ingredients used, there on the rug beneath his knees. He read its meaning at once; Il-Adib had extended a sacred blessing, offered enduring strength.

Irony again. Sario shut his eyes, wet his lips, then murmured words of lingua oscurra, broke the pattern, scattered branches and blossoms. Quickly he took from beneath its carved weights the fragile sheet of parchment, rolled it carefully, slipped it back into its protective rune-warded tube, then laid it carefully atop other tubes within the brass-bound thornwood casket.

"I will preserve the *Kita'ab*," he said, "not for what it is to Tza'ab Rih; not for what it is to the Viehos Fratos, ignorant of its truths . . . but for what it shall be for *me*." He closed the casket, reset the latch, briefly traced the carved glyphs incised in wood. Lingua oscurra, warding sacred contents. "My *Kita'ab*," he said. "My key to true power."

Sario laughed. Indeed, a chieva. Chieva do'Sihirro.

In silence he rolled up the thin, rune-woven rug that had so fascinated him, tucked it beneath his arm, carried it with the casket out of the tent.

Within minutes of his departure the body would be found, he knew, the tent destroyed. The old man had been visible outside of the fabric, but never the tent itself. Without the rug, without the lingua oscurra warding its presence, the house of Il-Adib now could be discovered.

A Tza'ab tent within the walls of the enemy, though its viper were slain, would not be tolerated.

Alejandro took her to the private solar granted the Duke's son within Grijalva walls, and told her the truth. He saw the color drain from her face, saw the imminent collapse of her legs, and caught her elbows before she could fall. At once he guided her to a chair and helped her settle into it with some degree of grace and self-control.

" 'Vedra," he said, "I am as shocked as you, but is it so bad a thing?"

One hand gripped the smooth pale column of her throat, naked of adornment. "Of course it is," she managed. "Nommo do'Matra, Alejandro—*my* painting to be presented to the King of Pracanza?"

He attempted humor. "Eiha, at least it speaks well of your work, no?"

"No," she declared. "It speaks well of nothing but that he has stolen something from you—and from me!"

"Eiha, yes, I suppose you might put it that way." He prowled around her chair, less amused now. Absently he clasped his meat-knife, drawing it a half-inch, clicking it home again. "But he is the Duke, after all, and what is mine is his."

"It was a gift to you."

"I commissioned it."

"I refused payment."

He smiled. "So you did."

Tightly she said, "Had I meant it to go to the Duke, I would have sent it to the Duke."

Alejandro laughed. "Arrtia's temperament? Not many would dare to criticize Baltran do'Verrada!"

"He deserves it for this, no?"

He halted his pacing, his clicking of the meat-knife, reassessed her agitation. *My poor arrtia—* " 'Vedra, amora meya, what would you have me do? Ask for it back?"

"You could."

Stony-toned. Stony-faced. He did not know how much was truly anger, how much was regret, how much was fear that her talent, good enough for him (though only because he insisted it was; she refused to believe him), was not good enough for the Duke. Nor for the King of Pracanza and the King of Pracanza's daughter.

Matra Dolcha, lend me strength. I would not hurt her, given another way. But neither do I wish to be hurt. He moved behind her chair, set hands upon her shoulders, took solace in the contact and offered comfort all at once. "I can't ask for it back. My father left two weeks ago, and the painting is with him. But I have only now had the courage to tell you." He sighed, feeling her stiffen into immobility; first the painting appropriated, now he confessed to not informing her at once. "And I should think— should *hope!*—it more important to you, to us both, that a betrothal is imminent, rather than the portrait has been appropriated."

"Stolen, Alejandro?"

He squeezed cold flesh gently, seeking familiar response. Thumbs caressed. "Does it mean nothing to you that I am to be married?"

Her head was bowed. Masses of hair fell forward, obscuring her expression, blinding him to her thoughts. But her tone was infinitely level, betraying nothing but acceptance. "Of course you will be married. So will I."

That stopped him. His hands stilled upon her shoulders, tightened. Coldness clenched his belly: abject, utter fear. "There is talk of that? A marriage for you?"

"There is always talk of it. For all women, most especially Grijalva women. And I am somewhat older than most who are already wed." He felt the choppy inhalation that made the shoulders tremble beneath his hands. "I am nineteen now . . . it is time I bore children."

It came without thought. "Bear mine." And knew the instant he said it, he wanted it very much. He leaned close, stirring ringlets with his breath. " 'Vedra, grazzo, I beg you—"

"*Grijalva* children."

It stunned him into anger, into pain. Would she do no more than mouth the family litany? Did no part of what he said move her? "Blessed Mother," he said curtly, withdrawing stiffly, "does it mean nothing to you at all that I am to be married to make another

Heir for Tira Virte, and *you* are to be married to make artists for Grijalvas?"

Saavedra laughed softly, and he heard desperation at last. "What else are we to do? Protest? Refuse? We are what we are, Alejandro . . . we were never meant to be anything else, anything more, since the day of our births." She stiffened beneath his touch. "After all, would you have me be your wife? A Grijalva chi'patro as Duchess?"

His hands encircled her neck, rested atop delicate collarbones as if he adorned her with the finest of all jewels. As perhaps he did: the love and regard of a man who would be Duke. "Nommo Matra ei Filho . . . were it permitted," he vowed in formal lingua, "so I would have it be."

A spasm passed through her. "But it isn't. It won't be. It *can't* be."

"No." He removed his hands, left her, circled now to face her. Onto one knee he bent, close enough that his breath gusted against the sheer fabric of her skirt. Into both strong hands he took one of hers, clasped it, kissed it, drew it to his heart, held it there. "I will never insult you with false promises of what cannot be. But I will honor you as I may, as it is within my will and power to do."

She was very white. There was nothing in her now of the girl beside the fountain two years before, flinging soaked ringlets away from her face to grin at him in delight, in an unself-conscious display of the generosity, the honesty of spirit that made her remarkable.

Nothing in her, this moment, of the girl he had fallen in love with that day beside the fountain, though he denied it much too long for reasons he could no longer recall.

Blessed Mother, make her see how very much I care. Eiha, he denied nothing now. He wanted it all; if he could not have precisely *all,* he would demand what was left. "Marria do'Fantome," he said clearly.

Color spilled into her cheeks. Gray eyes grew enormous, blackened by shock and candlelight. "The 'shadow marriage'? You, and—me?" Disbelief echoed it. *"Me?"*

"As real as it can be, far more than a shadow. All but the sacred vows recited before the Premia Sancto and Premia Sancta—"

"Before your father, your mother, all the highest of Tira Virte." She sighed, closed her eyes, removed her hand from his clasp. "They will never permit it."

It startled him. "Who? My father? My mother? The Ecclesia? Eiha, they will have little to say about it—"

"My family," she said bitterly. "The Viehos Fratos, who govern Grijalvas."

He blistered the air with an exorbitantly vile curse fully worthy of the streets.

Saavedra opened her eyes—those great, gray eyes, enormous and strikingly eloquent in her elegant, fine-boned face—and smiled sadly. "You serve the do'Verradas. I serve the Grijalvas."

It stung. "Am I not good enough for them?"

Tears glittered briefly. "I think you are certainly good enough, Alejandro. I think they see only that what they need of me are strong children, talented children, potent and fertile children who may sire and bear others. We can afford to lose no one, you see . . . there are so very few of us left."

He withdrew from her, rose from his knee, prowled again as a cat, walking the perimeter of the small, private solar. Meat-knife clicked blade against sheath lip. Boot heels scuffed first baked tile, then bright-hued rugs, setting serpentine wrinkles in them. And when eventually he stopped, turned, smiled, he saw the truth in her face at last, blatant as a sword blade: she was terrified to lose him, but certain that she would.

Blessed Mother . . . It hurt to see her pain, gladdened to know she cared as deeply as he. And now he knew what he could offer at last to assuage the mutual fear. *She will not lose me, nor I her.*

"Negotiations," he said crisply, certain of his course. "My father, with Pracanzans. I, with Grijalvas." He lifted broad shoulders in an eloquent shrug. "The key to successful negotiation is finding out what the other side wants, and—if it be possible—offering it, or something very like. Something more. Something they want so badly they will offer up precisely what *you* want."

Saavedra shook her head; in candlewash the ringlets sheened blue-black. "There is nothing," she said. "We are not rulers . . . we are not Dukes, or Heirs. And our living, earned from skills, is acceptable and honorable."

"Painters," he told her simply. "Superb, remarkable painters. Even their women, as proven by my father's intention to use your work to advance a betrothal." He smiled to see her astonishment; she had not thought of it so. "And what is there in this world that a Grijalva painter desires most?"

She understood perfectly. At once. She required no explanation. And did not hesitate even as the light of joy suffused her eyes and color tinged her face.

"Sario," she said.

Alejandro grinned. Laughed. Swept her up from the chair and embraced her, essayed a few steps of a popular danza, was gratified and emboldened by her echoing, exultant laughter, by her unfettered joy, by the magnitude of her response.

"Sario," he said.

Nothing more was needed.

⊷ ❈ NINETEEN ❈ ⊶

Saavedra stood at the open door of the tiny cell that had served her so long as atelierro, as the confines of her world, defying distinction, dictating inspiration, defining imagination. She had served and learned at once, for nearly all of her life; and yet now her life was changed.

Empty, the room—eiha, not utterly: the cot remained, the small window worktable, the basin and ewer, the nightpot behind the screen. Such things were the family's, not owned by an individual. There would be others for her now, grander though not so great as to mark her wealthy or noble. And a grander room as well, larger, spacious, boasting bigger, better windows for improved light. She supposed some felt it wasted on her—she would never be a Limner and therefore did not deserve the better quarters—but no one would protest. They understood the import of the Heir's interest, his patronage. For the first time in three generations a Grijalva had the ear of a do'Verrada.

"Ear," Saavedra murmured dryly, "and, I am certain they say, something entirely more."

She grinned fatuously. Indeed, patronage . . . save it was not for her work, not specifically so, nor for the work of other Grijalvas.

"For me." Though spoken softly, it echoed in the room.

Tentative at first, the slow blossoming of joy into exultation—afraid to commit herself; afraid admission would spoil it all—but then Saavedra, freed, laughed, and laughed again into the echoes of her joy.

"Alejandro do'Verrada . . . and Saavedra Grijalva."

There. It was said. Was *announced.*

She supposed—no, she was certain—that in the streets, in families such as Serrano, she was reviled as harlot. Whore. But among the Courtfolk it would not be for what purpose she served, but for her wholly undistinguished and notorious name. At Court, such things as this were common. Baltran do'Verrada himself never hid his mistresses. Gitanna Serrano had been in his bed for seven years, acknowledged and tolerated, as was Alizia do'Alva.

"But I am a *Grijalva.*" For that, they would revile her. Call her chi'patro. Deplore Alejandro's lamentably poor taste.

And the Ecclesia would be outraged! Sanctos and sanctas might drop dead in the streets!

Saavedra laughed again. She could find no portion that regretted what had kindled between them; eiha!—it had kindled long before consummation, which had proved neither of them entertained thoughts of unworthiness or hesitation. There was no part of her that flinched, that hid, that avoided contemplation; love had followed infatuation even before consummation. Now all of her exulted. Body and spirit thrummed with it.

Alejandro loves me. And then in an uprush of joyous disbelief and hesitant acknowledgment: "Alejandro loves *me.*"

It made not the slightest difference there would be no formal sanctioning beyond the vows they themselves made. Among the Grijalvas, where children were so vital, even brief pairings between men and women were considered very like a sacrament. Some married, some did not. It was not even unheard of for a Gifted male and a fertile woman to marry, despite his sterility; there were potent men who could impregnate the woman. There was no sense in denying a true bond between Limner and fertile woman merely for the sake of children. Sterility was not, after all, a *punishment,* but an indication of Giftedness. So long as children were born to Grijalvas, the parentage did not matter.

Saavedra herself had never known her father. A kind but physically weak man of poor health, reputed to be odd in appearance— plump and womanish—her mother told her the summer before Suerta Grijalva died of fever. Guilbar Grijalva was a family oddity, confirmed as Gifted, and yet inexplicably incapable of painting a proper *Peintraddo Chieva.* Late in life he most unexpectedly sired a child whom his wife swore was his: Saavedra, his only progeny in fifty-eight years of life. He lived longer than Limners, but more briefly than men lacking the Gift; Guilbar Grijalva's only legacy was to be known as different even within a family of those who were commonly accepted as so.

But her child, if one were born, would know its father, because its father would survive far beyond Limners or poor, sickly, *different* Guilbar Grijalva, and no one of the Viehos Fratos would suggest she marry or bed other men so long as she was the Heir's mistress.

Smiling, Saavedra put out a hand, caught the latch, pulled the door to. This part of her life was finished. Surely one day she would marry, as Alejandro would marry, but for now they were as one. And she would make it last as long as she possibly could, even with the aid of the Mother to whom she prayed with increasing gratitude and vigor.

Saavedra closed the door. Heard the latch click. Turned her back on what she had known to look instead upon what she *would* know.

For only a moment something other than joy crept in to sink a brittle barb into her spirit. *I must never tell Sario . . . must never say anything at all of the discussion Alejandro and I had regarding negotiations—and Lord Limners.* But then mentally she shook the barb away as a horse a biting fly; it didn't signify, was worth no contemplation and certainly no apprehension. Sario's prodigious genius was enough of itself to win him the position when Baltran do'Verrada died.

"More than enough," Saavedra murmured, and winced inwardly to acknowledge the folly in believing even for a moment she had played a part.

As she turned, thinking ahead to her new chambers, bells began to toll.

The long plank worktable in the huge, arch-ceilinged atelierro was cleared of all save the *Folio* and the thornwood casket. Sario set out a small copper bowl containing three items: blossoms of goldenrod, geranium, and vervain, for Precaution, Protection, and Enchantment. He broke them beneath his thumb, inhaled the admixture, then dropped the crushed blossoms into the bowl.

Next he opened the casket and began removing and uncapping leather tubes, methodically drawing from them the sheets of parchment, some tattered, some torn, some burned ragged at edges or marred by spark-charred holes. Carefully he unrolled and spread each upon the worktable, weighting them with such things as brush handles, pigment bottles, chunks of ruddy amber.

Sario studied them. The text, so carefully hand-lettered, meant nothing in essence save to serve as a book of prescribed behavior—compordotta—and misdirection. There was something to be learned of it, some small magics such as the Grijalvas knew, some acquisition of Acuyib's teachings and philosophies, but not what *he* had learned, what Il-Adib had taught. What he knew now, the truth of Al-Fansihirro, lay in the lingua oscurra, the shaping of the borders, the splendid illumination of each initial letter.

Next he turned to the *Folio,* the great prize of Verro Grijalva. He opened the leather cover, settled it flat upon the table, began to turn and examine each page. From *Folio* to *Kita'ab,* from *Kita'ab* to *Folio,* until he saw the pattern.

Broken, of course. There were gaps within the *Folio,* gaps with the pages retained for so long by the old man. Torn pages, half-pages, blood- and water-stained pages, marred in some cases into indecipherability. Missing pages, missing sections, so that where one left off and another began there was no sense at all, no completeness or clarity of language.

Broken patterns. They could never be remade. Too much lost, too much destroyed. But he knew more than any how best to fit together the triad of a triptych, even multiplied.

Time. It was what all of them lacked: Grijalvas, Gifted, Lord Limners, Viehos Fratos. Ironically those who lived the longest had the least to offer the family, being unGifted and therefore secondary, essentially powerless, meant for lesser things.

He was meant for greatness. And greatness required time.

Sario, sighing, brought the candles closer, set them upon the table. It was compromise: light, yes, but at a distance so as not to threaten what could never be replaced. Still, it was enough to see by, enough to make the gold and silver filigree glisten as if yet wet. As if but newly drawn.

In the silence of the atelierro, broken only by the whisper of parchment moved here, moved there, then brought again to *here,* Sario worked. The pattern could never be healed, but he could repair portions. And learn from them.

He smiled. So much learned in two years with the man. So much learned in eighteen years with the Grijalvas. Eighteen years together of such truths and magics as no one in the world could bear to know.

Such truths and magics as no one in the world could *learn* to know: he was the only one. Because it was not the arts of the *Folio* alone that was the true Grijalva Gift, or the arts contained in the borders that were the full *Kita'ab,* but what he made of them both. That pattern he wove from the parts into the whole upon the loom of his body: the crucible of the true Art and Magic, the old man had told him. He was in himself an Order. The sum of Sario's parts were woven into a whole, from Tza'ab, Tira Virteian, and Grijalva blood and bone to the unquenchable fire, the Luza do'Orro of his talent, and the inner vision of the Al-Fansihirro. One among many potentials, Il-Adib had said, but the only one with the nature, the talent, the blood and bone, the ambition, the ruthlessness, the willingness—and the *hunger* to be what he must be.

No one else. Not now. Only Sario. Only Sario knew. Only Sario could *be.*

He touched the ancient pages of *Folio,* that was *Kita'ab.* "Mine," he murmured softly. "All of it, only mine—"

He broke off as the latch rattled. He froze, twisting to stare hard-eyed at the atelierro door; and then laughed softly, because the latch, though unlocked, could not be opened. Not by hand, not by key, not by sheer strength applied by man or ram.

More of his doing. No one could learn it now. There were no other potentials. Il-Adib was dead, and Sario intended to share nothing of the knowledge.

The latch ceased rattling. "Sario."

Pleasure died. He waited.

"Sario."

He cast a glance at his work, at the open *Folio,* the additional pages, the bowl of blossoms.

"Nommo Chieva do'Orro, Sario."

In anyone's name, in any*thing's* name, he need not open the door. For this man, he would.

A second glance at his work. Hidden Language, hidden work, hidden knowledge and power . . . but he wished to share the *triumph* of his knowledge with another, with only one other; with this man who stood on the other side of the door. He would not share it all, but he would share enough.

Pride blossomed anew. *I have done what no other has.* And this man of them all would understand. Would regret his own lack of courage. This man had himself tested the limits of his family, but turned back. Sario had not. *There is much to be proud of.* And so he rose, went to the door, applied saliva to his fingers, smeared away the tiny words he had painstakingly painted around the latch.

The Hidden Language, hiding itself, but also the truth of the power. "Now," he said quietly, and stepped aside as the other lifted the latch.

Raimon Grijalva did not at once enter the atelierro. He looked beyond Sario to the worktable, murmured a prayer, then spoke more loudly, if without much force. "I am alone."

Sario smiled. "Of course, Sanguo Raimon. I would not have permitted anyone else to enter."

The lines incised in aging flesh deepened perceptibly. "Nommo do'Matra, of course not." Raimon walked directly to the worktable and did not glance around even as Sario shut the door. There was no time to paint the oscurra again; Sario set the bolt and locked it. "So." Raimon stood at the worktable, shoulders stiff beneath black doublet. "Have you become a copyist, then?"

Laughter was genuine. "You believe I merely *copy?*"

"Don't you?" Raimon leaned closer. "Am I to believe—" And then he broke off.

"Yes," Sario said, grinning, "I thought you would see it, given a moment *to* see." *Now he will know. Now he will see it.*

Silence, save for ragged, noisy breathing, and the subtle susurration of page moved atop page. "Matra Dolcha—oh, Blessed Mother—" A hand clasped the Chieva, kissed it, pressed it to his heart. "—Holy Son . . ."

"And Acuyib." Sario grinned, laughed. Elation burgeoned. "But I don't expect you are familiar with that name."

A spasm shook Raimon. When he moved at last, it was to turn awkwardly, to steady himself with one splayed hand set atop the table. "How could this be? The *Folio?*"

"*Not* the *Folio,*" Sario said, then gestured. "Eiha, yes, the *Folio*—but more. Other. We have been ignorant of truth, Sanguo Raimon . . . and cloistered fools, as much as the sanctas and sanctos!"

Raimon aged as all Gifteds: approaching forty, he appeared sixty. Youth was banished, vitality diminished, the warmth of his features replaced by a spare, hard-edged beauty that was born of suffering. The restless spirit that had made him Neosso Irrado, the impatience of his talent, had been contained and nearly quenched. A man yet lived inside, a powerful, brilliant man—one of the highest among them now, elevated the year before to Sanguo—but the knowledge of duty, of sacrifice, the acknowledgment of price, aged him in spirit as well as in body.

With evident self-restraint he asked, "What does this mean, Sario?"

Sario laughed aloud. He could not contain his jubilance. *See what I have done?* "That Verro Grijalva, who sent us the pages that became our *Folio,* sent us far more than a text to improve technique in our art and how to comport ourselves. He sent us the promise of power, the key to foreign magic, though he was ignorant of it. And so we accepted it as such, what we learned of it, but the key *we* saw was base metal, not true gold." Sario looked at the Chieva hanging at Raimon's throat, then touched his own, shut it within one hand. "It's more than *Folio,* Raimon. It's also *Kita'ab.*"

Refutation, sharp and angry. "That can't be."

"It is." Sario indicated the worktable. "Look again, Raimon. Recall that only a third of the text has been deciphered, ever . . . we skip those words we do not know, the sections we can't comprehend." He moved then, released his Chieva, moved to stand beside Raimon "Look here . . . this word, do you see it?" He indicated one in the bound *Folio,* indicated its like on one of the loose pages.

"Here, and here—and here. Throughout the *Folio,* throughout the other pages."

"I see," Raimon said colorlessly.

"That word is unknown to Grijalvas; has always been unknown. Until now." Sario permitted his finger to touch the inked letters for only an instant. "Acuyib, Raimon. That is what it says." It was simple for him now; he knew the language and its accents intimately. " 'Acuyib. Lord of the Desert, Teacher of Man.' "

"You *know* these things?"

"Grazzo, I was *taught* these things. Yes. And now I know them." He grinned, looking for pleasure in Il Sanguo's expression, in his tired eyes. "I know many things." *But not all of them will even you know.*

Raimon's face bled out into a bleached whiteness stark as printed canvas. "And how will you use these things you have been taught?"

"As you wish me to use them." Sario shrugged. "Your instructions were clear." *Where is the approval?* Urgently he said, "I was to do what was necessary to see that a Grijalva—that *this* Grijalva—"

He broke off. Outside the chamber, outside Palasso Grijalva, but a handful of streets away from the artisan's quarter, the great Cathedral Imagos Brilliantos began quite unexpectedly to toll its massive bells. In its wake other bells began also to toll, the bells of the Sanctias, the chimes of the shrines.

Now? Sario, as every living resident of Meya Suerta, understood perfectly the language of the bells. Shock assailed him; he knew it, knew the pattern of the bells, the dolorous tolling . . . he had never heard it before, never like this, never *just* like this, for the other dead do'Verradas had been only infants.

It will cease. But it did not. And the initial impulse, that first prayer of denial, altered. *Nommo do'Matra—let it be true—* Guilt. But the spasm passed. "Matra," he murmured. *Let it be true.*

Raimon sank to his knees. Bowed his body. Clasped his Chieva do'Orro. "Nommo do'Matra, nommo do'Filho—" Bells continued to toll. "—Nommo Matra ei Filho—" The world was made of bells. "Oh, Sweet Mother, Blessed Mother, Holy Son and Seed . . ." Raimon caught his key, carried it to his lips, then clasped it against his heart. "Grazzo—protect us. Protect us all."

Sario echoed it; such was expected. But he offered up an additional message. *—and grant his son even in grief the wit to see the worth of my work, so he may appoint me over another.* He paused. *Especially a Serrano.*

He felt—brittle. Breakable. On the cusp of shattering, if another person so much as spoke his name.

Of course, they did. They must. They had no other name, no other man, to whom to turn. There had been two of them, though the other far greater; he was lesser, insignificant: a lone and quaking sapling compared to the great sturdy forest.

Alejandro, they said. Coupled with an entirely new title and honorific.

Duke. Your Grace.

No, he longed to shout. *Neither of them is me.*

Both of them. And more. Alejandro Baltran Edoard Alessio do'Verrada, by the Grace and Blessings of the Matra ei Filho, Duke of Tira Virte.

He would break. They would break him.

Alejandro, they said. Begged. Commanded. Consoled. In the midst of questions, answers, comments. Accusations. Tears and shock and outrage.

"Are you certain?" he asked at last, and started them all into abrupt and ragged silence. He flinched away from hard and angry stares bitter as winter fruit. "Eiha—would there be cause to do it? Sense?"

"Political expediency," one of them answered, as if to a child. As he supposed he was, with regard to their jaded world. "Who can say for certain, save that it was done? There are factions, rivalries, enemies—even among the Pracanzans willing to listen to an embassy . . ." The conselhos muttered among themselves, speaking of tragedy and war. Of assassination.

"Are you *certain?*" He asked it again because he was utterly convinced his father would want him to be. Very, very certain. Baltran do'Verrada knew such things instinctively, from natural astuteness coupled with years of experience, but his son, his Heir—now Duke in that father's place—was certain of nothing at all save everyone at Court wanted to go to war.

—want ME to go to war— Because of course he would have to; Tira Virte's Dukes always led the armies into battle.

"I don't want a war."

Voices died out. He had shocked them again. Shocked himself as well; he had not meant to speak aloud.

"Eiha, I *don't,*" he said clearly. "No man should desire to go to war."

"Not even to avenge his slain father's honor?"

Alejandro winced. Indeed, there had been honor in Baltran do'Verrada. But so much more. *Wisdom, wit, certainty of purpose—* He swallowed painfully. *I am certain of nothing save I am unfit for this.*

"Your Grace," someone said; was it the Marchalo Grando, Lord Commander of the Armies? Perhaps so; Alejandro's eyes were oddly misted and he saw very little. "Your Grace, there are courses to be plotted, options to be weighed, decisions to be made."

Pent-up rage and fear and grief exploded from his chest. "Nommo do'Matra, will you *give me time?* Sweet Mother, but a son is told his father is slain, and within the hour you gather like herding dogs to drive him into war!"

In the wake of that, silence reverberated. Abruptly he could see. All. Everything. Comprehension shook him.

Painfully he said, "There *is* no time."

The Marchalo—*his* marchalo, now—took pity on him in tone if not in words. "None, Your Grace."

◆━ TWENTY ━◆

Sario schooled his face into obedience, into what was proper for others to see, although blind they remained. Confidence, yes; arrogance, no. Certainty of purpose, of his right to be there; but no smugness, no condescension. Pride was permitted—in moderation—because self-certainty was required; without either a painter was no more than a dauber, a copyist, a man sent to the road as an Itinerrario—which was of itself no insult, as it was honest work and often led to greater things—but for someone who believed his gift deserved far more it was nothing less than proof of mediocrity. And it was that belief which drove Sario out of the acceptance of such a thing as mediocrity—easy, effortless, *comfortable* mediocrity—into the perfectionism that conflated talent, technique, and Gift in the crucible of his soul.

He had donned clothing made specifically for the occasion, and which would, he knew, cause much comment. But it was an honest statement and one no Grijalva dared disregard or dismiss. While the others wore traditional dark hues, the quiet, drab colors affected by a family wishing to draw no attention lest it prompt offense, Sario boasted the brilliant, unmistakable green of his so-called "bandit barbarian" ancestors, and the Order. He had discovered the color suited him: he was desert-dark in hair, in eyes, in skin, and rich hues flattered. He had not affected the turban, however; it was one thing to quietly remind everyone of the ancestry shared by Grijalva and Tza'ab, quite another to invite additional overt hatred. And it was not only Grijalvas who attended the exhibition but also the principal families of Meya Suerta, the most powerful of the Courtfolk, the Premio Sancto and Premia Sancta, and Duke Alejandro himself.

Whereas Sario cared not a whit for anyone else, certainly not the Premias, he *needed* Alejandro, a man by all accounts nearly undone by grief, by his abrupt ascension, by the need for extreme expediency in all things, most especially the recovery of his father's body and the incipient war—and who was undoubtedly heavily influenced by the others.

Perhaps even by Saavedra . . . Sario looked for her in the throng. She was not a Limner and thus was not expected to attend, nor was her position as ducal mistress sanctified in such a way as to permit public dishonor to the do'Verradas—although there was now only a Dowager Duchess, no longer a wife to offend—but he had sent word inviting her. As one of the candidates displaying his work, he had the right. Everyone else of note would be there; *he* wanted Saavedra present. She of them all had believed in him from the beginning—and he desired her as much as anyone else to witness his glory.

His spirit soared abruptly. It would be he, of course. There could be no other.

There . . . Saavedra had come in the Galerria door, then stepped away into a corner as if to remove herself even while present. So self-effacing? When she was mistress of the Duke?

Sharply exhaled breath hissed between his teeth. His emotions were a complex welter of resentment, acknowledgment, jealousy, envy, acceptance, vindication, pride, and all measure of things he could not identify. But through the intricate, tight-knotted pattern ran one blood-red thread: she was and always had been *his* Saavedra, as he was and always had been her Sario—and now there was another who took precedence in her thoughts.

He shut his eyes. Around him swelled the noise of many, the potential conflagration of those who gathered to wait, to observe, to critique, to praise. Grijalvas, Courtfolk, members of such families as Serrano, do'Brendizia, do'Alva, do'Najerra, others.

Better for the family, he reminded himself. *Better that a Grijalva share his bed, even as a Grijalva paints for him.* But it took him like a barbed broadhead in his vitals, in his able but infertile loins, that Saavedra truly *loved* Alejandro, not that she shared his bed. *She should love ME.*

Saavedra saw him. Smiled. Bloomed: a desert-bred lily, fragile in appearance but immune to the searing heat of Tza'ab Rih, the miasmic humidity of the city; white-faced, black-haired, clothed in soft-carded purple-and-cream woven out of gaudiness into glorious subtlety.

She came at once to his side, to murmur praise of his appearance, to touch a hand to the rich patterned doublet of green silk, exquisitely cut, precisely laced. Beneath it the fine lawn shirt, high crimped collar embroidered and tied with real gold—he had spent extravagantly, convinced the occasion merited it—the gathered cuffs laced and embroidered equally. So as not to incite too much disapproval he had retained black as the color of his hosen, as well as for the soft-worked leather of his boots.

"You cut your hair," she said, smiling brilliantly. "I am so accustomed to seeing it hanging into your face, or tied back haphaz-ardly—now here is your expression for everyone to see, Sario. Promise me you will not scowl once, grazzo? You have a black, bitter scowl."

He wanted very much to display it, but restrained himself. "No scowl," he agreed, "and cut hair, yes. And infinitely proper com-pordotta."

Saavedra laughed. "Impossible! Proper? Eiha—never from you!"

Sario managed a tight smile. "At need, 'Vedra, I can be anything necessary."

That set a flicker of doubt into her eyes, and then it cleared. She laughed again. "Today you might as well be as you wish—people excuse the excesses of the talented." A gesture indicated the paint-ings on the wall before them. "For these, they will forgive you any-thing."

"Kindly said, 'Vedra—but no doubt you echo what is being told by friends and family to every candidate present here, and to those elsewhere also waiting to hear the decision."

" 'Kindly said,' " she agreed, "and also the truth. Matra Dolcha, Sario, you know what you are. *I* know what you are! So does every family candidate; don't you see the scowls cast your way?"

"Black, bitter scowls?" He smiled. "Yes, I do . . . and I thank you for your faith, 'Vedra—" Abruptly he broke off, caught both her hands, clasped them tightly. It was unplanned, unthought; in that moment he needed her very badly, so he might say what he should have said so many times before. "You have never failed me. Never. In all I have said, all I have done—even in what I *am* . . . eiha, I bless you for it, 'Vedra." He kissed the back of one hand, then the other. "I bless you for everything. Never doubt, Luza do'Orro, that I know what you have done; that I appreciate your friendship and support . . . and when I can, *if* I can, I shall re-pay you for all. Never doubt it, 'Vedra." He still clasped her hands tightly in his own, pressed them hard against his breast, against his golden key. "Nommo Matra ei Filho, nommo Chieva do'Orro. *Never* doubt it."

Her hands were cold in his. " 'Golden Light?' " she echoed. "Why would you call me that?"

"Because you are." He released her hands. "Always, 'Vedra— you have been there with me, shining as brightly as the golden light of our gift." He smiled. "Our Gift*edness*."

"I am not—"

He overrode her. "I have told you: the fire in one recognizes the flame in another." Sario looked beyond her, reasserted self-control. "And now at last he comes, our new Duke, for the Grijalva portion of his Paraddia Galerria—shall we watch as he examines the paintings, and try to predict his thoughts?"

Saavedra seemed almost to flinch. And then she smiled, though it lacked the unforced brilliance of her others. "As if there is any question!"

"Eiha, well—there is always a chance. Ettorio is not unskilled, and there is Domaos, Ivo, Ybarro . . ." Five Grijalvas, of them all. "And those of other families, even the Serranos; even, dare I say it, *Zaragosa*—" He smiled as he said it, knowing what he knew—*except the work is wasted, now!* "—and Alejandro may well reappoint his father's Lord Limner." He gestured qualification. "It's never been done, but it *could* be—"

"None of them, Sario. You."

It was declaration. It was expected. She never failed him.

Sario smiled, then stepped away from the wall upon which a select few of his paintings were displayed, so that Duke Alejandro, when he arrived, might view them without obstruction.

⚷

The scent of beeswax and cedar pervaded. Raimon Grijalva, bowed down before the exquisitely-painted icon—in Palasso Grijalva it could hardly be otherwise than exquisite!—with knees pressed into worn flagstones unsoftened by rug, heard the scrape of a footstep, the rattle of a latch. He murmured a hasty final devotion, kissed his Chieva, pressed it to his heart, then rose, turned, halted. "Davo!"

The older man's smile was ironic. "Did you expect someone else?"

He did. "Sario," he admitted, "come to tell me the result."

"It is as you expected. But did you doubt it?"

"No." Raimon released his self-steadying grip upon the velurro-draped table on which the icon was displayed. "Indeed, I expected it. Didn't you?"

Candlelight was unflattering to Davo's face. At forty-five he began to fail; clearly he would not see the fifty-one years of Arturro's lifespan, or the forty-nine of Otavio's, dead the year before. It was Ferico now who was Premio Frato—but they all of them aged, and Ferico, too, would fail before much longer.

Leaving Davo—or another . . . perhaps even me—

"I expected it," Davo admitted. "To me, there was no other choice. But—I am a Grijalva, and some would say I am biased."

Raimon arched brows. "There were four other Grijalvas among the candidates."

"Be not so ingenuous, Raimon . . . you are too old for such games, and it doesn't become you." Davo softened it with a smile, then sighed and collapsed upon a narrow bench beside the door. "Eiha, but I ache. I wish someone might discover a magical potion that could bring youth back to my joints." He massaged misshapen knuckles gently. "It is the marshes, by the Mother—I swear, it is the marshes." He settled his spine with care and returned to the topic. "There was no other Grijalva candidate who could in fairness be considered worthy of the appointment."

"And no other candidate *of any other family* worthy of the appointment."

"So. But there is talk already, Raimon. They say we influenced the decision."

Raimon coughed a laugh. "*We* did? Grijalvas? But we are no one, Davo . . . we are utterly insignificant in the politics of the city, of the duchy—"

"Of the bedroom?" Davo's face lighted briefly in sly amusement. "A Grijalva in his bed, a Grijalva in his Court."

"Then we are yet one shy of what the Serranos claimed," Raimon countered sharply. "Caterin Serrano remains the Premia Sancta. She still poisons the Ecclesia, building on their fear of us."

"But she wields less power now." Davo shifted again upon the bench. "We have gained much in a very brief time, Raimon, when one counts up the days of the pairing between Saavedra and Alejandro, and now Sario's appointment. We must be certain the opportunity is not wasted. Not after working toward it so very long."

"Sario is the first Grijalva Lord Limner in three generations, Davo. The appointment is less than two hours old, and already you decry him."

"Not *him,* Raimon . . ." Davo grimaced. "Eiha, yes, I suppose you might say so—but I don't mean to decry him so much as express concern. He is young—"

"And will serve the Duke longer because of it."

"Young in *self-control*—"

"That, he will learn. Has learned much already, no? Admit it, Davo."

"I admit it." The older man smiled. "You have been his champion for nearly as long as Arturro was yours."

"I required it. So has Sario."

"You have a gift, Raimon, the gift of looking beyond the heat that sears a man into charred bone to the more focused and there-fore less dangerous flame behind."

"There is nothing about Sario that is not dangerous," Raimon declared. "I know it, Davo. I champion him, yes, but I have never denied it. My argument has always been that only someone with the talent, the Gift, the technique—and the unrelenting obsession to prove the rest wrong, the determination to *defeat* the rest—could accomplish this goal. Many have tried, Davo . . . in three genera-tions, many have tried."

Davo's eyes were steady. "It might have been you. *Should* have been you."

He demurred instantly. "No. My fire was too small, too uncer-tain . . ." Raimon walked softly to the bench on the other side of the door and sat down, echoing the posture of the older man. "My de-sire was nothing more complex, nothing more demanding, than simple ambition. There is a difference between such things as ob-session and ambition. Ambition wants. Obsession *needs*."

"And thus will gain. But more than talent, more than Gift, far more than obsession is necessary to comport oneself properly—and to use the power at hand in the manner that serves the family as well as the Duke and his duchy." Davo's voice was infinitely quiet. "You were—and remain—the best for that task."

Raimon stared hard-eyed into the pallor of the tiny shrine within the Palasso; perhaps now with a new Duke, a new mistress, a new Lord Limner, things would change and Grijalvas might worship again in public. "But I also wish someone might discover some-thing to bring youth back to my joints . . ." He lifted his hands, ex-amined swelling knuckles; felt the stiffness in his spine. *Be not so certain I am graced with anything save my own share of obsession, if for my family instead of myself.* "It comes to us all, the bone-fever. It comes—and consumes us."

"And Sario?" Davo asked. "Will it consume him as well? Or shall he consume *us?*"

Raimon, brought up short, no longer felt the quiet ache in knuck-les, in spine. He lowered his hands to his thighs and looked at the man who, after Arturro, had helped to shape his soul.

"Sario learned very young how to make and wear a mask," Davo began. "An inviolate mask; not invisible, but impregnable. There is nothing of his thoughts in his face because the mask shields it, and though a man may read arrogance and ambition, those are not sins such as we punish; that is for the Mother." He resettled the weight of dangling Chieva against his chest. "But you, Raimon, never made a mask, and so there is none to wear." He looked now at the icon. "If I wish to know what Sario is capable of, if I wish to see guilt, sorrow, regret, the devouring fear—all emotions he will never exhibit—I have only to look at *your* face. And thus know all."

A chill settled into Raimon's bones. In that moment he thought surely the season had turned; was the bitter cold of bleak Sperranssia instead of the wet warmth of mid-Plagarra, named after the month of the plague.

"We have not sent one of us to Court for three normal generations, and even this came sooner than believed possible. He has now placed himself beyond us, and thus is beyond discipline no matter what he might do." Davo paused, closing one trembling, swollen hand over his Chieva do'Orro. "You are not."

It took effort to speak, and even then Raimon believed the voice issued from another throat entirely. "He is what we have made him."

"Eiha, I think not. I think Sario has made himself . . ." His voice was infinitely gentle. ". . . save for such encouragement and leave as was given by you."

Rising apprehension drove him to an impolitic answer. "We required *someone* like Sario!"

It echoed briefly, died away into candle-scribed pallor.

"*Like* Sario, I grant you—but not necessarily he." Davo shifted his feet; boot soles scraped against flagstones. "A flawed tool will break, and in the breaking may injure another. Perhaps many others."

" *'May.' "*

"When admitting the 'may,' one must also admit the repercussions of the breaking itself—if the 'may' comes to be."

Raimon set his teeth. "Holy Mother," he said hoarsely, "what do you want of me?"

Davo sighed. "Nothing more than you have ever freely offered, frato meyo. Truth."

Raimon's eyes burned grittily as he gazed upon the gilt-etched icon but three paces away. Arturro's work. "You came *here* for this." *Because of the icon. Because of Arturro. Because I could not lie, not here, not now, before the Mother.*

"Because you would never attempt to lie, and I had no doubt you would desire divine assistance." Davo gathered himself, rose with effort, turned stiffly toward the door. "In the Name of Our Blessed Mother and Her gentle Son, I give you this much, Raimon: on the day of our greatest triumph since Verro Grijalva destroyed the *Kita'ab,* nothing shall be done."

Raimon sat locked into immobility until Davo shut the door behind him, and then gave vent to the shudder that took him utterly,
the fear that racked him without mercy.

*O Mother, that Davo might have chosen another example than
the Kita'ab . . . might have used another phrase . . .* But he had not,
and so the irony of what the *Kita'ab* was, how it shaped every day
of Grijalva life, Grijalva compordotta, was now a spear made to
pierce through flesh to soul.

So. The rank of Premio Frato will never be mine after all.
Raimon slid off the bench. Stood up as an old man, as they said
Zaragosa Serrano stood: slightly stooped, shoulders shrunken,
bone-fevered hands curling into loose and strengthless fists.

He knelt again upon the flagstones before the icon. "I gave him
leave," he confessed. "I gave him leave to do as he would to make
himself Lord Limner . . ."

Flawed tool, Davo said.

". . . and so now he is appointed such by the Duke himself, may
You Bless his name and his seed, and my task is done. You are
wise, Sweet Mother, and always generous, and I question none of
Your divine compordotta—but if I may offer this, if you will permit me in Your graciousness, I will say only that if Sario works *for
the family* as well as for his Duke and his duchy, I shall count it
well done."

And worth any sacrifice.

❧ TWENTY-ONE ❧

Alejandro, seated stiffly in the chair that had been his father's, was entrapped in chambers with various conselhos all counseling him simultaneously. Shock and grief had dulled him into utter helplessness the first two days following the news of his father's death, but he was allowed no time for personal mourning: he had inherited a duchy along with the grief. Thus the conselhos, after professing equal shock and grief, recovered very quickly, far more quickly than he in their lust for vengeance, and gave him no time to sort out thoughts and emotions. They proposed war. At once. Now they demanded ducal response as immediately.

He shifted in the chair, conscious that its stiff, aged leather, stretched over two decades to suit the powerful, restive body of Baltran do'Verrada, did not in the least fit the equally restive but less mature son. Such power, such solidity, required time. *Yet they will give me none.* Alejandro moved again and scowled at the conselhos. *They cluster like wolves waiting for me to offer my belly!*

He had in short order discovered that hard-won courtesy and self-restraint gained nothing. He was their Duke, they all told him—with such frequency and vehemence that he believed perhaps they themselves needed to be convinced—but they gave him no ground to speak. Attempts at offering comment, at explaining himself, met with a resounding lack of response save for the occasional polite dismissal.

Frustration burgeoned. *They ignore me!* Although perhaps they would not when—*if*—he surrendered to the frustration and raw grief, as he had once before. But he preferred not to give over self-control; it served no purpose save to convince them he was incapable.

Eiha—am I not? His father, after all, had prepared him for little. Forty-three was not old enough to expect death in any but Grijalvas, and especially not in a man as vigorous as Baltran do'Verrada. No one had believed his nineteen-year-old son would inherit the duchy so soon.

Self-control was fragile, fraying with every moment; therefore he looked upon it as wholly providential when his new Lord

Limner was announced into the chamber, and every voice in the room broke off at once.

Holy Mother. Alejandro appealed, wiping a hand across a tense face as he settled once again into the cradling leather, *save me from these moronnos who look for my father in me.*

Sario Grijalva, still clad in the black and green he had worn to the ceremony that invested him with the position so many coveted, entered quietly through the paneled door into utter silence. He stopped. Waited. Let them look upon him, upon the Chieva do'Orro that dangled at his waist even as the keys and locks of the sanctas and sanctos dangled against bleached robes.

But so different, Alejandro thought. *What 'Vedra has told me of the Grijalvas, their rigid compordotta—Blessed Mother, but they are as different from us as those of the Ecclesia!* And wondered uneasily if his thought might be construed as heresy.

Someone shifted stance slightly, crunching boot sole against grit-coated stone flag. "Eiha," a voice murmured dryly, "it is not so much the popinjay as Serrano, eh?"

Someone laughed softly, and another man offered, "At least it is not wearing *scarlet.*"

Grijalva smiled acknowledgment, an acceptance of the challenge. "Nor will it ever." Deliberately he echoed the insult. "*It* detests the color."

Thus the posturing began. Alejandro, versed in the ways of Court if not in its political intricacies, marked the moment the conselhos closed ranks to bait. "And do you then fail to use it in your paintings?"

"No, conselhos," Grijalva demurred. "I use it with moderation."

"And will you never then wear it at all, even during Mirraflores?"

Alejandro, relieved beyond measure that Grijalva's arrival shifted the massed intensity from himself to another, waited expectantly. It was a test, he knew; Mirraflores, which marked the restoration of the Mother's fertility—and thus the fertility of Tira Virte—after the birth of her Son, was celebrated by the draping of vivid bloodflowers throughout the city . . . and by the wearing of them, real or of silk or colored paper, as personal adornment.

"With moderation," Grijalva repeated serenely.

Alejandro grinned. *'Vedra said he had wit.*

Also boldness. Grijalva swept the chamber with an assessive glance, marked out the clustered conselhos individually, examined each, then turned to his Duke with an elegant bow. "Your Grace. I freely confess that I am new to my duties and as new to these chambers, but if you will permit me, I may be able to offer a resolution to your present difficulty."

Better-spoken than expected—that will annoy them. Alejandro opened his mouth to answer, but a massive snort from the man closest to him preempted speech.

"*May* you!" Edoard do'Najerra, the late Duke's Marchalo Grando, cut crisply through the murmuring and whispers. "*You* may?"

"I may," Grijalva did not even so much as glance at the older, stout-built man, whom the late Baltran do'Verrada considered a close companion. "If the Duke—" The pause was minute, but considered. "—or *you* will permit me to speak?"

Dark brown eyes were turned from do'Najerra to the Duke, expressing no more than courteous patience. Alejandro, suppressing a brief startled smile, gestured awkward permission instantly. "Sweet Mother, Grijalva—be not so hesitant! If you can resolve this dilemma—"

"And dishonor!" do'Najerra thundered; he had trained his voice on the tourney field.

"—then I shall be most pleased," Alejandro finished pointedly. He shot the Marchallo a baleful glare. "What does it entail?"

"Merely that for which I am present, Your Grace." Sario Grijalva's smile was infinitely sweet. "I shall paint."

"Paint *what?*" someone shouted from behind the others. "And if that is the remedy you suggest, if you feel it more worthy than the honor of war, why not simply paint Duke Baltran back to life?"

Matra Dolcha— It shocked Alejandro. Shocked everyone. Even the man who had suggested it. Oddly enough, it did not shock Grijalva; Alejandro wondered absently if anything could. "Bassda!" He was distantly gratified to see that *this* time they listened. They even looked at him. "Bassda," he repeated. "Nommo do'Matra, that *is* what he is for, no?—the Lord Limner paints. And it is *with* paintings that such things as marriages are made, treaties recorded, *wars avoided.*" Now he had them. He nodded toward Grijalva, who waited in quiet self-possession a pace away from the ducal chair. "If he can settle this war by wielding a brush rather than a sword, I shall be glad of it. Nothing is earned in war—"

Mistake. It set them off again.

"Nothing but *honor!*" a man shouted: Estevan do'Saenza.

"Nothing but *land!*" cried another; Alejandro believed it was Rivvas Serrano, a distant relation to the now-dismissed Zaragosa.

"And lives saved, Your Grace," put in Edoard do'Najerra, remarkably sanguine in the midst of clamoring disbelief. "As well as regaining your poor father's abased body—"

"I can do that," Grijalva interposed.

Thunderous silence. Then a furious roar.

"*You* can do that!" Now even the Marchalo was angry. "So easily, then? Eiha—shall you paint the body here, and thus it *arrives?*"

A deep voice muttered, "Only the Mother has such power as this."

"Or a Grijalva wielding dark magic." It *was* Rivvas Serrano.

Alejandro thrust himself to his feet. "Bassda," he said sharply, sensing disaster. Saavedra had told him he had a fine grasp of command . . . eiha, perhaps he might borrow his father's if he yet lacked his own. "You are here in my presence, by my request, in my service—*you will not speak again unless I give you leave.*"

Shocked faces. Startled eyes. Mouths frozen in mid-word. But not a man spoke. He had not given leave.

"Grazzo." Alejandro resumed his seat with deliberation, keeping relief from his tone. He could not help but see the thoughtful reassessment in Edoard do'Najerra's expression. Emboldened, he turned again crisply to Sario Grijalva. "You can do this?"

"Restore your father to life? No. I have no such power, nor does any man." That was for Rivvas Serrano's benefit. "But regain his body? Yes. I can do this."

A growl arose from the mass of men. Rivvas shoved his way through the others so that he came to the forefront, staring furiously at the young man who had replaced his kinsman. "What have we said of the Grijalvas, Your Grace, but that they have recourse to such magics? He admits it—here before us all he *admits* it!" He flung a glance of loathing at Grijalva, then appealed to his Duke. "Your Grace, my own kinsman, Zaragosa Serrano, tried to present evidence to your late father—"

"There was none," Alejandro interrupted. "I heard of it, of course—who hasn't?" He shrugged, pleased that now they listened at least to part of what he said before erupting again. "Everyone knows Zaragosa was convinced the Grijalvas dabble in dark magic—"

"And so they do!" Rivvas thrust a hand in the new Lord Limner's direction. "He has admitted so, Your Grace."

Alejandro shifted his gaze to Sario Grijalva. *'Vedra claims he is clever . . . clever enough to evade this trap? Or am I stripped of my first appointment?* Which would damage him far more than simple inexperience already had. That much he knew of Court; he had to establish control, to establish his own way even with ruthless arrogance, before he lost them utterly. Tautly he repeated, "You can do this?"

"I can, Your Grace." Grijalva was unperturbed by the tense ripple of hostility. "It is a simple matter, you see—"

"Simple matter!" Rivvas shouted. "To conjure up a body?"

"To paint it present?" Estevan do'Saenza now took his lead from Serrano, stirring further concern. "Your Grace, surely you must see—"

"A simple thing." Grijalva's still voice undermined their bluster. A slim, dark hand brought into sight two sheets of folded parchment; Alejandro could not help marking the length of slender fingers, the trained, graceful motions of a man accustomed to precise physical control. "You see—it is here already. The body." Grijalva smiled faintly at Alejandro, who found himself smiling back without intending to. "What need is there of magic, dark or otherwise, where there are wagons to carry the dead?"

Silence. Even breathing was stilled as each man heard and comprehended what Grijalva suggested.

"Wagon?" someone murmured in stunned disbelief.

"A message accompanied the body." Into the tense expectancy, Sario Grijalva offered the papers to his Duke. "As I came to the door—" A nod of the head indicated it, "—I was given this for you. A message, I was told, explaining how Duke Baltran came to be killed—"

"Murder!" Rivvas cried, attempting to regain the moment.

"Assassination!" shouted do'Saenza, attempting to assist him.

"Perhaps so." Grijalva was unruffled; Alejandro envied him his composure. "Perhaps not. And perhaps the Duke should read the message to know; it is addressed to him, and I was told it explained all." He extended the folded sheets, inclining his head.

"Matra ei Filho—" Deliberation banished, Alejandro stood in a rush and grabbed the parchment from Grijalva's hand. He hesitated only an instant, then broke the wax and tore the papers open.

Disappointment extinguished hope. *But I can't—* He looked at them all, loath to admit yet another failure. Instead he appealed to his personal secretary, who had been his father's. Because of that link, the steadiness in Martain's eyes, Alejandro managed to recapture his father's tone of command. "Read these, grazzo."

Martain accepted and examined the papers. "Regretto, Your Grace—the language of the first is unknown to me . . . and the other is ruined."

"The language of the first is not unknown to me." Grijalva again. This time the disbelief was less explosive, the conselhos more restrained, but the murmurs that ran through the chamber were in no wise mitigated.

Alejandro handed the parchments back. "What do they say?"

Grijalva accepted the letters, groomed creases from them, scanned them quickly. "Yes," he murmured, "I know it. The language of Tza'ab Rih."

Edoard do'Najerra took a single long stride forward and tore the letter from Grijalva's hand. "Tza'ab Rih!" Clearly it was unbelievable, and as unacceptable. "No one reads that language. It is the enemy's tongue—"

"And the enemy has sent back your dead Duke." Sario Grijalva cast an apologetic glance at Alejandro. "It seems he went hunting near the border of Tza'ab Rih on the way to Pracanza, and met with an accident—"

"Treachery." The word was forced between Marchalo do'Najerra's clamped teeth. "Baltran was murdered. We know this. And now the Tza'ab admit it?"

"The Duke was *not* murdered." Quietly Grijalva recaptured the much-abused letters. "The accident was the kind any horseman might encounter. Duke Baltran, you see, was thrown from his mount." He shrugged. "Upon landing, his neck was broken."

"Lies. It was assassination."

"Was it?" Alejandro deflected do'Najerra's startled glare by looking instead at Grijalva. "Is that what it says?"

"And also that there were witnesses."

"The Tza'ab," do'Najerra stated flatly.

"Tira Virteians," Grijalva corrected. "The Duke's party accompanied him."

"Then why are they not here?" Alejandro asked before anyone else could; and someone would. "Why are we not brought word from those who were *with* my father?"

Grijalva gestured. "Duty, Your Grace—and yet more tragedy. The Duke's party accompanied him to propose a betrothal between you and the Pracanzan Princess—that duty they carried out."

Alejandro nearly gaped. "They went *on* to Pracanza?"

"Most of them. What it says, Your Grace, is that your father died moments after being thrown from his horse, but had time enough to command them to complete the embassy to Pracanza. That the interests of Tira Virte were best served by making the peace with Pracanza and binding it with the marriage." He shrugged elegantly. "Apparently the rumor of assassination was no more than that, Your Grace."

"Rumor!" Alejandro sat down abruptly. "Rumor . . ." He looked now at do'Najerra. "You would have me go to war on the basis of *rumor?*"

The flesh of his heavy face deepened in hue. "Would you have me fail my poor Baltran on the word of a *Tza'ab?*"

"It apparently was not meant to be merely the word of a Tza'ab," Sario said. "Two of the Duke's party accompanied the body with the aid of the Tza'ab, to see it safely back to Meya Suerta. But the party was attacked by border bandits. Some of the Tza'ab were killed outright, as was our own Dio Ormendo. Antoneyo Barza was wounded and died later on the way, but not before he wrote a note." He held up a smeared and tattered paper. "Unfortunately the paper became damp and the ink ran, but it is Antoneyo Barza's signature and seal . . . I must assume the Tza'ab brought this note to confirm their own."

"Trickery," do'Najerra rasped. "I don't accept my poor Baltran died in a fall from his horse. And it is too convenient that Barza's letter is ruined!"

"I can question the Tza'ab who escorted the wagon, if you wish," the young Lord Limner said, "but the bodies are here as well. Why not let the late Duke and Antoneyo Barza tell us the truth?"

Incensed, Marchalo do'Najerra challenged instantly. "And can you read a body as well as you read Tza'ab?"

Sario Grijalva did not look away from the furious, powerful man. "To paint the living," he answered quietly, "one must study the dead."

Saavedra's new room was not a room at all, but a *set* of rooms: three altogether. It startled her first that so much could be given to one person, secondly that they would give such to *her*. A small bed-chamber, a fractionally larger sitting room, and an airy, many-win-dowed chamber that opened onto a north-facing balcony overlook-ing the central courtyard with its gurgling marble fountain.

"Lord Limner's quarters," she murmured, drifting from one room to the other and to the other, astounded and delighted by so much light and spaciousness. "There, I think, for the worktable, and the easel should stand *there*—" And she broke off into guilty laughter, that she should so easily settle into such luxury.

So much to do . . . there was her trunk to unpack so that clothing might be freshened, personal things to set out, and of course the vast array of the requirements of her work: canvas, stretched and unstretched; papers; boards; stoppered pots of ground pigments;

boxes of brushes, knives, tools; rattling jars full of amber and gum acacia; sealed bottles of poppy oil, linseed, glue, inks; baskets crammed with favorite charcoals, chalks, dip pens . . . so *much* to find a place for— "—and so much room in which to place it!"

The door behind her banged open; a high-pitched curse accompanied it. She turned swiftly, startled, and grinned to see one of her many cousins trying to get through the door as arms overflowed with canvas, stretchers, boards.

"Here . . . Ignaddio, *wait!*" He did not. Things began to fall. "Ignaddio!" Hastily she caught and rescued that which also threatened to depart his arms, then bent to gather up what had already fallen. " 'Naddi, you should never try to carry it *all*. Bring smaller loads."

He stretched his chin to secure a heap of tattered canvas. "Takes longer. Where do you wish this to go?"

"In there." Gathering fallen papers, Saavedra angled her head toward the balcony chamber, now her atelierro. "Through there, 'Naddi—follow the sunlight."

As bidden, he followed. His voice was muffled by what he carried as well as the wall between them. "So—have they decided you are Gifted, to give you such quarters?"

Saavedra sighed. He knew. They all knew. "Eiha, would I tell *you?*" She sorted papers—sketches she wished to consider transferring to canvas or wood one day—and rose, careful of edges and corners. "If it were true, you would never believe it."

"No?" He remained in the room, out of sight. She heard the sounds of clinking bottles, a rattle of something else. "It would be foolish to deny it—our blood is closer than most, and I hope myself to be a Lord Limner . . ." His voice grew louder, clearer; he paused now in the open doorway, a slender and yet ill-defined boy, unkempt dark curls flopping down into hazel eyes. "But why should *you* be so blessed, eh? Duke's mistress *and* Limner?" He grinned, danced around her outstretched, jabbing foot, slipped past her and through the sitting room to the door giving way to the corridor. "And what would they call you?—surely not *Lord* Limner! Eiha, no, you had better look to your bed-skill, 'Vedra, if you wish to keep the Duke—what does he know of painting?"

He was gone, giggling, clattering down the flight of stairs to fetch more of her things, but Saavedra answered anyway. "He knows I am good." She reconsidered. "He *says* he knows I am good—but perhaps that is only kindness." She supposed it might hurt, but she was too happy for pain. " 'Naddi . . ." She raised her voice, though undoubtedly he would not hear; or would choose not to. "You had best mind your tongue as well as your lessons—or they will name you Neosso Irrado."

"And why not?" He was back, arms full of cloth-draped paintings. "The last one so named became Lord Limner!" His grin was quick, even as he struggled with stiff, painted canvas. "Shall I—"

"*Ignaddio!*" Saavedra was horrified. "Matra Dolcha, that you should stack them up like so much cordwood . . . 'Naddi, how *could* you?" She caught up and carefully lifted the draped painting on the top of the stack. "You know better, cabessa bisila!" She turned back the cloth with care. "Set out the others on the bed—*separately!*—so we may see if there is damage. 'Naddi, *why?*"

Now he sulked; at thirteen, he offended easily. "They smelled dry to me."

"What would you know of that?" Saavedra set the rescued painting against the wall and knelt to study it for damage. "Cabessa bisila," she muttered. "A potential Limner would never do such a thing." And then she frowned. "This isn't mine. 'Naddi—"

"It's mine." Stiff apprehension, and burgeoning hope.

"But—" Still kneeling, she twisted to look at him. Saw the pallor of his cheeks, the teeth worrying at bottom lip, the clenching of his hands in the soiled, tattered tunic. "Why?"

It burst out of him. "Because you *are* good, 'Vedra—everybody says!"

It was unexpected, and unexpectedly gratifying. She laughed breathily. "So, *everybody* says?"

"The moualimos. Some of the estudos." He twisted his mobile mouth. "Am *I* good, 'Vedra?"

"Eiha, of course you—" Saavedra halted. What he wanted to hear was not necessarily the truth, but what she offered *ought* to be. It was why he asked. " 'Cordo. Shall we critique it together?"

"Matra Dolcha, *no*." He reconsidered. "I mean—I think . . ." He stared hard at the floor, tunic hem stretched taut nearly to tearing. "I am afraid. Study it, grazzo—but tell me later what you think."

" 'Cordo." She knew that fear. With care she redraped the canvas. "But you need only have asked . . . there was no need to risk the paintings merely to gain an opinion."

Relieved that she would do as he wished, he paid little attention to her. Already he freed the stretched canvases on the bed of their protective wrappings. "This one is unharmed—I *was* careful!—and this one . . . *filho do'canna!*"

" 'Naddi! Recall your compordotta, grazzo. If you truly wish to be a Limner—"

"What *is* this?" His voice was raw with excitement. "When did you paint *this*, 'Vedra?"

"Until I see it, how can I know?" She shook dust from her skirts, walked to the bed. "That one—" She checked, shocked into silence.

Ignaddio's fascinated gaze moved from the painting to her face. "I didn't know you were *so* good, 'Vedra!"

It gusted sharply from her lungs. "But—that's *horrible*—"

Ignaddio nodded vigorously. "That's what is *good* about it!"

"No, no—" Stricken, Saavedra gestured the comment away. "Where did you find this? It isn't mine."

He shrugged narrow shoulders, staring again at the painting in unrestrained delight. "In the workroom."

"Which workroom?"

"The one where we put all the paintings packed to be shipped somewhere else." He was uninterested; such shipments were routine in a family of artists who painted so many copies. "I like how you have painted the hands so crippled, 'Vedra—and the lines of pain in his face—"

" 'Naddi!" She wanted to protest that the grotesqueness of the painting was not due such flattery, and yet she had to admit the artist's talent was more than talent. It was sheer genius.

"Who is it?" Ignaddio asked. "And why would he wish himself painted so?" Young he was, but already he understood that vanity often superseded truth.

"I don't know who it—" But she did. Abruptly, she did. "Filho do'canna." She collapsed to her knees even as 'Naddi laughed in gleeful delight to hear her swear. "Oh Matra, Blessed Matra—"

"Who *is* it, 'Vedra?"

She kissed fingertips, pressed them to her breast. "Nommo do'Matra ei Filho, let him not do this . . . let him never *do* this—"

"Who is it? Who has done what? Who shouldn't do this?"

The series of questions posed in a child's unbroken treble at last breached her horror. A trembling hand—her own?—reached out to tug at cloth, to cover the painting. " 'Naddi—"

"Who painted it, 'Vedra?"

"No." Now the hand settled on his shoulder, clasped tightly. "No, 'Naddi . . . no importada." She stood up unsteadily, guided him toward the open door. "Go, now. You have helped enough today . . . go and play, if you wish."

He balked. "But I want to *know*—"

"No." *You don't. No one should know.* "Go on, 'Naddi."

"But—"

"Do'nado," she said firmly. "It was nothing at all, Ignaddio—
just a poor jest painted by a moronno luna."

"*But*—"

She pushed him out, shut the door, leaned against it. A final
plaintive question came from beyond the wood; when she ignored
it long enough, Ignaddio went away.

Trembling, Saavedra straightened. Pushed herself from the door.
Went to the bed. Tore away the cloth to display the ruined hands
and tortured features of Zaragosa Serrano.

She had seen the painting before, in Sario's atelierro. She recalled questioning him about the border, the affectation that now
was in everything he painted.

He put this where I was sure to see it. He wanted *me to see it. He
wanted me to know.* Her belly cramped. Saavedra turned her back
on the painting, slid down to the floor, scraped her spine against the
bed. *I have always been his confidante, always understood him, his
need to express his Gift. And now he shows me this.*

She sat there staring blindly, collapsed upon hard stone flags . . .
aware of fear, of tears, of nausea—and an understanding at last of
Sario's terrible Luza do'Orro.

TWENTY-TWO

He spent himself as a man does who has not lain with a woman in too long: with a quick-struck and scouring immediacy that left him drained, not sated; that left him limp in body and spirit as wet linen. The woman beneath did not protest; she laughed softly, breathily, murmuring of a sword whose temper is tamed by a properly-fitted sheath . . . and he let her have it, let her flatter herself, let her believe she had kindled and quenched his best.

He moved then, shifting weight, aware of slick flesh adhered to his own—and knew instantly and with utter certainty that he had wasted himself, his seed; had thrown away that which could better be used for power.

It palled: fleshly contact, release, sheer physical need. He pushed away from her and rose, climbing free of tangled sheets and coverlet, unheeding of his nudity as he stood beside the bed. Sweat dried on him as she turned, shifted, propped herself up on one elbow.

"Go," he said. "Now. Adezo."

It shocked her. "But—"

"You have had all of me you shall have . . . what is left is mine, and there are better ways to spend it."

Astonishment now was anger. She tore back the bedclothes and climbed out, equally naked, equally uncaring. The epithet she used was framed in a mouth accustomed to such, and he laughed.

"Boys? Is that it?" She found and reached for smallclothes, yanked the shift over her head and tugged it across lush breasts and undulant hips. "Girl, followed by boy—as sweet vinho follows sour? Is that it?"

He said nothing. He watched her, marking the coursing of colors in her face: he had not studied scorn before, or humiliation, or such taut, restrained fury. All were tangible to him. *I must recall this . . . use this . . .*

She muttered again such vile commentary upon his person, his manhood, his poor and hasty industry that he grinned unrestrainedly, entertained by her vocabulary. Which infuriated her the more, and when at last she departed, she banged the door shut so forcefully he feared it might crack the lintel.

Gone. The smell of her remained, a cheap, thick perfume concocted of violets in an oil going rancid, and the undertang of lovemaking, of sweat, of spent—*wasted!*—seed. Yet naked, now dry, he stared at the bed and considered his emotions. That he was a man, he knew; that there was something worth more than the transient physical pleasure of copulation he was certain.

Transient pleasure . . . wholly unlike art that remained as alive, as permanently documented as that passing moment of physical bliss could not be, ever, as alive and real as art because art was of the body *and* the mind; and art, once completed, could never be extinguished by such trivial things as exhaustion, as infrequency, as the inability of a man under certain circumstances to raise the infamous sword.

Sario smiled. *That sword is worthless. It ages, sickens, grows lax. But the blade of true creation cannot be broken. Ever.*

Nor the one of power. He knew its name, its guises. And learned more each time he read of the *Kita'ab*, that was also *Folio*.

Meya Suerta, as most cities, began with small ambitions. But they had grown even as the city, and now the tattered hem of voluminous skirts covered much of the mellow land between the broken palisades of rising hills leading to the heights, and thick lowland marshes. Surrounded by orchards and vineyards, the walls and lesser dwellings of those who built beyond the city were buffered against depredations of the marshes, and yet the citizenry felt its incursions regardless. Most particularly Grijalvas, in their very bones.

Raimon paused near the fieldstone wall, noting idly how its spine had collapsed in places. The undulant sweep of stacked stone followed the line of the hills, separating vineyard from vineyard, orchard from orchard, so that grapes and olives did not offend one another; so that the citrus remained inviolate.

He walked the crown of a quiet hill, aware of exquisite rose-golden light that made him long for paletto and easel; aware also of impatience and growing expectancy. The quick-scribbled message had said nothing beyond that it was urgent he come. It was not from a Limner—there was no invocation of the Golden Key—but was nonetheless from someone who knew him, who knew where his interests lay.

When she came, striding up from the city with lifted skirts clasped into fists, he was startled. He did not know why he expected a man, but he had; and now she was here, all grown out of awkward adolescence into inarguable beauty, a warm, exotic beauty formed of the best of Tza'ab features and the best of Tira Virteian, so that she was not one *or* the other but wholly of them both.

Raimon did not understand why he had not marked it before, why it had taken Alejandro do'Verrada's interest to make him truly see her. Perhaps it was that she was so much younger than he . . . but no, youth meant nothing save promise to a man who died when not yet old. Perhaps it was that he had been distracted, dedicated to family goals and compordotta, to the Viehos Fratos, to Sario. Or perhaps he had been blind. Foolishly blind.

He smiled. He knew what lived within her spirit; it pleased him to see the exterior matched it.

She did not smile back. She reached the crown of the hill, dropped crumpled skirts, faced him poised so rigidly he feared she might shatter. "Do you know what he has done? Do you know what he *is?*"

Pleasure was extinguished. He opened his mouth to ask identification of whom she meant; closed it. He knew. *Blessed Mother . . . does everyone know what I have done?*

Fine cheeks were wind-glazed from the walk. "Can you stop him?"

That startled. "Stop him? Why? We have worked many years to place a Grijalva in his position."

She shook her head; thick ringlets, bound loosely back, massed across slim shoulders. "He isn't a Grijalva anymore. He's— he's . . ." She considered, gestured helplessness. "More. Less. *Other.*"

He turned away from her abruptly, staring across terraced vine-yards and orchards toward the dark smudge of marsh beyond. From there, Davo claimed, came the pestilence that afflicted them; the bone-fever that twisted joints into painful immobility and help-lessness. *Is it the fever that kills us so young? Some poison in our blood?*

"What will you do?" she asked. "What *can* you do?"

Is it the pigments we grind, tempered with bodily fluids to create the Peintraddos?

"You can't do nothing," she said. "You must do *something.*"

He did not turn to her. "I have done something. I helped create him."

"You didn't!" Skirts rustled against breeze-stirred grass as she came deliberately around to face him. "You as much as anyone have counseled proper compordotta . . . do you know the truth of it? Of him?"

"That he is capable of more than other Limners?—eiha . . . I know."

"For how long?"

He looked into her face, into fierce but frightened eyes. "Since the beginning."

"I will not accept that." Delicate color tinged the flawless clarity of her skin. "No one has known 'from the beginning.' Or surely he would never have been admitted to the Viehos Fratos, surely you would have done more than invoked the Lesser Discipline." Color deepened. "I recall Tomaz. Do you recall Tomaz? How he died?"

Startling himself as much as her, he caught her arm. "How much do you know, Saavedra? How much has Sario said of us?"

"Of you?" She shook her head. "He breaks no oaths, Il Sanguo—there are no secrets of the Limners I should not know, because we all of us are Grijalvas—"

She knows too much. He clamped her arm more firmly within his grasp. "That is not the question I asked, nor is it proper answer."

"Nor have you answered *my* questions," she countered sharply. "Nommo do'Matra, Sanguo Raimon . . . you say you helped create him. Do you know what you have done?"

"Lost control," he confessed, "if there was any I ever claimed." He released her arm abruptly, aware of the twinge in his knuckles. "I think there is more in his soul than even I believed possible."

Eloquent brows arched. "And yet you did not tell the others?"

Guilt scoured him into self-flagellation. "Better to ask, what *did* I tell the others."

Color fled her face. "That he was suitable. Oh, Blessed Mother—you *suggested* him! En verro—*you* supported him!" Wind plucked at ringlets. "He said there was only one he trusted, only one who believed in him."

"I believed him suitable, yes. And I believed it vital that he be given the opportunity to become Lord Limner."

"Why?"

That angered him. "Because one of us *had* to be!"

She flinched briefly from the sheer volume and vehemence of his shout, recovered ground. "Is it so very important that Grijalvas regain *now* what was lost?"

"Yes."

"No matter the price?"

He thrust between them one hand, displaying fingers that already began the transformation from powerful into powerless. "We know the price, Saavedra! It coils within our bones, waiting for the day when it may creep out into the light."

She checked, went on. "But if you knew he—"

Curtly, he overrode her. "How could I know what he might do? It was enough that he might not."

She shook her head. "I am a Grijalva. I was raised to believe as you believe, as Sario believes, that we should stand by the side of our Duke—"

"By the side," he emphasized.

"Yes, of course." And then she understood. "Do you believe Sario might want more?"

"I do not. He will not."

"But if he did—"

"How much time," he asked deliberately, "will you have to paint when you have borne a child? As you raise that child? As you bear and raise another?"

Though she said nothing, her answer was implicit in the tautening of her face. Little time. No time.

Raimon nodded once. "Above all, he must paint."

"En verro." Her voice was rusty. "I know—I've known all that he was since boyhood. I saw the Luza do'Orro—I saw it always, though others denied it; though they distrusted and disliked him."

"Called him Neosso Irrado." He nodded again. "So they called me. It seems a prerequisite."

She understood at once. "Then if *you*—"

"There are those who are," he said, "and those who shape."

"As you shaped Sario."

He offered no response.

"Why?" she asked. "Was there no other but he? Would there be no other suitable Limner perhaps a decade later?"

"These are matters for the Viehos Fratos—"

She cut him off neatly. "Make them mine, grazzo. I shaped him as much as you."

Wind ruffled his hair, stripped it from his face so he could hide nothing from her. "Because I wanted to."

She recoiled. *"That* is your answer? Your justification for allowing this to happen?"

Bitterness warped his laughter. "When a man cannot become what he himself desires, he may shape another to assume his place."

"But—"

"Bassda!" It burst from him abruptly, astonishing him as well as her. "I am aware of the magnitude of my failure," he declared, "and

its repercussions. Matra ei Filho—I was foolish, Saavedra, but not estupedio. Nor deaf. Nor blind."

Tears suddenly welled, were dashed away. "Neither was I," she said in a raw, bleak tone. "Neither *am* I, but I did no more than you. I did *less* than you!"

"Eiha, neither of us is to blame."

"No? But I am. I said nothing of the old man, the old Tza'ab, who taught him things."

"And I said nothing of the pages of the *Kita'ab,* and the truth of our *Folio.*" He saw her startlement. "Do you see? Assigning blame, assuming guilt, accomplishes nothing. Unless we care to share it, and thus dilute its focus."

Her exquisite face was devoid of color, stark as bone beneath soft-worked vellum. "I came to you so the Viehos Fratos would understand what he is. So they could stop him."

"How?"

"Peintraddo Chieva," she murmured wretchedly.

"Would you have us kill him? Cripple him?"

"No! Sweet Mother, *no*—"

"Then what, Saavedra? Invoking the Lesser Discipline did nothing to dissuade him."

"No," she said. "Ah, no, not that, not either . . ." And then she went whiter still.

"Saavedra?"

"His *Peintraddo*—"

"We have it. With the others. It remains in the collection of the Viehos Fratos."

She shook her head rigidly. "No . . . no, Il Sanguo—you have a copy."

"A *copy*—"

"I have the original." Her face was wasted. "He gave it into my keeping."

Breath gusted out of his lungs. "This abrogates all oaths . . . Nommo Chieva do'Orro, this is not possible!"

"It is. It was done. I have it. I have his *Peintraddo*." Wind stripped the coil out of a ringlet beside her ear, gave it back fecklessly. "Would a threat to it be enough?"

Bones ached in the fragile envelope of flesh. "For Sario? What do you believe?"

"I believe . . . I believe. . ." She shivered as gusting wind snapped her skirts away from her body, but he knew it was not that which caused the response. "I believe he would do what he thinks is necessary. That he would *be* what is necessary . . ." Tears bloomed, died. "He told me so."

" 'Vedra." He used the diminutive; saw it register. " 'Vedra, why did you come to me?"

She swallowed heavily. "Because I am afraid. For him. *Of* him. And because I love him." She gestured hastily, forestalling him. "Eiha, no—not the way I love Alejandro . . . not the way women love men whom they wish to marry, to whom they desire to bear children—it was never that way between us—" She checked minutely and he wondered if Sario could so freely admit the same. "—but in a *different* way, a way I don't understand, not truly, save to know it exists. Here." She pressed a hand against her heart. "I understand him, Il Sanguo . . . I see his light, his flame, I answer it—and he sees mine. Believes in mine." Bleakly, she said, "Sario always told me we shared the same soul."

Raimon could not offer what she required—Alejandro's embrace, his warmth, his love—but he offered what *he* could: hands clasped upon her shoulders, and such truths as he could muster. "Your soul is your own," he promised. "I see no blight in it, no disease that destroys its strength." He turned her toward the vineyards, the orchards. "You are not as the vines are, as the olives and the oranges, vulnerable to wind, to frost, to depredations of the insects . . . you are Saavedra Grijalva, gifted with talent beyond so very many, beloved of a Duke—and possessed of a soul no one else may share. That no one else, even Sario, may destroy in his own designs." He squeezed her shoulders briefly, suppressing a wince as pain bloomed in his fingers, then turned her back so he might look into her face. "I asked you before why you came to me. Is this fear of what he *will* do?—or fear for what he has done?"

"Both," she said as wind buffeted. And told him about the portrait of a maimed Zaragosa Serrano.

When she was done, when she justified her fear far beyond overwrought imaginings, he turned sharply from her. He saw nothing, no terraced vineyards and orchards, no fieldstone walls, no marshlands beyond a bright blurred haze of tears.

"Sanguo Raimon?"

So much I have done.

"Il Sanguo?"

So much as this, bred out of my own desire, out of my own design.

"Sanguo Raimon . . ." She paused. "I could not bear to see such talent extinguished."

He said nothing.

"And there is always Alejandro." He had given her comfort, Raimon realized. By sharing her fear, she took encouragement from him, from no longer being alone. "I could speak with Alejandro."

She could. More so than he could.

"Perhaps you could speak with Sario."

Why not? He had shaped him. Had shaped this woman as well, and her fear; he had done far more than ever he intended.

I wrought too well.

Davo had said it. A flawed tool, breaking, may injure another. Others.

Time, he realized. *All of it for time, because we claim so little. Had I waited—had I sought another boy—*

There was no other. There could be no other in Raimon's lifetime, who contained within one flesh so much that was required.

Mine to do, he realized. *Mine to undo.*

"Sanguo Raimon—"

He turned. Smiled brilliantly. Kissed his fingers and pressed them against his heart. "Nommo Matra ei Filho," he said, repeating the motion with his key. "Nommo Chieva do'Orro. It shall be seen to."

Hope kindled, as did color. Wind tore hair from her face and bared it, bared the magnitude of her relief. She murmured gratitude to Mother and Son, said it more forcefully to him, then smiled against the wind and turned to make her way back.

Raimon watched her go. *That much, I have done that deserved to be done. Wrought peace within her soul.*

If at the cost of his own.

◆TWENTY-THREE◆

Ignaddio had done exactly as directed: stacked paintings, panels, wood for stretchers and frames against the walls of Saavedra's new atelierro; piled jammed portfolios and sketchbooks, sheaves of unused paper in one corner; set out baskets and bottles and boxes into an ill-defined puzzle upon the floor, the worktable, even upon the lone chair. Saavedra herself, mired in the midst of sorting everything out of unfamiliar clutter into the equally cluttered arrangement she found comfortable and useful, did not at first mark the visitor's arrival; it required a pointed clearing of the throat before she heard, turned to see—and then she very nearly dropped the dented pewter tankard serving as brush holder.

"Alejandro!" —*Eiha, but he is glorious!*

Alejandro Baltran Edoard Alessio do'Verrada grinned his renowned grin, unself-consciously displaying the crooked tooth that was in adolescence considered a flaw, yet now was called charming. "I prefer you like this, I think, rather than Court-clad; it reminds me of the day we met."

She remembered it as well as he. She had reeked of oil and solvents set into grimy linen, bore paint and chalk dust beneath her nails—while tangled, unbound ringlets were soaked with fountain water. Aside from the water, her present appearance in the midst of dust-laden industry nearly echoed that day.

She clutched the mashed tankard. "But I'm *filthy!* You might as well send me off to the middens, or to the dyers, even the *tannery*—"

He took one long stride, appropriated the tankard and bent to set it down, then, disdaining dust and perspiration, swept her all of a piece into his arms. "Filthy, mussed, with paint upon your face—" He touched a smudge on her cheek. "—and the pungent perfume of spilled oil . . . eiha, I am besmirched. And inconsolably *desoladio.*" He kissed her. Hard.

Response was instantaneous. She had never known it quite so powerful before, an abrupt and unassailable awareness that nothing else in the world mattered in this moment *but* this moment, and what they could make of it.

"Door—" she murmured against his mouth.

"Closed," he answered, into hers.

"There is a bed in the other—"

"No," he said. *"Here."*

Amidst a tangle of unprimed canvas; the rattling of stoppered bottles; a basket of chalk tipped over to spill its contents in a rainbow across the rug; the tankard mashed yet again; his crushed and now-featherless hat—*here* it was.

Sario had caused to be made a massive upright chest with drawers and locks built into it: shallow, wide drawers that stored and warded finished and incomplete works. There were other chests, caskets, baskets, so many containers for the storing away of his needs. It took time to sort through, to sort out, to put away into an arrangement he found most appropriate and useful the tools of his talent, the tangible requirements of his Gift. Pots, bottles, vials, all sealed with wax, or cork, or leather; sealed also with lingua oscurra. Rims of tiny, indecipherable runes warded that which was vital, so that he need not find himself naked of the makings of power at any given moment.

Grijalvas learned many crafts as they grew and were taught; the family had survived the years after the Nerro Lingua not only by copying, by occasional commissions, but by serving the needs of artists and others. He as much as any of them knew how to mix, to make, to bind together the necessary ingredients for various crafts and recipes. He could make paper, bind leather . . . and so he bound the loose pages of Il-Adib's unintended bequest and made himself a *Kita'ab.* An infinitely brief, unfinished, private—and wholly personal—*Kita'ab,* that was also as much as it could be Grijalva *Folio.*

It took much time to sort out the past life of Palasso Grijalva he brought with him to the future life of the Palasso Verrada. He was given a wing all to himself so that he might tend his own requirements in such a way as to serve the needs of his Duke and thus the needs of the duchy. There were servants, of course, though he dismissed most of them; two he kept for convenience, because when lost within the work he often forgot to eat, to drink—and why not send another to fetch a tray to him rather than break his concentration?

Concentration was so vital, especially with the oscurra and borders that demanded his best, lest the magic harm *him* . . . it infuriated Sario sometimes that he needed to urinate. That too interrupted. But such things he would tend himself; he did not believe paying a servant to pee would relieve his own bladder. Although there were times he wished it were possible.

At present he did not require the nightpot; kneeling upon the rune-worked Tza'ab rug brought from Il-Adib's tent, Sario sorted papers. Papers upon papers: maps of Tira Virte, maps of Pracanza, maps of Ghillas, of Taglis, Merse, Diettro Mareia, even of Vethia, so far to the north of the world . . . he did not believe he could bear to look at another map, and yet he must. He was now Lord Limner; his task was to acquaint himself with treaties, wars, alliances, with family needs and family habits, with the interests of other Dukes and kings and princes, with their innumerable wives and children, even with their *pets*—because if he were to help shape diplomacy, to assist his Duke in creating history, he had to know everything.

"Matra," he murmured. "I cannot believe *Zaragosa Serrano* was capable of this—capable of anything beyond clothing himself in scarlet!"

A step scraped at the door. He had not shut it of a purpose; what he did was never undertaken without invoking proper protections—and he needed just now to convince everyone in the Palasso Verrada there was nothing for them to suspect of their new Grijalva Limner. Let them look upon him.

"And so Zaragosa clothes himself in it forever, no?" the other asked evenly. "The scarlet of shame, the reddening of fever-racked hands, the crimson of his blood as the leeches bleed him in hopes of healing an unanticipated and debilitating illness very like that which commonly afflicts Grijalvas."

Sario did not turn. He knew the voice, recognized displeasure bordering on contempt. "His talent was dead. His body might as well be."

"When the Matra decrees it so." Raimon Grijalva came further into the chamber. "Have you usurped Her place?"

Sario, who yet knelt with his back to the man, grinned, tended maps. "No doubt the Serranos would argue so!"

"And have they the right of it?"

So, it comes . . . Sario stacked one map atop the other: Ghillas conquered Diettro Mareia. Now for the genealogies, the complex lattices and laceworks of marriages, births, deaths, the endless inventories of paintings recording events . . . "I do what I must. I am, after all, of the Viehos Fratos."

"And?"

"And?" He shrugged, smiling, examined the multiple marriages of Baltassar of Ghillas written out so meticulously; how *could* a man bear to marry so many women? And how had so many managed to die? "Am I supposed to be other?"

"More, perhaps," Raimon said. "You have resources others do not, even those who are of the Viehos Fratos."

Oddly, he felt anticipation, not regret; and a stirring nearly as powerful as lust. "Does it trouble you, Raimon?" He set aside the Ghillasian genealogies, the inventories, turned instead to trade agreements between Taglis and Tira Virte. "Do you fear I will misuse what I know?"

Silence.

Sario smiled more widely. *There is pleasure in this—there is POWER in this.* Quietly he put aside the papers and rose, dusting knees. Turned: chain and Chieva glittered in candleglow. With schooled self-possession he confronted the only man he had ever and always respected. "You made me," he said clearly. "Grazzo, be precise in this—of *what* do you believe I am capable?"

Raimon's face was stark. "Anything."

Sario paused a moment—he had not expected the bald truth quite so soon—and then nodded. "Permit me to rephrase, grazzo— what do you believe I will do?"

"Whatever you choose to do."

Truth, again. From this man he expected nothing less, or more; events had moved more quickly than any anticipated, even he. Zaragosa had been meant to die, or to be dismissed because of illness, but Baltran's freakish death had put all into motion too swiftly. And, clearly, Sanguo Raimon had accepted what others couldn't or wouldn't imagine. Not yet.

Then he shall have truth as well. "Nommo Chieva do'Orro, Raimon, I swear this: I don't want to rule. Is that what you fear?"

The older man shook his head. "Even you comprehend that contesting for Tira Virte would throw the duchy into a civil war so disastrous it would destroy everything—and leave you with nothing worth ruling. Unless. . ." Raimon's expression was at once bitter as winter, sere as summer. "Unless it is that you serve Tza'ab Rih now."

Sario laughed aloud. "Eiha, they might wish it! They might even expect it—it was what the old man wanted—but that is not my goal."

"Then what is your goal, Sario?" Raimon paused, examined expression, posture, then continued. "Have you any that avoids usurping the Mother's Throne?"

So much pleasure now, so much anticipation. "Heresy—or humor! Which is it, Raimon?" Laughing, he spread hands wide. "To be what I am. That is my goal. To be Lord Limner to the Duke of Tira Virte."

"Why?"

"Because I was shaped to be so by men such as you."

Raimon took a single step, checked. "It was not *I* who began this—"

"No? Of course it was. Otavio and Ferico would surely have done more than burned three tiny holes along my collarbone—" Sario touched his doublet. "—in fact, I believe they might have suggested I be treated as Tomaz was treated, thereby forever quenching a fire they could not control." He shrugged easily. "I am as you see me. I might have been less, might have been more, left to my own devices—but now I am the man whom the Grijalvas view as savior—"

"Savior!"

"—because it is to me the Duke shall come, *must* come, to plot his plots, his policies, and the campaigns of the conselhos; to conduct trade and make treaties; to arrange to marry a woman, to get heirs upon her; to marry another if that one dies in the bearing; to commemorate deaths and births and marriages and thus more births and marriages, and possibly more deaths . . . to document *life,* Raimon! To record the history and change of a nation and her people." He paused, looking for comprehension in place of contempt in the other man's aging face. "That is what we do. That is our task. To unmask the world so others may know the truth and be bound by it."

"Your truth."

"We all of us make our own—or, in the name of coin, accept commissions to twist the truth as others will have it twisted."

"You will bring harm to no one."

He fears that—fears ME. "No one beyond whom my Duke requires harmed."

With elaborate irony and equally clear disdain, "Zaragosa Serrano?"

Sario sighed. "Do you truly care what becomes of him, Raimon? Eiha, I know you seek evidence I have become a monster—or threaten to become one . . . but why must you be so certain I shall? I am a *painter,* Raimon! All I have ever wanted to do is paint!"

Raimon's hands trembled, betraying his rigid posture from strength into weakness. "Then paint," he said hoarsely. "I give you leave to paint. As *we have taught you* to paint."

Sario smiled, offering such brutal honesty as he could: truth was truth. "But there are many teachers. Many moualimos. And not all of them need be Grijalva."

"That old man, the old Tza'ab you told me about—"

"—wanted to make me into a second Diviner." Sario shook his head. "Why is it so many men wish to shape others? Am I nothing but flesh to you? A bit of bone, arranged so; a hybrid hide, stretched over that bone *so;* a mind empty of all save what thoughts men put into it, men like you and Arturro and Otavio and Ferico because surely the boy could never think for himself! Surely he *mustn't.* Surely the boy must be controlled through the inflexible rigidity of compordotta, the rituals of dying men—"

"Dying men!"

Ignorance annoyed him. Refusal to accept truth stirred him to retort. "Viehos Fratos," he said curtly. "Arturro. Otavio. All the dead men. All the men who *shall* be dead, and soon: Ferico. Davo. Even *Raimon,* though he has a handful of years yet left to him—even as the bone-fever destroys his Gift." There was nothing now in him but a cold, abiding anger. "What is a Lord Limner but a man who lives forever?"

"He dies, Sario—they all of them die!"

"But not their works." Sario shook his head. "Who comes to our galerrias, Raimon? Who comes to see what we were, what we shall be? Eiha, no one . . . they come to commission us to *copy* the others, to copy the Lord Limners, because only the work of such men *grants* those men immortality, and only Lord Limners are granted the chance to have their work preserved for the immortal glory it is." He drew in a hissing breath. "And that is the family goal. *Not* to place a Grijalva beside the Duke . . . but to steal back the years that are stolen from us, to put them into our paintings because we can't contain all those years in our flesh without being devoured." He extended hands, displayed them. Slim, young, talented hands, tensile in beauty and strength. "I am nearly twenty. In the same span of years I shall be your age, and my hands, afflicted by the curse of our family, will be older yet. No Limner who must paint, no Limner with such hands, *may* paint. And so he dies."

"Sario—"

"We die, Raimon. All of us. And no one remembers. No one cares." He let his hands drop back to his sides. "Your way, the way of the Viehos Fratos, is to make a man whose *work* succeeds him. But that is a false life. An artificial life. You don't understand, you or the Viehos Fratos, the boys who hope to be Gifted . . . you don't understand at all. You have permitted your imaginations to become crippled, and you accept it as the Will of the Matra ei Filho . . . eiha,

I do not, I reject it. True life is *living*—and that is my goal. To live. So I may paint. A man's soul dies when his ability is stolen, as yours is now being stolen . . . but my soul will not die. I forbid it."

"Sario . . ." Tears stood in Raimon's eyes as he repeated in despair. "None of us lives forever."

"Perhaps not," Sario agreed, "when one accepts as inevitable that which is of the earth."

"We are *all* of us of the earth!"

"Not I," he answered. "I will temper myself as we temper paints: with binders . . . and my flesh that is pigment, my bone that is canvas, shall not die."

Raimon's face collapsed. The fine architecture of skull nearly pierced the brittle vellum of what once had been young, taut skin. "Blessed Mother . . . Matra Dolcha, Matra ei Filho—"

"Prattle your prayers," Sario said, "but this has nothing to do with Her or Her Son."

Anger kindled, took flame. The eyes yet were young, powerful in pride. "You would say so to me? To *me?*"

Resolution wavered, was renewed in a rush of conviction. "To you as Raimon Grijalva? To you as one of the Viehos Fratos?"

"To me as a man, as one who has befriended you, supported you, spoken for you—"

"Yes," Sario answered. "I say it to you in all of your guises. *I will do this.*"

Raimon's hand shut itself around his Chieva. "Even a Lord Limner is not beyond our means, Sario. If you make it necessary."

Sario laughed. "Because you have my *Peintraddo?*"

A glint of quiet triumph shone briefly. "We have the useless copy, as you made certain. But Saavedra has the true one."

"So." Very softly he asked, "Does she?"

And so it came at last, so it reached Raimon in pure truth and un-adorned simplicity: they none of them knew him. None of them at all. No man. No woman.

Gently Sario explained, "We are the finest artists in the world, Il Sanguo. Copying is as nothing. Not once. Twice. Thrice." He looked upon the one man of them all he had liked and respected, even honored, and realized he had grown beyond such things. Weakness he dared not tolerate. Weakness he would not. "You have betrayed my trust," Sario said, but felt no pain of it. That he was also beyond.

Raimon's body trembled. "As you have betrayed mine. To paint a copy of your *Peintraddo Chieva*—to paint *two* copies!"

"And you see how it serves me, frato meyo. How it keeps me

whole enough to paint, how it keeps me alive." Sario shook his head. "I will never be Tomaz. I will never be you. I will never again be threatened by anything done in the Crechetta."

The litany was begun. "It is our way—"

And ended. "Your way is outdated. I make a new way, now. No one else has the courage, the means, the capacity." Sario smiled. "Or the Luza do'Orro."

━● TWENTY-FOUR ●━

Alejandro stirred out of a drowse into wakefulness. Leather bed-ropes squeaked beneath the mattress. After the first and infinitely satisfying union on the floor, they both of them complained of impediments to a more leisurely and comfortable exploration—brush handles, the battered tankard, the gouging corner of a box—and so he at last allowed her to lead him to the bed. A second union followed, as had the acknowledgment that wine consumed before he came, the warmth of the day, the lassitude in his body, would combine to carry him off to sleep.

Saavedra had retorted tartly that it was good of him to wait *at least* until they were finished.

Now he was awake, smiling over that, but disinclined to rouse or to rouse her; he drifted contentedly, one naked hip pressed against hers while hair not his own enshrouded his neck. In such peace as he had not known since news of his father's death, he permitted himself to consider the ramifications of it more fully.

Death had made him Duke. It also extinguished his youth. Counted a man because of age, of size while his father lived, he was counted a boy *beside* that father by all who knew them both. Now Baltran was gone—and Alejandro invested. A forced and force*ful* entry into adulthood, but it was done. Duke Baltran was dead of the Mother's whim, his wife transformed to widow, his children made fatherless.

Alejandro felt a pang of grief, of desertion, of loneliness. His mother had retired to dowagerhood immediately and lived now at Caza Varra, one of the country estates; and eight-year-old Cossimia also was gone, sent to Diettro Mareia to be fostered until of an age to wed the Heir. That left only him, both son and brother—save now he was Duke instead of Heir—and it changed matters. Significantly. Life now was difficult, and no choice at all was simple. Each was fraught with potentials and possibilities, and dangers within each one.

"Merditto," he muttered wretchedly, turning to align his body more fully against Saavedra's.

She was not, after all, asleep. "What are you thinking about that makes you swear so desperately?"

He sighed into her ringlets. "Marriage."

"So." She paused. "Alejandro . . ." Her tone was oddly choked, half-serious, half-ironic, as if she fought not to laugh. ". . . will you forgive my rudeness, grazzo?—but perhaps you might consider thinking about such things when *not* in my company—" She twisted to face him, to look into his face. "—and *certainly* when not in my bed!"

He caught fire. From head to toe. Sweat stung armpits and groin. "Merditto! Moronno! Cabessa bisila!—" He flopped over onto his belly and pressed his face into the mattress. How could he have been so unthinking, such a witless monster?

She trembled against him, laughing in delight. "And everything else, as well—Blessed Mother, let *me* call you the names . . . is it not my right?"

"—moronno luna," he finished, lifting his still-warm face. "You should send me away at once!"

"Eiha, I could, but then I would lose you all the sooner, no?" She smoothed the firm ridge of muscle that weapons practice had set like a shelf of stone into his back. "I would rather keep you as long as I may . . . you *will* marry, amoro meyo, and then—"

"But not yet. Not yet." He sat up, shoving tousled hair—his—out of his eyes; depositing tangled hair—hers—aside so he would not catch it beneath him. "Forgive me for that, carrida . . . but meanwhile they will have me married, bedded, and presented with an Heir before the year is done; must you hasten it?"

"Poor Alejandro . . . am I supposed to pity you?" She sat up, tossed back disarrayed ringlets, sat against the wall. Her shoulders touched his, adhered. "Pity the woman instead."

He swiveled his head to study her, to consider—marked laughter in her eyes. "Canna!" he declared, without heat. "Heartless, selfish woman—"

"Heartless, selfish, *honest* woman . . . and I know you." She leaned, tipped her head against his. "I know you, Alejandro, and I know also she will be fortunate."

Laughter was banished. It was complex: pleasure and pain at once. "Eiha, carrida—were I not a Duke—"

"Then I would never have taken you to my bed!"

He grinned briefly, but repeated, "—were I not a Duke—"

"—and I not a Grijalva . . ." She sighed, catching his mood. "But you are, and I am, and this is the best we may hope for. And it is not so poor a thing, I think. Better than nothing at all."

Thoughts flowed like river water channeled by stones in a random pattern. "I don't think he loved her . . ."

"*Who?*"

"Gitanna Serrano. I don't think my father loved her. I think he *liked* her—"

"That is a beginning."

"—and I think she offered something my mother couldn't—"

"Mistresses do."

"—and I think he needed her in some way, some way I can't comprehend . . . perhaps to prove himself—"

"*You* are proven, en verro!"

"—to make himself a man in all respects—"

"And your presence evidence of that, no?"

"—because he was Duke of Tira Virte, and a Duke must be all things." Alejandro looked at her. "I would not wish to be like that."

"Duke?"

"All things."

"Dukes *are,* Alejandro."

"I can't be, 'Vedra. I am not my father."

"And that pleases me, amoro meyo. I have no wish to sleep with your father." She checked, touched his arm. "Regretto—I should not jest about the dead."

"But he is." He shrugged, aware of grief as yet unresolved, but not overwhelmed by it; her presence eased him. And knowing the death was accident, as Sario Grijalva had proven by examining the body and questioning the Tza'ab escort party, eased him even more. Dead was dead and worthy of mourning, but war was not a prospect he wished even to contemplate. Like a startled horse he shied from that, and yet admitted to her the other, because he could. "He is dead. Thus I am put in his place . . . and I am afraid."

After a moment she turned toward him, set the flat of her palm to his heart, pressed her cheek against it. "You are not alone in this."

"No. Grazzo do'Matra—and you." He leaned, kissed her soundly, sat back, considering other options. Once again he slipped through the rocks, carried to yet another eddy of consideration. "And there is another who will aid me . . ." Recollection urged him upright; cool wall was against shoulder blades. "Eiha, 'Vedra, you should have seen him! Should have heard how he spoke to them! Matra, I wish I had his courage—wish I had his poise! All those stiff, proud men, strutting like cocks in the henyard . . ." He laughed; he recalled it so well. " 'Grijalva,' they accused, as if it were epithet, and 'Grijalva' he said back, as if it were honor! Perhaps it will not be so bad after all, with his help." He turned to her. " 'Vedra—you know him better than I . . . has he always been like this?"

Troubled, she grimaced briefly. "Arrogant? Yes. Certain of himself? Yes. Certain of his value to any man who requires help? *Infinitely* yes."

He assumed an expression of mock astonishment. "And you call yourself his friend?" Alejandro clapped a hand to his breast. "Eiha, that would wound me!"

Dryly she said, "Nothing wounds Sario."

He let the levity go. "Then perhaps that is best."

Something in his tone caught her. "Alejandro, does it worry you so much?"

"That I am Duke? Yes. Infinitely." He sighed, plucking at bedclothes. "I am not ready. Not prepared."

"You have men to counsel you, men who served your father."

"Fools," he said curtly. "All of them, save . . ." He smiled a little. "Save the man you recommended. The infinitely arrogant one so certain of his value."

"Alejandro . . ." Her tone was strange, as if she meant to say something; abruptly she dismissed it. "He *is* arrogant. He *is* certain of himself. And he is talented far beyond any man alive."

"Then I am safe, no? I have you to counsel me in the night, and him to counsel me in the day. I am well-served indeed!"

She cast him a sidelong, troubled glance. Then abruptly caught his hand in hers. "Alejandro, promise me something . . . promise me you will be your own man." He stared at her, astonished by the vehemence in her tone. "You may be frightened—so would I be!—but you have a good heart, Alejandro, a great and generous heart, and you are not a fool. Be certain of yourself, not in what others believe. Unless you agree with it."

"Of course . . ." He smiled warmly, adjusting his hand so he clasped hers now. "Have faith in me, carrida . . . I require *counsel,* yes, but I shall make the decisions."

She studied him, weighed his words, then sighed relief. A brilliant smile lighted her face. "Then all shall be well. But this once, if only this once, I shall make one for you: it is time you went back."

"Back? 'Vedra!—where are you going?" He pulled up the sheet rucked awry as she left the bed. "I thought you might show me more of your portfolio. You promised, en verro."

"En verro," she agreed, bending to retrieve his hosen; her shift. "But another time, I think."

"Saavedra." He had her now with that tone, forbade more evasions. "What is it?"

After a moment she shook her head. "Do'nado."

He reached out and caught a hand as she turned. "This comes because of him, no? Is there something you are holding back?" Apprehension spasmed, coupled with shock. "Is it that you and he—"

"*No!* Never." She shook her head. "Never."

Alejandro frowned. "*You* suggested him, but even without your suggestion he was the only possible candidate. I saw that at once. Everyone agreed except the Serranos, and that was expected." He grinned, recalling their displeasure; banished it and shrugged. "Had you and I never met at all, he would have been named. There was no other choice."

"Eiha, no." She managed a smile, though the bloom of it wilted too quickly. "That he would never permit. Not with such fire, not with such *need.*"

It was a tangle he did not wish to pursue. Not now. Too many other duties required him. "There," he said, summoning his father again. "Bassda. Sario is Lord Limner, and you are my mistress. So it is, and so it shall be. Bliss."

"Bliss," she echoed sourly, and tossed his hosen at him.

Kita'ab. Folio. By either name, by any name: *power.*

One candle lighted the chamber, the Crechetta—they could not prohibit or prevent his presence in it, even if they wished to; he was of them as well as of Al-Fansihirro—banishing all shadows save those most ingenious; and he read by its light, a meager light unequal to such glorious inked and painted illumination made into borders, into lingua oscurra; and for the illumination of the truth, the way, the answer to questions he had never known to ask, because a man asks nothing when his imagination is crippled.

It angered him, that those who reared him lied. Fairness argued they did not even yet understand it *was* a lie, any of it, still lost within Grijalva ritual born of Tza'ab rites, but he was not inclined to fairness *or* argument and recognized it purely as falsehood now. Acknowledged it. Despised it.

So much yet to learn. Nearly two decades as a student of the family, two years with the old man, the estranjiero who offered him as much as an Al-Fansihirro could: the key to power, true and *rooted* power, power so integral to Tza'ab Rih that even now, more than one hundred years after Verro Grijalva captured the *Kita'ab,* its potential for rediscovery, rebirth, made one old man live in the heart of the enemy and wait for the fleshly vessel that could be recognized, reclaimed, reshaped.

His jaws clamped. *Will no one let me be? Can no one see that what I am is what I have always wanted to be?*

Not Duke. Not of the Viehos Fratos. Not even Premio Frato. Merely—painter. And Lord Limner, so he could defeat death by forcing the world to acknowledge his work, his Gift.

Yet now there was another way. His work would live on, as intended, but so would Sario Grijalva.

Tension ran from clenched jaw through neck and shoulders. *Meek as sheep, these moronnos . . . they pray to the Mother and thank Her for Her generosity and blessing, when what she truly offers is Her divine backside! Body dead by fifty; talent killed by forty? No. No!*

His Gift would not allow it, or his talent, his ambition. Too much yet burned in him, too much yet needed to be freed . . . two more decades was nothing, nothing at all, when weighed against the scope of his Gift, the lightscape of his vision. He needed *time.*

Needed youth.

He read by the light of candleglow, by the illumination of the pages of their *Kita'ab* and his; by the illumination of oscurra and imagination at last kindled into true Luza do'Orro, the golden light of comprehension.

"Let them die," he said. "Let them permit themselves to fail at forty, to die at fifty. And I will *watch them.*"

He would. He could. While the *Kita'ab* lacked pages, it did not lack all answers to all questions he had learned at last to ask.

Sario stared into candleglow, letting the fixity of his gaze merge and bleed out light and shadow until nothing was distinguishable beyond the faint gleam of gilt upon ancient paper. One elegant, eloquent finger gently traced out the pattern inked onto the page two hundred years before. "It is enough," he said. "It must be, and it shall be."

He had said it so many times, prayed it so many times, declared it so many times to himself, to Saavedra; even, once, to Raimon.

A smile grew, broke into a grin, into laughter. For the first time in his life he believed long-dead Verro Grijalva was, after all, a hero. Believed, and blessed him, for providing the answers to questions he had not known how to ask.

He blew out the candle. One faint, final glint of gilt, of gold, of power.

It must be. And it shall be.

He walked alone through the city's streets, unmindful of shadow, of darkness, of danger that lived in such, breeding desperate men out of despair. Let them come; Raimon did not care. And because of that, none came. Footsteps scraped, scratched, approached furtively, retired. He was left alone to walk the streets, to welcome darkness and death, and yet the latter did not come.

At last he passed out of squalor into security, save for those would-be bravos who challenged even security for a greater prize, and then into a pool of lamplight that spread like spilled ale around his feet, dappling cobbles and limning the way to the Sanctia.

He lingered, trapped like an insect in amber, wondering if anyone would melt him into a resin suitable for use in binding powder into paint, into creation . . . and then smiled to think of himself like that, ground powder made into a man by the talent and ambition of the painter.

Sario. Sario was like that.

It swooped back then, stooping like a raptor upon powerless prey, as Sario stooped on Il Sanguo's protestations.

Il Sanguo. What were they but two words set together? Rank, yes, in his society, within the family, but wholly manufactured by such men as he counted himself among, an artifical system designed to keep order, to control compordotta. Art was so demanding, so consuming a master that without a system of discipline imposed upon its practitioners nothing would be accomplished beyond abject chaos. Art for art's sake, no more; no goal, no ambition, no focus for the light, the Luza. It would serve no one, left to its own devices; would merely exist, unstructured, unrealized, and therefore unappreciated—and the men who created it would die unsung, their vast talents unknown, unseen, unappreciated.

To die young, with glorious works stacked away in a locked, forgotten atelierro, was a true punishment, a true discipline of the damned. And if Sario fought that, if Sario meant to transcend what they all of them faced, Raimon was uncertain he could truly blame him.

And for that *he* would be punished.

Lamplight glimmered. He turned to it, seeking admission, confession, comprehension, absolution. And went in, where he would be welcomed as a man in need—or turned away because of his name, with need refuted.

As he passed through the door he closed a hand around his Chieva, thinking to slip it within the collar of his doublet where it would not be seen, for surely without its presence no man—noviciato, initiato, sancto, Premio Sancto—would know what he was.

Grijalva. Tza'ab. Both.

Chi'patro.

But he released the key and left it there after all, shining in the light; no man should hide what he is. And was gratified nearly to tears when the sancto, coming forward from dimness to greet him, marked the Chieva do'Orro, knew it, smiled. Then extended a welcoming hand.

TWENTY-FIVE

Just in from sword practice, from wrestling, from smacking with and being smacked by age-polished staves, Alejandro reeked of his own industry. The doublet was shed in the tourney yard, left to a servant to fetch; now he wore no more than a loose cambric shirt soiled by sweat and the grime of the hard-packed dirt yard, sleeves rolled back to scraped and battered elbows; laces unlaced, or torn free to dangle haphazardly; billowy folds adhered to chest and spine. Hosen were shredded at both bruised knees from an unintended and painful obeisance, though he had got his own back; and his hair, slicked away from his face by a quick sluicing of water from the rain barrel, straggled damply.

He might have gone at once for a bath, to soak away aches and dirt, but he had been waylaid from his path by Martain bearing a letter, and the schooled blankness of expression on his secretary's face alerted him. That expression, coupled with the quick-scanned contents of the letter, served to chase all thought of a bath from his mind. Because of it, he now sat in a chair in the atelierro of his Lord Limner, reeking of his efforts, with rump settled on the edge of leather and elbows planted against taut thighs with booted feet equally planted, while splayed, rigid fingers channeled riverbeds into damp hair.

The clever, infinitely arrogant young man who seemed older than he but was not, was less effusive in his concern. In fact, Alejandro was not certain his Lord Limner was concerned *at all.*

He looked up, glowered, scoured hair out of his face with unkind fingers. "Surely you must see," he said sharply. "Don't you?"

Sario Grijalva, poised at an easel, arched a brow. "That depends," he answered. "En verro, I see that you are upset . . . and I don't question that you should be; it is not my place to do so—but must news of this sort thrust you into despair?"

Alejandro scowled more blackly yet. "I would not expect that of you."

A lock of dark hair straggled loose of leather tie, curving forward like a wing to echo the line of the Limner's jaw. "Because I am your servant?"

Curtly Alejandro snapped, "Because you care for Saavedra." He paused. "Or so I have been led to believe."

"And so I do. And if I believed this a threat to her, I assure you I would share your concern." Grijalva paid fixed attention to his work a moment, nodded approval, then continued. "But where there is no threat, no man need waste concern."

Alejandro snapped stiffly upright in the chair. "Filho do'canna! You see this as of no moment?"

Grijalva considered that, then set down his paletto, his brush, and perched himself upon a stool to give over full attention to his exasperated Duke. He in his own way was as unpresentable, smeared with paint if not sweat, clad in clothing donned for comfort, activity, and the expectation of getting dirty. "A man might rejoice to know that a king considers him worthy enough for a princess."

"And so my father's final task is completed. The suit is accepted." Alejandro collapsed into the chair again, flopping against leather. Broad hands depending from arms ridged with sinew dangled in eloquent assertion of futility and despair. "What am I to do?"

"Marry her, Your Grace."

Alejandro scowled. "What about Saavedra?"

"Does it matter?"

"To me! As it should to you!"

"Why? Did you expect me to fall to the floor in despondency and helplessness?" Grijalva bared good teeth briefly—*better than mine!* Alejandro marked in annoyance—and continued before his Duke could frame a retort. "You could refuse, Your Grace."

It was preposterous. "And hurl insult at Pracanza? Undo what my father began? Perhaps begin a war my conselhos would prefer, while I at the same time must *rely* on their biased counsel? Merditto, Grijalva, you understand nothing!"

Grijalva shrugged elegantly. "Then marry her, Your Grace."

Alejandro, who had grown to inhabit a body too powerful for elegance, itched. He scratched at hair drying into unkempt spikes. "I am not opposed to marriage, en verro . . . nor even specifically to the Pracanzan princess, whom I do not know, have never met, have not even *seen*—"

"They are sending a portrait, Your Grace. Perhaps when it arrives, you will feel less concerned."

"Why?" Alejandro, growing belligerent, was not disposed to courtesy. "If she is beautiful, am I then expected to be pleased above that which is expected of me in what is otherwise done strictly for politics?"

"As a painter, Your Grace, I am somewhat acquainted with the response engendered by a portrait. A lovely woman or a handsome man solves many worries, Your Grace."

"Nommo do'Matra, Grijalva—I have to *live* with the woman, not merely gaze upon her painted face!"

"Why not?"

Alejandro froze. "What do you mean?"

"I mean merely that often a man and his wife do not cohabit beyond the necessity of getting children."

Alejandro knew about that. He recalled all too clearly a memory of his mother, dressing for his infant sister's naming ceremony, speaking most bitterly about Gitanna Serrano.

Discomfited by the image, he shifted in the chair. "Is that fair? That all wives should be used only to bear children, then forgotten in favor of a mistress?"

"Fair, Your Grace?" The Lord Limner frowned consideringly. "To whom?"

"To the woman! Merditto, Grijalva . . . if the man goes elsewhere, sleeps in another woman's bed, what is it to the wife but insult?"

The answering tone was mild, without color of any kind save quiet, idle inquiry. "Then Your Grace will pension Saavedra off? Bestow upon her a distant country estate even as the late Duke bestowed such upon Gitanna Serrano?"

Furious, insulted, frustrated beyond thought, Alejandro lurched out of the chair so dramatically it screeched across stone flags to hook a leg on a rug. "By the Mother, Grijalva—" And stopped. *What am I to do? Insult my new bride by keeping a mistress, or insult Saavedra—and make myself miserable!—by sending her away?*

"So." Grijalva hunched now on the stool, hooked heels over a rung and rested his chin upon clasped hands. "How may I help you, Your Grace?"

"There *is* no help for this."

"There is. The proper man may provide a remedy . . . and you selected me to *be* the proper man, no?"

"But . . ." Alejandro frowned. "What can you do?"

Grijalva laughed softly. "Paint."

"But how is *that* to make a difference? You document everything, that I know, but what can you do for this? Paint me out of love with Saavedra, and *in* love with the Pracanzan girl?"

The painter considered it. "If you wish."

"Merditto! Don't mock me! This serves nothing, Grijalva."

"Then I will offer another answer."

"*What* answer? What answer is there? Unless you may find a way of painting this woman into acquiescence that I have a mistress—eiha, I know my father had several, but I also know how it hurt my mother!—or if you may find a way of painting Saavedra to always be mine, there is nothing you may do. And none of these things *can* you do!"

Grijalva shook his head. "We do more than you believe, Your Grace. We are painters, but also diviners." His quick smile was odd, yet was banished too quickly for examination. "We paint the truth. We paint falsehood. We paint a man into presentability, a woman into beauty, so that a match may be made. We paint a couple who have been at war for decades, yet by recapturing the love, honor, and respect in painted images we remind them of what once was, and they *remember*. We flatter, Your Grace; we take instruction as to how we should begin, proceed, complete; we make and unmake, recreate and reclaim every part of the world." He lifted one shoulder in a slight shrug. "The portrait sent with your father was painted with the eyes of love, with the heart and soul of a woman who had bound herself to you. No one else would have made such a likeness, would have presented you as *she* sees you . . . in such a way that the Pracanzan princess also saw you. And answered."

Alejandro drew breath, gusted it out. "Then paint me Saavedra with those same eyes, with that heart and soul, so that I may never lose her."

For one moment, Sario Grijalva's poise deserted. And then was reestablished. "To do that, Your Grace—"

"—the painter should love Saavedra." Alejandro did not smile. "Then such a task should be within your abilities, yes?"

Grijalva's face was white as new linen. In the eyes dwelled cold anger, a bitter anger, and loss beyond comprehension.

Trembling from a complex tangle of emotions he could not begin to identify, among them jealousy, frustration, desperation, Alejandro do'Verrada put one foot in front of the other and reached his Lord Limner, stood beside his Lord Limner, looked into the unmasked face, the eyes of passion, of obsession. "She says you believe yourself of infinite value to a man in need. Then let it be agreed, en verro, that I am a man in need. You shall thus apply yourself to this task and *prove* that worth."

After a moment, Grijalva took up his brush again. Steady of hand, he began to paint. "I can do that, Your Grace."

At the doorway Alejandro paused, turned back. "I will never give her up. And you will never again suggest that I should."

Eventually he answered, "Your Grace, be assured that when I am finished no man living may ever suggest such a thing."

⊶ ⚷ ⊷

The boy crouched like servant, like supplicant. His attention was wholly focused on his task, so deeply lost that he did not hear her come to him, or stop; was not at all aware of her presence even as she waited. He merely knelt upon the courtyard tile beside the fountain and sketched, chalk dissolving into powder against poor-grade paper spread atop weather-pitted tile.

A stray breeze lifted mist from the fountain, carried it to dust her face with moisture. To Saavedra it felt good; to the boy it brought with it frustration. "Filho do'canna!" he hissed, and hitched himself and his paper around so that his back warded his work against importunate wind and water.

He saw her then, and his face blazed. "How long have you been standing there?"

"Momentita," she answered. She looked beyond his embarrassed, self-conscious face to the work itself. "Sario."

Ignaddio nodded, sat up, did not look at her face, as if afraid to see her expression communicate disapproval or disappointment.

Saavedra studied it, marking technique, the first suggestion of style as yet unrecognized. "He has an expressive face, no?"

Ignaddio hitched a shoulder.

"Have you spent much time observing him?"

"Before he went to the Duke." Now he was anxious, no longer avoiding her eyes. "You *knew* it was he!"

"There is no question of it." She smiled to see his relief. "You have a good eye for line, though your perspective requires work."

"How?" He stood up hastily, dragging the paper from the tile. "How may I improve it?"

No protest. No defense. Simply an inquiry into how he might improve. *Eiha, he will be a good learner.* "Do you see this line here? The angle here between nose and eye?" He nodded. "You have drawn them too perfectly—no face is truly balanced. One eye is set higher, one lower . . . one is set closer to the bridge of the nose, so; the other is not so close." She touched a fingernail lightly to the indicated lines. "Do you see? There. And there."

"I see! Eiha, 'Vedra, I *see*—" He caught his breath. "Will you show me?"

"Ah, but it is for you to do. I have told you what I see, now you must see it for yourself, and correct it." She smiled, recalling how swiftly Sario demonstrated corrections and improvements by *doing,* not by asking. *I will not do the same with 'Naddi. He deserves to make his own mistakes, and correct them in his own hand.* "You must always be hungry, 'Naddi . . . to improve technique, your talent, you must always be hungry."

"I *am* hungry!" he said. "There is so much left to learn, and no matter what I do, it seems the moualimos are always adding more." He sighed, heaving narrow shoulders. "Rinaldo says I may never catch up."

She knew what that meant. "Rinaldo undergoes Confirmattio soon?"

"In a week." Ignaddio stared down at his powder-smeared hands, clasping paper and chalk. "They will send him to the women in six days."

Saavedra restrained the impulse to set a comforting hand to his cap of dark curls; a boy on the cusp of manhood did not wish to be treated by any woman as if he were still young. "Your turn will come. I promise. Perhaps in *two* weeks, and then you will not be behind Rinaldo by much time at all."

It did not placate. "But I am *older!*"

"Are you?" She affected surprise. "I thought it otherwise."

He shook his head vehemently. "*I* am older. By two whole days."

Saavedra shaped her sudden grin into a smile; he would take offense at anything more than mild humor. "But surely there are things you do that are superior to his. Color, perhaps? Perspective?"

"No, you have just said my perspective needs improvement." It was stated as fact, nothing more, which spoke well of his attitude. "And he mixes colors better, also. But the moualimos have said I have a good eye for shadow." He grinned proudly. "I used Sario's painting of the exterior of the Cathedral Imagos Brilliantos for a model; the moualimos say he captured the shadows of the arches and the belltowers far better than anyone."

"Eiha, in art he is not so poor an example to mimic," she agreed, "but recall that his compordotta was far less advanced—and far *more* troublesome!—than yours."

Ignaddio was not impressed by that. "If I could be as he is, I would suffer any punishment they wished to give me for poor compordotta."

" 'Naddi!"

His eyes implored her. "I want to be *good,* 'Vedra. I want to be as he is, to be Lord Limner and serve the Duke. Isn't it what we train for? Isn't it what *you* would train for if you were a man, and Gifted?"

It took her like a blow. She defined herself by her art first, her gender lastly, but even by art she was defined a woman because she could never be more than she was: female, and not Gifted. Talented perhaps, but meant for no more than a man who was proved fertile, and thus incapable of the true-talent that those of the Viehos Fratos must exhibit, or a potential Lord Limner.

Sario swears I am Gifted. She shut her eyes. *Matra ei Filho, if I were—*

"What would you be?" Ignaddio asked. "Gifted, or no?—if you were a man? If you could have a choice?"

She prevaricated. "It's a choice I will never have to make."

He persisted. "But if you *had* to."

To be male, and Gifted, meant she would become one of the Viehos Fratos, would tend to the family, to compordotta, to such things as agreeing to, ordering, or undertaking the Chieva do'Sangua. To destroying genius.

She had already helped kill a man. She did not believe she could ever make that choice, take that life, again.

And yet a choice between being good, or being better, was no choice at all.

"Bassda," she muttered, "you ask too many difficult questions!"

Ignaddio sighed. "That's what the moualimos say, too."

"Then it must be true. En verro." She indicated his sketch. "Complete that, 'Naddi. It is well begun. Think on what I have said, consider how you would begin differently, and bring it back to me. I would like to see it when you are finished."

All the world was in his eyes. "I will! Don't forget!"

"No." She smiled as he darted away for fresh paper. "No, I won't forget; there is too much of me in you. But *you* will have more opportunity."

And then she knew her choice made after all. Opportunity. One might or might not fail, but when the opportunity to *try* was taken away, one would never know at all if there was merely technique in one's work, or talent.

Genius was another thing, but that was beyond her comprehension. Sario had and was genius. *She* was a woman, was good, was perhaps gifted—but not Gifted.

Trust 'Naddi to show her the truth.

"Matra Dolcha," Saavedra muttered. "You may become Neosso Irrado without even trying!"

TWENTY-SIX

The lath-and-plaster door. Fourteen steps, twice. The tiny closet from which a man could see, if he crouched down and peered through a slit between wall and floor, into the Crechetta.

Raimon did not crouch. He did not peer. He merely mounted the final step, ducked his head against the low ceiling, then escaped it by sitting down.

Better. With feet upon a lower stair, and head not so threatened, he could breathe.

Worse. He could also think.

And so he thought. He sat perched upon the floor in the closet above the Crechetta, and remembered back down the years to the time he had been punished and sent to dwell in darkness while the burn on his wrist seared his soul as deeply as his flesh.

In the Sanctia there had been peace. Though he could not tell the elderly sancto everything—his oaths as Gifted, as one of the Viehos Fratos, forbade it—he told him enough to be as truthful as one could be. To his credit, the man had neither expressed shock, disgust, nor ordered him out of the Sanctia. The sancto merely listened, allowing Raimon to purge—and then quietly explained there was nothing he might offer a man who could not be wholly truthful.

Davo had said he was. Davo had, in the family shrine, suggested he be nothing but what he ever was: truthful. But there were truths, and *truths;* he would not honor his oaths if he told the sancto everything, even in the sight of the Mother and Her Son, nor would he honor the Mother and Son in whose names he had sworn his Grijalva oaths.

Therefore he was twice-damned, twice condemned, and worthy of punishment. Perhaps, to be symmetrical, of *two* punishments.

Only one mattered.

Raimon turned back the sleeve of his summer-silk doublet, untied and unlaced the cuff of his shirt and peeled it away. The wrist now was bared; in the nearly nonexistent light creeping up from the open door below no scar could be seen. But he saw it. Felt it.

Holy Mother, how it burns.

He had throughout his life been honest by his lights, and *for* his light, his *Luza do'Orro*. Punished for it, also, for his determined attempt to be more, to be *other*, than was allowed. But the punishment, the Discipline, had not been limited to the slight blemishment of his *Peintraddo* that also burned his flesh, but to time, and time to think; to consider who and what he was, who and what he might be, and how he might become it.

In punishment, in the closet above the Crechetta he had sought and discovered a new truth, a painful truth, the kind of truth that did more to quench his fire, to extinguish his light than any physical punishment.

Gifted. Good. But not great. Not good ENOUGH.

It had nearly destroyed him, that truth. Even as it did now.

He knew who and what he was. And it was not enough. All he would *ever* be, all he had become, but it was not enough.

Sario had known. Sario had become. Sario *was*.

Everything Raimon was not, nor could ever be.

Truth: In the name of his own failure he had shaped boy into adult, gifted into Gifted, limner into Limner—and man into monster.

Sario Grijalva was everything they had prayed for, had worked for, had made. But also more. And other.

Truths: *Folio* was *Kita'ab*. *Kita'ab* was destruction.

Laughter was quiet, and ugly. Until the tears came.

Sario was most particular about the way the room was arranged. He instructed Ignaddio, who had come to watch, where to shift furniture, pile books, distribute the small items such as a pot of flowers; a drift of silk cloth across a velurro-and-leather chair; a basket of fruit; a tapestry shawl; the copper-clad iron lantern, albeit unlighted during the day; a half-melted ruby-hued candle stub in a clay cup; a flagon of wine and two crystal glasses, both freshly poured. And he also had the boy shut and latch the shutters.

"Why?" Saavedra asked, watching the meticulous industry as she sat crosswise in a chair, silky velurro skirts sliding like water from her knees as hair over shoulders and breasts. "Don't you prefer the light?"

He busied himself with setting up his easel, selecting the charcoal he would use to sketch in the first details, envisioning parts of the painting that would make the whole. "Light may be painted in later."

"No—I mean, don't you want the light by which to *see?*"

He barely glanced at her. "For now, no. Perhaps later. I'm seeking shadow for this." Ignaddio made a sound of delight, and Sario looked at him curiously. "This meets with your approval?"

"Eiha, *yes!*" the boy cried, red-faced in pleasure mixed with self-consciousness. "They say you are the best at handling shadow, and that is *my* best, as well."

"*Have* you a best?" He did not look at the boy now, still concerned with preparations.

"Sario!" Saavedra chided sharply, shooting him a glare of displeasure.

It brought him up short, spilled him into abrupt and discomfiting realization. *So . . . she protects yet another eager boy.* But he went on without indicating his brief consternation. "Eiha, 'Vedra, we all believe we have a 'best,' but often it is no more than mediocrity."

"How would you know?" she challenged instantly. "You have never viewed any of his work."

"Should I?" It pleased him to see such color in her face; he would recall it, paint it that way. "What do I know of such things? I am not a moualimo."

"But you *could* be!" That from the boy. "And—and I would be most honored—"

"Of course you would." Sario cut him off; Saavedra's expression suggested he would pay for that. "But I am Limner, not moualimo—and Lord Limner at that—"

"He knows that," Saavedra snapped. "Why else do you think he wishes to learn from *you?*"

The emphasis made it sound entirely horrific. Now beyond the first unpleasant shock, he found it all rather perversely amusing and fascinating that she neglected her protection of him in favor of someone else, another boy who wanted very much to be better than good. Sario wasn't wholly certain how it made him feel, that acknowledgment.

"There are things I can teach, and things I *may* teach, but none of them just now." Sario looked again at the boy, marked the anxious hope in eyes and expression. "Ignaddio . . . 'Naddi?—" A nod confirmed the diminutive. "—there is much you must learn before I could teach you. It was a thing I didn't understand very well at your age, either, but it was true; an artist must learn the rules before he transgresses them."

"*You* never did," Saavedra remarked pointedly.

He decided then it *did* hurt, that she should desert him in favor of another. Quietly Sario found the proper charcoal, fit it to his hand, nodded. " 'Naddi, you had best go for now. Surely you have classes."

"None just now." The boy smiled winningly. "*This* can be my class—and I will stay out of the way! I promise!"

"Do you like it when others watch you work?"

Ebullience faltered. "No."

"There will be time later. This is merely the preliminary sketch, you see . . . later there will be paint, and time for questions."

Ignaddio looked from one to the other. "You only want me to go because you mean to argue."

It astonished them both; Saavedra bit into her lip as Sario frowned fiercely to suppress imminent laughter. "Indeed," he answered gravely, and Ignaddio was so taken aback by being told the truth he merely blinked and acquiesced without further comment. Sario grinned at Saavedra as the boy left. "You see? Your sulks and black scowls are obvious even to that boy."

"He has seen none of them before," she countered, "unless *you* are the object of discussion."

"Am I often?"

"More often than *I* prefer!" She sought, found a stray hair, smoothed it away from her face. "Must you be so cruel to him? He wants very badly to be like you."

"Or *be* me." Sario smiled. "It's now attainable, 'Vedra, the appointment as Lord Limner . . . what once was only dreamed is now truth, and all the boys will think they have the talent to take my place."

"Quite natural, no?"

"Of course, as it should be. But they are fated to be disappointed. I make no plans to be replaced."

"You will be one day. You *must* be." She gestured. "In ten years, fifteen, your knuckles will begin to swell, to lose flexibility . . ."

"Will they?"

"Unless you have found a cure for the bone-fever, I think so!" She scowled. "Have you?"

He grinned. "Eiha, no."

She contemplated his expression. "For a man who comprehends very well that his hard-won position must be given to another in twenty years, you seem uncommonly content."

"Twenty years is a long time, 'Vedra."

"You have never believed so before! You always decried the fact that all the Limners failed by forty, died by fifty—"

"And so I still do," he agreed, "but that does not prevent me from enjoying my position for now." He waggled a hand at her. "We discussed how you should stand . . . so *stand,* grazzo."

Saavedra did not move. "You were unconscionably rude to 'Naddi."

"No more rude than any moualimo was to me. 'Vedra—will you stand as we discussed?"

"Must you treat him as you were treated? If you resented it so much, then surely—"

"Perhaps resentment is a part of the training. It did make me hungrier."

"And *an*grier."

"Which most likely is a part of the recipe also." He looked at her patiently, waiting. When she did not alter her stance, he made an inquiry. "Do you mean for us to begin today *at all?*"

Saavedra, still scowling, muttered in frustration. "Can't you just begin a sketch without me? There is the background that doesn't require me at all, and—"

"I want it this way," he said firmly. "I want to capture every bit of you, from beginning to end."

"Why?"

He sighed elaborately. "Perhaps I should ask you why you required *Alejandro* to be present for every single moment as you painted him."

She clamped her mouth shut. Color rose in her face.

Sario smiled sweetly. "Grazzo. Now, will you take up your position?"

"I thought you wanted to argue."

"I thought we *had.*"

"Eiha, no—this was nothing. A skirmish." She did not seem quite so irritated now, as if the boy's departure and their habitual bantering eased the situation onto less turbulent ground. "Ignaddio wants nothing more than for someone to approve of his work."

"Do you?"

"He is promising."

"Many are promising, 'Vedra."

"From many come the few," she countered. "You were one of many also."

"But no one else," he said, "stands where I do today."

"Oh, no?" She arched expressive brows. "I do—save at this very moment I sit. But that can be changed. I need only to rise, no?"

He offered her the grin she had sparred for, baited for. "You, too, were promising."

"No more? Eiha, I am desoladia!" One hand pressed her heart, mocking him. "I rather believed there were yet techniques I might still master. But now you say I *was* promising—"

"I dare say you remain so," he said, "but you will not permit me to judge if there is worth enough to teach you . . . if there is Gift in you, although I know there is. But you are afraid."

"Worth!" She thrust herself from the chair, standing now on the other side of the table. "You think I have none because I will not succumb to your barbs and blandishments? Because you have convinced yourself I am somehow Gifted, despite the fact no Grijalva woman has *ever* been Gifted, and blame my reluctance on fear?" She shook her head. "Nommo do'Matra—you were always arrogant, but this transcends it! You are not the Son, Sario, to sit upon the Throne beside the Mother!"

"En verro," he agreed, "but there is indeed a throne, and I stand beside a Duke."

That blow struck home. He saw her recoil, albeit slight; marked the stiff tension in her shoulders, the taut line of her arms as she planted hands upon the table to brace herself.

"There!" he cried, before she could shout at him. "This is how I should paint you: Saavedra Grijalva, poised on the brink of foul language! Foul, scathing, *powerful* language, enough to send me to my deathbed, no doubt!" He laughed at her. "Eiha, 'Vedra, have I stirred you to true anger? Do you fear I will lose myself in such luxury and the trappings of power that no more shall I be your little Neosso Irrado?"

"You *have,*" she said in a deadly tone. "You have already lost yourself, Sario."

"And what of you?" he countered. "Have you lost me? Or did I lose you first?"

She blinked. "I don't—"

"—understand? But you do. You understood and accepted it the day you permitted yourself to bed Alejandro do'Verrada."

Her face was very white. "And you? Did you not turn from me first, on the day you permitted yourself to study with that Tza'ab estranjiero?"

"I learned much from him."

"Too much."

"Enough to please our new Duke. Am I not Lord Limner?"

"That took me—" And she stopped. As if someone from behind had thrust a spear through her spine.

It required no time at all; he had never been slow of wit, nor lacking in knowledge of conspiracies and the will to discern them.

The initial retort died so quickly he might never have thought it. In his fist, abruptly, charcoal snapped.

One of her hands pasted itself to her throat, as if to wrench free the cords that gave her voice. The other very tightly gripped the edge of the table, so tightly he saw the blood-blush and white striations in her unpainted fingernails, the rigidity of locked knuckles.

He was both surprised and gratified that she made no attempt to renounce what she had begun to say, that which was, left unsaid, implication enough to answer unasked questions. Explanation was not required.

Empty. Curiously *empty*. Or perhaps the shock would come later. "So," he said quietly, "shall you assume the pose we agreed upon?"

She was white to the lips. "You *still*—"

"—wish to paint you? Eiha, of course. It is for Alejandro, and I serve my Duke in all things."

The hand at her throat shifted, passed from neck to breasts, to abdomen. And rested there. Intimately. "If—if you think it wise . . ."

"Wisdom has nothing to do with a man's desire to have his amora painted, Saavedra. That is vanity. And possession." Sario sought, took up another charcoal, "Adezo, Saavedra, please assume the pose."

⇒•TWENTY-SEVEN•⇐

Martain diffidently uncrated and unwrapped the swathed rectangular parcel, then carefully set it upright on an armless chair. It was not a proper easel, but would do; certainly well enough that Alejandro and everyone else in the chamber might look upon the painted woman and see her worth, though her value was incalculable when one counted not only the dowry but political gain also.

"So." It was Edoard do'Najerra, the argumentative Marchalo Grando. "Pracanza sires beauty."

Alejandro looked at him sharply. *Too eagerly said* . . . and others in the chamber, moving to approach, to examine, murmured impressed agreement as swiftly.

"His last task!" do'Najerra said, raising his voice so that all might hear. "Baltran's final concern was for his son's welfare, and the future of the duchy!"

Agreement, approval, tribute. Alejandro wanted very badly to scowl, but kept his expression bland as watered wine.

"Belissimia," do'Najerra pronounced with vigor, indicating the portrait.

Agreement. Approval. Tribute.

Blessed Mother, lend me patience . . . "It is agreed," Alejandro said lugubriously, "that the woman is beautiful."

"And a princess," do'Najerra added; to that wholly unnecessary observation his Duke did at last cast a mildly irritated glance, and the Marchalo Grando had the unexpected grace to color, to cough, to become fascinated by a nonexistent scuff on a perfectly-tended boot.

"And a woman," Martain murmured for ducal ears only; after years of service with Baltran do'Verrada, and half as many spent prying the Heir's comfit sticky fingers off various letters, he had the right of familiarity.

Alejandro grinned briefly, then trimmed it back to a slight, meaningless smile offered to the others. "We shall consider," he said, "and contemplate, and in all ways weigh the worth of the alliance between Tira Virte and Pracanza."

"But, Your Grace!" Do'Najerra forgot all about his boot. "Your

Grace—your father had already done so . . . I recall quite clearly discussing the advantages of such a union!"

"*You* may have discussed them. I never did. I was not consulted."

"Your Grace, this was what your father desired! This is what he set out to Pracanza *for*—"

"And what he *died* for, en verro!" Rivvas Seranno. Of course.

Agreement, unmodified by approval or tribute. Alejandro clamped his teeth tightly shut. One upraised hand quelled the murmuring; it was Estevan do'Saenza who was slow to still, standing next to Rivvas Serrano. *I would do well to separate them,* Alejandro thought, *much like a moualimo separates unruly estudos.*

He gifted them all with a steady smile of unflagging self-confidence. Watching Sario Grijalva handle the twenty men with such ease had offered inspiration. "The world is different now than it was but weeks ago, when my father lived—"

"En verro!" Serrano declared vehemently. "Matra Dolcha, the day those bells were tolled . . . Nommo Matra ei Filho, I thought my heart would break!"

Alejandro raised his voice. "As I said, the world is different now, and we must not forget that one small change may alter the significance of events—"

"*Small* change!" Estevan do'Saenza, collar cutting into fleshy throat, took on a most unflattering hue. "You call the death of Baltran do'Verrada a *small change?*"

"Within the world, weighed against the scope of all the duchies and principalities and kingdoms, yes," Alejandro said. "We are a small duchy, important only to ourselves."

The indrawn breath of shock multiplied by twenty astounded conselhos became the noise of catastrophe. Alejandro realized it and cursed himself, caught Martain's slight movement from the corner of his eye, forced himself to relax. *I need Grijalva here with me. He is better suited for this than I.* But Grijalva was elsewhere, and the new Duke had no one but himself. *What would he do in my place?*

He answered himself swiftly and took two strides to the painting propped against the chair. "Do you doubt me?" he asked, so quietly they had to silence themselves to hear. "Do you doubt the wisdom of a man who must weigh his present and future against his father's past?" Now he loosed the restraints on his tone. "Eiha, you should not; I would suggest that the King of Pracanza is just this moment reevaluating *me!*"

That caught them. They had none of them thought of that.

"And perhaps he shall find me wanting, no? I am not my father, as you have all been at pains to remind me . . . and perhaps the Pracanzan king thinks less of me as Duke than he might as Heir to a man in his prime—do you believe it possible? Do you think he might reconsider and ask for the portrait back?" He dropped one hand to loosely grip the frame. "Is it not possible that Pracanza may decide I am not worthy of this admittedly beautiful woman?" He shrugged. "After all, a man who cannot lead his conselhos into common cause in something such as *this* can hardly be counted on in matters such as war." He paused. "No?"

It roused them all into protest: of *course* he was worthy; of *course* he could lead them into common cause; of *course* Pracanza would believe him ideal for his daughter.

Quietly Martain murmured, "You have them, Your Grace."

As quietly, "Do I? Good." Alejandro grinned brilliantly, and the men in the chamber responded as predictably as any crowd would to the dazzling good looks and high humor of the man who so closely resembled the ruler they had lost.

And then Rivvas Serrano made a comment about the Pracanzan painting, about the Pracanzan artist, and reminded them all that the current Tira Virteian Lord Limner was a Grijalva—a *Grijalva!*—who was expected to facilitate the documentation of all matters relating to their city and their duchy.

Triumph faded. "Merditto," Alejandro murmured as quarreling broke out afresh.

"Your Grace." Serrano, followed by do'Saenza, worked his way to the front of the multi-hued cluster of men. "Your Grace, forgive our presumption, but we must in all honesty admit our deep concern with the man you have selected to be Lord Limner."

"Your concern," Alejandro began, "runs only so deeply as your jealousy of the Grijalvas, who have supplanted your own family."

"Your Grace!"

"Eiha, be not so dramatic in your reaction, Rivvas. I may not have sat upon my father's lap during councils, but I have *ears,* do I not? I know very well how deeply runs the enmity between Grijalva and Serrano."

"For just *cause,* Your Grace."

"For no cause!" Alejandro shot back. "For no cause in which

you—or anyone—have provided evidence!" He shook his head. "Merditto, Serrano, you are all of you cabessas bisilas! And I am expected to listen to your counsel? How? *Why?* What is there you may offer me save recriminations born out of jealousy and fear?"

"Your Grace." This time it was Edoard do'Najerra, solid of frame, stolid of temper. "Your Grace, do you blame us for concern? We knew Zaragosa, were accustomed to Zaragosa—"

"Accustomed enough that you held him in contempt," Alejandro retorted. "Or have you forgotten all over again that I have ears?" He clasped one, tugged it twice, then released it. "I think it far too soon to judge Sario Grijalva beyond what he has yet done, which comprises very little other than the mere *insignificance* of halting a war . . ." He let that make itself felt, saw the verbal slap register. ". . . a wholly unnecessary war that surely would have killed many of us, and as many Pracanzans; a war which all of you supported on the basis of a rumor." He looked at no one now save do'Najerra. "I trust him at this moment more than I trust you, Marchalo, in regard to the ability to divide truth from falsehood, and with just cause." The latter for Rivvas Serrano. "He has been named, has been acclaimed, is Lord Limner. *Accustom yourselves to it.*"

Do'Najerra held himself in tight control. "Your Grace, there is concern that they might rise to overtake us. Forgive me, Your Grace, but even your mistress—"

"—is a Grijalva. Indeed." Alejandro swept them all with a scathing glance. "Can none of you count? Do you forget overnight the facts of our past? In my father's time there were *four* Serranos of vast and abiding influence: Lord Limner, mistress, Premia Sancta, conselho." He looked directly at Rivvas. "Only two left, after so many years . . . eiha, do you see the sun setting over Familia Serrano?"

"It's not that, Your Grace."

"No? Then what is it, Serrano?"

Rivvas did not shirk it. "Magic."

Alejandro fell back a step in mock astonishment. "I had forgotten! *Dark* magics! Yes!" He turned, slipped behind the chair, clasped each top corner of the frame. "Rivvas, what *kind* of magic? Evil, I must suppose, for you to use it against him . . . well then, of what is he capable? We've already established he cannot paint a dead man back to life, en verro—what, then? Shall we invite him to paint *this* woman to life?" Alejandro indicated the painted image with an elegant gesture. "She is truly alive, after all, *if* in Pracanza. Why not save the time otherwise wasted on a long and arduous journey and merely have him *paint* the Pracanzan princess here . . . why not have him mumble some words, breathe powder over the image, and conjure her into being? No? But, Rivvas—you want so very badly to convince me he can do evil things with this magic . . . eiha, what would you have him do?"

"Make himself Duke," Estevan do'Saenza said sharply. "If the Serranos are correct and Sario Grijalva *does* know magic—"

"Then he would have to kill each and every one of you in addition to me," Alejandro said. "And possibly even every citizen of the city, no?" He shook his head. "Do you truly believe it is possible for one man to usurp control of an entire duchy?"

"Verro Grijalva might have."

"Verro Grijalva died saving his do'Verrada Duke from assassination in the aftermath of war." Alejandro did not look, though everyone else did; behind him, on the wall, hung the massive original of Piedro's spectacular *Death of Verro Grijalva.* A similar painting by another Grijalva, Cabrallo, hung on the opposite wall. "And *Sario* saved his particular do'Verrada Duke *from* war, which often is nothing more than mass assassination, no?"

They clustered yet, breaking only slightly into small clutches of like-minded men. Estevan do'Saenza and Rivvas Serrano remained partnered; Edoard do'Najerra stood alone, as always; others grouped themselves in twos, threes, fives. And waited, for what else their Duke might say.

Weighing me . . . eiha, it is time I weighed THEM.

Alejandro left the chair, the painting, and went out among them. He knew well enough how to intimidate by sheer size; he was taller than all but the Marchalo Grando, and even that man was no taller than he. Alejandro had marked it in his father, though he never understood why it should matter. Now he saw it did, and employed it as he sought out each man, looked into his face, let him look into *his,* then nodded slightly. He let them see what he did, let them squirm and shift and trade glances, let them wonder what he thought. Eventually he returned to the chair, to the painting.

"You don't know me," he said quietly. "I accept that, and I understand also that you are frightened and confused; Baltran do'Verrada is not a man lightly viewed or easily replaced. I accept *that.* I welcome that, en verro: he was a man among men, but wholly of himself." He drew in a deep breath, let it go slowly.

"Time," he said, "I ask only time. Grant me it, as I will grant it to you, and we shall make our way together."

Rivvas Serrano stirred. "But—"

Edoard do'Najerra turned on him. "By the Mother," he said in deep disgust, "can you not look beyond the length of your nose? He is a *Grijalva*. In twenty years he will be dead, or dying, and we will have this to do all over again!"

Alejandro opened his mouth to protest—it was not the sort of endorsement he would have preferred—then shut it. At this juncture anything would do, if it silenced them. And after all, it was true.

Twenty years . . . how would I feel if I had only twenty years to rule? And realized, unhappily, that he did not truly wish to rule for twenty *hours*. Not if he had to argue with conselhos moronnos every day.

Alejandro sighed and looked at the portrait of the woman he was expected to marry. *Thank the Mother for Sario Grijalva, who will help me enforce their compordotta—and bless the Mother more so for Saavedra, who will help me embrace mine!*

Raimon paused outside the door, put his hand to the latch but did not grasp it, drew in a breath that filled the depths of his belly, filled his head with air and light, then opened the door and went in.

His mind ticked them off as he stepped into the Crechetta and shut the door. He did not even need to look; he saw them in their customary places, albeit Ferico inhabited the chair once filled by Otavio, once filled by Arturro. Raimon had known no other Premio Frato personally, though he could count off the names. All the portraits, the *Pentraddos Chievas*, hung in the Galerria Viehos Fratos, a private locked chamber prohibited to anyone else, so no Gifted Grijalva might ever forget who had the shaping of their family and their world—and the risks to himself if he abrogated honor and servitude.

He wore customary black, though there was no rule of compordotta specifying such a thing. And his Chieva, glinting in candlelight. Vigorous hair brushed into quiescence. It silvered now from black into white, though he doubted he would live long enough to truly be white-haired.

They had left a chair for him at the foot of the massive table. Raimon moved to it, grasped the carved wooden finials, did not grimace as his grip sent a twinge of pain through sore knuckles. He stood there, straight-spined, and let them evaluate the color of his spirit, of his soul.

Neosso Irrado. Once. Many years before.

Sario would smile at them . . . but there is none in me to give them, nothing in me but fear, and anger, and the knowledge of failure.

No man looked away, askance, aside. Nine surviving Viehos Fratos—he was tenth, Sario, eleventh—sat at the table and waited for Ferico to begin.

But it was Davo. And that frightened Raimon as nothing had.

"Nommo Chieva do'Orro," he said quietly. "No more than that, Raimon. Truth. In the name of what we are."

And so he told the truth. "He is more. He is other."

"To what degree?"

That, he could not answer. And told them so, told them also there was no proof, only rumor. That although Sario himself alluded to improprieties, no evidence could be offered. There was none.

Not even the *Kita'ab,* Raimon knew, for no man among them would believe their *Folio* other than what they and their ancestors had believed for years: a manual of artistic instruction, detailed in all ways of technique, recipe, and behavior save for those pages that were missing . . . and as they could not read all that was text anyway, it made no difference what did not exist. What mattered was what *did* exist. Of Sario's intent Raimon knew nothing, merely that the Limner's compordotta suggested he knew things no other did. But implication alone could not convict a man without evidence.

What he had was not evidence: *Folio,* that was *Kita'ab,* but Sario merely *claimed* it was; a suggestive painting of Zaragosa Serrano, but bone-fever, despite its pronounced predeliction for Grijalvas, was not uncommon in Serranos any more than in any other family; a peintraddo that was not after all *Peintraddo,* but an ambitious man, an obsessed man, would not permit anyone to hold the key to his destruction, of talent or survival.

Chieva. Always a Chieva, of one sort or another. Chieva do'Orro. Chieva do'Sangua. *Peintraddo Chieva.* So many keys, so many locks, so many hidden doors.

The *Folio* itself was a door. Perhaps Sario had found a key in the other pages. Perhaps Sario himself *was* the key.

More. Other. Sario Grijalva was not as they were, and never had been. And Raimon, convinced of one certainty: that the man who was so different, so obsessed—he who was *more,* and *other*—

might become what no other had achieved in three generations . . . and so he commited himself into that brotherhood, that conspiracy, of which neither of them spoke, save for one day in the closet above the Crechetta.

"It is believed," Davo said, "there was complicity. That compordotta was neither honored nor employed."

Raimon gripped the finials more tightly. Complicity, conspiracy. He denied neither, but answered with truth. "Sario has always made his own compordotta. It is an element of his personality."

Ferico spoke for the first time. "This element is not permitted."

The truth, no more. "Permission has never mattered to him."

"And why is that? Is he better? Is he apart?"

"One might argue so," Raimon said quietly. "He is Lord Limner."

"But did he achieve it through compordotta, or no?" Ferico persisted. "There are *reasons* for compordotta, as you well know, and reasons why we must control it so closely, so inflexibly, giving way to no excuse. The *Peintraddos* alone, misunderstood by those not of the family, would mark us as capable of committing evil."

Davo took it up in Ferico's stead. "Those rumors have persisted for years," he said, "despite efforts to discredit them. The Serranos, in particular, have been most diligent—imagine if they had knowledge of the *Peintraddos!* We would be persecuted. Rooted out. There are those in the Ecclesia who already suggest we should be, and the Premia Sancta herself saw to it we were prohibited from worshiping in public—though Duke Alejandro now has rescinded that bit of lunacy." He shook his head. "Compordotta exists for a wholly legitimate reason, as each of us comprehends. We Limners walk a cusp such as no other walks, even other male Grijalvas. We are impaired by infertility, a stunted lifespan, the sheer decay of physical ability . . . and we are also impaired by rumor and false beliefs. It would take so very little to destroy us, you see. Alejandro may rule absolutely, but such rule came upon him early and unexpectedly; he is young, untried, tentative, inconsistent. He might seek guidance from the conselhos as a group, or from any one of them. And if that one is strong enough to gain Alejandro's confidence, and if that one views us as a threat . . ." Davo gestured. "You are a clever, insightful man, Raimon. Explanation would be redundant."

The rebuttal came instantly. "But there is Sario at Court. The Grijalvas have a voice there, *despite* its deplorable compordotta!"

"And that is why we can do nothing to him," Davo said gently. "Without us, you have put the piece into play, Raimon. The game now must be completed. We dare not take from the board anything so vital as Sario, despite that in him which we abhor. A Grijalva is better than no Grijalva—and yet we dare not assume it is enough. Caterin Serrano remains Premia Sancta, and Rivvas Serrano remains a conselho. So long as there is a single Serrano so close to the Duke, we dare not grow complacent. The cusp remains."

"Then why am I present?" Raimon asked. "I have no power among you, nor ever will now, and Sario listens to no one. If you believe I might be able to mitigate his arrogance, control his compordotta, I fear there is nothing to come of it. I have indeed put the piece into play, and it makes its own course from here. I myself have been taken off the board."

"And so you have served your purpose," Ferico said. "Your usefulness is finished. There is no work for you among us now; Baltran's death and Sario's appointment came too early. We were not prepared then, and we are not prepared now. All came too swiftly."

"That is not my fault," Raimon said. "Blessed Mother, but Duke Baltran's death was an accident. It might have happened two years ago, or ten years from now—"

"In either case," Ferico said, "we would have had time to properly prepare a candidate for his Heir, or Alejandro's Heir, or that Heir's son. It is all a matter of time, Raimon, as it has always been—but your support placed Sario in a position such that only he could be fairly considered, with no time left to us at all." He glanced at the others briefly, then looked back at Raimon. "I think we are all in agreement that had you not proved so eloquent a supporter, in all likelihood he would have been subject to Chieva do'Sangua well before Baltran do'Verrada ever departed upon his journey to Pracanza."

"You can't punish a man for his talent! For his Gift!"

"No," Ferico agreed. "Only for compordotta we believe dangerous to the family."

"Then why am I called here?" Raimon asked.

"Because it reaches farther than that," Davo explained quietly. "You enabled him."

"Then it is my compordotta we're discussing!"

Ferico's gaze was steady. "You are a clever, insightful man, Raimon. Explanation would be redundant."

Only his grip upon the finials kept him from falling to his knees.

He clung tightly, disregarding the pain, and tried to compose himself. *Until the words are said—*

"Nommo Matra ei Filho. Nommo Chieva do'Orro." As one, save for himself. And Sario.

Always Sario.

TWENTY-EIGHT

Sario was immensely pleased: the painting went well. After multitudinous complaints about his stringent posing requirements, Saavedra had at last grown silent and simply let him work. Therefore it was with more than mild annoyance that he looked up to scowl at her as she made some small sound.

"What is it?" he asked crossly, and then, "Matra meya, what's happened to your color?"

She gripped the chairback. "How can I know?" she asked, scowling. "My eyes are in *my* head, not in yours."

"This won't do," he said. Then, sharply, "No, no—'Vedra! Don't move *now!*"

"I am going to sit down." And she did, seating herself with some care on the chair he employed as part of the composition.

Exasperated, Sario set down his brush. "Do you mean me to be an alla prima painter?" he asked. "I had thought fa presto, at *least;* I would prefer to take my time rather than be forced to complete this from start to finish in a single session! After all, you required Alejandro's presence for *weeks.*"

Saavedra smiled thinly. "But you have never said I might be an alla prima painter myself, have you?"

"You *could* be—if you allowed yourself to believe it, and others to confirm it. Then they would permit you to paint as you wished. Alla prima, fa presto, or in sections requiring weeks, as you will."

She put the back of her hand against her brow briefly, then stroked hair out of her eyes. "Sario, why is it you are so opposed to children?"

"I'm not."

"You are. You have no kind words for them, ever."

"Children are an impediment. You yourself have said Ignaddio's constant interest interrupts your own work, and he is not even *yours.*"

"There is no question that children may interrupt, and even perhaps impede—but there is hostility in your tone."

"For you," he said plainly. "For your sake, 'Vedra, and the sake of your talent, your *need* to paint. You know I believe you are

Gifted, and yet your reasoning behind not permitting me to test you is that you could not possibly *be* Gifted."

"I can't be—and you know why, Sario."

"It is *because* you are a woman that I know, 'Vedra. You are—different. I can see it in you. How many times have I said the Light recognizes itself?" He spread his hands illustratively. "You see? You are a Grijalva, a woman, and therefore must bear children . . . forsaking altogether—and willingly, from the sound of it!—your Luza do'Orro." He scowled. "Do you know how many men would sacrifice anything for your potential?"

"I *have* no potential beyond what I already am!"

"Because you have been taught since birth there is nothing for women. Eiha, but this infuriates me! You supported me in all things when I transgressed, and yet you will not permit me the same service. I know what you are, I know what you can *be*—if you would only let me test you, to confirm that you, too, lay claim to the Gift and all it entails!" He glared, moved nearly to tears. "Why, when I wish to do something for you instead of *to* you, do you resist me?"

"Sario—"

"We have shared so very much from the beginning, 'Vedra—and you want to take it all away from me. All of it." He sat stiffly on his stool and stared fixedly at the unfinished painting. "You are all I have ever had."

She stared hard at her hands a long moment, then finally said very quietly, "Things change, Sario."

"Indeed. So do people."

Her features were pale and pinched. Shadowed circles beset her eyes. "I never meant to hurt you."

"With the truth, such as you discern it?" His smile was bitter, wintry. "I know what I am, Saavedra . . . and I know how hard I worked to become it. You would be a liar to suggest someone else deserved the appointment, with or without your—aid."

She didn't smile. "En verro."

"So." His chest was tight, knotted up; with effort he relaxed. "You remain determined to throw away your talent in the name of children."

"I *want* children, Sario."

"They wish you to want children, and so you do."

"That isn't it at all."

"Of course it is. They put this in your head so you *think* you want children, so you will never consider your talent."

"And my Gift?" She smiled briefly, then shook her head. "Sario—is it that you cannot sire any?"

"Thank the Mother in Her wisdom for that!" He kissed his fingertips, pressed them against his heart. "I want nothing to do with children. I want only to *paint,* not to train up an infant!"

She examined him a long moment, weighing his words, his tone, his expression. "Eiha, that is probably as well," she said eventually. "You would not be a good father."

It astounded him that she could make such an all-encompassing judgment. "How do you know? Why do you say that?"

"Men who detest children rarely make good fathers—unless, of course, they truly do want and like them, and merely lie about it."

It was ludicrous, all of it. "Bassda, 'Vedra! I have come to paint you, not discuss procreation." He took up his brush again, gestured incisively. "Assume the pose, grazzo."

"I'm tired," she declared; indeed, she *looked* tired. "I want to sit here and rest—paint something else, Sario. The lantern. The decanter. The *fruit.* None of them is tired, nor will they complain that you make them stand too long." She cocked an eye at the fruit. "Of course, none of them is *standing . . ."*

"Bassda," he muttered. "Matra, but you try my patience."

"Then be an alla prima artist," she suggested sweetly. "Surely you have both vision and ability to paint all at once, from beginning to end, and will be as content with it after one session as you would be with weeks of work."

He growled deep in his throat, intending to say something more, but he had lost her. Her attention clearly was fixed on someone else; and then he heard the footstep in the door.

Ignaddio. Of course. Proving his contention that children impeded work.

" 'Vedra?" Ignaddio piped. " 'Vedra, you are to go out."

"Go out? Go out where?" Sario asked sharply. "No, you will *stay.* I cannot have the work disrupted yet again!"

Ignaddio dipped his head. "Regretto, Lord Limner, but it's the Duke. He's waiting in the courtyard, by the fountain."

"Matra Dolcha!" Saavedra leaped up from the chair in a flurry of rose-colored skirts and black ringlets.

"Merditto," Sario muttered as she ran out the door. He scowled at Ignaddio, scowled at his brush, scowled at the work. "How can he expect to receive his commission if he keeps stealing the subject?"

"May I see?" Ignaddio asked.

"No, you may not see. I permit no one to see a work in progress."

"But you said once the preliminary sketch was done—"

"Bassda! You try me, ninio." He waved his hand in a gesture of dismissal. "Go. *Go.* Find Diega for me—look in the laundry, grazzo—and send her to me. We have business, she and I."

Ignaddio's eyes widened. "But—I thought you couldn't—"

"Couldn't what, ninio? And what concern is it of yours what I can or cannot do, or what I may or may not *wish* to do?"

"Do'nado," Ignaddio whispered.

"Indeed, do'nado. Adezo, go. Send Diega to me. Then take yourself elsewhere, or I shall never even once examine your portfolio."

And as he had never even once suggested he ever would, the implied threat had the desired effect. Ignaddio departed.

Saavedra stepped beneath the arched, vine-draped entrance leading from a small walled garden into the central courtyard and stopped short. Alejandro stood but yards beyond her, gazing fixedly into the fountain and wholly oblivious to her approach, the sound of her footsteps obscured by the gargle and spray of cascading water. His was a pure, clean profile of such striking clarity she realized all at once she must paint him again, and very soon. Too often portraiture was of a full-face pose, or perhaps three-quarters profile—she wanted the profile itself, as if it bedecked a coin: the high brow partially obscured by unruly hair, still wavy in adulthood; the clean bridge of the nose, as yet unblemished by weapons practice or a misplaced wrestler's hold; the chiseled hollow between nostrils and upper lip; and a mouth she knew intimately enough that she blushed to think of it. The chin beneath was pronounced enough to establish a hint of stubbornness, but also of character; and it was far better to have more chin, she thought, than less.

She moved toward him. Her shoes crunched now on gravel and he turned, banishing the profile entirely, but Saavedra did not care. There were esthetics she appreciated in any of his postures, in the lifting of a brow, the quirking of his mouth, the quick snapping gesture of a thick wrist and broad hand in dismissal of a point of argument he found abruptly insignificant, even if it be his own.

Not in the least inhibited by the notoriously flawed grin, he bestowed it upon her freely, then caught both of her hands as she joined him at the fountain. Spray bathed his face, now hers; it mingled as they kissed. But within moments his expression altered from tender to serious, and she knew he had not come out of simple desire for her company.

Saavedra tugged him down beside her as she perched upon the curving bench surrounding the lowest basin, disregarding wind-drifted spray. "Tell me."

He made no attempt to prevaricate. "Caza Varra," he said simply. "I must go there."

She shook her head. "I don't know it."

He scraped a bootheel against a stone flag, digging at an edge as if he would pry it up. "It's one of the country estates. My father took us there during summers when he could get away." He sighed, plainly ill at ease, digging more vigorously. "My mother is there now. She has retired from Court, from all public life."

Saavedra laughed, clamping a hand on one of his knees to prevent him from excavating further. "A loving and dutiful son should go see his mother, no? Lest she make her displeasure known!"

"Eiha, yes, I suppose there is that." He caught the hand, clasped it, lifted it to his mouth, kissed it gently. "Forgive me, carrida . . . I beg you, forgive me—but I must go to my mother to discuss an impending betrothal."

It stabbed only distantly, as if she had formed calluses in preparation for this moment. "Yours."

"Mine."

When she could manage it without clamping down hard enough to score his flesh with nails, she squeezed his hand. "Eiha, we knew this would come. He went there for this purpose, your poor father." Courtesy forbade her adding that he had also taken her painting of his son, which now resided in the court of Pracanza's king.

"But not so soon!"

"Not so soon," she echoed. "No. But it has come now, and we must make the best of it." And then false courage evaporated, along with the brisk tone. "Bassda! I am no conselho trained to diplomacy and evasion. Let me say what I feel, Alejandro . . . that I am angry and frightened and jealous and hurt and confused and bitter and posessive and I want to cry, all at once!" She drew in a painful breath. "But that gains me nothing beyond a splotched face, red eyes, and a swollen nose—and then you would never wish to look at me again and you would look only at your Pracanzan beauty—" She broke off. "*Is* she beautiful?"

Clearly disconcerted, he made no answer immediately.

"Merditto," she muttered. "She would be. Matra Dolcha, what else? The daughter of a king, a dowry rich beyond imagining, trade potential that can only aid Tira Virte, fertility, I am certain—likely she will be fecund as a rabbit!—your mother will undoubtedly adore her, *and* she is beautiful!" She looked at him through a glaze of tears. "And now I am crying anyway because I can't help myself, and you'll go away the sooner!"

"Meya dolcha 'Vedra . . ." And he did as she both wanted and expected: embraced her, held her close, comforted her fears as only he could, with warmth and nearness and words that made no sense nor needed to, so long as he said them.

"Regretto," she said into his shoulder when she could speak again. "I meant never to do this. I *despise* women who do this."

"But I love this one, and she may spoil as many of my doublets as she wishes."

"It's weak."

"It's many things, all of them painful and none of them weak. And I also am all of the things you claimed to be in that lengthy, uncompromising, and unceasing string of words you consider epithets so vile I flinch to hear them."

She managed a choked laugh. "Do *you* want to cry?"

"At this moment you are crying enough for two. I'll wait."

This time the laughter was easier. "Until when?"

"When my mother adjusts the fit of my meticulously tailored clothing, smooths back freshly-brushed hair that is already in place, cups my jaw and tells me what a fine mennino I have turned out to be after all—en verro, the very *image* of my father!"

"You are. Both of those things."

"I am the image of Alejandro do'Verrada, whomever he may be. One day I may even know myself."

She smiled, but it died. "When shall you go?"

Alejandro sighed. His heel sought the flag again and began to dig. "This afternoon. A rider was sent out. Caza Varra isn't far, and she expects me tonight."

Saavedra sat up. "Then you had best go." Without success she tried to smooth the tear-stained, creased velurro of his doublet. "And change before you leave, or she will know some woman has been crying into your fine clothing."

"I expect she may do it herself, once she knows I mean to marry."

"Then suggest to her—stop digging, Alejandro, or you'll have *all* the stones up!—suggest to her she use your other shoulder. I am an arrtia, no?—symmetry is important."

He embraced her again, laughing softly into her curls as he gathered her close. "Meya dolcha amora, don't fear I will forget you, or cast you off—if for no other reason than you tend your stonelayer's work so well! I promised you the Marria do'Fantome, and you shall have it. When I am back, I will take the proper steps."

"When you are back from announcing to your mother you mean to marry the Pracanzan girl? Don't be a moronno, Alejandro, there is no time for that now." She made a placating gesture. "Later, perhaps."

It did not suit. "But it must be done before she arrives! Merditto, 'Vedra—can you imagine the outrage if I entered into a shadow marriage after I married her in the Ecclesia?"

"Before is better?" She shook her head. "Alejandro, I know you meant it when you said it, and I bless and honor you for it . . . but perhaps you should reconsider, in view of what has happened. *Then* no one imagined your father would die . . . you are Duke now, and things are complicated."

"I meant what I said, 'Vedra."

"I release you from it."

Something that wasn't humor glittered briefly in his eyes. "I will make the arrangements today before I leave for Caza Varra."

"You *can't!*"

"No? I am Duke. I can do what I wish precisely *when* I wish to do it." He rose then, kissed her soundly, turned to depart.

"Alejandro?"

She heard the scrape of gritty tile beneath his boots as he swung back. "Yes?"

In bewildered curiosity, "What are you going to do?"

"Take the first steps toward having the Marria do'Fantome legitimized."

"How?"

"By having it painted by the Lord Limner."

She surged to her feet. "Alejandro—*no!*" But as he registered baffled surprise at her vehemence, she realized she could not explain. What existed between her and Sario was so intangible as to be impossible to define. Not love, not true and passionate love such as she and Alejandro shared, of the heart and soul and body, but of the spirit, of that which shaped their talent, their gifts. *No man who does not share it can ever understand.* And so she shook her head. "Do'nado," she said. "Go and do as you will."

It was enough. He inclined his head, kissed fingertips, touched them briefly to his heart, then opened and extended his hand to in-dicate the blessing included her as well.

"Matra," she murmured as he went from her, crunching across gravel. "Matra Dolcha, let me be wrong . . . but I can see nothing of this but an ending. No man, newly married, should cleave to his mistress."

And no mistress, loving that man, could give him up freely.

⊷ TWENTY-NINE ⊷

Alejandro pounded up the stairs after gesturing away the young man who appeared to direct him; he thought by now all of them should realize he at least knew his way to Saavedra's quarters, if little else within the sprawling Palasso Grijalva. At the top of the stairs he went straight to the door that opened into the sitting room, passed through it to the atelierro, and found Sario Grijalva standing at an unshuttered window staring out into the courtyard.

The Limner turned even as Alejandro stopped short at the easel, examining the uncompleted painting. His focused determination bled away into awe as he gazed at the painting. "Matra Dolcha! I was not expecting *this*."

"No?" Grijalva's expressive face was pinched and pale; the flat line of his mouth was severe, as if he feared to speak lest he spit. "Well, I am not satisfied with it. I shall begin again."

"Again! But why? This is glorious!"

"It is a mere daub. It does not please me." Grijalva left the window and moved to the easel, sweeping a cloth over the image. "I shall begin again."

The swift appraisal and dismissive declaration set Alejandro back. "But surely if *I* am pleased—"

"Grazzo, Your Grace, but this is what I have trained for all my life, no? Permit me the chance to admit it is not my best work . . . I would never interfere with the ordering of your duchy."

All his intentions came back redoubled. "But I *want* you to," Alejandro said on a rush. "Is it possible?"

Grijalva blinked, clearly astonished. It was the first time Alejandro had ever seen him so. "You *want* me to—interfere?"

"Can you do that?"

The mixture of expressions crossing Grijalva's face followed one after another so instantaneously that Alejandro could not begin to name them all. And then he settled on one: sublime self-confidence. "Have they set you to this, Your Grace? Out of fear for you, for Tira Virte?"

"Has *who* set me to this?"

"The conselhos. Perhaps Marchalo do'Najerra, Conselho

Serrano, Conselho do'Saenza . . ." Dark eyes were limpid. "They have made common cause, no? To mistrust and undermine me?"

The laugh was startled out of Alejandro in a quick, choked blurt. "But this is your opportunity to undermine *them*."

White-faced, Grijalva turned away abruptly, returned to the unshuttered window, and stared out again. The line of his shoulders was rigidly set, his neck unbending, every minute inflection of his posture cried out his need for careful voyaging, for a discernment of what truths lay beneath the too-obvious surface.

This is none of it going as I expected . . . Sighing, Alejandro went to the chair behind the table and hooked it close with one booted foot, then dropped into it backward, spread thighs embracing the chairback. He folded his forearms across the rim where velurro was brass-tacked to wood and rested his chin upon them. Choosing his words with care, and their inflection, he said merely, "You will serve me in this."

Grijalva's brittle posture grew more inflexible yet.

"You will," Alejandro said, finding it easier now to be as firm of spirit as tone. "I wish to find a way to make certain no man among the conselhos may undo what I desire done, and that is to make certain Saavedra Grijalva remains my mistress for as long as we wish it ourselves." He paused, studying the soiled folds of shirt that hung from the stiff line of Grijalva's shoulders. "I am to marry the Princess of Pracanza, and I would honor Saavedra and her family as much as I am able."

At last Grijalva moved. He swung around as if he held a sword, as if he expected attack. His eyes were alive in his face, burning with an intensity Alejandro found disturbing. "You would *honor* us?"

That annoyed. "I have said so."

"Then make certain no one in all of Tira Virte may harm us!"

Annoyance diffused into puzzlement. Alejandro frowned. "You have the Ducal Protection."

"And it is worthless, Your Grace." Grijalva's smile now was neither pleasant nor sublime, even if he did recall the required honorific. "You know the Premia Sancta poisons the Ecclesia. One never knows when she may convince the Premio Sancto to join her."

Alejandro gestured sharply, dismissively. "That is over now. I declared it so."

"For that you are honored and blessed, Your Grace—" Perfunctory courtesy, no more. "—but do you see how it is with us? At this moment we Grijalvas have reclaimed two of the primary positions any of us may hold, by your will and grace, but there remain others who would see us thrown down from there; would, given leave, have us broken entirely."

Offended by the blithe dismissal of the power of his word, Alejandro sat stiffly upright in the chair. "That will not happen."

"Your Grace . . ." The expressive face with its blade-straight Tza'ab nose now was troubled. "Your Grace, there are ways men have of making certain they get their desire even if ordered not to."

"Then aid me in this, Grijalva! I have no intention of seeing you thrown down from your position, or Saavedra sent from me; nor do I wish to see your family broken. Find me a way in which no man may cause this to happen, be he Edoard do'Najerra, Rivvas Serrano, or Estevan do'Saenza." He paused reflectively. "Though, en verro, neither of the latter two are of such stature that they might accomplish it. The Marchalo *might,* but he is content enough at the moment to let you die in twenty years—it is a detached way of defeating the enemy." He sighed, chewed briefly at a cracked thumbnail. "Though I cannot promise it might *remain* that way."

"You are Duke," Grijalva said, as if he tested. "Your word is law."

Merditto, is he blind? He removed his thumb. "My word is the word of a young, untried, admittedly frightened Duke who would sooner have his father alive again and in this role than be in it himself. And they know that. They prey and play upon it." Alejandro sighed again, deeply, and rested his forehead against the rim of the chairback, letting tacks bite into flesh. Muffled by stuffed velurro, he said, "I am Duke, you are Lord Limner. We need one another, although few understand that." He lifted his face again. "Therefore I ask you to aid me in this, that we may, between us, protect your family."

Grijalva turned back to the window. He blocked much of the light; Alejandro could see little but silhouette. "There is perhaps a way, Alejandro."

He barely marked the familiarity. "En verro?"

Grijalva nodded. "If *each* mistress were to come from my family . . ."

"Each? You mean—forever?"

The words came more quickly now, with crisp declaration. "Let it be agreed that Palasso Grijalva and only Palasso Grijalva will supply the Duke with his mistress. A *confirmed* mistress—the one to whom he offers Marria do'Fantome." Grijalva turned sharply, gesturing further illustration. "That need not bind a man to only one woman, Your Grace—you and your Heir and *his* Heir and all the Heirs to come after may entertain whatever women you choose to—but only one woman, one *Grijalva* woman, would ever hold the rank." He spread slim, eloquent hands. "One wife, sanctified by the Ecclesia; and one mistress, 'sanctified' and *confirmed* by Marria do'Fantome."

"That gains me Saavedra," Alejandro said. "What does it gain you?"

"Not *me*," Grijalva said. "Do'nado—beyond the knowledge that my family's future is secured."

"And that is enough for you?"

Grijalva laughed softly. "I am Lord Limner. It is all I ever desired in this life . . . but my responsibility is to my family—" His pause was very slight. "—and of course to my Duke, for Grijalva Lord Limners, as much as the tragic Verro himself, have *always* served do'Verradas."

Alejandro considered it. He played out as many ramifications as he could conjure in his mind, knowing very well how others would react.

He smiled, taking fire. "Twist their tails," he murmured, seeing it, and the smile kindled to grin, to laughter, "eiha, *how* it would twist their tails!"

"And would go far to establishing your own rule," Grijalva added. "You are not your father, may the Matra bless his name—" Briefly he kissed fingers, pressed them to breast. "—and it is time they accepted it."

Alejandro thrust himself up from the chair. "Done!" He nodded vigorously, grinned; the world was whole again, bursting with promise. "Paint it, Lord Limner. Document this edict. Confirm this position. And when I am returned from Caza Varra, I will have it known to all the conselhos, all the Courtfolk—even to Serranos!— I mean to offer Saavedra Grijalva the Marria do'Fantome."

Sario Grijalva's expression was strange. "That," he said, "is more than Gitanna Serrano ever had."

"Or the Premia Sancta?" Alejandro laughed, then said: "Pluvio en laggo." He shrugged. "We make a new lake, you and I, with fresh rain besides." Alejandro shoved the chair back toward the table. "I must go. Tend to this, Grijalva, and you shall have my permanent protection in all things. For as long as you live."

"Twenty years? Twenty-five?" Smiling oddly, Grijalva hitched a shoulder. "Eiha, what does it matter? Much may be done in so little time."

"Begin now," Alejandro commanded—it was effortless, now

that he was certain of his course—and strode out of the room briskly.

⚷

The corridors, grazzo do'Matra, were empty of others. On a fine day such as this most went out into the city, or set up easels and sketchbooks in the colonnades surrounding the inner courtyard, or went into the gardens. Lessons were taken away from Palasso Grijalva entirely, so that estudos had the opportunity to take instruction at the specific sites the moualimos discussed. Raimon recalled such occasions in his own life, as estudo and moualimo both.

Deep inside the walls, light was not a given. In the outer corridors high arched windows permitted sunlight to illuminate the chambers, the cells, but in the heart of Palasso Grijalva, grown large despite the harrowing of their numbers, dimness and darkness pervaded, and shadow.

His soul was as dim, as dark, as shadowed. Bitterness was banished; rage dismissed. It was done. The words said.

He walked stiffly, as an old man. It was age, but escalated, the age of a man twice his years, were he anything but Grijalva. But more even than age, than the depredations of bone-fever.

Nommo Matra ei Filho. Nommo Chieva do'Orro.

Through the inner corridors, through dimness and darkness, and shadow, into the light of acceptance, of peace, of willingness. He was only helpless in so much as he permitted it, and he did not.

At the doorway he paused. He unlocked, then set his hand to latch, lifted, and went in.

Galerria Viehos Fratos. Where brothers and uncles and cousins, and all manner of ancestors, contemporaries, stared out of painted images as if they yet lived.

No sons. No fathers. That was denied such as he.

Peintraddo Chieva. Each one. Save one.

A copy. One of several. How clever. How sublimely prescient. And Raimon for the first time in his life truly envied Sario, for having the courage to know himself far more than any man alive, and to look beyond his immediate goal to the long-range repercussions.

Clever Sario. Gifted Sario.

Sario Grijalva, in whom burned a fire, a Luza do'Orro so bright, so incontestably brilliant as to blind a man. And to kill a man. As many, Raimon suspected, as he viewed necessary.

He went to his own face and gazed upon it. There was no doubting, even now, that it was his, did a man look from the painted face to the living. But younger, infinitely younger, less worn, less used, less shaped by the events of the latter years of his life; shaped of fifteen years only, not forty-one, full of hope and humor and certainty of purpose.

Certainty of purpose, that he among them all might become Lord Limner.

Nommo Matra ei Filho. Nommo Chieva do'Orro.

He had not become. He had made.

He sighed so deeply as to empty his lungs of air, his heart of apprehension. "Eiha," he said, "what does it matter? They will do it themselves, as we did to Tomaz . . . as perhaps we should have done to Sario."

Nommo Matra ei Filho. Nommo Chieva do'Orro.

He took down from the wall the *Peintraddo Chieva,* to touch again the image, the brushwork, the pigments and binders and resins and varnish, the recipe of the *Folio* that was in truth *Kita'ab,* that was he: Gifted, Limner, of the Viehos Fratos; that *had* been he before Sario.

Raimon Grijalva shut his hand around the Golden Key hanging from its chain. Then adjusted his grip and plunged the Chieva through the heart painted beneath the clothing.

Sario stood before the unfinished painting Alejandro had so admired. He was distantly pleased that the Duke had been so impressed, but that reaction also stirred in him a measure of condescension, condemnation: it was not his best. But Alejandro could not see it.

"No," he said tightly, "I will not permit it to be so. No man may judge my work save me, because no man can know what of myself I put into it."

Into this, little. It lacked the ingredients Alejandro himself had commanded: the eyes of love. No, he had painted it with the eyes of jealousy, of resentment, of impatience. And it showed. To him.

"Lord Limner?"

A small voice. A female voice. He turned and beckoned her in impatiently. Diega. A Grijalva, but little more; she was meant to bear children to unGifted males. In her hands was clasped a small clay pot, stoppered and sealed with wax.

"There." He indicated the table. "Have you the other?"

She placed the pot on the table, then backed away. She shook her head.

He knew she was afraid of him. Eiha, he had required it; what he requested of her was to remain private. He had assured it by agreeing to paint a miniature of the man she professed to love to ensure he would love her, though he did not tell her how—bound with Tza'ab lingua oscurra so that the man would forever welcome her affections. He wondered if she thought of what she truly asked; if she grew weary of the man she would nonetheless have him until one of them died.

"No?" he asked sharply. "You clean her chambers, you wash her linens—can you not do so simple a thing?"

Diega shook her head again. "Lord Limner, her courses have ceased."

"Ceased! But—" It robbed him of breath, the abrupt comprehension. For a moment he gaped like a fish gulping air instead of water; then Sario shut his mouth so tightly his teeth protested.

Alejandro's child. Of course.

How could this *not* happen?

He had ignored it, because there was no child of their pairing— until now. He had ignored the images of bedsport utterly because the work had consumed him, and because he had been *able* to ignore it—until now. They were private people, Saavedra and Alejandro, and shared the fire of their passion with no one else.

Alejandro's child. Growing beneath her heart even as Sario painted her. Even now.

He became aware then of Diega, waiting stiffly. With effort Sario forced a smile. "Eiha, then it cannot be helped. There is cause for joy, then, no? A bastard do'Verrada, son of the Duke himself?" He paused. "Or daughter. One must not forget that women have some uses. *You* do, no?" He favored her with a smile that drained the color from her face. "Eiha, you may go. And be certain that you shall have what you want of—Domingo?"

"Alonso."

"Of course. Alonso. Forgive me." He nodded. "Come to my rooms at Palasso Verrada in ten days, and I will have it ready for you."

She wavered. "Ten days?"

"Can't you wait until then?" She forbore to answer. He had frightened her very badly. "Five days," he amended. "But no sooner than that, for I have other tasks."

She bobbed her head, waited for dismissal; he gave it impatiently.

As she left, he realized he trembled. For only a moment he wondered why—had he not accepted the truth?—and then the pain of renewed acknowledgment stooped upon him and took him so deeply in his vitals that he fell awkwardly and unexpectedly to his knees, gripped doubled fists into his belly, bent and bent and bent until his head touched the floor.

He rocked there, like a child; wanted to spew food and wine and pain out onto the floor until he was free of it all, free of grief and futility and fear, free of tears, of the emptiness that wracked him, of the knowledge that she had accepted it before he, had seen it, acknowledged it, had *embraced* it, even as she embraced Alejandro do'Verrada.

There was no crueler pain he could imagine, than to know the only one who shared his Luza do'Orro, his Gift, could so thoroughly, definitely, reject it. And him.

Blessed Mother, but he had accepted she would never sleep with him. That was no longer of any moment; his art was all, and though he would occasionally take such release as perhaps he wished or needed, it was more vital that he not spend himself profligately, not waste the power.

Eiha, it was not that at all. It was that she left him alone so entirely, that she turned from him when he most needed her to find his way among the enemy; that she spent *herself* in the arms of another man, and now carried his seed.

Fertile seed, that had taken root.

His own never would. Never could offer her what apparently she believed was worth the sacrifice of her Gift.

He, who had broken every oath, every vow made of such bindings as would result in the destruction of his Gift if he permitted them the opportunity, was left alone even by Saavedra, who had never once failed to support him, to guide him, to sacrifice herself in the name of his Gift.

She extinguished his light. Clouded his vision.

She might as well have burned his true *Peintraddo Chieva,* even as she had burned Tomaz's so many years before.

Evisceration, unflagging and systematic. She took from him his pride in achieving the goal he most wanted by admitting it was *her* doing, not his, that gained him that goal. She took from him his knowledge of cleverness in avoiding the only power a man might hold over him, the potential destruction of his hands and eyes by the alteration of his *Peintraddo,* by accusing him of changing, of madness. She took from him her absolute and unadulterated support of him, of his talent, of his Gift. And she bore another man's child, when he could sire none that might inherit his Gift, his Light.

It was not a thing of Grijalvas, inheritance; Giftedness was unstudied, unknown beyond that it existed, and infertility was welcomed for what it betokened. But in the world he now inhabited, the vast and boundless world of Dukes, of conselhos, of foreign courts and kings, he was no man in their eyes at all, merely a boy who painted. Whose loins were empty of fertile seed. And who could, by their lights, never prove his manhood.

It mattered to them. And thus it mattered to him, because it must.

Sario unbent and gazed blankly up at the unfinished portrait. With the eyes of love, Alejandro had commanded. Eiha. Therefore let it be so.

Nommo Matra ei Filho. Nommo Chieva do'Orro.

He rose, shook out the sleeves of his shirt, began to pack up his things. What he would do was best undertaken in his own atelierro, as it was equally undertaken in his own heart.

THIRTY

Saavedra came upon Ignaddio crouched in a corridor, bundled up as if he were forgotten laundry. Legs were crossed, doubled up, pulled tight against his chest; elbows hooked his knees, but forearms stretched vertically to grant his hands the freedom to clutch hair, to drive fingers into the tousled curls and snug tightly, tight enough to threaten his scalp. His spine brushed the wall only momentarily, and again, and again: he rocked, if slightly, if with quiet, unceasing economy, with utter, abject grief.

" 'Naddi!" She swept down, skirts fanning across the broad flags of the corridor floor. "Blessed Mother, what is it?"

He stiffened beneath her hand, stilled, then turned to her, releasing his hair to grasp at skirts instead, to set his face into their folds and sob unremittingly.

Matra Dolcha—is it Confirmattio? Had he failed? She threaded fingers into hair, cupped the crown of his skull against her palm. "'Naddi . . . Ignaddio—you must tell me."

He cried the harder, a harsh, racking sound that brought tears of empathy to her own eyes. One hand groped for her upthrust knee, capped it, clung. And when at last he raised his head and exposed his face, she saw grief coupled with horror.

She knelt fully now, cradling the back of his skull in both hands. "You must *tell* me, 'Naddi!"

"The door," he said. "—was open . . . I went in . . . I wanted to look at the *Peintraddos*—" He gulped a sob, worked hard to regain self-control. "It was *open,* 'Vedra, I swear it wasn't locked—and so I went in . . ."

Peintraddos. She knew how desperately he wanted to be Gifted. "The Galerria Viehos Fratos?"

He nodded jerkily. "It's always been locked—this time it wasn't. And I wanted to look . . . I wanted to imagine my own *Peintraddo* hanging up there one day—"

"As it may," she said, then flinched inwardly. "Unless—"

"And *he was dead.*"

Breath gusted from her. "Dead? Who?"

He gulped another sob back. "Il Sanguo."

"Raimon—"

"I found him—he lay there, 'Vedra, all sprawled, all bloody—" His face convulsed briefly. "And his Chieva was bloody, too."

"Matra ei Filho . . ." She felt cold. Ill. "Blood, 'Naddi?"

"On his breast, on his Chieva, *everywhere* . . ." He clutched her skirts into white-knuckled, shaking fists. "'Vedra—his *Peintraddo* was pulled down, pulled down from the wall . . . and there was a hole torn through it!"

But nothing was ever permitted to happen to the *Peintraddos.* Sario had been most plain. Such paintings were put away, locked away, warded against any accident so no harm could come to the Limner. So much risk was involved that they took great care that *nothing* happened to the *Peintraddos.*

Saavedra fell back then, collapsed against the wall so firmly her shoulder struck it painfully. "Not Raimon . . . not Sanguo Raimon—eiha, Blessed Mother, Gracious Mother—*not Raimon*—"

"Why would he do it?" Ignaddio asked, fighting not to wail. "Why would he do it, 'Vedra?"

Raimon. Not Ferico, who might die in a week or a year. Not Sario, who might be victim to Chieva do'Sangua if he did not alter his compordotta—

The flesh rose up on her bones. What she said she did not know, did not hear. But Ignaddio did, and it frightened him. "'Vedra— 'Vedra, don't . . . don't *say* that!"

"But it is," she said, so clear in mind, in certainty, that the world around her was distant. "It *is* his fault, 'Naddi! It must be! For no other's sake would Raimon do such a thing. For no other man would he be placed in such peril that he saw no other way." She caught him to her, hugged hard. "Eiha, that he should do that—that you should *see* it . . ." She released him. "Regretto—that you should have seen such a travesty!"

Tears had stopped, but his face was still damp. "They sent me away."

"Who did?"

"Davo. The others. They came when I shouted . . . they sent me away because I had gone in where I wasn't supposed to, but also because I saw . . . him."

She nodded. "And now I must do the same." She shut her eyes, swallowed down the knot of pain from her throat, felt it lodge in her chest. "I must go. I must go to Sario. He should know . . . he should be *made* to know . . ." She scrubbed impatiently at her own share of tears. "They sent you away only so they could tend him properly, not because you didn't count. En verro. And now I must go, too—but I promise to come back later; I'll come to you, and we can go together to the shrine and pray for his soul before the icon."

He nodded, blinking rapidly.

"Sweet 'Naddi . . ." She doubted in this moment he would take offense at her words. "I am so sorry it was you who found him." Saavedra disengaged, rose from the floor. "I am so sorry for all of it."

And she left him there, wan of face, forlorn in posture, and felt the first knot of *something* in her belly that was neither child, nor sorrow, nor pain, but a cold and abiding anger.

⚷

Providential, Sario decided—or perhaps appropriate!—that he should only two weeks before prepare an oak panel for such an undertaking as this. The boiled linseed oil, carefully and repeatedly applied, had penetrated completely, so that no excess remained, and it had taken the thin layer of lean oil paint perfectly. The surface was ready for him.

The panel was large, begging a landscape, or a life-sized portrait. No easel would hold it; he had ordered it set against the wall, where it dominated the chamber, the atelierro of the Lord Limner. But he turned from the panel. Later. For now there were other concerns, other requirements of the task.

Ingredients he pieced into a large copper bowl: bluebell, for Constancy; white chrysanthemum for Truth; cress, for Stability and Power; fennel to lend Strength, to Purify, to defeat Fire; fern, for Fascination; fir, for Time.

Sario nodded. Thank the Mother—or Acuyib—that the old man had taught him the language, the lingua oscurra, so that he had learned the Tza'ab magic. Now, coupled with the Grijalva Gift—eiha, he was unlike any other Limner in the world! And always would be.

More yet: honeysuckle, for Devoted Affection; lemon blossoms, for Fidelity; lime, for Conjugal Love—he would not deny her that after all; white rose, for Worthiness; rosemary, for Remembrance; thyme, for Courage, a walnut leaf, for Intellect. And hawthorn, for Fertility.

All of these things: *Saavedra.* He would dilute nothing, for to do so would be a falsehood, and in this he desired only Truth.

Urine he had, from Diega. The other ingredients he would procure himself: blood, sweat, saliva, hair. He would recognize the moment, seize it, take what was required. But he could begin already. She was as he was: different. A woman was made of parts and pieces even as a male. Perhaps in Saavedra the tempering of Tza'ab blood with that of Tira Virte, with the changes wrought by the Nerro Lingua, coupled with her gender made her a female version of himself. She had her own Gift, her own Light. He had seen it.

And he would use it.

Sario set out also a clean marble slab, the muller on which he would temper ground pigments into paints; a paletto knife, jars and stoppered pots of pigments, of wine, milk of figs and oil of cloves, of poppy, linseed, saffron; a clutch of glass vials, brushes, a pot of wax, the charcoal he would use to sketch in the lines that would create from the inner vision the outer, the reality of Luza do'Orro.

Already he envisioned the border.

He stopped, counting out his needs. And glanced up in surprise as the door latch was lifted, the door was thrown open, as Saavedra herself came into his atelierro.

At first she could say nothing. And then she said everything and all at once, so that she could not tell if any of the words fit together into a whole, into something that made sense. She thought they must, somehow they must, because he was stirred out of an odd immobility and inner detached awareness into comprehension.

And he said nothing.

"Filho do'canna," she said at last, when nearly out of breath. "It should have been *you* in the Galerria. Should have been *you* who plunged his Chieva into his *Peintraddo!*"

"But why?" he asked. "If it's my death you want, that would not have accomplished it. That is not my *Peintraddo*."

The audacity of it astonished her. "No, that's true . . . *I* have it!"

"Do you?" He barely shook his head. "If you would be certain, go to it and destroy it. And then come back and vilify me more."

Shock upon shock. "Then it was a copy—a *second* copy—"

He was white around the mouth. "I am particularly gifted at making copies. It was all we were permitted to do for so many years."

"Sario . . . Sario—he's *dead!*"

He frowned abruptly. "Regretto—I am not being properly sorrowful, no? Not giving him proper honor—such *shocking* compordotta . . ."

And then she saw the grief in his eyes, in the unnatural immobility of his posture. How he held himself so stiffly, with such absolute rigidity that she did not know how he might ever move again.

"Did you know?" she asked. "Did you ever once *believe* he would do such a thing?"

"I believed in myself," he said softly, "as he required me to do." His face was harrowed. "Eiha, 'Vedra—he must have known. And I suppose I did also . . . and yet did nothing to prevent it."

"They must have meant to destroy his *Peintraddo*."

"No—not destroy it. Destroy *him*—Chieva do'Sangua." He took up and clenched into a fist a paletto knife. "And so another sacrifice is made."

"For you." She wanted to spit. "So much, in your name."

"My Gift," he murmured. "For my Luza do'Orro." He looked at her then, stared at her. Extended his hand. "'Vedra, grazzo—can you offer me no comfort?"

"In this? Why should I? It was yours to do or undo, Sario—you chose to do it."

He shivered once, enough to set the paletto knife to spasming in his hand.

She bared her teeth. "I want you to suffer."

"I do."

"Suffer *more*."

"Eiha, 'Vedra—Blessed Mother, Gracious Mother—" He shut his eyes, lifted the paletto knife into the air. "And so my Gift fails me, and I can't bring him back—can't paint him back . . . it isn't *possible*."

She feared then he might harm himself, might use the paletto knife on himself. And for all her anger, she could not deny his own measure of grief. He had never lied to her.

"Sario—Sario, grazzo . . ." She moved to him, put out her hand. "Give me the paletto knife—"

He whipped out his free hand, trapped her wrist in it, wrenched it over so the palm was exposed. And brought the knife down in an abrupt, slashing move that opened the flesh of her fingers.

"You're Gifted," he hissed. "Remember how Raimon burned a painting that had only a portion of the ingredients? This is the same, only this time it's you who will manifest the damage. So I can prove even to *you* what you are."

Saavedra was abruptly freed as he twisted away, reached toward the easel, the painting upon it. She staggered back, stumbled into a chair, over it, upset it, fell. Skirts were crumpled around her knees as she braced herself against the floor, one hand sliding in blood.

"Matra—" she gasped. "Matra ei Filho—"

Blood, *her* blood, splattered across the painting with a snap of his wrist, flung across the image of herself. She saw the spatters, saw the drips, saw how it marred the image, blended with the colors. "What are you doing?"

"I have said from the beginning you are different," he declared. "Nommo Matra ei Filho, but you are like no other. I cannot say what has caused it anymore than I can say what has caused *me*—was it our parents? The spark that kindled conception? Something in the blood?"

"I'm just a *woman*."

Sario laughed. "Perhaps that is it. Perhaps that you are a woman, and claim the Gift as I do—"

"I can't!"

"—combined with the blood, the talent, the heritage—"

"I'm not what you think I am!"

"—because the bodies are different . . . whatever it is that makes us male as opposed to female—"

"I'm not *like* you!"

"Attend me," he said sharply, and scratched blood and paint away with a ruthless thumbnail.

Saavedra cried out. Her shoulder *burned*.

Sario spun on her. "Look at it. *Look* at it, Saavedra."

It burned and burned.

"Not at the painting," he hissed, "at your shoulder!" And before she could move, could make an effort to escape, he was on her. Hands scrabbled at the neckline of her gown, tugged it away, exposed the shoulder. "There," he said. "Look, *look* at it—and tell me again you aren't Gifted!"

A scrape. A peeling back of a layer of flesh so that blood stippled fluid. As if a man's thumbnail had gouged into flesh, as his had gouged into blood and paint.

The wail escaped her, brief and broken.

"Admit it," he said. "Nommo Matra ei Filho, nommo Chieva do'Orro—*to which you are entitled*—admit it!"

"I carry a child," she said on a rush of expelled breath. "I carry a *child*—it can't be! *I* can't be!"

"In this there are no rules," he said. "How can anyone simply decide a woman who is Gifted may not also be fertile?"

"I *can't* be!"

"You are . . . as I have always known, you *are*."

"Alejandro—"

"Gone—whining to his mother, no doubt. It is for you and I to sort out, 'Vedra. As it should be . . . as it has always been."

He was too close to her. She scrabbled awkwardly on the floor, aware of blood on the hardwood as she pulled herself away from him. "Let me go . . . Sario, let me go."

He laughed. "I don't hold you here. Grazzo, *go*. Go and think upon the truth."

She struck out then, smashed the palm of her unbloodied hand across his cheek and set nails, so he would bleed as well.

He made no attempt to stop the blood, to explore the gouges. He sat before her, crouched as a supplicant, and grinned. "You are. Like me."

"Monster," she whispered, and saw the kindling of anger in his eyes.

"Gifted," he said. "No more, no less. And other. Different. What I have learned from Il-Adib and the *Kita'ab*."

"Bassda," she gasped. "Bassda, I will hear no more of this." She pulled herself away, caught at the chair, levered herself up to one knee, one foot. "Whatever you may be, I am not like you. In no way. I will *never* be like you . . ." It was hard to move, so hard; she felt ill and old and cold and weak. "—*not* like you—am not, will never be—"

He moved then, startling her anew. This time when he caught her shoulder it was not to pull away her sleeve, but to trap her, to push her back awkwardly against the wall. And he came down upon her, held her there, employing unanticipated, tensile strength to keep her.

"This once," he said against her mouth. "I don't love you, 'Vedra—not in that way . . . but we are the same, we are bound, we are linked, we share the Luza do'Orro—"

She twisted, tried to wrench her head awry, but his mouth came down regardless, touching first the perspiration across the top of her lip—and it was wholly without love, without passion or desire that he kissed her; was nothing more than obsession, posession, the enmity and rage of a man who has relied on a ruthless determination and alien compordotta to make himself into something more. Something other. No matter what it cost.

Even Raimon's life. Even her innocence.

And then he released her. Fell back, laughing, barely flinching as she spat first into his face, then again onto the floor.

"Grazzo," he said. "Grazzo meya, nommo Matra ei Filho."

Shaking, nearly unable to remain upright, Saavedra pulled herself to her feet and made her way to the door. She caught the jamb there, clinging as hair tumbled into her face, as a torn and forgotten sleeve bared the telltale mark of a thumbnail that had never touched flesh, only paint.

"You *are*," he said.

She ran. From him. From herself.

Sario frowned. She had not had the presence of mind to close the door, and what he planned required secrecy. He got up, aware of aches, of bruises to be, of the sting of her outrage across his cheek. Blood. It was not his he needed, but hers. And she had supplied it.

He went to the door and closed it, set the latch. More than a lock was needed, but he would tend that. For the moment there were other more pressing matters, needs to be attended.

Quickly he gathered the glass vials, pried away the wax sealant, removed the cork stopper. He took a clean absorbent cloth and patted his lips, drying them of perspiration; then shredded the cloth and tucked threads into a vial. Then he took up paletto knife, cleaned it, knelt on the floor. With meticulous care he set the second vial against the hardwood and used the knife to coax spittle into it. When it was full he stoppered it, turned to a third. Blood next: two and one half vials, no more; he dared not scrape up wood, which would pollute the ingredients.

The vials he placed into the copper bowl. He then retrieved the clay pot Diega had brought him, placed it upon the table next to the bowl.

Urine. Blood. Saliva. Sweat. Not all, but enough.

Sario sighed, dabbed a cuff against the bloodied scratches, then stopped short.

A careful search divulged what he hoped for: a snarl of hair trapped in the filigree of his Chieva. Three strands, four, coiled into ringlets.

He worked swiftly and with absolute concentration, trimming a lock of his own hair, trimming hers, then binding the commingled human hair with that of sable onto a slender wooden handle. He sealed the bristles, made the brush; wet it with his own saliva, then uncapped the smallest jar. Smiling, he carried brush and jar to the door, and knelt. With swift economy he painted gilt-hued oscurra around the latch, so no one might open it.

When that was completed he returned the jar to the table, washed the new-made brush in solvents, dried it, then removed the blood-spattered, scratched painting from the easel and set it aside.

"Now," he murmured. "Adezo." He stood before the oak panel, examined its readiness by eye, by touch. Then took up an unused soft rag and wiped the surface entirely clean.

Alla prima. Begun and finished in one session.

He had no more time. Time was always his enemy.

THIRTY-ONE

In her chambers, Saavedra stripped and washed, paying particular attention to her face, to the places he had touched her, to the scrape on her shoulder. She did not wish to touch that, but it was no more than it appeared. She found it both distressing and illuminating.

This is what they do. This is how they commit Chieva do'Sangua. Only they painted, *re*painted, an image out of health and youth into decrepitude and age, from a proud, promising boy into an aging man afflicted with bone-fever twisting his hands, with milk-fever blinding his eyes.

Her hands were whole, her eyes. She was in all ways the same, save for the scrape upon her shoulder—and knowledge.

Trembling she put on fresh shift, fresh gown, spread bandaged hand across her abdomen. He knew. Sario knew. She had told him. Even Alejandro knew nothing, nor anyone else save perhaps the women who washed her linen; it was improper compordotta to announce an impending birth until four months had passed, for as sterility afflicted males, so did early miscarriage afflict females. Reaching four months did not assure certainty of birth or survival of the infant, but there was more safety in it, and so the custom had become a ritual.

The mirror gave her truth: hollow about the eyes, taut around the mouth, pale of flesh, but whole. Nothing showed of her knowledge. Swiftly she tied back ringlets, then went to find Ignaddio and share prayers for dead Raimon in the Grijalva shrine.

* * *

Sario worked swiftly, with certainty, murmuring lingua oscurra, giving way from the knowledge of what had occured to what must; employing precisely what Alejandro had commanded him to employ, but of his own will, his own doing, his own Gift and Light. The original plan was disregarded, as was the original if incomplete portrait; he worked now completely separated from anything he had done before, making this wholly fresh, wholly new, unlike anything he or anyone else had done before him.

A woman, standing in the middle foreground, behind a table but not obscured, as if poised to move away from it. The table itself, in near foreground, was only partially visible, its image carried off the bottom of the panel, extended to the left and carried off again; movement was imperative, and the suggestion of it. Thus a man looking at the painting saw mostly the edge of the table, not its surface, and that edge carved into interlocking patterns, a border, leading the eye. On the table lay books, vellum pages, a lighted lantern; an earthenware bowl of fruit; silver pitcher. And a closed *Folio,* its aged leather binding set with gold and gemstones.

Behind the woman, in the background, windows, the high and arched embrasures cut deeply into thick walls, all honey-hued curves and shadowed, deeper hollows, with shutters folded back. Beyond the windows, through the arches, the sky beyond, fading from twilight to evening, from the colors of sunset to the tones of night, rich and dark and encompassing. On one deep sill a new candle, tall, fat, honeycombed, twelve hours delineated by gilt-painted, incised rings. Its light but a blur, painting a warm patina over the honey-hued, clay-smoothed surface of the wall.

On the other sill, also behind her, a mirror set upon a small easel, silvered glass framed in gilt and pearls. A memory-mirror, a luck-mirror, gifted to a lover in celebration of Astraventa, when the stars fell from the sky.

To the extreme right, nearest the edge of the panel, a door, iron-studded, iron-bound, consuming the foreground. Shut. Latched. But not locked. Not barred.

And the woman: behind table, before windows, illuminated by candle, by lantern, caught between light and shadow. One hand, a long-fingered, slender hand, barely touched the gem-set leather binding of the *Folio,* as if she intended to open it; yet the poised posture suggested interruption, a startled expectation that made the *Folio* after all unimportant, forgotten.

The other hand, equally long-fingered, equally eloquent, was dropped to brush her abdomen, as if to cup it, to ward it. She faced the viewer and yet turned away also, caught between stillness and movement. Her head was uplifted, in motion, turning from viewer to door. The fine bones of the face illuminated by lantern light, by an inner, joyous light of anticipation, as if she knew a man was at the door, a lover, the father of her unborn child. All the fine bones, *all,* knit of chiaroscuro, hollows and shadows and lines and relief, tilted, turning, limned by love: hers for him, his for her, and none of it Sario's.

He paused in his muttering, his painting. Caught breath. Went on.

The sheen of pale bare flesh above the low, straight line of her gown, an ash-rose gown; the stippled scumble of flame-illumined velurro, laced taut against breasts, against ribs, against abdomen; the still-slender abdomen as yet unbloated by pregnancy; the low, straight, slash of neckline, high enough in bodice only to hide swollen nipples, reaching from side-seam to side-seam so that the sleeves, ruched and quilted to stand above shoulders, were laced onto the merest strip of fabric rising from the bodice.

The deep bell of the skirts, fold upon fold of heavy velvet, vertically fretted by light, by shadow. Divided by the table, begun again beneath it, what could be seen of it. And the tumbled mass of ringlets, swept back from her face to expose it save for one or two fallen strands, fallen coils before the ear, another dangling to bare shoulder—and yet another near an eye, begging for readjustment by a lover's tender touch.

Swiftly, so swiftly; there was so little time.

Color, tone upon tone, warm, cool, light, dark, mixed to form the whole. He tempered upon his muller, adding oil as necessary, wine as needed. Applied black pigment to the marble so it would not taint fresh color . . . rubbed it clean, took up the brush, began again to paint.

Detail to nose, to just-parting lips, to gray and brilliant eyes; even to lashes, to the hollows of her ears, the clean vertical line of neck from uplifted jaw to the first downswept curve into horizontal shoulder. The blush of light, here; the deeper stillness of shadow, there.

Saavedra: posed, poised, caught. Waiting for Alejandro.

<hr />

Ignaddio's cell was as hers had been, bereft of that save what came with it, and what he put into it: himself, imagination, inspiration. A narrow cot, strung with rope; a chest for clothing; a table near the window, with ewer and basin. And the clutter of his craft.

Saavedra paused in the doorway. He had left it open, as if wanting to hear the first footstep of her approach; but if he did, if he marked her approach at all, or her presence, she could not say. He sat upon the bed, shoulders bowed, head tilted downward.

" 'Naddi," she said, and he turned. She saw then he had been drawing: a sheet of wood-heavy paper upon a board, a piece of charcoal, smudged face and filthy hands. He set them aside as he saw her. "Eiha, no—don't stop. If you wish to draw, do so—I can return another time."

"I've been waiting for you," he said.

She wondered if she had been so long, first with Sario, later in her chambers removing the taint of him. "Regretto," she said. "Shall we go now?"

He stood up, shaking out of eyes a lock of fallen hair. "What will they do with him?"

She thought he meant Sario, then realized he meant Il Sanguo. "Give him passage," she answered, knowing it was not what he asked, and yet she had no answer. She had never known a Grijalva to take his own life by any means; had not known save for Sario what was done at all for a Sanguo who died.

Raimon had not died. Raimon had perverted what was forbidden by the Ecclesia, unknown within the family.

"Shall we go now?" she repeated. "We'll talk to the Blessed Mother, ask intercession, pray for the peace of his soul."

Ignaddio nodded, rubbed grimy hands on his tunic, thus transferring the dust, and was no cleaner for his efforts. A second toss of his head swung hair out of his eyes; she saw deep worry in them.

"What is it?" Saavedra asked.

He stared hard at the floor. "I am to undergo Confirmattio next week."

Inwardly she flinched; it was done to discover Giftedness, and just this moment she wanted nothing to do with such undertakings. "Eiha," she heard herself begin calmly, "is this not what you wanted? First Rinaldo, now you. Not so far ahead of you after all, is he?"

He refused to look at her. "I don't want it now," he said. "I'm afraid."

Once she might have sent him to Raimon, to ease his fears; but Raimon *fed* them instead. "Because of what happened?"

He nodded. "He had years left to him. *Years.*"

In the house of Grijalvas, even boys thought of such things.

Saavedra sighed. "We may never know why, 'Naddi—" She did. *She* did. "—but we must not let it affect our own lives beyond proper mourning. If you are Gifted, you will be needed. Perhaps— perhaps you are meant to be his replacement."

His head came up sharply in shock. "Replace *Il Sanguo?*"

"No," she said after a pause, "no, no one shall replace Il Sanguo. But perhaps you can learn from what he taught, and help his memory to be honored."

Ignaddio nodded. "That I would like to do."

"Then come." She did not extend a hand; he was aware of dignity again. "We'll go to the shrine."

After only a moment's hesitation, the boy preceded her out of the cell.

<hr>

His voice was counterpoint to his heartbeat, rising and falling as he recited the Hidden Language. So much detail now: the grain within the wood of the door, the table; the intricacies of the carved border along the edge of the surface; the rich glint of gemstones fixed into the leather of the *Folio,* set aglow by lantern; the text and illumination worked into the vellum pages; the lacework of honeycombed candle, lighting itself, the window, the folded shutter; his small copper bowl now set in the sill, holding such plantstuffs as bluebell, white clover, rosemary—and, in private jest, a drift of peach blossoms, for Captivity.

And lingua oscurra. In light, in shadow, in flame, in darkness, in the folds of her skirts, in the coils of her hair, in the border of the table, in the woodgrain of the door, in the binding of the *Folio,* in the text of vellum pages.

Oscurra. Everywhere.

<hr>

Saavedra didn't know if the shrine brought peace to the boy, if the icon offered surcease against his fear and grief. For herself, it offered some measure of renewed hope, realization: that she was Gifted after all, unaccountably Gifted, did *not* mean she must accept the tenents of the Limners. She could never be one of them, never of the Viehos Fratos, never a Grijalva who shaped compordotta and family goals. She was herself, nothing more, nothing other; leave that to Sario, to be shaped of different needs. To wish to shape other folk and *their* needs.

Ignaddio sat beside her on the bench set against the wall. The shrine was small, barely large enough to hold more than six men, but in that moment it loomed large as a cathedral. No bells. No sancto, no sancta. Merely a velurro-draped table and an icon upon it, the wooden panel painted by, it was said, Premio Frato Arturro, who was himself now dead, as Raimon was now dead; Arturro who was, they claimed, everything but father to the boy.

Boy. Raimon had not been a boy for years. She had never known him as a boy. He had always been older, Gifted, one of the Viehos Fratos.

Saavedra wondered if Arturro knew. If Arturro welcomed Raimon, or if self-murder would turn the Premio Frato against his estudo.

Ignaddio stirred. "May I go, 'Vedra?"

She started. "Eiha—of course you may go. I don't mean to keep you here beyond your wishes." She touched his hand briefly. "I will stay a while, 'Naddi. Go on."

He nodded and stood up, turned to the door. With his hand on the latch he looked back at her. "You didn't mean what you said, did you? About it being Sario's fault?"

She drew in a breath to give her a moment, and strength. "It's very important to you that he be forgiven, no? That *I* forgive him?"

Ignaddio looked at the floor fixedly, then lifted his eyes again. "He's Lord Limner," he said. "It's what I want, too—but if what you say is true . . ."

If what I say is true, I have forever spoiled your dream. When it isn't even the position at fault, but the man in it. That much she could offer: an ending to his worry.

"I was angry." That was truth. "Angrier than I have ever been, 'Naddi—I make no excuses for it. But I will also offer you this: that sometimes in anger things are said that shouldn't be."

He worked that out. "Then you didn't mean it?"

"I said things I shouldn't have."

Ignaddio wanted to ask more, but saw swiftly enough he might not hear what he wished. And so he took what was offered, what he could shape to mean what he wished, and left the shrine.

"Poor 'Naddi," she said. "All our fine ideas have been shattered today: a Limner takes his own life; another is accused of abetting that. But I can't help it: life is *never* fair."

Neither fair to a boy, despairing of his dream, nor to a woman despairing of innocence.

"I want it back," she said, looking at the icon. "I want that innocence *back*."

But she had lost it so many times. In the closet above the Crechetta, witnessing Chieva do'Sangua; in the Crechetta itself after burning Tomaz's *Peintraddo*.

All for Sario. But as much for herself, because deep down, deep inside, far back in the hidden, forbidden places, she had longed for the Gift that made him so different.

So much more. And other.

He said she was. He *swore* she was.

Saavedra stood up abruptly from the bench and walked the four paces to the table. There she knelt, there she bowed her head. "Forgive me," she begged. "Forgive me!"

He labored over the chain, detailing every link. All of it oscurra, all of it Tza'ab script, all of it tiny, perfect, precise. Link after link, rune after rune, word after word after word. It depended from her neck, bisected the swell of breasts, of bodice, dangled to her waist. Above the hand that gently warded abdomen he painted the key, also of oscurra, its shape the shape of his own.

He stopped then. Gasped. Shook himself out of stupor, out of the trance of Al-Fansihirro, of concentration so absolute as to render him not of the world even though he inhabited it. He set down his brush of a sudden, dropping it heedlessly to smeared marble muller; staggered back, back; pressed the heels of his hands against his eyes, ground, smeared, scoured; breathed loudly and raggedly in the silence of the room.

Blessed Mother, Great Acuyib . . .

He had spent himself badly, pouring all that he was into what she would be. Spent the talent born of Grijalva, of Tza'ab, of everything he was. More. Other. Different.

So little left—

And in the admission of his efforts his hands began to tremble, his body to spasm, his teeth to click together. On the floor it seemed safer; he knelt there, shivering, retching, and heard the faint chiming of the links of his chain. He shut his hand upon the key, felt its shape, its weight, its solidity.

Fear flooded abruptly. Had he sacrificed it?

He climbed to his feet, reeled, approached the panel, searched the painted key and links. *Identical.* Save his own was hard, pure gold formed of natural and manmade links, not of oscurra.

Relief blossomed. He spun away, muttered a prayer to dual deities, went to lean weakly against the wall. So much done—so *much* done in so brief a time.

And something left to do.

He slid down the wall, feeling the faint bite of hand-smoothed clay as he collapsed upon the hardwood, hearing the scrape of cloth against it, smelling the stench of his industry: blood, urine, semen, sweat.

Sario shook. *I have done all save the last.*

Paint, solvent, oil, wax, the pungency of plantstuffs, the incense of guttering candles.

Felt the shuddering of his heart beneath unquiet flesh.

And breath choking him as if he died of Plague.

Trembling hands worried hair into a wilderness of spikes and sweat-stiffened curls. Beard stubbled his jaw; his wrists scraped against it as he drew his hands down along the contours of his harrowed features. He caught the Chieva again and clasped it, shut it up within his hands, locked fingers around it.

Wait. Wait.

It was not achieved yet. He could still undo it.

Wait.

He would not. Dared not.

Tears welled. Spilled. Shivering, he lifted the Chieva do'Orro to his lips, kissed it, pressed it hard against his breast, and thrust himself to his feet in one abrupt motion. He walked swiftly to his table, took up the tiny brush containing his and Saavedra's hair, dipped it first into urine, saliva, blood, and lastly into pigment still smeared upon marble muller.

He leaned close to the portrait, biting deeply into his lip in intense concentration, hesitated—then crisply signed his name into the latch upon the door leading into Saavedra's cell.

Kneeling before the table, before the icon, Saavedra believed at first the candle had gone out. She looked up, marking the sudden dimness, the pallor of the shrine, but saw through a hazy glaze the faint glow of lighted candle.

Within her chest, her heart hammered. Startled, she pressed both hands to her breast. Against her palm she felt the uneven beating, the thump and retreat, the too-swift hastening, the lagging.

She could not draw breath. Could not *breathe*—

"Matra—Matra Dolcha—" It gusted from her, taking her final breath. Empty of air, lungs labored.

Saavedra stumbled up. Grasped the table, caught cloth, tugged it away so that the icon moved, but did not tip. And then she lost her grip, lost the cloth entirely, could not grasp the table beneath.

She threw back her head in a silent wail of fear, of utter incomprehension.

One hand clutched at her abdomen, the other at the icon as she fell, the painted wooden panel, Arturro's masterwork in praise of the Matra ei Filho.

Her hand passed through it. Through varnish, through paint, through binders, through oils, through the wood beneath. As she fell she did not rock the table, did not upset the icon, nor pull down the velurro.

She smelled oil and wax and blood, the pungency of aged urine, a drift of fern, of fennel, a trace of peach blossom.

Felt as she fell the weight of a chain on her neck, the cold touch of metal against warm and living flesh.

And then the weight was gone, the cold touch of metal; and flesh was neither warm nor living but mixed upon a muller, painted onto wood.

THIRTY-TWO

In the sultry warmth of summer, Alejandro shivered. "Do you—" He stopped. Swallowed. Found breath and strength, from somewhere. Began again. "Do you know what this says?"

Grijalva nodded.

"That—that—" Again he halted. Again read the words on the page held in trembling hand. And, again, began. "—that she wishes to grant my wife—my *true* wife, she says—the love and honor of a true husband, and not a man of divided heart?"

Grijalva nodded.

"You know this? That it says this?"

Grijalva offered nothing.

"But it can't be *true!*"

"Your Grace."

Not disagreement, compassion. Merely confirmation.

Alejandro's outcry was framed of pain, of anguished denial. Frenziedly he tore the paper to shreds, then threw the scraps to the ground: supreme rejection of evidence, or truth. "I will have her back. I will. Do you hear it? *I will.*"

Tonelessly: "Your Grace."

"Find her. Find her at once! You are a Grijalva, her friend—" His face spasmed. "—her kinsman, and closest companion . . . *find her.* I am Alejandro do'Verrada, by the Grace of the Mother and Son, Duke of Tira Virte, and I *will* have her back!"

Grijalva held his silence.

Silence defeated. The Duke was again no more than a man. "Nommo Matra ei Filho, this can't be." It was. He knew it. Knew *her.* "Sario—Sario, tell me she wants me to come fetch her . . . I, myself, to fetch her, to prove my love and devotion . . ." Of a sudden he looked down at the scattered scraps and cursed himself for destroying what was, the Limner said, written in her own hand. Through tears he begged, "Tell me."

Grijalva shook his head.

"Filho do'canna, Limner, *say* something! Sweet Mother, you stand there with your mouth sealed up like a corpse, pale enough unto death . . . can you say nothing? Make no explanation? Offer no suggestion?"

Grijalva at last graced his Duke with more than an honorific. "Her letter made it clear: she is not to be found. Not to be brought back. You are not to search for her—because it would be futile."

"Futile." The Duke sat down all at once, collapsing into the chair his father once inhabited. "Futile."

"She will not be found, Your Grace."

"You must know something, Limner. You know things. Limners know things."

"Not what you wish me to know."

He slid out of his chair, knelt, took up the first scrap, then another, thought to mend the letter, to paste it back together.

Futile.

"I can't," he said unsteadily. "—can't—do this . . . Grijalva, I can't *do* this. Not without her. She is to be *here,* with me . . . she is to be my mistress, my *wife,* confirmed according to the rite of Marria do'Fantome. You told me so. You showed me the way." He gazed down upon the two scraps of paper he clutched. Released them. "I can't do this without her."

"You are not without her, Your Grace."

He snapped his head up. "What?"

"Without her in flesh, perhaps, but not without her in spirit." Grijalva gestured to the wall, to the shrouded panel set against it. "I freely give you what is left of her, Your Grace . . . *all* that is left of her, so you may have her forever."

Alejandro stared at the concealing cloth. "Is that—" His throat closed painfully. "That is Saavedra? The portrait?"

"It is Saavedra." A hint of a smile. "Indeed, the portrait you commissioned, Your Grace. So she would never leave you."

Holy Mother, but it hurt. "She *has* left me!"

"In flesh, perhaps. Surely not in spirit." Grijalva lifted one shoulder in an elegant shrug. "Perhaps she lied in part—women do, Your Grace, as suits their needs—but there is truth in this." He paused. "Every truth, Your Grace."

Dazed, Alejandro waited.

"So long as you have the portrait, you shall always have Saavedra. But you must tend the painting as if you tend her flesh."

"I can't," he said, and tears rushed into his eyes yet again. "Nommo Matra ei Filho, how am I to bear this?"

"You will, Your Grace. You are the son of Baltran do'Verrada, and your task is to rule Tira Virte."

"Without her?"

"You *have* her, Your Grace; Nommo Matra ei Filho, I promise

you that. You need only guard it most carefully, as if you guarded
your life, your loins, your duchy."

He rose. Stared at the shrouded painting. Then gestured sharply
with a snap of his wrist. "Take it away."

"Your Grace?"

"Take it away. Put it somewhere. Be rid of it. I will not look
upon it."

Grijalva's face went corpse-white. Dark eyes blackened to fill
his face. "Not at *all?*"

"I can't."

A gust of breath issued from Grijalva's mouth. "Eiha, I understand . . . here, then, I shall assist you—"

Alejandro took one step to halt it, stay it, prevent it—but it was
too late, the shroud was lifted and pulled aside, the portrait was his
to see.

"She's waiting for you," the Limner said. "Do you see it?
Look closer. Here she waits, passing the time until you come—
and here you have only just arrived, unseen but heard . . .
see how she begins to turn, to look? See the delicate
color of her face as she recognizes your step? See how the *Fol—*
the *book—*is left unopened; how she forgets all in the realization that you are there, just *there,* on the other side of the
door? See how she means to rush to the door and lift the
latch, to admit you in good haste?" Dark, desert-bred eyes
were strangely opaque. "It is all there, Your Grace. All.
Saavedra. For you."

Trembling beset him. What he felt, how he hurt, was private, not
even for his Lord Limner. "Go," Alejandro said. "Adezo. *Go.*"

Grijalva made as if to turn, stopped. Gestured slight but eloquent
inquiry. "Shall I have it carried away, Your Grace? Shall I keep her
for myself?"

That stabbed. He could barely speak. "Leave it."

"Of course." The Lord Limner inclined his head. "Your Grace,
regretto—forgive me for such presumption. But you are not alone
in this. You have her still . . . and you have me."

"Nommo do'Matra—*go—*"

Alejandro heard the soft steps, the lifted latch, heard it click into
place.

Alone. Alone.

Matra Dolcha, he could not bear this.

Alone.

Could not.

And knew he must.

Sario departed Alejandro's presence and went at once to Palasso Grijalva, made his way up the stairs, to the rooms she had inhabited. The rooms where he had placed all of his paintings, such as the one of Zaragosa, that might provide evidence of his power, or a means to bring him down. He would paint more, of course, but there were other places for them to be hidden. What he had been was gone. For now the paintings of his past were where no one would ever find them.

He shut her door from the corridor, then took from leather scrip a small brush and a pot of paint. Unsealed, unstoppered it. Dipped the brush into it, withdrew, began to paint.

The door was a panel smaller than the other, but he did not intend to paint it all. Only what was required.

Lingua oscurra, born of Tza'ab Rih even as he had been. Fitting. *Children of the Desert,* Il-Adib had called them; had meant them to be. But they were not, either of them. They were Grijalva. Chi'patro. And Gifted.

He painted oscurra into the woodgrain, set a border around the edges, signed his name beneath the latch. And when Ignaddio came up the stairs and asked what he was doing, he did not do more than cap his little pot, clean his brush upon a rag, tuck both into his scrip.

"She asked me to do this," Sario said quietly. "Before she left, she requested this." He shrugged. "Who can predict what fancy will take a woman?"

Shadows cradled Ignaddio's eyes. "Why did she leave?"

"Because she loved the Duke, but he is to marry the Princess of Pracanza."

"She could have stayed here!"

"Eiha, some things are too bitter, too painful for women to bear." He turned toward the stair. "Will you come? I thought I would walk through Galerria Viehos Fratos; would you like to accompany me?"

The boy's color ebbed, then rushed back. "With *you?*"

"Eiha, it is not so much."

"You're Lord Limner!"

"And so you would like to be." Sario smiled to see the sudden blush, put a hand upon the thin shoulder and guided him toward the stairs. "Is that so poor an ambition? I think not. I think it a worthy goal."

Ignaddio descended the stairs, twisting to look back over his shoulder. "Do you think I could be? Ever?"

"Oh, I do believe so . . . but only if you *survive!*—mind the stairs, mennino, or you will break your neck." He smiled easily. "And that would be a terrible sorrow for both of us."

Ignaddio gripped the rail more firmly. "For me, eiha, I suppose. But—why for you?"

"Because I need you."

Now the boy missed a step, caught himself. One more and he was down, and there he turned swiftly. "Why? Why would you need *me?*"

"Because there is much of me in you, if also a surfeit of innocence. But that can be altered . . ." He laughed softly. "Have I utterly stunned you, 'Naddi?"

The boy nodded mutely.

On the final step Sario halted. "I need your youth. I need your strength, I need your talent, your Gift, your flesh, your Luza do'Orro. Because one day mine will fail."

Ignaddio's voice rose to a broken squeak. "I'm *Gifted?*"

"You are."

"But—how can you know? I haven't undergone Confirmattio yet, and you've seen none of my work"

"Bassda." He touched a shoulder briefly. "It is in me to know. And I do. The Light recognizes itself in another."

"But—"

"But. Bassda. Come with me to the Galerria; if you would begin your lessons, they are best begun today."

"Merditto," Ignaddio muttered, and then reddened. "Regretto . . . but—how long will it take? To know what you know? Will I ever?"

Sario guided him gently down the corridor. "You are thirteen, no? Eiha, let me say only this: in fifteen years' time I will be thirty-five and you twenty-eight . . ." He nodded; smiled inwardly because he told the boy everything, *everything,* yet would not be understood. A perverse jest, and ironic. "By then, I feel certain. Perhaps later it will require fewer years, but for now, fifteen. To be safe. In fifteen years I will be irreplaceable, and Alejandro will know the truth—he must know, eventually!—but he can't dismiss me *because* I am irreplaceable . . . and so he will learn to use me, to rely on me absolutely, to *require* me—and it will all become an infinitely simple matter." He looked down at the boy. "Can you wait fifteen years, 'Naddi? To be a Lord Limner?"

The boy's eyes shone. "Fifteen years is a very long time, Lord Limner."

"But such things as I will teach you require time—if you are to be me. And I am to be you."

The words within words bewildered Ignaddio. "But—I *can't* be you! Can I?"

"Eiha, perhaps not—perhaps I exaggerated." Sario made a dismissive gesture. "But I most certainly can be *you,* because I know how."

"How?"

"Lessons," Sario explained crisply. "Lessons learned from an old estranjiero, a *Folio,* and a few reclaimed pages of a most holy book." He smiled. "And now let us proceed to *your* lessons, and in fifteen years you will know absolutely everything I know. I promise it."

Ignaddio stopped short. Thrust his young, unformed chin into the air. "Make an oath of it."

Sario laughed, then inclined his head. "As you would have it." He lifted his key to his lips, kissed it, pressed it to his heart. "Nommo Matra ei Filho. Nommo Chieva do'Orro."

Ignaddio Grijalva broke into a brilliant grin of such magnitude it illuminated the corridor.

It eased the soul, that smile. *It will be well. It must be, and it shall be. And all of it worth it.*

He cast a glance over his shoulder, but could not see the stairway. Could not see the door.

Eiha. In time, neither would anyone else.

"Lord Limner?"

Sario prodded a narrow shoulder. "Bassda. We have work to do."

Always the work. Always so much. Always so little time.

Unless one were Limner. Gifted. Chi'patro.

And willing to *use* Luza do'Orro, not to extinguish it.

In the absence of day is night; in the absence of sound is silence; in the absence of light: darkness.

I did not plan for this, anticipate this, dream of this. No one would, save a madman; and I can't truthfully say he *planned for it at first, or even in the middle . . . only at the end. For reasons I can't know, save for speculation, though I'm certain he offers one. A single clever sentence full of explanation, of witty justification, explaining the* need *for such action.*

No need. Save his own.

No fear, save his own, perhaps; for what I could say to one who would listen? Who might then respond with threat, with harm?

But no one will ever know. He need explain nothing, and Alejandro will never think to threaten, to harm.

It came upon me all at once. Engulfed me utterly. Blotted out my world and created another, at his behest. His requirement.

Gift. Curse. In both there was conception, gestation, birth. I was progenitor once, though now I am prey, victim to magic, to power no one, not even those who are Limners, might comprehend. And what I—even I—can't properly describe.

Neosso Irrado. But he is more. Is other.

That some call gift, I must name nightmare.

What have you done to me?

GALLERRIA 1261

The vaulted foyer of Galerria Verrada was as coolly serene as he remembered, and as soothing in its early morning silence. But it smelled different. The current Grand Duchess, Gizella do'Granidia, had introduced a fashion from her sweltering southern home: glazed white porcelain pillars, high as a man's head and slender as a woman's corseted waist, pinhole-punctured in Tza'ab-like geometric patterns and stuffed every third day with fresh jasmine and rose petals. Set in every window recess, the pillars gave off only a faint odor now, but as the day wore on, the sun's heat would fully release the fragrance. An affectation, but he had to admit its practicality. The hotter the day, the heavier the sweat—and the stink—of the privileged visitors. Yet the hotter it became, the richer the masking scent would become.

An elegant solution to an inelegance; still, he found it effete. Without exception—but for a few Serrano mediocrities—the pictures here had been painted amid the sharp smells of blood, sweat, semen: crude and earthy smells that permeated canvas and colors. Long gone, of course, worn away by rainy winters and torrid summers, by cleanings, by the sighs of those who stood here in awe of Grijalva genius. It was too bad; the reality of power ought to be recalled in the smell of the paintings. Then he smiled at his folly. No one but ruling Grand Dukes ever knew the source of the magic, and not even they understood its real scope. That was how it must be. He had arranged that a very long time ago.

All in all, though, he much preferred the pungent scent of paint—not surprising, as he had recently finished mixing a full array. The wax- and oscurra-sealed pots rested safely in a locked coffer of his atelierro above the wine shop, ready for use. Never again would he wait until he'd found his next host. Once, he'd been so physically weak after the bleeding that the transfer had nearly been ruined. (Although once the spell was cast, feebleness had worked in his favor; restraining the worn-out old body had been simplicity itself.) Each time since then, he had come home prepared.

He had also learned not to wait until his current host began to age. He'd made that mistake two lives ago. So contented had he been with Oaquino's posting at the elegant Court of Ghillas that the years had slipped past unnoticed. Then, one shocking morning in early spring, a hip joint stabbed so sharply that he could barely rise from his silken bed. Oaquino had been but forty-two, and the swift onset of age had caught him unawares. The journey back to Tira Virte had been an agony of physical pain and mental anguish, the relocation into a healthy eighteen-year-old cause for profound relief.

Oaquino—and after him Ettoro, who'd developed the bone-fever at the ridiculously young age of thirty-five—had also taught him to check bloodlines for early death and inbreeding. Dioniso, his current host, came from excellent stock and at forty-one looked and felt ten years younger. This time he intended to give himself years and years to pick and choose and find exactly the right young man with exactly the right traits. Through the centuries, his specifications had become most exacting indeed.

First and foremost, the boy must possess good ancestry and excellent health. He must be an acknowledged talent, so that the slow revelation of real genius would not excite comment. He wanted a good-looking boy as well—and cringed to recall that graceless gawk Renzio, a choice that had been no choice at all due to his advanced years and urgent need. No more Renzios; he refused to be stuck again inside an ugly man for twenty years.

Recently he'd added family connections to his list of desired attributes. His first hosts had been mainly from lesser branches of the vast Grijalva tree. He'd reasoned that comparative anonymity was a good thing; he could pass more or less unnoticed as he accustomed himself to his new lives. And the fewer people intimate with his chosen incarnation, the fewer who must be deceived while he made the gradual changes of personality necessary to bring past behavior in line with his own character. Grazzo do'Filho, teenaged boys were *expected* to be unpredictably skittish, and adolescent artists in particular were moody en tudo paletto.

But family connections had become important to him. Dioniso was of an influential line that had produced two Lord Limners and a Ducal Mistress in the last fifty years. The advantages of position were obvious—worth the extra effort to find and worth the extra work of fooling family and friends. Dioniso was on the short list for every plum assignment; when he had expressed a desire to be posted to Niapali, authorization had come within days. Best of all, whenever he returned home, he was warmly welcomed and celebrated and given the choicest rooms available.

Though when making his selection he always hoped for a personality similar to his own, it didn't matter all that much. He'd become adept at subtle alterations in character. And if the strain of acting a part became too great, or friends grew puzzled by the changes, there were two convenient options. First, he could volunteer for a few years of itinerant duty, the shit-work of the marginally talented Grijalva. Galling as it was, the bolt-hole had served him well in several instances. Time spent as an Itinerarrio earned marks for service as well as provided a cushion of years between memories of who "Zandor" or "Timirrin" had been, and who he *really* was.

His other option was, of course, a suggestive or even fatal painting or two done in his atelierro above the wine shop. But he disliked the trouble of collecting specimens—a disgusting process at best, and occasionally dangerous.

He paused within the Galerria's great bronze doors while an assistant curatorrio rattled through a chaotic desk for a copy of the latest guide sheet. Absent from Meya Suerta these twelve years, he wanted to know whose work was currently fashionable, what changes had come to the arrangement of paintings—and what the historians were writing nowadays about his portrait of Saavedra. An acknowledged masterpiece, a priceless work of genius, a delight to anyone lucky enough to behold it—and, he grinned to himself, the despair of student Limners who could never hope to equal even the tiniest featherstroke of his brush on canvas.

At last a page of heavy paper was given him. Beautiful work, he mused idly, expert fingers judging rag content, artist's eye approving the typeface. He hadn't exercised his paper-making skills in—oh, a century or so. Perhaps he ought to take it up again as a hobby.

Closely printed on both sides, with the Grand Ducal Seal at the top, the guide sheet began with a brief reference list of Tira Virte's rulers and the Lord Limners who had served them. He nodded his thanks to the curatorrio, thinking with an inner chuckle how shocked the youth would be to know that the greatest Lord Limner of them all, and likewise the painter of most of the important and all of the finest pictures in the Galerria, was about to take a tour of his own works.

He strolled slowly along the tiled floor, pausing before paintings with which he was long familiar, pretending studiousness for the benefit of a group of silent sanctas half the Galerria away. Every so often he stopped in honest interest before a *Treaty* or *Marriage* painted by someone he'd known. Old Bennidito had really had a way with color; he'd forgotten how Tazioni could make trees look as if a breath would visibly and even audibly rustle leaves; no one, not even he, had ever outdone Adalberto for exquisite rendering of the drape of a shawl along a woman's arm. He nodded wordless tribute to long-dead colleagues, generous in his own genius, able to acknowledge theirs.

He passed the sanctas with a nod. They looked like a herd of dried-up dun cows: skinny, big-eyed, darkly tanned from incessant gardening that fed only a tiny percentage of the poor—but at least provided roses for Grand Duchess Gizella's scent-pillars. They recognized the salute with abrupt dips of white-wimpled heads, lips tightening at the sight of the Chieva do'Orro hanging from its chain around his neck.

Like all Limners who wore the Golden Key, to the Ecclesials he was an object of disgust. Sterility was unnatural, an abomination to a Faith based on the fertile Mother and Her Son, and thus a sign of divine disapproval. He'd always wondered how the Ecclesia reconciled this with the abundant fecundity of Grijalva women and the proven virility of unGifted Grijalva men. Perhaps the attitude was merely the last fierce-held remnant of the years of the Nerro Lingua, when the Grijalvas had suffered more deaths than any other family in Meya Suerta; this had been seen as a mark of divine retribution for having sheltered the chi'patros. He lost himself in reverie of his first life for a moment, remembering that old canna of a Premia Sancta, Caterin Serrano, and her banishment of all Grijalvas from the shrines and Sanctias she controlled. Alejandro had taken care of *that,* but the animosity remained. To the sanctas and sanctos of Tira Virte, the Grijalvas were an affront that centuries of service to their country had done little if anything to mitigate. Condemning them were their chi'-patro origins as bastards of infidel outlaws, their rumored magic, their power at Court, and especially their scandalous personal lives—and most especially of all, the Mistresses. The family was tainted, root, branch, and stem; the Ecclesia had not changed its attitude since Duke Renayo and Duchess Jesminia returned to Meya Suerta with fourteen ladies-in-waiting pregnant by Tza'ab outlaws, the twenty chi'patro children of those outlaws, and the corpse of Verro Grijalva. As he passed the silent sanctas, he wondered what the official line would be on the reality of Grijalva art—let alone his uses of it. The thought made him smile, and the women turned away in renewed scorn of one who dared a pleasantry to those who loathed him and all his kind.

Dismissing the sanctas from his thoughts, he stopped before a *Birth* by Guilbarro Grijalva—or, rather, attributed to Guilbarro, for of course it was his own work. He let slip a sigh as he contemplated it. A rare masterpiece, even for him. The only daughter of Cossimio I was surely the loveliest baby ever born. Painting her and her beautiful mother had been one of the great joys of his lives. He recalled it so clearly: gambas playing softly in the recesses of the summer-shaded arborra, iced drinks served whenever he flicked a finger, Grand Duchess Carmillia aglow with happiness, her baby daughter laughing the whole time. And there little Cossima was, as sweet and lively as on the day he'd finished the last rose in the vase at her mother's elbow. The child sat on Carmillia's knee, both of them dressed alike in simple white linen and a rainbow of ribbons. A golden cage rested on a pedestal beside them; noting Cossima's fascination with the birds, at some point he had opened the cage to let them fly about the arborra. He could hear her giggles still. Delight had nearly distracted him from quick-sketching her excited little face and the smile on her mother's lips. Both expressions looked down at him now, perfectly captured, looking as if painted yesterday. Very fine work, indeed. Adorable little Cossima . . . how he would have loved to have painted her *Marriage*.

But she had died of a fever before her fourth birthday. And within a year of completing this picture, Guilbarro himself was dead. Cossima's *Birth* was the only work of his in the Galerria—and the guide sheet commented on how sad it was that so promising a talent had been lost so young.

A corner of his mouth turned down. He could have done so much as Guilbarro. Clever, handsome, with all the right connections, he'd already taken the initial steps toward becoming Lord Limner. The *Birth of Cossima* had, in fact, been his audition.

Scenes from the past cast dark veils over the portrait of the laughing baby and her radiant mother. A hunting accident; a broken leg from which Guilbarro was recovering nicely—and then disaster. Some fool of a sancta mixed pain medication incorrectly. It was discovered within two weeks, but by then the damage had been done. He was well and truly addicted.

They'd tried to wean him from it. But even had the withdrawal worked, his ambitions were finished. No Lord Limner could be made vulnerable by addiction to liquor, gambling, sexual habits, or drugs. The potential for subornation was too great. Even if the medical establishment avowed him free of it, the danger of relapse would always be there. Neither the do'Verradas nor the Grijalvas could countenance a Lord Limner with a drug habit in his past.

The agony of that life's ruin very nearly matched the agony of never having *quite* enough of the drug. He could neither think nor work in such a state. But he understood his choices all too well: he could suffer through the cure and survive and never become Lord Limner, or he could abandon this life and assume another.

Guilbarro's younger brother Matteyo saved him—and in the saving condemned himself. He couldn't bear remembering, but suffocating memories swept like thick tapestry curtains across his vision. Desperation led Matteyo to procure drugs enough to augment doses that became weaker every day in the attempted cure. Devotion caused him to bring Guilbarro his paints, a canvas, a mirror. The hell of it was that the self-portrait was Matteyo's idea. *"Paint yourself into being well again,"* the boy said. *"You're good enough, 'Barro, you can do it. I know you can."*

Oh, he had. He had. Despite shaking hands and drugged dreaminess, he painted Guilbarro. And when the work was done and the time came, he actually explained the process. *And Matteyo agreed.* By painting Guilbarro to the life, he had painted Matteyo to his death.

"I'm a mediocrity, all the moualimos say it. But you're a true genius, 'Barro. You deserve your chance to be Lord Limner. The world deserves to see your work. I don't matter. You do."

And so it had been done. He'd Blooded the paints with Matteyo's help, and killed Matteyo with a quick, merciful thrust of Saavedra's golden needle in Guilbarro's painted heart. Easy enough to call it suicide: despair at tragic circumstances, agony of withdrawal, and so on. Easier still to weep when Guilbarro's corpse was discovered, with Matteyo vanished from it. Selfless, generous, loving Matteyo: the only one he'd ever regretted.

Two days later, with the body safely buried, he wept while he tore the Guilbarro portrait to shreds. A month after that, within the fresh and healthy fifteen-year-old body, ready to honor the boy's devotion by becoming Lord Limner not just for himself but for Matteyo, too, he found himself under arrest. Someone had discovered Matteyo's illegal purchases of drugs; the boy was accused of assisting Guilbarro's suicide. The irony had escaped him at the time, and caused no more than a bitter grimace now. The thought of Matteyo still hurt too much.

Convicted of the lesser charge—though Matteyo's branch of the family was influential, the scandal required a name to hang it on— he was banished. The remote and arguably civilized barony of Esquita was a misery of empty hills and emptier minds, whose ruler required cosseting because of his one asset: iron ore. Not for sixteen long years did he return to Meya Suerta, not until word came that Matteyo's mother was dying. The Grijalvas appealed to Duke Cossimio I, who allowed him to come home for the death watch: the bond between mother and son was the most sacred in the Faith. As she lay dying, he found Timirrin and began the next painting—began, too, the displays of frantic grief that accounted for Matteyo's suicide soon after his mother's death.

He blinked a blur from his eyes, still thinking of Matteyo, and saw again Cossima's sweet little face. Almost two hundred years since he'd painted her plump fists reaching for the bright-feathered birds. Though visitors to the Galerria sorrowed over her tragedy, they left remembering her laughing black eyes and her mother's joy. Such was the power of sheer artistic skill, nothing to do with magic.

No picture of Matteyo hung at Palasso Grijalva for the family to remember him by. A portrait existed, though no one would ever see it. He reminded himself that when next he visited his atelierro above the wineshop, he must paint another sprig of blue-flowered rosemary, for remembrance, near the section of the *Peintraddo Memorrio* dedicated to his loved, lost Matteyo.

He walked on past several generations, and stopped before a huge picture by the greatest Lord Limner who had ever served Tira Virte: Riobaro Grijalva. No fewer than eleven paintings here were Riobaro's. As he regarded the *Marriage of Benetto I and Rosira della Marei*—she of the all-powerful banking family—the smile returned to his lips. Not because the portrait was a masterwork (it was), but because every minute of his life as Riobaro had been a masterwork.

Timirrin's life had been quiet. He studied, taught, copied what he was told, and kept to himself for eighteen placid, uneventful years. The final five of them, however, he'd spent watching and marveling as Riobaro grew from talented fourteen-year-old to accomplished Limner of nearly twenty. Riobaro had been perfect from the day the Confirmattio had proved his sterility. After Timirrin's existence as a nonentity, power was calling again. And

Riobaro *was* perfect: tall, long-limbed, heart-catchingly beautiful, with melting dark eyes and full lips and riotous black curls that didn't begin to gray until his forty-fifth year. All his line were long-lived (for Gifteds) and he had excellent connections at Court, his mother's half-brother being Lord Limner. Best of all, he was a passionate admirer of the work of Sario Grijalva. His style was as nearly identical to the revered Lord Limner's as he could make it; even in childhood he had copied and recopied all the available paintings. Happily, he was born into a time when slavish imitation of long-dead Masters was approved. No one tried to dissuade him from his ambition to be the next Sario.

His wish was granted.

When Riobaro's uncle died in 1115, Riobaro was the only possible candidate to replace him. The widowed Duchess Enricia liked and trusted him, and was pleased that her young son's regency council now included a man who shared her own prime objective: the gold-filled coffers of the Principio della Diettro Mareia. They were determined to see Benetto married to the Principio's heiress.

Trade treaties were negotiated that Riobaro went to Diettro Mareia himself to paint. He took with him drawings of Benetto and brought back similar drawings of Rosira. The pair were in love with none but each other practically from the cradle—and he hadn't even had to use his magic to do it. Yet while everyone waited for the children to grow to marriageable age, Riobaro did use his art and his arts as necessary to cement ducal power in the provinces. Tira Virte thrived. And when Benetto reached his majority in 1122, becoming Grand Duke in fact as well as name, the Lord Limner made sure that the Grijalva selected as his Mistress was a close relation to himself. As marriage to Rosira della Marei neared, he also made sure that Riobaro's cousin Diega Grijalva sent her lover on his way with a smile and many excellent memories—even as she clutched the deed to a manor house and a large tract of Casteyan forest that had been her lover's parting gift.

Riobaro died, universally mourned, in the fifty-third year of his age and the twenty-fifth year of his service as Lord Limner. He had guided Tira Virte not only to greater prominence but to true greatness; his was a painterly gift seen once in five generations; he was beloved of all the do'Verradas and all his countrymen (with the exception of the provincial barons he'd brought to heel, but they kept their mutterings to themselves). Of all Lord Limners, Riobaro was the only one to have an official portrait within the Galerria Verrada.

Moving along to regard it now, the man who had been Riobaro let another sigh escape him for that perfect life. Too bad he hadn't been able to follow through with another one just like it, but he'd reckoned without the sexual vigor of Domaos' body and its helpless physical passion for Benecitta do'Verrada.

The daughter of Benetto and Rosira was a walking scandal from the day she first put one foot in front of the other. The terror of her servants, the despair of her mother, the torment of her younger brother, she was also the incomparable jewel of her father's indulgent heart. Gazing up at her *Marriage*—a painting he had not done and in which no one ever noticed her husband—he reflected once again that with her, he'd never stood a chance.

Poised to begin another brilliant career as Lord Limner, he had been completely thunderstruck by Benecitta. Bold and beautiful, nineteen years old to his supposedly mature thirty, she had decided that if her brother had a Grijalva Mistress, it was only fair that she possess a Grijalva Lover. The man who would surely be named Lord Limner when Riobaro's successor died was, to her mind, the perfect choice. Domaos—not as devastatingly handsome as Riobaro but not painful to the eyes, either—fell headlong into her trap and her bed. Knowing he ought to have known better, astounded that sex could have such powerful magic of its own, still he carried on a two-year affair with her in total secrecy. Not since Saavedra had a woman fascinated him so. The danger of discovery only added spice. Benecitta never knew of the crimes great and small he committed to ensure that secrecy, even while cursing himself for a reckless fool.

Then her father announced her betrothal to a fiercely proud baron whose attractions were measured in square miles of vineyards. Benecitta was perfectly willing for the marriage to take place—so long as Domaos was posted to her new home as resident Limner. Torn between passion and prudence, eventually he found courage enough to decline the honor. He couldn't go on bespelling or killing people who saw what they shouldn't—and Benecitta's betrothed had sharper eyes than most. But it was Baron Fillipi do'Gebatta's vast experience of women—far vaster than even three previous wives could account for—that proved Domaos' undoing. The baron's taste ran to virgins; he knew one when he bedded one; Benecitta definitely was not. The morning after the wedding, he stormed through Palasso Verrada to the Grand Ducal chambers and ripped the *Marriage* portrait into many, many pieces before it was even dry.

The union was annulled. Benecitta was packed off to the

strictest and most remote Sanctia in Tira Virte—"I hope she learns humility, for compordotta is obviously beyond her!" as her infuriated mother put it. Domaos lived in dread for days—while frantically painting a self-portrait—before the Grand Duke finally realized the extent of his daughter's "friendship" with the Limner. Domaos was seized one midnight, taken in chains to the border, and forbidden to set foot in Tira Virte again.

Mere thought of those years made him shudder. It was one thing to travel from court to court, city to city, painting *Marriages, Births, Deeds,* and *Wills.* An Itinerrario was an honored guest, a precious gift from Tira Virte, and well-paid besides. But an uncredentialed roving painter was shunned. Domaos eked out a marginal living in Ghillasian and Niapalese towns where anyone who could draw a straight line with a ruler became the local archivist—and who did not appreciate the arrival of a Grijalva Limner, disgraced though he was. Competition for every commission was intense, pay was despicable, Domaos was constantly watched while in the presence of young ladies (a rare occurrence; the scandal was common knowledge), and the work humiliated one who had twice reached the pinnacle of his profession.

In twenty-one years he gained not so much as a glimpse of another Grijalva. Because they were precious commodities, they did not travel without armed escort. He could not waylay one on the road. He was cut off not only from his country but from another life to replace this miserable one.

Finally, at the astounding age of fifty-three, with his health failing and his desperation growing, he wrote to Benetto's son, now Grand Duke Benetto II. The reply came back with a delegation of two Grijalvas and a sancta well-schooled in medicine: Domaos could return home to die.

As for Benecitta—she had been forgiven years ago. Her father loved her too much *not* to forgive her, though at his Grand Duchess's urgings he did leave their daughter incarcerated at the Sanctia for nine long years. But in 1162 Benetto was in an expansive mood—his Heir had just wed the colossally wealthy Verradia da'Taglisi—and so agreed at last to the pleadings of Count Dolmo do'Alva to free Benecitta. The count, no more proof against her allure than Domaos had been, had loved her since their youth. Theirs was the *Marriage* from which she flirted down at all and sundry, as captivating at thirty as she had been at nineteen.

Matra ei Filho, he thought, shaking his head. The painting was nearly a century old, he hadn't seen her since their final impassioned night together, and she'd been dead over forty years—yet he could still feel the helpless coil of desire in his belly. Amazing woman.

No, he *had* seen her again. She'd visited Domaos at Palasso Grijalva as he lay dying—to tell him she forgave him, if you please. So much for humility.

Odd that he hadn't recalled her visit until now. Then again, he'd been so feeble that he barely had strength to prepare his paints for the portrait that gave him Renzio Grijalva: a sixteen-year-old mediocrity in whose lanky, graceless, plain-faced body he'd spent a blissfully quiet twenty years.

But no more Renzios. His requirements were set, and this time he would give himself the leisure to make the perfect choice. It was time he became Lord Limner again—especially if the more recent pictures in the Galerria were any indication. Dreadful stuff, barely competent, cloyingly sentimental, the palettos made up of mint-greens and cherry-pinks so sweet his teeth ached. He must become Lord Limner before artistic standards sank beyond hope of recovery.

He walked on, bored by what he saw, irritated by the process he knew was to come. It was so annoying, the balancing of one need against another. The boy must be young enough to provide a goodly long time in the body, but old enough to be Confirmattio. He must be talented and far enough along in the training to evidence adult mastery, but not so individual in his style or set in his ways that the inevitable change to complete genius would be too great for credence. So many adjustments that must be made each time . . . so much brilliance that must be hidden, sometimes for years, until it was excusable by maturity . . . so many classes that must be endured again and again, taught by moualimos moronnos who barely knew purple from puce or a rose from a rhododendron . . . so much dissembling and deception and deference. Nommo Chieva do'Orro, it was hard sometimes, very hard!

And sometimes, for years at a stretch, he forgot why it was necessary.

For Saavedra, certainly. For the day when he would finally free her, and she would finally be his. Had she yet realized her mistake? Eiha, he could wait. Because there had come to be another reason, and on the occasions when he was most brutally honest with himself, he knew that reason to be far purer than even love.

He had painted five thousand canvases, ten thousand. There remained in him thousands more. His Gift must not be lost, not before he had fulfilled it. He would *know* when he had created absolute and ultimate perfection, the one masterwork that would justify everything he had done in the name of—and through the medium of—his Limner Blood.

But not yet. Not just yet. Despite all the inconveniences of establishing a new life, despite the inevitable decline into age and the fear of not finding the right host—*that* painting still waited for him. It would be the culmination of his many lives, and his truest immortality.

Saavedra waited for him, too, inside a painting that in his youth he had thought was the finest he would ever do. How foolish he had been! Only look at what he'd painted in the last three hundred years! How she would marvel, and weep for sheer joy, when he showed her the final masterwork—and she would know at last that love was nothing compared to the splendor of his genius, his Gift.

The centuries had taught him that. He had come to know himself and to understand the jealousy that had caused it all. He'd forgotten what Alejandro looked like, but he could still see Saavedra's face as she beheld his work, with that in her eyes which loved its beauty and loved him for its creation. He had mistaken the look she'd given Alejandro as something to rival her love for him. But it wasn't the same. Not the same at all. Her feelings for Alejandro were mere carnal urgings, not the supreme transcendence only his art could engender in her. The do'Verrada Duke had held her body in his arms for a little while—but *he* held her deepest soul in his hands forever.

As he walked slowly past gilt-framed mediocrities and occasional competencies, he wondered when he should release her. Soon? During this life? The next, when he was young again? Eiha, no. Not until he had painted the perfection that would be his love-gift to her, finalizing his claim on her spirit.

But at least he could go to her now, and promise that one day he would be ready. Ignoring the page in his hand, he strode to the far end of the Galerria, intent on the place her portrait had always occupied. True, he had not seen it in over a hundred years—had not trusted himself to view her face. But he was older now; he understood everything; he owed it to her to tell her so, even if she could not hear him.

Gone.

She was gone!

In her place was an insipid picture of Renata do'Pracanza in her old age, backgrounded by the sere pallor of the wasteland Alejandro had dug her out of to become his Duchess.

He spun on one heel, ready to shout down the coffered ceiling in fury. How *dared* they remove his painting?

In the next instant he calmed himself. It was surely in a workroom being cleaned, or getting a new frame, or had been taken to Palasso Grijalva to be studied as the masterpiece it was by awed young Limners who could never hope to equal it.

He promised himself to ask—discreetly—when he returned to the front desk. For now, he directed his gaze to the *Duke Alejandro*. It used to hang in his own chambers in Palasso Verrada. Night after night he'd considered stabbing that proud chest. Burning those long fingers that wore a luminous gray moonstone ring in memory of Saavedra's eyes. Acid-scarring that handsome face, blackening that crooked front tooth, painting all the exposed skin with symptoms of sifilisso.

Killing him, as he so richly deserved.

Alejandro. He stood there in the prime of his years, a plain curtain of dull black velurro behind him, his beauty all the more compelling for the bleak backdrop. Beside him, every other do'Verrada appeared either a barbarian or a beribboned bravo. His physical beauty was both of the warrior and the poet. His consciousness of worth—so hard-won!—combined with his genuine modesty so plainly in his face that even the clumsiest Limner could have painted his portrait and been hailed a genius. But there was also in his green-flecked eyes and in the curve of his lips a terrible grief that no one but Sario could capture—and no one but Sario had caused.

"You were what I made you," whispered the former Lord Limner to his Duke. "Because of me, you gained the wisdom they all praise. With me at your side, you thwarted all who opposed you, fought when you had to, made peace when you could, and did all that had to be done for this land we both loved. But you were the man *I* made you. Without me, you would have ruined yourself over her. I saved you from that. Because of me, you became a legend."

And Alejandro had known it. He repressed a smile at the memory of himself on what everyone thought was his deathbed, withered hand clasped gently in fingers still strong and supple. He and his Duke had both been only thirty-four years old.

"Fare you well, old friend," Alejandro murmured, tears brilliant

in his fine eyes. *"Everything I've accomplished—I could never have done it without you."*

Nice of him, Sario thought at the time, to admit it.

A few days later, the worn-out body died, and he watched with wide, carefully awestruck eyes as the great Duke came to pay his respects.

"The painting we discuss this morning is a work by Oaquino Grijalva, called Il Cofforro. Can any of you tell me the origin of this nommo do'arrtio?"

Called Il WHAT?

His head snapped around. Seven Grijalva boys, none past Confirmattio, were seating themselves on the floor beside a vastly populated picture Sario didn't remember painting—either as Oaquino or anyone else. He edged closer, glancing at the work: his, en verro, abruptly recalling the hours he'd spent mixing exactly the right color for the incredible wig worn by Pepennar II of Ghillas, a shade of red never seen in nature.

"Eiha?" barked the moualimo. "Why Il Cofforro?"

When did they think that *up?* He folded his arms and repressed a glare.

"Dirado? Can you answer?"

A boy's voice piped up, "Moualimo Temirro, it's because all his pictures have such peculiar hairstyles."

He winced. Fashions in Aute-Ghillas in 1210 had been uniquely absurd.

"Wrong," snarled Temirro—who was beginning to remind Sario of Otavio. "Anyone else? Cansalvio?"

"It was the way he did hair, Moualimo," another boy said in a smugly superior tone.

"Indeed? So he plaited all those wigs with his own hands, did he? Arriano, perhaps you can be more precise?"

The youngest of them, scarcely nine years old, gulped. "He—he *painted* the hair very well, Moualimo. On the canvas, I mean. It looks so real you could—you feel like you could curl it around your finger."

"The Hairdresser"! Still, he supposed he ought to be mollified by recognition of an effect he'd worked very hard to achieve. Matra knew that Ghillas in those days fifty years past had provided ample chance to perfect it: all those massed curls and coiling braids, intricate crimps and cascading wigs. . . .

"Hmph," grunted Temirro. It was all the acknowledgment any

boy ever got for a right answer, Sario felt sure. More and more like Otavio, he thought, and hid a grin.

"We've established Oaquino's claim to fame—his only one, I might add. You'll have noted, I'm sure, that his placement of figures in this *Treaty* is exceptionally awkward, if not actually ridiculous."

I'd like to see anyone get twenty-seven people into one painting when no two of them would consent to be in the same room with a third, and four of them were assassinated before I even finished the damned thing!

But it seemed someone had come to his defense. He caught the tail end of Cansalvio's question about how hard *was* it to make all those people stand still long enough to be painted?

"Moronno! You think all were present at the same time? Recall which *Treaty* this is!"

They fell silent. He racked his own brain trying to remember. He'd painted it, he ought to—oh, yes. Pepennar had rounded up his fractious vassals—some of them nearly kings in their own right—and forced them to sign a treaty of undying friendship and mutually profitable trade with Tira Virte. The friendship had died with Pepennar twelve years later; the trade had survived. Trade always did.

But now he knew why these boys were studying this particular painting: Ghillas, it was strongly rumored, was angling for the betrothal of its Princess to the current Heir. This was unheard-of, that Tira Virte's huge and powerful northern neighbor would actively solicit a marriage rather than wait in regal disdain for Tira Virte to come begging. Talk also had it, though, that Don Arrigo was resisting this honor with all his might, for he deeply and genuinely loved his Mistress, even twelve years into the association. *Eiha, the do'Verrada passions,* he thought acidly, *and the Grijalva beauties—ever a dangerous combination. . . .*

The boys had taken sketchpads out of their satchels and were dutifully lining up to take a brief but intense look at the painting. He knew this drill well; he'd been through it often enough, and would endure its tedium again. Each boy would choose something specific about the picture and attempt to reproduce it. For older boys, the lesson was to attempt something not yet mastered: the flow of drapery, the shadows thrown by vast candle-masses of overhead lustrossos, the arrangement of background figures not touched by direct light. These youngsters would merely repeat lessons already taught back at the Palasso by copying something they already knew how to do from the work of a recognized master—even one called Il Cofforro, whose only real talent was for doing hair.

One of the boys merely glanced at the painting when it came his turn. He sat back down on the floor, hunched over his sketchbook, and with breathtaking rapid strokes outlined the entire composition. Sario's brows arched. *Arrogant little merditto,* he thought, smiling in spite of himself. He spent the next minutes pretending to admire a *Marriage* by Grigarro—a rival of Oaquino's—then strolled over to Temirro and introduced himself.

"Itinerarrio Dioniso?" A tentative smile touched the old man's face—wrinkled and age-spotted, though he could not have been fifty. "Son of Giaberta?"

He nodded—dangerously; he had no idea of "his" mother's name. "She's well?"

"Healthy as a two-year-old filly, for all that she's sixty!"

This was not welcome news. "Saluto!" he replied heartily, to the old lady's health. "Does she still live in the Palasso?" he asked, praying that she did not.

"No, more's the pity. Wed to some twice-widowered lordling with a hundred children and a thousand square miles of Joharran desert. I miss her. It's ten years, and we correspond regularly, but I miss her. Go see her, she'll be glad of—*Rafeyo!*" he barked all at once. "Chieva do'Orro, what are you doing?"

The ambitious stripling looked up from his work, but not with fright. There was defiance, but also something deeper, something he'd seen in his own eyes—*his own eyes*—centuries ago. He always experienced a twinge of guilt when he took a boy whose eyes burned this way. Who knew but what he deprived the world of a genius to rival his own? Still, the feeling always passed. His Gift was the greater. His Gift must be served. If the boy possessed the fire of a Neosso Irrado, better to quench it before it could truly rival Sario.

And, en verro, it was infinitely easier to choose someone whose fire already shone. He needn't pretend half so much.

Rafeyo rose from his place beside Arriano, showing a grace unusual in one his age. Most boys of thirteen or so battled constantly against elbows and knees and feet that never seemed to do as told. But Rafeyo's movements were lithe and supple as he approached Temirro.

"What's this?" the moualimo demanded. "What's this, then?"

"The *Treaty of Aute-Ghillas.*"

"The whole painting?"

Rafeyo nodded.

"Was the assignment to sketch the whole painting?"

"No, Moualimo Temirro."

A slow, controlled inhalation. "Then, if you would be *so* kind, explain why you have done precisely that!"

Rafeyo's face was yet a muddle of childish softness around the sharpest of Grijalva noses. But, practiced at such extrapolation, Sario saw the promise of fine looks. More, he saw the certainty of fire in that hasty but perceptive sketch. He even heard it in the man-child voice when Rafeyo at last framed his reply.

"A painting must be viewed as a whole, not an assemblage of parts. I can't separate out one thing from the composition as if I were a milkmaid straining curds." He paused, deliberate in his insult as he tacked on, "—Moualimo."

He had barely bitten back another grin when, at Rafeyo's next words, he was ready to strangle the boy himself.

"Most of it *is* curdled, in fact. If you'll look closely, you'll see I've changed it. It's much better now."

Temirro seized the sketchpad, ripped the page out, and held it up to the *Treaty*. There was barely time to note that several figures had been moved and most of the Throne Room's tapestries were omitted when, with a snort, Temirro tore Rafeyo's page in half. "Sit down," he growled, "do as you're told."

Rebellion flashed in Tza'ab-black eyes, and sheer fury at seeing his work—*his work!*—destroyed. But Rafeyo was still just a child, and his future until his Confirmattio was in Temirro's gnarled hands. He did not bow, he did not yield, but he did sit down and do as told.

"Miserable little wretch," Temirro muttered. "His mother's fault, of course. But for your ears alone, Itinerarrio, he's among the best I've ever taught."

"Eiha, it won't do to let him know that for a few more years, though." He was still stinging from the slight to Oaquino's work—criticism from a thirteen-year-old boy!—but knew he must make the effort to be casual with the old man.

"If I had my way, he'd *never* know how good he is. I've seen things from him you'd swear were done by an Aguo or Seminno or Sanguo!"

"Truly?" His interest in the boy increased. "One of us?"

It was more than a query about his painterly talents. Temirro understood and shrugged. "Not yet Confirmattio. If he becomes so, I hope he learns the rights and wrongs of it before he learns too much."

Sario nodded at this likewise oblique reference to magic's power. A few moments later he excused himself and walked back to the bronze doors, musing about young Rafeyo all the length of the Galerria. Sunlight now baked the jasmine and roses within the scent-pillars, and he was sure the odor would cling to his clothes. Repressing a sneeze, he handed the guide sheet back to the assistant curatorrio and took a half-dozen steps before remembering to ask about the portrait of Saavedra.

"Oh, you mean *The First Mistress?* Permanently removed to storage. Grand Duke Cossimio's mother didn't much like it—or maybe it was his grandmother, I forget. But it hasn't been on display for years."

"It hasn't?"

"I don't think it was even uncrated during the last cleaning—but someone might've done that for the inventory in 1216—the one ordered by the Nazha Coronna." When Sario continued to look as blank as a virgin canvas, the curatorrio explained, "Tazita. Grand Duke Arrigo II's Mistress. What she ordered was done, and done at once." Though he was far too young to have known her, there was genuine and awed respect in his voice for the force she had been.

"I remember," he replied, though he did not; he'd been out of Tira Virte for most of the Uncrowned Grand Duchess' rule.

"But as regards the painting, if you want specially to see it, perhaps I can ask—"

"No," he managed. "No, I was just curious. It—it's something of a legend." He'd been about to say, *It was a favorite of mine.* Which could not be if no one had looked on it in so many years.

"And a legend *she* is," sighed the curatorrio. "Sad story. Very sad. I think that's why it was removed. Yes, I'm sure of it. Cossimio's mother it was, Grand Duchess Verradia—she came here as a young bride, wept when she heard the tale, and it was taken down."

"How . . . compassionate . . . of her," Sario said through gritted teeth. "Dolcha mattena, curatorrio."

He raged in silence all the way to the steps of the Portalla Granda. Some sentimental idiot of a girl had shed a few tears over Saavedra's "sad story" and *that* was the reason no one had seen his masterpiece in so long? The crowning achievement of his youthful art and magic, the instrument of his revenge in oil and blood and oak panel, had not been seen by *anyone?*

He should have known. For an artist of his caliber, he had been singularly blind. The evidence had been right there in front of him, and he hadn't seen it. *The First Mistress* was longer and wider than the *Duchess Renata* now occupying the space—yet no telltale darkness around the replacement indicated where a larger painting had once hung. It had been missing so long from the Galerria that faded wallpaper had been replaced. Taken down and forgotten, except when a Grand Duke died and complete inventory was taken of his possessions. . . .

Sudden sunshine blinded him in earnest, and the sneeze that jasmine and roses had sired was finally born. He wiped his eyes and his nose with a square of silk from his pocket, prosaically distracted from trancelike fury.

Eiha, what did it matter who saw or didn't see the painting? *He* knew it was unequaled. *He* knew the sweet taste of his vengeance. What did anyone else matter?

Eyes adjusting to the fierce blaze of noon, Sario crossed the Zocalo Palasso and made his way home—reminding himself that, as he settled into teaching and the occasional commission, he really must keep track of young Rafeyo.

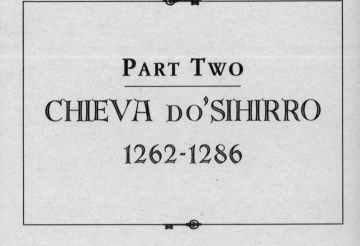

PART TWO
CHIEVA DO'SIHIRRO
1262-1286

PART TWO

"*. . . and* then—and *then*— what do you think happened?"

A dozen children bounced and wriggled on blankets flung on the lawn. "Tell, tell!" one chanted; "Did he win?" cried another; "What about the princess?" demanded a third. "Please finish the story, 'Chella, please!"

She sat laughing in their midst, lovely as the spring morning and painted in its colors: eyes of iris-blue, sungold hair, skin pale and soft as new roses, wearing a gown the sweet green of spring leaves. As she resumed the tale, and the knight battled enchantment while the princess struggled against a wicked stepmother, the servant who watched from a doorway conducted her own war against tears. Agnetta had raised the girl practically from the cradle, and regarded her now with love aching in her bones. Mechella was so young, so beautiful, so innocent and trusting—and so soon to be the wife of a man she had adored since girlhood, a man Agnetta feared would break her heart.

Had Queen Mirisse lived, there would be someone to consult about her misgivings. But the good Queen was dead these fifteen years, leaving behind a royal husband who yet grieved for her, a little daughter whose only maternal affection had come from a maidservant, and a son deprived of such tender influences entirely. King Enrei, second of that name in Ghillas, was a fond father but overburdened by cares of state; after his wife's death he had agreed with his ministers that the six-year-old Crown Prince be given a masculine household to educate him in his future position. The King's sister had for fifteen years ruled these men as well as the ladies assigned to Mechella—no difficulty in recognizing the source material for the wicked stepmother of the current tale! Hatchet-faced Princess Permilla could often be heard in the children's wing of the palace declaring that "It is a *king* we are making here!"—as if a little boy was batter to be stiffened into dough, pounded into perfection, and crammed into a baking tin marked *Enrei III.* Permilla was as rigorous with Mechella in a different way: she attempted to mold her niece in her own rigid image. Praise be that she had failed. Praise also that last year when

Mechella came of age, Permilla had been eased out of authority over the girl.

Replacing their mother's single-hearted love with the fawnings of inferiors and the protocols of Princess Permilla was not the wisest thing the King had ever done. But both children survived, possibly due to hereditary stubbornness that pitted willful nephew and niece against mulish aunt. By her own lights, Permilla had failed with both of them and the fault was all theirs. Agnetta could have told her—had a Princess of Ghillas demeaned herself to personal conversation with a servant—that the children would have done anything to please her if only she had shown them a little of the maternal love they had lost.

Now, at twenty-one, Crown Prince Enrei was quite full of himself. He'd been tumbling chambermaids since the age of fourteen (despite dire warnings, for Ghillas had an unhappy history of royal bastards), and lived for blood sports. Liberation three years ago from Permilla had set him running wild to pursue all the delights open to a man young, handsome, rich, royal, and universally admired—at least to his face. Still, he possessed a good mind and a kind heart, and it was confidently hoped that he would settle down, do his duty, and marry. Eventually.

Mechella, on the other hand, was all eagerness to wed. She was everything a father could wish—royal or not. Only Agnetta knew how desperately unhappy she had been since her mother's death, how she hid it, and how deeply she needed to be loved. With worried eyes Agnetta watched her Princess now, wondering if next spring her precious girl's smile would be as bright, her laughter as easy and carefree. She had heard things about that land across the Montes Astrappas, and feared the lightning they were named for that would separate her from her darling forever. Tira Virte was a place barely civilized by Ghillasian standards, despite its airs and graces and the proud propagation of the Grijalva Limners' art. It was the Grijalvas who worried Agnetta—but not those who were Limners.

Mechella finished the triumphal conclusion of the tale to a rousing cheer, and just in time, too: the tutor who schooled servants' offspring finally located his wayward charges and shooed them back to class. He did not scold Mechella, of course—who in the palace ever could, ever had? (Always excepting Permilla Pruneface.) Indeed, as Mechella pleaded the beauty of the day as an excuse for stealing his students for an hour, the tutor's stern expression softened to a smile. Seeing this, Agnetta's worry abated slightly. Who could fail to adore this girl?

Answer came from unhappy experience in her long-ago youth: beauty and charm and innocence were useless when a man who ought to adore his bride was instead deeply enamored of his mistress.

Alone now, Mechella extended long legs to stretch, reaching her arms high overhead as if to embrace the warm spring sun. Agnetta knew there was scant time for what must be accomplished before noon—a complete change of clothing to what Mechella laughingly termed Court Finery Second Class—but despite the need to hurry, Agnetta let her be. This was the last of her girlhood; soon the adult chaos of celebrations, preparations, and farewells would begin.

She was so young. Too young.

At length the servant bowed to necessity. Approaching Mechella, calling her name, she ached anew at the ardent excitement of the lovely face turned to her.

"There's news?"

Of her own misgivings, Agnetta was blunt. "The Grijalva has returned from Tira Virte—and your father is as happy as a pup wagging two tails."

The next instant Agnetta was being whirled across velvety manicured lawn and Mechella was singing with laughter.

" 'Chella! Stop that, I'm dizzy—"

"So am I! Isn't it perfect? I'm to marry Arrigo do'Verrada!" She kissed Agnetta's wrinkled cheeks, her own smooth skin flushed with joy. "We'll marry and have a dozen children and be the happiest couple in the world!"

Matreia e Filei, I hope you are right, my darling. Extricating herself from the jubilant dance, she caught at Mechella's hands. " 'Chella, listen to me. Is this what you want? Is *he* what you truly want?"

The Princess laughed again. "Agnetta! I've been in love with him since his state visit! For all these five long years I've dreamed of nothing else! But Papa's been so stubborn—I told him when I turned eighteen that I was ready to marry, but he kept putting it off—" Headlong chatter ceased. Abruptly suspicious, knowing Agnetta's every expression far too well, Mechella demanded, "What's wrong? Tell me what you're thinking!"

This she most certainly would not do. She knew what Mechella did not: that amenable as Arrigo's parents had been two years ago to the alliance, Arrigo himself had balked. Not even Lord Limner Mequel's own portrait of Mechella last year had moved him toward a betrothal. What had changed his mind? Or perhaps the right question was *had* it changed?

Eihia, to the Flames with his mind! What about his heart?

Mechella made a face that mocked Agnetta's sour look. "You're thinking of that Grijalva woman, aren't you? Don't worry, Enrei explained it all to me."

"He *did?*" gasped Agnetta, vowing to wallop the Crown Prince herself if he'd revealed anything that might hurt his sister.

"Eihia, yes," Breezily now, mimicking the sophistication of her elders: "All do'Verradas take such women as their official Mistresses. It's a traditional arrangement with the Limner family." A little-girl giggle escaped. "Enrei likes the idea of an official Mistress!"

"I'll just bet he does. What else did he say?"

"First of all, when the Heir is betrothed, the Mistress retires from Court with gifts of property and jewels and all that." She dismissed the Grijalva with a negligent wave of her hand. "The do'Verradas are very generous. Second, the Mistresses are always barren, so there's no danger of a bastard claimant to the throne. We know what trouble *that* can cause! Third—and I think Enrei will use this with Papa—it's much better to have the Heir keep to one woman rather than cause scandals chasing noble virgins at Court, or tavern wenches who might not be very clean." A vague frown informed Agnetta that her innocent darling had no idea that "clean" referred neither to laundry nor to bathing.

Mechella's expression turned mischievous. "Finally, Enrei says, think how lucky the wives of the Heirs are, knowing their husbands know *everything* about pleasing them in bed!"

"'Chella!" But the admonishment was automatic, and she couldn't help a smile. Annoying as he sometimes was, the Crown Prince actually made a good deal of sense. Still . . . "I'd like to be present when your brother presents this Mistress notion to the King. Birthday fireworks would be nothing to compare!"

They laughed and started for the terrace of the Pallaiso Millia Luminnai, where tonight every one of the Thousand Candles would be lighted in the grand ballroom when the news was officially announced. Mechella chattered all the way to her suite: how handsome Arrigo was, how charming, how accomplished at music and hunting and chess (which Mechella had labored to learn after his visit), how wise a ruler he would be, how much she desired to help him in his duties, how she yearned for children, how she hoped to be accepted by his people . . . and on and on, all with a sweet ingenuousness that wrung Agnetta's heart.

She listened in silence, telling herself that if this marriage was what Mechella truly wanted, then all speed to the wedding. She did not say that the kindness of a grown man to the fifteen-year-old daughter of his royal host had nothing to do with what would happen between them when they were husband and wife. Agnetta knew herself hopelessly prejudiced, but in that moment of spring with her Princess outshining the sunlight, Agnetta could believe that when it was written, this tale, too, would have the happiest of endings. Faced with such goodness and such determination to love and be loved, how could Arrigo do'Verrada do otherwise than adore her—she who was so young and beautiful, so kind and gentle, so innocent and trusting . . . .

". . . and so insipid it beggars the imagination. And they expect me to *marry* this infant!"

Tazia Grijalva cast a quick glance at the tall, uniformed figure pacing the morning room of her little caza in the best part of Meya Suerta. Any other woman would have told him to sit down and stop carving up her carpets with his ceremonial spurs. But Tazia had never in her life been like any other woman—not even any other Grijalva woman.

"She's very pretty," Tazia said. "I've seen the portrait."

"She's well enough, I suppose." Arrigo gave a shrug that made the gold braids of his epalettos dance and glitter. A handsome man, he appeared to best advantage in the green tunic, black trousers, and high black boots of the Shagarras—an honorary captaincy in a regiment that for the last century had done nothing more militarily strenuous than stand sentry at Palasso Verrada. The deep color of the tunic brought out the gold flecks in his brown eyes, and the epalettos lent pleasing width to his shoulder. But although he was just thirty, the wavy black hair was a touch thin at the crown of his head and his devotion to long hours outdoors had put tiny lines into the tanned skin around his eyes. More serious were the twin furrows of discontent framing his full lips. She knew their source. He was in a uniquely painful position: an intelligent, capable, dedicated man who had nothing to do but wait for his father to die. This, more than his years, had marked his face, this terrible knowledge that he was fully prepared to serve his people while also knowing such service could only come when the father he loved was dead.

It had been Tazia's task these twelve years to make him forget as often as possible, to keep those lines from deepening any further, to cheer him when he was depressed, to applaud him in those duties his father allowed him to perform—to *love* him. This she had done, and gladly. But soon the work would fall to another woman. A pale, pretty, innocent girl from a foreign land who neither knew Arrigo nor understood him. And if the Princess failed in her charge . . .

"She's so *blonde*," he continued, striding back and forth as if still on the parade ground. "It's almost unnatural."

"Arrigo!" Tazia laughed and set down her embroidery. "Surely you're not suggesting she dyes her hair! Carrido, don't be so silly. Every family has its characteristic looks. We Grijalvas have our distinctive noses—some rather more distinctive than others, to be sure! No do'Verrada daughter stands more than an inch over five feet tall. It's the trait of the Ghillasian royals to be very very pale. Which reminds me, you must warn her about how fierce our sunshine can be."

"I don't *like* blondes. And she's a bore—barely educated—"

"I hear she's been studying our dialect—and chess, too," she added archly.

He gave a derisive snort.

"You *are* being silly. She's very much in love with you already, and only twenty." *Eighteen years younger than I—Matra ei Filho, young enough to be my daughter!* Banishing the thought, she said, "The girl is only trying to please you."

"*You* please me."

Crossing to her chair, he snatched the needlework from her hands and his eyes possessed her in the uncanny manner of all the do'Verrada men. It had taken her breath away from the first—she who was so intent on being his Mistress that until she met him she hadn't even considered what it might be like to be his lover.

"You, and none other," he added softly.

She flowed up into his arms, knowing she should not. It was time for her wean him from her as delicately as she knew how, for kindness' sake. But the Princess would have him soon enough. Tazia would relinquish him because she must, but until then she would take and enjoy what was still hers alone.

And yet . . . and yet.

Later, while he dozed with his head cradled between her breasts, she wondered whether she must truly give him up forever. Some of her predecessors—most notably the grandmother for whom she was named—had resumed the Marria do'Fantome after the death of their Grand Duke's wives. Not that she wished any harm to Mechella—Matra Dolcha, no! But could they not share his life, his loving—and his power?

Grandmother Tazita had done so. Hers was a life to be envied. The perfect Mistress's life. After producing a child for the family—

a daughter, Zara, who was Tazia's mother—Tazita became the Mistress of Arrigo II before his marriage to Nadalia do'Joharra. When the Grand Duchess died, Tazita resumed her position and held it for twenty-one years until her Grand Duke's death. In Grijalva lore, Tazita was known as Nazha Coronna: the Uncrowned. Even during his marriage, though faithful to his wife, Arrigo II made no political move without consulting her. After Nadalia died, he would have married Tazita had it been allowed. Now, a mere thirty-one years after her death, she was a legend.

Her portrait in the Galerria Grijalva showed a smiling young woman, black hair curled and braided in the elaborate fashion of the time, voluptuous figure encased in a velurro gown of Verrada sapphire blue cut so low her nipples were nearly exposed, a blood-red ruby on a gold chain clasped around her creamy throat. But Tazia remembered her grandmother as she had been in her sixties: hair gone silver, soft curves melted away by the illness that would eventually kill her, the jewel lost in a billow of lace hiding her scrawny neck. All that remained was her glorious smile, given to her six-year-old namesake as she said, "If you are very good, very obedient, and very clever, you might have a handsome do'Verrada of your own one day. After all," the old lady added with a twinkle in her black eyes, "your full name is Tazita, just like mine, and the newborn Heir is another Arrigo, is he not?"

What Grandmother had not told her, and what she had discerned for herself over the years, was that whereas goodness and obedience were all very well, the main thing was to be clever. The recurrence of names was an omen, but fate did not necessarily cooperate unless one nudged it now and again.

Matra ei Filho, how clever she must be if she wished to rival her grandmother's career! The only time Tazia had ever mentioned the coincidence of names, Arrigo arched a brow and remarked that it would be nice if he could have *something* to call his own. Educated by his father's tutors, replacing his father as captain of the Shagarra Regiment, patron of his mother's pet charities, owner since his eighteenth birthday of the Heir's Jewels and suite at the Palasso and of the hunting lodge at Chasseriallo, and on and on—no wonder he wanted to have *something* to call his own. Tazia had never again referred to their becoming a second Arrigo and Tazita. Instead, she set about making him feel himself unique in the annals of Tira Virte. In this she had succeeded for twelve years.

But now he would marry. If he was not the first do'Verrada to wed the daughter of a king, at least he would be the first to wed a Ghillasian. Tira Virte had been attempting a marriage alliance with the powerful northern kingdom for two centuries. The schemes of the late Lord Limner Pedranno and his successor Mequel had finally borne the desired fruit. Mechella was not just a Princess of Ghillas, she was *the* Princess of Ghillas, the only royal female of marriageable age and a dizzying dower prize. The money was substantial, of course, but the real benefits were free access to Ghillasian ports, reduced tariffs, and favorable prices—and more to come when Mechella made King Enrei a grandfather. But, most importantly (although most obliquely to everyone but the Grand Duke and the Viehos Fratos), a Limner would be credentialed and permanently installed at the Pallaiso Millia Luminnai in Aute-Ghillas, complete with a cadre of copyists. What a Grijalva saw, he could paint; what he could paint could be used.

Tazia had a general knowledge of how vital a Limner was at Aute-Ghillas because her son had shared with her all he had clandestinely discovered about Grijalva secrets. Rafeyo was just fourteen, even now undergoing Confirmattio, and though his sterility was not yet beyond doubt, he had always been utterly sure of what he was. Tazia was proud of him, and prepared to become even prouder, but the truth was that Rafeyo's birth had been a mistake.

In four Confirmattios she had escaped pregnancy. Then, in 1247, lack of suitable girls compelled her—at the age of twenty-four!—into service one last time. Infuriated when her fourth cousin Renallo fathered a child on her, she bore her son in bitter resentment. His birth accomplished one thing, however: she would never again conceive. For this she was grateful to the boy, for at least he had spared her the process that would have rendered her barren, a mysterious procedure all Mistresses underwent to prevent any bastard do'Verradas.

Tazia began with resentment, progressed to impersonal gratitude, and gradually developed a vague interest in her son, but mothering him was left to her own mother, Zara. Tazia was too busy recovering her waistline and ensnaring Arrigo to bother with the child. If she thought of Rafeyo at all those first ten years of his life, it was with the remote curiosity of a much-older sister who wonders how a little brother fares.

Recently they had begun to spend more time together. He was a handsome boy, his burgeoning talent was a credit to her, and Arrigo not only didn't mind his visits, he actually liked Rafeyo. Arrigo would make a good father, she thought, brushing her lips to his thinning hair and picturing his children as cozily friendly with her as he was with his father's former Mistress, Lissina.

Once a week Rafeyo came to Tazia's caza and told her everything in his head. When he discovered certain things or overheard certain others, she knew about it shortly thereafter. She encouraged him to investigate, cautioned him not to be caught lest he be marked as Neosso Irrado, and anticipated the day of his Confirmattio—when her value to the family would increase for having produced a Limner. It wouldn't be long now before that happened—of the three girls he'd bedded this winter, none had become pregnant. One more, and Rafeyo Grijalva, only son of the Heir's Mistress, would be Confirmattio.

Sometimes, after the enforced intimacy, young couples fell in love and later married, especially if a child came of the bedding. Renallo had briefly tried to court Tazia after she turned up pregnant; his wooing had lasted only as long as it took her to say five words: "I intend being Arrigo's Mistress." Rafeyo would never be so foolish as to become enamored of any of his bedmates. He knew his duty to his mother and his talent. No Lord Limner ever married; Tazia couldn't imagine Rafeyo wanting to. He was hers, and she smiled with the pleasure of anticipating herself mother of the Lord Limner. . . .

Nazha Coronna, mother of the Lord Limner.

She supposed she ought to be shocked by her ambition. But as she stroked the rippling muscles of Arrigo's back, she had only a mental shrug for the boldness. Why should it not happen that way? It was eminently practical and would make everyone happy. Arrigo would be a find Grand Duke. Tazia was a perfect Mistress and understood Court politics inside out. Rafeyo was Gifted and had the talent to use it. The three of them would accomplish wonders.

As for Mechella de Ghillas—everything Tazia had heard about the girl indicated she was rather stupid and totally ignorant of governance. Court life might suit her, but Court politics would not. With enough babies to keep her busy, she'd hardly notice Arrigo's absences. Tazia was willing to share for the sake of appearances. With Arrigo's heart in one hand and Arrigo's power in the other, and her son as Lord Limner to aid and abet the whole, she could afford to be generous.

The years spread out before her in shining splendor. Rafeyo would become Confirmattio, learn all there was to learn about the Limners' art—and tell Tazia every detail; Mechella would have lots of babies; Arrigo would do his duty by providing those babies while missing Tazia so dreadfully that *he* would propose she return and become his Nazha Coronna; and Tazia herself . . . hmm. Perhaps she, too, ought to marry. Nothing like a wealthy, complacent husband to deflect gossip while Mechella came to terms with reality and Tazia established her position so firmly that none would dare gossip. Yes, a husband. She even had a man in mind.

It would happen as she wished, with a minimum of effort and fuss. Within five years all would be arranged to Tazia's satisfaction and the greater good of Tira Virte.

Because, when it came to it, no matter how pretty Mechella was and no matter how many babies she gave Arrigo, it was Tazia he loved. What woman, lovely and fecund though she be, could compete with that?

THIRTY-FOUR

The Ghillasian capital, Aute-Ghillas, eagerly anticipated the forthcoming arrival of Don Arrigo do'Verrada. Don Arrigo, who anticipated his forthcoming marriage with nothing approaching eagerness, was going to be a little late arriving. The gist of this—gently and diplomatically phrased—brought a heartfelt cry from Princess Mechella.

"But when? *When?*"

King Enrei frowned, irritated by his daughter's frets. Lucky for the girl that only her family was there to observe. They in turn were observed by the professional eye of the Grijalva Limner, who told himself that a portrait capturing the moment would be less than flattering.

The King, slightly squint-eyed from too much time spent studying documents, was not attractive when annoyed. A flush extended from lace collar to fair cheeks, across a hooked nose all the way up to a freckle-peppered pate revealed by scanty golden hair. In the Limner's opinion, he would have benefited from his royal predecessor's penchant for wigs. The Crown Prince, lounging in elegant boredom by a window, was clad for the hunt and looked as if his sole competency in life was the daily murder of helpless woodland creatures. An older Princess sat prim-lipped in a corner, looking simultaneously smug and sour. The lovely Mechella simply looked miserable. And mulish. Who would guess that such an expression could appear on that sweet face? Her father gave her a glance that ordered her to alter it; the Limner hid a grin, knowing that the King feared he would paint a warning to Arrigo.

"Carridia," said the King to his only daughter, "I know you're disappointed. But I'm sure he won't keep us waiting long." The tone and the knotted brows indicated that mere Heirs to Grand Dukes did not keep Kings waiting at all.

The Limner assayed yet another low bow, with yet another flourish of the soft arrtio's cap: Grijalva gray with three plumes dyed Verrada blue. The number and color of the feathers told all and sundry that he was an Itinerarrio as clearly as the Chieva do'Orro on its long chain meant he was a Limner. Only a Grijalva would know that the length of the feathers—a whole foot each, and damnably difficult it was to manage them sometimes, too—indicated his membership in the Viehos Fratos.

"Gracious Majesty," he said, knowing his Ghillasian *r* was nicely gargled for a foreigner, "Don Arrigo charged me specifically to humble himself before his bride. It is an unhappy fact that even the most vital personal concerns must sometimes be superseded by affairs of state." Reaching inside his jacket, he produced a blue leather pouch glistening with the gold Grand Ducal Seal. "His Grace bade me give unto the Princess' hand this token of apology, loving affection, and hopes for the future."

King Enrei nodded permission for him to approach across the throne room's pink marble floor. Bowing again, he said to Mechella, "These are Don Arrigo's own words: 'Please accept this poor trifle, and if I am to be forgiven this delay, please wear it when I come to you, so I may know your feelings at once.'"

He opened the drawstring. Into her palm spilled a clanging chain of beaten silver ovals set with balas sapphires he judged to be worth over two thousand mareias.

There was nothing wrong with the King's eye for jewelry. "'Trifle'? His Grace apologizes rather expensively," he remarked in dry tones.

The Crown Prince grinned irrepressibly at his stunned sister. "Be sure to make him feel guilty often, 'Chella. You'll end up with more jewels than the Empress of Tza'ab Rih!"

Taking the liberty of giving the young man a wink, the Limner said, "In fact, Highness, this once belonged to the Empress Nooria al'Assadda, from whom it was—shall we say, 'liberated'?—after the Battle of Shagarra Plain." Turning once more to the girl, he added, "It would be an honor and give me great personal pleasure to paint Your Highness wearing these jewels before His Grace arrives."

She watched him carefully, blue eyes outshining the gems she completely forgot as he promised Arrigo's presence. "Soon, Itinerrario Dioniso? Very soon?"

He made a graceful gesture of one hand. "What man, knowing such a woman awaits him, would delay an instant longer than absolutely necessary?"

She blushed charmingly, and the jewels trembled a little in her fingers. Her prune-mouthed aunt flashed her a look that said her own hands would clutch this "trifle" white-knuckled whenever it wasn't clutching her skinny neck. He made a mental note to gift the old stick with a few spare baubles to soften her up. He already knew, with regret, that his Anthalussan gelding was about to join the Crown Prince's string of hunters in the cause of sweetening Ghillasian tempers. There remained only the problem of how to slather the King with enough honey to smooth over Arrigo's delay. Damn the fool for balking at the marriage, and costing Tira Virte so much by way of bribes to soothe these justifiably affronted royals.

Then he had an idea. Aute-Ghillas had been without a painter since old Bartollio Grijalva died twelve years ago. One provision of the marriage contract was a supply of limners for the nobility, plus a Court Limner—and only the Grijalvas and Grand Duke Cossimio would know the difference signaled by the capital letter. Arrigo wouldn't arrive for at least a week; the time could be spent and the King's annoyance assuaged by execution of a portrait. *Several* portraits, he told himself glumly as he regarded once more the distinctly uninspiring aunt, unless Arrigo got his ass into the saddle soon. Mechella would be a delight to paint. Pretty girls always were. An equestrian portrait of the Crown Prince, of course. As for the King . . . eiha, there were ways of hiding baldness.

If the royals were pleased—as was the duty of a Grijalva acting on behalf of a Grand Duke of Tira Virte—Arrigo might even be welcomed as planned instead of being kept waiting as retaliation. There were a million excuses for delaying a wedding: needlework, banquet, decorations, guests, a shy bride (not a factor here, he thought wryly)—he'd seen them all in the course of his lengthy career. The Ghillasians must be made happy, so that they would make Arrigo happy, so that Grand Duke Cossimio and Lord Limner Mequel would be made happy—which they most emphatically would *not* be if Arrigo felt insulted enough by retaliations for his tardiness to cancel the whole thing. If talk told true, he was inclined to cancel anyway.

The things I do for the do'Verradas, Sario—now Dioniso sighed to himself, and began the necessarily roundabout conversation that would lead to hours and hours spent painting a portrait of Princess Prune-face.

The boy and girl stood side-by-side, listening. The door slammed at their backs. The bolt grated metal-on-wood. The lock clicked. Footsteps moved on to the next chamber. Motionless, not touching, staring at the leather-webbed bed, they waited until the last thunk of wood and clang of metal signaled the last imprisonment and the footfalls died away down the corridor.

The girl spoke first. "You know what to do?"

"I know what to do," the boy snapped. "You're my fourth, after all."

"No guarantee of competence," she pointed out, crossing to the bed. Above it an arched recess in the wall held an icon with a candle on either side. She reached over and in the last sunset light through high windows lit both wicks. "One for you, one for me," she muttered. "With the Mother and Son watching as if we were Initiatos in a Sanctia cell. I wonder if They approve."

"Does that matter to you?"

"Would it matter if it did?" She began unlacing her bodice. Her skin glowed in the dimness, a complexion dusky-dark even for a Grijalva, revealing more than the usual concentration of Tza'ab blood. "This isn't exactly how I wanted to spend four months of my life. I'll do my sacred Grijalva duty, but don't you dare get me pregnant." Tossing the bodice toward a corner, she added, "And I won't put up with anything strange, 'cordo?"

He unbuttoned his smock and hung it on the door hook. " 'Cordo. Let's just get it over with."

"Such enthusiasm." Naked to the waist, she flung her blouse after the bodice and untied the waist-tapes of her skirts. "Honesty's a good start, I suppose, especially for two people locked in together for the next three nights."

The chamber did resemble a stark Sanctia cell: bed, washstand, no rug or even a painting here in Palasso Grijalva, except for the watchful icon. At least it was cool despite spring's unseasonable heat. Whitewashed walls six feet thick were windowed eight feet up on north and south, providing a cross-breeze through silk mesh screens. A feeble gust fingered his hair as he straightened from shedding sandals and trousers.

"You've nothing to worry about," he told her. "I won't put my brat in your belly. I know what I am."

"Clever mennino, to know what the Viehos Fratos don't!"

"I'm not a little boy," he replied sharply as he removed his shirt.

"That's what you're here to prove. I haven't seen much evidence yet." She said it in a tough voice, deliberately insulting. But he was man enough even at fourteen to hear that her anger and bitterness had nothing to do with him, and so was not insulted.

Plain gray skirt and white underskirt puddled at her feet. She kicked the garments after the blouse and bodice, stretched out on the bed, and leaned back on her elbows. She had a fine body: high-breasted, slim-waisted, hips richly curved. But most Grijalva women were her equal or better, and she was nothing out of the ordinary. Head tilted to one side on a long neck that was her best feature, she asked, "Are you really that sure about yourself?"

"I've known all my life."

"If you say so." With a shrug, she lay back. "Come on, then. They inspect the sheets each morning. At your age, you'll be expected to perform at least twice a night. That's supposed to be the best thing about this for us girls."

As the varied noises of passion began to escape high windows and echo in the hall outside, he set about the task of proving himself in absolute and efficient silence.

After, she rose and went to the washstand, soaking a towel in the basin. As she wiped sweat from her body, she admitted, "You're no amateur. But you don't enjoy it much either. I'm not *that* ugly, you know."

"I think you're very pretty." He turned on his side to watch her, head propped against one hand.

She tossed him a wry grin over her shoulder. "A bit of advice, amico. A Limner paints the foul as well as the fair, so learn how to flatter—especially women. Start with whatever she's proud of—with a little practice, you can always tell. Move on to what she thinks is an imperfection—you'll know what it is if you're clever—and then lie like a Tza'ab rug."

He grinned at the challenge. "You have a lovely neck."

She gave a start. "How did you—"

"It's in the way you hold your head, and that little gold necklace is just the right length to emphasize it." He laughed. "As for 'imperfection' "—I don't have to lie. Your breasts are perfect."

Rallying, she retorted, "Had vast experience of breasts, have you?"

"The first girl's were like overripe melons. The last had none at all."

"Not bad," she conceded. "But remember that comparisons are risky unless you know the ins and outs of private rivalries." After rinsing the towel, she brought it over to him. "Here—feels good in this heat." A voice cried out down the hall, manly baritone cracking to boyish soprano. "Not as good as *that,* though. Cansalvio's enjoying himself. I recognize the squeak."

He scrubbed chest and underarms. "What a tragedy if *he* turns up Limner! I've more talent in one thumb than he has in his whole body."

"Matra Dolcha! So sure of that, too? How do you know so much?"

"You don't live at the Palasso."

With a frown: "No, with my mother and stepfather in his caza outside the city. What's that to do with—"

"If you lived here, you'd hear me spoken of."

Dark eyes widened mockingly. "What a strain such genius must be!"

He blushed, but in annoyance and not for shame at his arrogance. She'd find out—they'd all find out—once this stupid Confirmattio was over and he joined the ranks of the real Limners, the only true Grijalvas.

She tossed the towel to the floor beside the discarded topsheet for the servants to take for washing tomorrow morning. Perching at the foot of the bed, knees hugged to her breasts, she said, "Another piece of advice. Think as highly of yourself as you like—who knows, you may be right to do so—but hide it from the Fratos. They're a jealous lot. When they find a true talent, they're both thrilled and furious."

"I've learned that," he acknowledged. "But how do *you* know it?"

"My brother. Half-brother, really. We're both Menninos do'Confirmattio. Mother was only sixteen when she had Cabral, twenty when I was born. Then she married Master Jonino—he owns copper mines in Elleon—and took us with her. I've lived all my life outside the Palasso and I suppose they forgot about me. But my brother returned for his education. He's not a Limner—I have a niece around here somewhere—but he's a great artist all the same."

"I'm sure," he said politely.

She wasn't fooled. "You think talent is reserved exclusively for the steriles? Anyway, I thought his contribution to the family would be enough. But there was a shortage this year, and somebody remembered me, so here I am—worse luck."

He nodded, knowing that again she meant no personal insult to him. "Four girls needed, but only three suitables. Trinia's mother, grandmother, and aunt died in birthing, so she'll never even be bred. Filipia's line hasn't produced a Gifted in three generations. As for Pollia . . . eiha, let's just say she's painting with an imaginary brush."

"See how delicate and tactful you can be?" she teased.

"Grazzo millio," he thanked her in kind, suddenly liking her quite a bit. "So you're here to do your Grijalva duty."

"Their idea of it, not mine." She shook her head, black hair swirling in a thick cloak around her shoulders. "If you're as sure about yourself as you say, then I've escaped. I want babies only by the man I love and marry."

He arched his brows in exaggerated shock. "Fall in love, marry, *then* make babies? I've never heard of a Grijalva with merchant-class morals!"

"Sneer all you like," she snapped. "Four of you silly little arrtios I've had to bed, four months of my life wasted either in wallowing with one of you or waiting to be told to—while they hold their breath to see if I'm pregnant! And if I were, there'd go another year while I bore the child!"

He shrugged. "That's what Grijalva women do."

"Not *this* Grijalva!" she shot back grimly. "If you can't under-stand it from my side, consider yourself. You know who your mother is, but your father—the Fratos know, of course, but in real terms you might just as well be one of the original chi'patros. Which doesn't matter inside the Palasso, but wait until you're out in the larger world. Sanctas and sanctos watching you sideways as if you've got purple skin and five eyes."

"Who cares about them?" he scoffed.

"We don't, but the rest of the world does. They mimic those sideways looks so everyone knows they share the Ecclesial disap-proval of our disgusting, immoral, unnatural existence."

"Eiha, I see what you mean. But it makes no difference to Limners. We're too valuable."

"Haven't you *ever* been outside the Palasso? Limners are in the world most of all! Talk to my brother Cabral about it one of these days—you could learn a lot from him, even if he *isn't* one of your exalted brethren," she added tartly.

"Do you feel sorry for me?" The concept amused him.

"Yes," she answered forthrightly. "For all of you. At least Cabral and I had a family. *One* mother, *one* father, without a thousand half-siblings and cousins and suffocating numbers of other rela-tions—none of whom care merditto about you until and unless you turn up Gifted. What did you have but a cot in the crechetta while sharing one woman's breasts with another baby? And then there's your so-called education," she continued, angrier by the moment. "Art, art, art—and forget the rest. For instance, what do you know about the sciences?"

Straight-faced, he replied, "Enough to mix paint solvents with-out causing an explosion."

"It's not funny! They teach you just *enough* without worrying whether or not you understand it! *Enough* history not to insult for-eigners with your ignorance. *Enough* literature to babble a few poems to entertain nobles while they sit for their portraits. *Enough* about horses so you won't fall out of the saddle—stop laughing! Don't you see how they keep you in prison?"

"Regretto," he apologized, because he did like her despite her silly ideas. "I was just remembering my riding lessons."

"Ah, but you're one of the *lucky* ones, or so you think! You're Gifted—and may the Gentle Mother have mercy on those who aren't! A life spent as a drudge, making bad copies of other men's masterpieces—"

"Bassda," he said tolerantly. "Everything you say is true, and nothing you say makes me the least bit sorry to be what I am. En verro, I'll tell you why no one will look sideways at *me* and I'll never sit in the copyists' drudge room." He smiled, savoring the moment. "I'm Tazia's son."

"Tazia!" She blinked, and in a completely different voice said, "Arrigo's Mistress! Matra ei Filho!" His pride dissolved at her laughter: sharp, derisive, full-throated in its mockery. "You truly think your ambition will survive the Ghillasian marriage?"

Stung at the insult to Tazia, he said, "Arrigo adores my mother. He may send her from Court for a while to placate his bride while she has a few babies, but Tazia will return. And I'll be at her side."

"About twenty years old, fully trained, and ready for Lord Limner Mequel to hand over his brushes?" Eyeing him narrowly, her face anything but pretty now, she asked, "What if Arrigo starts adoring his wife instead?"

He shrugged. "Lissina is always at Court. She and the Grand Duchess are close friends."

"But who *wouldn't* love Lissina? She's a jewel, and everyone knows it."

"Which didn't prevent everyone from being shocked when Gizella named her daughter after her husband's former Mistress—and even made Lissina one of Lizia's Sponsors!"

"So you think there'll be a little Tazitia in Mechella's nursery one day, do you?" She didn't wait for an answer. "Eiha, everybody's terribly cozy at Court, I agree. But it's an unusual arrangement and Gizella's an unusual woman. I've met her. She's sweet and kind, and she genuinely *likes* Lissina. What if Princess Mechella doesn't like Tazia?"

He said nothing, having already said too much. What the Princess liked or didn't like mattered not at all. Frankly, having seen her portrait, he wondered if she even had a full paletto of brains with which to understand the situation. In her vapid blue eyes had been no hint of intelligence to match Tazia's. True, she was lovely—if you liked washed-out blondes—but no threat to Tazia's vivid dark Grijalva beauty.

"The future," his companion said at last, "should be fascinating. But for now, my Lord Limner, if it's all the same to you, I'd like to get some sleep."

" 'Cordo." He hid relief, not wanting to hurt her feelings. If she'd met Grand Duchess Gizella, she could have Court connections that might be useful one day. Besides, she was the very first person to call him "Lord Limner." He'd remember that—maybe paint it one day as a personal memento for her. The thought made him grin to himself.

"Sleep is just what I need," she was saying. "I was up late last night studying, and—" She broke off as another series of grunts, moans, and cries signaled duty done down the hall. "—and I doubt tonight will be very restful! *Why* must some people announce it so loudly?"

"Trumpeting like a Grand Ducal Herald," he agreed, and together they laughed, humor restored.

She lay beside him, not touching him. The breeze had died down and it was too warm to sleep skin-to-skin, especially with someone who'd been a stranger three hours ago.

"What do you study?" he asked all at once, wondering if she was one of those Grijalva girls who fancied themselves artistically gifted.

"Hmm? Oh—plants."

"For medicines?"

"Perfumes."

"En verro?" He decided to make much of her boring little hobby. She might be useful, she'd been fun in bed, and he liked her. And there was the brother, Cabral. One could never have too many Grijalva allies, even unGifted ones, if one desired to become Lord Limner. "It sounds difficult and complicated."

"I mix scents the way you mix colors. It's how I met the Grand Duchess. I created a special fragrance just for her."

"From roses, I'll wager. It's said she loves them."

"I used a base of rose, yes. Always white, she won't have any other. Then some grasses, valerian, a few other things."

His painter's mind instantly translated the items into their symbology: I Am Worthy of You, Submissiveness, Accommodating Disposition. From all he'd ever heard, that was Gizella to the life.

"You ought to make a perfume for the Princess," he said suddenly.

"As a wedding present? That's a wonderful idea! Perhaps one day your mother will want something special, too."

He ignored the hint, merely saying, "Mmm, she might enjoy that," thinking that Tazia would not be Tazia if she did not smell of the Elegance of yellow jasmine mixed with the Gladness of myrrh and the Sweet Temptation of apples. Turning onto his other side, he pretended to fall asleep. But it occurred to him, and he smiled to consider it, that the Princess's perfume ought to be blended mainly from almond oil, for her Stupidity in marrying a man who belonged to Tazia Grijalva: Nazha Coronna, mother of the next Lord Limner.

THIRTY-FIVE

To Dioniso's everlasting astonishment, Princess Mechella ordered him to paint her in her wedding gown—leaving space enough beside her for Arrigo.

"You'll have to paint this picture anyway," she said, "and the sooner it's finished, the sooner we can all go home to Meya Suerta."

Amazing enough to be summarily commanded (he, a Grijalva Limner—one might even say *the* Grijalva Limner); but she had all the precise details in mind, too. She knew every symbolic flower she wished included, how she wanted to stand and hold her head and hands, the background, even the time of day. Obviously, she'd been planning this for years. Thus once more the girl showed steel beneath the roses-and-sunshine sweetness. Dioniso bowed graceful homage to it, hiding a grin for the shock awaiting Arrigo, and told himself that as Lord Limner in his next life he'd have a merry time of it with Mechella as Grand Duchess.

In her snowy bridal finery she was sheer splendor from diamond tiara to pearl-encrusted slippers. Miles of thin, airy white silk fell from her tiny waist like the petals of a rose, each edged in cobwebby lace. A starched underskirt supported the delicate material. The bodice mimicked a rosebud, tightly furled layers at the waist rising to cup surprisingly voluptuous breasts before lapping onto her shoulders in little sleeves sewn with pendant teardrop pearls. Just where the petals parted at her breastbone the initials *A* and *M* intertwined were embroidered in gold.

She'd planned the dress for years, too.

Accustomed to luxury, witness to three centuries of aristocratic display in six different countries, still he was stunned by this tall, golden-haired Princess in her wedding gown. When he bowed to her, it was with the genuine humility an artist must feel in the presence of beauty he is lucky enough to commit to canvas.

The long hours he spent sketching and then detailing her were infinitely preferable to the interminable days he spent with Princess Permilla.

She proved flighty over the posing of her person. Each of her suggestions was a disaster. In the robes of the Order of Ghillas, at an open window with gardens spreading to the horizon, she looked like a tour guide. In the robes of a Patron of the University, reclining in her salon surrounded by devotional books, sacred icons, and three hideous little yapping dogs, she looked equal parts scholarly sancta and kennel keeper. In her own interpretation of the colorful Ghillasian national costume (silk and satin substituting for linen and wool), seated by an ornate fountain, she looked like a parched plant in a painted pot set out by a worried gardener for watering.

At long last he called on every scrap and shred of diplomacy he possessed to persuade her that no background could do justice to her innate presence, no pose could convey her instinctive grace, no symbolic costume could encompass her wide-ranging intellect. He asked her to wear a plain white gown, stood her in front of a plain white plaster wall, and presented her with a small but respectable fortune in very old, very rare blue Tza'ab glass beads. Earrings, necklace, hairpins, and bracelets had been meant for Mechella; he told the old prune this quite bluntly, adding that no matter how much trouble he brought on himself, as an artist he could not bear to see the azure mystery of these small crystalline miracles worn by any woman lacking the rich depths of character he perceived in Permilla's eyes.

"The jewelry and the Princess mutually enhance each other," he concluded. "Nothing else can *deserve* to be in this painting."

She not only bit, she swallowed whole. The sketch took him half an hour. Permilla retired to her chambers positively stuffed with smugness.

Then it was time for the Crown Prince.

He had two choices: *Crown Prince, with Horse* or *Horse, with Crown Prince*. When young Enrei arrived in the stableyard with the biggest stallion Dioniso had ever seen, he knew which it must be. The youth was thrilled with the preliminary drawing, and even more impressed when Dioniso released him from his posing after only fifteen minutes so that he was free to take the monstrous horse for a gallop. Watching him ride off, Dioniso considered it not a matter of *if* he would break his royal neck, but *when*.

This left only the King himself, and because there was as yet no formal portrait of Enrei II in all his regalia—there having been no limner at Aute-Ghillas in the year of his coronation—this picture proved easiest of all. King, Throne, Robes, Crown, Orb, Scepter: he'd done a score of them and could have mixed the cobalts and madders in his sleep. He was signing *Dioniso Grijalva* at the bottom by the end of the afternoon.

Wonder of wonders, Arrigo arrived the next day—only fifteen

days late, and just in time to reap the warm and welcoming benefits of Dioniso's work. Mechella was, of course, not allowed to greet him with the rest of the family. Their first official meeting as betrothed husband and wife would take place in full view of the Court the next morning. But as Dioniso took a late-night stroll to clear the final brushstrokes of Princess Prune from his head, he witnessed an affecting moonlit scene in the private royal garden.

Mechella's shining head was unmistakable. So was the glitter of gold braid on Arrigo's Shagarra uniform. Running toward him, she stopped just short of flinging herself into his arms. He stood his ground and bowed. They exchanged a few awkward phrases Dioniso could not hear. There was a brief, nervous pause—and then Arrigo offered her his hand. They walked like shy young lovers to the seclusion of a hedged retreat, and were lost to his view.

So much for Tazia?

"Limner," came a trembling voice behind him, and he spun around. An elderly servant stood there, twisting work-roughened hands by the silver light of the waning moon. In common accents, and slowly—as if she didn't believe a Tira Virteian would understand the King's Ghillasian—she said, "Limner, I beg you—tell me he will be good to her!"

"Of course he will," he began.

She shook her head vigorously. "No! Speak to me not as a man who serves a prince, but as a man who knows another man—and a man who knows his own kinswoman. Will the Grijalva loosen her hold? Will my precious girl have a chance to make him love her?"

Dioniso was moved by the woman's devotion. "I think she will," he replied, honestly as far as he knew. "Don Arrigo is ready to marry and have sons. He knows his duty, and she is its delightful embodiment." With a smile for the old woman, he finished, "Only look at your Princess. She's a rare beauty, charming, young, a delight en tudo paletto—and the Grijalva is nearing forty, old enough to be Her Highness' mother!"

This did not seem to bring much comfort. "Look after her," she urged. "You have painted her with rare understanding, you must have seen into her soul and been moved. Advise her, caution her. She *is* young in the ways of women like the Grijalva."

"Surely you'll be there to do all that."

"No." Tears ran down her wrinkles like spring snowmelt through streambeds. "I have been forbidden."

"By Princess Pru—Permilla," he corrected himself, and when

she nodded confirmation of his guess he went on, truly shocked, "Is the poor girl to take none of her own people with her?"

By long tradition, brides were wed in their own countries and escorted to the border by a regiment or so of their own military. At that point the new husband's officers and men took over guardianship. But the girl always was attended into her new country and home by her own maids, menservants, and the like.

"I haven't had the heart to tell her yet. It is declared that the instant she marries him, she is Tira Virteian and must surround herself with—with strangers who don't know her or love her, courtiers interested only in advancing themselves, barbarians—"

"We are at least marginally civilized in my country," he observed dryly. "Be easy in your mind, carridia matreia. If she is alone, Don Arrigo will be even more tenderly disposed to protecting her. There's nothing like a beautiful girl who is also vulnerable to make a man feel strong and powerful. And soon enough she will have true friends, you may count on it. No one could resist her charm and innocence for very long."

She wrung her hands again. "That's true, that's true," she fretted. "But promise you'll look out for her. Please, Limner, I beg you in the name of your own dear mother who loved you as I love my darling 'Chella!"

He filed the diminutive away for Arrigo's use while trying to recall his mother's face. Impossible; and, after more than three hundred years, not surprising. He remembered her name—Felippia, and a vague scent of citrus tea. That was all.

"Be easy," he repeated. "Princess Mechella is everything Don Arrigo could wish for. He is no fool, to scorn perfection when all that most noble husbands can hope for is as short as possible a list of imperfections."

"Promise me!" the servant insisted.

He saw no harm in avowing that he would indeed keep watch over Mechella. It was only prudent for one in his current position to do so, and as for his future position as Lord Limner . . . He sent the old woman back indoors, and if she was not entirely happy, at least she no longer wept. But her distress made him curious enough to wander the gardens for an hour or so. At length he was rewarded with the sight of Arrigo with his arms about Mechella, her face turned ecstatically up to receive his kiss.

Do they miss me? Wonder where I have gone? My friends, my family, the moualimos—Alejandro? What does he think? That I have

run away, deserted him, betrayed him—no, he would never be-
lieve—but Sario could make *him believe—Matra ei Filho, I could*
not bear it if Alejandro thinks me false!

When I am freed, I will go to him, tell him—but not until I have
dealt with Sario, who claims to love me and yet has done this hor-
rible thing to me—to my child—eiha, poor mennino, poor little one
inside me—

Your papa waits for us, corasson meyo, carrido meyo, he waits
for us out in the world—

And so does Sario. So does Sario. . . .

"And so you are Confirmattio! I'm so proud of you, Rafeyo!"

Tazia did not embrace her son; she couldn't recall ever having
done so, and to do so now probably would have shocked him stu-
porous. But she gave him her laughter and her applause, and he
basked, blushing, in the praise.

"You will learn Grijalva magic—and the rest will become fathers," she went on, pouring the wine Arrigo had sent her from
Ghillas. Handing a glass to Rafeyo, she said, "You may find this a
little dry, but it's time you educated your other palate, too!"

He grinned at the pun and ran a finger down the crystal flute to
test the temperature. "Is it cold enough yet? I only just arrived."

"Carrido, do you think I haven't counted the days until your last
girl would resume her bleeding? This has been on ice since last
night!"

"You, at least, never doubted me!"

"And now no one else will either." She toasted him. "Saluto ei
Suerta!"

"Sihirro ei Sanguo," he replied, and they drank.

" 'Magic and blood'?" she asked, arching a brow.

"It's how Limners toast each other. I heard it for the first time
last night." He rubbed the back of his neck ruefully. "I heard it a *lot*
last night, in fact. All the Limners in residence gathered to welcome me, and each toasted me in order of rank, so . . ."

"You must've drunk barrels! I'm surprised you can even walk
this morning. Eiha, the recuperative powers of youth. Now, tell me,
Rafeyo," she said, leaning forward, "when does it begin? When
will it finish?"

"I'll study with—" He paused. "Tazia, forgive me, but is it really
safe to talk here?"

She gestured around the small, windowless room. "Months ago
I had this chamber redone floor to ceiling so you and I *could* have

a safe place to talk. I've had complete faith in you for much longer than it took to chill the wine."

His dark eyes widened—his father's eyes, long-lidded and thick-lashed; odd how as he grew older she saw less of herself and more of Renallo in their son, but he was growing to manhood and perhaps it was to be expected. Whatever his physical resemblance to his father, Tazia knew the boy's heart was hers. He proved it by giving her a dazzling smile. *Her* smile, she told herself proudly, *her* gift of the Gift that had made him a Limner.

"You did all this for me? For us? Grazzo millio, Mama!"

She could have counted on her fingers the times he'd called her that. And suddenly she knew it was a word she must encourage. The holy bond between Mother and Son, the most sacred in the Faith, sweetly repeated in herself and Rafeyo. She gave him her warmest smile, the one she'd practiced again and again in a mirror in the weeks before her first meeting with Arrigo, and Rafeyo returned it delightedly. A fourteen-year-old was no more proof against it than an eighteen-year-old had been.

"Only you could have thought of such a thing," the boy said, his gaze roaming once more about the room. It was one of those cramped, inconvenient spaces common in Meya Suerta's older houses, used for storage or pantry for wine served to afternoon guests. The room had been gutted of shelves and cupboards, nearly doubling its size. Vents had been cut into the ceiling, their outlets on the other side of the house to prevent use by eavesdroppers. Heavy brocade hangings and a thick rug soundproofed the chamber. The furniture was sparse but fine: sofa and chair upholstered in sapphire silk, carved wooden table topped with green marble, and a tall silver candlebranch in a corner. The door had a double lock.

Reassured of privacy, Rafeyo detailed the next few years of his life. He would spend many months with the masters of watercolor, ink, pencil, chalk, charcoal. At the same time he would learn from other masters methods of preparing and using paper, parchment, silk, linen, plaster, wood. Only then would he be taught oil on canvas, and with these lessons would come tutorials from each of the three great masters.

"Do you know what they're called?" he asked, practically bounding in his chair with excitement. "Il Aguo, Il Seminno, and Il Sanguo!"

"Everyone's heard the terms," she reminded him. "I must say they always struck me as rather bizarre."

"You don't understand! Aguo is tears, saliva, and sweat. Seminno is—"

"—semen," she interrupted. "So?"

"That's where the magic is, Tazia! They mix the paints with all those, and with blood, and because all of them are part of a Limner's body, and Limners have the Gift, and know all the words and phrases and the special mental disciplines—" He paused for breath. "—the magic goes into the paintings!"

She sat back on the sofa, stunned. There were rumors, of course; mutterings around the Palasso, mostly, because everyone feared Grijalva power too much to speak in the open of magic. Even the Ecclesials kept their mouths shut, though their eyes flung daggers. But Tazia, ambitious in the only way open to a female Grijalva, had ignored anything to do with painting.

Until now, when her Limner son explained it to her.

"Oil must be the most powerful, because they teach it last. Think of it—paints mixed with a Limner's blood, on a canvas prepared with his sweat and tears and the words of power—"

"Do you truly know this, Rafeyo?" she demanded. "Or are you only guessing?"

"I know it as truly as I've always known I'm a Limner," he replied solemnly. "I learned something earlier this spring. I couldn't come tell you about it because of the Confirmattio. Do you remember last year when the nephew of the Baron do'Brendizia died in prison before he could come to trial?"

She nodded. "He killed himself rather than expose his family to such disgrace."

"It wasn't suicide. A Grijalva killed him. Maybe even Lord Limner Mequel himself!"

Involuntarily she glanced around the room as Rafeyo had done a little while ago. Heavy wood and thick brocade calmed her. "Go on."

"Brendizia was arrested for being drunk and disturbing the peace. But that was just an excuse. How many Courtfolk are ever thrown in jail for having a good time at a tavern? What he was *really* guilty of was plotting to convene the Corteis."

"I'd heard something of it," Tazia said, which startled Rafeyo, just as she intended. In truth, she had heard nothing of the sort, which she had no intention of admitting to her son, and the shock of hearing it now set her heart thudding. She must pay more attention to what was being said, or she would be useless to Arrigo. She must invite more of those boring old cows to tea, strengthen her contacts among the nobility—and to do that, she must wed very soon to the nobleman of her choice.

"Eiha," said Rafeyo, "someone found out what he was doing.

There was evidence against him. After he was arrested they searched his rooms in the city and found papers, letters, everything they'd need in a trial."

"Names of other conspirators?"

"Nothing so lucky. He wasn't very clever, but he wasn't completely stupid either. They could've tortured it out of him, though."

"A nobleman?" she gasped. "A Brendizia?"

He shrugged. "A traitor is a traitor. Anyway, they could've tried him, and jailed him for a while, but he'd be sure to use the trial to his own purposes, denouncing Grand Duke Cossimio and calling for freedom and a legislature to assemble and so on."

"The baron would die of mortification," Tazia declared with a certainty based on ten years' acquaintance with that irascible nobleman. "If rage didn't kill him first," she added thoughtfully. "What a scandal. A Brendizia! Certainly they had to execute the foolish boy."

"Quietly. And use it to warn anybody with the same ideas," Rafeyo finished, nodding.

"Yes, of course, but how?"

"Somebody painted him dead."

This time Tazia actually slumped into the sofa pillows, shocked beyond words.

"It's possible," her son told her. "He was found dead of 'natural causes,' but really it was an execution. I don't know yet how it's done, but I'm positive it *was* done." He caught her gaze, long-lidded eyes glittering. "Do you see what this means, Tazia? Do you know what we could *do* with this?"

She recoiled inwardly from the fevered glee in his eyes; outwardly she merely nodded. But because he was her son, even though she had not raised him, something in him responded to what she was certain she had not revealed. He drained wine down his throat in a gulp, and spoke quickly.

"Not really paint anybody *dead,* of course, but I'm sure there are things we could do, magic that would make them think what we want or do things—"

"Yes, of course," she said almost mindlessly.

"Don't you see it? That puling Princess of Arrigo's wouldn't stand a chance against you, Mama!"

The word triggered something in her, something that made her brain lurch into motion again. Not maternal instinct; no, when he named her his mother, he reminded her that he and she were inextricably linked. "Rafeyo! Promise me, promise you'll attempt *nothing* until you're one of the Viehos Fratos!"

His young face registered something akin to betrayal. "But that'll take so *long*."

"You can wait. Rafeyo! Obey me in this! You must know everything, be as wise as you can in all the ways of Grijalva magic, before you can use it to our best advantage. What if you were caught? Worse, what if you were harmed by magic you didn't yet fully understand? I couldn't bear it if anything happened to you. You *will* be Lord Limner one day, Rafeyo, don't be impatient, don't become the talk of the Palasso as a Neosso Irrado. It will all come to you in time, I swear it."

He bit his lip, no longer an ambitious young man yearning for power but a boy-child yearning for his mother's love. "You believe in me that much?" he asked softly, almost shyly.

It made her acutely uncomfortable, the way she'd felt when her mother Zara had brought him here just after Arrigo established her in this caza, and Rafeyo ran to her on unsteady legs crying out, "Mama!" After an awkward hug, she'd sent him to the kitchen with a servant—and told her mother to prevent similar displays in the future.

Now she reached over to touch his wrist. "I have *always* believed in you." She let her fingers trail down to his fingers, caressing them lightly, tenderly. "The hour you were born, I looked at these hands—so tiny then, so fragile, but such long, beautiful fingers!—I *knew* I had given birth and life to a Lord Limner greater than Mequel or Sario or even Riobaro!"

"You did," he replied fervently. "We both know you did. I'll make you so proud of me."

"I already am. But you must promise, Rafeyo. Attempt nothing until you know precisely what it is you do."

"I promise."

After he left her, she sat quite still for some time, eyes closed, in her safe but stifling little room. *I must find a way to get some air in here, it's horrid now that summer's coming.* Telling herself that she went in search of a breeze, she locked the door behind her and went upstairs to her bedchamber, calling on the way for another bottle of wine.

As she waited for it, she undressed, pacing, thinking of the other news of the morning: Mechella's first appearance in Meya Suerta had been delayed. Custom dictated that a do'Verrada collect his bride, come home and introduce her to the city, then journey north to the castle of Caterrine for a period of seclusion, during which it was his duty to impregnate her. But Arrigo, sending excuses to his parents through Itinerarrio Dioniso, had taken the girl directly to

Caterrine. Official gossip said it was to spare her the capital's summer heat and stink. Unofficial gossip—always more reliable—asserted that he wanted his charming child-bride to himself for as long as possible and indeed could scarcely keep his hands off her.

"That puling Princess of Arrigo's wouldn't stand a chance. . . ."

Tazia slid her arms into a white silk bedrobe, knotting the sash loosely around her waist. A servant arrived with the wine and was dismissed. She stretched out on the daybed before the louvered windows, drinking Arrigo's gift and wondering who among her Grijalva cousins she might persuade to a subtle interrogation of Dioniso. Perhaps one of her sisters, though they had all loathed each other from childhood. But she must find out if Arrigo had truly fallen in love with the girl.

Eiha, she was *supposed* to want that, wasn't she? His happiness in marriage, an advantageous alliance, Cossimio and Gizella satisfied, the people rejoicing, merchants enriched, Grijalvas entrenched at Aute-Ghillas, lots of little do'Verradas in the ducal nursery, the succession assured. It was her patriotic duty to wish Arrigo in love with his new wife.

His blonde, beautiful, innocent, adoring, *twenty-year-old* wife. . . .

She lay there in the coolness high above the most fashionable avenida in Meya Suerta, drinking wine and thinking about the do'Brendizia nephew painted dead in his prison cell.

⸻◈ THIRTY-SIX ◈⸻

Arrigo did not bring his bride to Meya Suerta until autumn. The intervening weeks were punctuated for Tazia by social calls, though not as many as had been customary during her tenure as Mistress.

Her visitors fell into three categories. First, those who made sure she knew the latest from the lovers' nest at Caterrine. Some gossiped to pay her back for twelve years of social supremacy. Some came out of curiosity over her reaction. An innocent few, assuming her affection for Arrigo to be as generous as Lissina's was for his father Cossimio, presumed she would want to know that her former lover was happy. The gossips, the vengeful, and the curious arrived in a state of anticipation and went away disappointed. The innocents, however, had their every expectation met: she was all smiles and sweet words for Arrigo's newfound joy.

The second sort of caller were admirers who, thinking her fair game now that Arrigo was well and truly wedded, wished to experience her charms personally—for private gratification or public boasting or both. These departed in frustration, not due to any overt ploy of Tazia's but because in near-constant attendance on her was a visitor who was a category unto himself: Count Garlo do'Alva.

He came as a suitor, and two days before the public announcement that Arrigo and Mechella would be home for Providenssia, Garlo and Tazia were quietly and privately married.

He was a tall, personable man, at forty-seven in his late prime, his build as powerful as his stringent personal compordotta. His black hair was thickly silvered, a striking contrast to dark brown skin—which, it was rumored, he owed to more than a dollop of Tza'ab blood. He had married the great heiress Ela do'Shaarria half his life ago, gotten three sons on her, and buried her in 1260. Needing neither heirs nor riches, his requirements in a second wife were beauty, conversation, familiarity with and influence in Court politics, and sexual sophistication. Everything, in short, that he had not experienced in his first marriage. In Tazia Grijalva, he found them all and more besides.

The newly-wed Count and Countess do'Alva journeyed north from Meya Suerta to his ancestral castello in time for Providenssia.

They missed encountering the newly-wed Don Arrigo and Dona Mechella on the road by mere hours. Whether Garlo planned this to spare his bride sight of her replacement, or whether Tazia planned it to spare Arrigo's bride sight of herself, in all quarters it was agreed that the thing was gracefully done.

Even though it was also agreed that Tazia could have shown up naked in the road and Arrigo wouldn't have noticed.

Arrigo was equally adept at timing. He arrived in Meya Suerta and introduced Mechella to his people on the very day of Providenssia, in the midst of harvest celebrations. With a fine sense of the dramatic and with the connivance of the Premia Sancta, he sneaked his wife into the Cathedral Imagos Brilliantos through a side door just before his parents' ceremonial entrance. Mechella's first curtsy on Tira Virteian soil was thus to the living embodiments of the Mother as Provider of Grain and the Son as Crusher of Grapes: Grand Duchess Gizella in glittering ripe gold and Grand Duke Cossimio in splendid wine-red with the dark ruby ring of his ancestors glowing from his finger. If the older pair symbolized autumnal riches, young Arrigo and Mechella were the promise of next year's spring in vivid do'Verrada blue embroidered with grape leaves (his) and new wheat (hers).

Those lucky enough to witness the scene went wild with joy. Even the most exaggerated reports of Mechella's blonde beauty were found to be lacking, and in a society that worshiped art she was seen to be a living masterpiece. The choirmaster, grateful for the Premia Sancta's timely warning, signaled his hundred adolescent boys to sing "Blessed by Thy Loving Smile," a hymn of thanksgiving more suited to nuptials than the seasonal favorite "Thy Gifts of Golden Grain." The refrain echoed to the vaulted ceiling and the crowds outside sang along, filling all the city with music.

After the service, the two couples walked down the nave and ascended to the Presence Balcony. The Zocalo Grando was packed; people even hung from the statue of Don Alesso do'Verrada atop the great central fountain. His descendants and their wives waved and smiled, acknowledged the cheers and singing, then toasted each other and all citizens with glasses of wine while servants in Verrada blue and junior Ecclesials in dun and brown distributed small loaves baked from this year's first grains.

The procession back to Palasso Verrada was on foot. The route was cleared—gently, at Cossimio's order—by the Shagarra Regiment. Garlands and swags of leaves and sheaves were everywhere: hung from lampposts, from tiled eaves, from lintels and shop signs, from the neck of every person on the streets. Those people close enough to Mechella to exclaim in wonder at her rare, fair northern beauty also saw that while she smiled and looked about her with excitement, she seemed a little pale and clung tightly to Arrigo's arm.

The popular verdict: she was with child. And indeed this proved to be the case, though formal announcement did not come until that evening when the torches were lighted and a second, more boisterous procession wove through the streets, with singing and dancing and thousands of bottles of last year's wine.

Arrigo told his parents first, as was proper. Mechella blushed becomingly when, the moment the four were alone in the private Grand Ducal suite, he said, "Papa, Mama, I present to you Mechella—mother of your grandson!"

"So soon?" Cossimio roared with laughter. "Quick work, boy!"

"Isn't that just like a man?" Gizella made a face at her husband and went forward to embrace the girl. "They think *they* do all the work of making a baby, when in reality their task lasts only a few minutes!"

The Grand Duke let out a guffaw to tremble the rafters. "'Zella! Arrigo's a strong young buck—half an hour at least! And I know you're not speaking from your *own* experience!"

"I'll thank you to keep a decent tongue between your teeth, Cossi!" To Mechella, who had crimsoned, she added, "Men! Eiha, carrida meya, I'll keep you here only a little while, and then you must rest." They sat on a velurro-covered sofa and Gizella clasped both Mechella's hands. "Arrigo is moronno luna to have paraded you all that way among thousands of people intent on getting a look at you. You must be scared half to death."

"Not at all, Your Grace," Mechella responded bravely but not quite convincingly. "I was glad to see them, and glad they wished to see me. I hope they'll like me."

"Bound to," Cossimio said, "and don't worry your pretty head about it for an instant." Flopping into a chair, he undid the buttons of his heavy red robes. "Matra ei Filho, this heat! Arrigo, have someone fetch us cold drinks." As his son moved to the bellrope, he went on, "You just be your own sweet lovely self, gattina, and they'll adore you. They ask only a smile and a kindness—'Zella can tell you all about what a Grand Duchess does, for she does it to perfection."

Mechella, who had never in her long-legged life been called "kitten," smiled at her husband's father. To her surprise, his gaze narrowed above his thick black beard and he studied her most minutely.

"I must say," he told her at last, "you've nothing to worry about in the smiling department. Your picture doesn't half do you justice—and won't Mequel have fits when I tell him so!" This sent him into another braying laugh, after which he glanced at Arrigo with that same taut, evaluating look. "You left a Grijalva behind at Aute-Ghillas?"

"Itinerarrio Dioniso, to finish up some portraits. He'll be back soon, I think." Entry of a servant with a tray of iced drinks and small cakes interrupted him. When the family was alone once more and Gizella was busy pouring and parceling, Arrigo went on, "I think Candalio might do as the permanent Limner. He's about my age, and very accomplished."

"Who? Oh, the one who painted the *Deed* to Caza Reccolto this spring when we gave it to—"

"Do you prefer almond cakes or walnut, Mechella?" the Grand Duchess said smoothly.

"Almond is my favorite," she replied. "Grassia—no, that's the wrong way to say 'thank you,' isn't it?"

"You'll learn very quickly, I know," Gizella said. "Our 'grazzo' does multiple duty as 'thanks' and 'please' and 'you're welcome'—probably because we all talk so fast we can't be bothered with more than one word for all three concepts!"

Mechella laughed lightly. "Most Tira Virteians *do* speak very quickly, like fireworks or shooting stars! And I've noticed that it's because you take out syllables here—or Ghillasians add them, I've never discovered which. Do you know, Arrigo?"

"Probably a little of both, 'Chella," he answered with a smile.

" 'Chella! What a sweet version of your name!" said the Grand Duchess. "I'd been wondering what to call you."

"My mother used it."

"You lost her a very long time ago, I know, and it's very sad. But I hope you'll allow me to be just a little motherly toward you, 'Chella. I always wanted lots of daughters, but managed only one."

"One was enough," Cossimio observed pointedly. "Not since Benecitta has there been a do'Verrada with a six-foot personality inside a five-foot body."

"I told you about Benecitta," Arrigo said to his wife. "The great family scandal. I'll show you her portrait in the Galerria tomorrow."

"Most do'Verrada women are very short," Gizella explained further. "Our Lizia just tops five feet, and Cossi's aunt was even smaller. I don't know why that is, because the men are quite tall. You'll stand out by standing up straight, carrida, and I hope your girls take after you!"

"It might be like the Grijalva Gift," said the Grand Duke with a shrug. "The men have it, the women don't. Now that I think on it, Candalio isn't the best choice for Aute-Ghillas, Arrigo. Terrible reputation with the ladies."

"It was only a suggestion," Arrigo said rather stiffly.

"Close cousin of—um, Zara Grijalva, isn't he?"

"Yes." His voice was wooden now. "Of Zara Grijalva."

Gizella rose in a swirl of golden satin. "If you're going to bore us with politics, we're leaving. Come, 'Chella. I'll show you your rooms and you can have a nice rest before dressing for dinner. Has Arrigo explained our duties of the evening? I'm afraid we'll be up rather late."

She escorted Mechella from the salon on a wave of pleasant chatter. Up a flight of stairs, down three corridors, and past a dozen Shagarra sentries, they finally reached the Heir's private apartments.

"I had it all redone," said Gizella. "I hope you like it. Here's your bedroom, with bath and dressing room between it and Arrigo's. A private sitting room and office for each of you—"

"Office?" Mechella sat on the huge bed, all hung with blue and green with silver stitching, and flooded with white lace.

"You'll have a secretary to manage your engagements, which will include official duties, charities, and various social functions. But you needn't worry about that now—or indeed until after your baby is born. Everyone will understand if you keep to yourself until then."

"But I *want* to do it all! I'm Arrigo's wife now, I know I have responsibilities, and I'm looking forward to them."

"I'm sure you are, and I'm sure your training was the very finest. But here in Tira Virte—eiha, pregnancy excuses one from all that. It's a very holy time in a woman's life, 'Chella. Like the Blessed Mother, all her strength goes into nurturing her child."

"Yes—yes, of course, I only meant—"

"I know, dolcha meya." Gizella patted her hand. "But don't worry one instant about anything at all. Everyone will expect you not to be very visible for a while."

"I hope my baby is a boy," Mechella said fervently. "I want so much to be everything Arrigo wants—and everything you and the Grand Duke and all the people expect—"

"Carrida mennina! You heard Cossi. Just be yourself. He and I

love you already, and it's certain Arrigo adores you! I had only to
see his face to know it. I nearly wept there in the Imagos to see him
so happy, and I have you to thank for it."

"Your Grace—"

"Gizella if you must, 'Zella if you like—" She giggled suddenly,
like a little girl. " 'Zella and 'Chella! How dreadful!"

The Grand Duchess' laughter was infectious. "At least it's accidental! There's a family in southern Ghillas named deLosia, and
they named their three daughters Rosia, Tamosia, and—"

"Zosia!" Gizella guessed, crowing as Mechella nodded. "Let's
hope the poor things get married as soon as possible!"

"Rosia did, just before I left—" Laughing so hard she could
barely get the words out, she finished, "—to Baron deProssia!"

When both women had caught their breath, Gizella said, "Why
do people do such things to innocent children? Bad enough to pass
along a family trait like huge ears or a cast in one eye, but—really!"

"What do the Grijalvas pass along to their children? What did
the Grand Duke mean about them?"

"Nothing very important or interesting. They're clever painters,
some better than others. For instance, the one you met at Aute-
Ghillas, Dioniso—he's said to be brilliant at portraits but terrible at
landscapes. Lord Limner Mequel—you'll meet him soon, he's a
wonderful man and he'll paint your baby's *Birth*—he can sketch a
rose with a pencil on any old scrap of paper, and you'd vow you
could smell its fragrance! Almost all the Grijalvas are talented, but
each has a special gift, just as the rest of us do."

"I see. I thought perhaps the reference was to Tazia Grijalva.
Arrigo's Mistress."

Gizella blinked several times. "What? Her? Surely you're not
concerned over something that was over long ago?"

"Thank you for not denying that he was . . . involved with her,"
Mechella said with simple dignity. "No, I'm not worried. I'm only
curious. Will—will she be at Court?"

Gizella shrugged. "The Grijalvas and the do'Verradas have an
arrangement stretching back hundreds of years. There used to be a
family called Serrano, a very long time ago, which competed with
the Grijalvas. But the Grijalvas are so obviously the superior artists
that the Serranos faded away. Anyway, this arrangement is a political one, with the Grijalvas supplying not only the Lord Limners
for Tira Virte, but also a nice, pleasant, pretty young woman to—"

"I know," Mechella said. "My brother Enrei told me all about it.
And it does seem very sensible."

"Yes, it is, and it's worked out very well for all concerned. Why, Cossi's former Mistress, Lissina, and I are very good friends. Delightful woman, you'll like her, too. Are you tired? Would you like to talk about this later?"

"If you've time, I'd prefer to hear it now."

"Eiha, as you wish." She tilted her head to one side, a little smile on her face. "When I first came here from Granidia, a new young bride like you, Lissina helped me through the maze of protocol among the Courtfolk with all the sweetness of a sister. You're young and beautiful, Arrigo chose you as his wife, and you're the mother of his child. No mere Mistress can compete, I assure you from personal experience!"

Mechella stared at her hands. "But—but if she still wants him—"

"Mistresses know that once the Heir marries, their time is over," Gizella said firmly. "For the sake of their own standing in the world, they don't make a fuss or do anything silly. And every do'Verrada is tender of his bride's feelings. Cossimio told me he'd send Lissina from Court, but I told him not to be absurd, we'd already become friends and she was about to marry the Baron do'Dregez so she'd be here anyhow, and why make a fuss? I knew he loved me."

"Gizella . . . I don't think I'm as good and kind a person as you are. I don't want the Grijalva woman anywhere near me—or Arrigo."

"Perfectly understandable, but I think you'll find your worry is all for nothing. Tazia knows her duty and her place. Now, be easy in your mind about all of it, carrida, and let me send your maid in to help you out of those stifling clothes. I'll wake you in time for dinner. Afterward we show ourselves at the balcony during the procession through the streets. It's very pretty—torches blazing, people singing and dancing—" She giggled again. "My first Providenssia here, Lissina and I borrowed our maids' dresses and sneaked out to mingle with the crowds. How we danced, and with such handsome young men! And, do you know, one of them turned out to be Cossi!"

"En verreio?" Mechella laughed.

"En verro," Gizella corrected, smiling. "He and I were both very young, and months of uninterrupted Court life had us both longing for escape. We hadn't let on to each other, you see, for fear of causing disappointment. The very next day he took me to Chasseriallo, our hunting lodge, and all autumn we lived alone together with only a single servant! You were raised at a much grander court than this, so you're used to all the duties and pressures, but there may come a time when you need Chasseriallo. It belongs to Arrigo now, and he loves it and takes any excuse to visit. So you bear that in mind, carrida." She got up from the bed, smoothed her skirts, and began taking pins from her upswept dark hair. "I'll send in your maid now."

"I—I haven't one."

"What?"

"Aunt Permilla said I must become Tira Virteian in all things. And I agree with her," she said determinedly. "I'd be very grateful if you'd help me choose my servants—and advise me about clothes and correct my accent and—"

Gizella sighed. "Lissina did all those things for me. Except the accent, of course—I was born in Castello Granidia! But Lissina is unique, and I suppose we mustn't expect the same from Tazia. I would never have allowed her to become Arrigo's Mistress if there was anything wrong with her character, but she's no Lissina."

The maid's name was Otonna. She was a broad-faced, cheerful girl, immediately likable, extremely efficient. When she had come, unlaced Mechella's bodice, wrapped her in a silken bedrobe, and departed, the new Dona lay back on the lacy bed and reflected on her introduction to her new family, her new home, her new people. If it all bore a delicate patina of joy and wonder due to the love she bore Arrigo and the promise of bearing a son, there was yet a dark blemish of rust: Tazia Grijalva. She was no Lissina, warmly welcoming to her former lover's bride; and Mechella was no Gizella, bred and born in the country, accustomed to its traditions.

Still . . . she *was* young, Arrigo did love her, and she carried his child. What barren, aging, cast-off Mistress could possibly compete?

THIRTY-SEVEN

"No hope for it," said Grand Duke Cossimio to Lord Limner Mequel across the vast conference table. "It'll have to be Arrigo."

The Grijalva frowned. "Your Grace, with respect—"

"Yes, yes," Cossimio interrupted. "Just married, wife pregnant, new life, and so on. But I can't go myself, none of the Courtfolk will do, and I can't send just a Grijalva, he wouldn't have the necessary access. Arrigo can take the Limner to all but the private discussions. Besides, it'll be good experience for the boy. I won't live forever, you know."

"Nor I," Mequel mused, "and my time will end much sooner than yours. So I suggest that a few of our most promising young painters accompany Don Arrigo to Diettro Mareia. It will be good experience for them, too."

The Grand Duke harrumphed. " 'Quellito, you know how I hate to be reminded that you won't always be around to rely on."

"We've done good work together," the Lord Limner said with a smile. "This Ghillasian marriage, averting trouble with Taglis and Friesemark—"

"Not to mention that fool nephew of do'Brendizia's," Cossimio added, frowning. "Did we ever catch any of his confederates?"

"A few. They were dealt with. Nothing for you to bother about."

"Call up the Corteis—what stupidity! Legislate everything from taxes to treaties! Haven't we done well by the people, Mequel? Haven't we kept them at peace? Given them prosperity? What more do they want?"

"It seems that the very conditions we created have birthed ingratitude."

"Eiha, a man who works all the day to feed his family has no time or energy for politics."

"Precisely, Your Grace. But one who is well-fed, warmly clothed, with a stout floor underfoot and a snug roof overhead—"

"Make them rich and they start thinking up ways to get richer," Cossimio concluded in disgust.

"Yet I doubt they'd risk that wealth—or their snug roofs—in

pursuit of electing a Corteis. They'll spend a nobleman's money sooner than their own. The Brendizia boy's inheritance vanished that way, you know."

"No, I hadn't known. Moronno! Keep an eye on the younger generation, Mequel. It's not just money but influence and leadership they want. No Tira Virteian worth the salt in his soup would follow some merchant even a single step." Decisively stacking documents, he added, "I'll tell Arrigo this evening that he's off to Diettro Mareia. You choose a few Limners to go with him, and a competent one to do the paintings."

"I'd been wondering about that," Mequel confessed. "Not who to send, for I've a few ideas, but what ought to be painted."

"If Arrigo succeeds, then only the usual interiors, I think, for keeping an eye on our dear Principio Felisso. If he hashes it, we may need something more elaborate."

With quiet casualness, Mequel said, "The Principio is a devoutly religious man."

Cossimio's dark eyes sparked with interest. "That's right, he is. After I sent that icon, he shipped me fifty cases of his best wines. An icon that didn't quite do what I intended," he reminded Mequel irritably. "Or we wouldn't be in this position now."

"Granted. But Pedranno was at the end of his life and his powers, and perhaps did not work with all the skill that made him Lord Limner to begin with."

The Grand Duke frowned. "Is that what you're afraid of? That you're getting old and won't be able to work anymore?"

"It has crossed my mind. With Pedranno's example preceding me . . ."

"You're only forty-two!"

"He was but a year older when he painted the icon."

"I won't hear of it. You're stronger than ever, 'Quellito."

"Your confidence honors me, Cossi," he said softly. "But soon— oh, not this year or even next—but *soon,* my powers will begin to fade. When they do, I'll tell you. Long before that I'll have a new Lord Limner for you."

"I won't allow you to retire," the Grand Duke warned. "And I won't touch your damned portrait or allow *you* to touch it either! Don't you ever ask me to stick pins in your picture or whatever it was my deplorable ancestor the first Cossimio did to kill Lord Limner Timius."

"He did so at Timius' request, as a favor. The Lord Limner was terrified of growing old and feeble."

"*I* say it was murder!"

"A merciful death, by the hand of a friend."

Cossimio scowled horribly, thick black eyebrows nearly hiding his eyes. "Mequel, you know how well I love you. I hope you love me as much. But I still say it was murder, and I won't hear any more about it—or do anything like it for you!"

"En verro, I will never ask of you what Timius asked of his Cossimio. But times were different then. . . ." He trailed off, then shook himself. "This question of the Diettro Mareian pictures is as yet unresolved. I like the idea of another icon, something the Principio will live with constantly, pray before on his knees at night in his own bedchamber."

"Keeping faith with us as well as with the Faith," Cossimio said, nodding. "Be careful, though. I think his wife has her suspicions. Remember when her uncle connived with the Tza'ab?" He grinned suddenly, white teeth bright between mustache and beard. "One of your better efforts, amico meyo! Painting the old boy ulcerated with the symptoms of sifilisso until he owned up to our Embajadorro, and then a miraculous 'cure'!"

"We can't use the same sort of technique on the Principio, then. His wife would note the similarities. Pity."

Cossimio thought it over, then nodded. "A *Peintraddo Sonho*. For a religious man that would do very well. See to it, Mequel." Rising, he placed documents in an iron-bound coffer and locked it. "I'm off to pry my son out of his wife's bed. I must admit, Arrigo is a damned fortunate man. She's a charming girl, and staggeringly beautiful—when she's not green with morning sickness. Any word on how Tazia's taking it?"

"She continues in Casteya at the do'Alva estate, silent. I can make enquiries if you like."

"No, no. Let the woman have her dignity—and her rich new husband! Arrigo seems to have forgotten all about her. I recall being just as callous about Lissina when first I wed 'Zella."

Mequel smiled. "Not callous. Merely in love."

"Still am!" The Grand Duke laughed. "Arrigo looks to be repeating my good fortune. It would please me if Mechella and Tazia could become friends, but that's up to them, I suppose.

By the way, do you think we could use Mechella to sound out the wives and sisters of potential traitors in the nobility?"

"She was raised at a royal court, she must understand how to use social occasions for political purposes. But she shouldn't be asked to work for us until after the baby is born, I think."

Cossimio nodded vigorously. "Only then can we be truly certain of her. I'll have no repetition of Duchess Elseva—loyal to the do'Elleons, her father's spy for the first years of her marriage—dreadful woman."

"The births of her sons changed her mind."

"Exactly. Nothing like her own flesh as Heir to interest a mother in a country's future. And speaking of futures, consider it a Grand Ducal Edict to live at least another twenty years." He placed a large hand on Mequel's shoulder. "I need you too much."

The Lord Limner bowed his head submissively, a little smile playing around his lips. "I'll try, Your Grace. But how will you punish me if I fail?"

"That's not funny, 'Quellito."

⚷⚷

Has Sario shared what he knows? Are any of the Viehos Fratos aware of what he can do? It would give such power to the Grijalvas, this mastery of true magic—the Serranos would be left in the dirt, Tira Virte would defeat anyone who dared challenge us—but he would be careful what he told, and they, knowing, even more careful of how it was used—Matra, such power—we Grijalvas could become Dukes if we chose—

Eiha, not with our chi'patro blood. Not with the Ecclesials opposing us. They barely tolerate our existence. If we were to attempt anything political—

He would never give up the deepest secrets. Never. And even if others knew, could any of them paint me from this prison? Would they, knowing I am here by Sario's hand? How much do they fear him?

Merciful Mother, You who bore a Child, who but You would dare have mercy on me?

⚷⚷

"Must you go?"

"My father needs me." Arrigo didn't add *"At long last!"*; it was not something he wished to admit to his bride of scarcely six months. He went on sorting the clothes his servant had laid out for inspection, throwing rejects onto a chair. Uniform of the Shagarra Regiment, yes; uniform of the Sea Guards, no—the redoubtable sailors of Diettro Mareia would laugh themselves silly at Tira Virte's pretensions to a navy. But the uniform reminded him of one reason why the journey must be undertaken now. "I hate leaving you, 'Chella, but I have to get there and back before the sea becomes too rough."

Eyes round with fear, Mechella clasped both hands beneath her chin. "The sea—oh, Arrigo, I hadn't even thought—couldn't you go overland?"

"And take five weeks about it—each way!—instead of only one?" He smiled over his shoulder at her. She curled in a deep chair, silk-and-lace bedrobe frothing around her body and framing her pale face. "Travel by sea is perfectly safe until the Nov'viva storms, and I'll be home before that."

"Home," she said glumly, "to a bloated, hideous cow."

He crossed to her and took her fisted hands in his, kissing each whitened knuckle. "Home to my beautiful, adorable wife." Kneeling beside her, he pressed one hand to her belly. "I fancy I can feel him. He gets bigger and you get lovelier every day. By the time I get back, you'll be so dazzling no one will look at you without—"

"—without wondering how anyone so fat can even walk!" Giggling, she leaned over to kiss him. They were in his half of their shared apartments, and tonight they would share his bed—passionately, for when he returned her pregnancy would be too far advanced for lovemaking. Her kisses began to kindle his desire for her, and once again he marveled that they had not spent a single night apart since their marriage. He'd never suspected he would become so besotted by this girl, so infatuated with her long body and her golden hair—so unlike Tazia! Suddenly he wondered what it would be like not to have Mechella beside him all those nights in beautiful, romantic Diettro Mareia. When this anticipated lack of her enflamed him further, he got reluctantly to his feet, for he must finish the packing.

"Promise you'll be sweet to me, Arrigo, when I look like a cow about to have twins."

"Even if it looks like triplets," he teased, and she laughed again. "The last person who called me 'sweet' was my mother, when I was about five years old."

"Oh, but you look just like a little boy in the mornings, with your hair all rumply and your eyes all soft with sleep."

"With not *enough* sleep! And whose fault is that?"

"I can't help it that I love you so much—" Her guileless blue eyes took on a sly glint. "—or that you're such a wonderful lover. Whose fault is *that?*"

"Yours. You inspire me. Which do you think, the gray coat or the tan?"

"The tan. It puts little gold sparkles in your eyes—or is that my fault, too?"

"Stop looking at me that way or I'll never get this finished. And it all has to be ready by morning. I leave tomorrow night."

The playful gleam vanished from her iris-blue eyes. "So soon? Oh, Arrigo!"

"There'll be plenty for you to do. You won't miss me too much."

"I'll miss you terribly! Don't be angry with me, but it frightens me, being here without you. All these people—your mother has been so kind, and I'm very grateful, but without you here to guide me I'll feel so alone!"

"Everyone loves you, 'Chella. Remember what my father said? Just be yourself, and no one will be able to resist you."

"But it won't be the same as being at your side. What am I to do if they ignore me once you're gone? I'm still so unsure about protocol, and manners. I pronounce things wrong no matter how hard I try. What if I do something that's not right?"

"Don't work yourself into a state, carrida, it's bad for the baby. You are Princess Mechella of Ghillas. No one will ignore you. And whatever you do *becomes* right."

"I'm Dona Mechella of Tira Virte now," she stated proudly. Then, in a smaller voice, "Ghillas seems very far away."

Arrigo applied the standard marital remedy for unhappiness. He swept her up into his arms, carried her to the bed, and made love to her amid a sea of silken sheets the exact color of her eyes.

Hours later, as she lay fast asleep in his arms, he reflected that there was much to be said for a young, beautiful, loving wife. Mechella's shy and innocent sensuality, her eager attention to his instruction in the arts of love, her gratitude—these were new in his experience, and sweetly intoxicating. Still, as he stroked the delicate skin of her long back, he felt a fleeting pang of longing for Tazia's bed. He missed her familiar scent and warmth, her sure knowledge of him, the comfortable fit of his flesh to hers. Twelve years. . . .

His hand slid between Mechella's belly and his own hip

to stroke the swell that was his child, the first of many strong sons. And daughters, too, pretty little girls with Mechella's golden hair and delicious giggle. His wife, his Dona, his Grand Duchess, mother of his children. He slept, smiling, certain that when he was far from home his dreams would be of Mechella.

THIRTY-EIGHT

The populace of Diettro Mareia turned out in huge numbers for Arrigo's arrival. From the port to the Ressidensa Principeia, crowds lined the streets waving bits of sapphire-blue cloth and cheering Arrigo's horseback progress. He was touched and pleased—until he realized that their shouts were not of "Don Arrigo" but "Dona Arriga": their way of naming his wife.

He laughed and shouted to Dioniso Grijalva at his side, "I think I'm a disappointment to them!"

"It had been rumored she'd come with Your Grace!"

And so it proved. Principio Felisso della Marei met him at the top of the Ressidensa steps, and they had barely exchanged formal kisses before he said, "But where is your fascinating wife?"

"Regretto, Highness, she was unable to come with me. She very much wanted to, but my father is concerned for his grandson."

"Ha!" bellowed Felisso, beaming all over his wide, wonderfully ugly face. "You hear that?" he yelled to the crowd. "Not half a year wed, and he's already got her with child! A cheer for Dona Arriga and her son!"

Dioniso sidled over and, his mouth an inch from Arrigo's ear, advised His Grace to show the portrait. Arrigo nodded. Dioniso snapped his fingers at a brace of Grijalvas, who between them carried a huge velurro-wrapped painting. Its unveiling brought another tidal wave of sound. Felisso sucked air in through his teeth—the local expression of admiration, which Arrigo found singularly vulgar. A moment later Arrigo himself was sucking air in earnest; Felisso had dealt him a powerful fist in the ribs—the local expression of congratulation, which Arrigo found singularly painful.

"Madreia ei Filhio, Cousin, I wonder you leave her bed at all!"

Deprived of breath and speech, Arrigo managed a smile.

Dioniso—who, not having been introduced, did not yet exist as far as the Principio was concerned—shattered protocol but proved himself worthy of the Embajadorro's cap Cossimio had given him before this trip. Bowing low amid the crush of nobility, he shouted at the Principio, "While Don Arrigo has compelling reasons to stay in Meya Suerta—" Much sucking of air as they all paid tribute once more to Mechella's portrait. "—his friendship for Your

Highness demanded that you have the earliest opportunity to admire Dona Mechella!"

"Friendship?" Another genial buffet, this time to Arrigo's shoulder. "He wants to torment me, more likely! A portrait instead of the real thing! Quella Bellissima!"

Breath recovered at last, Arrigo attended to compordotta. "Cousin, I bring to your notice Embajadorro Dioniso Grijalva, my personal assistant."

Now that Dioniso existed, he could speak more freely. "I'm glad your Highness likes the painting. A very nervous young limner is standing over there trying to hide his anxiety about its reception. Cabral!" A Grijalva stepped forward, bowed, and did not straighten until Dioniso introduced him. "The young man who painted this masterwork—though admittedly no one could ever paint an unpleasing picture of Dona Mechella! His name is Cabral, Your Highness, and these others are our kinsmen Zevierin and Rafeyo, Grijalvas all."

"Fine work!" Felisso said heartily to Cabral. "Welcome to Diettro Mareia! Now, you walk that picture all the way around the terrace here so they can get a good look at her, but don't you dare let anybody touch it! My steward will tell you where to hang it!" He paused to admire Mechella's image once more, hissing prodigiously. "Grandia Bellissima! You *are* intent on torturing me, Cousin!"

Inside, down a short hallway and up a long flight of steps, Arrigo found himself in the presence of the Principia Felissa. She allowed him to kiss her forehead, responded with the antiquated lips-and-heart salute that was used only at great holidays nowadays in Meya Suerta, and enjoined him to call her by her personal name, Rosilan.

"Cousins should not be so formal, eihia?" she asked with a flirtatious wink. "I won't keep you, for you must be tired from your journey. We dine privately tonight, just the three of us, and you can tell me about married life."

"I was hoping for some advice about just that, Cousin," Arrigo replied with a smile. "You have so happy a union—and so many children! Though to look at you, I would never believe you had *one* child, let alone eight!"

"Nine," Felisso corrected. "You've made a good start, Arrigo. Just go on getting her pregnant!" So saying, he dealt his wife a hearty slap on the backside. She laughed and sank a fist into his substantial belly, and this was Arrigo's introduction to the rulers of Diettro Mareia.

Rosilan was as beautiful as Felisso was ugly: she with honey-colored skin, he dappled with freckles; she dainty of figure and features, he like a wine cask on short legs, with a nose that took up the majority of his face. But their eyes were the same hazel-green, and their hair was the same curly dark auburn, and their hands were alike in that the thumbs were oddly elongated. The similarities were unsurprising, for their mothers were sisters and their fathers' fathers had been brothers. The presentation of their brood—four sons, five daughters, all auburn-haired, all plain as peasants, and none showing the slightest sign of intelligence behind their hazel eyes—was Arrigo's introduction to the dangers of inbreeding.

Later, alone with Dioniso in one of the Ressidensa's suffocatingly ornate suites, he said, " 'Cousin' I may be to the Principio, but Grazzo do'Matra the relationship dates back four generations! Did you *see* their litter?"

"Litter, indeed, Your Grace—that should've been drowned mercifully at birth."

Arrigo reclined in a long, low, preposterously carved and gilded chair. "Tell me, if it's not too intrusive, how do the Grijalvas avoid the demonstrable perils of consanguinity?"

"We keep excellent records, Your Grace," was the laconic reply.

"Yes, but—after all these centuries of mating Grijalva mainly with Grijalva . . ."

"There are the occasional unfortunates," Dioniso admitted. "But because the truest Gift descends in the female line, it is possible to marry outside the family and still produce a talented painter."

"So there's an infusion of new blood every so often? Very wise. I hadn't known that about your women."

"On this journey, I will tell you several things you do not yet know about the Grijalvas."

There was that in the Limner's voice that made Arrigo glance up. "Things my father knows?"

"Things only Grand Dukes and the Viehos Fratos know."

"Such as?"

Dioniso hesitated, as if he'd already said too much, then shrugged. "For the present, I may say only that it would be helpful if you and the Principio exchanged personal tokens at some point. A lock of hair, perhaps."

"A—?" Abruptly he remembered that Tazia always insisted on cutting his hair herself, carefully gathering the clippings for immediate burning. His laugh sounded nervous even to him as he said, "Surely you don't believe old superstitions!"

"Facts, Your Grace. With a brush made of the Principio's hair, it will be possible to paint an icon to inspire faith with us as well as with the Mother and Son. The Grand Duke mentioned to you that such an icon, painted to the Principio's tastes, is my duty here."

"Yes, but—"

"Usually collection of . . . personal effects . . . would fall to a Grijalva, and you would be unaware of it. But I believe you deserve to know such things."

"Before I become Grand Duke?" Arrigo sat straight up. "Tell me at once, Dioniso—is my father ill? Does he have only a short time left? Is that why you—"

"Your father is in perfect health, Grazzo do'Matra, and with Her blessing will live many long years."

He exhaled in relief. "Then why are you telling me such things?"

"I don't agree with the Viehos Fratos that Heirs should be kept ignorant until succession. How much more good you can do for Tira Virte if you *know!*" He paused again. "I have broken certain vows by telling you even this much. I hope you won't think that any vows to *you* will be broken as lightly."

"No, no, not at all," Arrigo said distractedly. "You do this to help me and our country, and I'm grateful. I'll remember it."

"By your leave, then, I'll go make sure the portrait is hung properly. These Mareians are notoriously clumsy of hand and eye." He gestured with a grimace to the vulgar display around them, and Arrigo laughed.

Dioniso bowed himself out, taking a moment in the hall for a private chuckle. Then he hurried to the gallery, not only to educate the servants in how to hang a painting but to begin the education of Rafeyo.

What Rafeyo learned that afternoon about the respect due Grijalva art was augmented that evening by a lesson about the obligations of a Grijalva arrtio.

With Don Arrigo dining privately with the Principio and Principia, the rest of his little delegation was free to seek their meal at one of the city's best restaurants. Dioniso—drawing on the experiences of another life—recommended the Fructio di Marei, telling his Grijalva brethren that one could hear better rumors elsewhere, but they were after gusto tonight, not gossip.

"And the gusto here is said to be superior even to the Quattrei Astreia," he told them as they entered the establishment, a small cavern of a room hung with gleaming brass lustrossos that glistened candlelight onto fine glassware laid out at the dozen tables.

The innkeeper, overhearing his food praised beyond the most celebrated restaurant in Aute-Ghillas, beamed and escorted his Grijalva
guests to the best table—exactly as Dioniso intended that he
should.

The innkeeper flourished huge squares of snowy linen onto each
lap. Bending close to Dioniso's ear, he whispered in very bad Tira
Virteian, "Quattrei Astreia not so good now?"

"As good as ever it was—I was there this year."

A long, satisfied sigh. "Bonnito Gusto, amiccio meyio!"

And good eating they had. Dinner consisted of seven exquisite
courses, each presented by the innkeeper himself while his wife
and the wine steward debated vintages and a strolling gamba
player serenaded them with favorites from Tira Virte. Cabral, who
had grown up outside the Palasso with a stepfather who adored dining out whenever he was in town, was impressed; Zevierin and
Rafeyo were overwhelmed. A simple appetizer of bread topped by
olives and mushrooms was followed by bowls of creamy herbed
rice, fish stuffed with almonds, and a lightly dressed salad of
greens and fruit to cleanse the tongue before the beef was served.
This came in medallions fanned with sliced potatoes and red
onions drizzled with a spicy-sweet sauce. After apple tartlets,
cheese and biscuits, and tiny cups of strong black coffee, the feast
ended with the innkeeper's wife pouring short glasses full of clear
liquor, each nestled in its own little silver tub of ice.

The three older men took it on themselves to further Rafeyo's
culinary education. Dioniso lectured on wines, Cabral on meats
and cheeses, and Zevierin on the intricacies of sauce. The tendency
of every growing boy to inhale his food was scowled out of Rafeyo
with orders to savor every mouthful or he'd offend the innkeeper.
But what awed the boy most was not the meal or the wines but the
deferential service and the respectful nods of patrons who recognized the Grijalvas by their distinctive gray feathered caps.

"At home," Rafeyo confided in a whisper, "only the Fratos are
treated so. I feel like a Lord Limner!"

And behaved as if he were. But his dignity was at last defeated
by the clear liquor that ended the meal. Deceptively smooth on first
sip, he didn't notice the pepper flavoring until it grabbed him by the
throat. When he finally stopped coughing, he wiped his eyes and at
Cabral's urging drank a whole glass of water straight down.

Dioniso leaned back in his chair, a smile on his lips. "Don't look
so downcast. You disgraced no one—not yourself, or us, or the
Grijalvas, or Tira Virte. In fact, it's a great compliment to this

house that you nearly choked to death on their homebrew. They may even give you a bottle."

Rafeyo looked alarmed, then grinned. "I'll be sure to accept politely—and then give it to an enemy!"

"Remind me to stay on your good side," Cabral chuckled. Nodding to his left, he said more softly, "That's an interesting turban that woman has on."

"A Tza'ab?" Rafeyo's eyes went wide. "Here?"

"Of course not." Dioniso didn't even give the woman a glance. "Turbans are current fashion here. But I agree, Cabral. It's interesting. I noticed it earlier."

"Why?" Rafeyo demanded. "I think she's ugly."

"Not shy, are you?" grinned Zevierin, a Limner about Cabral's age. "The headdress indicates growing taste for things Tza'ab, which Tira Virte supplies to all other nations the way it supplies limners—through a strict monopoly. Now, this control of popular Tza'ab goods would make our merchants even richer than they are—if Principio Felisso hadn't begun secret negotiations with the Tza'ab Empress."

"Bypassing our monopoly," Cabral finished, "and breaking a treaty that goes back a hundred years. We're here to persuade the Principio otherwise."

"It's kind of boring, though, isn't it?" the boy asked. "I mean, painting a treaty to stop a war is one thing, but—"

"Not one to waste your energies on anything less than the grand canvas either," Dioniso observed. "Do you have any idea how much Tira Virte makes off import taxes on Tza'ab rugs, cloth, jewelry, glass, and pitch?"

Rafeyo did not.

Cabral gave a shrug. "Much Grijalva work has to do with such 'boring' things. You don't paint to serve your own talents, Rafeyo, you paint to serve your country and your Grand Dukes." All at once he nudged Zevierin. "Stop gaping at that woman over there, or I'll tell my sister."

Zevierin blushed darkly and glowered. Cabral grinned at him.

"Who are you watching?" Rafeyo asked. "Is this one pretty?"

"Very. Two tables away. Don't turn and stare, Rafeyo, it's not polite. Besides, her husband is with her, and worships her."

Dioniso brushed crumbs off the tablecloth. "The gamba player has been performing for them alone when he hasn't been gracing us—and he won't take any money from them for it. So, Rafeyo, what can you tell me about them? Quick glances only."

His gaze darted over his shoulder a few times. Hesitantly, he began, "They're married, but not very long because they're still crazy in love."

"Such cynicism! What else?"

"They don't often come to such expensive places. Their clothes are nice enough, but she's not wearing any jewels and he's not comfortable—like he's afraid he'll spill something that won't wash out. I think they might be celebrating something—their first anniversary?"

"Not bad," Zevierin complimented.

"But not correct either," Dioniso said. "It's not their first anniversary, she's not wearing her bridal coronet. That's traditional here. By his expression, they've just found out she's going to have a baby."

Cabral snorted. "You're right. There's no mistaking that stupid grin."

"Just like Don Arrigo," Rafeyo muttered.

"You judge your do'Verradas harshly," Zevierin observed. "Tazia had her twelve years with him. It's time he married and fathered a Grand Duke."

"But he *did* have that same stupid look on his face," the boy insisted, and the other three exchanged glances acknowledging that wine had had its usual effect on the very young.

"Cabral is quite correct, it's common to expectant fathers," Dioniso said. "As if they'd accomplished a major miracle by getting a woman with child! Now, if it was you, or me, or Zevierin, it *would* be remarkable!"

Rafeyo giggled; Cabral smiled, not minding that he was not Confirmattio; Zevierin's expression turned wooden before he glanced away.

Dioniso continued, "So they're not rich enough to be regulars here, they're deeply in love, and she's pregnant. How would you paint them?"

Before Rafeyo could reply, the young man picked up the hitherto ignored account tally—and blanched.

"Uh-oh," Cabral murmured. "He can't pay the bill."

The young man visibly gathered his courage and summoned the wine steward. There followed the sort of dispute rarely if ever seen in so elegant an establishment. Though conducted in rapid-fire Diettro Mareian, the Grijalvas were able to gather the gist of it. The bottle ordered was *not* the excruciatingly costly vintage listed on the tally. The wine steward showed the label; the young man looked slightly ill.

"The steward's mistake, of course," Cabral remarked. "Look at his face. It's a common enough ploy to increase the cost of the meal, though this waiter must be inexperienced, to choose this couple."

"So?" Rafeyo asked, owl-eyed.

"So," Cabral finished, "*somebody* has to pay for the wine, and if not this boy, then the waiter. And he's obviously not impressed by young love."

"The gamba player is," Zevierin said.

"They're talking too fast. I can't get more than six words in ten," Rafeyo complained.

Cabral obligingly translated. "The gamba player tells the wine steward to own up to the error. Refusal. He offers his own tips to cover the wine—which our young friend is too proud to accept. And now here comes our host to investigate."

The lovely young wife was crimson with impending tears; her equally humiliated husband was grimly determined as he explained their circumstances to the innkeeper. Cabral continued his commentary.

"We were right. They've saved for this night since they married, to celebrate their first baby. The wine steward again denies any mistake. He's lying." Cabral blinked suddenly. "Matra Dolcha, sixty-eight mareias for a bottle of wine? That's more than their whole dinner cost! What do you think, Dioniso?"

"I think I am a very lucky man." He groped in his pockets, then swore. "Merditto! My pencil case is in my other coat. Cabral? Zevierin?"

Rafeyo dug a hand into a pocket and came up with a small sketchpad and two bits of charcoal. "Will this do? Are we going to pay their bill?"

"In a manner of speaking. Eiha, I haven't had this pleasure in quite some years. Cabral, clear the table."

Zevierin rose. "The needlework pillows hint at an embroidery frame or two upstairs, I'll go ask."

"Good," Dioniso said absently, glancing around the room with a critical, evaluating eye.

"But what are you doing?" Rafeyo asked plaintively.

"Shh," said Cabral, eager eyes fixed on the charcoal stub in Dioniso's fingers. "Watch."

"Watch *what?*"

"Shh!"

Dioniso swept away the last of the crumbs, pursed his lips, then nodded to himself and began to wield the charcoal with sure strokes. Tables, chairs, ceiling beams, polished lustrossos, arched kitchen doorway—all took shape with breathtaking speed. He even incorporated the stains on the cloth into the composition. A splash of red wine became the flowers on the serving bar; a spot of sauce turned into the pewter platter hung on the far wall.

People were drawn in just as quickly, their characters portrayed as accurately as the knots in the planks of the floor. The innkeeper, his wife, the gamba player; the haughty woman in the Tza'ab turban, a boisterous family of six at the corner table; couples shyly courting and couples long married; a group of wealthy merchants enjoying an evening away from their wives (their expensive mistresses were diplomatically drawn in at another table). And, of course, the young couple in all the joy of their expectations. The wine steward was conspicuous in his absence. Cabral began to chuckle and ended laughing aloud with Rafeyo and Zevierin, who had returned with an embroidery frame.

"Bassda!" Dioniso snarled in mock fury, grinned all over his face. "How's a man supposed to work in all this racket?"

The Grijalvas were making the only noise. Everyone's neck craned to see what the Limner was up to. Those near enough to witness the miraculous transformation of a white tablecloth into a work of art whispered of its progress to others farther away.

At last Dioniso stood back. He surveyed his work for some moments, added a line here, a smudge there, and signed it. He whisked the cloth from the table in a swirl and held it up for inspection. Patrons exclaimed on recognizing themselves, and applause soon followed. Lively, evocative, in a minimum of strokes Dioniso had captured the room and those in it as only a Grijalva master could.

Cabral bowed to the innkeeper. "I trust this will cover everything?" he asked, and Zevierin groaned at the pun.

Befuddled with bliss at having a genuine Grijalva of his very own, drawn in his very restaurant on his very tablecloth—and perfectly aware that it was worth twice the cost of a whole case of the disputed wine—the innkeeper babbled incoherent thanks. He then ordered the wine steward to bring a bottle of the vintage in question to the Grijalva table.

Zevierin held the embroidery frame up to the cloth. It encircled less than a quarter of the drawing. "A bedframe might work," he complained. "Did you have to draw *everybody,* Dioniso?"

"Dioniso?" The innkeeper squinted at the signature. "This other name is—"

"Yes, I know." Handing the cloth over, Dioniso crossed to the young couple. The husband stammered, trying to protest; the wife, beyond speech, caught Dioniso's hand in both her own, liquid brown eyes eloquent of her gratitude. Smiling down at her, the Limner said, "You've done me a great service tonight, one I wish to repay."

He freed his fingers and plucked a clean napkin from a nearby table. Spreading the linen out, he sketched a charcoal portrait of the startled pair as they had looked for most of the evening: gazing raptly at each other, giddy with joy.

"Will you do me the honor of accepting this?" he asked when he finished. "I regret I won't be in Diettro Mareia when your baby is born, for surely the child of such handsome parents would be a marvel to paint. Please allow me to give you this small token of my hopes for your continued happiness and a fine, healthy son."

Zevierin snatched up the napkin. "Now, *this* fits!" He stretched it over the inner circle of wood, eased the outer circle into place, tightened the brass screw, and gave it into the girl's trembling hands. "And it's signed 'Dioniso Grijalva,' which means it's a personal gift. You really can't refuse, you know," he ended merrily. "He'd die of shame if you rejected him!"

The young husband recovered himself and with dignity said, "Master Dioniso, if the child is indeed a boy, he'll bear your name. We are in your debt."

"No, you aren't," Cabral told him. "That's just the point." To the room at large he explained, "You've just witnessed the continuation of a Grijalva tradition. One night in 1123, Lord Limner Riobaro was dining in a restaurant nearly as fine as this. It turned out that some young students near him were given someone else's roast by mistake—" He cast a speaking look at the mortified wine steward. "—and couldn't pay for it. Rather than insulting the students by paying in coin, Riobaro drew a picture on a tablecloth and presented it to the innkeeper. It still adorns the wall there in Castello Joharra."

"Castello Granidia," said Dioniso, who ought to know.

"Ah," said Cabral, with a bow. "In any case, ever since, any of us lucky enough to see a similar situation pays tribute to the great Lord Limner by doing as he did, and signing his name to the picture."

Dioniso bowed to the blushing girl. "So you see, it's both a privilege and an honor for me to draw this picture. I thank you for the opportunity. En verro, *I* am in *your* debt."

Later, when they were weaving their way through the streets back to the Ressidensa, Rafeyo proved himself a very sentimental drunk. "That was *beautiful*," he kept saying, leaning on Zevierin's shoulder. "Jus' *beautiful*."

"We know," Cabral said patiently. "You've told us. Several times."

"It *was*," the boy insisted. "Even *looked* like R'baro's work!"

"By custom," Dioniso said, "we try to use his style."

Rafeyo nodded owlishly. "*Jus'* like 'im."

"Damned close," Cabral agreed. "Maybe the shadows weren't quite Riobaro, but the signature was perfect."

The man who had once been Riobaro arched a brow.

Rafeyo came to his defense. "Was *jus'* like Ri-o-bar—*ohhh!*"

Zevierin spun the boy away from him and held him at arm's length, but too late. Selections from a seven-course dinner and a great deal of wine and homebrew ended up on Zevierin's brand-new boots. "Merditto!"

Dioniso and Cabral laughed as Rafeyo collapsed into Zevierin's arms and slowly slid down his length to the cobblestones. Refusing to ruin their own clothes by helping to pick him up, let alone carry him, they laughed harder when the young Limner hoisted the boy across one shoulder like a sack of rags for the paper mill—and the completely unconscious Rafeyo continued his disgraceful performance down Zevierin's back all six blocks to the Ressidensa.

Dioniso reflected with regret that he must remember caution in drinking; Rafeyo obviously couldn't hold his liquor worth a damn.

THIRTY-NINE

When Principia Rosilan showed up for weekly worship in the gigantic Ecclesialla della Corrasson Sangua wearing a Tza'ab turban, Arrigo suspected he was in trouble. He was sure of it when Principio Felisso commented on how delightfully it suited her.

She tossed her head to set the golden tassel dancing flirtatiously. "I suppose fashions in Tira Virte have long since embraced and discarded Tza'ab follies. But it's all new to those of us in Diettro Mareia."

Meaning, of course, that there was a growing demand for all Tza'ab goods, and Tira Virte's monopoly on trade in them was resented. In the Ecclesialla, the day's Recitassion reinforced the message. A sancto with a deeply sonorous voice read the tale of the farmer who, owning the only bull in the area, charged exorbitant fees for the animal's services. On the night of Fuega Vesperra, the spring celebration of conception, the greedy farmer dreamed of a cow weeping in despair for lack of a calf. Claiming that the gentle brown eyes were exactly those of the Mother in the village Sanctia's icon, the chastened farmer thereafter sent his bull to service the local cows free of charge.

It was a standard Recitassion for news of an important pregnancy—the royal bull fulfilling his duty to the nation by siring the next generation—and could have been interpreted as a salute to Arrigo and Mechella. But the farmer's monopoly on the bull and the staggering sums he charged before his change of heart were more to Felisso's point. Arrigo sat, and listened, and fulminated.

Just in case he hadn't understood, dinner that evening was served by all nine ugly little della Mareis, just as a Tza'ab host's offspring served honored guests. They wore matching suits of black-and-red striped Tza'ab cloth and the long pointed toes of their Tza'ab slippers were decorated with tiny silver Tza'ab bells. Yet as unsubtle as the display was, the term "Tza'ab" was never mentioned.

Arrigo returned late to his chamber, head still clanging with all those irksome little bells, and summoned Dioniso.

"Paint the icon," he ordered. "I don't give a damn how it's done. Get a lock of his hair yourself—and one from the Principia, too.

Stick pins in them to get their blood if you like! I want that icon painted *now,* Limner."

Dioniso bowed to the Heir's impatience. The next morning Rafeyo got "lost" near the Principio's bathroom. That afternoon Zevierin presented a flagon of perfume (distilled by Cabral's sister Leilias) to the Principia's personal maid, with whom he had been purposefully dallying these several days. That evening in Dioniso's chamber, Rafeyo produced a vial of the princely urine and Zevierin handed over twenty long strands from the princessly hairbrush.

On the fifteenth and final day of Arrigo's visit—with goodwill blooming like roses and the words "Tza'ab" and "trade" still unmentioned in the same sentence—Arrigo said his farewells and presented his cousins with two icons.

The first was for Rosilan, a dainty glory of soft colors and tender brushwork depicting the smiling Mother in the first days of Her pregnancy, surrounded by nine children. (There was no resemblance to any of the nine ugly little della Mareias; that would have been heretical as well as an aesthetic disaster.) In a sunny outdoor scene, set in an orchard with pines in the background, the Mother sat on spring grass with a wreath of blue-flowering rosemary crowning Her brow. In Her lap was a basket of plums, symbolizing the coming fruition of Her womb. Her smile was directed at the one little boy who held a plum in his hand, signifying that the Child to be born was male.

The icon painted for Felisso was altogether different. The youthful Son was presented as a scholar dressed in plain dark robes, seated at a desk in a candlelit Sanctia cell. His head was slightly bent over a book, but His gaze lifted to look the viewer straight in the eye. His expression clearly said, *"You are there only because I am looking at you"*—an uncanny trick of the Limner's art. On the desk were two white vases filled with flowers, and a ripe red apple. Outside the ivy-twined window behind Him, a landscape washed in moonlight showed a line of white poplar trees and a glimpse of forbidding desert sands beyond. The contrast of golden candleglow and silvery moonlight alone made the icon a masterpiece. But there was greater significance to the painting, as Dioniso readily explained to the Principio—who nearly sucked the white off his teeth in admiration.

"Your Highness, inside the Sanctia, faithfully guarded by ivy at the window, is the steady light of civilization. Outside, the arid night of ignorance is lighted only by the inconstant moon. The poplars and the desert beyond represent time—though cruel and inexorable outside the Sanctia, it cannot touch the Son or His Truths, as symbolized by the Apple of Knowledge."

Dioniso did not say that these symbols had other meanings and that bound into both icons were other significances.

Felisso declared he would have the icon placed in his bedchamber, where every morning on waking he would see it and recall the duty of a civilized prince to keep time and ignorance from blighting his people. Arrigo smiled, Dioniso bowed, and the Tira Virteians took their leave—after the Principio extracted Arrigo's promise that next time he would bring his fascinating wife.

"I wish we'd brought her this time," Zevierin said as they were taken to the port by carriage. "All she'd have to do is wear anything that wasn't Tza'ab, set an instant fashion, and—" He winced as their conveyance, nowhere near as well-sprung as the gilded vehicle Arrigo rode in ahead of them, jounced over a crater in the road. "—the whole problem would be solved."

"Women do have their uses," Rafeyo said airily, a boy's attempt at casual sophistication that made his three companions hide smiles.

The lack of a formal treaty bothered Cabral, and he said as much while they unpacked Dioniso's gear in the Embajadorro's private cabin. A stiff afternoon wind was blowing, and although seas were rather high, the ship's master was confident they would outrun the coming storm. They were less than an hour underway and already the prow dug strongly into massive waves, the pitch and roll making every movement problematical. But young muscles and total imperviousness to seasickness kept the three younger Grijalvas upright. Dioniso, however, sprawled on his bunk, eyes squeezed shut in silent misery.

"Cossimio won't be pleased," said Zevierin in response to Cabral's worries. "He expects a grand *Treaty* canvas to hand in Galerria Verrada."

Rafeyo gave a snort. "The result is the same as if there were a treaty. No more illegal trade with the Tza'ab."

"But no painting," Cabral reminded him. "And therefore no public record."

"I'll tell you another thing he won't like," said Zevierin, folding a few clean shirts into a drawer. "Diettro Mareia has not one but two beautiful new Grijalva icons. Cossimio's very possessive about us, you know."

Dioniso rolled over—not quite voluntarily—and opened his eyes. "Happily, Arrigo will have to explain it to him, not I. Go away and let me suffer in peace. Go on, out!"

Cabral grinned and placed a basin on the floor in easy reach.

An hour later, Rafeyo crept into the darkened cabin with a pitcher in one hand and a candle under glass in the other. The light pained Dioniso's eyes.

"I brought you something hot to drink," the boy whispered. "They say it'll calm your stomach."

He considered telling Rafeyo to go away. But, as he'd hoped, a bond was forming now that would serve him well in future, and here was another chance to foster it. The same was true of Arrigo; when Mequel retired or died and Rafeyo was of an age to become Lord Limner, Arrigo would remember that the Grijalva he'd liked and trusted—and who'd told him so many interesting things—had liked and trusted Rafeyo.

So he drank a cup of the minty-sweet potion while Rafeyo emptied the metal basin, and after a little while he did feel better.

"Grazzo." Leaning back on the pillows, he cradled the warm cup between his hands. Only a twinge of the bone-fever, and only because he felt so generally dreadful. He had just turned forty-two; Dioniso's line was strong and long-lived, for Limners; he had nothing to worry about. "Sit and talk with me. You've a hundred questions in your eyes."

There was a quick flash of a smile—charming in the child's face, it would doubtless become more so in the grown man's. Dioniso had never met Tazia, but if her smile was anything to compare, it was no wonder Arrigo had been reluctant to marry.

"I've been dying of curiosity ever since I sneaked that vial out of the Principio's night chamberpot! Disgusting!"

"The youngest always gets the worst task. But you didn't demand an explanation, which was very wise of you in foreign surroundings. Sit, Rafeyo, and I will answer your questions." As he had answered some, but not all, of Arrigo's. He sipped again, sighing as steam warmed his face. "Let's begin with Principia Rosilan's icon. Oil on wood, neither potent in themselves, but because the work was done with brushes made of her hair the icon has certain strengths—of suggestion only, but enough to the purpose. You'll learn relative degrees of power and how to call up your own magic later. For now, tell me about the symbols."

Rafeyo perched on the edge of a chair, lithe young body swaying instinctively with the roll of the ship, his laced fingers clasped between bony knees. Dioniso made note of the posture for future reference as the boy answered. "The Mother sits on grass, signaling Submission. But I don't think the Principia is the obedient type."

"Not in the slightest, which is why I added the plums."

A frown; a sudden grin. "Fidelity! And a whole orchard of them, not just the fruit in the basket—that'll work even on her!"

"So we may hope. What else?"

"Rosemary for Remembrance, but what's she supposed to remember?"

Gulping back another twinge of seasickness, he drank more tea and replied, "The Mother wears Diettro Mareian peasant dress. I wish the Principia to recall that she herself affected that style—considerably grander, of course—in her patriotic youth. Her current taste for Tza'ab costume—"

"—will go away!" Rafeyo interrupted.

"No. But her former preference will now compete. And when she decides she likes her native costume more, her happiness will have nothing to do with the icon. There's nothing a pretty woman loves more than setting a new fashion." He nodded thanks as Rafeyo poured another cup of tea. "Tell me about the pine trees."

"Pine trees?"

"Eiha, perhaps you haven't gone that far yet. Pine signifies Magical Energy—again, note that I used an entire forest! Because I had access only to a brush made of her hair, the painting itself must compensate."

Rafeyo didn't understand, but asked the right question anyway. "Why not use something stronger?"

"She has experience of such work. Not her personally, but a relative. It was necessary to be subtle. Now, I don't expect you to comprehend the Principio's icon, so I'll explain it to you."

"I know bluebells for Constancy, and ivy for Faith."

"But not, ultimately, with the Son. You're about to interrupt me again by saying dandelions signal Male Potency. Quite true. Felisso will see the power of the masculine mind and loins—and his own fathering of those nine gruesome children. Which reminds me to remind Mequel to tell Cossimio that no do'Verrada daughter must even consider betrothal to one of those hideous little apes. I won't have the family looks ruined."

Rafeyo laughed. "Weren't they frightful? Can you imagine being Court Limner there, and having to paint nine *Marriages?*"

"Spare me," he replied with a shudder. "My stomach is delicate enough as it is. But we were speaking of the humble dandelion—which also stands for Oracular Vision. Felisso is a devout man. The vision in his dreams will be of Tza'ab sands that are no part of the civilized precincts of the Sanctia."

Black eyes huge, Rafeyo whispered, "You mean—will this icon

make him *dream* things? Why? What is there in the painting that—"

"This you'll also learn in due course. The apple will call up a dream. The Principio will believe it a vision, and have no more to do with the Tza'ab. It's known as the *Peintraddo Sonho,* the painting of a dream."

The boy mulled this over. Then: "There was a smell about both icons. Not oil paint or wood, but something else."

Dioniso smiled, very pleased. "You have a good nose. It was vervain, the scent of Enchantment, rubbed into the wood back and front before I even made up my paletto."

Again he was quiet. At length, and very humbly, he said, "This is much more complicated than I ever suspected."

"But you *have* suspected. It's a poor excuse for a Grijalva who doesn't guess much of the truth before Confirmattio."

"How much truth *is* there?"

"More truth, and more power, and more magic, than any of us ever suspect."

Awed, Rafeyo breathed, "We Grijalvas are more powerful than anybody in the world!"

He'd been expecting this—indeed, had led the boy to it. All young Limners said the same thing after their first glimpse of magic's reality. Over the years Dioniso had learned that the answer always given them was true. He said it to Rafeyo now, wearing his most solemn face.

"We use that power in service to the do'Verradas, who protected the chi'patros when we would have been cast out. They saved our lives when a populace crazed with terror of Nerro Lingua would have murdered every last one of us."

"But if we wanted to, we could be—"

"No," he said severely. "Never." Pushing aside the memory of Raimon and Il-Adib and the night hours when he himself had not only thought this thing but plotted its accomplishment—before he'd learned otherwise.

"But why?" cried Rafeyo.

"We are of Tza'ab blood. The chi'patros had less standing than the lowliest camponesso on the poorest farm in Tira Virte. That blood can never be cleansed from us, according to the Ecclesia."

"You don't *believe* that, do you?"

"Of course not! But others do, and if we ever tried to take power, we'd perish. Even a hundred Viehos Fratos painting a thousand paintings could not influence all the people who would oppose us.

So we use the power we are given, and do not reach for power that can never be ours."

"But—"

"We are a part of Tira Virte, but we are always apart from it."

Rafeyo bit both lips, then burst out, "All because of the Ecclesia's self-righteous—"

"All because it would be foolish even to try." During his stints as a moualimo within Palasso Grijalva, he'd drilled that into his young charges. Not only was it smart politics, and simple fact, but he dreaded that one day some Neosso Irrado would ignore even more rules than he himself had done, and thereby bring the Grijalvas down with a fatal crash.

To Rafeyo he continued, "And consider the Grand Duke, who has direct power over all Tira Virte. Even with an army of conselhos, he must squint over account books to make sure he's not being cheated. His home is filled with scheming Courtfolk on whom he must keep constant watch. He must worry about keeping wealth and power—and extending both if possible. He marries as he is told to, and lives a life circumscribed by the most rigid compordotta."

He stopped, hiding a smile, for Rafeyo was imagining himself Grand Duke of Tira Virte. By the expression on his face, he was shackled to a gigantic ledger with twenty knife-wielding barons at his back—and one of the della Marei grotesques as his wife.

Rafeyo's eyes were huge with horror. "But—I'd never get to *paint!*"

"Not often."

"It's *much* better to be us!"

"I've always though so," Dioniso said dryly. "A Grijalva Limner is honored *above* all the nobility by the Grand Duke. The family takes care of the money, and whatever you need is provided. Palasso Grijalva is a haven occupied only by us. You may marry whom you choose—or not marry at all, as you choose. Our compordotta is not the degenerated mockery it has become in society, all elaborate manners and mannerisms to hide vulgarity and licentiousness, but retains its truest form: a sense of honor. As for power . . ." He smiled. "We are free to do what our blood commands us to do. *Paint.*"

"Which is the greatest power of all," Rafeyo said. "But—doesn't it bother you that you had to paint what Don Arrigo told you to?"

"It's part of the service we owe. You'll come to understand this, and cherish the opportunities it gives you. Although I was *ordered* to paint the icons, and there were certain requirements for each, the creation was mine. This is the joy of what we do, Rafeyo—to impose our own vision and talent and Gift onto a set form, to make a masterwork of the lowliest *Birth* or *Marriage*."

Rafeyo left soon thereafter, with much to think about. Dioniso finished off the tea, lay back in a bunk that mercifully had settled to a mild cradle-rocking, and fell asleep smiling.

—❖ FORTY ❖—

The new year of 1263 arrived with due celebrations from which Mechella was grateful to be excused. Through the winter she was so ill and listless that Arrigo feared for the child. Eminent physicians arrived, clucked like gossiping chickens, opined that nothing ailed her but a difficult pregnancy or perhaps the weather—and presented their bills.

As spring neared, the bigger Mechella got, the better she felt—and she was so big that twins were indeed rumored. Her energy was such that she volunteered to oversee the planning of the children's celebrations for Astraventa: her favorite holiday.

Mechella's first contribution to the religious and social life of Tira Virte—beyond rare appearances since her marriage—was to add a Ghillasian touch. Rather than simply hand out little mirrors with which to "catch" falling stars during Astraventa, children would hunt for the mirrors on the Palasso grounds. Her steward nodded enthusiasm in her presence and groaned once he left her, for not just special mirrors but repairs to the gardens would be charged to her privy purse.

The innovation was a great success. By the last sunset glow on the day of the festival, while parents were served cider and star-shaped cakes indoors, hundreds of little boys and girls scampered laughing amid the flowers and shrubbery to seek hundreds of little wooden-handled mirrors decorated with ribbons. Prizes clutched in grubby fists, they ran to the courtyard fountain where Mechella tied the ribbons to hundreds of little wrists. Sweets were distributed as they waited in wriggling anticipation for the "starry wind."

Night fell; the yearly shower of sparks across the sky began, and all the mirrors turned skyward to catch a bright speck of light. The Palasso walls reverberated with joyous shrieks of success. Parents emerged from indoors to collect offspring giddy with too many sweets and the thrill of having captured a star. Mechella stood at the top of the steps, smiling as the good people of Meya Suerta bowed their respects and thanks.

Then she saw a little girl shuffle past, crying, her mother attempting in vain to soothe her. Mechella descended the steps and

knelt, awkward in her bulk, and took the sticky hand that held the
mirror.

"What's the matter, mennina?"

"Din't catch'un," the child sobbed. The mother, dumbstruck by
Mechella's notice, tried to pull her daughter away. Mechella shook
her head, smiling.

"Maybe you blinked," she told the girl, "and didn't see it. Let's
try to find your star." She tilted the mirror this way and that to
search, her free hand deftly unpicking a tiny Tza'ab glass bead
from her spangled gown.

The child peered earnestly into the mirror, frowning, "Issin'
there," she whimpered.

"Maybe if we turn it this way—oh! Here it is!" And she pretended to pluck the faceted glass bead from the girl's hair. "No
wonder you didn't see it!"

"Mama! Mama! My star!"

"You know what I think?" Mechella placed it in the child's
palm. "It got lonely for the dark night sky where it used to live, and
saw all your pretty black curls, and decided that's where it wanted
to be—not caught in any old mirror."

Clutching the "star," the girl hurtled off to show her friends.
Mechella pushed herself to her feet, breathing hard, and smiled as
the young mother whispered, "Grazzo millio, Dona." She dipped a
curtsy before hurrying after her daughter.

With children and parents gone, it was time for the formal ball.
Elsewhere in Tira Virte, more than dancing would mark the festival. Astraventa celebrated procreation, the starry wind symbolizing
the gift of life. Soon there would be many weddings, for on this one
night even unmarried couples were licensed to "seek falling stars"
in every glade and glen, and a child born of Astraventa was a great
blessing. Mechella's brother Enrei had once told her the festival
was nothing but an excuse for illicit lovemaking. But Mechella
preferred to believe the pretty folklore: stars found shelter in
women's wombs that night, and babies born of Astraventa had very
special souls.

Whatever might occur after the ball for the Courtfolk, the holiday's more rustic aspects were nowhere in evidence at Palasso
Verrada that evening. Scores of elegant nobles wore so many crys-
tals and brilliants and sequins and diamonds on their black clothes
in imitation of the night sky that it seemed all the constellations had
descended to earth to dance.

Mechella, who loved to dance, was mortified by her heavy-foot-
edness. She intended to spend the evening sitting on a sofa until

midnight, when fireworks would send stars upward into the sky, returning what the night had given. But Arrigo insisted she take the floor at his side. She was positive she looked absurd; when she told him so, he only laughed. And as he whirled her carefully across the ballroom, she suddenly discovered she felt light as a feather. So she danced with him, and with his father, and several of the more important noblemen, and the commander of the Shagarra Regiment. At length, pleasantly tired, she settled on her chosen sofa to recover her breath. Arrigo, having done his duty by the other ladies, brought her a cool drink and leaned down to whisper in her ear.

"See Dirada do'Palenssia's diamonds? Fakes."

"No!" she exclaimed, scandalized.

"I swear it. And I further swear that the Countess do'Brazzina's breath could fell a horse. Worst of all was Baron do'Esquita's sister. She trod on my feet four times. Clumsy as you are, dolcha, at least *you* didn't break my poor toes!"

She dissolved into giggles. "Arrigo! You are a *shocking* gossip!"

"Oh, but I saved the best for last. You've noted, I'm sure, Zandara do'Najerra's spectacular figure? Well, she owes her waistline to iron corseting and her impressive bustline to cotton padding!"

"Eiha, you could hardly avoid noticing *that*. She pushed it against your chest every chance she got!"

"Mechella!" he scolded, mimicking her tone, and joined her in laughter.

A murmur ran through the crowd just then. From the corner of her eye Mechella saw the conductor lift his baton with frantic haste and urge his musicians to a loud and lively tune. Couples resumed the dance floor, but necks craned as they strove to observe something happening near the ballroom doors.

Amid the shifting dancers Mechella glimpsed a tall, distinguished man escorting a slender woman toward Cossimio and Gizella. The man's somber black coat was spangled across the shoulders with brilliants, as if he'd been caught outside in the starfall. The woman positively glittered, her stars in the form of a diamond necklace. White-fire gems, indubitably real, dripped across bare neck and shoulders all the way to swelling breasts that owed nothing to dressmaker's artifice. Neither did her trim waist require breathless lacing. High-piled black hair was unadorned except by candlelight; rose-red lips wore a faint smile made challenging by the arch of her brows. Dark eyes ignored everyone in favor of the Grand Duke and Grand Duchess, as was proper—but somehow

Mechella knew the woman had taken due note of every face in the room. Including hers.

She looked up at Arrigo, intending to ask the woman's name. But then she knew. It was in his eyes—startled, admiring, angry, briefly lit with desire. Mechella felt the sting of tears. How *could* he allow that woman back at Court? But when he glanced down at her, and she saw him grope for words—he who was always swift and supple of speech—his anguish melted her heart. It wasn't his fault. He hadn't known. Her hurt became fury at the Grijalva's arrogant presumption and sheer bad manners.

Her voice was soft and composed as she said, "I see the Count and Countess do'Alva have arrived."

Gratitude for her calm glowed in Arrigo's face—and admiration, too. "And almost late enough to be insulting. My father hates tardiness, especially when he gives a party." With hardly a pause, he finished, "Would you care to dance, 'Chella?"

She knew it for an offer of escape, and loved him for it. To spin gently in his arms, to forget the rapacious gaze of the Courtfolk, to postpone the inevitable meeting. . . .

No. She would sit right here and wait for the woman to exhibit her shabby compordotta for all the world to see by approaching her with some paltry excuse for being late. She let the crystal-embroidered shawl drop from her shoulders, revealing her own full breasts and the exquisite circle of tiny diamonds around her own throat, and smiled up at her husband. "Only if you're willing to carry me!"

He grinned. "Father let Lizia stand on his boots when he was teaching her to dance. I'd do the same for you, but—"

"But the toes broken by do'Esquita's sister would be crushed beyond repair!"

And so they were laughing when Tazia, Countess do'Alva, came to pay her respects with the whole Court watching. There was little to see. A curtsy, a few murmured words no one overhead, a graciously smiling Mechella, a perfectly composed Arrigo, and a coolly beautiful Tazia. Nothing more.

However, Grand Duchess Gizella was observed to sigh quietly and close her eyes in what was interpreted as a brief prayer of thanks. Lissina, Baroness do'Dregez and Cossimio's former Mistress, glided unobtrusively to her cousin Mequel's side, and mere moments later the Lord Limner was dancing with Tazia. The Grand Duke missed the whole thing in conversing with the Count do'Alva.

It was all a terrible letdown. The avidly anticipated meeting was over, and the only fireworks of the evening came that midnight.

The next day was another story.

In the do'Alva caza, situated in the newest and most fashionable quarter of Meya Suerta, Tazia was besieged with callers. Most remembered to congratulate her on her marriage before turning to eager discussion of the previous night's ball. Count Garlo put in an hour's dutiful attendance in his wife's reception room. Lissina, who'd been through much the same thing years ago, kindly arrived early and stayed late to help Tazia fend off the more pointed verbal darts. She also let it be known that the Countess would henceforth be privileged to sit on charitable committees overseen by herself and the Grand Duchess. Nothing like Gizella's name to squelch gossip.

But Tazia needed no assistance in once again frustrating those who had come to dine off her discomfort. By evening half Meya Suerta joined the Grand Duchess in a sigh of relief; the other half sighed for disappointment.

Publicly, Tazia was a model of modern compordotta, the elegant art of correct behavior. Privately—that evening, alone in the soundproofed room of her own now-empty little caza—she paced and wept and cursed both Arrigo and his pale, pregnant bride.

"Canna!" she raged. "Witless idiot! How dare that stupid cow simper at me!" She threw a silver box of sweets; the muffled thunk against the thick tapestry was distinctly unsatisfying. "And that condescending pig Arrigo!" A gilt wine cooler followed the box with equally ungratifying results. "I'll carve that smirk off his face with a butcher knife!"

At last she collapsed on the sofa, exhausted, her nose running and her eyes burning and her head feeling as if it would explode like last night's fireworks. After a time she rose and went upstairs to collect a few personal items—her excuse for visiting her old house. The mirror showed the damage wrought by tears; that, and the damage wrought by the years, succumbed to the cosmetics on her dressing table.

"A true Grijalva," she told her reflection bitterly. "Paint is magic in our clever hands!"

But it would be such a long time before Rafeyo learned enough Grijalva magic to be of use to her. Until then, she was on her own.

A heavy crystal bottle of perfume smashed into the mirror, and at last she began to feel better.

A few days after Fuega Vesperra, Dona Teressa do'Verrada was born. The labor was surprisingly easy after the difficulty pregnancy, almost as if the baby was quick into the world to apologize.

Regretful as he was that the child was not a boy, Arrigo nevertheless was enchanted by his tiny fair-haired daughter. That evening he stood alone on the Appearance Balcony to announce the birth, the cheers of the populace ringing sweetly in his ears. When, ten days later, the child and her mother went to the Cathedral Imagos Brilliantos for the first time, the people of Meya Suerta turned out in even larger and louder numbers.

Palasso Verrada was inundated in gifts. Hothouses of flowers, orchards of fruit, baby clothes enough for an entire province, mountains of toys, libraries of books—one room and then two and then four were set aside for the display of presents from foreign rulers, the Courtfolk, the lesser nobility, merchants, ambassadors, craft guilds, and commoners from every corner of Tira Virte. One thing alone marred Teressa's arrival: Lord Limner Mequel had taken ill, and could not paint her *Birth*. The task fell to Dioniso Grijalva by Arrigo's specific request, and the portrait that came from his brushes was one of the loveliest ever done. At its completion, a small army of copyists went to work, reproducing every stroke to be sent to foreign courts and ranking nobles.

Mechella's first venture outside after the Ecclesial ceremony was to visit Mequel at Palasso Grijalva. This caused a sensation, for no do'Verrada had set foot there since Duke Alejandro paid his respects after Lord Limner Sario's death. Mechella's concern for Mequel was seen as further evidence of a warmly affectionate heart, and her visit produced an immediate improvement in his condition.

She caused more amazement by asking to tour the workshops. Dioniso was her escort from classrooms to copy hall—where eighteen portraits of her daughter, all lined up and ready for crating, gave her a sudden fit of giggles.

"Regretto," she apologized. "They're beautiful, and I mean no insult. It just occurred to me how Teressa would feel, seeing all those babies that look exactly like her!"

The Limner smiled politely. "Perhaps you'd like to see the Galerria?"

"I'd love to, but I've stayed too long as it is, Teressa will miss me." After a moment's hesitation she went on, "I know your original will hang in our Galerria, to look at whenever I like. But babies grow up so quickly, and . . ."

Correctly interpreting her expression, he asked, "Would you like one of these copies for your private rooms, Your Grace?"

"Could I? Oh, but if I did, someone would have to paint yet another copy."

"No importado. It's good practice for our youngsters."

She walked slowly among the easels, pausing here and there to look more closely at this painting or that. Finally she returned to a particular copy. "They're all wonderful, but this one is closest to your original."

"The artist will be honored, Your Grace."

"I'd like him to deliver it personally, so I may thank him."

"Cabral will attend you at your convenience."

Dioniso escorted her from the workroom along a low, drafty corridor that he described as being one of the oldest parts of the Palasso, built before Duke Renayo's bequest four hundred years ago. "The age of this section is seen in the barrel vaulting and blind arcades—so termed because the stone walls between each set of columns block the view. There are always two columns to honor the Mother and Son—" He broke off. "But I'm boring Your Grace."

"Not at all," she lied. "Who are the people in the portraits along the—what did you call it? Blind arcades? Shouldn't the pictures be in your Galerria?"

He shrugged. "The people are of minor importance, or the paintings themselves are not up to standard."

"Minor to whom, Dioniso?" she asked indignantly. "Certainly not to those who loved them! And whose standards? The limners who did the work surely did their best!"

He bowed sincerely. "It is the unique gift of Your Grace to see people, not politics and paint. I knew even in Aute-Ghillas that you would bring gifts to Tira Virte that have nothing to do with your lovely face, your dower, or your children."

"It's kind of you to say that," Mechella said, surprised by the way he saw her. "But I wish I understood more about other things. I know nothing about your art, for example. You Grijalvas are so vital to our country, I want so much to know all I can about what you do."

"When Cabral brings the painting, perhaps you can spare some time to walk with him through the Galerria Verrada. He's quite knowledgeable, and a much better speaker than I!"

And so, several days later, Cabral Grijalva presented himself and his copy of *Birth of Teressa* at Palasso Verrada. After he directed the hanging of the picture in Mechella's sitting room, they went to the Galerria for her first lesson in art.

". . . and here you see another example of chiaroscuro in the play of sunlight and shadow over Duchess Enricia's wedding gown."

" 'Chiaro—'? I should have brought a notebook," Mechella sighed. "I'm afraid I'm terribly stupid about remembering all this."

"Not at all, Your Grace," Cabral replied instantly. "I'm the one at fault for trying to tell you all of it at once. No wonder the Viehos Fratos keep turning down my request to teach."

She dimpled. "If you can teach me, you can teach anyone, and I'll tell them so if you like! But why won't they allow it?"

"I do not have the Gift," he said simply.

"How can you say that? Ignorant as I am, I knew right away that your copy of Dioniso's painting was the best of them all!"

"Your Grace's praise is more than I deserve. I should explain that there are two sorts of Grijalva. The first are like me—a certain amount of ability in original work, and sufficient skill to mimic real talent." He paused, then admitted diffidently, "I had the honor of copying your *Marriage* last year."

"Did you? I'd love to see it."

"It was sent to Merse. We don't have much trade with that country, so true talent wasn't required. The copy was only a courtesy. You see, the real Limners have an almost magical touch. See here, how Duchess Enricia's skin looks as if you could feel the warm softness of her cheek? I can't do that. And I could never teach anyone else how to do it either."

"Have you tried?"

He seemed taken aback. "It isn't permitted. I'm only a copyist. Oh, I do original work in my spare time, when I'm not needed elsewhere, but I'm not good enough to waste paint on."

"You're just as good as the rest of them—better!"

Cabral shook his head. "I do not have the Gift," he repeated. "My friend Zevierin, for instance, is an extremely accomplished Limner. His copy of your charming little Teressa will be sent to Your Grace's father, the King." He smiled. "But *mine* will be seen by you every day, and to me this is the much greater honor."

Mechella spread her hands in a gesture of helpless confusion. "I suppose you Grijalvas have your reasons for the way you do things, but it seems to me your talent is wasted, not the paint you use. May I ask one last question before you go?"

"I am at Your Grace's service as long as you wish."

"Two questions, then. First, how can anybody tell when one limner has this Gift and another doesn't?"

"All Grijalva boys are tested. Those who succeed are taught differently from those who fail, according to the precepts laid down three hundred years ago by the great Lord Limner Sario."

"Some of his pictures are here in the Galerria, are they not?"

"Yes. He did some excellent work, for his time. But his most important legacy is not in his paintings but in the system he devised for nurturing talented young Limners."

"Of which you do not feel yourself to be one. Eiha, Cabral, I disagree. And my second question proves it, for I would like to ask if you'll teach me about painting. The Grand Duchess is forever escorting guests through the Galerria. If I knew more, I could free her from having to repeat herself so often! She's been so sweet to me, I want to help her however I can."

Cabral bowed low. "It would be an honor and a pleasure, Your Grace. But I must warn you," he went on with a quiet laugh, "that you'll get a large dose of history along with art. All Tira Virte's past is on these walls."

"That's another reason I want to learn," she confided. "I'd remember the history so much better by hearing about the people and looking at their faces. Would twice a month be too often? Would it take you too much from your work? I can."

"I will be here every day if you wish it."

"Oh, any more often than once a week and I'd never remember a thing! And next time I promise to take notes!"

FORTY-ONE

That summer saw Mechella's entry into all the delights and pitfalls of Court life. Gizella and Lissina kept careful eyes on her, but soon realized that not only was the girl newly confident now that she'd borne Arrigo a child—even if it was only a girl—she was so charming that even her rare mistakes made her more beloved.

True, her education was not extensive nor her understanding deep, but she was so humble in her desire to learn that the stodgiest scholars endured her ignorance with smiles. She tended to a slightly glazed expression when politics were discussed, but she was a divinity on the dance floor. She had scant notion of where each noble's estates were located, but she always asked after the children and grandchildren by name. Her notes thanking this countess or that baroness for a wonderful dinner were written in a childish hand, but with such innocent sincerity that even her spelling was instantly forgiven. And her face, her figure, her jewels, and her clothes were the envy of every woman in Meya Suerta.

Arrigo nearly burst with pride whenever he looked at her. When they toured schools, village fairs, Sanctia hospices, or guildhalls, the people chanted her name even more loudly than his. Everywhere she was deluged with irises, her favorite flower. When it was rumored she had a fondness for almonds, baskets of them appeared whenever she did. She was seen wearing a Casteyan lace shawl, and the camponessa who had made it as a wedding present grew very rich in commissions for wealthy noblewomen. Mere days after she donned an embroidered apron to tour a feeding kitchen for the poor, every woman in Meya Suerta with any claim to fashion sported a similar garment.

In one thing alone did Mechella displease Arrigo: she loathed Chasseriallo. Thinking to give her respite from the constant round of parties, balls, and charity work, he arranged for a week's stay at the lodge in autumn. The moment they arrived, she began to cough. By next morning she was running a fever and spent the whole time in bed. Moreover, she had nightmares: moss festooning the oak trees wrapped around her throat, the torpid river suddenly became a torrent that swept her away, the little chirruping tree-frogs swelled to the size of horses and crashed through the roof. At length he had pity on her nerves and took her back to Meya Suerta. But he couldn't help remembering times spent here with Tazia—she who waded hip-deep in the river to fish beside him, she who loved the dark mystery of the trees, she who joined him in hunting and wild rides over the hills and the ancient bathtub every evening. . . .

Disloyalty to Mechella shamed him. As she recovered her spirits in Palasso Verrada, and became once more the lively, adorable girl he'd married, he forgot Tazia. Almost.

By Providenssia Mechella was pregnant again, and even more ill with it than the first time. She took to her bed and canceled her engagements—not that any of her official appearances with Arrigo had any real import. At farm fairs, he judged the horseflesh and she the baked goods and embroidery. They attended ceremonies blessing a new mine or mill or medical facility. They dined with the Drapers Guild, the Vintners, the Clockmakers, the Linen Merchants, the Goldsmiths, the Corn Factors. She enjoyed it all, even the boring speeches, for there was always the promise of talking to people and hearing their concerns. And they told her everything, from worry about a child's broken wrist to their views on trade with Taglis.

But Arrigo fretted. He had thought his marriage would change things. With a wife to assume some of the social burden, he had thought he'd be free to work with his father on matters of state. He knew his ideas were good ones. For instance, Tira Virte ought to be selling wagonloads of gorgeous Casteyan furs to the cold northern kingdom of Merse. Opening one market, Arrigo reasoned, would eventually open others. But Cossimio shook his head. Trade in luxury items was no way to establish Merse's dependence on Tira Virte; political cooperation was gained through fear of losing an essential supply of foodstuffs or minerals, not cloaks for the wealthy. Further, the Merseians didn't adhere to the practice of painting rather than writing treaties, so how could any business be done with them?

Arrigo understood this painting angle better than his father suspected, but revealed nothing of his knowledge. The information Dioniso had given him about Grijalva art not only made sense and explained many historical puzzles, but worried him as well. No aspect of governance or foreign relations could be trusted unless a Limner painted it—and this gave entirely too much power to the Grijalvas. Seeing no way around this entrenched power, Arrigo decided that if it could not be curbed, then at least he would make certain he had his own Grijalvas from now on.

And so he encouraged Mechella's art lessons with Cabral, and met with Dioniso at least once a month, and wondered when the time would be right to include the Count and Countess do'Alva in the small entertainments he hosted at Palasso Verrada. Now that Mechella was pregnant again and too exhausted to attend, he felt he could issue the invitation. Besides, what gossip could come of a gathering of a dozen or more people? It wasn't as if he were summoning Tazia to an intimate midnight supper. And he was no longer in love with her anyway.

One thing had definitely changed since his marriage. When he appeared alone now in public, disappointment showed on every face. Gifts were always for Mechella; flowers were always her adored irises. Arrigo began to realize how deeply she was loved by the people of Tira Virte. *His* people. It was gratifying, of course, to have her such an overwhelming success, but annoying when they called her name and demanded to know why he hadn't brought her with him, even though they knew she was again pregnant.

The first time it happened, he held up a hand for quiet and the Gemcutters Guild fell silent in their huge tapestried Hall. Smiling, Arrigo said in a voice that carried all the way to the painted rafters, "Regretto, but Dona Mechella was not feeling well enough tonight to join me, though I can't say that I entirely regret being the cause of her indisposition." There were cheers and laughter; someone cried out, "Good to see a man who enjoys his work!"; someone else yelled, "This time a son!" Arrigo grinned, and told his wife about it the next morning when he presented her with the guild's gift: bracelets of a dozen different stones, one for her and one for Teressa. Mechella blushed, and they laughed together.

He used the same little speech several times to similar effect. But one day no one laughed, and a voice called out, "If it was you suffering to bring the next Heir into the world, you'd not be so quick to joke on it!" The woman was immediately silenced by her mortified husband, and red-faced officials of the Woodworkers Guild apologized profusely, but a chant rose in the courtyard outside as Arrigo left the building: "Me*chell*a! Me*chell*a!" He didn't tell his wife about it, and never used the witticism again.

The day after it happened, a group of nobles and their wives came to the Palasso for an afternoon of music and conversation. Arrigo welcomed his guests, saw to their comfort, and kept his countenance when Tazia arrived alone.

"Garlo's deep in consultation with his stewards—something tedious about the crops. But he insisted I come today. I hope it's all right."

"It's kind of you to join us," Arrigo responded, and directed her to the wine and cakes before turning to welcome the next couple. It didn't occur to him until people sat down for the concert that he and Tazia were the only ones lacking their spouses. The chairs had been arranged in pairs with small tables between them, each husband and wife together. Arrigo sat alone. So did Tazia.

The music was provided by the latest sensation: the eight-year-old daughter of Baron do'Varriyva. Little Clemenssia's artistry with the gamba was nothing short of extraordinary. She entered with perfect aplomb, enchanted them for an hour, and then was taken back home by her mother for an afternoon nap. Listening to her, watching her small clever fingers dance across the strings, Arrigo was struck not only by her precocious brilliance but by the incongruity of a nobleman's daughter evincing a talent other than for needlework or flower arranging. Clemenssia had a genuine gift, and her parents were at virulent odds over allowing her to pursue it without being subject to the usual strictures on a highborn girl to get herself married as soon as possible. Arrigo wondered what might have befallen him if he'd had a gift for music or literature or even painting, like the Grijalvas—and gave sincere thanks to the Mother that he did not. He couldn't imagine the misery of wanting desperately to pursue one course when duty compelled him elsewhere. It was bad enough wanting to do what he'd been born for and knew he would excel at, and not being allowed to do it.

After Clemenssia's performance, the company broke into small groups to chat. Arrigo drifted, ever the affable host, gathering the latest gossip. This ought to have been Mechella's task, freeing him to talk politics with the men.

At length he found himself at the refreshment table, where a footman poured more wine into his glass. All at once he heard Tazia's voice behind him.

"Poor child, her father's winning the battle for now. Although my cousin Lissina and I intend to join the fray on Clemenssia's side."

"Charming as her playing is," replied the Countess do'Najerra, "her duty is to marry. With a few children underfoot, she'll soon forget all about the gamba."

"How can you think so!" Tazia exclaimed. "It would break her heart to give up her music. It's one thing to be born to a duty you want to perform, and quite another to be forced into it when your heart's life lies elsewhere."

"Nonsense," snapped the other woman. "She's eight. How can she know what she wants? And why should she have the pleasure of choice when the rest of us don't?" She paused. "But of course *you* did, Tazia. Or were you, too, merely doing your duty?"

Arrigo felt his breath stop. Was this what Tazia had endured since their parting? He composed his expression, and turned; Zandara do'Najerra was so flustered by the sight of him that she nearly dropped her sweet-laden plate. He gave her a precise count of three to meditate on her blunder, then said blandly, "Just the lady I hoped to see! Zandara, my mother would take it as a great favor if you'd join her hospital committee. They plan a new children's wing, and no one has more experience of children than yourself. How many little brothers did you raise?"

"Seven, after my mother died, Your Grace, and six sons and three daughters of my own."

"And another expected, perhaps?" He gave her rigidly corseted waistline a casual glance. She turned crimson and set down her plate. "Eiha, my mistake. I'd heard a rumor, but rumors are so often wrong, aren't they? May I tell my mother you'll oblige her?"

Stiff as her stays, she replied, "I'm honored, Don Arrigo. I'll consider it not only my duty but my pleasure."

"How lucky," murmured Tazia, "to combine the one with the other."

Arrigo betrayed not a hint of his amusement, but Tazia had known him a very long time, and when she glanced up at him with twinkling dark eyes he was hard put to keep a straight face. The Countess do'Najerra, knowing herself overmatched, excused herself and left the two former lovers alone.

"That was very naughty of you," Tazia observed.

"She deserved it, the silly cow. Does that sort of thing happen often?"

"Not as often as I'd like. I rather enjoy outwitting them. Though it would be more fun if they had more wits." She gave him a smile and started to walk away.

"Don't go just yet. We haven't had a talk in a long time."

"Would it be proper? Oh, don't frown so. I only meant that word might get back to Dona Mechella, and she might not understand that there's nothing between us."

"There used to be a great deal between us—which is why half these women would go running to Mechella with the tale of our conversation if they could."

"I heard she wasn't feeling well—again. I hope she gets over it soon. I'd hate for her to miss another autumn and winter social season."

"I'll convey your kind wishes for her health."

"Now you're frowning with words! I'd better leave before people think your awkwardness means something it doesn't."

"Why shouldn't I have a casual chat with an old friend?"

She laughed lightly. " 'Friend' if you must, but spare me the 'old'!"

"You'll never be that." He sipped wine. "Did you mean that about taking little Clemenssia's side against her father's matrimonial ambitions?"

"Certainly. You heard for yourself, the child is uniquely talented. Why should she be forced to marry if that's not her will?"

He gave a shrug. "She's only eight. She doesn't know what she wants."

"You agree with Zandara?" Her elegant brows arched. "Eiha, I suppose putting duty above personal preference is bred into you do'Verradas."

"And into you Grijalvas?" He lowered his voice. "Was Zandara right about you?"

Her lashes swept down in sooty shadows on her cheeks. "You know she wasn't, Arrigo. You *know* it! Now let me go, please."

Her steps were a little too swift as she walked to her chair and snatched up her shawl. He knew everyone was looking. But by the time she joined the group at the windows she was all charm and smiles. Such was her duty now, as the Countess do'Alva.

And her pleasure?

Did she love Garlo? Odd that he'd never asked himself that before now. Nearly a year since her marriage, and he'd never even been curious. It hadn't occurred to him what she might be going through as the discarded Mistress. Surely the same had not happened to his father's Mistress! But Mechella had not befriended Tazia the way Gizella had done with Lissina. That was wrong of her, he decided. And he was at fault, too, for becoming husband and father had occupied him so totally that he hadn't even wondered if the woman he'd once loved was happy.

He finished his wine and held out his glass for more, cursing himself for coldness and heartlessness. He'd make it up to her, he vowed he'd see to it that she was as respectfully treated and as admired as Lissina.

And in this he required Mechella's cooperation.

That evening, while she picked listlessly at her dinner tray from the shelter of her lacy bed, Arrigo explained the Countess do'Alva's predicament and his desire that Mechella assist in remedying it. Then he sat back in his chair with every confidence of his wife's instant acquiescence.

"No!" Mechella snapped. "I won't! How can you ask that of me, Arrigo?"

"All you need do is follow my mother's example," he said patiently. "It isn't easy for Tazia—"

"Don't say her name in my presence!" She pushed herself higher against the snowbank of pillows. "And don't ask me to feel sorry for her either!"

The notion of anyone's pitying Tazia struck him even more forcibly than Mechella's outrage, so much so that he simply failed to react.

"That woman was your Mistress for twelve years! How could you even think I'd want her in the same room with me, let alone—"

"My mother—"

"I'm not your mother! I'm your wife! What if it were the other way around, and I'd had a lover I wanted you to befriend so his feelings wouldn't be hurt?"

He laughed at that. "You're being ridiculous. Women don't take lovers."

"Grijalva women do! And so have women of your own family—Benedetta, or whatever her name was—Cabral told me all about her when he showed me her portrait!"

"Benecitta, and she's nothing to do with this." She was being completely unreasonable; he gritted his teeth and returned to his best, most rational argument. "My mother never had the slightest difficulty being kind to Lissina."

"Do you know what your mother told me the very day I arrived here? She said that woman was no Lissina!"

Rising, he glared down at her. "She has a name. Tazia do'Alva. I suggest you start using it, because you'll be meeting her rather often from now on."

Mechella began to cry. "Arrigo—please, *please* don't ask that of me, not now when I'm so ill carrying your son—"

"You said *last* time it would be a son, and it wasn't." Her gasp told him he'd gone too far. Bending down, he took her hand and kissed it. "I didn't mean that, carrida. I adore Teressa. And I adore you. That's why all this is so absurd. What threat could Tazia ever be to you?"

"Your mother said th-that, too," she sniffled. "Oh, Arrigo, please don't let's fight about this. I can't stand it, my nerves are in shreds."

"Regretto, carrida meya." He stroked her loose golden hair, and after a time she calmed down and knuckled her eyes like a child.

"Then—then you'll send her away?"

"What?" Arrigo pulled back as if she'd hit him.

"I don't want her here! Not when I'm so hideous. Please send her away, Arrigo, I'll never ask anything else of you again, I swear it."

Coldly, he replied, "To send her away would be to admit publicly that I still have feelings for her that could threaten you. Did you think of that? Do you ever think about anything or anyone at all other than yourself?"

She covered her face with her hands and wept bitterly. But he was already gone.

FORTY-TWO

The first storm of autumn brought near-disaster to Galerria Verrada. The wind clattered a roof tile into a gutter, blocking it and exposing a section of tarred paper that worked loose and ripped away. When the rains came, wood and plaster were soaked by water backing up from the clogged gutter. Drip became trickle; trickle turned to stream; by mid-afternoon a torrent gushed down into an attic everyone had forgotten existed.

When the flood was discovered, crafters risked their lives in the wind-lashed rain to cover the roof, replace the tile, and clear the gutter. Servants frantically began to mop up the water flowing down the attic stairway to a storeroom where lesser art treasures were kept. More servants hustled paintings out of harm's way into the Galerria. Grand Duke Cossimio himself took crowbar in hand to pry open crates, horrified at the potential damage to his family's heritage. Grijalvas were summoned immediately. Lord Limner Mequel, recovered from his illness, was first on the scene, and when he saw the sopping ruin of Yverrin Grijalva's beautiful *Betrothal of Clemenzo I and Luissa do'Casteya,* his eyes filled with tears.

Happily, this was the only major casualty. All other damage was confined to water-warped frames, some spotting, and a few smudges here and there, all easily repaired. The greatest danger was mold, a familiar enemy in Meya Suerta's humid climate and one the Grijalvas knew how to fight. Easels were brought and the paintings at risk were set in the Galerria to dry. All others were propped against walls until new crates could be made for them.

Thus the entirety of the do'Verrada collection became available for Mechella's education. Cabral was assigned to the Galerria until rescue operations were complete, and she took him from his work quite often to discuss pictures that hadn't been seen in generations. *Births* and *Marriages* of do'Verrada relations; *Deeds* for various Grand Ducal properties; *Wills,* landscapes, icons, portraits of the Lord Limners—all were there for her education and pleasure.

"That's only a copy, of course," Cabral explained as they admired the *Lord Limner Timius Grijalva.* "The original is in our Galerria with the other portraits of the Lord Limners. And if you're about to say that they all look alike—eiha, you'd be right! We're inbred, we Grijalvas. It's rare these days that someone is born with hazel or gray eyes, or fair skin, or something less than the distinctive Grijalva nose." He touched his own nose ruefully. "I'm one of them, pitiful thin thing that it is!"

"And with greenish eyes as well! At least that makes you recognizable among all your cousins," she teased. "What's the standard Grijalva type, then?"

"Mequel," he answered promptly. "A few inches over medium height, black haired, dark brown eyes with long lashes, dark skin that never sunburns—"

"I could wish for that. I've acquired quite an amazing collection of hats!"

"Grijalva skin with golden hair? No, Your Grace's coloring is perfect as it is."

"Eiha, I'm glad Teressa is staying blonde—at least I'm not the only one in the Palasso anymore! What are all these paintings over here?"

He sidled past a scent-pillar in the crowded Galerria, knelt, and flipped through canvases leaning against the wall. "Ah, I recognize these. Some of the earliest Grijalva works. This one is the *Birth of Renayo,* Duke Joao's little brother, who died when he was four. See how it lacks the framing runes? Those didn't come into fashion until Lord Limner Sario's time, about fifty years later."

"He changed a great deal about the way Grijalvas paint, didn't he?"

Cabral gave her a smile over his shoulder. "You see, Your Grace doesn't need to take notes on my interminable lectures!"

"Is that a challenge?" She regarded the *Birth* with eyes newly educated in distinctions of style and composition. "It looks almost primitive, doesn't it? But I thought all the *Births* of that period always included the mother. Why isn't Elseva do'Elleon—" She broke off with an annoyed little shake of her head. "Of course. Renayo was a boy, and to paint his mother with him would be heretical."

Cabral nodded. "Scenes of a mother with her son are confined to religious paintings. So little Renayo is all alone in this portrait. But—now, where did I see it?" He sorted canvases and pulled out a small portrait of a woman in blue holding a naked infant girl. "Joao's sister and her daughter," he announced.

She searched her memory of the family genealogy. "Caterin and . . . Alanna?"

"Alienna," he said. "But that's very good, Your Grace. Nobody remembers Caterin nowadays."

"Except for her portrait, she might as well not have lived at all. That's sad, Cabral. Very sad."

"Not at all, Your Grace. *Because* of this portrait, she lives forever."

"Trapped in a painting—as we all shall be one day," she replied with a little shrug and a smile. She drifted away from the works spread out before her to a painting with its back to the Galerria. "What's this one? It's not damaged, but it's set apart as if waiting for a curatorrio to work on it. Help me move it."

Together they turned the huge framed wooden portrait around, leaning it against the nearest scent-pillar. Mechella ran down her mental list of identifying characteristics—runes, colors, pose and placement of the figure, floral and herbal symbology, clothing, and so on—but this painting was like none she had ever seen before.

Along the border was a wealth of runes in gold paint given depth by black shading to the left of each sigil. The portrait itself was complex in composition, and odd with it as well, for there were more runes and patterns on the edge of the table in the painting, barely visible beneath a gold-fringed green drape. A mirror on an easel behind her, a painting within the painting over her right shoulder, part of a velurro curtain in a corner—still, one saw the young woman, not the things that surrounded her.

She was dark-haired, gray-eyed, beautiful in the way most Grijalva women were. She leaned intently over the table, the pearls swagged at her bodice seemingly caught in mid-motion. One long, slender hand lay flat beside a large book, the other reaching toward a small lantern as if she wished to adjust the light. The volume's gem-set leather binding was barely hinted at, a mere glimmer of colors and gold, for the book lay open on the table for her study.

To her left was a formidable door: iron-studded and iron-bound, but neither locked nor barred. Behind her, arched windows were set deep into thick walls, shutters folded back to admit the first dawn sunshine of a fine spring day. On one sill was a fat candle about six inches high, only just snuffed, a threadlike mist of smoke trailing upward from the blackened wick. Fine, delicate work, that—Mechella had never seen anything like it before. Yet even as her gaze roamed the painting, she realized that *she* was choosing the direction of her contemplation, that there was no discernible flow of shape and color and angle and line through the portrait. The pose of the woman's hand did not draw her eye to the other books on the table; the silvery sheen of dawn found no echo in the silver pitcher glistening with condensation; the shadows cast by the lantern on ash-rose gown and pallid cheek did not repeat in similar shadows around the earthenware bowl of fruit. Cabral had been teaching her the interior geometry of paintings, but this had none as far as she could tell.

Mechella found it difficult to look at the work with her intellect. Indeed, it was nearly impossible to look at anything but the woman's face. The graceful head lifted as if distracted from her studies, lips set in a defiant, determined line, dark curls slightly disarranged as if she'd raked her fingers back through her hair before reaching toward the lantern. And she had the most compelling, intelligent, tragic eyes Mechella had ever seen in any face, living or painted.

All at once she heard Cabral gasp.

"Matra Dolcha! It's Saavedra!"

"Who?"

He gaped at the painting, his skin gone grayish and his hazel eyes huge. Mechella touched his arm and he gave a violent start. "Oh—I beg Your Grace's pardon, I just—it's *her!* I can't believe it. No one has seen this painting in a hundred years!"

"But who *is* she?" Mechella asked again, astounded that a painting could give him such a turn.

"Saavedra," he repeated almost reverently. "Sario Grijalva's masterpiece."

A work by one of the greatest Lord Limners, undisplayed, unseen for a century? "Why isn't it hanging in the Galerria?"

Shaken, Cabral took a step back as if the mere sight of the portrait might burn his eyes. "I—I don't know."

She was coming to know him for an honest, open man, and therefore knew he was lying. "Of course you know, Cabral. There must be a story to this picture. There are stories about all of them."

"Are you growing tired, Your Grace? We've been in here for hours—"

"My Grace feels just fine, Cabral. With this baby I'm sick in the evenings, not the mornings. And the next time you want to distract me, don't be so clumsy about it. Tell me the story of this Saavedra. It's a lovely name."

He sighed in defeat. "She was a Grijalva—Sario's close cousin, in fact. Legend says she was almost as talented as he was—or as any man of our family has ever been."

"She sounds a little scandalous," Mechella said with a smile. "A woman Limner! What happened to her?"

Cabral swallowed hard, not taking his gaze from the painting. "Saavedra fell in love where she shouldn't have, and rather than see her lover marry someone else she disappeared from Meya Suerta—from Tira Virte, in fact. He searched for her, but no trace was ever found. Sario painted this portrait so that her lover had something to remember her by."

A sad enough tale, but hardly of an impact to cause Cabral such amazement. Mechella examined Saavedra's face again. Some subtlety of expression in the gray eyes resonated inside her—not recognition of the family similarity of most Grijalvas, but emotion speaking to kindred emotion. Mechella felt bewilderment draw her brows together. She had nothing in common with this woman's beautiful tragic eyes. . . .

"Chieva do'Orro, you found her!" Lord Limner Mequel hobbled over, supported by a gold-topped cane Cossimio had given him to aid his halting steps. "I've been looking for her these four days!"

Mechella smiled. "I'm glad to see you so improved, my Lord."

"Nothing like work to put new strength into even the most recalcitrant bones, Your Grace," he replied with a bow. "Cabral, I must steal you now. Get someone to help you take *The First Mistress* upstairs to be recrated."

" '*The First*—'?" Mechella's stomach clenched in a way that had nothing to do with her pregnancy. Her gaze flew to Cabral. He wouldn't look at her. And no wonder: Saavedra's abandoned lover had been Duke Alejandro do'Verrado!

She chided herself for a fool. No picture would be here at the Palasso, even in storage, that didn't have some connection to the do'Verradas. Suddenly the tale was not sad but insulting: a reminder of that other Grijalva woman who now called herself a Countess.

As casually as she could, Mechella turned to the Lord Limner. "Why did she leave Alejandro?"

"No one knows." Mequel folded his hands atop the cane; the long fingers were as yet straight and strong, untouched by the bone-fever that was slowly crippling his legs and spine. "Some say she was banished by Alejandro's conselhos, some say she left voluntarily, and some even say she was murdered." He gazed at *The*

First Mistress with thoughtful dark eyes shaded by thick lashes. "They say many things, but no one knows for certain."

Mechella experienced reluctant pity. The emotion angered her—as if she were feeling sorry for that other Mistress who deserved nothing but contempt. But then she abruptly understood why instinct prompted compassion and fellow-feeling. Before she could stifle the words, she heard herself ask, "Did anybody ever say that she was pregnant?"

Both men caught their breaths—Mequel a bit painfully as he moved in to study the painting, muttering to himself. Cabral joined him. Mechella only watched, not saying why she knew it to be the truth. It was quite simple, really: it was why Saavedra seemed familiar. It wasn't the shape of her mouth or nose or the color of her hair or anything else Grijalva. Despite the defiance in that set mouth, despite the poignancy of those luminous pale eyes, there was in her face that inexplicable *something* that Mechella had seen in her own mirror.

"I think she had to leave because she was pregnant with Alejandro's child," Mechella said. "Bastards are never welcome. And at that time the Grijalvas were—how did you put it, Cabral?"

"Consolidating their position at Court," he mumbled, casting a wary glance at the Lord Limner. Mequel shrugged; it was only the truth, after all.

Mechella continued, "So if she was carrying a child, she'd be dangerous not just to the do'Verradas but to her own family. Perhaps she left on her own, or was taken away by force—but perhaps she really was murdered."

"It would explain much," Mequel mused. "The story has it that she and Alejandro were wildly in love and he would have wed her if he could. If a child was expected, then he would have had honor on his side. What true compordotta used to be, that combination of right behavior and justice and integrity that the Serranos never possessed. . . ." Suddenly he bent closer to the border framing the painting. "Cabral, look at this sequence. Have you ever seen anything like it before?"

Stiff as the oak panel Saavedra was painted on, Cabral replied, "I know little of the oscurra, Lord Limner."

"Oh, that's right. You're not—eiha, enough," he said hastily, wincing as he straightened up. "I'll have to study her before she's put away again. Take her up to my office above the Galerria, Cabral."

"And cover her up with something," Mechella said suddenly.

Mequel gave her a curious look that turned to admiring approval. "She does have rather amazing eyes, doesn't she? I'd hate to walk into my office and be startled into a fall by that fierce look of hers. Sario was a genius, no doubt of it, but this painting is . . . different."

Mechella hadn't meant anything of the sort; she merely wanted no one else to see *The First Mistress* and be reminded. She listened to their plans for shutting Saavedra away, wishing it was that easy to be rid of the Grijalva woman who had followed in Saavedra's footsteps.

The arrival some weeks later of Arrigo's sister and her three children set all Palasso Verrada into an uproar. Mechella, meeting Lizia for the first time, felt queasy not just from her pregnancy but from shyness; Cossimio and Gizella adored their only daughter, Arrigo thought his two-years-elder sister had hung the stars, and indeed the whole Court turned out to welcome her, even though she arrived at midnight during a thunderstorm. When the family was private and the children sent off to bed, Mechella ventured a compliment on how glad everyone was to see her.

Lizia laughed and kicked off her shoes. "Eiha, they turned out in force only because nobody's seen me in so long! They want to look at the damage done by the wilds of Casteya!" She tossed the black widow's veil from her face and propped her wool-stockinged feet on a stool near the fire.

"Expecting you to look like a wrinkled crone of seventy," Arrigo grinned, bringing her a tankard of mulled wine. "How clever of you to look scarcely fifty!"

She put out her tongue at him. He threatened to pour the drink on her head. Their mother clapped her hands sharply in automatic reproof, then burst out laughing. "Eiha, 'Chella, you see what I endured when they were children!"

"Still are," the Grand Duke said in mock disgust. "Not a day over ten, the pair of them." He frowned suddenly, all the humor draining out of him, even his mustache drooping. "Are you quite certain you're happy at the Castello, guivaerra meya? It's so far from Court."

"Oh, Casteya's quite civilized these days, Patro. I don't even have to wring the chickens' necks myself anymore. Amazing what a do'Verrado dower will do for declining grandeur." She drank wine and sighed, wriggling her toes. "It's good to be here, all the same."

Lizia had wed Ormaldo do'Casteya at nineteen in a marriage of convenience that became a love match. She'd once told Arrigo that because there was no one else interesting in Casteya, she'd been obliged out of sheer boredom to fall in love with her husband. When Arrigo reported this to Mechella, he had wryly added that not only had Ormaldo been ridiculously easy for his sister to love, she hadn't known an instant's boredom from the day the Count took her to his run-down wreck of a castello.

"She was never one for parties and dances. She helped with Mother's charities, of course, but when she married Ormaldo she finally discovered what she was meant to be: a Marchalo Grando commanding the army that reclaimed Castello Casteya from wrack and ruin."

The marriage produced three children—Grezella, Maldonno, and Riobira—before Ormaldo died of a wasting disease, aged only forty-three. Lizia, eleven years his junior, had shut herself and her children up in their restored castello since his death three years before. But now Maldonno, Count do'Casteya, was old enough to become a page at his grandfather's Court. So to Meya Suerta they had come.

Next morning, bright and early, Lizia brought her children—still in nightclothes and bedrobes—to see their baby cousin. They dutifully expressed admiration for Teressa, then occupied themselves, with considerably more enthusiasm, playing in the nursery.

"And now that the children are out of the way," Lizia said, settling on the edge of Mechella's bed, "their mothers can have a nice cozy talk. I'm so glad to meet you at last, carrida! You're all that Arrigo told me in his letters."

"And you're everything everyone says you are," Mechella responded, trying to smile. She was feeling very shaky this morning after a late night last night, and with the Iluminarres holiday coming up, she knew she needed all the rest she could get.

"The one thing to believe," Lizia said with a wink, "is that I am indeed short of person *and* of temper! You leggy creatures don't know what it is to look up all your life—my neck aches constantly. The only reason I'm not black and blue from being stepped on is that I make so much noise people *have* to notice me. Now, tell me all the latest gossip."

Mechella knew that there was only one topic of general discussion these days: the Grijalva woman. Arrigo had said nothing about her for weeks, and no one could talk about her in Mechella's presence, of course, but she wasn't a fool. The woman was still at Court, though by mutual silent agreement an arrangement had formed between Mechella and Arrigo: if the Countess do'Alva was to be present at any function, Mechella would be absent from it. Arrigo could have either his wife or his former Mistress at his entertainments, but not both.

"Eiha, what a frown!" Lizia exclaimed, and Mechella gave a start. The tiny Countess snagged an apple from the breakfast tray and munched on it as she continued, "I have informants—everyone does—but they don't know all the ins and outs the way a do'Verrada must. I assume you've established your own little system for gathering information?"

Mechella shook her head.

Lizia was shocked. "You must! Rapidia! How else will you know what's really going on? I'll lend you a few of mine until you can find your own."

"I'd rather not," Mechella said primly. "I have no interest in gossip, and it seems like—"

"—spying? You'll be Grand Duchess, you have to know what goes on. My mother has Lissina, of course—" She stopped, gave Mechella a searching look, finished the apple in a gulp, and tossed the unbound black hair from her shoulders. "So that's it."

"I beg your pardon?"

"The Grijalvas. Eiha, don't look so stiff and formal and Ghillasian! We're rather free in our manners here, and I've always said what's on my mind and don't intend to stop at this late date. Think me rude and graceless if you like, but we're going to do what Mother says you and she did right off, and that's talk about Tazia."

A year ago Mechella would have been overwhelmed into meek silence. Now she gave Lizia a cold stare. "I find her a boring topic of conversation."

"Eiha, I can tell. That must be why at the very sound of the name your eyes turn to ice. I'll tell you what Mother probably didn't. Arrigo was eighteen when Tazia began the chase. A year later, she caught him. Men are still boys at that age, and—"

"I have no interest in—"

"—and a boy is no match for a clever woman," Lizia went on inexorably. "She made him think he couldn't live without her. But now he knows he *can,* and very happily, too, so she's no danger to you. But there's something you must understand, Mechella. Father doesn't give Arrigo much to do. He likes being Grand Duke too much to give up any of the fun of it, even to his Heir. I hope when Maldonno comes of age and is ready to take on Casteya, I'll be more gracious about sharing! But the point is that Tazia knew this, and used it. She made Arrigo feel important, essential, that even the most trivial official engagement was meaningful. And of course she was quite lovely then, and experienced in bed, which always appeals to a young man. She made him feel he was the most fascinating man and wonderful lover in Tira Virte."

Mechella cried, "And you tell me I have nothing to fear from such a woman?"

"I tell you my brother is deeply in love with you, much more so than he ever was with Tazia. It's in his letters."

"What brother writes to his sister about his mistress?"

"Arrigo has always told me everything."

"Then tell *me* how I can send that woman from Court! I've begged him to, but he—"

"That's asking him to banish his youth. No man wants to do that. And, en verro, I think that hearing his young, beautiful wife complain about a woman he doesn't love anymore would flatter any man."

"But why does he need to hear it?"

"Because that's how men are," Lizia replied with a shrug.

Mechella shredded a slice of bread onto her plate. "I hate knowing she's here, I know it's part of what's making me so ill. But Arrigo won't send her away, he won't stop inviting her here—what can I do?"

The Countess sighed. "You have several courses of action open to you. First, accept her. Not as my mother did, of course. Tazia is—"

"—no Lissina, yes, I've been told," Mechella said impatiently. "I can't pretend to like her, I just can't."

"You could make Arrigo swear never to see her alone, and believe him—no matter what."

"I—I'd *have* to believe him, wouldn't I?" Mechella whispered.

"Or die of jealousy." A grim note crept into Lizia's voice. "But there's another choice. Turn a blind eye, make your own life and power."

"Wh-what do you mean?"

"Tazia is a grasping kind of person. I never much liked her, though I never told Arrigo so. From what I've heard—and you'd hear it also if you'd done what you should to make certain you hear—she's only biding her time before she chases him down again. Her husband won't mind. Garlo's interested in power, which is doubtless why she married him."

Mechella stared. "You mean—if she and Arrigo—Count do'Alva would—"

"You innocent child," Lizia sighed, "half the wives at Court have lovers. And possession of a Grijalva wife whose lover is the next Grand Duke would secure the do'Alva fortunes."

"That's despicable!"

"That's life," Lizia answered with another little shrug of delicate shoulders. "Whatever you decide, I advise you to gather people around you anyway, persons you trust and who'll be useful to you. Make yourself powerful. I had to, when Ormaldo became ill, or his cousins would have stolen my son's inheritance and ruined all that we accomplished in bringing Castello Casteya back to life."

"Make myself powerful? How?"

"Don't you see that in some respects you already are? The people adore you. Don't ever underestimate—carrida, are you feeling well?"

Mechella lurched out of bed, breakfast tray flying, and barely made it to the sink.

When she emerged, the room was tidy and Lizia was gone and the maid was waiting to help her into clean clothes. Mechella cursed feebly and wished she had the Lord Limner's determination to work no matter what his physical maladies. But Mequel's infirmities were mere pain, nothing at all like the trials of pregnancy.

She was ashamed of herself for disparaging the man's suffering. And as she recalled Lizia's words about how the Grijalva woman had captured Arrigo, she realized that she must emulate Mequel's courage or lose her husband. *She* must be the one to make him feel essential to Tira Virte; *she* must be the one to tell him he was a perfect lover; *she* must be the one he could not live without.

She was pitiably certain she couldn't live without him.

Her maid stood nearby, fidgeting. "What is it, Otonna?"

"Will Your Grace send word to Palasso Grijalva canceling today's lesson?"

Cabral—she'd completely forgotten Cabral. *"My mother has Lissina, of course. . . ."* Cabral could be a beginning. But first she must take herself strictly in hand.

"No, I'll get dressed now, I'm feeling much better." She paused seeing Otonna with new eyes. "Have you any sisters or brothers, Otonna? In service like you, I mean."

Showing not the slightest puzzlement at the question—indeed, with a gleam in her eyes as if she'd been waiting for this for months—Otonna replied, "My mother had four daughters, Your Grace. Primavarra, she's head maid to the Grand Duchess. Yberria cleans the Grand Duke's private rooms. Varra does the same for the Palasso offices of four conselhos."

Spring, Winter, Summer—and her own Autumn; all the seasons of the year, and all the important rooms in the Palasso. One day she might even find this funny.

"You were listening at the door."

"I was, Your Grace, and I can't say it shames me." Her soft lips thinned and her plump chin lifted; it was a camponessa's face, broad and plain as the earth, and as wise. "Dismiss me for it, but this whole year I've been waiting for just this moment. Primavarra, she's my twin, when she heard about *that woman* coming back, she said to me, 'You tell her Grace that when she needs us, we'll be ready.' I've told all my sisters how good and kind you are, all innocent and unknowing of the nasty ways of the Grijalvas."

Mechella was well and truly startled—at first by the torrent of words, more than she'd ever heard at one time from Otonna, and then by their meaning. "You don't trust the Grijalvas?"

"Not a bit." Otonna folded her arms over a well-filled bodice of Verrada blue. "It's not decent, giving over a young man to an older woman who's meant to—to do what they do, which is keep Limners powerful at Court. Why, the Blessed Alesso who died freeing us from the heathen Tza'ab, he'd put a stop to it were he alive, and that's fact. It was that slinking Sario who trapped the do'Verradas into generation after generation of scandal, and he used Saavedra to do it!"

"He did?"

"He did! He gave her willingly to Duke Alejandro, bringing him to the Grijalvas instead of to the Serranos—so Sario could be made Lord Limner! And then when she vanished, he painted that picture so poor Alejandro would always have her Grijalva face before him, and when Alejandro's son came of an age for it, he was given a Grijalva woman for a Mistress as a seal on the bargain that made them Lord Limners one after the other, with the Serranos nowhere to be found!"

"I see," Mechella said faintly.

"The sanctas and sanctos have the right of it about the Grijalvas," Otonna continued, "but even they don't dare challenge them—and that's worrisome, Your Grace, when even those who speak for the Mother and Son stay silent. And *that* one—Varra's husband, he's master of Don Arrigo's horses, many's the time he went to Chasseriallo, so he's in a position to know about *her*."

Mechella nodded, confounded by this unsuspected view of the Limner family. "Yet you've said nothing to me before."

"Eiha, Your Grace had to learn on her own, Primavarra said to me, and she had the right of that as well. She was always the quickest—out of the womb before me, into service first of us four, and risen high in the Grand Duchess's favor as well."

Forcing herself out of bed, remembering Mequel's painful movements and wishing for half his bravery, Mechella asked, "But what about Cabral Grijalva?"

"As Your Grace's eyes and ears inside their Palasso?"

Mechella gave a start at how easily the maid followed her thoughts. "I was thinking of it, yes." How horrified Aunt Permilla would be to hear her ask the opinion of a servant. And how far away and thoroughly irrelevant Aunt Permilla was now.

"Eiha, there's Grijalvas and Grijalvas, aren't there? Proof enough in the sisters Larissa and Margatta, cherished friends to our blessed Duchess Jesminia. And Baroness do'Dregez, Lissina Grijalva that was, she's a fine kind lady with nothing but goodness about her. And Mequel isn't so bad, though he *is* one of the odd ones."

"Odd?"

"As I say, there's Grijalvas and Grijalvas. Yberria's husband, he's their cook, he said when I asked that Cabral isn't one of the unnatural ones—meaning those squint-eyed painters who can never father a child and put strange magical signs all over their pictures, and also the women who have one baby after another in hopes of getting a painterish son, just like prize horses bred for hunting."

In her year as Arrigo's wife, she hadn't even thought about what the Ecclesia or the commoners or anyone else thought of the Grijalvas. Limners were simply a fact of life in Tira Virte. Surely the sterile Limners couldn't help what they were—and Mequel was one of the dearest men she'd ever met. As for the other painters, they worked on behalf of Tira Virte, not themselves. Still, she agreed with Otonna's judgment of Grijalva women although a highborn wife was in much the same position when it came to it. The getting of a son was Mechella's primary responsibility, too. It put her on similar footing with the Grijalva brood mares. And she didn't like it at all. She must be worth more than that—mustn't she?

Otonna said, "But Cabral's on your side, see if he isn't, and against his own Grijalva kin if it ever comes to it. And how is it I know this?" She smiled. "Only that he painted a copy of Your Grace's *Marriage*—and has been in love with you ever since."

Mechella sat down very hard on the bed. *"Cabral?"*

"En verro, and anyone without Your Grace's sweet innocence would have seen it weeks ago. But don't ever let on that you know. Eiha, there's the hour chime, I'll have to hurry the lads with the bath water. Will Your Grace wear the lavender or the pink today?"

☞ FORTY-THREE ☜

Four days later, Arrigo and his sister welcomed their guests—twenty-two titled parents and their forty noble offspring, aged ten to thirteen—to an afternoon of puppetry and games nominally hosted by Count Maldonno do'Casteya. The gathering, ordered by Cossimio and organized in haste, would serve to make known to his adolescent peers the Grand Duke's grandson. From the ranks of the boys would come his friends; one of the girls might become his wife. It was devoutly hoped that Maldonno, raised in a ramshackle castello and as much a stranger to elegant silks as he was to the great names he met that day, would begin to see that he had a position to uphold. He simply could not run wild through the Palasso, and he must learn his role in society—as the unfortunate incident of the pony in the Galerria proved (though Mequel laughed uproariously when he heard of it, Cossimio was not amused).

Lizia, equally accustomed to casual manners, was as uncomfortable at the party as her son. "I don't see why this is necessary," she complained to Arrigo between arrivals. "He's always been free to do as he likes without all this formality stifling him—unlike all these little hothouse flowers! Matra ei Filho, it's just like when we were children and Mother gave all those hideous parties, which you hated as much as I did, don't deny it!"

"Had to be done, then and now," Arrigo said, not without sympathy. "Calm down, Lizi, I've invited a few who aren't 'hothouse flowers.' Tazia's bringing some cousins."

"What? Are you mad? Grijalvas rubbing shoulders with do'Brazzinas and do'Varriyvas? The least we can expect is a score of black eyes! We'll be lucky if they don't all leave!"

"No one will leave." He turned to greet an approaching baroness and her sweating, lace-collared twelve-year-old son. After Lizia made the proper noises and the pair joined the party, he went on, "They're not stupid. Someday one of those Grijalva boys will be Lord Limner."

"How nice for one of them," she snapped. "And speaking of Grijalvas, I've been meaning to talk to you about Tazia. You're making Mechella very unhappy, you know. Or *did* you know?"

"Leave my wife to me," Arrigo responded sharply.

"And your former Mistress? Shall you leave her to her husband?"

Stiff-lipped, he replied, "Stay out of it, Lizia." Then, catching sight of a familiar mane of glossy black hair, he said, "And here's the Countess now." With her middle stepson and six other boys—including, he saw with a start, her own son, Rafeyo.

Verradio do'Alva, a scrawny sullen-faced boy in a silver satin jacket, was completely overshadowed by the sturdy, plainly dressed Grijalvas. After directing the youngsters to the games and refreshments, Arrigo smiled at Rafeyo and said how good it was to see him again.

"Just don't tell him how he's grown!" Tazia winked at her son, who blushed and made a face. "Or that he's ready to grow one of those silly half-beards that are the fashion with young men these days. Such talk makes me feel old enough to be his great-grandmother. I must say the sight of the Countess isn't helping. You look twenty-two, it's positively depressing."

Arrigo chuckled. "You've hit her in her vanity, Tazia—"

"No, she in mine!" Tazia laughed. "That must be your son over there, Countess. He has the fine Casteyan look of his father about him."

"We all think so," Lizia answered, thawing a bit.

Arrigo said, "Rafeyo, you must be well into your studies by now. How are you enjoying life as a Limner?"

"Very much, Your Grace. It's quite challenging."

"I gather you've been brought along to supervise the younger cousins?"

The boy replied with another grimace.

"And at Dioniso's suggestion," his mother continued, "he'll make some sketches as practice, and a memento of the occasion."

"Delightful idea," Lizia said. "I'd like to have one, if you don't mind, Rafeyo."

"Honored, Countess," he bowed.

"Lizi," said Arrigo, "I think everyone's here, and even if they aren't, I'm dying of thirst. Shall I bring you something to drink?"

Thus he escaped with Tazia to the refreshment tables. Plates of fruit were predictably untouched; plates of sweets had been just as predictably demolished. Seven gigantic crystal bowls held variously flavored lemonadas dyed improbable colors, and Tazia pointed hesitantly to a garish purple. Arrigo laughed while the servant grinned and dipped a cup for her.

"It's only plum juice," Arrigo said. "And not bad, really."

"I foresee frightful experiments in kitchens all over Meya

Suerta. All these children will want something green to drink the way it was at the Palasso!" She sipped, nodded approval, and went on, "And no wine, not even for the adults. Very wise. I take it you remembered what happened to you at age fourteen during Mirraflores?"

He groaned.

"All Meya Suerta heard you up on the balcony, drunk as a brace of barons and singing at the top of your lungs!"

"How indelicate of you to remember so clearly what I swear I don't remember at all! Have one of these cakes, the pastry cooks have a new recipe."

"No, thank you—and we really must stop meeting like this, always at a table laden with sweets. Arrigo, you're ruining my waistline!"

"You're babbling," he observed softly. "I've never heard you do that before, Tazia."

"I could say the same of you," she replied just as quietly, just as mindful of the nearby servant. "Arrigo—"

"Is it getting any better?"

"If you mean am I still beset with caustic countesses and baronesses with barbed tongues—not so much anymore. Thank you. If you mean—" She broke off and looked away.

"Tell me." When she shook her head, he urged, "Tazia, tell me!"

"If—if you were asking if it's getting any easier being without you, the answer is *no*." Raising her face to look him in the eye, she finished with a bright social smile. "You're very kind to give Rafeyo such notice, I'm grateful. I should go look at his sketches. If you'll excuse me?"

"No, I will not excuse you. I—"

A small gasp from the servant made Arrigo's head turn. His wife was hurrying through the doorway of the music room, heading straight for him and Tazia with an expression of worry and fear on her pallid face.

"Arrigo—" Mechella didn't even see Tazia. "There's dreadful news," she whispered. "You and Lizia must come at once."

"What is it? Teressa? My parents?"

"No, no, they're well. It's—"

She saw Tazia. Her cheeks flushed and her whole body went rigid with loathing. Tazia met her gaze for a moment with something indefinable flickering in her eyes, then looked away.

Concerned and annoyed, Arrigo said, "People are watching,

Mechella. You've upset everyone. Why didn't you send a servant? Tell me what's wrong, so I can set their minds at rest."

With a last hate-filled look for Tazia, she said, "There's been a terrible earthquake in Casteya, in the foothills of the Montes Astrappas. Hundreds are dead, perhaps thousands—"

"And my father has sent for me to help him." *At last!*

"I don't know, I haven't spoken with him. I only heard by accident, on my way to the Galerria. Some servants were talking, one of them had taken the courier up to your father. I came as soon as I could, to tell you and Lizia—"

Arrigo swallowed anger. The servants had known before he did! His father was even now planning rescue efforts, commanding food and workers and medical help for the stricken area, while he, the Heir, the next Grand Duke of Tira Virte, stood in a room filled with children.

He glanced around for Lizia. The man whispering urgently in her ear was his father's personal aide. There was no alteration in Lizia's expression as she heard the news, only a twitch in one cheek, a brief clenching of one hand. Fiery as she could be, she knew how to conceal her thoughts and emotions in front of others. His gaze slid to Tazia—her face was as smooth as his sister's—and then to Mechella.

"Go to your father," Tazia murmured. "He'll need you."

Arrigo couldn't help a bitter retort. "Will he?"

Mechella surprised him then. "Of course he will! I've already sent word that you'll be there immediately. And—Arrigo, I hope I've done right in this—I ordered our carriages made ready. They'll hold a lot of food and blankets and medicines, and they're much faster than wagons."

"Well done, Your Grace," Tazia said, nodding approval. She might not have spoken for all the notice Mechella took of her.

"Everything should be ready by first light, Arrigo. We'll leave—"

Lizia was making the announcement, serious but calm, alarming no one: minor temblor, minor damage, no reason to cancel the entertainment, understand that we must leave you now, go on enjoying yourselves—

Arrigo stared at his wife. " 'We'?" he echoed incredulously. "'Leave'?"

She looked him straight in the eye, not upward, as Tazia had to. "We must help in any way we can, and how can we know what's needed unless we're there?"

"Your Grace." Tazia was frowning. "I'm aware that you don't

know about such things, but one earthquake is almost invariably followed by another. In your condition you really mustn't think of such a journey."

Mechella rounded on her, blue eyes flashing. "How dare you tell me what I must and mustn't do! These are our people, and we're going!"

"Your Grace!" Tazia shrank back with the shock.

Before anyone could say anything else, Lizia's heels clicked angrily toward them across the tiled floor. "What are you waiting for?" she snapped. "Arrigo, Patro wants us at once."

He suspected that it was only Lizia, Countess do'Casteya, whose presence had been commanded. Nodding to Tazia, he took his wife's arm and his sister's, and together they left the music room. But he glanced back over his shoulder at Tazia—abandoned, alone, eyes wide with worry for his safety and hurt at Mechella's rebuke. Arrigo suddenly found himself in the grip of powerful and conflicting emotions.

Tazia knew the risks of the journey to Mechella and the child, and the danger of further tremors, and she was afraid for them—for *him.* Mechella cared more for the people than for any danger to their unborn son. She didn't know enough to be frightened. Eiha, but she was right. These *were* their people, and it was their duty to help. She understood that with the instincts of a Princess of Ghillas. Tazia did not. Yet it had been Tazia whose first words were that his father would need him, though Mechella had arranged the journey even before hurrying to tell him of the disaster, showing a presence of mind and a practicality he had not hitherto looked for in her. Still, her furious reply to Tazia's justifiable concern was inexcusable.

What it came down to, he told himself as he assisted his pregnant wife up the stairs, was that Mechella had reacted as the royalty she was: duty first, personal concerns unimportant, her only thought their people's need. But Tazia—

Tazia's every thought was for him as a man, as Arrigo—for his very personal need to be of use, and for his safety. . . .

"Can't spare you," Cossimio growled at him across a conference table littered with maps and lists. "I want you here, taking over my other duties until this is resolved."

"But—"

"No argument! I've had enough of that from the conselhos! Not enough this or that or the other damned thing to send to Casteya's aid—we'll just see about that! I'm the Grand Duke and when I want a thing done, Nommo Matra ei Filho, it *will* be done!"

Gizella said soothingly, "That's why your father needs you here, Arrigo. He must go himself to the warehouses and granaries, otherwise—"

Arrigo couldn't give up just yet. "I could be doing that on the way to Casteya. There are storehouses along the route, and things wouldn't have to go as far."

His father scowled mightily. "And I say you stay here. Lizia has to go, Casteya's hers, but not you. You'll take my regular duties, end of discussion."

Arrigo intercepted a glance of sympathy from his sister. He refused to acknowledge it. Mechella stared in silence at her laced fingers in her lap, all the spirit gone out of her. She wasn't willing to fight for what she knew to be their rightful duty as Don and Dona. Not that this surprised him; in the past year she must have learned how futile it was to argue with Grand Duke Cossimio II when his mind was made up.

The next morning she did not send for her maid to prepare her bath and dress her. Arrigo, enquiring of Otonna as to whether his wife intended to remain in bed all day—again—received nothing more than a shrug and a few words professing ignorance of Her Grace's plans. So Arrigo was as surprised as anyone when a courier came in at noon with a message from Lizia: the caravan of carriages taking her and supplies to Casteya was also taking Mechella.

Cossimio shouted curses for half an hour until Gizella got him laughing over how they'd misjudged their shy, self-effacing 'Chella. Reassured by Otonna as to her health, they were impressed by her determination and took it as evidence that she now thought of their people as her own. Cossimio decided to make a gesture of sending the courier back with messages attempting to dissuade her from the journey. But gesture he intended it to be, for Meya Suerta was applauding Mechella on every corner and zocalo, and drinking her name in every tavern. So the note did not contain a Grand Ducal Command that she would be compelled to obey—or which, disobeyed, would force him to chastise her.

Another note left the Palasso shortly thereafter. Late that night, still half-blind with fury, Arrigo slipped out a garden gate and went alone and unobserved to Tazia's old caza. She met him in the empty hallway, a lamp in her hand. He sat with her on the staircase until nearly dawn, then returned to the Palasso resigned—if not to his wife's spectacular display of disobedience, then at least to substituting for his father while Cossimio concentrated on the crisis.

"Show that you're willing to listen and help when everyone else is not. The others are doing very noisy and obvious things, Arrigo.

The hard part was left to you. Your father has no time for the day-to-day business now. You do, and he trusts you to do it. The people will remember. They may take her to their hearts as kind folk welcome a stranger, but you're part of their souls. You'll be the one to keep Tira Virte functioning in this emergency. You'll show that you care for *all* your people. Now, go home and get some sleep, Arrigo. You'll need it."

Mechella didn't think of it as disobedience. After all, the Grand Duke said that *Arrigo* must stay in Meya Suerta. He hadn't even said Mechella's name.

As it happened, Arrigo was wrong about her royal instincts. Had Mechella examined what compelled her, she would have recognized it as the next step in a path mapped out by her own childhood. Deprived of her mother, she had played the maternal role by telling stories to servants' children at Pallaiso Millia Luminnai. Her husband had given her a daughter of her own, but he had also given her a whole nation to care for, and until now she had spent her time learning its needs while scarcely aware that she *was* learning. This journey of hers would end—though she had no way of knowing it—with her involvement in every aspect of Tira Virteian life when she became its Grand Duchess. And Tira Virte would return her love a thousandfold.

All that she knew now was that she must go to Casteya and do what she could to help. She felt well enough for any journey. She worried about her baby, but Arrigo's carriage was the newest and most comfortable in Tira Virte, and the ride was amazingly smooth. There were physicians in their party who could take care of her, and Lizia to keep a close watch on her for weariness, and she simply *couldn't* stay in Meya Suerta when her people needed her.

She spent the long days of travel poring over hastily scrawled inventory sheets with Lizia, making plans based on news from Casteyan messengers sent to intercept them. She and Lizia thought themselves prepared for whatever might await them.

They were wrong.

Their arrival at the first mountain village flattened by earthquake brought bitter tears neither woman would shed. Where once there had been houses, shops, a smithy and a mill and a little stone Sanctia, there was nothing now but ruin. Roofs of tile had collapsed all the way down into basements; roofs of thatch had, on falling, turned the candlelit homes beneath into infernos. The first sign of life Mechella and Lizia saw was a huddled gathering in the graveyard beside the wreck of the Sanctia. Rescuers had spent days digging through the rubble, hoping for survivors but locating only corpses. They had been digging graves, too, but wasted no time or effort on coffins; even in late autumn coolness there was danger of disease. The dead were buried without even a winding sheet, for every scrap of cloth was needed for bandages and every blanket for protection against the chill nights. There was no refuge from the cold, not even in the village Sanctia, which had burned to the ground. Arrigo's steward had packed a spacious tent for Countess Lizia's use, but when it was learned that there was not a scrap of shelter to be had in all the village, the two women agreed that it should be used for the injured. They would sleep as they had on the road, in their carriage.

"We've had word, Countess," said the weary sancto, who had miraculously survived the destruction of his Sanctia, "that Castello Casteya was only mildly shaken, Grazzo do'Matra."

Bleakly, Lizia said, "Grazzo for what?" And she looked eloquently around her at the disaster.

Mechella trailed Lizia in stunned silence, ashamed of her ignorance. Lizia knew some basic medicine, enough to clean and bind wounds and discern which injuries required the physicians who had come with them. Mechella knew nothing about such things. Lizia, savior with her late husband of a tottering castello, knew what could be rebuilt and what must be abandoned; she could glance at a heap of broken stones and know if it was safe to dismantle or too dangerous to touch. Mechella knew nothing about this either. She saw only devastation that wrung her heart. But Lizia showed little emotion, and instead gave brisk orders that were always obeyed. Mechella felt useless, and knew how futile was her presence here.

Yet that evening as they sat in their carriage, sodden with exhaustion and staring at the meal served on Arrigo's silver-gilt traveling service, Lizia smiled at her and said, "You're more help than I thought you'd be."

"I'm hopeless and we both know it."

"At the things I'm good at, yes. You can't wind a bandage without snarling it, and to you one pile of fallen stones looks just like any other. But haven't you seen their faces? You don't even have to speak. You just look at them, touch their hands—it's as if their pain and fear are living things you cradle in your arms. Understanding and sympathy—they're qualities I don't possess."

"And of no practical use. It was stupid of me to come."

"Eiha, that's just it, carrida. You don't have to be here and they know it, but you came anyway." Lizia sank into the butter-soft suede upholstery, sighing. "Matra Dolcha, I'm tired. And there's worse to be seen further on."

Mechella leaned toward her in the lamplit carriage. "Lizia, tell me what I can do. I'm not good at any of the things you know so much about. There must be *something* I can do besides talk to them and hold their hands."

"It's the one thing they need that I can't provide. Mother can, but I'm more my father's daughter, as you've undoubtedly noticed," she finished wryly. "I'm too tired to think, Mechella. Let's try to sleep."

On the second day Mechella discovered how she could best help. Lizia lost track of her midmorning and had no time to look for her until late afternoon. She found Mechella in the cleared-out hollow of a cobbler's shop, surrounded by children, telling them a story.

Lizia hated to disturb them, but it was nearing dinnertime and Mechella had to eat and keep up her strength. Arrigo had said she'd been sickly while carrying Teressa and was again in delicate health, though there was little evidence of it now. Lizia's own pregnancies had been characterized by a ravenous appetite; even if Mechella's were not, she had to eat.

On the walk back to the carriage, Mechella told Lizia what she'd learned. Most of the children had lost either mother or father. Some had lost both. One little boy had been trapped for two days, shielded by his mother's slowly dying body. Another broke his arm falling out of a hayloft where he and his five siblings were playing; he alone had survived the earthquake. Twin girls barely four years old were found in the street outside a house; their father lay dead inside, killed by a collapsed beam, and no one knew how the girls had escaped. One brother and sister were alive only because their uncle had carried them to safety. When he returned for his sister and her husband, a wall toppled and all three adults died.

"At first I thought I'd just keep them out of everyone's way, and make sure they didn't play in dangerous places. But then they started talking to me, Lizi. Almost every child in this village is a tragedy. Some have no family left alive. Do you think—would it be all right if I tried to find homes for them?"

"Duchess Jesminia," Lizia murmured. " 'Chella, I think that would be a very good thing."

So in that village and in a dozen more over the next twenty days, Mechella gathered children to her side. She talked to them, held them while they cried, told them stories, gently coaxed their names and circumstances from them. And as each community began to recover and think about the future, she carefully matched each orphan to a new family.

Lizia's reference to Jesminia reminded Mechella that the beloved Duchess had championed the chi'patro children of long ago, but this was a completely different situation. However, recalling who had taken in those children, she had an idea. One night in their darkened carriage, wrapped in furs against the mountain cold, she asked Lizia about it.

"An excellent point," was the thoughtful reply. "Although I've never heard of such a document. Usually orphans are taken in by cousins, no matter how remote. This time whole families have been wiped out."

"Then it would be better to make the adoptions legal?"

"I believe so. And at the same time we can protect their property, such as it may be. These children are still their parents' heirs. We should establish ownership as soon as may be, before anyone can argue about it."

"Lizi! Surely no one would steal—"

"My innocent, wouldn't they just!"

"Then we'll store the proofs at the Sanctias."

"Brilliant! And if someone wants to buy the land to rebuild on—better a business than an empty hole along the street—the Ecclesials can decide if it's a good offer—"

"—and hold the money for child's future," Mechella interrupted excitedly, "the way part of my dower is being held for Teressa!"

"Better than brilliant!" Lizia laughed. "And to think you said you were useless! You can write to my father tomorrow."

"I—I don't think I'd better."

"You're not still worried about that silly note he sent? 'Chella, if he were really angry and really wanted you to return, he would've said so, believe me. I know my father. But maybe you should write to Arrigo instead. This will give him something to do."

Mechella was glad Lizia couldn't see her face. "I—I don't dare, Lizi. He really *is* angry with me. I haven't heard from him since we left Meya Suerta."

"Eiha, it was a naughty trick you played, but he knows by now how much good you're doing." She paused. "He and Patro are worried about the baby, of course, but you're not very far along yet and you seem healthy as a horse."

"I feel *much* better than I did with Teressa."

"It's my opinion that pregnant women shouldn't be coddled,"

Lizia said forthrightly. "Shut up indoors, allowed no exercise except a turn in the gardens, nothing to do but knit and fret—being useful and doing things is infinitely better for one's mental state as well as one's health. But I *do* worry about these conditions, 'Chella."

She smiled in the darkness. "Don't be. I'm warm, dry, comfortable, and everyone takes such good care of me. Most of the time I forget I'm pregnant."

"Eiha, then I won't send you back even if Patro *does* order it. You're a great help to me here, and Arrigo will be pleased when he learns of it. And this new idea of yours—you'll have to write him at once."

Mechella shifted within her cocoon of furs. "I haven't sent him any letters at all. I don't know how he'll react if I—"

"Not in all this time? 'Chella!" There was a rustle of blankets and the scrape of a match that lit a lampwick. "You put pen to paper this instant!"

The resulting letter, composed under Lizia's stern gaze, was at once stiff, wistful, and apprehensive. It was sent next morning by courier. Mechella lived in anguish awaiting Arrigo's answer. It came several afternoons later in the form of a carriage emblazoned with the Grand Ducal Seal, rolling into another landscape of rubble that had once been a thriving town. From it emerged Cabral Grijalva, four junior Limners, and—in charge of doling out canvas and paint—Cabral's younger sister, Leilias.

There was no letter from Arrigo or Cossimio. Gizella's was the signature on the note Cabral presented to Mechella. The Grand Duchess had penned heartfelt words blessing her and Lizia, entreaties for them to stay safe and well, the approval of the new Premio Frato Dioniso of their plan, and assurances that the children were fine though missing their mothers very much.

Mechella read, handed the page to Lizia, and said quietly, "I'm glad you're here, Cabral. I've a list of what we need. You'd best get started."

~•~ FORTY-FOUR ~•~

Dioniso took possession of the Premio Frato's quarters with mixed emotions. It was the highest he had risen in the Grijalva ranks for a very long time, but it was not as high as he intended to go in his next life. Besides that, he had rather liked his predecessor, Agusto: a fine painter, a stern teacher, and a sardonic wit that made light of growing infirmities so that no one knew how truly ill he was up until the very day of his death.

Artistically, Dioniso was exactly where he wanted to be. Where he *needed* to be. As Premio he would pass judgment on everything and everyone—and especially on how the estudos were taught. The decline of painting would be reversed. He had sworn it. He would bring art back into line with his own genius, so that when he took Rafeyo in a few years, he would be hailed as the greatest since Riobaro.

Politically, he was also excellently placed. It wasn't quite as good as being Lord Limner, but that could wait. Still, as Premio, he would have access to the Grand Duke whenever he liked, and to Arrigo and Mechella. What he had begun on the journey to Diettro Mareia had been nicely furthered by the painting of Teressa's *Birth;* he would continue in this manner, doling out bits of information to Arrigo and ingratiating himself with Mechella through his art. This notion of hers to paint the inheritances of the Casteyan orphans had met with his approval, and he'd personally selected those who would do the work. Rafeyo was, of course, among them—resentful at this squandering, as he saw it, of his talents. But the goodwill he would establish with Mechella would be invaluable in the future.

There was the boy's fierce loyalty to his mother, the discarded Mistress, to worry him—but as much as Dioniso might want to paint Rafeyo into liking Mechella, he could not. Any alteration in behavior would be remarked on. And anyway, how much damage could he do in only a few years, when he would be almost exclusively at Palasso Grijalva learning his craft?

The ceremony installing Dioniso as Premio Frato was a subdued one, out of respect for the earthquake victims up north. After a solemn ritual in the Crechetta, during which he received the begemmed golden collar of his new office and vows of obedience of the other Limners, he went out into the torchlit gardens to be formally introduced to the rest of Palasso Grijalva and hear their congratulations. Normally there would have been a grand banquet, but it suited him not to spend the whole night drinking and feasting. He had another errand.

Accordingly, once all was quiet in the vast warren of the Palasso, he slipped out a back gate and made his way to his secret atelierro. The paints were a matter of moments to mix; he need only add one detail to the figure of Dioniso in the *Peintraddo Memorrio:* the collar of the Premio Frato.

It was the work of an hour. Afterward, he mixed other colors and painted in another sprig of rosemary for dear Matteyo, whispering, "It was not in vain, frato meyo. I *will* become Lord Limner again."

Then he sat down at the table, running his fingers through the thick Tza'ab rug atop it, and contemplated the dead white bone of his own skull.

Fifty or sixty years after Sario's "death"—he'd forgotten when he'd done it, and it didn't matter—he had opened the grave one midnight. Nearly all the flesh had rotted off, so he hadn't experienced the shock of seeing his own half-decomposed face. Taking skull from spine, leaving all else in the grave, he'd brought it back here and cleaned it with acids to get rid of the last bits of skin. It rested now on this table, a reminder of what he had been, what he had done, what he would do—and what fate did *not* await him.

Taking it between his two hands, he stared into the empty eye-sockets and smiled. For others, this was the end of all things: a hollow skull where once a brain had been, grinning teeth bared with no soft lips to cover them, cold bone unwarmed by flesh and skin and thick black hair. He alone had escaped this destiny.

He, and Saavedra.

It had been fashionable in the last century to paint a skull into the *Peintraddo Marria,* where the newly married couple stood young and proud and wealthy, all their lives before them. The memento morta, the skull, was intended as a reminder that youth was fleeting, pride was mere vanity, and wealth could not buy freedom from this inevitable fate.

He had freed himself from it. Himself, and Saavedra.

Cradling his own skull between his hands; thinking thoughts that had once sparked within this now-barren arch of bone; gazing into the emptiness where long ago he had looked into living, terrified eyes that no longer had anything of Sario in them, but instead Martain—no, *Ignaddio;* he had been the first. He glanced up to the

Memorrio, and for a few seconds could not identify which one Ignaddio was. Ah—there, the clothing gave it away, the style of centuries ago.

He returned his gaze to his own skull, seeing it for what it was: a memento viva, a reminder of life.

His life. Saavedra's life.

Soon. The twinge in his fingers, brought on by the atelierro's chill, reminded him that there were few years left in this body. But then would come Rafeyo—strong, handsome, clever, extremely well-connected Rafeyo—and when *he* was added to the *Memorrio,* it would be with the gorgeous robes and jewels of the Lord Limner on his shoulders.

And then, perhaps, he would bring Saavedra from her painted prison, and—

—and live a life together, and then die? End as spiritless meat and bone in separate graves, all thought and feeling and brilliance and magic gone forever?

Shuddering, he set down Sario's skull and left the atelierro.

"She's not at all as you said," Leilias Grijalva told her brother as they walked through what had been a prosperous market town. "Did you see her face as she read Gizella's letter? And she didn't even ask about Arrigo!"

"Why should she, when his silence tells her all she needs to know?"

Leilias shrugged. "You said he's annoyed, but she's doing him nothing but good here. They'll rule one day. People will remember her work on their behalf."

"*Her* work. Not his." Cabral kicked at a stone, hands jammed into the pockets of his heavy gray woolen jacket. "He sits in his father's place, hearing disputes about ore shipments and the price of seed corn and a hundred other useless things that could just as well be done by the senior conselhos, while *she*—" He broke off abruptly.

Leilias said nothing for ten or twelve steps. He glanced down at her and frowned. She wore the despicably superior expression she used to when they were children and she'd been listening at keyholes. Growling at her, he demanded, "Don't you have to inventory the brushes or something?"

"Now, you know very well that's only my excuse for coming along on this little outing. At *your* suggestion, I might add! But she seems to be doing very well without us. I must say I'm surprised to find her competent at something other than childbearing."

He glared. "Mallica lingua!"

"Find a more original insult, frato meyo," Leilias said merrily. "Everyone knows I have a sarcastic tongue! What I was going to say is that it's in Meya Suerta she'll need our help. Especially now that Arrigo is visiting Tazia again—alone, and, he believes, in secret."

"What?" Cabral grabbed her arm. "What have you heard?"

"I had it from someone at Palasso Grijalva, who had it from someone in Arrigo's service, and I'm not going to tell you anything else until you calm down." She shook herself free of his grip. "What use will you be to Mechella if you can't keep your countenance for five minutes and go around rattling your own sister's teeth out of her head?"

Cabral's jaw clenched so hard that a muscle in his cheek jumped. After a moment he said, "Has Arrigo resumed with Tazia?"

"It's only a matter of time. He won't like it when Mechella comes home a heroine. And you know Tazia—all honey and oil to soothe his hurts."

Cabral shook his head. "If he begins again with Tazia—Matra ei Filho, it'll kill her," he whispered.

"Eiha, we'll just have to see that it doesn't. That's your plan, isn't it? To protect her against Tazia and her little whelp Rafeyo?" She shrugged, righting her cloak. "Which reminds me—did we have to bring him along? He's got talent, granted, but he makes me nervous."

"Premio Frato Dioniso's idea. If we'd left him at home, someone might have suspected something."

"And so it begins," Leilias murmured. "Suspicions, rumors, denials—what's believed, thought, felt, guessed, known, unknown—and who's on whose side. It will split the family, you know. Those for Mechella, those for Arrigo, and those who don't want anything to do with the whole mess. Poor Mequel. It's *his* health we ought to be concerned about."

"No mention of 'poor Dioniso'?"

"It's anybody's guess as to whose side *he's* on."

"His own." Cabral kicked another rock.

Leilias paused before the Sanctia, razed yesterday after Lizia determined that no part of it was salvageable except the belltower. "What a ruin! Reminds me of Tavial's *Siege of the Tza'ab Castello*."

"Tavial didn't paint that," her brother replied absently. "Sario did, before the siege even took place."

"Another clever Grijalva. Don't you wish we were clever enough to paint these villages back into being? That would be *real* magic, not that 'power of artistic genius' nonsense people credit us with."

Cabral said nothing. But if Leilias knew anyone in the world, she knew her brother. This time it was she whose hands grabbed his shoulders, her voice low and tense as she demanded, "What is it? Tell me!"

"I don't *know* anything, really—" But he met her eyes, dark hazel like his, and she caught her breath.

"Are the rumors true? The whispers?"

He shrugged her off. "You mean the ones that stop when a woman like you or a mere limner like me comes into a room? I'm not sure, Leilias. But since I've lived at the Palasso—" He stopped, then with seeming irrelevance said, "Rafeyo makes me nervous, too, and not just because he's Tazia's son. There's something about his eyes. . . ."

"He's always been an arrogant little mennino," she mused.

" 'Always'?" he echoed. "How do you know?"

Leilias looked him square in the face. She said nothing more. She had no need to.

"Matra Dolcha!" Cabral ground his teeth. "Last year was his Confirmattio!"

"We talked a bit, and I almost liked him for a while—in a way. It was his suggestion that I make a perfume for Mechella's wedding gift. But now that he's a Limner—there *is* something about his eyes, you're right. As if he knows exactly what he wants and is only biding his time, laughing behind his hand."

"Just like his mother."

"I'd guess they're after the same thing, in the end."

"You stay away from him," he warned suddenly.

"No need to say *that* twice! After the Confirmattio, Cansalvio blushed and stammered, and the other two at least looked sheepish if they saw me around the Palasso. Rafeyo stared me right in the eye and *winked!*"

"If he comes near you again, I'll break every bone in his hands!"

Leilias patted his arm, a smile hovering around her mouth. "Grazzo, frato carrido, but I can take care of myself. Save your righteous wrath for Mechella. She needs protecting much more than I."

Three mornings later a caravan of wagons arrived from Meya Suerta. Mechella was struggling with a heavy box in the back of a wagon when two large hands grasped it for her.

"Allow me, Your Grace," said Cabral, hefting the wooden crate to the ground.

"Grazzo, Cabral—just don't scold," she said, wrinkling her nose. "Help me with the rest?"

The supplies included food, clothing, blankets, tents on loan from the Shagarra Regiment, and six boxes labeled "From the Children of Palasso Grijalva." These proved to contain toys, and Mechella exclaimed in delight at the dolls and games and painted wooden horses and knights. In one box was a note addressed to her and signed by Premio Frato Dioniso.

> In you, Dona, the Mother blesses Tira Virte beyond our deserving. The children here hope these small gifts will bring smiles where smiles are needed.
> Your humble servant,
> Dioniso

"How sweet of all your little cousins to give up some of their toys!" She held up a pair of porcelain dolls with silk-thread black braids. "These are just what I need to keep the children busy. I'm running out of stories to tell!"

While Cabral stacked boxes, she called over a few villagers to begin distributing blankets and food. Suddenly, without warning, the ground quivered underfoot. Mechella lost her balance—more from fright than the severity of the temblor—and would have fallen had Cabral not caught her up in his arms.

"It's all right," he said. "It'll stop in a moment."

She was biting both lips between her teeth. Her skin was milk-white and her blue eyes were huge and she was rigid with terror against his chest, but she did not cry out. When the shaking stopped, she bent her head to his shoulder and let out a long, shuddering sigh. She wore a scarf to protect her hair from dirt and dust, and he turned his cheek to it, wishing it gone so he could feel that wealth of sungold silk against his face.

He let her go. She gripped the side of the wagon for support. He rather felt like doing the same. She was dressed no better than a camponessa and she smelled of sweat and garlic and she was pregnant with another man's child—and when she gulped down her fear and smiled at him he thought he would fall on his knees at her feet.

"I—I was told this would happen," she managed in a small voice. "But it wasn't so bad, was it?"

"Nothing compared to what destroyed this village. Are you all right, Your Grace?"

"Yes. I won't be so silly next time, now that I know what to expect. I—"

" 'Chella? Oh, here you are!" Lizia came striding up, a long sheet of paper trailing from her hand. "Eiha, you're a real Casteyan now—you've been through an earthquake! Not much of one, but it still qualifies. Now, come with me. Rafeyo has an idea."

This idea proved to be the solution of how to paint the adoptions while legalizing property rights. The boy spread out a sketch on a fallen slab of building stone and explained.

"I had some problems in composition—these will be very awkward pieces, which annoys me—but that won't matter to these people as long as the paintings are legal. In the old days we used to do a *Will* as a series of scenes inside a connecting ivy vine for fidelity. I propose to use the same pattern. We paint the child in the middle. The old name is symbolized to his right, in this example by the two pears in his right hand for Pirroz, which puns with piros—that means 'pear,' " he added condescendingly to Mechella.

"Go on," she said evenly.

"The new name goes on the left—in this case a simple pebble in his palm, for his new family have been stonemasons forever, which is why their name is Piatro. As for the section of orchard the Pirroz boy inherits from his dead father—behind on the right, as seen from the main road with all landmarks clearly visible. The village house was harder. There *is* no house anymore. But when I inspected the location from the rear, there's a direct line-of-sight to the Sanctia. It's the only thing in the village left standing." He leaned back from the sketch. "So. We end with four elements: child, old name, new name, and inheritance."

Cabral frowned. "What if you can't find a convenient pun?"

"I've read through the list. They're all pretty obvious." He shrugged. "All componessos are named for their occupations or characteristics—Anjieras, for instance. The family came here from somewhere else and the name 'estranjieros' stuck."

"You've solved our problem most cleverly, Rafeyo," said Mechella. "Grazzo."

"It wasn't that hard—if you don't mind clumsy painting."

Not a hint of a *Your Grace,* still less of respect. But Mechella only smiled, and Cabral cringed within that she wasted that glorious smile on this boy who hated her.

"I don't agree, Rafeyo," she said. "Look at the way you've sketched the boy—as if he's cradling the pears in memory of his dead parents, and yet holds the pebble as if he's been given a diamond. This is much more than a legal document, Rafeyo. It's the work of a true Limner."

Cabral inspected the sketch again. Mechella was right. Despite Rafeyo's contempt for the commoners he was now obliged to paint—no glorious grand canvases here, he thought, remembering the boy's ambitious words in Diettro Mareia—this work had been done with great sensitivity. Cabral felt a surge of pride in his family that could produce such instinctive artistry even with minimal efforts—and an entirely different warmth that Mechella had absorbed so much of his own teachings about that art.

Rafeyo did something unexpected then: he met Mechella's gaze for a long, assessing moment, lowered his lashes, and murmured, "Grazzo millio, Dona Mechella."

Thus were the orphans painted, all of them dumbstruck that actual Grijalvas were drawing their pictures, and the finished portraits were given to the local Sanctias for safekeeping. Mechella met with each surviving sancta and sancto, outlining their duties toward each child and family. She always finished with, "I shall expect a report each Penitenssia and Sancterria—more often, if you like or if there's something special to tell me. I'm deeply concerned with the welfare of these children and your village. I hope you'll do me the honor of accepting this toward reconstruction of your beautiful Sanctia—it isn't much, but it will get you started on your building fund."

Winter approached, and the day snowclouds threatened over the Montes Astrappas Lizia announced that they had done as much as they possibly could. The injured were recovering, the dead were buried, the orphans placed with families, the paintings finished, and there were enough walls with roofs on them to shelter diminished populations until spring. Roads only just cleared of tumbled boulders would soon be rendered impassable by snow.

"And besides which," Lizia finished, eyeing Mechella, "you're getting bigger by the hour. Cold food, no bed, and unspeakable sanitation I will tolerate—barely!—but *not* the sight of my only sister with her back naked to the wind because she's too pregnant to lace her gown!"

They went home by way of Corasson, an estate long held by the

Grijalvas. On the journey there, Mechella heard its history from Lizia, and did not much like the tale.

In 1045, Clemenzo III became Duke of Tira Virte at age eighteen. The next year he fell violently in love with Saalendra Grijalva—much to the annoyance of her family, which had another girl in mind for him. But he would have none but Saalendra, and they conducted much of their affair at an estate halfway between Meya Suerta and Castello Casteya.

"Which was at that time famous for its splendors," Lizia sighed. "Clemenzo's grandmother was a do'Casteya, so he had cousins at the Castello who welcomed him whenever he and Saalendra wanted some fresh mountain air. But he was a rather odd man, en verro."

Odd, because he had ideas about including lesser nobles and even merchants in government. Like his great-grandfather Alejandro, he saw them as a counterweight to the great counts and barons, and made known his intention to reconvene the Corteis. He also resolved on war with Pracanza rather than endure any more border skirmishes—or marry the princess offered as peacemaker as Renata do'Pracanza had been offered to and accepted by Alejandro. When Clemenzo was assassinated in 1047, some thought the greater nobles were responsible and some that Pracanza was behind the crime. But it was also said that Clemenzo had been murdered—and Saalendra with him—by persons acting in revenge for the rejected Grijalva girl.

Whatever the case, Clemenzo's brother became Cossimio I, and in 1049 the exquisite Corasson Grijalva became his Mistress. They also spent much time at the estate where his brother and her cousin had been so happy. In 1052 he purchased it for her, and there they lived the whole year round. There was no more talk of expanding the government or of war with Pracanza. Affairs of state bored Cossimio and he left everything to his conselhos—who, fortunately, included the highly capable Timius Grijalva, Corasson's half-brother, who would one day become Lord Limner.

Then, in 1058, Corasson died in a riding accident. Shattered, Cossimio returned to the capital and buried his grief in work. Shortly thereafter he wed Carmillia do'Pracanza—younger sister of the princess proposed as his brother's bride—and ruled for another thirty-seven years. He never again set foot within twenty miles of the estate, renamed Corasson by the Grijalvas to whom it now belonged, and when he died, his *Will* specified that his heart be entombed with his dead Mistress. Duchess Carmillia, who never even heard Corasson's name mentioned—let alone suspected her husband's deathless devotion to another woman—ordered his heart removed from his corpse as he had wished. Then, with her own hands, she flung it into the deepest swamp in Laggo Sonho.

"What a horrid story!" Mechella exclaimed.

"It has its deplorable aspects," Lizia allowed.

"I wish you hadn't told me. I'm sure I won't sleep a wink inside such a dreadful place."

"You mustn't blame the house, 'Chella. Corasson is really quite wonderful, though we won't be seeing it at its best time of year. And it's quite comfortable for all it's so old. A place for lovers. . . ." She sighed, and after a moment continued softly, "Ormaldo and I spent a few nights there right after we were married, on our way to Castello Casteya. I think I began to fall in love with him then."

With her first sight of Corasson, contrary to all expectations, Mechella also fell in love. All the house's unsavory associations went clean out of her mind. Every spindly tower and fanciful crenellation, every winter-bare climbing rose and venerable oak, every arched window and rounded turret enchanted her. It was like the castles of her childhood in Ghillas, though it lacked moat and drawbridge because it had never been meant for war.

"I don't recall the original name or who built it," Lizia said as the carriage rattled up the drive. "You'd think all these towers and turrets would make it look ridiculous—like a manor house trying to give birth to a castle. But instead, it's beautiful."

Cabral handed them down from the carriage. "It gives me great pleasure to welcome you to my family's most charming property," he said with a smile. "But it must be a quick welcome without a tour of the grounds—I think it's about to rain."

It did rain, and for three solid days, miring the roads in mud. Mechella spent the time exploring the lovely old caza with Leilias, whose sharp tongue both shocked and amused her.

"It's a rather scandalous place, even aside from its history," Leilias said as they admired the dining room's painted ceiling— which featured scores of scantily clad youths and maidens draped languidly and sometimes licentiously around a sylvan glade. "Cabral says the pair in the middle are supposed to be Clemenzo and Saalendra. Personally, I've never entered a room here without wondering if they or Cossimio and Corasson made love in it!"

"In a *dining room?*"

"It's a big table," Leilias drawled, and Mechella giggled despite herself. "Dusty, too," she went on, tracing an idle design on the wood. "Nobody lives here now—just a steward and the farm workers. Their houses are down the road. Poor neglected Corasson."

Mechella wandered along the row of ladderback chairs, inspecting the flowers embroidered on the seat cushions. No two were alike. "It's sad for a house that knew such joy to be empty now. Doesn't anybody ever visit? I thought perhaps the Grijalvas use it the way the do'Verradas use Caterrine."

"That's another thing about this house. No child was ever conceived in it."

"Now you're making fun of me! All the Mistresses are barren!"

"No, Your Grace, I'm serious. Servants are always getting pregnant, correct? But not one has ever done so under this roof. They've been questioned, believe me. Each time they swear the lovemaking happened in the barns or the woods or one of the cottages, but never here. You'd almost think there was some kind of spell to prevent it."

Mechella laughed. "I could make a story of it—the first lady who lived here was a nasty, wicked woman who decreed that any woman who got with child under this roof would be put to death. She made a pact with an old witch or wizard to ensure it."

"Because her husband had a roving eye and was a scandal with the servant girls in every other house they'd ever lived in," Leilias contributed, entering into the game.

"Very good, I hadn't thought of that." Mechella stood at the head of the table, fingers clasping the heart-shaped finials of the master's chair. "Anyway, she let all the servant girls know what fate awaited them. But of course love will not be denied, and so when one of them turned up with a big belly, she had her executed."

"As a witch," Leilias added, "for only another witch could cancel the spell on the house."

"But as time went by, the terrible woman found she'd made a terrible mistake. She got the wording of the spell wrong, and instead of limiting her curse to the servant girls, she'd made a mistake and said *any* woman. So of course she never had any children either, as punishment for her wickedness."

"And so it remains to this day, that any woman living at Corasson who wants a baby must get one elsewhere than under this roof!" Leilias concluded, and applauded.

They continued on their tour of the house, Mechella dying to ask if Arrigo had ever brought Tazia here, but she couldn't bring herself to say the words. Much as she liked Leilias—for herself as well as for being Cabral's sister—she could not discuss such personal things.

As they strolled a dank hallway to the music room, Leilias said casually, "The last do'Verrada visit here nearly ended in disaster.

There was a fire in the stables and Grand Duke Cossimio's father almost died trying to save his favorite hunter. He decided he hated Corasson and bought Chasseriallo, and no do'Verrada has set foot here since."

So Mechella's question was answered without her having asked it. Arrigo had never even been here. That there was at least one place in Tira Virte that he had never seen appealed to Mechella; she could share with him something new to him about his own country. For the rest of the rainy morning she paid close heed to details of design and decoration, the better to describe Corasson when she got home.

The trouble was, the more she saw of Corasson the more she felt she *was* at home. She loved the architecture, so reminiscent of the great castles of Ghillas. She loved the warm grace of the interior, neglected though it was, with private and public rooms alike proportioned for daily living, not ceremonial grandeur. She loved the wealth promised by roses and herb gardens and trees, and the charming little pocket gardens snuggled into odd angles of the house. But most of all she loved one thing: the instant she saw Corasson, the moment she entered it, she could picture herself there. Herself, Arrigo, and their children.

Corasson had not been constructed for war; neither, despite Lizia's impressions, had it been intended for lovers wishing solitude. It had been meant for a family. One had only to tour the sixteen bedchambers of the second floor to know that the private quarters were designed for a husband and wife and large, happy brood.

It was a shame that the Grijalvas—who were nothing if not a large family—had never put Corasson to its best use. To Mechella, the house cried out for a loving couple and lots of children with their nurses and tutors, toys on the stairs, ponies in the stables, dogs underfoot, laughter and games and even temper tantrums—all the cheerful chaos of a country home. Mechella had never known such things herself or observed them in other people's houses. She imagined that Lizia had led that kind of life at Castello Casteya while Count Ormaldo was alive; she suspected something of the same at Palasso Grijalva (surely so, with all those children running about!). But Corasson, meant for a family, languished in lonely emptiness.

"Cabral," she said one evening as they waited in the dining room for Lizia, "would your family ever consider selling Corasson, do you think?"

His brows climbed above startled hazel eyes. "Sell?"

Down the table, Leilias gave a small, half-choked laugh.

"Forgive me, Your Grace. It's just that the Grijalvas have been trying to get rid of it for two generations!"

"Now you've done it," Cabral scolded, grinning.

"What's she done?" Lizia asked, striding through the double doors to her chair. "Pass the plates. I'm starving, and I can't wait for those boys of yours to join us."

"I want to buy Corasson," Mechella explained.

Cabral said, "And my moronna of a sister just told her it's been for sale with no buyers these last fifty years!"

Lizia crowed with laughter. "What a bargain you'll get, 'Chella! What a trick to play on the Viehos Fratos!"

Sighing, Leilias said to her brother, "The Countess has never forgiven us Grijalvas."

"I've never understood why," he said innocently. "It wasn't Aldio's fault that little Dona Grezella picked the lock on his paintbox—"

"—having decided that all my gowns would look better with red flowers!" Lizia complained, black eyes dancing. "Aldio had the gall to say afterward that my daughter showed a real eye for color!"

"Aldio," Cabral said earnestly, "has ever been a shrewd critic."

With a snort of appreciation, Lizia turned to Mechella. "Listen, carrida, if you're serious, then I'll have my steward stop here on his way to Meya Suerta next month. He can survey the home farm and tell you if the place can turn a profit. You'll need a structural survey, too."

Lizia plotted the purchase of Corasson as single-mindedly as a Marchalo Grando planned a battle. She made lists and estimated prices and debated alterations and repairs. All Mechella could say in response, with a glance at the rain-wrapped window, was, "Eiha, at least we're sure the roof doesn't leak!"

But if she was initially amazed by Lizia's enthusiasm, that night she remembered what Lizia had said about making her own power and place, and her joy dimmed just a little.

They left Corasson two mornings later. After long hours being jostled in the carriage, with wheels spewing fountains of mud from every rut in the road, Mechella was deeply grateful for the sight of the wayside Sanctia where they would spend the night. As she stretched the stiffness and aches from her limbs by pacing the length of the lamplit nave, Cabral approached with a large sheet of paper in his hands. It proved to be a detailed sketch of Corasson.

"Rafeyo's work," he explained. "He got bored waiting for the rain to stop, so he went out in it and drew this. I thought you'd like to see it."

"He really is very talented, isn't he? I must thank him for the gift."

"It's . . . not exactly a gift," Cabral said awkwardly. "He was showing us his portfolio. He condescended to discuss with me the difficulties of architectural painting."

"I see." She walked to a lamp hung from a pillar and inspected the picture. "He's *very* good. I can almost see the roses getting ready to bud in the spring. Would he lend me this if I promise to return it once Don Arrigo has seen it?"

"I'm sure he would, Your Grace."

She hesitated. "Does . . . does Rafeyo still hate me, do you think?"

Lamplight gilding his green-flecked eyes, Cabral said quietly, "No one who spends two minutes in your company could do otherwise than adore you."

She took refuge from astonishment in a swiftly summoned smile. "That's sweet of you, Cabral. But I'd settle for his not despising me."

"Your Grace—Mechella—"

Whatever he might have said was lost in the silvery chiming of bells summoning all within hearing to partake of the Sanctia's bounty: a simple meal preceded by a brief ritual of thanks. The elderly resident sancto shuffled into the nave, followed by a few noviciatos, the Grijalvas, and finally Lizia—late as usual. By the time all were assembled and the sancto began singing the ceremony, Cabral was gone from Mechella's side and she had almost—almost—recovered her calm.

Still holding the sketch of Corasson, she glanced down the row of worshipers to Rafeyo. She had noted that although Grijalvas did all the proper things during Sanctia ceremonies, most of them resented the Faith that cast them as sinful beings a step removed from heresy. Most hid it; Rafeyo was ostentatious in his contempt. When the small First Loaf was passed around, from which each person was supposed to take a token bite, Rafeyo stepped back a pace and folded his arms across his chest. After an instant's confusion and a frown from the old sancto, the Loaf went from the young Limner on Rafeyo's left to Leilias, on his right.

Mechella had tried to ignore his disrespect for her; he had his grudges just as she had hers, and she surmised they were fairly equal in strength. But she could not ignore his callous rejection of the symbolic sharing of life's gifts—gifts that included his substantial talent. She recalled hearing Leilias talk of the boy's ambition, that it was not impossible for one of his superior ability to reach it. As Mechella saw the tight disapproval on the old sancto's face and the flinty challenge in Rafeyo's black eyes, she vowed that this self-righteous Grijalva would become Lord Limner over her dead body. It had nothing to do with his mother—not very much, anyway. She simply refused to countenance a person like Rafeyo anywhere near her family.

Mechella listened to the litany of thanks to the Mother and Son, let the morsel of bread dissolve on her tongue, and whispered a small prayer for the health and long life of Lord Limner Mequel.

~~◆~~ FORTY-FIVE ~~◆~~

When Mechella and Lizia arrived in Meya Suerta late on a gloomy, overcast afternoon, preparations for Penitenssia were underway. As the mud-spattered carriages were dragged by exhausted horses through the streets to Palasso Verrada, everyone in the city stopped work to cheer. They paused on ladders where banners were being hung; they clung to the tall poles of the street lamps with decorations dangling from their hands; they emerged from bakeries and butcher shops—aprons white with flour or crimson with blood—to wave and yell and sing blessings on the two ladies.

Groggy with weariness, waking too abruptly from an uneasy doze to an inexplicable uproar, Mechella trembled. "What's happened?"

"They're calling for us." Lizia nudged her with an elbow. "Tidy your hair, carrida, I'm about to open the curtains."

Mechella raked her fingers through a few snarls, then gave up with a wince. "I'm a wreck, Lizi. *Must* I be seen like this?"

"Yes."

Lizia parted the heavy tapestry curtains. Mechella held herself from shrinking back in fright from a horrible panorama. Beyond the living faces crowded close to the carriage were skulls, hundreds of skulls. Festooned with black ribbons, they grinned from every lamp post and lintel and eave. Full skeletons danced high above the street from wires strung roof-to-roof. Every window was draped in black, with what seemed the unearthed contents of whole cemeteries nailed to the casements.

Penitenssia, she told herself frantically, clinging to Lizia's hand and trying not to show her fear. *It's Penitenssia, that's all, just readying the city for the holiday—*

But the horses were as skittish as she, startled by the danza morta figures overhead. The carriage lurched. Mechella cried out.

"She's injured—"

"Our Mechella has been hurt!"

"Matra ei Filho, preserve her!"

"Fetch a physician before the baby is lost!"

Righting herself with Lizia's help, Mechella tried to reassure the

crowd. She smiled and waved and called out that she was perfectly
fine. But the rumor wildfired and a great moan shuddered the street.

"Matra Muita Dolcha, mercy on our Mechella!"

"I vow by my family's icon to give this month's profits to the
poor if only our Dona Mechella and her child are spared—"

"I vow my silver cup to the Sanctia—"

"Find a physician! Quickly!"

Amid the screams of grief and the promises to the Mother and
Son a man's strong voice shouted, "Make way! Make way!"

"Cabral!" Mechella recognized his beard-stubbled face as he
struggled to the carriage, shouldering people aside. When he
reached the window, she clutched at his extended hand. "Cabral,
tell them I'm all right, tell them—"

"You'll have to show yourself!" he yelled over the din.

She cringed against Lizia. "I can't!"

"It's that or the people will run mad and the horses will bolt, and
then you *will* be in danger! Hurry, Mechella! Do you want everyone to be trampled?"

"Do it," Lizia ordered. "I'm too little, they'd never see me. Open
the door and stand up. I'll hang onto your skirts, Cabral will keep
you steady. Rapidia, 'Chella!"

And so, bolstered by Cabral's strength, she stood in the opened
doorway of the carriage and at the sight of her the people bellowed
with joy. She lifted a hand to wave; incredibly, the gesture silenced
them. She glanced wildly down at Cabral, who nodded encouragement, eyes shining.

"Good people—" she began. And then she saw their faces, the
individual faces of her people straining toward her, concerned and
joyous and anxious and loving.

"My people," she corrected herself. And the roar of delight that
was their answer echoed all the way to Palasso Verrada—

—where Arrigo stopped in the middle of a sentence to the
Blacksmiths Guild, and listened with a thousand speculations rampaging through his mind. The bellow resolved into a chant, one he
had heard before, and just as he identified it, the guildmaster cried,
"Dona Mechella is home! Grazzo do'Matra ei Filho, our Mechella
is home at last!"

"Merditto! You should've seen her—parading through the streets
in front of the carriage, with Lizia up on the box with the reins in
her hands!"

"Eiha, Lizia handles horses better than she does her children," Tazia murmured, knowing Arrigo would not hear her. No one else would either; her caza was as deserted tonight as a graveyard at a pauper's funeral. And as cold.

"She walked—*walked!*—all the way to the Palasso, people singing and holding up their babies as if mere sight of her could bless them all their lives!" He paced stiffly, front door to the staircase where she sat, staircase to wall, wall to front door. "My Ghillasian Princess of a wife, in a dirty gown three sizes too small and some camponesso's lice-ridden cloak on her shoulders, with her hair in tangles and Cabral at her side grinning like an idiot—"

Tazia shifted on the bottom step, fisting her hands between her knees. She'd heard the whole tale this afternoon from Rafeyo, of course—whose expressions of disgust had been hymns of adoration compared to Arrigo's tirade.

"—and *I* had to stand on the Palasso steps with Father and Mother and all the conselhos, watching this performance as if I approved of it! When she finally arrived—merditto, like a Marchallo at the head of an army of rabble!—I had to kiss her and make much of her and stand there for half an hour while they all yelled themselves hoarse over her! First she sneaks away like a thief, now she comes back like *this!*"

Taking the small lamp from the floor beside her, Tazia rose and looked up at him. There was more gray in his hair; small wonder, with the cares of the nation on his shoulders while his wife made a public spectacle of herself.

"I'm freezing, Arrigo."

His boot heels thudded to a stop on the floorboards. "Haven't you been listening? Don't you understand what she's done?"

"Of course. She's come back to you."

He glared. "Is that all you can say?"

"She's come back to you," Tazia repeated. "And you have come back to me."

She took his hand and led him to the little room hidden beneath the stairs, and lit the candles behind the upholstered sofa, and locked the double locks of the door.

━━●━━

Penitenssia was at once the most solemn and the most riotous holiday of the Ecclesial calendar, serving to clear away the old year and give joyous welcome to the new. The date shifted a bit each year, for the third day must always coincide with the first day of luna oscurra, moondark.

Dia Sola was, as its name suggested, for solitary contemplation of sins. No one ventured out except in dire emergency. The city, draped in black, lay empty and silent but for the skeletons strung above the streets, twitching in their death dance, rattling in the winter wind.

The second day, Dia Memorria, was dedicated to ancestors. Small offerings of water and wheat were placed on newly tended graves. The dead who had no living descendants were propitiated with bits of paper drawn with the sigil of the Mother and Son secured by pebbles at the headstones. All Meya Suerta stayed awake until midnight, keeping watch by black wax candles for stray spirits that had accidentally gone unhonored that day.

On Herva ei Ferro, women stayed indoors weaving special charms on iron pins from grasses cleared from the graves. The complex patterns—each family's was different, taught mother-to-daughter for generations—formed knots signifying the protection given by the dead to the living in gratitude for remembering them. While women wove charm after charm, men built effigies of wood and straw and iron nails. Figures of people and animals were draped in black cloth painted with the white outlines of bones, topped by skull masks symbolizing sins and misfortunes. At dusk these apparitions were paraded through the streets with the Premia Sancta and Premio Sancto leading the way, intoning prayers. By nightfall everyone crowded into the Cathedral Zocalo, where the effigies were secured on poles anchored in hay bales. In absolute silence, in a night unlit by torches and empty of the moon, the people confronted grinning spectral images of Greed, Jealousy, Anger, Sickness, Adultery, and a dozen others. By an eerie trick of special white paint, the skeletons glowed in the dark; most children had nightmares for weeks afterward, and behaved themselves scrupulously long into spring.

From dawn until noon on Dia Fuega, adults came to pin bits of paper to the effigies. Sketched on these were the last year's troubles—anything from a major illness or bad luck in business to an unhappy love affair or the theft of a cow. In the afternoon children wearing charms their mothers had woven pelted the effigies with stones and offal.

Then, with the twilight rising of the first fragment of the moon, the Premia Sancta and Premio Sancto stood with the Grand Duke on the steps of the Cathedral to declare the old year finished. The images were set alight. In the graveyards, all the little pieces of paper were ignited and the pebbles retrieved for fortune telling while the blazing effigies burned away the old year and cleansed the world for the new. Back in their homes, families exchanged gifts and a feast was laid out. And if celebrations spilled into the streets and lasted until dawn, it was only natural after solitude and contemplation of sins and the fright of those stark glowing skeletons.

That night, too, all the guilds gathered in their halls to hear who had won the prize for the finest work of the year. Woodcarvers and carpenters, potters, glaziers, tanners and cobblers and saddlemakers, goldsmiths and stonemasons, coopers, wainwrights, and especially Grijalva Limners—masters of every craft waited nervously for the outcome of fierce competition. After the victors were announced, the names were read of apprentices who had earned the rank of master. The very best had the honor of accompanying the guildmaster and the winner of the competition to the offering of masterpieces at Palasso Verrada.

Penitenssia was Cossimio's favorite holiday. Not only did Gizella throw a terrific party on Dia Fuega, but he received the most splendid gifts imaginable. He reveled in evidence of Tira Virte's superiority in all crafts. But that night Cossimio did something completely unexpected, extremely cunning, and wildly popular. He announced that this year the finest work of every master in Meya Suerta, which would have gone to him, would be presented instead to their beloved Dona Mechella in gratitude for her selfless service to Tira Virte.

Dona Mechella's blushes lasted all during the formal gifting. Don Arrigo, standing at her elbow, smiled and smiled. If that smile wavered occasionally . . . eiha, he was worried that she would tire herself by staying up so late. Before Casteya her condition had not been noticeable, but now she was very pregnant—and glowed so with it that rumors of illness were scornfully dismissed. Surely it was nothing more than demonstration of husbandly devotion that made Don Arrigo take the first opportunity to urge her upstairs to rest.

There was nothing wrong with Mechella's health. In retrospect, she was ashamed of herself for ever having felt ill. Mequel was right: one simply decided that one had too much to do, and in the doing forgot to be sick. And she had learned that she could do much more for her country than simply bear its next Heir. In fact, life would be just about perfect if only Arrigo didn't wear such a grim face when they were alone.

The morning after Dia Fuega, while she sat in bed admiring all the lovely things spread all over her room, Arrigo entered to inform her that he would be celebrating his birthday elsewhere than at the Palasso.

She regarded him in dismay. "But—I thought we'd spend the day together, you and Teressa and I—"

"Plans were made while you were gone," he said, picking up a gorgeous lace shawl. "I had no idea when you'd return. It would be unforgivably rude to cancel. This is very fine, isn't it? Each sunburst picked out by one gold thread—subtle, yet richly done. Much better than that gaudy stuff they make in Niapali." Running the shawl through his fingers, he went on, "What will you do with all this?"

"What do you mean?"

"We have plenty of tapestries and vases—what's this thing, a salt cellar?—and Matra knows you have more than enough jewels." He nodded at a box open to reveal gold earrings shaped like tiny irises, a diamond dewdrop on each. "Father spends days deciding which pieces he can bear to part with for the usual charity auction."

"I know," she said quietly. "I remember from last year. Not to criticize your father, but I think the crafters expect us to keep their gifts and use them."

"You intend to keep *all* of it?" He used a corner of the shawl to polish a button on his Shagarra uniform; he was on his way to a review in honor of his birthday. "That's hardly of a piece with your new reputation for good works."

After a moment of mindless hurt, Mechella decided she hadn't really heard him say so cruel a thing. "I plan to ask your father what the usual proceeds are from the auction, and give the same amount to the Ecclesia schools."

His brows arched. "So much for your privy purse! With the Casteyan expenses added to what you spend on clothes, you'll be out of money within the month."

More sharply than she intended, she replied, "You forget that the balance of my dowry will come when I bear a son for Tira Virte."

"But your dowry goes into the do'Verrada coffers, not your own," he countered.

"My father will be generous to me as well when I give him a grandson."

"I'll have to tell that to *my* father so he can stop worrying about the cost of rebuilding those wretched villages."

"There'll be enough," she retorted. "Don't worry. And plenty left for something else I had in mind—" She hadn't meant to tell him this way, but it all came tumbling out. She waved one hand to encompass all the marvels: stained-glass lampshades, carved rocking chair, tapestry, brass lustrosso, rosewood clock, a dozen more gifts. "All this will go to Corasson."

"Corasson?"

"I'm going to buy it, Arrigo."

"Matra Dolcha! Wherever did you get such a ridiculous idea?"

"We stopped there on the way home and—I want it, Arrigo. I want to live there—when we're not here at the Palasso, I mean." Although just why she had wanted this so much, she couldn't quite recall just now—not with Arrigo staring in frank astonishment.

"The Grijalvas will never sell it."

"They've been trying to get rid of it for fifty years. When my son is born, my father will—"

"*Your* son? Didn't I have anything to do with it? And what if this one's another girl?"

"This baby is a boy."

"That's what you said last time." The gold-shot lace snagged on his signet ring; untangling it, he went on, "Do you know Corasson's history? It was built by the Serranos before their ruin at the hands of the redoubtable Lord Limner Sario. Every Serrano who ever lived there died an unnatural death on the way to it or from it—a fall from a horse, an overturned carriage, murdered by bandits, heart seizure, all manner of sudden tragedies. And you want to *live* in that horror of a place?"

"They didn't die *at* Corasson. It's not the house's fault." She leaned toward him, hands clasped on drawn-up knees. "And perhaps we're just what's needed to turn Corasson's luck. I want us to have a home of our very own—"

"We would, if you didn't hate Chasseriallo so much."

"I don't hate it, I just—oh, Arrigo, Corasson is such a beautiful house—"

"I've never seen it," he said with a shrug, and she felt a surge of joy: Leilias had told her true, the Grijalva woman had never taken him there. Corasson would be *theirs,* hers and his. But her happiness died as he finished, "Eiha, if it amuses you to scheme about buying it, do so. But I tell you the Grijalvas will never sell."

"You don't *want* me to have it!" she blurted. "You don't want us to live there! You want me to stay in the Palasso!"

He looked even more surprised, as much by her tone as her words. "I thought that would be obvious. You're my wife, mother of my children. You belong at my side, not at some remote, ramshackle—" Suddenly he let out a sharp laugh. "Of course, that's it. Lizia infected you with the fever that made her rebuild Castello Casteya from the ground up. This is her doing."

"Only in that she suggested we visit Corasson on the way home! It's *not* ramshackle, it's wonderful, and I'm going to buy it, and there's nothing you can do about it!"

"Isn't there?" He took exactly one step toward the bed, fist clenched in fragile lace. Then he checked his temper with visible effort and gave another careless shrug. "We'll discuss it another time. I'm late. Kiss Teressa for me."

The door slammed behind him.

Beside her was a little rosewood clock, a lovely thing of richly carved wood surmounted by an enameled copper rooster that flapped its wings and chirped each hour. Her fingers closed around it and she very nearly flung it at the closed door just to hear the crash. But she couldn't destroy a master crafter's work—and it would look so beautiful on display at Corasson.

She threw a pillow instead.

An instant later Otonna entered from the dressing room. She snatched up the pillow and plumped it with casual efficiency. "So there'll be no day with the family, Your Grace?"

"Stop listening at keyholes, Otonna. It's impertinent."

"I'm afraid I'm to blame," said another voice, and Mechella turned to see Leilias Grijalva appear from the dressing room. "I came by to return the things you lent me on the journey, Your Grace—we didn't mean to listen, en verro—"

Mechella felt the annoyance drain out of her. Fingering the little rooster's rainbow wings, she said listlessly, "It doesn't matter. The whole of Meya Suerta will know by tonight that he isn't spending his birthday with me."

"Your Grace." Leilias approached with soft footsteps. "Had you thought—forgive me, but—surely you know whom he *will* spend it with."

Shocked, she stared at the two women. In both faces was heartfelt sympathy; not pity for her stupidity—though she knew she should have realized at once where Arrigo would be—but genuine compassion for her and real anger for Arrigo.

"Where?" she demanded. "Tell me where they'll be!"

⟜ FORTY-SIX ⟜

"Insult me, will he?" Mechella fumed in the darkness of her carriage—hers, not Arrigo's, a gift from Cossimio that combined the efforts of the best saddlers and wainwrights and blacksmiths in all Tira Virte, with the paint still drying on the Grand Ducal seal stenciled onto its door just yesterday. "Patronize me, treat me like a child—he wants me here in Meya Suerta, of a certainty he does—to stifle gossip! As if I countenance this relationship and signal it by staying in the same city with *that woman!*"

Leilias heard this with shock, dismay—and a sneaking little thrill of enjoyment. "It's not Don Arrigo to blame here, Your Grace, not entirely," she amended. "You must realize what a clever woman she is. And how ambitious for herself and her son."

"He's as bad as his mother!" Mechella spat. "Both of them nasty, stinking little merdittos!"

Leilias blinked; she hadn't thought Mechella knew that word. But she put aside startlement and set herself to turning Mechella's anger from Arrigo—with whom she might still make a successful marriage—to Tazia.

"The great good you did in Casteya, that's what she played on. It was *you* doing it, you see, not him. She made it seem to him as if this was your fault, that you'd done it deliberately to make him look the fool."

"He could have come with me! He could have defied his father!" Suddenly she sank wearily into dark blue cushions. "No, of course he couldn't. He had more important duties, he's the Heir. It's one thing for me to do it—I'm the foreigner, they've all commented on my odd ways, I know they have—"

"No one has ever done so, Your Grace. And you're no longer estranjiera in Tira Virte. The people love you."

"Do they?"

"You *know* they do! Eiha, you have only to listen to them cheer your name—"

"She probably used *that* against me, too."

"As I say, she's very clever." Bracing herself against a jounce of carriage springs, Leilias wished for some light so she could see Mechella's expression and choose her words accordingly. "Her cunning is something you must be ready for. I might be able to help if I knew what you plan."

"It's enough that you came with me tonight, Leilias. I'm very grateful."

"I still wish you'd tell me what you intend."

With a kind of fatalistic grimness, Mechella replied, "I intend to help my husband celebrate his birthday, of course. Why do you think Otonna spent all day letting out the seams of my best gown?"

Tazia's tenure as Mistress had yielded not only the caza in town but a small manor house built especially for her. Caza Reccolto was aptly named, for it was the final harvest of her twelve years with Arrigo. She was the official owner, but on her death it would revert—like Corasson and all the other properties given to Grijalva Mistresses through the centuries—to the family. Caza Reccolto was about a hundred years old, a half-timbered building in the shape of a *T* for Tazia; Arrigo's idea of a tribute, Leilias supposed. The crossbar was the front of the house, fully three hundred feet from one side to the other; the rest of the letter was invisible to the rear. As Mechella's carriage turned into the drive, Leilias saw that the place was ablaze with lamplight at every window like a Sanctia greeting the Birth of the Son on Nov'viva. The music of gambas and gitterns and flutes could hardly be heard for the laughter echoing out the front door—open, even though it was winter, to let in enough cold air to offset the heat of all those lamps and all those dancing, drinking, laughing guests. As Mechella and Leilias descended from the carriage—to the slack-jawed befuddlement of the footmen—Mechella nodded regally to the youth who leaped forward to assist her up the steps. Leilias gulped down a lump of apprehension and followed.

Once inside, any other woman would have been compelled to spend at least ten minutes repairing the damage of an hour's drive to her hair, clothes, and makeup. Mechella, golden and glowingly beautiful, merely paused in the hall to glance in a mirror and tweak a curl back into place. She wore a gown of raw silk, woven gold in one direction and silver in the other. The point of the low-cut bodice was decorated with a fabulous Tza'ab pearl brooch, drawing the eye to perfect shoulders and full breasts. Tiny pleats provided the necessary fullness at the raised waistline. Soft curls cascaded down her neck, held up by the dainty tiara of pearls that had been her father's wedding gift. The gown shone like one of those antiquated suits of armor on display at Shagarra Barracks; Mechella was well-girded for war.

Leilias watched her walk calmly toward the source of the loudest music and laughter. The rustle of silk skirts sounded like the warning of distant thunder; the subtle glitter of the material was like flashing gold-and-silver lightning. War, storms—Leilias shook her head, her anxiety redoubled with the images scattering through her mind. She crept forward, telling herself it was her duty to listen. Although it was a very good thing that Mechella was acting instead of *re*acting, Leilias wasn't sure she was wise enough yet to make her actions the right ones. By the abrupt hush and the stutter-scrape of gamba bows, she knew Mechella had been noticed. Gliding closer to the ballroom door, she heard Tazia's bright call.

"Your Grace! How marvelous!"

"I hope I haven't come too late and ruined the surprise," Mechella replied, with such cool aplomb that Leilias joined the footmen in an imitation of an astonished goldfish.

Even more bizarre, Tazia fell in with it. "You're exactly on time—and by the look on his face, we've well and truly surprised Don Arrigo!" Leilias wished mightily that she could catch a glimpse of the man's face as Tazia went on, "Forgive me for stealing Her Grace away for a few moments. She really must have something hot to drink, it's shockingly cold outside tonight."

"I'm quite comfortable, I assure you."

"I insist. Back to the music! And if anyone says anything *really* interesting while we're gone, I'll be furious!"

The two women came across the ballroom threshold and onto the chessboard-tiled floor smiling. The smiles stayed intact even when Tazia took hold of Mechella's elbow. Then Mechella yanked her arm from the grip and commanded icily, "I require privacy."

"What I have to say to you isn't for the gossips, don't worry," Tazia snapped. "This way, down the hall."

Leilias followed, silent as a ghost, past other guest-filled rooms where gilt lustrossos blazed above eye-popping silence. The long hall was a galerria unto itself, every available wall surface occupied with a painting—landscapes, still-lifes, nature studies, even a few maps, but only one portrait. Tazia herself, of course, recently done and done twice life-size by her son Rafeyo, whose signature was in the bottom corner. Leilias paused to curl her lip at the huge image of Mechella's rival, then hurried down the hall.

She held back at the kitchen door, flattening to the plaster wall as cooks and kitchen maids prudently fled. Then she inched closer and craned her neck for a full view of the battle.

If Mechella was dressed for it, so was Tazia. *Over*dressed, Leilias thought acidly. The brocade gown was too busy: huge blue flowers, writhing green vines, no two blossoms or leaves alike, as if an untalented Grijalva had gotten drunk before slopping paint all over a canvas. But Leilias had to admit that the lace shawl was a marvel, sunbursts delicately outlined in gold thread. Tazia's tiny, tightly sashed waist made Mechella look enormous, but she couldn't compete in regal bearing. In height either—though heeled slippers and upswept black hair brought her within a few inches. Leilias wondered if short women really thought such things fooled people into thinking they were tall.

They faced each other in the red-brick kitchen across a massive wooden table laden with tiers of pastries. For several moments neither woman spoke. Then Mechella leaned forward, fists braced on knife-scarred wood. Tazia tilted her head to one side, arms folded, the exquisite shawl slipping a bit from bared shoulders.

"Well? Be quick, I have guests waiting."

"I have no interest in anything you could say to me, but I advise you to listen carefully to what *I* am about to tell *you*."

"And that might be?" Tazia asked, faintly smiling.

"Stay away from Court."

The smile widened.

"Go back to your estates. Go on a journey—preferably to Merse, and the longer you spend there the better. Go anywhere at all. But leave Meya Suerta and don't come back."

"*This* is what you drove an hour here to tell me? You could have put it in a letter—phrased less offensively, too. Then again, I've heard your spelling leaves your correspondents baffled at best."

"Offending you is the very last thing I care about. I give you until the Sperranssia holiday to make your arrangements."

"You *give* me?" Tazia gave a gay little chirrup of laughter, as if she had never enjoyed anything so much or found anyone so deliciously droll in her entire life.

Mechella's cheeks flushed. "Interrupt me again and I'll order your packing myself—now, tonight. Believe me in this, you *will* leave Court."

"And if I refuse?"

"You forget yourself."

"To the contrary, I know *exactly* who I am. Don't you?"

Mechella's back stiffened. She stood straight again, fingers clenched. "I know *what* you are. We have a saying about women like you in Ghillas."

"But we're not *in* Ghillas." With an air of patient sweetness, Tazia said, "Tell me, I'm curious. What precisely do you think you can do to force me into this exile you speak of?"

"A conversation with your husband would suffice."

Tazia burst out laughing. "You ridiculous creature!"

"How dare you!"

"Next you'll tell me I'll pay for this, or I haven't seen the last of you, or some other tired old cliche. No wonder you bore poor Arrigo to distraction!"

Mechella was quivering with rage. "Chiras!" she hissed. "Canna!"

At the obscenities, Leilias knew all was lost. She shut her eyes and leaned her forehead to the wall, not wanting to hear any more.

"The least you could do is learn proper enunciation." Suddenly the amusement vanished from Tazia's voice. "Sow, am I? Bitch? We have sayings in Tira Virte, too. 'Merditto alba,' for instance. Literally, it's 'white shit'—but the real essence of it is a little different. And entirely appropriate to the high and mighty Princess of Ghillas. What 'merditto alba' really means is that you think your shit doesn't stink."

There was a brief, deadly silence. Then, in a voice as cold as stone, Mechella enquired, "What was it again? Merditto *Alva?*"

Leilias didn't understand the crisp ripping sound she heard next, but the angry swish of silk warned her to hurry back down the hall, where she waited as if she'd been there the whole time. Flushed and furious, Mechella strode by without seeing her. Leilias ran to keep up, hoping she'd have the sense not to confront Arrigo.

Confront him she did, but not in the way Leilias feared. A brief pause in the hall to regain control, a squaring of her shoulders, a smoothing of her hands down her gold-and-silver skirts—and from the salon doorway Leilias saw Mechella glide sedately toward her mortified husband, place a hand on his arm, and lean up to kiss his cheek.

"Bonno Natallo, carrido," she said, her accent flawless. Then, turning to the shocked and secretly delighted guests—who would all dine out on this for months—she produced a smile to outdazzle the blazing lustrossos. "Forgive me if I don't stay. I only wanted to surprise Arrigo as arranged. Have a lovely evening—no, dolcho meyo, you needn't see me home."

Leilias half-strangled on repressed laughter. He'd stay, all right. She'd left him no choice. He would stay, and endure every bright social smile that hid rampaging speculation, every sidelong glance of sly amusement. And so would Tazia—once she recovered from Mechella's parting shot.

But minutes later in the dark carriage, when they were clear of the torchlit drive, Mechella burst into tears.

" 'Chella, you mustn't," Leilias soothed, stroking the golden curls. "She knows now you're someone to be reckoned with, you showed her for the bitch she is—don't cry, 'Chella, please."

"You h–heard?"

"Every single syllable—which you pronounced perfectly, by the way. Especially when you called her 'merditto Alva'!"

Mechella gave a choked little laugh. "That *was* a good one, wasn't it?"

"Brilliant! Now, dry your eyes. We must put you to rights before we get to the Palasso. You'll have to go past some guards, and they're dreadful gossips."

Mechella shuddered. "Gossip! No one will talk of anything else for the next year! He doesn't love me, he never d–did—they all know it, Leilias, they all laugh at me and p–pity me behind my back."

Leilias wanted to shake her. "It's either one or the other, they can't do both. You can make yourself into what she called you—a ridiculous creature—and they'll have every right to laugh. Or you can make yourself pathetic, and they'll be justified in pitying you. Or . . ."

"Or what?"

"You can show them all the woman you showed Arrigo tonight."

"Oh, Leilias—that was the hardest thing I've ever done!"

"Nonsense. Keeping yourself from clawing that woman's eyes out—now, *that* must've been damned near impossible!" This time Mechella laughed more easily, so Leilias added, "Is that why you had your hands clenched so tight? Your nails must've sliced into your palms!"

They reached the Palasso near midnight. Descending from the carriage, Leilias nearly tripped over a trailing length of lace. By lamplight she saw the pattern: sunbursts outlined in gold. Mechella saw the direction of her gaze and gathered the material in both hands as they went up the steps.

"He gave her my shawl, Leilias," she whispered, forlorn as a child. "*My* shawl. It tore when I grabbed it off her shoulders, but I just couldn't bear it any more, seeing her wear what my people gave to *me*—"

"Let me take it to the maker, I'm sure it can be rewoven good as new."

"Oh, I couldn't! She'd know I'd been careless of her beautiful work, I'd be too ashamed."

Which, Leilias reflected as she coaxed Mechella to give her the lace, was one of those vital details that would make the tale of this night resound to Mechella's credit. It was reminiscent of the way her Grijalva cousins sketched out the composition of a painting. Telling little touches here and there were minimal in and of themselves, but taken altogether these unpretentious truths added validity to a portrait. First the lacemaker, then the lacemaker's friends, and then all Meya Suerta's common folk would know about this night exactly what Leilias *wanted* them to know—and embroider the whole story as finely and creatively as this shawl. The Courtfolk would hear—and possibly believe—Tazia's version. But the *people* loved Mechella.

"I'll take care of it," she assured Mechella, and smiled to herself. "Shall I come up with you? No, I see Otonna is waiting. Dolcho nocto, Your Grace. Try to sleep. Everything will be well, I promise." Eiha, yes, she would see to *that*.

***

By early afternoon Dioniso had heard two conflicting but equally diverting versions of the previous night's scandal at Caza Reccolto. So the portrait of the future was taking shape, he mused, and it was time he began adding his own brushstrokes. He knew just where to start.

The boy was all alone in the atelierro allotted to those currently studying with Il Aguo. Rafeyo sat on a stool half-turned from the door, an empty easel before him and sketches spread on the floor at his feet. Of water there was plenty: tears of angry frustration were knuckled away at regular intervals as Dioniso watched. But not a drop reached the pencils scattered any whichway on the nearby table.

His first impulse was to tell the boy not to waste his substance. It had been a long time since Dioniso had used his own tears; they'd been difficult to come by for decades. But he stayed silent while marveling at the emotions of youth that could so easily produce that precious moisture.

He cleared his throat to alert Rafeyo to his presence. The tousled dark head turned, a frown marring his features. In the time since Dioniso had first seen him, he had grown much taller and the severe adult lines of his face had emerged through boyish softness. But the eyes that regarded him resentfully were those of a thwarted, sulky child.

"Never tell me that at your age you've already run out of ideas, Rafeyo."

"They want formal drawings of Corasson. It's not *my* idea."

"That's our lot as Limners. We paint what we're told." He bent, picking up a sketch by one corner, trying to recall exactly what

Rafeyo would have learned by this point in his training. With the changes Dioniso had already made in the way the boys were taught . . . enough, perhaps. But he was about to learn more.

Rafeyo kicked at the table, and pieces of stone crockery rattled. "Heard it before—that we have to use every chance to paint something really special. But everybody else gets to paint whatever they want—look at all those boring old things put up for best of the year! And the winner! Imagos Brilliantos on Astraventa—Premio, I could do better than that in my sleep!"

Dioniso's lips quirked; precisely his own opinion, but it wouldn't do to say so. It was a treacherous balance, establishing authority while fostering familiarity. Besides, as Premio Frato he had cast the deciding vote for the abysmal painting. It had been necessary to gain its influential maker's support. And he'd refined his thinking over the last weeks; should the Grijalva "best" decline in quality these next few years, the talent of "Rafeyo" would be all the more noticeable. So he'd allowed the ghastly piece to win the prize.

The boy was still complaining. "And they won't even let me *near* oils yet—when they know that's what I'm meant for!"

"Eiha, let's see what you can accomplish with pencils."

"Pencils!" he snarled. "Little girls draw stick-figures of their dolls with pencils!"

"But little girls aren't asked to execute the picture that will drive up the price of Corasson when Dona Mechella opens the bargaining." Rafeyo's frown deepened, confirming that he'd heard all about last night. Dioniso smothered a grin. "All you need to do is make it pretty—she won't notice any of the finer points."

"And let anyone see my name on an inferior work?"

"Indignation is an asset, but don't overdo it. Pencils or not, it's an honor to be chosen to draw this. If you're clever enough, reminder of Corasson's beauties will fetch us a better price. Our purse is in your hands, Rafeyo."

"Wonderful," he muttered. "They only picked me because I was there and got bored and sketched the filthy old pile."

Dioniso sighed. "If I show you something useful, will you keep quiet about it?"

Sullenly: "Show me what?"

"I suggest that you stifle your wrath at the injustice of not winning for year's best initiato. Patience. At not quite sixteen, you've time."

"The moronno who got it is only ten months older than I!"

"Too bad," he replied without sympathy. "You've been weeping large and bitter tears over it, to no avail. Squeeze out a few more and I'll tell you how to use them."

Fresh rage and humiliation stung new tears to Rafeyo's black eyes, just as Dioniso intended. He caught them on the tip of a pencil labeled Serrano Brown—eternal reminder of the family he had long ago systematically destroyed for the sake of his Duke, his country, and art—and, not incidentally, the Grijalvas. The magic produced by these few droplets of water would be mild at best, but he had an idea.

"Now, Corasson must look its best, 'cordo? Therefore you will work as if it were spring, not winter. Climbing roses in full bloom and fully leafed trees are worth a few hundred mareias."

"But this is to be nazha coloare—"

"The limitations of monochrome can be overcome. Warm and soften the composition by using browns and grays more than black. You can get around nazha coloare with faint suggestions of red and yellow in the roses, green in the trees and grass—more of an *instinct* that color exists than the certainty of its presence. Do you see what I mean?"

"I—I think so." Rafeyo began to look interested. "It takes a delicate touch to do something like that. Show me, Premio Dioniso?"

Rafeyo learned quickly. After two false starts soon crumpled and tossed away, the boy tacked up a fresh sheet of fine paper and, after a glance at his strewn sketches, began to draw.

Dioniso watched, gratified, as the outlines of Corasson took shape in muted grays. He noted the mannerisms of the boy's concentration: one ankle wrapped around a leg of the stool, lower jaw thrust forward, an occasional tap of the pencil on the front teeth. The young body moved with enviable grace when he leaned back for perspective or selected another pencil—at which times he invariably licked his lips.

When he reached at last for the Serrano Brown, Dioniso stopped him. "Wait."

"What for? You've broken my rhythm!"

"You'll get it back. Your tears are on this pencil, part of its substance now. Use it carefully—for what you felt as you wept will linger in every line and shadow it draws."

Rafeyo eyed him narrowly. "You mean even without scents worked into the paper?"

"Even so. Pay attention. You could use this brown for any number of things—define a highlight, suggest a shadow, contour, shape. But what you felt with those tears will be felt by any person who stands at Corasson in the exact place you use the pencil."

He had the satisfaction of seeing the boy so stupéfied that he very nearly lost his balance on the stool. It took Rafeyo a couple of tries to find his voice; when he did, he rasped, "How, Premio? How is this possible?"

"For now you need only accept that it *is* possible. Think about Corasson, Rafeyo." He made his voice low and lulling, the kind of tone that could seduce a woman from her virtue or a boy into his magic. "How it will look in the spring, who might walk through a door or beside a wall or beneath that big oak tree. . . ."

The Serrano Brown hovered, darted forward like an arrow to define the rough bark of the oak on the south side of the house.

"Is it *exactly* as it was?" Dioniso murmured. "Does it match not only your sketches but your memories? Consider the slant of spring sunlight. Is this as true a rendering as if it *were* spring and you were drawing the tree from life?"

Rafeyo hesitated, drew in another line here, another shadow there.

Dioniso murmured soundless words learned centuries ago; they would not be as powerful here as if he drew with his own substance, but they would add just enough to Rafeyo's work to make a difference.

"Are you certain this is how it will be?" He leaned forward, his face just above the boy's shoulder, his cheek nearly touching Rafeyo's cheek. "What do you feel?"

Trancelike—so very close to the real thing, an amazing accomplishment of sheer instinct in one so young—Rafeyo said slowly, "Angry . . . it's so unfair . . . they patronize me, treat me as a child . . . I want what I was meant for . . . the canvas . . . the oils. . . ." He gave an anguished sob. "Chieva do'Orro, I want to *paint!* They won't let me, they won't give me a chance—"

Dioniso inhaled the scent of his breath: chamomile from afternoon tea, basil from stew served at lunch. They would do. Magical Energy and Hatred. With these and his emotions of rage, resentment, and desperate longing for what he did not possess, encounters beside that oak tree at Corasson might prove entertaining.

Pulling back, Dioniso breathed a few more silent phrases before replacing the brown pencil with black in the boy's unresisting fingers. "Touch the tip to your tongue before each stroke," he whispered. "Yes, that's it. Now finish the tree."

Considering the limitations of monochrome, the result was uncannily lifelike. But now, of course, the oak did not match the rest of the picture. Dioniso waited for Rafeyo to come out of his haze—

shaking himself like a puppy in from the rain—before he spoke again.

"Do equally good work on the whole or they'll know you're up to something."

The harsh command startled Rafeyo. "Wh–what?"

"Look at it!" Dioniso snapped. "One absolutely magnificent tree trunk—and a whole page of inferior scribbles! I've seen better graffiti from the charcoal stub of an alleyway Qal Venommo!"

"It is *not* inferior! It's just not finished yet! I'll show you, you just wait."

"I am as accomplished at that as I am with oils—which, if you continue so impatient, you will never learn from *me*."

All the defiance washed from the dark eyes. "You mean—*you* would teach me?"

How he had always loved that look in a young man's eyes: awestruck, eager, humble and proud all at once . . . eiha, it had been such a long time . . . the Luza do'Orro was there in Rafeyo, and a joy to behold.

Rousing himself, he replied. "*If* you demonstrate enough talent—and produce a work that significantly increases the price we get for Corasson!" He decided to smile, and was rewarded with a brilliant grin. Yes, a handsome boy, with everything else he required besides. "I'm bored by the Viehos Fratos," he went on confidingly, "and I intend to take on a few select students. Only the most promising, of course."

"Me and who else?" Rafeyo asked, his natural arrogance reasserting itself in the implication that none of his fellows was as worthy of Dioniso's time.

"Arriano, perhaps."

"Eiha, *he's* all right. Just not Cansalvio!"

"Do you think me a fool, to waste my teaching on such as he?" It was, truth to tell, his favorite aspect of each life: choosing talented young men, giving them the benefit of his genius, creating a group of Limners who had his teachings in common and who later would form his next life's own personal faction among the Grijalvas—for of course his next life was always lived in one of those special estudos. To his choice, he said, "I take only the best. When you've finished this, we'll speak again about truly finishing it."

"With magic."

"Not much, but enough." He paused, composing his face into grim lines. "Rafeyo, should you be tempted to try this on your own, don't. I'll know—the Viehos Fratos know everything sooner or later—and not only will you never study with me, you will never hold a brush in your hand as long as you live."

Rafeyo nodded—too quickly. "I know enough to know I don't know enough to do this on my own, Premio."

"Send word when you think this is done. And tell no one what you've learned, not even your mother."

Rafeyo caught his breath. "How did you—"

"I told you. We find out everything sooner or later."

FORTY-SEVEN

In the late spring of 1264 Mechella was delivered of her second child, a large dark-haired boy she called Alessio Enrei Cossimio Mequel. The absence of his father's name in the list was not lost on anyone. She damned the gossips and named him as she pleased, as was a mother's privilege.

The birth of his son's son meant even more to Grand Duke Cossimio than the assurance that his line would continue into another generation—for at Alessio's birth he suddenly discovered how much fun it was to be a grandfather. Lizia's children had spent their early years at Castello Casteya, so he had missed his chance with them. Though he was fond of Teressa, his booming voice and bristling beard frightened her and she was only now learning not to be shy with him. But little Alessio cooed whenever his grandfather appeared—and moreover was Cossimio's very image (but for the beard, of course). Arrigo and Lizia looked very little like the Grand Duke; Alessio was a copy in flesh of the *Birth of Cossimio III* hanging in the Galerria.

This fascination with his new grandson made his conselhos complain—with justification—that he was neglecting his duties. In truth, he spent the bulk of each day dawdling in the children's quarters, which now took up half a floor of the Palasso and housed all five of his grandchildren. When told by Lord Limner Mequel—diplomatically, and not without sympathy—that pressing affairs of state required his attention, Cossimio gave an annoyed snort but did not glance up from tickling Alessio's bare belly with a feather.

"Let Arrigo do it. He got enough practice after the earthquake." Then, recalling that being Grand Duke was fun as well, he added, "But don't let him make any decisions. I'll review recommendations and decide things myself. Look at this, 'Quellito! He's smiling at me!"

"Your joy in your grandson is a lovely thing, Cossi, but—"

"That's just what he is to me—pure joy. I won't miss Alessio's first words or first steps, not like I did with my other grandchildren. It's too bad you'll never know this, old friend. Tell you what—you be his Zio 'Quellito. There, you see, he likes the idea—he's laughing!"

The Lord Limner decided not to point out that not only did any child laugh when tickled, but that an infant Alessio's age understood no ideas other than wet, sleepy, and hungry. Mequel simply surrendered to the inevitable and joined Cossimio at the cradle. A pocket yielded a clean new brush, and he drew its silkiness over the baby's cheek. Alessio crowed, burbled, and belched.

"A disgusting sound for a future Grand Duke," Mequel observed. "And the smell won't do at all—he needs a new cloth. But you know, I can see the attraction of the rest of it. So small and helpless, and those big eyes staring up at one . . . I suppose even in an old eunuch like me, the instinct survives."

"'Eunuch'!" Cossimio laughed and slapped his shoulder—carefully, for Mequel's bones were more brittle by the day. "I'm not so far gone in my dotage that I don't remember Dorrias, Felissina, Yberra, Ollandra, and Tomassa—not to mention those lively redheaded twins from Ghillas! And that little Pracanzan who almost made you a *real* eunuch when she caught you with your sixth cousin!"

"Cossi!" Mequel grinned. "Such scandalous talk in front of an innocent child! And don't you go telling him tales about me when he gets older. What will Alessio think of his Zio 'Quellito then?"

Cossimio's expressive face lost all happiness. He picked up the baby and cuddled him, gazing over the downy head at his friend. "When he gets older, and you're not here—that's what you meant, isn't it? I thought I'd forbidden—"

"And I replied that I would do my best," Mequel responded gently. "I will, Cossi. I promised you."

"Here," he said abruptly. "Hold him."

"I'm not very good with—"

"I said *hold him!*" Cossimio thrust the child into his arms.

It seemed instinct really did function even in a sterile Limner who would never know fatherhood, for he cradled the child most comfortably and naturally. He touched his lips to the curly black hair and smiled.

Gruffly, Cossimio said, "Stay like that. This time *I'll* paint the picture, Lord Limner, in my mind, so I can see you and him like this whenever I close my eyes. Just in case you do the unthinkable and fail to keep a promise to me."

"Cossi—" Much moved, Mequel found he was stammering. "It

isn't—I know I said—but it's not for me to—" He cleared his throat and ended, "I'll try. You know I'll try."

"That's all I ask. 'Cordo?"

Alessio waved a fist in Mequel's face. He rubbed his cheek to the tiny, perfect fingers, allowing himself—just this once—to feel the true depth of his regret that he would be dead before this child reached his fifth birthday.

"'Cordo," he answered softly. "I *will* try."

. . . and will it still be spring when I am freed? If I am ever freed? He has given me a lamp and a candle against the night, and water to drink, and trees outside the window—but there is no scent from the wick or the wax, no savor to the water, no sound of wind in the leaves. Not even he *could paint the wind. . . .*

Will it still be spring? The same *spring? A year from now, ten years, twenty—*

Why didn't he simply steal this life beneath my heart, rather than steal living from me? He could have taken my baby's life without taking me from the living world of spring and scent and taste and wind—

Will he free me before he dies?

Or has he found a way to cheat Death as well as Life?

Every summer all who could afford it fled the stifling, muggy heat of Meya Suerta. They went east to the seaside, north to the Montes Astrappas, west to the lofty hilltop city of Granidia, and even as far south as the shoreline of Shagarra where one could dimly see the sands of Tza'ab Rih on the horizon. Wherever the wealthy went, it was with one thing in mind: a cool breeze.

That summer, despite reports of the occasional vibration underfoot in Casteya, half the Court found excuses to go north, for they were sure of finding at least one night's welcome at Corasson along the way. Some came out of friendship for Mechella, bringing gifts for her lovely new home. Others came out of curiosity, wishing to see the almost forgotten monument to Serrano pride where so many do'Verradas had disported themselves with their Grijalva Mistresses. A few came to spy for Arrigo, for he had not joined the rest of the family at Corasson. He still had not forgiven her for buying it.

King Enrei had been extravagantly generous at the birth of his first grandson. He was also exquisitely specific about the uses to which the money should be put. A third of the impressive coffer of gold mareias went to education; another third built the long-desired children's wing onto the hospital in Meya Suerta; the remainder went to Mechella herself. She used most of it to buy Corasson. Arrigo, remaining at the Palasso to attend any little matters that might arise, was almost daily subjected to reminders of King Enrei's munificence. The vigorous young sancto who oversaw Ecclesial schools submitted plan after plan for improvements on old buildings and construction of new ones. The conselhos responsible for health and public works inundated him with lists and architectural renderings and schedules and estimates for the hospital. The ladies of his mother's various charity committees sent letters about the schools and letters about the hospital and never failed to call down blessings on Enrei's name. Neither did any of them—sancto, conselho, nor lady—fail to thank Arrigo for fathering a son and for marrying the living miracle that was Mechella.

"I begin to understand," he told Tazia one night, "why women complain of being valued only as brood mares. I was never so loved for anything I did as when I played stud to a Princess."

That he could show some humor about it was a relief to Tazia—and confirmed her timing. He'd been ready to return to her. He needed her. Slowly, through the winter and spring, as they resumed the comfortable relationship, his temper improved and he relaxed and she was sure the lines in his face were softening.

Tazia and Arrigo did not meet every night, as they used to during their twelve years together. But every day messages went back and forth by the hands of trusted servants, regarding everything from the day's doings to choice gossip to expressions of love and desire. Sometimes they met at her town caza; sometimes she slipped into the Palasso by a back stair. Twice that summer they sneaked away to Chasseriallo, and a dozen times to Caza Reccolto. With most of the Courtfolk gone from the capital, there were few to observe and act the informant, but they were careful all the same.

Arrigo's friends sent him letters about Corasson. Clouds of dust as room after room was cleared and cleaned and decorated. Cossimio and Gizella doting on all five grandchildren. Teressa prettier every day. Alessio growing apace. Maldonno's riding now expert. Grezella caught kissing a kitchen boy, Lizia laughing herself silly over it. Little Riobira embroidering pillows for the salon with Lissina's guidance. And Mechella: gracious hostess, loving mother, radiant with delight in her happy family home.

Tazia was receiving the same nauseating news. Steeling herself one night as she lay beside Arrigo in his bed, she said, "You'll have to go for a visit, you know."

"Hmm? Go where?"

"Corasson."

Grunting, he rolled over and reached for a winecup on the bed-side table.

"Just for a few days. Bring her a picture or a tapestry from the Palasso collection, be devoted son and husband and father—and then come back to me."

"Why should I make that long, dusty journey at this late date? Summer's nearly gone—and it's been so perfect, Tazia, I don't want to waste a moment of it at Corasson."

"But you must go, or people will talk."

"Let them. I don't care anymore."

"You have to care, at least for a while. Listen to me, carrido meyo." She sat up and lit a candle so she could see his face. "Your work after the earthquake showed your father you can fulfill his duties. Now that he's so besotted with Alessio, he'll be glad to give you real power, especially after the brilliant work you've done this summer. He's sixty-eight this year, an age when a man is ready to relinquish some of his burdens and enjoy the years he has left to him. You'll be doing him a favor, Arrigo, giving him more time to spend with his grandchildren."

"If only he'd see it that way!"

She drew in a careful breath. "Shall I tell you how he *does* see things? Cossimio adores his wife, and to him this is an indication of true manhood. He sincerely loved Lissina, but he worships your mother. So until you have officially been given power enough—"

"I have to keep our secret, and play the devoted husband." He made a face and settled back into mountainous pillows. "Which means going to Corasson for a visit. And after I have this power, Tazia? What then?"

"Rafeyo will be seventeen next year. He's outstripped all his class and Premio Frato Dioniso tutors him privately—a great honor. Mequel won't last much longer, but we only need him until Rafeyo is fully trained. Two years at the most. And then—"

"Dioniso," he mused. "I like him. But he's past forty, too old to become Lord Limner when Mequel—" He paused for a swallow of wine. "But as head of the Fratos, Dioniso will have great influence over who becomes the next Lord Limner. And Rafeyo is his special student. Very clever, Tazia."

She let herself smile demurely. "I thought so, and I'm glad you agree. With official influence in government, Dioniso's friendship, and my son as Lord Limner, you can accomplish wonders, Arrigo!"

"But not for another two years," he reminded her. "And where does Mechella fit in?"

"I think her purchase of Corasson indicates she doesn't *want* to fit in."

"The people think she hung the moon and all the stars. They won't take it kindly when I openly reinstate you. Eiha, neither will she!"

"Do you think I'll enjoy any moment you're with her? But you must get another child on her, Arrigo. More babies distract her."

"I'd rather get a child on *you*." He fumbled behind him to replace the goblet, ignoring the shatter of glass as he missed and it hit the floor. "Shall we do that tonight, Tazia? Shall we make a baby?"

"Oh, Arrigo—if only!"

"Tonight we can, carrida," he murmured, drawing her into his arms. "You and I are married, as we should have been years ago. We're young, and deeply in love, and ready to make a dozen children—the first of them tonight."

"Oh, Arrigo. . . ."

Dioniso surveyed his small class of favored youths, pleased by their attentiveness even in this heat. They knew what an honor it was to be taught by him. How much more awestruck they would be, he thought with a hidden smile, if they knew who *really* taught them.

Rafeyo was fulfilling every promise. Arriano, two years younger and not quite so talented, was repaying Dioniso's tutelage with a marked increase in confidence and a corresponding growth in perception. Gutierrin and Tiodor were clever in their way, but useful more for their family connections to high-ranking Viehos Fratos than for their artistic abilities. Dioniso could wish for another truly gifted student, someone for Rafeyo to compete with, but he worked with what he had.

This was to be a lecture, not a demonstration. After making sure everything he needed was on the table before him, he poured himself a glass of cool lemonada and began.

"Paint in a day to last a century—this is the rule of the fresco. We begin by clothing ourselves in the compordotta of the fresco. That is, Enthusiasm, Reverence, Obedience, and Constancy." He paused to smile. "To speak of more practical matters, wear something you don't mind spoiling, for the first part of the process is very messy."

He went on to describe how one soaked a wall and coated it with coarse plaster—two parts sand to one part lime. "The Serranos," he added with a sneer instantly mimicked by his estudos, "used to hire masons to do this. The stink of the lime offended their delicate nostrils. But we are not so effete, and we do our own work from start to finish."

The drawing for the fresco having already been done, a small needle was used to prick holes along every line. He held up the golden needle Saavedra had long ago given him for the purpose, then tucked it back into its case and held up a loosely woven bag of charcoal dust.

"Lay a coat of fine plaster on the day's section, press the sketch against it, and strike this bag lightly over the whole. When you peel off the sketch, your design will be outlined in black dots on wet plaster. Now time is of the essence. You must paint before the plaster dries, so the pigments bond with the lime. You have about six hours."

A groan from Arriano, who was old enough to know how quickly the hours could pass, elicited sideways glances from the younger ones who still thought themselves indefatigable, infallible, and invincible.

"For the coarser work, your brushes will be made of the bristles of a white hog. For the finer, bear or sable—although the new brushes made of seal fur from Friesemark and Vethia are becoming highly prized." Dioniso held up examples of each, then continued, "Mineral pigments are best, things such as ocher, burned grapevines, lapis lazuli, mixed with water. Avoid white lead. A Serrano—" Again the sneer. "—once used it to paint the Mother and Son. The lime turned white to black and the Son's swaddling clothes looked as if He'd been soiling them for a month."

"Appropriate to a Serrano painting," Rafeyo murmured. "They're all shit anyway."

Dioniso grinned as the students laughed, then rapped his knuckles on the table for their attention. "The rest of the guidelines—formulas, pointers on technique, and so on—may be found in your books. I will see your sketches in three days for the rebuilt Sanctias in Casteya. If any of them please me, their makers may assist in this important commission, and paint their frescoes on an inconspicuous wall of an insignificant Sanctia."

"And in later years," Arriano said, eyeing Rafeyo sidelong, "people will make pilgrimages to his wall and say what a genius he was, even at sixteen!"

Rafeyo made a face at him—nothing more dire, for the boys were friends even if competitors—and intoned, "*No* wall graced with a Grijalva fresco could be insignificant—even an *Arriano* Grijalva wall!"

Smiling, Dioniso dismissed his little group to plan their proposed frescoes. When they were gone, he climbed the stairs to the Premio Frato's suite, telling himself it was ridiculous to think that there seemed to be more and more steps every day. He was as spry as ever; his joints did not hurt any more than they ought to at his age; his fingers were yet straight and strong; his mind was as keen and his perceptions as shrewd as they had always been.

And yet . . . and yet this body was growing older every day. Every single day. He sank into a large, overstuffed armchair beside a window, letting the hot afternoon sun bake into his bones, and fought back memories of panic.

To grow old . . . to feel pain in every limb . . . to watch his hands twist and gnarl like tormented tree roots . . . to know his senses were losing their sharpness and his mind its quickness and his body its health and strength. . . .

No. Not this time. Dioniso came of good stock. Healthy. Long-lived—for Limners.

And there was Rafeyo. He was here, available, within easy reach of hands and magic and paintbrush. There would be none of the horror of being Matteyo or Domaos, exiled far from Tira Virte, without hope of a strong young Grijalva for refuge.

But he remembered. Chieva do'Orro, the pain, the terror, the solitude, the dread—! He remembered all those things with a physical anguish, as if every painting he had ever Blooded in more than three hundred years was being simultaneously pricked with needles and seared with candleflames.

Eiha, ridiculous! He roused himself with the reminder that only those few paintings Blooded as Dioniso could harm him. The others were dead paint on dead canvas, painted by dead men. Only *this* body, this blood, had power over him.

And this reminded him of something else he must attend to very soon: the cataloging of every magical painting Rafeyo had done or would do until the day came. No stray pieces of Rafeyo's substance, on paper or canvas or frescoed wall or even so much as a scribbling in his sketchpad, to provide a painful future surprise.

Chieva, it was so complicated, this business of living forever.

Cabral stood back from his easel, scowling. Mechella, singing softly to Alessio to keep him from fussing, glanced up. Seeing the limner's expression, she made a comical grimace to imitate it and began to laugh.

"What a dreadful face! Smile at once, you'll scare the baby!"

"I'm not good enough," he muttered. "I shouldn't be painting this, I haven't the skill. You should've asked Dioniso or Zevierin, a real Limner—"

"I don't want Dioniso or Zevierin to paint this portrait, I want you." A breath of a breeze quivered the trellised roses above her head, scattering a few more petals onto her thin lacy gown. "Now, stop being so silly and paint!"

"I tell you I'm not good enough!"

"Nonsense. Mequel did the official version. I want one for myself, and you painted my copy of Teressa's *Birth,* so it's only logical that you should paint Alessio, too."

"But this isn't a copy!" he exclaimed, flinging his brush onto the grass. "If you'd only let me work from Mequel's portrait—"

"If I did, the picture wouldn't be *yours,* the way *you* see my son. Cabral, pick up that brush and *paint!*"

"Best obey her command, Cabral," said the last voice Mechella had expected to hear at Corasson. She turned to see Arrigo strolling toward her with a smile on his face and a huge bouquet of wildflowers in his arms. "As I've learned to," he added, bowing playfully. "You commanded my presence, Dona, and here I am."

"Arrigo! At last!" She transferred the baby from her lap to the blanket and scrambled to her feet. She ran across the lawn to throw her arms around her husband. "I'm so glad you've come! There's so much I want to show you—"

"Careful, carrida, you're crushing the flowers!" But in the next instant he bent his head to kiss her.

Cabral moved tactfully away, calling his sister to come take the baby upstairs for his nap. As Leilias approached, Mechella drew away from Arrigo and smiled: joyous, breathless, bright enough to outshine the summer sun. Taking the flowers into her arms as Arrigo bent to pick up their son, she said, "See how big he's getting? And you won't know Teressa, she's grown at least a foot and she's brown as a sparrow!"

Cabral busied himself packing up his paints and gathering brushes for cleaning. Arrigo, jiggling the infant in his arms, came over to look at the unfinished portrait.

"It's excellent, and she's right. Pick up your brush and paint, limner," Arrigo smiled.

"I thank Your Grace, and I shall do so tomorrow."

"Oh, no," Mechella protested. "Tomorrow we're going exploring. There's so much to see, and Alessio fusses if I'm not with him the whole day long, so I'll have to steal your subject from you, Cabral. You'll love Corasson, Arrigo, I know you will."

"I'm sure of it," he replied.

Mechella laughed, perfectly happy now that he was at her side again. Corasson was complete. Leilias stepped forward to take the baby, but Arrigo shook his head.

"I've missed him. His nap can wait. But it's sweltering out here, 'Chella, let's go inside for something cold to drink." Together they crossed the lawn and entered the house by the garden doors.

Leilias studied her brother's face for a long moment. "Is it worth it, Cabral?'

"I don't know what you're talking about."

"Yes, you do."

"What if I did?" he burst out. "Would you warn me about what's in my eyes every time I look at her? I could grind that lying chiros into sausage meat and stuff him into his own foreskin!"

Leilias blinked; Cabral was rarely rude and never profane. But she couldn't help a sudden giggle either, and the words, "Merditto en chosetto seddo!"

Cabral snorted at the old country saying. "Shit in a silk stocking? You flatter him!"

"Eiha, the lying chiros had at least one good idea. I think we both need something very strong poured over the last of that nice, cold, white Casteyan snow down in the coldroom."

"I'd rather bury him in it."

"Easier, but not as creative. I liked your first plan best."

At summer's end, Lizia took her two daughters home to Castello Casteya. Maldonno and the rest of the family returned to Palasso

Verrada in time for Providenssia. Arrigo met them in the inner courtyard. He had left Corasson after only six days, pleading the pressures of government. Mechella parted from him most bitterly beneath the gigantic oak on the south side of the house, and watched weeping as he rode away with his retinue. Now, seeing him smile a warm welcome home, she could not help but think of the angry words exchanged that day.

"You've barely arrived and now you want to go? All I want is for us to be happy here, and you won't even give us a fair chance!"

"It's you who's not being fair. I was meant for this work from my birth—all I want is to be of use to my people."

"Our people! And stop lying to me, I know why you're so anxious to return to Meya Suerta! It's not the power and position you want so much and don't yet have, it's that woman—and you'll never really have her, don't you see?"

"You are ridiculous, Mechella. Let go of my arm, they've brought my horse and it's time to leave."

She watched Arrigo dandle Alessio in his arms as they all went inside, and could have burst into tears. Kind Gizella, attributing her looks to weariness, told her to go upstairs and rest. Escaping gratefully, Mechella locked her bedchamber door and flung herself across the vast bed. But the tears wouldn't come, and the burning of her eyes wouldn't go away, and she pummeled a pillow with her fists with fury at what Arrigo had done to her.

Yet—what had Lizia said about making one's own life? And Leilias, about showing the world the woman Arrigo had seen that night at Caza Reccolto? How she wished either friend could be here with her now.

But Lizia was at Castello Casteya, Leilias at Palasso Grijalva. Otonna would listen. Still, clever as she was in the use of her wits and her relations on Mechella's behalf, Otonna was neither a do'Verrada nor a Grijalva. Mechella needed someone intimate with power and politics. Lizia was unreachable—but not Leilias.

The Grijalvas were flattered—though some were suspicious—when Mechella announced that Leilias would join her suite as a lady-in-waiting. This singular honor, from a woman whose husband's renewed Marria do'Fantome with another Grijalva was an open secret, renewed comparisons with Duchess Jesminia. Admired for her beauty and goodness, beloved for her care of orphaned children, with a Grijalva in her household as friend and companion just as Jesminia had befriended Larissa and Margatta

Grijalva—though Duke Renayo had remained faithful and devoted to the end of his life, which would not be said of Arrigo. . . .

Lord Limner Mequel was not blind. Tradition held that when the Heir was born, his mother's portrait was painted for the Cathedral. Mequel used the same pose and background as in the only full-face image of the beloved Duchess—Liranzo Grijalva's unfinished *Duchess Jesminia at the Ressolvo*. The same luminous glow of stained glass windows framed Mechella, although her own golden hair was halo enough. At the festival of Imago, the painting was hung next to those of the other living do'Verradas. Mechella was officially Tira Virteian at last.

All that winter she complained to Leilias that her picture saw more of Arrigo than she did. Apart from family dinner twice a week, after which he dutifully spent the night in her bed, he was always anywhere but at the Palasso. She knew he wasn't with the Grijalva woman, who was wintering with her husband at Castello Alva. If the lovers met at Chasseriallo—Arrigo was forever going there to hunt—no one heard about it. Mostly he attended meetings, conferred with the conselhos, and in general earned a reputation as tireless, dedicated, and fully capable of ruling Tira Virte all by himself.

Which he did not.

Cossimio, back in the capital after a summer of leisure, felt in need of some work again. All foreign relations were conducted by him; all matters of high justice; all trade negotiations; all disbursements of public funds. Arrigo was left with settling petty squabbles, reviewing the tax rolls, and supervising construction of the new hospital wing—named for King Enrei II of Ghillas. Arrigo did not deputize for his father at holidays and social gatherings, for Cossimio appeared in his customarily prominent role at all such celebrations. In fact, Arrigo missed the party of the season: a banquet given by Mechella in honor of Cossimio's sixty-ninth birthday at which Maldonno, wearing for the first time the blue-and-gold of the Grand Duke's personal suite, acted as his grandfather's squire. Arrigo did not attend, having left two days earlier to dedicate the new memorial to Alesso do'Verrada in Joharra.

This was done at his father's bidding, and Cossimio didn't even miss him. The visit was meant to judge intimations of unrest in the southern provinces. On his return, Arrigo told his father the blunt truth: swift response to Casteya's urgent need had provoked disgruntled envy. Why, the Joharrans asked, had the catastrophic sandstorm of 1260 not produced such quick and generous aid?

"The difference," Arrigo finished, "is attributed to Mechella."

This statement he presented as he would a verdict sent up by the law court left to lie on the table for Cossimio's examination. It was true, and it was a danger. From the do'Verradas came all bounty, and to them was owed all loyalty. Mechella, innocently enough in her desire to help, had become a threat.

To Arrigo's fury and frustration, Cossimio didn't see it that way.

"Mechella, you say? Then I'll send her on a progress, to show the south that she cares equally for them. Arrange it, Arrigo, and go with her. The roads will be reliable again by Fuega Vesperra. Leave then, and stay away until Sancterria—when we'll all spend another fine summer at Corasson. This autumn you can take her up to Elleon for the same purpose, and everything will work out just fine."

Thus Arrigo became the man who accompanied Dona Mechella to Joharra. And Shagarra. And every market town and farming village in between. With each ecstatic welcome given their Dolcha 'Chellita—along with presents as grand as a lapis necklace and as humble as a basket of almonds—Arrigo's temper worsened. Joharra held a parade and a service of thanksgiving in the Sanctia Matra Serenissa. Varriyva named a new school for her. Brazzina renamed the town's central zocalo in her honor. Shaarria declared a three-day holiday to celebrate her visit. Shagarra gave a city-wide banquet with fireworks. At last, one evening in his mother's own home of Granidia, his resentment boiled over.

He had watched her smile and laugh and hug children and converse with everyone from the lowliest servants to the barons and counts who couldn't tell her often enough how they and all their people adored her. But in Granidia they knew *him*. He'd spent many summers here as a boy and youth, and the people welcomed him back with a warmth even greater than the homage they gave Mechella. The road up the hillside was lined with cheering throngs, and once within the massive walls the narrow streets reverberated with his name. At the peak of the hill was the castello he had played in as a child with a score of do'Granidia cousins, and they all turned out in force to embrace him into the family fold.

That evening, replete with good humor, he entered Mechella's bedchamber to find her still dressing for what Count do'Granidia, his mother's uncle, had described as a rustic country dance. With a slight frown for her tardiness, Arrigo poured himself a goblet of wine and sprawled in a chair to wait. He was always waiting on her these days.

Otonna fussed with the laces of an embroidered bodice, Leilias with the flounces of a tiered skirt—gaudy camponessa clothes given her on their arrival, which Mechella had received with as much delight as if they'd been the finest and most fashionable silks. When she spun around from the mirror, loose hair flying in wild golden curls and skirts flaring to show the length of slim bare legs, Arrigo slammed down his empty winecup and glowered.

"You look like a peasant."

Her blue eyes widened. But where once she would have flinched and begged his pardon and changed her attire immediately, now she merely turned away from him, saying, "I find these clothes charming."

"I said nothing about the garments. I said *you* look like a peasant."

Their gazes met in the mirror. A lengthy moment of real malevolence was broken by a nervous choking sound from the maid. Nearby, Leilias's eyes shot black daggers.

"Get out, both of you," he said.

"Stay where you are," Mechella ordered.

He rose from his chair. "It's the instinct of a peasant not to care who overhears what should be private between husband and wife."

"Husband!" She spun on one bare heel. "You haven't been that for half a year!"

"And have you been a wife? You're merely the woman I married and got children on."

Though this struck home—he saw it in her face—she rallied with remarkable speed. "If that's how you think of *me*, then I suppose you consider that Grijalva your true wife! Either way, you're living a lie!"

"Your insight surprises me, Mechella. Yours is the seeming—hers, the substance."

Trembling, she said, "If only there was a way to stop living the lies—"

"Perhaps we can arrange it," he suggested.

"Never will she take my place! Never!"

"You must know by now that never could you have taken hers."

There was another terrible silence before the rosewood clock chimed and the rooster flapped its rainbow wings. Arrigo flicked imaginary lint from his dark blue jacket.

"You've made us late—again." Swinging around, he caught sight of the two stricken servants and frowned. "Gossip as you like. It won't be believed. This is my mother's home, these people are my close kin." He smiled. "Besides, everyone knows how devoted I am . . . to my *wife*."

FORTY-EIGHT

Leilias was Zevierin's lookout that night. Most of Granidia was either at the "country dance" or at similar entertainments in the little grassy zocalos honeycombing the city. Those few who were on the winding streets, especially after midnight, thought she and Zevierin were fellow revelers on their way home.

"Hurry up, it's taking too long," she hissed, glancing over her shoulder. They were in a deserted alley between Ruallo Vacha and Ruallo Cordobina. On one side cattle were slaughtered for meat; on the other, skinned for leather; offal from each was thrown into the alley refuse bins. The stench was unbearable.

"Just another few lines," Zevierin promised, tossing long, straight black hair from his eyes. "Qal Venommo isn't very complex, but it's damned dark and I'm not used to working in charcoal on brick."

"Grown too exalted for the simpler things, have you, my fine Master Limner?"

Zevierin only grunted by way of a reply.

At the mouth of the alley dogs snarled, scrabbling through the offal. Leilias flinched and again urged Zevierin to hurry.

" 'Cordo, 'cordo," he muttered. "It's done."

She squinted in the darkness. "What does it say?"

"Nothing. It's all done in pictures, not words."

"Well, then, what does it show?"

"Allowing for imprecision caused by lack of light, haste, and the inferior materials—"

Warningly: "Zevierin!"

He grinned at her, a flash of white teeth in his dark face. "Tazia on horseback, digging in her spurs. The horse bears an uncanny resemblance to Arrigo."

She clapped a hand over her mouth to stifle a giggle, but it escaped anyway. "Zevi! You didn't!"

"Do you want people to get the idea or not? Where shall we go next?"

She took his hand and they hurried from the alley, wary of growling dogs. Back on a main street, she paused under a lamp to examine the hand she'd held. He tried unsuccessfully to keep it from her.

"No, let me look. Why are your fingers so sticky?"

"Why do you think?" He dragged a scrap of cloth from his pocket. "Come on, I want to finish at least four more before I faint from loss of blood."

"Blood?" Stricken, Leilias stared as he wrapped the cloth around his hand. In the stinking alleyway, she hadn't smelled it— she who blended perfumes and could tell the scent of an Astrappa Bianca rose from a Pluvio Bianco at twenty paces with her eyes shut.

"Zevi," she whispered. "Why?"

"Later I'll tell you what we Limners *really* do." He shrugged slender shoulders, a rueful smile quirking his rather plain, long-nosed Grijalva face into something suddenly much more interesting. "For now, find me a good wall, preferably plastered smooth. Brick is absolute flaming merditto to work on."

The next morning, as sunlight penetrated the steep and twisting streets of Granidia, outraged cries and derisive laughter began to ring out. "Qal Venommo!" the well-informed assured their friends—"poisoned pen"—as in every neighborhood people gathered to gawk, point, and believe the hilarious and occasionally salacious drawings that had appeared overnight as if by magic.

When Arrigo found out, he summoned to his presence all the Grijalvas—limner *and* Limner—currently in Granidia. Of the twenty-nine, eleven had witnesses that they'd been at home all night in their beds, twelve had similar witnesses that they'd been at one or another of the dances, six had been at Count do'Granidia's ball, and the remaining six were so feeble they were hardly able to climb a flight of stairs, let alone spend the night racing all over the tortuously sloping streets.

Arrigo glared at Cabral and Zevierin, the two Grijalvas Mechella had insisted on bringing with her. They were his prime suspects, of course. But he'd seen the latter several times at the ball, dancing with Leilias; the former wore the look of someone who has spent the previous night getting very, very drunk. Indeed, one of the do'Granidia servants had been questioned earlier, and he affirmed that Cabral had sent with clockwork regularity for yet another bottle until shortly before dawn.

But a Grijalva had done this—this—this *insult* to the Heir of Tira Virte. Even the cleverest amateur hand could not have worked such vicious slanders in the inimitable Qal Venommo style. A Grijalva had done it. And he knew their accursed vows would keep them silent about which one until the day they died. Not even Dioniso, who was his friend; not even Rafeyo, who was Tazia's son; not a single damned one of them would have revealed the culprit. And Arrigo knew it.

"Very well," he stated flatly. "If I am not to know which Grijalva did this, I will certainly know which Grijalvas will *un*do it. The able-bodied will take up brushes. *Scrub* brushes. And if I find one hint of a charcoal line on one wall of Granidia by sunset. . . ." He let the threat trail off unspoken.

"Your Grace."

He rounded on a stoop-shouldered Limner whose fever-ridden bones benefited from Granidia's fierce sun. "What?"

"Begging Your Grace's pardon, but the work cannot be washed off."

Another Limner nodded. "I had a look before I came here, Your Grace. It's—a kind of charcoal that doesn't respond to solvents of any kind."

Zevierin cleared his throat. "He's right, Your Grace. I, too, inspected a drawing, and—"

"Nommo Matra ei Filho! Paint over it, then!"

Hours later, sweating in the harsh noon sun, Cabral paused to press his thumbs against his aching temples. Zevierin looked up from mixing another bucket of white paint. After this day, Granidia would glow like alabaster. In places, anyway.

"Why don't you rest for a while?"

Cabral eyed him. "And *again* let you do the work I should have done?"

"Are you getting heatstroke? You make no sense, Cabral."

"Don't I? How'd you hurt your hand?"

Zevierin replied serenely, "As I told Don Arrigo when he asked about it, I scraped it on the stairs up to the watchtower. Those walls really should be smoothed over, they're like glass shards."

Cabral was having none of it. "Zevi, how did you hurt your hand?"

"The truth?" He grinned. "Leilias bit me."

That wrung a laugh from Cabral. "Don't you wish! Matra, I thought I'd fall over when Arrigo told you to be more careful of your precious Limner's hands!"

Zevierin poured out two cups of water. "I only hurt the left, which doesn't matter much."

"You took a stupid chance last night. Did my sister put you up to it?"

"I don't know what you mean."

"All the real Limners knew the instant they saw that bandage."

"I'm *sure* I don't know what you mean."

After a moment Cabral shook his head. "You're a fool, Zevi. But—grazzo millio."

"In fact," Zevierin said thoughtfully, "I'm absolutely positive I don't know what you mean. But you're welcome anyway."

For another twelve bright spring days Arrigo escorted Mechella on the rest of the arranged tour. In Dregez, the last town of any note on the road home to Meya Suerta, Baroness Lissina and a delegation of Grijalvas awaited them. At the death of her husband, the manor house and home farm became hers alone. It was confidently expected that she would will it all to the family, as every other Mistress had done before her. At that time a Grijalva with wife and children would be chosen to oversee the property. It was also secretly hoped that the Grand Duke would ennoble this Grijalva as the new Baron do'Dregez. Because Lissina was healthy as a horse and came from a line whose women lived to a ripe old age, it was assumed that Arrigo would be that Grand Duke. Therefore, certain forward-looking Grijalvas came from Meya Suerta to help Lissina welcome the Don and Dona to Dregez.

As in Granidia, Arrigo was greeted first, rather than as an afterthought. He was wanted for himself, not just for the woman at his side. This was true of the ranking citizens, anyway; the common camponessos still shouted only for Mechella, but Arrigo could ignore that as he was made much of by a score of fawning townsfolk and a dozen flattering Grijalvas.

He knew what the latter wanted, of course. Tazia kept him well-informed about the inner workings of her family. He was not swayed by the display, and would decide to grant the title of Baron do'Dregez or not as he chose. Still, self-serving as their attention was, he basked in it.

Mechella knew the Grijalva plan, too. Leilias and Lissina explained it to her the first evening of the visit as they sat in the Baroness' cheerful little salon overlooking an ornamental fountain. Dregez was constructed in the classic Hassiendia style: a two-storied hollow square with a courtyard garden in the center and a balcony running along all four sides. Its charm for Mechella was in its world-within-a-world feeling, though Leilias was much more taken by the profusion of aromatic herbs growing in beds and boxes amid the brick paving. Dregez was too hot even in late spring for many flowers, but hardy desert herbs thrived.

As the evening light faded and the three women listened to the plaintive notes of a gittern being played beside the fountain, Lissina also revealed in strictest confidence what no one would know until after her death. In keeping with what she and Baron Reycarro had agreed on, her will left Dregez to Riobira do'Casteya, younger and near-dowerless daughter of Lissina's beloved namesake, Lizia.

On hearing this, Leilias laughed until she choked. "The Viehos Fratos will have a collective seizure!"

Lissina nodded. "It's a good thing I'll be dead when they find out."

"Eiha, cousin, I promise I won't let them dig you up and stick you with their paletto knives!"

Mechella found none of this amusing. "But why Riobira? It's wonderfully generous of you, and she's a delightful child and very deserving, and of course you must do with your property as you like—but surely your family—"

Lissina shook her head. "Unlike Corasson before Your Grace bought it—"

"I thought we'd agreed to do away with titles!"

The former Mistress smiled her lovely, translucent smile. "Regretto, Mechella. I was about to say that Dregez has always been highly profitable. I think it unwise for the Grijalvas to have that much wealth—connected to a noble title as well." She rose and refilled their glasses with iced lemonada flavored with a few drops of the newest import from Merse, a clear liquor distilled from some sort of berry. It lent a nice tang to the citrus, and one could drink quite a bit of it without becoming giddy. "Also unlike Corasson, whose owner died before her *Will* could be painted, Dregez will not go automatically to the family if I can help it. It pleases me, and my dear Reycarro, to dower Riobira as befits a do'Verrada granddaughter. Lizia named her for him, you know—his full name was Reycarro Riobiro Diegan do'Dregez. And I love the child as if she were my own."

Leilias made a face. "What's all this mysterious motherly glow every woman but me seems to feel?"

Mechella smiled. "You'll find out one day, believe me. What I wish to know is how this can be kept secret. After all, a Grijalva will be needed to do the painting."

"That's why I've told you this," said Lissina. "I need a Grijalva, one I can trust, who isn't thick with the Viehos Fratos. I've settled on Cabral." When two pairs of brows arched, she explained, "One hears things. But I didn't like to borrow him without asking you, Mechella."

"You may borrow Cabral anytime you like. Would tomorrow do for the preliminary sketches?"

Leilias shook her head. "Not Cabral."

"Whyever not?" Mechella asked indignantly. "Are you saying he isn't competent or trustworthy?"

"Of course he is—and he'd laugh as much as I did at this joke on the family ambitions. He'd do anything you ask, you know that. But a *Will* painted by him won't work. It won't be—binding."

"He's a Grijalva."

"But not a Limner." Her tone supplied the differencing capital. "It was explained to me recently. Those like Cabral, capable of fathering children, are incapable of painting certain kinds of pictures. One potency precludes the other, if you get my meaning."

Lissina frowned. "I don't, and I'm not sure I wish to. These are matters for Grand Dukes and Grijalva Limners, not for us."

Mechella did not share her opinion. "Who told you this, Leilias?"

"Zevierin."

"I see." After a moment's keen scrutiny that made Leilias want to squirm, Mechella continued, "As it happens, Zevierin is with us on progress. I trust him as fully as I trust Cabral. Will he do, Lissina?"

"On your recommendation, of course. Grazzo, 'Chella," she added, almost shy with the diminutive. "You've eased my mind of a great burden."

Lissina showed them to the pretty bedchamber allotted Mechella and said good night. Otonna had readied the room with all the little things brought along as reminders of home: framed pencil portraits of Teressa and Alessio drawn by Cabral, an embroidered pillow worked by Riobira, a few favorite books, the rosewood clock. As the maid unhooked Mechella's bodice, Leilias tried to excuse herself. Mechella asked her to stay. Leilias hinted that she was tired. Mechella seemed not to hear.

"Will that be all, Your Grace?" Otonna asked as she finished brushing out Mechella's long golden hair.

Leilias said sweetly, "Have you an appointment with that good-looking steward—what's his name, the one Lissina trusts with everything?"

Mechella laughed. "Otonna! Serving me doesn't extend to falling in love with someone who can supply you with information, just because he *can!*"

"Eiha, Your Grace, I confess it—his information interests me not at all!"

"I'm glad to hear it." She paused, weaving her hair into braids with her own hands. "Speaking of acquiring knowledge . . . Leilias, how 'recently' did Zevierin tell you about the Limners? One day ago, five days ago—or the night you and he ran all over Granidia scribbling on walls?"

This time she did squirm. "Your Grace, I don't know what—"

Mechella giggled. "Otonna, did you see the one of that woman as a sow so old the butcher turned up his nose and the tanner wouldn't even take her for her hide?"

"A masterpiece, Your Grace," the maid chuckled. "But my own best favorite had her captain of the good ship *Tira Virte*—sailing straight into the Corrazha Morta off the Niapali coast. Zev—regretto, I meant to say *whoever* drew it—gave a true feel for why a sailor's courage dies on sighting those rocks!"

"I missed that one," Mechella lamented. "How many were there in all, Leilias?"

"I'm sure I don't know, Your Grace."

Iris-blue eyes laughed at her in the mirror. "Eiha, too bad. I suppose no one else would be able to tell me either?"

"I doubt it, Your Grace."

"Just as I thought."

They were in a dusty village half a day out of Dregez when it happened. Otonna was the first to see a too-swift movement in the crowd, but she was far from where Mechella and Arrigo stood on the Sanctia's narrow porch. Leilias, on the lower steps with the delegation of Grijalvas, was jostled by the rippling effect of someone shoving through the crowd. Cabral saw the small disruption and frowned. Mechella noticed it, too, from the corner of her eye, and glanced away from smiling attentiveness to the alcaldeyo's welcoming speech on behalf of his village. At that moment a strange spherical object, iron-gray and trailing a feather of white smoke, arced into the air.

Someone screamed. Arrigo pushed past the two resident sanctas to wrap his arms around Mechella and propel them both stumbling into the open Sanctia doorway. The flowers in her arms went flying and she tripped over the hem of her gown, Arrigo's steely embrace her only support. There were more screams, a crack of metal on stone, and then acrid smoke stung her nose and eyes. Arrigo pulled her farther into the Sanctia. She struggled against her husband's grip, freeing herself to wipe tears from her eyes.

"Are you all right, Mechella? Are you?"

"Y–yes," she said shakily. "What happened? What was that?"

"Stay here, I'll go find out. But if it's what I think it was—" He shook his head grimly. "Stay here."

Through the open doorway she saw a cloud of thin smoke. Beyond it, people fled in all directions. The elderly sancta lay on the porch, the young one kneeling at her side weeping. Village notables choked and coughed their way down the steps. Arrigo was nowhere in sight.

"Your Grace!" Cabral was with her suddenly, his eyes red and streaming with tears. " 'Chella, are you hurt?" When she shook her head, he mumbled a prayer of thanks. "Come into the sunlight and let everyone know. Half their panic is because they think you're dead."

"Dead?"

"Rapidia, Your Grace, before they trample each other."

She stepped out onto the porch, coughing as some of the dissipating smoke again stung her throat. At sight of her, the young sancta cried out to the Mother and Son in gratitude. Others called the news that their Dolcha 'Chellita was unharmed, and slowly the scene calmed down. It was just as it had been on her return from Casteya: her presence was enough.

"Where's Arrigo?" she demanded of Cabral.

"I think he's helping chase down the culprit. As for what happened—" He didn't finish, for Leilias had elbowed her way to Mechella and a moment later Otonna flung her arms around her mistress, sobbing.

"Oh, Your Grace, I thought for a certainty we'd lost you!"

"I'm perfectly all right—or would be, if you'd stop strangling me." She smiled and wiped Otonna's cheeks.

A few Grijalvas took their turn reassuring themselves of Mechella's safety. Their reddened eyes overflowed with involuntary tears. At last Arrigo ran panting up the steps.

"The filho do'canna got away," he snarled. "Did anyone see the thing hit? And where did it end up?"

The village alcaldeyo, trembling from his pointed red velurro cap to his shiny green leather boots, tottered up to where they stood. "Your Grace, someone kicked it out of the way, I didn't see where—oh, Dona Mechella, forgive us!"

"Forgive you for what?" she asked blankly.

"No one saw where the iron ball went?" Arrigo swore under his breath. "Eiha, in the manner of assassins, it's probably long gone. No evidence."

Leilias gasped. "Assassins?"

"It was a Tza'ab device, called by them *na'ar al'dushanna*—'fire and smoke.' Either this one didn't work exactly as planned, or it was only a warning." He dragged his sleeve across his forehead to mop up the sweat. "They stuff chemicals into a sphere with a wick attached. When it's lit, the smoke can be an irritant or a lethal poison."

Mechella swayed with shock. Cabral steadied her with an unobtrusive hand at her back. She hardly noticed.

Leilias said, "The sancta took the worst of it. But she'll recover. They've taken her to her chambers."

Cabral spoke quietly. "I believe you're right, Your Grace. It was both a failed device and only a warning. There was little smoke, and what there was did no serious hurt."

"But why would someone do this?" cried Mechella. "Who could hate us so much?"

"Not here," Arrigo said gruffly. "Come, we'll find someplace private within the Sanctia where we can talk. Cabral, attend us. Leilias, unpack some wine, Her Grace is too pale. And Otonna—washing water, at once."

"Oh, Your Grace," moaned the alcaldeyo. "This was the work of a moronno luna, no one to do with our village—you must believe this—"

"Of course we do," Mechella told him. "Go and wash the sting from your poor eyes, Maesso Birnardio. Would it be all right if we stay the night here? I'm far too upset to continue our journey as planned."

"Stay—" He pressed his fists to his tear-stained cheeks. "But we have no castello nearby, not even a proper caza. Nowhere fitting for Your Grace to place her head—"

"In Casteya last year, I slept in my carriage. Even a bed of hay in someone's barn would be more comfortable than that!"

"A barn—yes, we can do that." He started off to arrange it, caught himself, turned to bow to Mechella, again to Arrigo, and finally scurried from the Sanctia steps, wiping his eyes all the way.

"*Are* you hurt?" Arrigo asked worriedly of his wife.

"No. But we must show these good people that we don't blame them and feel safe in their village. Besides, if they catch this person, I want to ask him myself what complaint against us could make anyone do such a thing."

A short while later everyone's eyes had been rinsed as a precaution and they sat in the Sanctia schoolroom drinking wine from chipped pottery mugs. Speculation about the attack got them exactly nowhere. In Cabral's opinion, it was Tza'ab doing. Arrigo pointed out that this could be what they were intended to think. Knowledge of the *na'ar al'dushanna* was not limited to the Tza'ab, though they were the only ones cowardly enough to use it. Neither could anyone come up with a reasonable explanation of why this had occurred.

The pursuers returned to report that the culprit had utterly vanished into the hills, where he undoubtedly had a horse waiting. Of the instrument of mayhem, nothing had been found.

"So he had help," Arrigo concluded, "someone who snatched it up and thereby removed all the evidence."

"Which may mean," Zevierin said thoughtfully, "that it had some sort of identifying characteristic that would lead us back to its originator."

"Eiha, that's possible. But we'll never know."

That night Arrigo and Mechella slept in the Sanctia's best bedchamber—"best" in that it had a frayed rug on the stone floor, and a window with a silk-mesh screen to let breezes in and keep insects out, and only slightly worn linen sheets on the narrow bed. She dismissed Otonna and brushed out her own hair; he similarly released his own servant for the night and hung up his own clothes on the wooden peg at the door. She watched him from the bed, wondering what he was thinking.

"Arrigo . . . you saved my life."

Not looking at her, he said, "The damned thing wasn't deadly, Mechella."

"But you didn't know that," she murmured.

A shrug was his reply.

"What you did was very brave, and very quickly done."

"Nothing of the kind," he snapped. "What did you think, I'd take the opportunity to be rid of you?"

Her hand clenched around the silver handle of her brush. "I'm only trying to thank you. Why must you speak so cruelly?"

At last he turned, naked to the waist, and met her gaze. ~~mething~~ in his eyes softened, eased—became more like the man ~~loved~~ since girlhood. "Forgive me, 'Chella. I suppose I'm ~~by~~ this than I thought. That someone would do this— ~~een~~ so much worse—"

"You mean we might both have died." She set down the brush and extended a hand to him. "Arrigo—please hold me."

A shard of the old wry humor touched his mouth. "Carrida, that bed's so narrow it's either hold each other or fall on the floor!"

⚷

"Did you hear, Premio Dioniso? Did you?" Rafeyo burst into the atelierro, glowing with excitement.

"You're shouting, how could I fail to hear? But I assume you mean what happened three days ago."

"You really *do* know everything, don't you?"

But admiration for Dioniso's sources of information was short-lived; Rafeyo went on to babble at tedious length about Arrigo's courage, quick wits, and steely determination to find those responsible for this outrage. Dioniso wondered when—or if—Rafeyo would consider that this bravery of Arrigo's had as its result an uninjured Mechella. Perhaps he would also figure out that the instinct prompting Arrigo's actions revealed much about feelings he still cherished for the mother of his children, if not for his wife.

Eventually the boy ran out of praise, and they began the day's lesson. As he watched a series of meaningful flowers take shape in Rafeyo's sketchbook, he idly added up years. It might not be much longer before he could cast off these forty-five-year-old bones that despite his care of them were beginning to ache. Maybe he could find an excuse to be at Corasson this summer; the heat would soothe him, and he could surely find a few ways to discredit Mechella.

Her favor was no longer his object. With Tazia's star once more ascendant and her son his choice for his next life, he would be a fool indeed to assist Mechella in any fashion, direct or indirect. She was, quite simply, of no importance whatsoever.

The *na'ar al'dushanna* had been a calculated risk—would Arrigo act the hero?—but it had been impossible to let the Qal Venommo go unanswered. Dioniso had too much invested by now in Rafeyo as the next Lord Limner, and by extension in Arrigo as the next Grand Duke with Tazia as his Mistress, his Nazha Coronna. Their self-evident schemes for power dovetailed as sweetly with his own as the four sides of a well-constructed frame.

Thus Dioniso couldn't afford to have Arrigo look the fool, as the Qal Venommo had depicted him. Thus the frightening but harmless little incident of "fire and smoke," perpetrated by a couple of camponessos paid and painted into treachery. The formula had been taken from the *Kita'ab,* mixed in his atelierro above the wine shop;

he'd forgotten how much fun it was to blend things other than
paint. And the long, stuffy day of waiting for the compound to gel
had allowed him to select the perfect spot for Rafeyo in the
Peintraddo Memorrio.

Eiha, Dioniso's lot was cast with Rafeyo and Tazia and Arrigo.
He wished Mechella no harm, but recognized now that she had always been and always would be utterly useless to him.

FORTY-NINE

Investigation of the incident near Dregez proved fruitless. Grand Duke Cossimio was heard to curse without repeating himself for a full twenty minutes, and then flatly forbade the autumn tour of Elleon.

"But we *have* to go!" Mechella fretted, pacing her sitting room at Corasson. As was now usual, Grijalvas surrounded her. Leilias sat by the window, blending little vials of perfume; Cabral lounged in a chair, working on sketches; Zevierin stood at an easel, painting magic into Lissina's *Will*. None of them appeared to be paying the slightest attention to Mechella.

"Doesn't anybody see it but me?" she exclaimed. "How will the people of Elleon feel when they're slighted?"

"They'll understand," Cabral said absently, trading one pencil for another.

"They might, but *I* don't!" she declared, and swept from the room to lodge another complaint with Gizella.

As the door slammed behind her, Zevierin put down his brush. "What *I* see," he murmured, "is the hope in her eyes."

Leilias nodded. "When Arrigo is away from Tazia, he begins to remember why he used to love Mechella."

"Indeed. I'm surprised she's not with child again."

"Eiha, it was only those last few nights on the way home to Meya Suerta. The question is, is it for the best to bring them back together? Could they be happy if Tazia was gone from their lives? Would he forget her?"

"I wouldn't bet the Palasso on it," Zevierin told her. "One must take into account the acclaim Mechella receives in all quarters. That wears on his nerves. Although his recent heroism has done wonders for his sore pride—and his standing among the common folk, who praise him constantly for saving their Dolcha 'Chellita."

"The trip to Elleon could include a stay at Caterrine," Leilias mused. "To remind him how happy they were in those first months of their marriage."

"And possibly result in a third child. Yes. But they've got to come back to Meya Suerta eventually, you know—where Tazia will be waiting."

"But if she were packed off to Castello Alva—"

Zevierin began to put away his paints, potent with magic. "Perhaps, but there's the matter of Rafeyo. He's well on the way to becoming the next Lord Limner—may the Mother give Mequel another ten years! Dioniso sings Rafeyo to the skies, his work is excellent—"

Her lips curled in disgust. "And Rafeyo lets everyone know it, too!"

"He wouldn't take kindly to any efforts to paint his mother out of the picture. And you *can* bet the Palasso that once he's Lord Limner, he and Arrigo will return her officially and permanently to Court."

"So it will start all over again." Leilias turned a baleful eye on her brother. "Have you nothing to say about this?"

"Nothing." He continued to ply colored pencils on paper.

"You're supposed to be clever—Mother always says so, at any rate. Can't you see a way out of this?"

Cabral sprang to his feet. "You, Zevi, Mechella—all you do is *see*. You don't *hear*." So saying, he slid the sketch into a leather portfolio—Ghillasian green, a birthday gift from Mechella—and stalked from the room.

Leilias found her voice again after a couple of minutes. "What did *that* mean?"

Zevierin did not reply. Assiduously cleaning brushes, he watched his hands wipe many-colored magic saturated with his blood onto a cloth that later he would soak with the brushes in a huge tub of water. Once, while still an estudo, he forgot to warm the water first, and the shock of icy cold through his veins sent him shivering to bed for two days. The tub of water would be poured down a sink, drain into the river, and eventually find its way to the sea. He wondered idly how many minuscule particles of Grijalva magic yet clung to rocks and mud and plants along the way, how much of it drifted in the endless depths of the Agua Serenissa and the Marro Mallica. . . .

"Zevi! Answer me!"

"Hmm? Oh." He turned to her, wishing he could paint himself brave enough to tell her he loved her. The hell of it was that marriage to him would be a perfect solution for her no matter what she felt about him. He was a sterile Limner who could never give her a child. When Mechella took her into her household, the family had stopped pressuring Leilias to become a wife and mother. But they'd start their demands again soon. She was twenty-three, well past the usual age for marriage and children, and every Grijalva woman was expected to contribute at least one baby to the family line. He knew how Leilias felt about becoming a Grijalva brood mare. But he didn't want her to marry him to escape that. He wanted . . . what he could never reveal to her. Ever.

"Leilias," he said quietly, "what Cabral hears and we do not is, I think, something I just said. About painting Tazia out of the picture."

A wax-sealed vial slipped from her fingers and rolled across the carpet. It occurred to him that with her knowledge of scents, she would make the perfect Limner's wife. Odd that he'd never thought of that before.

"You can't be serious," she breathed. "Cabral couldn't have meant—"

"Both of you know about the magic now. I've broken every oath a Limner swears by telling you. Hasn't it crossed your mind that it could be done?"

She shook her head so vehemently that her hair came loose from its pins. "Nobody has that much power, nobody!"

"I do," he said bleakly.

"But—Zevi—"

"It's in that painting, as long as I'm alive." He gestured at the *Will,* almost finished on the easel. "I'm twenty-five. Lissina's seventy-one. She—" He paused as Leilias' eyes widened in disbelief. "Didn't you know she was that old? It's one of the ironies of being a Grijalva that our women so often look much younger than they are and live to be ninety, while our Limners are old at forty and usually dead before fifty. Lissina doesn't know about the magic, and you say she showed no interest in hearing even the most rudimentary of explanations."

"She sounded as if it frightened her. She said she didn't *want* to know."

He shrugged. "It's an attitude encouraged by the Viehos Fratos. Not everyone has your consuming curiosity. The point is, it's a fair bet that I'll outlive Lissina and this painting will be binding and there's nothing anyone can do about it. But lingua oscurra—these runes around the edges—will enforce the magic even if I predecease her. Which is possible, of course. And *that* is how much power any one Limner possesses, Leilias."

She leaped to her feet and stood shaking at the window. Zevierin wanted to paint her just as she looked in that moment:

black hair wild around her shoulders, the lines of her slim, strong body revealed by sunlight through the thin yellow silk of her dress.

When she spoke, there were tears in her voice. "Don't talk about dying, Zevi, I can't bear it. And don't talk about painting something terrible happening to Tazia—it's horrible—nobody should have that much power."

"No more will be said of it," he assured her. "Cabral might want to, and I wouldn't blame him if he did. But in an odd way, he can feel safe in the wanting, because he's not a Limner and he can't *do* anything about it."

"Neither could you," she whispered. "Even though you hate Tazia as much as we do, you could never—"

Unsure if she said this because she believed it or because she needed to hear him confirm it, he told her, "I could make an excellent case for it, but I would never do it."

"I know that. But what of Rafeyo?"

Zevierin shook his head. "There are reasons why he will never—"

"What could keep him from doing anything he wants to Mechella once he learns enough about being a Limner?"

He hesitated, then told himself it was as easy to be pricked for a painting as a sketch. "There's something else Limners are forbidden to speak of, and please don't share this part of it with your brother."

And he told her about the deepest of all Grijalva secrets: the *Peintraddo Chieva,* the self-portrait reeking of blood and magic that every Limner painted as his master's piece. She heard it with fear and dawning comprehension and a horrified fascination, and a look on her face that chilled him to the heart.

"Rafeyo won't really know what he's painting when he paints it," Zevierin said. "None of us do. The demonstration of its power is . . . convincing. All magical paintings are ordered and sanctioned by the Fratos—"

She shook herself. "Or the Lord Limner, which is what Rafeyo will be."

"Even Mequel answers to the Fratos. All Lord Limners do. If Rafeyo did anything, they'd know it by its magic and act accordingly to punish him."

Some of the tension left her body. "Then Mechella is safe. Rafeyo doesn't know how to do such things yet, and by the time he discovers his real power, his *Peintraddo Chieva* will exist as a threat to prevent him from harming her."

"Even if he lacks morals or ethics—and I suspect he does—the threat will suffice." The memory of pinpricks sending agony through his shoulder was thrust away. "Believe me, it will suffice."

Leilias pounded a clenched fist against the table. "I wish I *had* gotten pregnant by him!"

Strange how his mind kept working even though the shock of it seemed to stop his heart and breath.

Of course Zevierin knew she'd been called for a Confirmattio. Of course he knew that. And of course Rafeyo had undergone the test. Zevierin had simply never matched up the dates before. Or perhaps he had, and deliberately forgotten.

Rafeyo had slept beside Leilias. Rafeyo had made love to her—no, he told himself savagely, Rafeyo had used her body to prove his own magic, blind to the greater magic of her soul.

"Pregnant?" He made himself smile. "With Tazia's grandchild?"

Leilias gave a shudder. "Matra, what a repulsive idea! I should've just strangled him when I had the chance, and been done with it."

"There's a thought," he agreed.

Cossimio made it a Grand Ducal Command: Mechella was not to set foot in Elleon without his express permission. Faced with this edict, she could only bow her head over her unopened morning letters and obey.

After his witnesses—his Grand Duchess and his Lord Limner—departed Corasson's breakfast room to read their own correspondence, Cossimio said, "I'm sorry to be so severe, gattina. But I know you by now. Anything less than a direct order, you'd wriggle your way around it. Not that I disapprove of your spirit! But don't begrudge me your safety, carrida."

"You're sweet to worry. Perhaps we can go in the spring."

His booming laugh rattled the crystal. "If not, there'll be open rebellion in Elleon! I told you Tira Virte would love you, didn't I? The very first night I saw you. None of us can do without you. Not me or 'Zella or the children or Arrigo—did I tell you his letter says he'll be here in just a few days?"

"Will he? I haven't heard from him."

"Eiha, I've probably just ruined a surprise. That's a Grand Duke for you—can't keep a single secret that's not his own! You'll be sure to be properly astounded, won't you, gattina?"

Mechella smiled; Cossimio was hard to resist. Certainly Gizella found him so—this summer, as last summer at Corasson, they behaved like young lovers.

After a pleasant morning in the gardens, with the Grijalvas painting what they pleased and the do'Verradas doing nothing more strenuous than turning pages in books, everyone retired to nap away the midday heat. Then Otonna came to Mechella's chamber, waving a letter of her own.

"Beyond amazing, that's what my sister writes—but it's the truth all the same, that woman and her husband and all their sons are on their way to Castello Alva—including that merditto Rafeyo! And Don Arrigo's bringing them here! To Corasson!"

Sick with shock, Mechella shrank into a cool pillow. Here, he was bringing that woman here. "He can't," she whispered. "He *can't*."

What a fool she had been. His instinct to protect her from danger. Those few sweet days—and especially nights—of the journey back to Meya Suerta. His regret that he must stay at the Palasso for a little while. His promises that he would very soon join the family at Corasson, promise after promise all summer long. But very soon it would be Luna Qamho, and the first wheat shorn and sheaved. Lies, all of his words were lies.

Arrigo *lived* a lie.

Gizella had long ago counseled accepting that woman at Court. But that woman was no Lissina. Lizia had suggested several alternatives—and Mechella's own instincts had almost blindly directed her to the path she must follow. Her own life, her own place, her own power.

"No," she said softly, and Otonna halted in the middle of her bitter maledictions. "She will not set foot here. Not in Corasson."

"Your Grace?"

Wonderful, really—how easy it made everything, how calm she felt now that she knew. Glancing at the slack-jawed maid, she smiled. "If I have to tear it down stone by stone and set fire to every stick and stitch with my own hands, that woman will never get so much as a glimpse of my Corasson."

Otonna was speechless. A historic occasion; Cabral or Zevierin ought to commemorate it with a painting. But Mechella's Grijalvas had decided to roam the countryside after luncheon, the painters seeking landscapes to render for the new drawing-room mural, Leilias seeking flowers for her perfumes. Mechella wished for evening, when they would return and tell her what to do, how to keep that woman from crossing the threshold of her beloved Corasson.

No. Her own life, her own place, her own power. Corasson was her beginning. She owned it, loved it, had made it her true home. It was Arrigo's tragedy that he preferred to live a lie with that woman rather than a true life with her.

She remembered the tall, handsome, charming young man she had first loved. Fifteen, she'd been: lanky and clumsy and adoring. She could see herself and him as clearly as if a Limner's brush had painted them both and the portrait was right before her. And when he'd returned to the Palaisso Millia Luminnai, and kissed her in the moonlit garden—she could see that, too, from the sparkle of his epalettos to the coronet of a Princess of Ghillas that bound her hair. At Caterrine, at Palasso Verrada, at village fairs and guildhalls and ceremonies in the Cathedral Imagos Brilliantos; so many images of herself and him.

And none of them real.

Only one painted picture existed of the two of them together: a blond girl in a white bridal gown, a dark man in a green Shagarra uniform, newly handfast and full of confidence that they would be happy.

Who knew but what they might have been. She had fallen in love with Arrigo twice, once when she met him and once when she married him. Now she wondered why. And if he had ever loved her at all. It seemed stunningly appropriate that she had ordered Dioniso to paint her into the *Marriage* before Arrigo had even arrived in Ghillas; hers had been the heart-whole commitment, hers the eagerness to make a marriage. Now that marriage was no more than paint and perhaps a few stray fibers from a brush on canvas. Not even a Grijalva Limner could bring to life the seeming when there was no substance.

It hurt. She could not pretend it didn't. Something in her whispered that if only he would send that woman far away and make amends, she would forgive all and try once more to be happy.

But whatever he might do or say, she didn't think she could fall in love with him again. Not again.

"Your Grace," Otonna finally managed, "how can she be kept away? She comes with him and with her husband. To turn her away would be to insult them all."

"I don't know yet. Leave me now, I have to think."

"Three days it will be before she arrives like the Nerro Lingua—"

"I know that! Don't you think I know that? There must be some way to keep her out!" Hearing her voice rise, she took several calming breaths. "Go, Otonna. I need to think."

Arrigo and his party were delayed several days at a Sanctia when Garlo do'Alva's middle son announced with staggering suddenness that he intended to dedicate his life to the Ecclesia.

Verradio, eighteen and legally able to make his own decisions, gave his worldly goods to his two brothers and his servants, donned the coarse brown robe of a noviciato, and refused to leave his cell no matter what his father threatened. Horrified and furious, Garlo tried everything short of forcible entry and kidnap, refraining only because Tazia pleaded Verradio's cause.

Arrigo, observing all this with a mixture of amusement and amazement, was confounded by Tazia's eloquence in the young man's defense. As a second wife who would never bear a child of Garlo's blood and whose own son had no claim on the do'Alva fortunes, she could have no personal interest in Verradio's relinquishing his inheritance. The resident sancto, though grudging as all Ecclesials were to credit a Grijalva with any finer feelings, approved her championship of the young man.

What Tazia could have told Arrigo—and didn't—was that Verradio had presented her with a simple choice: support him against his father's wrath, or see draft copies of her letters to Arrigo published in every city, town, village, and hamlet in Tira Virte.

The night before he announced his entry into Ecclesial life he invited her to a private conference in the Sanctia's shabby little herb garden and showed her a damning sample. It was a page of lascivious praise for Arrigo's most personal attributes, much crossed-out and reworked until the effect of uncontrived passion was perfected.

"The Qal Venommo in Granidia will be nothing to this. Arrigo and my father will recognize your handwriting, even if they deny publicly that you wrote it. What will Arrigo think when he finds you must *practice* your 'spontaneous' love letters?"

Tazia sat down very hard on a stone bench, the garden spinning around her.

Verradio grinned. "None of you care what Mechella thinks— en verro, nor do I—but the people adore her. If this and its little friends are published. . . ." Verradio tucked the page into his tunic. "You really ought to burn such things. You never know who might come across them in the trash—accidentally, of course."

"Merditto!" Tazia spat. "Prodding through the garbage like a chiros!"

"You'd know about offal, wouldn't you, Tazia? Your every footstep stirs up more of it, your every breath is poisoned."

"I know you hate me," she said dismissively. "But how can you do this to your father?"

"I don't just hate you. I loathe you. I despise you. I curse the day my father wed you—and I curse him for shaming the do'Alva name by taking a whore to wife. I hope to cleanse myself of such feelings here in the bosom of the Sanctia, without your daily presence to remind me of how deeply I abhor the very sound of your name."

She rose, paced the broken stones of the walk, wrung her hands together. "If I take your part in this, Garlo will never forgive me!"

"Probably not." Verradio laughed. "But think how much good you'll do yourself and your family with the Ecclesia!"

Garlo allowed his second son to enter the Sanctia. He had no choice, but acted as if he did. His other sons, Zandor and Diegan, pretended solemnity as they rode out the gates, but secretly rejoiced in their brother's triumph—and envied him his escape. Tazia kept her mouth shut and her eyes downcast, lest she give way to fury. Rafeyo, in whom his mother had confided, added Garlo and Verradio to his list of persons to be dealt with once he was Lord Limner. Arrigo thought the whole incident absurd, but in deference to everyone's feelings kept his opinion to himself. They had lost four days on the journey to Corasson, and he was eager to arrive— eager to compel Mechella and Cossimio and Gizella and all the rest to accept Tazia into the family as Lissina had been accepted long ago.

One day's ride from Corasson they were met by a courier sent to inform them that the whole family was in mourning. Word had come to Mechella only yesterday that her father was dead. Arrigo immediately galloped off with a few guards, wanting to reach Corasson as swiftly as possible. Garlo and Tazia were left to decide for themselves whether or not they wished to intrude on the family's grief. Arrigo didn't phrase it that way, of course, but it was clear that on this journey to Castello Alva, the Countess would not have the pleasure of forcing Mechella to receive her. Just as clear was Arrigo's disappointment that his little ploy to bring his Mistress to his wife's official notice had failed.

Tazia was furious with Verradio for tricking her, and furious with Garlo for behaving as if she did not exist, and furious above all with Mechella's moronno father for dying. Eiha, this chance had been lost, but a time was fast approaching when Mechella would count for nothing in Tira Virte. The people could adore her all they liked. What mattered was that Arrigo adored Tazia. She resigned herself to circumstances and resolved to use these weeks to work her way back into Garlo's good graces. Damn Verradio—and damn King Enrei!

Garlo composed a formal letter of condolence over his and Tazia's signatures, delivered by his eldest son Zandor and, at Tazia's insistence, Rafeyo. The reply that eventually reached Castello Alva was addressed to the Count alone, written and signed by Leilias Grijalva "for Dona Mechella." The slight was deliberate—Garlo was an important man, distantly related to the do'Verradas—and he knew precisely whom to thank for the insult and why. Tazia returned to the sodden summer heat of Meya Suerta soon thereafter, alone.

Relations between Arrigo and Mechella were even worse. She refused to see him when he arrived. She refused to see him the next day. At last he ordered Otonna to unlock the door and stand aside. She did, eyes narrowed, saying, "You'll recall it later that I warned you."

Alone with his wife in her bedchamber, Arrigo took a few steps toward the velurro sofa where she sat hunched and miserable. Lissina had told him she'd been weeping for days. She looked it. Her golden hair was snarled and unwashed; as she looked up at him, he saw that her blue eyes were swollen with tears.

Gently, with compassion for her grief—for he'd liked Enrei and one day his own father would die—he said, "I'm so sorry about your father. I share your sorrow. He was a good man."

"Don't speak to me in cliches," she whispered. "Don't speak to me at all."

" 'Chella—"

Her voice was barely audible, as if grief had crushed the breath from her. "How dare you talk of my father? You promised him you would make his daughter happy."

"Mechella, you're overwrought. This is a terrible loss, I know."

"You betrayed him, you betrayed me. How could you even *think* of bringing that woman here?"

Arrigo took a few steps toward her. "Carrida, let me hold you."

"Aren't there beds enough in Meya Suerta? Or did you want the thrill of mounting your whore in your wife's own house?"

Leashing his temper, he said, "The pain of your loss is very great, but I can't allow you to speak that way about the Countess do'Alva."

"What you can or cannot allow has no meaning in my house. Get out."

"Don't be ridiculous. I'm your husband."

"No." She rose slowly, shaking hands fisted in wrinkled black skirts. Her lips curled back from her teeth and she said, "No, you're only the man I married, who got children on me."

"Mechella, I came to console you."

"You came because *not* to come would show the world what you truly are!" Anger gave her breath and bearing. She flung her hair back over her shoulder and glared. "Get out, Arrigo. Don't ever come to Corasson again—unless you *want* everyone to see you turned away at the door!"

"You wouldn't dare!"

"Try it, and find out!"

Arrigo tried once more. "You're too upset now to make sense. I'll come back when—"

"If you come back, I'll have my Shagarrans throw you out!"

He laughed. "I'm their *captain,* Mechella!"

"And *I'm* the one they love and serve!"

His temper slipped its chain. "And this love no doubt includes servicing you in bed!"

She neither flinched nor gasped; she laughed at him. "Grazzo for the suggestion! Any three of them would be more use to me sound asleep than you ever were wide awake!"

Arrigo crossed the room in three long strides, reaching for her.

"Touch me and I'll scream," she hissed.

Calling on every scrap of self-control that had ever kept private turmoil from public exhibition, he said, "I recall a night not long ago when you *begged* me to hold you. I tell you now, Mechella, I'd rather lie down in a trough of Plague-ridden vomit."

"Get out!"

"Gladly." He pivoted on one heel and strode to the door. With his hand on the crystal knob, he turned to look at her one last time. "I never loved you, Mechella. I married you only because my father commanded it. I bedded you wishing you were Tazia. And when my father is dead and I am Grand Duke of Tira Virte, only one door at Palasso Verrada will open to you: the door to the sewers. Dolcho nocto, Mechella—ei dolcha viva en Corasson, for you'll live the rest of your days here alone."

"In a hovel, rather than with you! But not alone, Arrigo—not alone, I assure you!"

"En verro?" He smiled. "And what will all your adoring people think, when their Dolcha 'Chellita acts the whore?"

⊷⊶ FIFTY ⊷⊶

Cossimio and Gizella took the children back to Palasso Verrada a few days later. Lissina lingered just long enough for Zevierin to complete her *Will*—still a secret from everyone but him and Leilias and Cabral and Mechella—then took her leave with much cautionary advice to her kinswoman about protecting Mechella's health in this time of her grief.

"They mourn differently in Ghillas," Lissina said on the front steps, drawing on her gloves as the carriage rolled toward her. "King Enrei will have a state funeral and all his Court will be in mourning for a full half-year. Mechella will grieve long after that, of course, but it's worst for her right now. And we allow only a few days of private sorrow here in Tira Virte, so people will say she's overindulgent if she shuts herself away at Corasson, but I suppose that can't be helped."

Leilias nodded politely, wondering what Lissina could know about grief. In her soft brown eyes was compassion for Mechella's pain, but at well past seventy, her face had fewer lines than Lord Limner Mequel's. Hers was not a face meant for suffering; recalling the outlines of her life, Leilias decided that suffering had recognized this and passed her by.

But a moment later she was thoroughly ashamed of herself as Lissina gave a quiet sigh and murmured, "I remember when my Reycarro died . . . six days later I had to attend a ball for the King of Taglis, when I could barely lift my head from my pillow. . . ." She swallowed hard and shook her scarcely grayed head. "Eiha, that's a long time ago. You must see to Mechella's welfare, Leilias. Write to me and I'll come at once if you think I can be of any help."

Later, Zevierin sat beside Leilias in Mechella's private salon, listening to the silence. At length, he said, "It's not just the death of her father she's mourning."

"One minute she weeps like a child, and the next like a woman whose heart has broken. It's over, Zevi. For Mechella and Arrigo, there's no hope."

He reached for her hand, holding it to his heart. "I feel so guilty. For us, it's only begun."

"I know. It's terrible to be so happy when she's—I've been try-

ing to find the right time to tell her about us. To give her something
she can be glad of for a little while. She's trying to get used to losing her father and her husband while I'm try to get used to having
everything."

"Are you certain you want me?" he murmured. "I still can't believe it—when you came to my room the night before we heard
about King Enrei, I—"

"Don't babble, Zevi," she scolded fondly. "I'm certain that I've
always wanted to be able to love someone. I'm just not certain why
it should be you!"

"Be serious," he urged. "I need to know, Leilias. In twenty years
I'll be forty-five, and old."

"So? In twenty years I may be a grandmother." Wrapping her
arms around his waist, she leaned against him and teased, "Does
the thought of making love to a grandmother horrify you?"

A few breathless minutes later, he sternly forbade himself her
lips long enough to ask. "Are you certain about children?"

She laughed low in her throat. "I thought you'd topple like a
pine tree when I told you I want babies. What do you think, am I
too old for a Confirmattio?"

"Leilias," he warned.

She made a face. "Oh, very well. Serious. The difference is that
it's not the Viehos Fratos ordering me to have children, it's *my*
choice. But only if you'll be their father."

"In heart and in spirit and even in blood, I'll never think of your
children as anything but mine," he vowed.

"I'll pick somebody kind and clever and talented, somebody
who looks like you." She nuzzled his cheek. "Mechella told me
when we were in Dregez that one day I'd understand about wanting to be a mother. She didn't know that for me, it came because I
want so much for you to be a father."

"I wish—"

"No, don't." She stopped his words with a finger on his lips.
"You can't, you're a Limner. Maybe our sons will be, too. But let's
wish for the things we know we can have—things like being happy
for the rest of our lives."

"A certainty," he said, tightening his embrace. "We're going to
be completely, wildly happy."

Leilias laughed. "Insanely happy!"

"Nauseatingly, by the sound of it," Cabral remarked from the
doorway. "Do shut up, both of you, before I lose my breakfast.
Zevi, unhand my sister. Leilias, try to stop pawing him for a mo-

ment. Mechella wants us. Otonna said she asked if everyone was finally gone, then said she'd meet us in the rose garden."

They waited for her in the morning sunshine, the first crisp breeze of autumn rustling the oaks. Green lawns spread to rose-covered walls, laced by beds of white and yellow roses at their fullest bloom. The fragrance was exquisite—and so was Mechella as she glided across the grass. Her simple gray silk dress was of the drop-waisted Pracanzan fashion, her bright hair in a single braid over her left shoulder. Days ago she had told Otonna to throw out every single stitch of clothing that held even a hint of the deep do'Verrada sapphire blue.

They rose from their chairs to greet her. She sat down below a trellis festooned with white roses, folded her hands in her lap, and addressed them as formally as if they were conselhos in conference.

"I apologize for interrupting your morning. I've come to some decisions that I wish to share with you. First, my father's funeral took place mere days after his death, so there was never any question of my going to Aute-Ghillas to attend. But I *will* be going to my brother's coronation after the half-year of mourning is completed. Grand Duke Cossimio has agreed to my request. I will be his sole representative and will go alone—that is, with a large escort of my Shagarrans but without Don Arrigo or the children. I expect that a few Grijalvas will accompany me as well, but that can be arranged at a later date."

She paused for breath, and smoothed her skirts over her knees. "Secondly, except for state occasions when my presence is required, I will no longer live at Palasso Verrada. My children will stay here with me until such time as they're old enough to take their places at Court. The Grand Duke allows this—though he thinks my withdrawal to be temporary. He and the Grand Duchess are welcome at any time to Corasson, of course—and the Countess do'Casteya and the Baroness do'Dregez. But if Don Arrigo attempts to enter, my Shagarrans have orders to remove him."

The Grijalvas kept their faces perfectly still. Mechella's tiny smile indicated that she noted this before she composed herself again and continued.

"Of the nobility, those who are welcome will know it. Those who are not will have the decency to stay away. Which brings me to you. Each of you must decide without thinking of anyone but yourselves whether or not you wish to stay here with me." Cabral surged to his feet; Mechella lifted a graceful hand. "No, don't say anything yet, hear me out. I want you here. But I also want you to understand that Corasson will be a Shadow Court at best. There will be no real power or influence until Alessio is much older. To that end, I would appreciate any advice you can give me about tutors for him and for Teressa, and people to include in the households I'll establish for them in a few years, and those who can advise me about political matters. I—"

"Stop it!" Leilias burst out. "You're not reading a speech—"

"En verro, I am," Mechella admitted. "I practiced it all day yesterday. It was the only way I could get through it. Let me finish, Leilias, and then you can take me to task for treating my friends like strangers."

Zevierin shook his head. "If you're going to insult us again, I'd rather not hear the rest. As if we wouldn't stay here with you!"

"I knew you'd say that," Mechella told him with a faint smile. "There's not much more. I was about to say that I trust you to recommend people I need to educate my children and myself. I also want to know who among the nobles, conselhos, merchants, and Grijalvas I can count on as friends—and especially I want to know who my enemies are." She paused and sighed. "I've been childish about many things. Instead of spending these last three years— Matra, nearly four!—learning the ways of Court, I thought my husband would guide and protect me. I was wrong," she finished simply. "I need your help."

Leilias slid from her chair to kneel at Mechella's feet. "You have it. You know that. Whatever you need, whatever any of us can do—"

"Get up at once!" Mechella scolded fondly. "I hope you know what you're doing, Zevierin, by marrying so much fire and passion!" They gaped at her; she laughed softly. "Did you think me sunk so deep in my own troubles that I'd be blind to my dearest friends? Even though you tried to hide it—for shame, trying to fool me! Do get up, Leilias, and let me hear from Zevierin and Cabral."

"You know my answer," Zevierin said.

"And mine," Cabral grated, turned on his heel, and strode off.

"Eiha," Mechella sighed. "Now I've offended him. You Grijalvas—more prideful than kings!"

By custom, foreign rulers were gifted with a painting commemorating their accession. Because the new King of Ghillas was

Mechella's brother, Dioniso proposed and the Viehos Fratos agreed on two pictures: one official, one personal. The former would be on display in some useful room—a council chamber, for instance—and the latter would probably end up somewhere in the new King's private suite. Both paintings would be steeped in symbolism all educated persons understood, and in magic known only to Grand Dukes and Grijalvas.

Dioniso, having done a portrait of Enrei III as Crown Prince, was Mequel's resource on the official painting. Pencil studies and verbal commentary on Enrei's personality were accompanied by the advice that if a horse was not prominently featured, the young King would stash the painting away someplace where it could not influence him and would do Tira Virte no good at all.

Dioniso painted the personal portrait himself, using it to teach Rafeyo several more things in advance of his fellow estudos. He also intended it as a kind of seduction into portrait painting, for Rafeyo showed an alarming preference for landscapes and architecture. This would not do at all. A Lord Limner put people in his paintings, not barns and cornfields and castellos and water mills.

The new style of landscape painting did not please Dioniso in the slightest. Low horizons with vast swaths of sky had been reversed; now the lands sprawled in marshy greens or desert golds beneath thin slices of cobalt sky. People were no longer perfect miniatures; instead, distant figures were suggested by a few swipes of color meant to convey the impression of a camponessa's full skirt, a man's dark cloak, a broad-brimmed straw hat. Worst of all, mathematical balance had been abandoned in favor of randomly scattered shapes with little relation to each other. Grijalva art must be strict in form because it must be strict in function, and Dioniso's every instinct screamed against loosening the rules with experiments that weakened the composition and therefore the magic.

Still, even the deplorable landscapes now in fashion were preferable to the execrable still-lifes. "Still" they definitively were—"life," they certainly were not. Nature had never produced such fruits and flowers as some Grijalvas were now painting: without blemish, perfectly symmetrical, and about as mouth-watering as the cold glazed ceramic they looked like. Every Limner painted dozens of still-lifes as a necessary part of his training, to learn how to place the symbolic flowers and fruit, herbs and trees, that anchored magic. But these pieces—meaningless exercises in trivia, every one of them, demonstrating nothing beyond the contrived architecture of a pile of fruit or the natural geometry of a flower.

As Premio Frato, Dioniso had influence. But he was too busy and his hands were too old to produce masterworks enough to turn his Limners from their useless meanderings in landscape and still-life. When Rafeyo became Lord Limner—a few years, no more, Mequel couldn't last forever—he would work those young, strong fingers to the bone if necessary to save Grijalva art.

But before that time came, there was a portrait to do, and he used it to fascinate Rafeyo with the possibilities. The formal painting—Mequel's first equestrian composition—contained all the usual elements. Cedars for Strength, yellow lilies for Peace, sage for Wisdom, and all the other indicators of kingly virtues. Dioniso had Rafeyo delve into more obscure symbolism from the *Folio*—Dioniso's own copy, annotated with tantalizing notes from the *Kita'ab*. One in five hundred Limners knew the old Tza'ab symbology. Careful inquiry told Dioniso that Mequel was not among them.

The Envy of a brass hand-mirror; the Folly of the blue rose; the Arrogance of a crown studded with black diamonds—of which stones there were exactly two in the known world, one of them in distant fabled Zhinna and the other on the gouty finger of the Empress of Tza'ab Rih. These symbols and more were emphasized by an unvarnished pinewood frame reeking of Magical Energy. The effective range of the painting was considerable; one could smell the pine from every corner of Dioniso's large atelierro in Palasso Grijalva.

The painting itself was a unique triple portrait: full-face in the center, right and left three-quarter profiles on either side. The unusual study was something Dioniso had been contemplating for a long time, and was a permissible experiment. Wherever it was hung, whichever way young Enrei faced, the magic would influence him. Left side Envy, Anger, and Pettiness; right side Folly, Arrogance, Stubbornness, and Inconstancy.

"Matra!" grinned Rafeyo. "If he paces back and forth, he'll go mad with confusion! But what if he looks at it straight on?"

Dioniso only smiled.

One morning Rafeyo arrived in the atelierro to find a sheaf of mingled wheat and hawthorn painted upside down over Enrei's handsome head. Tying these symbols of Wealth and Fertility was a white ribbon. The boy turned to the master, one finger pointing an accusation at the painting.

"You just gave him all the personal riches and all the children he could ever want!"

Dioniso laughed. "Look closer at the ribbon, and tell me what you see."

Rafeyo squinted. "Edged in silver at the top, gold at the bottom . . . triple knot tying the sheaf together—but the highlights are all wrong."

"Possibly because they're not highlights," he responded dryly. "They are runes, the lingua oscurra, barely discernible as such. I'll translate—these don't appear in the standard glossary. 'Thrice casting/Bind lasting/Ribbon's reach/Cancels each.' Note that the ribbon frames Enrei's head and drops below his shoulders."

"Then—" Rafeyo frowned. "You mean it cancels all his riches and his children?"

"At the very least it will make both more difficult to come by."

What Dioniso did not say was that by painting Enrei as close to sterile as he could without the essential materials to hand, he had done everything possible to make Mechella's children her brother's only legitimate heirs. The advantages to Tira Virte of a do'Verrada on the Ghillasian throne were many and manifold. But Rafeyo, loathing Mechella, would not see them. He was much too young and too ignorant of politics to look beyond his hatred of the woman who had tried to take his adored mother's place.

The boy's face had lit like a torch. "You're not just a master— you're a genius!"

En verro, he would miss this boy. . . .

"Jonino's nephew is wasted doing the bookkeeping for the copper mines." Leilias scrawled a notation onto the lengthening list of persons suitable for Mechella's new household.

"Jonino?" Zevierin asked. "Oh—your stepfather. What will he think of a Grijalva in the family?"

"Moronno, he *married* one, didn't he? Why shouldn't I?" She chewed the end of her pen, grinning at him. "You're nervous about meeting my parents, aren't you?"

"Not in the least."

"Liar. The nephew—what *is* his name? Eiha, never mind. Anyway, he plays the gamba, and his wife's not half bad on the gittern, if I recall. So there's our mathematics tutor and bookkeeper for the estate, plus two music teachers! Now, what's left?"

"Languages and religion." Zevierin tapped a fingernail on the desktop, staring out the window with a smile; he'd caught sight of Mechella and Cabral on their usual daily walk, and they were walking much closer together than usual. "I think I know where we can get both in one person. Do you remember old Davinio?"

"The groundskeeper at Palasso Grijalva? Never tell me he's a linguist *or* an Ecclesial!"

"No, but his grandson turned out to be both. Sancto Leo is a fairly good friend of mine, in fact. We debate the damnation of the Grijalvas on occasion."

Leilias drew back, aghast. "You'd bring a prating, self-righteous, Grijalva-hating sancto to Corasson?"

"You misunderstand." He laughed at her. "*I'm* the one who takes the high moral position, while young Sancto Leo defends us despicable Grijalvas. Does a good job of it, too. I'll introduce you when next we're in Meya Suerta—for Penitenssia, I assume? Or is Mechella determined to stay here all winter?"

She was so determined, failing a direct order from Cossimio. She said as much to Cabral as they hiked back up to the house through the stubbled fields of the home farm. Iluminarres approached, when fires were lit in the shorn cropland to summon rain in preparation for renewed fertility. The wind was growing colder, the days shorter, but Corasson lay ahead of them up the hill. Home.

"I'm hoping Countess Lizia will stay a few weeks on her way south," Mechella said. "And the Brendizias have promised to ride over for Imago, so we'll have to plan something special." She paused as they reached a fence. "Why are you smiling?"

"Because you are. Didn't you know?"

"Sometimes it feels like it, but. . . ." She shrugged. "Help me up."

He lifted her to the top rail. She swung around to face Corasson, giving him a swift view of wool stockings and stout shoes caked in rich earth. He climbed up beside her, thinking wryly of the delicate silks and sumptuous velurros of her Court clothes. Pulling from his jacket pocket the notepad and pencil no

Grijalva ever lacked, he began to draw Corasson, backlit by the setting sun.

They sat quietly for a long while, the only sounds the scratch of his pencil, the whinnies of paddocked horses, and the chirps and whistles of passing birds. At length he cast a sidelong glance at her and grinned.

"Why do people who can't draw always look at artists that way?"

"Was I looking?" she asked. "What way?"

"As if searching for something in our faces that shows why we can do what we do. Something in our eyes, the shape of our lips—or the way we comb our hair, for all I know! As if there's some mysterious exterior physical feature that could explain interior talent." He filled in a shadow on the sketch, then chuckled. "And they *listen,* too—even if we're just talking about the weather or wondering what's for dinner."

"Chieva do'Orro," Mechella responded. "That Golden Key all the Limners wear. That's what we're looking and listening for."

"Eiha, but that secret doesn't really exist. If anyone ever did find it, he certainly wouldn't talk about it! I know I wouldn't, if I were a Limner."

"None of you would, not even Zevierin." She picked at a splinter on the wooden fence rail. "Is Leilias really going to—how did she put it, go shopping?—for a man to father her children?"

"Yes. If she and Zevi want to be parents, that's their only option."

"It's strange. But no stranger than anything else about you Grijalvas." She smiled. "If I look deeply into your eyes, and listen to every word you say for the next fifty years, would I even begin to understand how it is that you can put a few lines on paper and have them look like Corasson?"

"I fear you'd be bored in less than a minute, Dona Mechella. Whatever it is that makes me an artist, I can neither show it to you nor explain it."

"I could never be bored with you, Cabral." She smiled, adding, "When would I find the time to be bored with anything? Mequel's advice about working in spite of illness is just as appropriate for grief. If I fill up my life with other things, then I haven't time to be sad."

"Yet I see it—here, and here." He dared to brush his fingertip across the air an inch from her mouth, her brow.

She said nothing for a long moment. Then, wistfully: "Can you paint me happy, limner?"

"Mechella . . . let me try. Please let me try."

"Cabral." She took the pencil and paper, let them drop to the ground. "I think," she murmured, "that you shall not need these to do it."

←→ FIFTY-ONE ←→

At the Grand Duke's request, Mechella spent Penitenssia in Meya Suerta. Arrigo's renewed Marria do'Fantome with Tazia was no longer an open secret; it was a public scandal. Cossimio was livid, Gizella heartsick. Lissina counseled patience. From Casteya, Lizia sent her brother a letter precisely six words long: *Moronno! Have you lost your mind?* Mequel, forty-five this winter and so stiff and sore that he rarely left his chambers, tried to ignore the whole disaster. The conselhos were silent. The gossips wallowed in every detail. And everyone—privately, nervously, reluctantly—began to choose sides.

For Mechella: the common folk of Tira Virte.

For Arrigo: the bulk of the aristocracy and most of the merchant class.

For Mechella: Cabral, Leilias, Zevierin, many of the Grijalvas related to them—and Lord Limner Mequel.

For Arrigo: Premio Frato Dioniso, the Viehos Fratos, and any Grijalva connected by blood to Tazia—even her sisters, who despised her.

Mechella's fifteen-day visit for the winter holiday made the thinnest of gruel for the gossips' nourishment. She and Arrigo shared their usual suite at Palasso Verrada, performed social and religious obligations, spoke pleasantly to all, and were much seen in public with their two young children. Her radiant looks were commented upon; his attentiveness was remarked. Cossimio dared to hope. Lissina warned against it. Tazia wisely caught a cold and confined herself to her husband's fashionable caza in town. Garlo, still not on speaking terms with his wife, sent the Grand Duke a plausible if transparent excuse for staying at Castello Alva. In the absence of a command of the type given Mechella, Garlo was safe in refusing to lend the dignity of his presence to the proceedings in Meya Suerta. The year turned from 1266 to 1267, Mechella went home to Corasson, Tazia recovered from her indisposition, and Arrigo told his parents in person and his sister by letter to mind their own business.

Mechella did not appear in the capital again until the spring. When she made her entrance—unheralded, unexpected and unannounced—at the Grand Duchess' Fuega Vesperra ball, a gasp escaped every throat. Even Arrigo, turning to see what the fuss was about, looked stunned. She seemed a slender column of starfire come down from the sky at Astraventa and only now gracing them with her brilliance. Her masses of golden hair were held in place by diamond-studded hairpins. Her gown was of glowing silvery gray: daringly low at the neck, shockingly narrow in the skirt, impertinently showing her lovely ankles. Most startling of all, her arms and shoulders were entirely bare of gloves, sleeves, or indeed anything at all but for a splendid diamond necklace and bracelets. The shawl draped from her bare elbows gave off subtle glimmers of gold from a sunburst pattern of rare beauty.

She greeted everyone with brilliant smiles and charming words, but her progress through the crowd was soon seen as a straight line to her husband. When she reached his side, she laid a languid hand on his arm and whispered in his ear. His complexion changed color. He gave her a look of astonishment. She smiled, tugging gently at his sleeve. He mumbled an excuse to the Count do'Palenssia and escorted his wife from the ballroom to a location unknown—while speculation ignited in everyone from Grand Duke Cossimio to the fifth-chair gamba player.

Tazia do'Alva, dancing at the time with Premio Frato Dioniso, was seen to lose her footing. Dioniso later made it known that he had been unforgivably clumsy and stepped on her hem. No one believed him.

What Mechella whispered to Arrigo was, "Come with me this instant or I'll have Zevierin paint your portrait—with all the symptoms of sifilisso." Where she led him was to a little antechamber on the second floor, equipped with a sofa, a table, an elaborate candlebranch, a cheery little fire in the hearth, and a lock.

"Have you gone mad?" he demanded as she closed the door behind them. "What's this nonsense about paint?"

"Don't pretend you don't understand. You have your Grijalvas, carrido meyo, and I have mine. And that's where this discussion will begin."

"We have nothing to say to each other."

"I don't agree." She rubbed at her head as if her diamond-studded hairpins hurt, her fingers disarranging a few carefully scrolled curls. "Oh, that's better. Sit down, Arrigo, and listen." She tossed a few pillows on the floor, sat on the couch, carelessly bunching her silk skirts, and patted the upholstery beside her. He stood stiff-backed near the locked door. "Don't be so silly, Arrigo, I want to discuss the children."

He folded his arms, eyeing her suspiciously. "What about them?"

"You're their father, and they love you—though I'm sure I don't know why. But I won't have them hurt any more than can be helped by anything that happens between us. Therefore I propose that we share them equally."

"No."

Mechella shook her head, sighing her sadness. "You see? This is just the sort of thing I'd hoped to avoid. Matra, but that fire is warm!" She let her shawl of gold-threaded sunbursts drop to the floor. "Undo your collar, Arrigo, you must be roasting."

"I won't let you take my children—and neither will my father."

"I think he'll find my proposal fair. You may have them both during the winter here at the Palasso. They love you, and they love their grandparents and Lissina, and they must learn how to be do'Verradas. But from Sancterria to Providenssia, they'll live at Corasson. Your parents have taken to spending the summers with me, which means that almost all year they'll be seeing the children every day."

He leaned a shoulder against a tapestried wall, unhooking his collar as she'd suggested. "You could've chosen a more comfortable place for this. By the sound of it, we'll be here a while. Now, if I understand your proposal, you want the children for more than half of each year? You call that fair?"

"I'm their mother. And summers at Corasson are much healthier than in Meya Suerta. You'll have Teressa and Alessio for five months every winter and spring, Arrigo. I think that's quite fair."

"What if I don't agree. No, let me guess. You'll have Zevierin paint warts on my nose. What foolishness!"

"If you know half as much about Limners as I do, you know it's anything but foolish." She massaged her head again, dislodging more curls. When she resumed speaking, her voice rang like steel on stone. "I should mention there is a condition to this arrangement. If you allow that woman anywhere near my children, I'll take them and never give them back. For Teressa and Alessio, she does not exist. I mean this, Arrigo. If they spend a single moment in her company—"

He smiled pityingly. "And how could you possibly prevent it?"

"Oh, I won't have to. *You* will. Because you know what a Grijalva Limner is capable of."

He gave in to nervous habit and began to pace. The little carved oak table had the misfortune to get in his way; he kicked it over, kicked it again deliberately, and spun to face her. "You have your Grijalvas," he said grimly, "and I have mine."

She laughed to herself, as if at some private joke. "Yes, I have my Grijalvas. It seems we are at an impasse—except for one thing." She rose lithely and cupped her breasts in her palms. His brows shot up as she slid her hands down silvery-gray silk to her flat abdomen. And smiled.

"You—you—"

"Don't splutter, Arrigo, it's unbecoming in a future Grand Duke. Aren't you happy to know you're going to be a father again?"

"Chi'patro!" he snarled.

Another secret laugh, as if he'd said something very funny. "If by that you mean 'bastard'—eiha, not in the eyes of the world, carrido. You and I and the father—whoever he may be—are the only ones who will know otherwise."

"Who is he? Whose bastard is it, Mechella?"

Stroking her belly, she pursed her lips and gave him a sidelong glance. "No, I don't believe I'll tell you," she mused. "Just imagine it, Arrigo. You won't look at any handsome Shagarra officer or fine young nobleman again without wondering if *he* might be the one. But you'll never know who fathered this child. And the world will believe it was you."

"Impossible! You're already pregnant—"

"Do I look it?"

"Everyone knows I haven't touched you since—"

"Everyone knows we're alone together right now. How long have we been in this room, Arrigo? Ten minutes? Fifteen? Quite enough time for the necessary."

He choked on the sweetness of her smile. "No one will believe that I—"

"Won't they?" She tossed her loosened hair from her eyes, and diamond-headed pins tinkled to the floor like shards of rainbows. "Countess do'Shaarria's dear old uncle just told me I'm the loveliest woman who ever set foot in Palasso Verrada. You're only a man, Arrigo—and my husband, with a legal and sanctified right to enjoy my beauty. Who could blame you for being unable to resist me, especially after a long separation, especially after I murmured so seductively in your ear?" She laughed. "Who could look at *me* and believe you faithful to your whore? How old is she now—forty? Forty-two?"

"Tazia won't believe—"

"Do you think I care?" Mocking humor vanished and she glared at him. "What she believes is your concern, not mine. I'm twenty-six, and I won't spend the rest of my life like a cloistered Initiata in a Sanctia at the back of the beyond!"

"So you'll play the whore instead!" He went for her, grabbing her bare shoulders, shaking her until her hair fell completely from its pins and cascaded down her back. "Who is he, Mechella? *Who?*"

She wrenched away from him, breathing hard, hate and disgust seething in her eyes. "You've been to Corasson. Dozens of handsome young men—my Shagarrans, my footmen, my stable hands, my farmers—or perhaps it was a visitor, some charming nobleman or merchant—anyone at all! You can't bully it out of me, and you can't make any of my people tell you!" With both hands she raked her hair back from her face, laughing at him again. "The only one you can be absolutely certain of is Zevierin! But be certain of this, too—he's just as much mine as all the others. You'll never know who my child's father is, Arrigo! Never!"

"I won't own to your bastard! I'll deny it, denounce you—divorce you!"

"I think not. You made a fatal mistake. You forgot the people you were born to serve. They love *me*. Not you. Call me a whore and my baby a bastard, they won't believe you. Not after I walk out of this room tonight looking like this."

She let him look at her: tumbled hair and flushed cheeks, silvery skirt all wrinkles, the marks of his fingers on her bare shoulders and arms. Horrified comprehension scrawled itself across his face as his gaze flickered around the room. Strewn pillows, table upended, lace shawl on the floor by the sofa—

"They will believe *me*," Mechella said softly, maliciously. "When the time comes, you'll welcome your third child just as you did the first two. There will be no denial, Arrigo. No denouncing. No divorce."

"I will *ruin* you," he breathed in a voice that shook with loathing. "You'll never sleep another peaceful night for wondering how I'll ruin you."

"Try," she invited serenely. "You have your Grijalvas, marrido meyo—but never forget that I have mine."

She swept past him, a smile on her lips, and unlocked the door. There was a footman outside, carrying a tray of used glassware; a maid was just down the hall with an armload of fresh sheets. They would do very nicely.

"Carrido, we've been gone simply hours!" she called lightly over her shoulder. "It's terribly rude!" She paused, knowing the servants were now listening. "Is my gown done up in the back? I don't know what I'll do about my hair. Really, Arrigo, did you have to take out *all* the pins?"

She heard him choke, and laughed gaily as she started down the hall. When she neared the maid she pretended to give a start. "Oh—could you do me the most tremendous favor? When you have a moment, could you fetch my shawl? It's in that little room down the hall. I really must hurry back to the ballroom—bring it to me there. Grazzo."

The girl would see the disarray of the antechamber, draw the intended conclusion, and—with the footman to back up her story—tell every servant in the Palasso that Don Arrigo had simply been unable to keep his hands off the spectacularly beautiful Dona Mechella. By noon tomorrow all Meya Suerta would believe the tale. And that suited Mechella just fine.

She ran down the stairs, heart racing. Fifty feet from the ballroom entrance she stopped, reaction trembling through her. That she, Princess Mechella of Ghillas, could have said such things to such a purpose—and enjoyed it so thoroughly! But she was no longer that callow girl. She was Dona Mechella of Tira Virte, the next Grand Duchess, and she would say whatever was necessary to protect herself. More, she was pregnant with the child of a man who adored her, and she would do anything to protect him and their baby.

How she wished for Cabral's strong arm now! Or at least Leilias' knowing smile and a wink of encouragement. But she was alone, and must see this through on her own. The worst of it was over—for, contrary to what she'd feared, she hadn't felt the slightest pity for Arrigo at all. Let him live his chosen lies; this one she would shove down his throat.

Once again flinging her hair back, she took a deep breath and entered the ballroom. The first person she saw was Lissina, whose gaze darted once and then again to Mechella's bare shoulders, as if she had not quite believed what she saw there the first time. Lissina was too tactful to mention the reddened fingermarks, but Mechella knew what she was thinking.

What they were *all* thinking, what they could hardly avoid thinking when Arrigo returned. Red-faced, his hair disheveled, the top button of his tunic done up wrong—Mechella felt her cheeks turn crimson at the picture he presented, and was glad everyone thought her embarrassed. En verro, her face was burning because she was trying very hard not to laugh, especially when his mother adjusted his collar for him as if he were five years old. The appearance of the maid a short time later, smirking as she handed over the shawl, was the crowning touch. Mechella thanked her, glanced around as if abashed, and pulled the lace up around her shoulders.

Her immediate personal reward was a single glimpse of the Grijalva woman's face halfway across the ballroom. Stark with shock, thin-lipped with rage, she looked every one of her years and then some. Arrigo started toward the woman, was seen by her— and was instantly presented with a view of her back.

The smile Mechella gave Lissina was pure dazzlement as she said innocently, "I do hope I didn't miss the fireworks."

⊶⊷

When Cossimio and Gizella arrived at Corasson for the summer, Mechella announced the happy news.

"And at Fuega Vesperra!" The Grand Duke chortled. "The very celebration of conception! How clever of you to have arranged it, 'Chella!" he added with a broad wink.

She blushed—easy enough, recalling the true circumstances of conception—and did not correct his impression of the timing. By her own calculation, it had happened during the glistening night of Astraventa. Not that that she and Cabral had shattered Corasson's reputation of having no babies conceived beneath its roof; they'd celebrated the holiday with appropriate rusticity in a willow-veiled glade. This child was one with a special soul come from the starry sky to be nurtured in her womb. Mechella glowed as if the spark of this child lit her from within—the child of the man she loved, who genuinely loved her. The only stain on her happiness was that once her brother learned of her condition, he absolutely forbade her to attend his coronation this autumn. In his letter of congratulations he told her flat out that he would be crowned King with her or without her, his Grijalva would send her a dozen paintings of the whole lengthy ceremony, and if she thought he wouldn't order his border guards to send her home to Tira Virte, she was vastly mistaken.

> *For until I get an Heir of my own, 'Chella carridia, if the child you carry is a boy, he will be King of Ghillas after me. So stay home!*

"I just hope the baby's late when he comes and small when he does," Leilias privately told her husband. She had said the same thing at least three times a week since Mechella had told them she was pregnant.

They were out walking in the hills, collecting herbs for Leilias' perfumes—and Zevierin's paintbox. Expert botanists each, though for entirely different reasons, they learned much from each other: she from him the magical properties of the plants, he from her better ways to extract and distill their essences. She was alternately fascinated and appalled by his descriptions of how certain spells, spoken when in a certain state of mind, activated and sealed magic in a painting. One kind of flower would soak up such-and-such a magical influence while another wouldn't and a third required another set of words entirely—all of which a Limner had to memorize from the *Folio*.

Plucking up a fistful of vervain, Leilias said, "If there was only a plant I could brew up and you could spell and then we'd put it in everybody's food, so they'd believe that a baby born several weeks early *can* weigh eight pounds and have a full head of hair!"

"Stop taking the roots as well as the stems," he scolded. "You'll denude the whole forest of next year's growth. And worry about Mechella's baby when and if you must."

"*Somebody* has to worry, because Mechella certainly isn't! As for Cabral—" She snorted. "My besotted brother drifts about wearing the silliest expression I've ever seen on a human face. Swear to me, Zevi, that when I'm pregnant you won't look such a fool."

He promised solemnly, then began to laugh. "I'm sorry, I can't help it. You remember when we went to Diettro Mareia a few years ago? Mechella was pregnant then, and Rafeyo kept saying what an idiot smile Arrigo wore. I'll wager it's not on his face now!"

Some days before Cossimio and Gizella arrived, Mechella sent a letter to her husband, sweetly phrased, officially informing him that he was to be a father. It was Arrigo's bad luck that the courier—who had strict instructions to deliver the envelope to him in person wherever he might be—found him in the Grijalva's public gallery with Tazia and Rafeyo.

They were planning a special showing—*By Sun and Moon: Two Centuries of Landscape Paintings*—to provide Rafeyo with experience in the curatorial duties of the Lord Limner. Premio Dioniso was said to be quite irritated by his choice of subject.

Rafeyo was wheedling a few paintings from Arrigo when the courier was escorted into the long, narrow little Galerria. "If you'll lend us Yberro's two *Granidia Sunrise* pieces from the Audience Chamber, that will fill out his period very nicely. I'd love to have something by Riobaro, but he wasn't much for landscapes."

"You've grown so in your work," Tazia smiled, "that you could probably paint one, sign his name, and have everyone believing it was his!"

As Rafeyo rolled his eyes, Arrigo laughed. "She's your mother, it's her sacred duty to embarrass you." Nodding thanks to the courier, he glanced at the wax seal on the envelope, frowned, and tucked the letter in his pocket.

"Begging Your Grace's pardon," said the courier, "but Her Grace said to wait for a reply."

"Tell her—" He broke off. "Very well, I'll read it here."

Tazia touched her son's arm, and together they moved away, pretending interest in self-portraits of long-dead Limners currently on display. The Galerria Picca was a project initiated thirty years ago by Gizella and Lissina. Because the Verrada was closed to commoners and the Grijalva was closed to everyone but blood kin, the two ladies felt it only fair to provide the general public with a place to view their country's art. The exhibition changed every three months, drawing on the inexhaustible family collection and occasionally those pictures owned by the do'Verradas. The experience of being curatorrio to an exhibit was invaluable for the young Limners, some of whom would go on to advise foreign courts and private collectors on the subtleties of placement, lighting, and preservation.

Three mornings a week, schoolchildren were guided through the Picca by incredibly patient docents, who gave them paper and colored pencils to contribute their own "masterworks" to the Grijalva collection. Truly talented children were invited to take formal lessons, and sometimes even become limners. Three afternoons a week, the general public was admitted. And at least twice a month Limners gave evening lectures on particular paintings or artists. No visit to Meya Suerta by Tira Virteian native or touring estranjiero was complete without an afternoon at the Picca.

Tazia and Rafeyo were gazing at Riobaro's *Self-Portrait at Eighteen* when Arrigo spat out a curse. Tazia turned in time to see him fling the letter to the floor and storm from the room. The courier bent to retrieve the envelope and single page.

"Give it to me," Tazia said.

"Her Grace—"

"—will never know unless you tell her, which you won't. Give it to me."

"Regretto, Countess, I cannot."

Gently, she asked, "Do you know who I am?"

Though he kept his gaze downcast, he revealed himself by a tightening of the lips as if he'd downed unsugared lemonada. "Yes, Countess. I know who you are."

Rafeyo solved the problem by snatching the letter from his hand. A bottom corner tore; it didn't matter. There was only a brief paragraph on the top of the page, Mechella's childishly round signature halfway down.

"Grazzo," Tazia said sardonically to the courier. "I'll make sure this finds its way to Don Arrigo's desk. You may go."

Rafeyo added, "You might as well go all the way back to Corasson. I rather doubt there'll be any reply."

The man shot a swift glance of loathing at them both, and walked away.

"Impudent camponesso," Rafeyo remarked. "Eiha, what does the chiras do'orro have to say for herself these days?"

"She begs to inform her beloved husband that the evening they shared at Fuega Vesperra—Matra, the moronno can't spell anything but her own name!—the evening produced a happy outcome. She—"

Tazia strangled on a gasp. Rafeyo put a steadying hand on her arm. "What is it?"

"Merditto! The filthy sow is *pregnant!*" She crushed the page in her fist. "He *lied*—the filho do'canna *lied* to me! He said it wasn't what it seemed, he never touched her except to shake the wits out of her—"

Thoroughly bewildered, Rafeyo said, "But I thought you *wanted* her to have more babies, to keep her occupied."

"And do you think I *meant* it?" she snapped. "He is *mine,* Rafeyo—he swore he'd never touch her again—damn him! I won't have it, I simply will not have it!"

"Mother, please—calm yourself. It's you he loves."

"Don't you understand? He saw her, he wanted her, and he took her! Merditto, practically in public on the ballroom floor! Don't you pay attention to anything but your stupid paints? He lied to me, he betrayed me—and she's laughing at me right now, I can hear her!"

"She doesn't want him anymore. You said she doesn't."

"Oh, don't be such a *man!* Of course she doesn't want him! She did it to humiliate *me!* She lured him off and came back looking as wanton as a Niapalese whore!" She looked around wildly. "A pen—I need a pen—"

He produced a pencil from his jacket. She snatched it and dropped to the floor and, smoothing the page on the blue rosette tiles, scrawled one scathingly obscene sentence.

"You take this to him. Do it now. Find whatever sewer he's in and give this to him!"

"Of course, but—" He took the paper and tried to help her to her feet. She fought him off, her face crimson and her lips pinched white. "Mama!" he cried, alarmed.

"Do it! Now! This minute!" She glared up at him, on her fists and knees on the floor, a crumple of topaz silk and mortified pride. Her breathing was ragged, her black eyes ferocious. "You're my son. Defend me!"

Blindly, he strode from the Picca into the street. Somehow he found his way to Palasso Verrada; somehow he found words to tell a footman that he must deliver a message from the Countess do'Alva to Don Arrigo. Somehow he climbed the stairs to the private quarters without stumbling to his knees as his mother had done.

Arrigo had lied to her, betrayed her. Rafeyo saw the magnificent paintings lining the hallways and staircases, all of them done by loyal Grijalva hands for lying, betraying do'Verradas. All this beauty, all this genius, at the service of a man who could do this to Tazia.

His mother. On her knees. His mother, from whose body he had taken life, from whose body Arrigo had taken pleasure for as long as Rafeyo had been alive. Arrigo cared nothing for Tazia's humiliation. She meant nothing more to him than one of these paintings on the walls: another magnificently beautiful Grijalva for him to possess.

And Rafeyo was compelled to serve this man. One day he would serve him as Lord Limner.

And Mechella, too. Grand Duchess of Tira Virte. She, too, he must serve.

It was her fault. Oculazurro corassonerro—the old saying, first used by Casteyan camponessos of the blond and brawny northerners who raided their lands long ago, fit Mechella perfectly. Blue eyes, black heart. If she'd never come to Tira Virte—if she'd been content to bear children and raise them and be sensible—if she'd never been born—

If she died.

He must serve Arrigo. He had no choice. Besides, it wasn't Arrigo's fault. He was only a man. It was Mechella's fault this had happened. When she was away at Corasson, everything was perfect between Arrigo and Tazia. Mechella was to blame. And if she went away permanently. . . .

He must serve Arrigo. He had no choice. Lord Limners served Grand Dukes.

But he would never serve *her*. Never.

He gave the folded, crumpled page to Arrigo's servant. "For His Grace's hand only," he managed. "From the Countess do'Alva."

"I'll see he receives it."

"Unopened."

Affronted, the man drew himself up and haughtily slammed the door in Rafeyo's face.

He was beyond caring. As he descended the stairs two at a time, words came into his head, his lips moving on them like a sancto chanting his devotions.

Never serve her. She's to blame. It's her fault. Never serve her, never—

And with the words and the soundless litany came an idea.

He was out in the street, sunshine glaring in his eyes, before it took shape—a sketch only, a swiftly drawn *fa presto* study for a much more elaborate piece. But he saw it, and not even all the blank spaces that were his ignorance could prevent him from laughing aloud.

Ignorance was a temporary condition. Il Aguo, Il Sanguo, Il Seminno—they would teach him. Premio Dioniso would teach him more. He would use all of it. He would start now with things he knew must be included, things he could already do, and as he learned new things, he would fill in those empty spaces. He, a true Grijalva, would create such magnificence and such beauty as had never before been seen.

But no one would see it except him: its creator and its destroyer.

⊷ FIFTY-TWO ⊶

The summer of 1267 was the most wretched in all Arrigo's life. Never in the history of Tira Virte—all four hundred and forty-eight years of it, back to the day Renayo do'Verrada had been proclaimed Duke—had an Heir been treated so.

Betrayed and rejected by the woman who had once adored him. Thrown out by the woman he adored. Rendered powerless by his father, no longer delegated even the most trivial of duties. Deplored by his mother. Castigated by his sister. Barely tolerated by his people. How had this happened to him, who had been their darling, their Neosso do'Orro?

He went to Chasseriallo and stayed there, despite the turgid heat of the riverlands in summer. He spent his days endlessly pacing his chambers and his acres, and his nights alone in his broad silken bed—wondering who had been and probably still was in Mechella's.

As for Tazia . . . she was an unhealed wound that caught in his chest with every breath. He would not beg to be heard; he would not implore her to believe. Yet that summer taught him as nothing else could that he loved her, wanted her, needed her—and should have married her.

How perfect it would have been. He could have lived his own life, been of use, carved out a place for himself. With Tazia at his side openly and legally he could have worked wonders. Children wouldn't have mattered, Lizia's son Maldonno could have inherited.

Instead, he'd done everything he was supposed to do. He'd taken a Grijalva as his Mistress. He'd given her up. He'd taken a Princess to wife. He'd fathered a son to inherit the Grand Dukedom and a daughter to bargain away in marriage. He'd helped Cossimio to the fullest of his abilities in every manner permitted him. He'd cared for his people.

And yet *this* had happened to him.

He was thirty-six years old and his life lay in ruins.

He found escape in a long-standing invitation to return to Diettro Mareia, not as a visiting noble but as a friend of Principio Felisso. He booked passage on a merchant ship, intending to stay at least a month. But a scant ten days into his tour of the country-side—escorted by Felisso and featuring every winery and high-class brothel in sight—a courier caught up with him, bearing a letter from Tazia.

Arrigo rode night and day to the nearest port, caught the first ship, and paced the deck all the way across the Agua Serenissa. Tazia met him on the quay of Tira Virte's main eastern port. The Countess do'Alva was unrecognizable in the do'Verrada sapphire worn by senior servants at the Palasso; she dropped a curtsy and gestured to the waiting carriage. Therein, she pulled the curtains despite the sizzling heat and they made love for thirty minutes.

Tazia was no fool. Recognizing even through her fury that Arrigo was her only chance for power, she took him back. And she had missed him, much more than she'd thought she would. They lived the last weeks of that summer at Chasseriallo, and to the Flames with what anyone saw or heard or thought or wrote in letters to Corasson.

A few days into the new year of 1267, Mechella was delivered at Corasson of Renayo Mirisso Edoard Verro, named after the first Duke of Tira Virte, her own long-dead mother, a favorite hero of Ghillasian history, and the courageous Grijalva who had been Duke Renayo's dearest friend. Little Renayo was said to be of average size, though surprisingly sturdy for a child born nearly six weeks too soon. But no one counted on their fingers or arched their brows, for the tale of Fuega Vesperra was well-known.

Zevierin painted the *Birth*. A copy was sent to Mechella's brother, King Enrei. Two copies were sent to Palasso Verrada: one for Cossimio and Gizella, one for Arrigo. All were painted by Cabral.

The Grand Duke unveiled his copy of the portrait during a special celebration. All the Courtfolk were invited to exclaim and admire before dining on eight courses accompanied by wines Arrigo had brought back from Diettro Mareia. It was remarked that Tazia spent quite some time staring at the painting of Renayo. The baby was blond and fair-skinned like Mechella and little Teressa, but had dark hazel eyes. He looked nothing at all like Arrigo.

After the banquet, Tazia found occasion to pass Arrigo where he stood by a window, a large glass of brandy cradled between his palms. All she said was, "I believe you." But later, when he slipped from the Palasso by a back stair and met her in the secret room of her empty caza, she was more eloquent.

"I am ashamed, carrido meyo. I am so ashamed! My jealousy blinded me to the truth. You couldn't possibly have done what she made everyone believe you'd done. I beg you to forgive me."

"Forgiven, dolcha." He sat beside her on the sofa and took her hand. "Forgiven the day I received your letter in Diettro Mareia. The fact that you came back to me even though you didn't believe me at the time makes it all the sweeter."

"You are a marvel of a man, Arrigo. I wish I was half as good a person as you are."

"Your goodness is in loving me."

"I do, dolcho meyo, with all my heart." She paused, stroking his fingers. "But I doubt even you could forgive *her* for what she's done. And to send you a painting of the child!"

"This party of my father's, it was a nightmare," he agreed. "All evening long, hearing people say how pretty the baby is, how much he resembles Mechella—"

"Her crime cannot go unanswered, Arrigo."

He thought for a time, watching her eyes. "One thing repeats over and over in my mind. She told me that she had her Grijalvas, and I have mine."

"You have me, and Rafeyo, and Dioniso—we are all of us yours, you know that."

"Rafeyo's learned a great deal. I know he's the special student of Premio Dioniso. And I know a few things about what a Grijalva Limner can do."

"Eiha?" she asked carefully.

"Would Rafeyo be willing to paint something for me? Nothing elaborate, nothing too serious. I'm not even sure what would be possible, or even appropriate."

"I—I don't understand. I never paid much attention to the painters."

"Dioniso painted dreams into an icon for Principio Felisso. Maybe Rafeyo could paint a few nightmares for Mechella."

Tazia snorted. "I'd settle for the Qal Venommo used against us in Granidia!"

"That was for the common folk. They'd never believe such things of their Dolcha 'Chellita." He spoke the nickname as he would a curse.

"If done correctly, they might. But Rafeyo's genius shouldn't be wasted on mere scribbling on walls. And Mechella deserves worse than to be embarrassed."

"Yes, but what? Of all the options possible, which would be the best?"

"Obedience would make a good start." She ticked off the list on his fingers. "Loyalty, chastity, submission—and a dozen or so more of the wifely virtues she so conspicuously lacks."

"Any change in her behavior would create suspicion—and she has *her* Grijalvas, too."

"None of them clever enough to cancel what my son can do."

"That's motherly pride talking."

"Arrigo—" She drew in a deep breath and slid even closer to him on the sofa. "Rafeyo tells me things. Dioniso has taught him far in advance of what his fellows are learning. He'll be Lord Limner within a few years. But we don't have to wait that long to do something about Mechella. With what he knows now, Rafeyo can bring her to heel." She met his gaze squarely and murmured, "Amoro meyo, he has, in fact, already begun."

Spring came early to Corasson that year of 1268, and never more beautifully. Climbing roses rewarded two years of tender care with masses of blooms that covered the house to the second-floor balconies. Every garden seemed eager to show itself equally dedicated to Mechella's pleasure; flowers burst from green leaves in colors profuse enough to render even a Limner drunk. Even the curious little pocket gardens tucked between wings of the house showed tiny white flowers in cushioning mosses. The days were so warmly sunny that the first outdoor lunch of the year was held the morning after Astraventa.

Mechella and Cabral had celebrated the anniversary of their son's conception with a reenactment of the circumstances. She was still rather stunned by their love; one hour she would feel as if she'd been married to him her whole life, and the next could be spent in passion so new and urgent it was as if they'd never touched each other before. Instinct told her that life with Arrigo could never have been like this—indeed, had she not escaped to Corasson and Cabral, she would have soured into a bitter and shrewish woman. She didn't understand why, but her Grijalvas did: Mechella was a creature whose purpose in life was to love and be loved. In her children, her family, her friends, and her people, she had found much of what she needed. But in Cabral she was wholly fulfilled.

That afternoon, with Astraventa still lingering in their smiles, they lounged with Zevierin and Leilias on blankets spread over the front lawn. The baby slept in Mechella's lap as his father tickled his nose with a new paintbrush. Renayo woke, yawned, and grabbed for the brush with typically long and well-shaped Grijalva fingers.

Cabral laughed. "Fifty mareias that he turns out to have a talent for art."

Zevierin sighed a vastly patient sigh. "A hundred that he won't know one end of a brush from the other."

"Men!" exclaimed Mechella. "Why is it, Leilias, that they look at a baby only to decide his future? Women are content to enjoy the present, helping a child grow and learn—"

"I *am!*" Cabral grinned. "I'm helping him learn about his birthright as a Grijalva."

Leilias pulled a face. "I'm more interested in his birthright as a de Ghillas. It pays better."

Mechella couldn't help giggling. "Wouldn't that be the most incredible thing? A de Ghillas and a Grijalva, with the surname do'Verrada, on my father's throne?"

"It's provisional only," Zevierin reminded her. "Failing any heirs of King Enrei's body. And *now* who's plotting Renayo's future?"

Cabral was trying to tug his brush from surprisingly tenacious infant fingers. "Your brother will marry and have a dozen children of his own. Although I admit it gives me a certain amount of truly vicious pleasure to consider the matter—Arrigo had a tantrum when he heard about the decree your brother signed. If it ever comes to pass, he'll have a seizure."

"But Cossimio and Gizella are thrilled," Mechella purred.

"They ought to be." Leilias reached over to feel the baby's diaper; still dry. "I suppose," she enquired sweetly of her brother, "that Arrigo's fits are your *only* reason for enjoying the notion of your son as King of Ghillas?"

Just as cloying in tone and expression, he replied, "My son and your nephew, Leilias. Be sweet to him, and he may make you a Princess one day."

"I'll take him over my knee if he tries!" she laughed.

Zevierin rapped his knuckles on the wine crate that served as a picnic table. "Enough, children. Whatever the future may hold, for now Renayo's a baby who's getting a sunburn."

Otonna was called over from the rose arbor where she and the farm manager—her sister Primavarra's husband's cousin's son—were finishing their lunch. The maid took the baby upstairs, cooing over him all the way, while the young man trailed behind her.

"Is he imagining certain things?" Zevierin asked quizzically.

"Himself, Otonna, and *their* baby?" Mechella stretched out with her head on Cabral's knee. "She's not serious about him. If she were, she'd go with him to his cottage once in a while, instead of always taking him to her own bed—beneath the roof of Corasson."

"The wicked spell still lingers," Leilias chuckled, ignoring the men's confused expressions. "But getting back to the subject of Renayo and the throne of Ghillas—"

"The claim is through me," said Mechella. "Arrigo's nothing to do with it."

"Or him," Cabral added, winking at her.

Leilias had more or less grown used to the freedom of their actions and speech. There was no danger of discovery, she told herself; everyone here was loyal. The lovers were circumspect when visitors came to Corasson. Not even sharp-eyed Lizia had suspected anything during her stay here. And in any case, the Serrano who had built the place had put in four hidden staircases, one of which led from Cabral's third-floor chamber down to Mechella's second-floor suite. There was no danger, Leilias repeated to herself. No one would ever know.

And even if they did, Zevierin could paint them into *not* knowing.

Her husband shaded his eyes against the sun, squinting down the drive. "What in the world is all that?"

"A wagon from Meya Suerta," said Mechella, not even bothering to look. "I expected it this morning."

"Not more furniture!" Leilias exclaimed.

"No," she replied, smiling mysteriously.

The cargo proved to be paintings. Zevierin and Cabral uncrated them, playfully chiding Mechella for banditry.

"They were all in storage," she said defensively. "Nobody wanted them but me. Mequel was kind enough to authorize my having them, and Cossimio agreed to let them out of the Galerria. En verro, I can't depend on my Grijalvas to provide pictures enough for all Corasson!"

"I should hope not!" Leilias said indignantly. "I have *much* better uses for Zevi's time!"

Shortly thereafter, the men went up to their atelierro for tools to repair a frame damaged in transit. Mechella opened another crate herself, and she and Leilias lifted out the portrait.

"Oh, Mechella! There's been a mistake—that's the *Saavedra*!"

"No, Leilias, there's no mistake. I asked for her." She stood back from the huge wood-panel portrait, sighing softly. "I used to hate this painting. But I've been thinking about her quite a lot recently. She and I have several things in common."

Leilias stared. "Such as?"

Gazing at Saavedra's beautiful gray-eyed face, she murmured, "We both wanted a man we couldn't have. We both carried the bastard child of a man we loved—a child impossible to acknowledge for who he really is. The difference is that although we were both caught in a web we didn't weave, I've broken free." She clasped Leilias's hand. "Something I never could have done without you and Zevi and especially Cabral. I see Saavedra and know how lucky I was to escape."

Leilias suddenly saw *The First Mistress* with new eyes.

"Look at her face," Mechella whispered. "She's caught and she knows it."

"Yes," Leilias heard herself say. "Poor lady."

"I'll never be able to live openly with Cabral or reveal that Renayo is his. But that matters so little compared to the happiness they bring me! Saavedra was never happy again. Whatever happened to her after this was painted—whether she left Tira Virte and had her baby or was murdered—she never escaped. I see her, trapped forever in that painting, looking just as she did centuries ago, and I pity her."

Only this woman, Leilias told herself, would pity the First Mistress. Only she would not blame her for beginning the tradition of Grijalva Mistresses that had been the cause of her sorrow. Only she would feel compassion, not hatred.

"Eiha," Mechella went on, smiling, "besides, it's a masterpiece, and nobody else wanted it, and something this lovely ought to be seen and admired. You know how I am about orphans!"

"And besides *that*," Leilias added, "in time, it will remind Alessio and Renayo of the tragedies Saavedra caused."

Mechella blinked in surprise. "I suppose so, although I hadn't thought of it that way. I don't want my sons to hurt their wives the way Arrigo hurt me. But you mustn't hold Saavedra responsible. *She* was the tragedy."

"And she's right," Leilias told her husband a few days later. They were riding south to Meya Suerta through the fullest glory of spring, just the two of them on horseback with nothing but their saddlebags. The freedom of it made Leilias recall Mechella's words about being trapped, and as she detailed the conversation Zevierin nodded agreement.

"Saavedra wasn't responsible, Sario was," he said. "The Mistresses were part of how he destroyed the Serranos—financially, artistically, socially—"

"I've been comparing myself to Saavedra, too," Leilias admitted. "And thanks to you, *I've* escaped. Have I told you yet today that I adore you?"

"Probably, but tell me again." He gave her a rueful smile. "I'll need to hear it rather often in the next month or two."

"That's nothing to do with you and me. I mean, it is, but—oh, you know what I mean." More severely, she said, "And don't you dare look so wistful. As far as I'm concerned, you're already the baby's father."

He made big eyes. "I only meant that I'm nervous about taking my place among the Conselhos."

"Liar."

Zevierin had been summoned by Premio Dioniso to the spring convocation. As Corasson's Limner, his status was just above Itinerarrio and just below Embajadorro, which entitled him to a seat on the council of the most senior Viehos Fratos. They, naturally, were determined to know everything that transpired at Corasson. Zevierin was equally determined not to tell them a damned thing.

The convocation would formally celebrate those who had become Confirmattio this spring, and then consider the lists of probable candidates for elevation to Limner at Penitenssia. All over Palasso Grijalva anxious young men would watch for any indication of their chances for this honor. Zevierin was not looking forward to having his every sneeze remarked on and his every facial twitch noted. He remembered most clearly what he and his fellow estudos had been like the last half-year of their training. Were they good enough? Had they learned everything necessary? Had the Grijalva Gift run true? And even if it had, did they possess talent enough to use it?

But people would study him not only as a Conselho but as Leilias' husband—for she was taking this opportunity to find a father for her first child. *Their* first child. Zevierin reflected that he'd be doing his share of scrutinizing faces: which man would she choose?

Their arrangement was not uncommon. Sometimes a boy and girl would fall in love when very young, or during their Confirmattio nights. If he turned up Limner, they married when his apprenticeship ended and a fertile Grijalva male sired her children. Zevierin and Leilias were an oddity in that they were both well into their twenties and everyone knew her opposition to becoming a "brood mare."

Most of the curious looks, though, would come because they were in high favor with Mechella. No one knew how power would balance out at Palasso Verrada. Those Grijalvas in Tazia's camp were supremely confident. Mechella's adherents among the family were more cautious. Zevierin wondered what they would say if they knew her younger son *was* family.

None of these matters were discussed at the convocation. The Conselhos reported on various family activities: this year's Confirmattio (two Limners and three disappointments); the Galerria Picca (an economic disaster, as usual, but the good will of the public was priceless to them), finances (excellent; the proceeds from selling Corasson had been invested in a wildly profitable iron mine), the condition of the Palasso (rain damage to the roof), and the storefront businesses in public document paintings (thriving, as ever). Then came reports from all Itinerarrios, read in a stultifying monotone by their director. Mercifully, there were fewer Embajadorros; their letters were bellowed out by vigorous, white-haired, deaf-as-a-brushpot Josippo, the only Conselho not a Gifted Limner, who had been overseeing Grijalvas in foreign courts for thirty-five years.

His roaring report from Ghillas was the first thing that interested Zevierin all day. Embajadorro Anderrio had been at Aute-Ghillas a little less than five years now, and had many interesting things to say about King Enrei III. Hearing his description of the young king's habits and character (one could not fail to hear it within the confines of the Crechetta; good thing the room was soundproofed), Zevierin suspected there would be no Enrei IV. Mechella's brother seemed incapable of making a decision about which horse to ride, let alone which noble virgin to marry.

Eiha, all the better for little Renayo, he thought, hiding a smile. The Viehos Fratos were delighted that King Enrei had selected his younger nephew as his heir—envisioning, as did the rest of Tira Virte, a blissful alliance leading to an ecstasy of profitable trade.

Zevierin tried to imagine what it would be like to be the uncle-by-marriage of a King.

There was one other claimant, an intricately connected cousin called Ivo. He had his supporters, but Mechella's son had more. She was remembered lovingly in Ghillas. Anderrio's report ended with the delicate suggestion that if Enrei asked for guidance, it should be given with all generosity and speed.

"Which translates," Zevierin told Leilias that night in bed, "as 'Don't let him do anything so colossally stupid as to make the Ghillasians reject Renayo just because Enrei chose him.' "

"Which further translates into, 'I want permission to do a few magical paintings for him if he really starts falling on his face.' " She sighed and rubbed her cheek to his chest. "I wish you could do one for me of a man who looks just like you and has all your best qualities."

"I note that you don't say *all* my qualities."

"Everything but your nose, carrido! It suits you perfectly, but imagine it on a poor defenseless baby!" She laughed and kissed what was undeniably the most prominent feature in his face. "If only you could paint a Grijalva with all my requirements, have him step out of the painting when we need him, and then go back into it until the next time we want a child!"

"Of all the clever things Grijalvas can do, creating life does not number among them. That's what we need women for—among other things," he added hastily as she sucked in an outraged breath.

On the second day of the convocation, after the Viehos Fratos had duly deliberated over the various reports, planning and policy were announced. Zevierin yawned through most of it. Then it was time for individual questioning: what had each Limner painted this year that could be considered even slightly magical? Zevierin had his answer ready in the time-honored formula: "Apart from the *Birth of Renayo,* I have painted nothing of Aguo, Seminno, or Sanguo." It was at least within speaking distance of the truth—he hadn't actually painted Lissina's *Will* at Corasson, only finished it there. But Premio Dioniso didn't call on him, or on anyone for that matter. Instead, he stood before his ornate chair with Lord Limner Mequel on one side of him and Il Aguo, Il Seminno, and Il Sanguo on the other, and lectured the assembly on the perils of recent trends in painting.

"Imprecision!" Dioniso said, his deep strong voice carrying the accusation to the rafters. "Inaccuracy! Inexactitude! All for the sake of a pretty picture!"

He strode to a huge easel, looking nowhere near his forty-seven years, and flung the tarp aside. Revealed was a fine painting of horses in full gallop across Joharran sands. Manes and tails whipped in the wind of their passage; hooves dug into the dunes or reached eagerly for still more speed; eyes black and glowing as hot coals were wild with the joy of freedom. During his training Zevierin had seen sketches that conveyed this same urgency of motion, but this was the first time he'd seen it in a fully realized oil painting.

"Isn't it *pretty?*" Dioniso sneered, contempt lashing at the Limners. "This is a *Deed* establishing ownership of these three stallions. See how their manes streak back in a blur of color! Feel the desert wind, hear the pounding hooves! Movement, sound, sensation—all evoked by mere paint!"

Marching to the other side of the room, with the self-portraits of every man here gazing down on him to double the living faces into a huge crowd, Dioniso tore the covering from another painting, this one a *Marriage*. It was at a different angle and farther from Zevierin than the other picture, and he could discern only the vague outline. Dioniso described it for them all.

"The fisherman's daughter marries the vintner's son. Her dress is embroidered with nets, his coat with lattices that support vines. Lovely, appropriate. Yet how does the Grijalva paint it? As a *landscape!* And of Laggo Sonho, of all the Mother-forsaken places! Where are wishes for happiness and love, children and wealth? The bridal pair are mere incidental figures in this *pretty* painting of a swamp in all its springtime splendor!"

Now Dioniso strode to his chair, and from beneath it grabbed a much smaller painting. As it was passed from hand to hand around the room, he gave his scathing commentary.

"A *Birth*—for a paying customer, no less, a noble family of Taglis! All the correct symbols are present—wheatsheaves for Riches, white lilac for Youthful Innocence, laurel for Glory, roses for Love, thistle for a Male Child, and so on and so forth. And so *pretty* it is, too! Eiha, *somewhere* in it is a child who will one day be a baron—but who can see him for the still-life this Grijalva has done? Was the baroness brought to bed of a baby boy or a basket of flowers?"

Somehow he managed to spear every Limner in the place with a look of utter disgust. "I won't tell you who painted these. I won't embarrass the artists—though they richly deserve it and I'd pin-prick a few of those painted fingers overhead if I thought it would do any good! What I want is to show you the degeneration that awaits if this trend continues.

"On what does our magic depend? Precision. On what does our reputation rest? Accuracy. On what does every policy and plan of Tira Virte rely? Exactitude. And what have these three Limners painted? A *Deed* where the items in question are nothing but streaks and blurs! A *Marriage* in which the bride and groom are but figures in a landscape! A *Birth* where the flowers and the fruit and the leaves and the sheaves make the child an afterthought!

"Yes, the pictures are *pretty.* Yes, the horses seethe with motion and you can almost hear and feel and taste the desert wind. Yes, this is a perfect rendering of where the young couple will make their home. Yes, there is a baby in there—somewhere. In themselves, these paintings perform their function—barely. But I defy anyone to look at this *Deed* of ownership and pick these three particular horses out of a herd!"

He turned his back on them and started for his chair, then just as suddenly swung around again. "Tell me what will happen when another *Deed* of property is painted, this one of a field or a building or an orchard, with the borders marked in blurs! Will such a document stand? It will not! And what about a *Peintraddo Sonho* to cure a little girl of nightmares? What if, instead of painting the frightened child in the precise attitude of sleep, she becomes a mere daub of color—a nightgown, a blanket, a suggesting of her black curls on the pillow? Will the protections in the painting and the spells for sweet dreams function? They will not!"

Dioniso walked to his chair and sat down, sweeping his gaze once more around the Crechetta. "Some of you will say it is permissible to paint *some* things in this new style. Things not of vital importance. Things that among people of good intentions would not be challenged. Who would question that these three fine stallions belong to the Count do'Granidia, or that this couple is well and truly married, or that this baby was born to a baron?

"But there are other paintings in which precision and accuracy and exactitude are essential. And I tell you that if such are ignored in *some* pictures, they will soon be ignored in *all.* Without precise rendering, magic does not function. Without accurate detail, the lingua oscurra does not work. Without exact attention to form and composition, power will not inhabit our paintings. And then, Fratos ei Conselhos, we Grijalvas will be out of a job."

Settling his formal gray robe of office around him, his gold-and-jeweled color glinting, Dioniso said in normal tones, "Now we will consider the list of those eligible for elevation at Penitenssia. Yvennal, read the names."

Zevierin remained stunned by the tirade all day long. As he and Leilias dressed to meet her mother and stepfather for dinner at a restaurant near the Zocalo Grando, he kept shaking his head over Dioniso's vehement eloquence.

"You'd think those poor Limners had purposely plotted the downfall of the Grijalvas," he said, knotting a length of crimson silk around his collar.

"Mmm."

"I kept waiting for him to order their *Peintraddo Chievas* taken off the walls so he could stick pins in their hands."

"Mm-hmm," she said, twisting another braid atop her head and pinning it in place.

"Not that I don't agree with his analysis, more or less. Nothing wrong with a pretty picture, but our work has to do so much more."

"Yes."

"Have you heard anything I've said in the last ten minutes?"

"Of course. Hurry and put on your jacket, Zevi, we're going to be late."

Outside the Palasso in the evening bustle of crowded streets, she hooked her elbow with his and murmured, "I don't like talking inside the Palasso."

After due consideration, he said, "Shall I paint a protection or six on our rooms?"

"They'd know—and wonder what we're hiding." She paused at a shop window, pretending to admire a display of clothes. "I heard something worrisome about Rafeyo today."

"So did I. He's to become a Limner at year's end."

"We knew that. There's worse." She pointed at a child's dress. "Wouldn't Teressa look adorable in that?"

"We'll buy it for her tomorrow," he promised, as aware as she that there were too many people close by. They continued walking and the homeward bound shopping crowd thinned, and eventually they felt safe enough to renew the conversation.

Leilias began, "I talked to Arriano this morning—he's as near a thing as Rafeyo has to a friend."

"The boy sees everyone as competition," Zevierin mused.

"Not Arriano, Grazzo do'Matra, who said some very interesting things to me today. He asked a few questions about perfumes, then slid around to the subject of Corasson. The roses, the forest plants, the herb gardens, just polite interest. Then he let something slip. He was curious, he said, because Rafeyo had told him how beautiful Corasson is at all seasons of the year. Zevi, Rafeyo was only there twice—once on the way back from Casteya and once when he brought Count Garlo's letter!"

"In winter and in late summer," Zevierin said thoughtfully. "And hated it."

"Which of the boys is lying?"

"Neither. No, I take it back. The only lie here is that Rafeyo thinks Corasson is beautiful. The rest is true, and we both know it."

Silently they crossed the great Zocalo in front of the cathedral, pausing to stare up at the statue of Alesso do'Verrada high atop the fountain.

Zevierin said, "So Rafeyo has been to Corasson several times. To spy for his mother?"

"Tazia doesn't give a damn what Mechella does or says or thinks. She's got Arrigo on a tight rein, the next Lord Limner is her son—why should she care what happens at Corasson?"

He reached into the fountain and splashed water on his hands, then slicked back his hair with the cool moisture. "Does he spy for Arrigo, then? To learn who Renayo's father is, because of the Ghillasian possibilities?"

Leilias shrugged. "What's done is done. Arrigo accepted the child publicly as his own. Whether he knows or not can't matter."

"Carrida meya, can you truly know so little about men?" He tucked his wife's hand into the crook of his elbow and they started for the street. "It gnaws at him. He doesn't want her, but the idea of anyone else having her—let alone getting a child on her—is more than he can stand."

She said nothing for many steps. Then, quietly: "Will it gnaw at you?"

"You forget, I'm not like other men." Meaning that because he was a Limner who wished to raise children, he would have to stand it.

"Not like any other man in the world," she said fervently, "and I thank the Mother on my knees for it." And, so saying, she kissed him full on the mouth. In public.

"Leilias!" A woman's voice, both shocked and filled with laughter, was seconded by a man's resounding chuckle and the words, "I *do* hope that's Zevierin!"

Zevierin blushed—absurdly—as his wife drew away and called

out, "Mama! Zevi, this is my mother, Filonna, and my father, Jonino."

The elderly man beamed with pleasure. But as warmly sincere as Leilias was in naming Jonino her father, Zevierin knew the implication of the words was meant for *him*.

⚡ FIFTY-THREE ⚡

Dioniso rubbed unguent into his aching knuckles, wincing at each movement. Spring rain, summer humidity, autumn winds, winter chill—it was all the same now. It all hurt the same. Pain was an enemy, dulling the mind. Constant, unremitting, not bad enough to require serious medication (even if he'd allowed it; he recalled Guilbarro's tragedy of addiction only too well), but too deep to ignore. A very long time ago (as Martain? Zandor? Someone he'd completely forgotten?) he had grown very old indeed for a Limner, and the pain had progressed just like this: from occasional unwelcome guest to constant and feared companion.

Two months ago at Fuega Vesperra the Grijalvas had celebrated their Premio Frato's forty-seventh birthday. Banquet, music, messages from all the far-flung Embajadorros and Itinerarrios, letter of congratulation from Grand Duke Cossimio, gifts—a celebration en tudo paletto, for it was understood if unspoken that he might not be alive next year to honor. Dioniso's mother, Giaberta—at sixty-three looking as if she were his slightly elder sister—had the decency to gift him with this ointment in private. A new recipe, she'd said, guaranteed to ease even the most painful aches. But hot needles still pierced the delicate bones of his fingers and the only improvement over the old medicine was that this one smelled better.

He capped the blue glass jar, damning the lid that must be twisted tight to preserve moisture, and leaned back in bed. It wasn't fair. He had so much left to do as Dioniso. As Premio Frato he could guide the Grijalvas as none other had authority to do. It was the highest he had risen since Riobaro. And there was so much yet to be done, that his vast years of experience had prepared him to do, that only he *could* do. Weren't they saying he was the best Premio the Fratos had ever had? Weren't they regretting that he wasn't just a few years younger?

Eiha, he'd done what he could. Corasson had been sold, and the money was turning a tidy profit. He'd found four possible candidates among the eight- and nine-year-old girls eligible to become Alessio's Mistress one day, for all that the boy was scarcely out of diapers. He had reorganized the Itinerarrios, simplified the pricing system of portraits-for-hire in foreign lands. True, idiots would still paint blurred and sloppy pictures, but at least he'd made everyone aware of the danger. Rafeyo, when Lord Limner, would build on what Dioniso had begun, enforce the rules of painting, and make the Grijalvas stronger than ever. It was necessary to the family, to the do'Verradas, to Tira Virte. Who better for the work than himself?

En verro, there was no one else who *could* do it. He was not just a Limner. He was *The* Limner.

And soon to be Lord Limner again. He allowed himself to dream a little, escaping the aches of this aging body in the anticipation of young strong bones, until reality sneered at him. Mequel showed every indication of living to be sixty. He was the same age as Dioniso, and stooped with it, but his hands were as supple as ever even if he could no longer walk without a cane. But the longer Mequel lasted, the easier it would be to put Rafeyo in his place when he died. The boy would be nineteen soon. With each passing season his reputation and influence would grow. Mequel, despite appearances, wouldn't live forever.

"Premio Dioniso?"

Pensierro, arrivierro, he thought wryly: to think of him is to bring him. "Come in, Rafeyo."

The door of his private suite opened and the boy—young man now—entered. He carried a covered tray from which sublime scents issued. "I've brought that stew the cooks always make for Sancterria. The sauce is pretty spicy this year, but I told them to make a milder version for you."

Another indignity of age: a contrary digestion. "Very thoughtful of you, amico meyo. Stay while I eat, and tell me how the preparations progress."

Rafeyo served, sat, and chattered. Dioniso wielded a fork on the thick succulence of venison sausages, chunks of beefsteak, and potatoes. He'd pay for the indulgence later, but right now he was grateful to be eating food that tasted like something.

". . . so everything is ready for the holiday. Premio, I have a question. Why do we celebrate so many festivals with fire?"

Dioniso chewed and swallowed a pepper before replying. "It sanctifies and purifies. It mimics the skyfire of the stars. It burns away the old to make way for the new. It destroys—and yet from the ashes new life comes, as when stubble is burned in the field. Fire is a holy thing." He grimaced. "And at Sancterria even the food is ablaze! Did you say this was *mild?* Pour me some wine, hurry!"

When his eyes had stopped tearing, he handed back the bowl

and asked to be told what Rafeyo had recently been working on till all hours of the night.

"I should've known you'd find out," Rafeyo sighed. "I've been practicing for the self-portrait. Just sketches so far."

"And which Lord Limner will be your model?"

This time he gave a start. "You knew I was going to use one of them as my pattern?"

"Your ambitions," Dioniso said dryly, "are not unknown. Nothing less than the pose of a Lord Limner will do for you. Which one?"

"That's what's keeping me up nights. At first I thought Riccian, but his cloak has all those draperies."

He knew the piece; he'd watched Riccian paint it. A dramatic pose, if flashy.

"I studied the ones from the last century, but they're awfully stiff. Except for Riobaro. Would it be all right if I used him?"

Dioniso had expected it. Not only was Riobaro's a fine painting, but he was the most revered Lord Limner in Tira Virteian history.

"It's a little presumptuous," he said, "though many a lesser artist has used it. You'll have trouble with the candlelight, however. Everyone does."

"I wanted to ask you about that. If you feel well enough this afternoon, could you come and advise me?"

"Gladly." He sipped the last of the wine. "I don't suppose you've used any magic on your sketches?"

Once more Rafeyo's eyes widened. "Just—just for the practice—"

"Don't look so nervous. I won't scold. You know something of what you're working with now. I trust you to be cautious with it."

"I will be, Premio. I promise."

"Cabral!" Mechella called down from the landing. "Come see Tessa in her new gown!"

He excused himself to the farm manager and took the stairs three at a time. Halfway up he stopped, pretending to stagger back stunned at the sight of the four-year-old. Clasping one hand over his heart, he bowed several times with many flourishes. "Bela, bela! Muito bela!"

Mechella knelt to whisper in her daughter's ear. Giggling, Teressa stuck out her gloved fingers, mimicking a great lady of the Court. Cabral advanced the last steps and bowed once more over the little girl's wrist. Then he hoisted her in his arms to dance her around the upper hall, singing a Joharran ballad at the top of his lungs. Three-year-old Alessio trotted determinedly behind them until Mechella swept him up and they began dancing, too.

"Matra Dolcha, what an uproar!" Otonna exclaimed. "Cabral Liranzo Verro Grijalva, you close your mouth this instant before you deafen us all!"

Teressa wriggled in his arms. "Better do it," she advised. "I have lots of names, too. When she says them all, she means it!"

"Of a certainty I do!" said the maid. "Now, you come along and let's take that dress off you before it gets spoiled—" Otonna cast a disgusted glance at Cabral. "—the way he's spoiled your appreciation of music forever!"

"You call that music?" Mechella teased.

Cabral set the child lightly on the floor—then grabbed Otonna to gallop her around the hallway. She spluttered and flailed, but when he finally let her go, they were both laughing.

Teressa crowed with glee. "Mama, now you dance with Cabral!"

"Later tonight, at the festival," Mechella promised. "Do as Otonna says, ninita. You don't want to ruin your pretty clothes."

"But I don't *like* nap!"

Alessio's jaw set mulishly. "No nap," he announced.

"A Grand Ducal Edict," Cabral murmured. "He's starting early."

Otonna shooed the children to their rooms. Mechella and Cabral followed to spend a few minutes admiring their golden-haired, hazel-eyed son, then went outside to inspect preparations for tonight's celebration of Sancterria. She had planned everything so that the guests—all the inhabitants of the nearby villages, her own people, and a few noble guests from estates in the area—would be completely surprised. From the front drive, Corasson would look as it always did. But when everyone came around back, they would gasp in delight at seeing the gardens all ablaze with light.

"There'll be a procession around the fields with torches," she told Cabral, "before we climb Piatra Astrappa to light the bonfire. They've cleared a dancing ground—everyone who plays any instrument at all will be there to provide the music."

"I never would have guessed," he joked. "The tutor and his wife have only been rehearing the orchestra all week! Today I think most of them were even playing the same tune."

"This from a man with a voice like a calf with colic!"

He tucked her fingers into the crook of his elbow as they walked. "Tessa looked adorable. An exact copy of your gown, I'm told."

"Cabral! It was supposed to be a surprise!"

He slanted a look at her as they neared the great spreading oak south of the house. "You've developed quite a taste for surprises, haven't you? I tremble to think what you'll do next."

"Eiha, a woman ought to keep a man guessing. Prevents his getting bored."

"Not in a million years," he assured her. " 'Chella, a letter from Zevi came today."

"Have they found the right man yet? I wish they'd come home. I miss them."

"They'll be back soon. The quest goes badly." He smiled. "En verro, my sister is a demanding woman."

"What else does Zevi have to say?" She sat on a little stone bench beneath the oak and looked up at him. "There must be something, it's in your face—and you never would have brought me out here to be private unless it was something important."

Cabral cleared his throat. "Eiha . . . that picture of Corasson, the pencil drawing—Zevierin tells me to destroy it."

"What? But why?"

"Because Rafeyo drew it." Taking the letter from his pocket, he opened it and read aloud to her:

> *It is a relief that the drawing is in our possession, not his. Still, you must dispose of it by the following means. Soak it in warm water until the paper disintegrates. Dilute the water by tripling its volume, then pour it down a drain.*

Mechella gave a nervous little laugh. "I never heard anything so silly! Destroy that lovely picture?"

"There's more."

> *I do not know if the drawing is Aguo, Seminno, or Sanguo. If it is, Rafeyo will feel a tingle of warmth from the water but probably not know its cause, and thus will not remark upon it. If it was not, he will sense nothing. But I beg you to take this precaution, amico ei frato, for talk here confirms his hatred of our dearest Lady and Leilias and I fear him capable of anything.*

"Zevi's run mad," Mechella said.

Cabral took a matchbox from his pocket and set the page alight. It singed his fingertips before he dropped it to the dirt and ground the ashes with his heel. Facing her again, he spoke words both grim and bitter. "No, 'Chella, he has not. He is in deadly earnest."

"But how could Rafeyo possibly—"

"I said that a letter *came* from Zevi. I did not say 'it was delivered.'"

She looked up at him blankly.

"It *came*," Cabral said, "into the atelierro upstairs. It's something Limners can do—accomplished ones, who know a place and can paint it with total accuracy, and into it paint a letter. We've communicated with our Grijalvas at foreign courts that way for years."

"Cabral," she breathed.

"The most spectacular example came when the Tza'ab were long ago massing for attack along the Joharran border. Duke Alejandro learned of it when a Grijalva spy sent just such a letter to Lord Limner Sario. Despite the warning, there was no possible way to get our troops there in time. So Sario consulted with all the Joharrans in Meya Suerta, and from their memories of the area painted a picture of the hills and dunes—*with an army standing on them.*"

"No—stop—Lissina was right, this is not for my hearing—"

"This army," Cabral continued inexorably, "of two thousand men in battle armor, appeared at sunrise across the distant dunes, just as Sario had painted them on his canvas. The Tza'ab were terrified into retreat. They didn't even approach to do battle, or send scouts to judge our strength—they simply fled. And they have never come so close to our lands again. But the Grijalva spy, inspecting these guerrieros do'fantome later that day, discovered that they were hollow. The armor was empty, the helmets—"

"No! I don't want to hear any more!"

"Sario was thorough in his depiction of the soldiers at the front of the army. They had faces. Hands. Fingers. He painted them precisely as the Tza'ab would see them from a distance, from the Tza'ab point of vantage. But they weren't *real*. And when the Tza'ab fled, and the spy reported this by another letter, Lord Limner Sario painted these thousands out of existence, leaving only the clean unspoiled sands in his painting—and on the Joharran border."

She was shivering in the shade of the huge oak, and he waited for a time until his own emotions were under control—the same horror, the same sick fear of power he'd felt when Zevierin had told him the tale. No one had ever painted such a picture again and it was utterly forbidden even to try, but *it was possible to do such things, and maybe even worse.* This was knowledge reserved only for Viehos Fratos and the Grand Dukes they served, and, as Lissina had cautioned, not for the likes of women or mere limners like himself.

At last he said softly, "I'm not a Limner—but Zevierin is, and he knows what Grijalvas can do. Sario worked that terrible painting in his own blood. When a painting is Aguo, Seminno, or Sanguo, it means that it is powerful and can be used even at a great distance. You didn't see Zevierin mix the paints for Baroness Lissina's *Will*. I did. Why do you think he had a bandage on his wrist for a week afterward? Mechella, he mixed those paints *with his own blood!*"

"He—he said he cut his hand on a paletto knife—"

He knelt, taking both her hands. Her fingers were cold; she believed him, though she didn't yet know it. "Do you remember when Tessa's little songbird died this winter, and she was heartbroken for days?"

All the soft rosy color drained from her cheeks. "Until Zevi . . . until he told her she might dream of her friend . . . and put a drawing of the bird under her pillow. . . ."

"And she *did* dream, and Sancto Leo told her it meant her bird was singing now for the Mother and Son. That's the gentle magic, Mechella. The sweetness of what a Limner can do. But there are other kinds of power." He felt her tremble, and kissed her palms.

"Wh—what could Rafeyo do to us?" she breathed.

"I don't know." He did, of course, and writhed at his own impotence to prevent it. "My precious love, if I had the Grijalva Gift in me, I would paint protections onto every wall of Corasson in my own blood. But I can't. I'm not a Limner. I can't protect you. We must trust Zevierin—a thing you know, or you wouldn't have insisted that he and only he paint Renayo's *Birth*. Our son is protected as long as Zevierin lives, while the blood flows in his veins." He laughed harshly. "I always wondered about that oath, the way it was worded. 'With true faith and in humble service I dedicate myself to my duty while the blood flows in my veins.' All of us swear it, but to a Limner it means more."

"And—Rafeyo?"

"Zevierin is worried, and with reason. Until Rafeyo paints his self-portrait, his *Peintraddo Chieva,* there will be no way of disciplining him. His blood will be in the paints he uses then, 'Chella. And Zevi says that a picture painted in a Limner's own blood—"

"Stop. No more," she whispered. "Don't tell me, Cabral, I don't want to know. Lissina *was* right. These are things for Grand Dukes and Grijalvas." With a shudder, she finished, "Do as he says with the drawing. I couldn't look at it now without being afraid. But don't tell me any more of this. Ever."

" 'Chella—"

"No!" She wrenched her hands free and leaped to her feet.

"Zevierin won't live past fifty," he said bluntly. "You'll need another Limner one day. I can never be what you truly need—"

"I need you as a husband, a father to my children—*that's* what you can never be, not openly, not before the world—ah, Matra, why is it we all want what we can never have?" She covered her face with her hands and fled into the house.

He stayed there on his knees for a long time, grappling with strange intensities of emotion: hate, despair, resentment, desperate longing for what he did not possess. Finally he pushed himself to his feet and trudged into the house. The drawing of Corasson was gone from its honored place in the dining room—torn off the wall, lying on the floor, the cords that had held it from the crown molding snapped. He cut a finger as he undid the frame hooks—glaring at the blood, hating it for not being Limner blood. For the rest of the afternoon he sat on a hay bale in the stable, watching in silent rage as the drawing dissolved in a huge tub of icy water. He left it cold on purpose, hoping the picture *did* have magic in it and that Rafeyo's teeth would chatter so hard he bit out his tongue and died of blood loss.

Does Sario gaze on me in my painted prison? Does he smile, does he laugh, knowing that he alone knows the truth? And . . . Alejandro? Does he weep, or curse, or cry out? Or does he stare in silence, hating me for leaving him?

Or does he never look on me at all?

I could look upon myself if I liked—there is a mirror, and I could see into my own eyes—but I'm so afraid of what I'll find in them. I am so afraid for myself, for Alejandro, for our baby—I fear Sario, what he has done, what he might yet do. . . .

He has left me a copy of the Folio—*as a torment, I am sure. Did he know it would open? Did he know the pages are written on as clearly as if he had penned each word himself? Indeed, it is his writing in the margin glosses. It must be a painted replica of his own copy. Does he wish me to know precisely how he did this to me?*

Or is it not torment but challenge to confirm his belief that I, too, am Gifted?

Could I use this book? Could I open one of my veins and find within it blood that would infuse mere paint with Limner magic?

Eiha, he gave me the book. But no paints. Not even a pencil to write with. If he had, I could have written on one of these pages and someone would see my words and—

But they should have guessed by now. Anyone seeing me within this framed prison would surely see that I have moved within it, that I am alive within it—

Only Sario gazes upon me. Only his eyes watch me while I go mad.

No. I will not go mad. I must be strong of mind and will and heart. For my child.

But I am so tired . . . two nights I have been here, two nights without sleep or surcease from this horror. No one has seen me. No one but Sario.

Matra Dolcha, when will he set me free?

The day of Sancterria, Tazia received Arrigo early in the afternoon at her old caza in town. He had a few hours free between his luncheon with the Silk Merchants Guild and the evening's festivities. They went out into the tiny garden behind the house to enjoy the sunshine. Tazia leaned back comfortably against Arrigo's chest, listening to the music of the bees. It was safe to relax here, shielded from prying eyes.

She had recently begun refurbishing her former home: taking back her own carpets and tapestries and furniture from Garlo's caza and castello, buying replacements for things discarded when she'd married. Soon she would resume her old life here and it would be just as it had been in the years before Mechella, when Arrigo had been entirely hers.

How often in those days had they done this: lazed away a soft sunny day on the square of lawn while bees dipped into new flowers and butterflies floated on a warm, languid breeze. Arrigo sat with his back to a tree trunk, Tazia reclining between his thighs, his arms enwrapping her and her head on his shoulder. She had never been so happy, and she smiled as she told him why.

"Rafeyo says the painting is ready."

"Mmm?"

"It only awaits your word. Whenever you please, Mechella will become as loyal and obedient as any man could wish." She laughed. "Just like a little trained puppy!"

A chuckle vibrated against her spine. "More boring than ever."

"But *compliant*. You must be careful not to order anything too contrary to her recent behavior for a while, Arrigo. Slide into it gradually. If there should be any sudden alteration—"

" 'Cordo, Tazia. We've talked about this before. You must admit, though, it would be amusing to command something really interesting. As punishment. She could host your next birthday ball," he suggested, then laughed aloud. "Better, maybe she ought to take to a Sanctia cell for a few years."

She winced; it reminded her of Garlo's wretched son, the cause of all her troubles with her husband. Garlo cared nothing for her renewed affair with Arrigo, but would never forgive her for the loss of Verradio to the Ecclesia. Perhaps Rafeyo could paint Garlo compliant, too. And Verradio silent forever. She wasn't sure exactly what could and could not be done. Rafeyo had been so busy with his painting and his classes and his special tutorials with Premio Dioniso that yesterday was the first time he'd come to see her in months.

Eiha, what she knew didn't matter. It only mattered what Rafeyo knew—and what he did with it.

Besides, she had plans of her own to pursue. Slowly, as if it had only just occurred to her, she said, "There *is* a way to punish her as she deserves. *You* could have another child."

"Not unless it was yours."

"It can be, in a way. I have a young cousin—"

He sat up, dislodging her from her comfortable nest in his arms. She turned to face him, putting all her yearning into her eyes.

"Arrigo, hear me out. Her name is Serenissa. She's my younger sister's child, born a year after Rafeyo and a Mennino do'Confirmattio, as he is. She's not quite eighteen, very bright and witty—and she even reminds me of myself in looks, the way I was at her age."

"You're still the most beautiful woman I've ever seen. But I won't do it, Tazia. Not if the woman isn't you. I promised you fidelity. That you didn't ask is all the more reason for me to give it. I couldn't make love to another woman, even one who looked like you."

"Not even for a child who would be ours?" she whispered. "Mechella's creature Leilias is wed to the Limner Zevierin—he's sterile, but they want children. She's at the Palasso even now, looking for a suitable father. Zevierin will treat her children as if he had sired them. He loves her that much. He wants her children that much."

"Tazia—carrida dolcha meya—" Arrigo drew her back into his arms, holding fiercely. "You are not only the most beautiful but the most generous and loving woman I've ever known! If you truly want this—"

"More than anything but your love, Arrigo. I swear to you I'll think of this child as ours, yours and mine. The cruelest thing I ever had to endure was that I could never bear you a child. But this way—don't you see—we could do what we've pretended so many times, make a baby of our own."

He was quiet for a few minutes, the drowsy hum of the bees and the sound of his heart the only things she heard. Then: "If you adopted the baby, wouldn't it take Garlo's name?"

"Never! I'd never give him legal rights over a Grijalva! He—or she—would be a fosterling, and remain a Grijalva. Only you and I and the mother would know that the baby is also a do'Verrada."

"Well, naturally it must be kept absolutely secret."

"Naturally," she agreed. All proof and documentation would be most secret indeed—until the time was right to reveal it. Her own adherents among the family would approve this. Mechella's sons would never take a Grijalva Mistress, having grown up prejudiced against the tradition by their mother. Such a smear on the canvas of Grijalva power could not be tolerated. A bastard would ensure do'Verrada compliance no matter what the vagaries of Mechella's sons. Tazia was sure she could explain it attractively enough to the important Grijalvas on her side so they would look the other way and break faith with an agreement dating back to Lord Limner Sario and Duke Alejandro. Even if she couldn't convince them— and she would judge the telling most carefully before breathing a word—*she* would have the child in her possession.

"—the next Confirmattio," Arrigo was saying, and Tazia tore her mind from delectable possibilities to find him much less stunned than before. "The child would be attributed to the boy whose place I take."

Much less stunned. It was insulting, how quickly he'd taken to the idea.

"The perfect solution," she told him. "But could we be sure of trusting the boy?"

"Eiha, there is that. What of the girl? Can she be trusted?"

"I'm sure of it." Tazia created laughter out of nothing. "Serenissa has always regretted that she was born too late to be your Mistress and too early to be Alessio's."

But Serenissa's daughter—and Rafeyo would use every scrap of magic he possessed to ensure that it *was* a daughter—would be of an age to seduce Alessio in twenty or so years. She laughed more easily, contemplating Mechella's face when she found out that her darling elder boy was sleeping with his own half sister.

Arrigo made the correct remark about being glad Tazia had been the one chosen for him, then returned to the logistics of getting Serenissa pregnant. As if Tazia hadn't already thought of everything—though it must appear to him that he'd worked it out on his own.

As she listened, guiding him subtly toward the conclusions she wished him to reach, she reflected that it really was rather touching, how it never even occurred to him that the lovely, fecund, dangerous Grijalva girl would have to die in childbed.

✦ FIFTY-FOUR ✦

Several hours before the Sancterria celebrations were due to begin, Dioniso let himself into Rafeyo's tiny atelierro and locked the door behind him. The room reeked of paint and solvents and stale urine from the unemptied chamberpot by the window. Well, naturally it hadn't been tended; Rafeyo kept the door locked. A pathetically easy lock it was to pick, too.

Rafeyo was not present. His sketches were: dozens of them, tacked up on the walls and spread out on the worktable. Dioniso was impressed in spite of himself by the boy's ability. On one wall were depictions of bygone Lord Limners in chronological order. It was, if nothing else, quite a fashion show. Starched neck-ruffs spread to outrageous widths before narrowing to white collars and then vanishing altogether; draped cloaks changed to long jackets, embroidered vests, and finally simple tunics; knee-britches (how he'd hated those!) were abandoned for trousers and boots. The only constants were the gray feathered cap and ceremonial collar of office. It had been such a long time since he'd felt that momentous golden weight across his shoulders, more satisfying than even the Chieva do'Orro at his breast.

Another wall showed several studies of Lord Limner Riobaro's *Peintraddo Chieva*. As anticipated, the candlelight had been troublesome for Rafeyo; Matra, he'd had trouble with it himself when he'd painted it. But Rafeyo was getting the feel of it rather nicely, as far as one could tell in a pencil sketch. Dioniso gazed for a long moment at the handsome young man—how wonderful it would be to be that young again! Eiha, soon. He could remember having worn that face. Perhaps if it had truly been his, Saavedra would never even have glanced at Alejandro.

On the worktable was the preliminary small oil on scrap canvas of Rafeyo himself in Riobaro's pose, gray drapery behind him and candle before him. Not yet filled out in detail, still it would suffice as a lure—*if* he had imbued it with magic. Dioniso bent to inspect it, squinting in late afternoon light through high attic windows. He cursed his slowly failing eyesight and his Grijalva pride that refused any palliative more conspicuous than a lens tucked in a pocket. Yet he saw the sign in the sketch: a tiny scratch on the back of the left hand, as if a fingernail had scraped across dried paint.

Cabessa merditto! he thought, shaking his head. The fool boy had even tested the magic. But his folly was proof of Dioniso's wisdom. Teasing Rafeyo down certain paths—not that he'd needed much urging; hinting at this and that—cautiously, for he was quick-witted; revealing just enough to make him hunger for more—certain that he would experiment on his own. What a wondrous thing curiosity was. How perfectly it complemented ambition, and put luster on the Luza do'Orro. He of all people knew this. He had lived his life by it. No surprise to anyone when Rafeyo continued to do the same.

He allowed himself to anticipate the moment. Rafeyo: young, strong, and his. Other men knew what it was to possess a woman's body for a few sweet minutes; he knew what it was to possess another's flesh for a lifetime. To feel bone and muscle and skin and blood and sinew, and make it irrevocably his own. Only he had felt such things. He was unique. He was Sario.

He smiled, reliving cherished memories—indeed, he could almost taste the sticky-sweet poppy syrup on his tongue. A mild dosage timed to take effect shortly after the transfer, it caused slight drowsiness, vague disorientation. He'd learned it was useful to make sure the abandoned host was befuddled; reliance on shock alone could be risky. One could never be sure of the resilience of any given mind.

As always when he dipped into bright remembered pleasures, he called up the darker colors of danger as well. He knew everything that would happen, everything he would experience. It had been twenty-eight years since the last time—nearly twenty-nine, he realized with some startlement—but he remembered everything. Including the dangers.

Only two things truly imperiled him. The first occurred during the instant the body died with the freeing of its spirit. The risk lay not in damage to abandoned flesh; it came when the soul had not yet been directed to its new home. Liberated from familiar matter, *something*—soul, consciousness, mind; he preferred to call it "spirit"—cast about in growing panic. It inevitably sensed the nearness of the shell it had so recently animated, struggling against the dictates of the lingua oscurra, trying desperately to reinhabit its former home. Forbidden this shelter, it sought the familiar in a painting from which it also must be blocked. Turning the spirit from blood it recognized was ever an act of sheer will.

But in the next instant came even greater danger. Denied its own flesh and even the whispering memory of it that was the painting, the spirit felt *hunger.* As many times as it had happened, as prepared for it as he had become, the reality forever awed him. Perhaps one day he would decide if it was wholly one thing, the spirit hungering to be incarnate—or wholly another, the empty body calling out to be filled. Whichever it might truly be, that moment was the crux: if he could not guide the spirit to the flesh waiting for it, it might escape him. Such required the strongest magic of all.

He had never yet failed. He would not fail with Rafeyo.

He was about to leave the atelierro when curiosity made him investigate the stacked canvases behind the door. If Rafeyo had gone against the decision of the Viehos Fratos—not to mention his own private strictures—and continued to paint those appalling landscapes, Dioniso would—

Landscape? Not technically. An architectural rendering, in Blooded paints that reeked from the canvas. Every malevolent symbol in the *Folio* and almost as many from the *Kita'ab* appeared in ribbon-wreathed lozenges around the edges, accompanied by runes so foul that even he was staggered.

His first thought was that Rafeyo was indeed a fool to have kept this at the Palasso. If anyone but Dioniso had discovered it—

Ah, but where else to hide it other than in damned near plain sight?

Dioniso was torn between fury and admiration. Clever boy! And twice clever to have cobbled together bits and pieces, hints and intimations, what he knew and what he could guess, from what Dioniso had taught him. He'd strewn insinuations freely, but never suspected the boy's hatred would provide such fertile ground. It would never do to let Rafeyo know how he had startled his master. Matra, even the stars were in their proper places!

It required no guesswork to know what Rafeyo intended with this perfect portrait of Corasson on the night of Sancterria.

"You go on without me, Arrigo," Tazia said. "I should put in an appearance at Baroness Lissina's reception. I'll join you later." She stood on tiptoe to kiss him in the late afternoon shadow of a poplar tree. "I have a lovely spot all picked out, nestled in a hollow of the hill where we can watch the sun rise. My cook is packing a breakfast."

"Sounds wonderful," he smiled. "I'll slip away from my parents during the Paraddio Luminosso."

"Eiha, change your shoes to boots first, carrido. If you march all night in those soft things you're wearing now, you'll be blistered until Luna Qamho."

He kissed her cheek. "I really must find a servant who looks to my comfort as tenderly as you do. Until later, dolcha meya."

If she was irritated at being cast as his most faithful servant, she gave him no sign. He left by a back alley, for they did not yet visit each other openly in broad daylight—the very last of the proprieties they observed. As she went upstairs to put on evening clothes she vowed that this last trivial bit of compordotta would not endure long. Once Mechella was brought to heel like a good little lapdog, Tazia would kiss Arrigo in public if she felt like it. The Grand Duke and Grand Duchess could scowl all they liked. Tazia would have Arrigo. And Rafeyo. And most of the Grijalvas. And a dutiful, obedient Mechella tucked away forever at Corasson. And, eventually, a little do'Verrada of her very own in the nursery.

She had to wait ten minutes for her footman to fetch a hired hack, then endured another ten minutes of bad springs and stuffy warmth on the ride to Caza do'Dregez across town. Lissina had for nearly thirty years held a ladies-only reception on Sancterria. Admission, by invitation only, was limited to the nobility and none but the wealthiest merchants' wives—for the price of gobbling down fruit ices in company with the Baroness was a generous "voluntary" contribution to Lissina's endless charities. As Tazia gave the butler the green leather pouch provided with the invitation for the purpose—suitably stuffed with do'Alva money—she wondered dismally if, on Lissina's death, she as a Grijalva Mistress would be expected to perform the same tedious duties.

Then she brightened. When Lissina died and the family inherited Dregez, she would suggest that the charities and this annual reception go with the title and lands. A tribute to dear Lissina, beloved of all. Pleased with herself, it was easy to charm and chat—even when she caught sight of Leilias Grijalva in the crowd. Their gazes met; Leilias was the first to look away.

As the sun slowly set, Meya Suerta began its revels. Torches would be lighted at the first sight of the evening star. Every business and residential block would have its own little fiery parade. The Cathedral Imagos Brilliantos would be circled by the sanctas and sanctos, Palasso Verrada by the family with the Premia Sancta and Premio Sancto, and Palasso Grijalva by everyone able to walk. After this would come a gigantic procession to the fields outside the city, where a bull, a stallion, and a ram would be driven between twin bonfires to represent every animal in Tira Virte. Music, dancing, and drinking would follow until the dawn.

All of which meant that Tazia could enter Palasso Grijalva, meet her son as planned, and afterward sneak away to meet Arrigo on the hillside, all unobserved.

Rafeyo took the Corasson painting from behind the door and set it on his easel. For a long while he simply gazed at it, a half-smile tugging his lips.

He had finished the last lines of the *lingua oscurra* only two hours ago; the prick on his thumb was a sweetly stinging reminder of that final effort of magic. With the words, the seal had been set on the painting even though the paint was not yet dry; they would be feeling it at Corasson by now!

Eiha, they were all outside, ever since sunset, lighting torches for the celebrations and sanctifications. Only those within the house would feel anything.

But not for long. Tonight. He would not wait another year for the stars to come back to the position shown in the painting. Who knew but that Mechella would add a seedling tree north of the house, or alter the flowers bordering the drive, or change the wooden trim to yellow instead of green. No, it must be tonight.

It had been laughably easy. Tell the Fratos he was spending a few nights at his mother's caza; tell them he'd taken a commission for a *Birth* or *Will* from someone living outside the city; tell them anything, and they believed him. Even Mechella's stupid orphans had been useful; he'd said that a picture he'd done had been damaged, and he must ride to the remote Casteyan village to do it up right again.

There were no nights at his mother's, no commissions, no trips to Casteya. But he knew the road to Corasson as well as he knew his own face.

This reminded him of the portrait he would soon begin. His own face, his own clothes—but Riobaro's pose, easy and dignified, lit by Riobaro's subtle and mysterious candlelight that had taken him so long to perfect. They'd all know whose *Peintraddo Chieva* he'd used as a guide for his own. He meant them to, meant to put them on notice. He glanced over his shoulder at the table where he'd left the oil sketch, but the lamplight didn't reach that far and he saw only the usual jumble of different papers and scrap canvas.

He set the lamp on the floor and resumed contemplation of his true master work. Corasson was reproduced down to the smallest

detail. All the ridiculous towers and turrets, mismatched crenella-
tions, climbing roses and oak trees and every damned rock and
flower—all of it in exact position. It had taken him a very long time
to get everything just so.

Coaxing the necessary information about magic from Premio
Dioniso had been simplicity itself. Dioniso the Great Premio Frato,
who thought himself omniscient! The old fool had never realized
that Rafeyo was storing up all the little threads of knowledge and
weaving them into the whole complicated tapestry that was
Grijalva art. Flattery here, wheedling there, a roundabout question
and a seemingly spontaneous leap of insight—Rafeyo grinned
widely and danced a few irrepressible steps over to the window.

The evening star had appeared, and the crescent moon above it
curved like the pregnant belly of the Mother. The star signified
sanctification of the Son in her womb, just as tonight all the land
and people and animals would be purified with torches imitating
starfire. All across Tira Virte the Paraddio Luminossos would circle
villages and towns and fields, and the animals would be driven between bonfires, and those in charge of public safety would flinch
with nervousness lest anything catch fire. Tonight, something
would.

The sky outside was nearly a match for the sky in the painting.
Only a little while now, until the moon rose just a little more and
the star glowed just a little brighter in the darkening sky. The urge
to dance his glee left him, replaced by a shivering—but of excitement, not that strange chill that had come to him yesterday. It had
seemed to originate in his lips and tongue and behind his eyes,
spreading down his whole body, making him fear he was catching
cold—and Limners feared illness of any kind, those intimations of
early death. But the shivers had passed after a few hours, and this
morning he'd woken feeling better than ever before in his life. And
why not? He had painted in oils, in blood, in sweat and semen and
tears and spit. In *magic*. This was what he'd been born for.

He returned to the painting, counting off minutes under his
breath. From his pocket he took a new, clean brush, dipped it in
lamp oil, lit it at the wick. A miniature torch to sanctify the painting of Corasson. To purify Corasson itself by burning it to the
ground.

"I really can't allow this, you know."

Rafeyo felt his knees give with shock at the sound of the
Premio's voice. It came from the corner shadows, and continued
with the cold inevitability of a Casteyan winter.

"Not that I care about Mechella. It's you I'm concerned for,

Rafeyo. You have no idea what will happen to you if you set fire to that painting." He gave a dry little laugh. "You know only what it amused me to tell you, and thought yourself oh-so-clever to guess the rest. Don't you realize I've watched you trace every little clue back to its origin and forward to its end? You have an expressive face, mennino, with remarkably passionate eyes. It's something I'll have to remember, and guard against."

"P–Premio—what—I don't—"

He stepped from the shadows, the lines of his body broken by the canvas he held in one hand. Rafeyo knew it for his own self-portrait sketch.

"En verro, it's not just you I'm concerned with. There's a painting at Corasson. A very important painting—the most important I ever created. I can't allow you to destroy it along with Corasson. And yourself, I might add."

"Mys–self—?" he stammered stupidly. "What do you—"

"Incoherence can at times be an admirable trait." He moved nearer, the oil sketch in one hand, the other extended toward Rafeyo, nearly touching him. "If you're attempting to ask what I mean by all this, allow me to show you."

Rafeyo felt his hand grasped firmly in the old man's disease-gnarled fingers. Panic thudded through him. He would be stopped—Corasson would stand—Mechella would live—all of it, all the work and the blood and the riding day and night, all for nothing—*nothing!*

Rafeyo lunged for the painting with the fire-tipped brush. The old man's grip on his hand kept him from reaching it. The flames passed near the painting but not near enough. He struggled, gained a step, leaned against the restraining grip.

Fire touched paint, and Rafeyo screamed.

He was yanked back but not allowed to fall. The old man's lean, cold arms wrapped him round, close and possessive as a lover. As the pain slowly eased, Rafeyo heard the chill inexorable voice again, again as if from shadows, for agony had blinded him with tears.

"Now do you understand? The demonstration with your *Peintraddo Chieva* is much less painful, only a pinprick. When you damage a canvas such as this one, painted with all these signs and symbols and runes, with everything a Limner can possibly put into it of his own substance, you suffer in your own body what you cause the painting to suffer."

It was true. Fire throbbed with every frantic heartbeat.

"Whatever is the most powerful fluid you use, this is how you will feel it. With tears, your eyes will burn. Urine, and you'll want to take a knife to your own manhood. But blood has precedence. And blood is in this painting of Corasson. As you now know, Rafeyo, this was a very foolish thing to do."

Pain was receding now, bearable. Fear replaced fire in his veins. He shook with it, terrified of this man with his cold, cold eyes.

Suddenly the crooked fingers released his hand and touched the tears that runneled his cheeks. Before he could react to the almost fatherly gesture, the fingers moved to the sweat on his upper lip. Then, swiftly, a thumb thrust between his lips and under his tongue, and came out slick with saliva. The moisture thus collected was daubed onto the scrap of canvas in the man's other hand.

"Grazzo, that completes the inventory. Except for semen, of course, but I've found that acquiring it is a disgusting process and not really necessary. By the way, you really ought to empty your chamberpot on a regular basis, Rafeyo."

His mouth was ash-dry, as if every drop of him had been raped away by that invasive thumb.

"You don't understand any of this, do you? Poor Rafeyo. Only a little while longer. Patience."

He'd heard that word often, but never accompanied by this particular smile. His gaze involuntarily shifted to the floor as a boot heel crushed the absurd little ceremonial torch. He felt as if his heart was extinguished in the same moment. His own heart; the wrong corasson.

Through wordless, mindless despair he felt his hand taken again, and his fingers were drawn across the last of the oscurra, smearing the paint. Destroying the spell.

"For all your efforts, an amateurish attempt. There are things in the *Kita'ab* that would smite Mechella where she stood. Now do you know what true power is, boy? Now do you understand what a Grijalva Limner is?"

A sob caught in his throat, strangling him, as his teacher and his tormentor began a low rhythmic murmuring, like a sancto chanting his devotions. All at once Rafeyo swayed on his feet as if not only his heart but his very being had been crushed. The old man's eyes were at once glazed and gleaming, watching something in the distance and yet focused fiercely on Rafeyo's face.

Curious. To be wandering. Drifting. Dissolving. Wayward spirit floating free, light and insubstantial as a feather—

No!

Casting about in sudden fear for hands to strike out with—

—voice to scream with—

—eyes to see with—

—heartbeat, breath, skin, bone, flesh, SUBSTANCE—

Something called to him. Bereft and terrified, he groped for the thing that was familiar, yet very weak in ways he did not understand—trying to clutch his own shadow. A wall sprang up—he could not see or feel it but he knew it was there, pulsing with a rhythm he didn't recognize. A rhythm rather like a heartbeat. . . .

Corasson! I must . . . the fire . . . where are my hands I need my hands I need the fire the burning my hands—

I know. I know you do. This way, Rafeyo. Come along. This way.

This time there was guidance. He lunged as he had for the painting of Corasson. And felt again the familiar casing of muscle and bone and skin clothing his soul—

Ah, so good to feel his body around him again, after that horrible lack. A supremely powerful magic had been used on him, and he was wild to know its name and uses and the means by which it was called forth. To do this to Mechella!

But how strange he felt. Dizzy, a little queasy, perspective altered as if he'd suddenly grown an inch or two in height. And his hands hurt. They hurt in every knuckle as he grabbed the back of a chair to steady himself. His muscles were sluggish. He couldn't understand it; a few moments ago he'd been taut with tension. His pulse was as dull as if drugged, when it ought to be racing with the last of his fear.

Still, the frightening aimlessness was gone, and he had substance again, bones and flesh and eyes. He used those eyes to look around in befuddlement.

A hand that was his own held up a framed canvas. Other fingers, also his, delicately displayed a needle. As the sliver of gold poised at the painted chest, he recognized what sort of painting it was, and the face within it.

By why would this man puncture the heart of his own *Peintraddo Chieva?*

He tried to move, to reach out, to stop what was to come. He looked down at his awkward, hurting, listless hands.

They were not his hands. They were gnarled and mottled and *they were not his hands.*

All the strength drained out of him and he staggered against the chair. He looked up and saw a face by lamplight.

The face was his own. His mouth smiled at him. But it was not his smile.

"Like looking into a living mirror," said his voice.

He had not spoken. The lungs and throat and tongue and lips he felt had not created speech. Yet he heard his own voice, issuing from his own mouth.

"Premio D–Dioniso—" And he flinched on hearing the deep tones, desiccated as old parchment, that came from his own throat. Not his own voice, not anything like his own—

"Sario." His mouth smiled at him. Not his smile. "And Ignaddio and Martain and even Riobaro—yes, even he. All Sario. But after tonight . . . *Rafeyo*."

"*Sario—?*"

He heard the voice that was not his, and looked at the hands that were not his, and at the painted face that was not his—and at the living face that *was* his.

Had been his.

When the needle pierced the painted heart, he finally understood. And, in understanding and in agony, died.

⚊⊶ FIFTY-FIVE ⊶⚊

Soothing the tension of Rafeyo's terror—rapid pulse and respiration, tremors, all the mindless responses to being for a time mindless—was the work of a few moments. It was like calming a frightened child, and indeed the words he murmured in his head as he stroked the new hands over the new arms and legs and chest were those of a loving father: "Hush, I'm here, don't be afraid, carrido ninito, I'm here now."

Sario stretched luxuriously, getting the feel of this strong young body. A little shorter than Dioniso, but he was only nineteen and probably hadn't finished growing. He inspected the hands by lamplight—the precious, supple hands—enjoying the long straight fingers and fine skin. Slowly, as if he at last explored the body of a coveted woman, he ran his palms over the new body. Rounded muscles of shoulders and upper arms; firm chest; flat belly; lean thighs—he laughed as manhood twitched and stirred, and on a whim caressed it to hardness. The swift surge of delight startled him. It had been years since he'd felt so urgent a response.

But with no time to indulge it, he took his hands away. All Rafeyo's sketches must be soaked to unidentifiable impotence. He had no way of knowing which of them had been bespelled. The paints with his blood in them must be locked away for the far future, when he would need them to paint himself out of Rafeyo and into another strong young man. But first the old wreck that had been Dioniso must be carried to bed. Tomorrow it would be sadly reported that the honored Premio Frato had died in his sleep of a seizure, probably of the heart. Which, in a way, he had.

Sario slipped the golden needle from the portrait and lit a match to burn it clean. Sancterria, he thought, amused; though the needle was long since hallowed by usage. Consecrated, for him, for having belonged to Saavedra—a gift from one of their cousins in hopes of encouraging embroidery rather than paint on canvas. She'd scorned it and given it to him for work on frescoes.

Through the heart with a golden needle that had been hers—it was both fitting, in memory of the pain she'd given him long ago, and merciful to Rafeyo. In the past he'd experimented with sliding it into the painting's head, but correct placement was tricky and sometimes produced only a violent headache. The abdomen he had used only once, and shuddered to recall it. Ignaddio, that had been; his first host, taken before he'd thought of the needle and used a paletto knife in the painted belly. The resulting mess stank to the skies and took hours to clean up.

Now he stored the purified, newly sanctified needle in a little silver box. He knelt beside the cooling corpse and undid the first buttons of the shirt, preparing to check for a telltale drop of congealing blood. Once, to his horror, the aged heart had burst at the touch of the needle and pumped blood all over his hands. Ever since (eiha, who had it been? Ettoro, perhaps), he'd kept a clean shirt handy just in case.

He was about to inspect the chest when the door opened behind him. Surely he'd locked it—yes, of course, and so had Rafeyo when he entered. But someone else must have a key. With sickening certainty, he knew who it was.

"Rafeyo!"

Tazia swirled into the room, white silk cloak and festive yellow gown rustling importantly. Sario tried to position his body to hide Dioniso, hoping the lamplight was dim enough. As he looked up, with startled dismay involuntarily—if appropriately—scrawled on his face, he wondered how it was possible for the same chi'patro blood that had created Saavedra's wistful loveliness to produce this woman. Tazia was beautiful, but there was an obviousness about her, a polished and disciplined perfection that could disgust, in time. She was inbred, overbred, the way lapdogs were too closely mated for looks without thought to temperament or intelligence.

Of this woman's ferocious character he had no doubts. As her gaze flickered to the painting of Corasson and then to the corpse on the floor behind him, she proved that brains at least had not been bred out of the Grijalvas.

"He caught you," she said quite calmly. "You should have been more careful. How did you kill him?"

"I didn't! He—he just—he was furious, and then he just died!"

She arched a brow, as if she *almost* believed him, then shrugged. "Eiha, he was close to fifty, and that's obscenely old for a Limner. He mustn't be found here. We'll have to take him to his room so it looks as if he died in his sleep."

"You always think of everything, matra meya." He knew instantly that it was the wrong diminutive, though her surprise turned at once to a smile.

"Of course I do, carrido. Here, I'll help. Did you finish before he came in?"

As they straightened out crooked limbs, he told her. Whined, actually; it was characteristic of Rafeyo when thwarted. "I don't know what happened. It didn't work. I did everything just right, I know I did—but it didn't work!"

Tazia shot him an angry glance across Dioniso's prostrate body. "If you did all of it correctly, why *didn't* it work?"

"I don't know!"

She sat back on the high heels of her gold-stitched slippers. "I can't say I'm not disappointed, Rafeyo. But you'll try again."

"But if I don't know what happened, how can I fix it?"

"You'll be an acknowledged Limner soon. Nothing will be kept from you then. You'll identify your mistakes—"

"I didn't do anything wrong, I know I didn't!"

"You will identify your mistakes," she repeated sternly, "and rectify them. And then you must paint as quickly as possible, because Arrigo has agreed to the thing we discussed."

"He has?" Sario hoped his expression wasn't too blank. He hadn't yet spent the usual long hours at a mirror, experimenting with control of a new face. And he was worried about controlling the body, too—the legs and the reach were shorter, the weight less, the poise of the head just different enough to unbalance him a trifle.

"He's quite eager," Tazia was saying, her voice sour. "And he won't like waiting until you spell his bitch of a wife to obedience. On the other hand, I'll have more time to work on Serenissa. Which reminds me, can you paint her amenable to bearing his bastard? It would help."

Sario reeled. A Grijalva bastard? Was she insane? Time sideslipped and he was once again the Sario he'd been born, learning that Saavedra was pregnant. Savagely he thrust away centuries-old emotion and fixed his mind on the appalling woman before him.

"Well?" she demanded. "Can you? And make it a girl?"

"I—I think so." Rising, he compelled his muscles to steadiness and reached down to help her up. Touching her was unexpectedly disgusting. "I should clean up in here and hide the painting. Can you get him into the hall? I'll be there in a minute to help."

"You want *me* to drag him? Eiha, 'cordo. But hurry."

Each of them took a leg and lugged Dioniso to the door. As Sario opened it, Tazia cast a last look at the painting of Corasson.

"She's nowhere to be seen in that. How can the magic work if she's not in the painting?"

He thought fast. Tazia obviously knew nothing of her son's plans for arson. "It's a special spell," he said. "It creates a whole atmosphere at Corasson."

Her black eyes went wide. "Do you mean that the very air she breathes would contain spells of obedience to Arrigo's wishes? How marvelous!" Alight with pride, she leaned over to kiss his cheek. He resisted the impulse to wipe his skin. "You never told me such things could be done. You've surpassed the greatest Limners, Rafeyo. Even Riobaro!"

"I try," he said, sketching a grin onto his face. "Drag him as far as you can. His rooms are down the stairs at the end of the hall."

"Don't be too long."

"You're wonderful, Mother. Did I ever tell you that?"

"I try," she replied, and winked.

⚷

"I don't like this," Zevierin said softly. "You had no reason to follow her from Lissina's except vague suspicion."

"Tazia looked entirely too pleased with herself to please *me*." Leilias walked boldly into the Limners' wing of the Palasso, where not even female servants were allowed, and started for the nearest staircase. "And I suppose it was 'vague suspicion' that made you tell Cabral to destroy that drawing!"

"Not that stair, it takes forever. This corridor is faster." He waited until she was beside him again, then caught lightly at her arm. "How can you be sure she's in the Limners' quarters?"

"Who else would she visit here but her son? Zevi, I wasted a lot of time finding you in that crowd outside. She may already have done what she came to do and left by now. We have to hurry."

"What do you think she might be doing?"

"How do I know?" she cried, frustrated, and flinched as her voice echoed. More quietly, she continued, "Why here, when she can see Rafeyo anytime at her caza? Why tonight, with everyone gone and the Palasso deserted?"

" 'Cordo," he agreed reluctantly. "The senior estudos are one floor up from the Viehos Fratos. Come on."

They climbed one flight and were halfway up another when they heard a woman's voice rise in some impressively creative cursing. Leilias froze at Zevierin's side.

"Tazia," she said with no sound at all.

"You were right," he whispered back.

They crept up the second flight and then the third, praying for silent floorboards as they followed bizarre scraping noises toward the Fratos' rooms. Turning a corner, neither was able to stifle gasps at the sight of the Countess do'Alva, hauling a body by its heels toward the stairs.

She glanced around, eyes wild and strange in the lamplight from down the hall. Her hair had come loose and her face was flushed, and rage flared in her eyes when she recognized them. Rallying quickly, she stood straight, let go the man's ankles, and with regal arrogance demanded, "What are *you* doing here?"

Zevierin stared at her, amazed. *She* was the one dragging a corpse. Then he saw whose corpse it was. "Premio Dioniso!" he blurted.

"I found him dead in the upper hall," Tazia said—too coolly, yet somehow not quite coolly enough. "I called out but everyone's gone. You two take him to his rooms and see him decently put into bed while I go for help outside."

"Of course," Zevierin said, as if he believed every word of it, and went forward to crouch by the Premio's head, fully aware of his wife's astounded eyes. He was sickened by the expression on the dead face: stark terror, hideous pain. Heart attack? Brain seizure? Zevierin hadn't the medical experience to know.

But he did understand the small bloodstain. The white shirt had tugged out of the belt as the body was dragged along, but it was easy to see that the drop corresponded to the left chest, just over the heart. Without conscious will he saw his hands rip open the shirt, buttons flying to rattle away in shadows beyond the lamplight. There—the little smear on bare skin—

"Murdered," he said thickly, not recognizing his own voice. "Premio Frato Dioniso was murdered."

Tazia backed up a few steps. "What? Impossible!"

Leilias bounded toward her, grabbing a double handful of costly silk cloak. The gold ties at the throat choked Tazia; she scrabbled to undo them and the slick white material hissed from her shoulders. Leilias dropped it and dug her fingers into the woman's arms.

"How dare you! Take your hands off me this instant!"

Leilias yanked her back toward the corpse. "What are you doing in the Limners' wing?"

"A question I could ask of you!"

"Why tonight?" She gave her captive a vigorous shake. Tazia tossed black curls from her face and glared.

"By what right do you interrogate me? Let me go!"

In a way, Zevierin had to admire her. Courage, cunning, arrogance, or sheer bravaddio, it was a remarkable performance. He got to his feet, certain that this sick weight of weariness in his bones was a preview of twenty years hence, when he would be old.

"Did you kill him?" he asked quietly. "Did you do it, or did Rafeyo?"

She struggled a moment longer against Leilias's grasp, then gave an incoherent cry and began to sob. "Rafeyo! It was Rafeyo!"

So much for courage. And Arrigo preferred *this* to Mechella.

"He did it, he's responsible!" she babbled. "He told me to come here tonight—I had to, he's a Limner, I'm afraid of what he might do if I disobey—he's told me things about your magic—terrible things! I went to his atelierro and there was Premio Dioniso, dead! I had nothing to do with it, nothing!"

Perhaps that much was true.

"Once out of his sight, why didn't you run?" asked Leilias.

A slight hesitation that said much. Then: "He's my *son*. I've protected him all my life—when you're a mother, you'll understand—it's your duty to help him, love him, no matter what! He's my only son, a mother loves her son no matter what he does—"

Frightened, but not frightened out of her considerable wits. Zevierin reconsidered his estimation of Tazia. And reminded himself to make his wife promise never to love any son of theirs like *this*.

"Where is he now?" Leilias rattled Tazia's teeth this time.

"Gone, I expect," Zevierin said, sparing Tazia the attempt to find a plausible lie. "We've certainly made enough noise to warn him. Can you hold her here while I find Mequel?"

"Certainly."

Leilias did something then that no Limner would ever do—no Limner, musician, goldsmith, or anyone whose hands were his life and livelihood. Zevierin watched in awe as his wife swung a fist at the Countess do'Alva's chin, with instantaneous and predictable results.

Further reminder: never, ever make Leilias angry.

Laughter and lamplight in every window and doorway. Roil of raucous bodies dancing, parting, swaying, staggering. Reek of alcohol sweat, pungent stink of pitch from burned-out torches, stench of cheap perfume. He slipped through the crowded streets like a shadow on strong young legs, kept watch with sharp young eyes. At the atelierro above the wine shop, clever young hands wielded the first key and subtle young fingers unpainted the second and the third.

And then he was safe.

He needed no light. He had known this place for hundreds of years. He knew where the *Peintraddo Memorrio* faced the wall, he knew the pattern of stains on the paint-blotched tarp covering it. Table here, chair beside it, easel there, trunk in a corner filled with paints and solvents and *Folio* and *Kita'ab,* stacked virgin canvases over by the shuttered window.

Musty sheets, moth-eaten blanket—a haven nonetheless. He curled on the bed and shook for a long time. Telling himself it was only the reaction of this body, this unfamiliar flesh that he could not as yet perfectly control.

No thread of sunlight wove him warning of the day. Sealed and blackened windows, thick wooden shutters over them, heavy burlap curtains over those, no breath of air. He was used to the closeness, to the dust and heavy air. His body was not. He couldn't breathe. The sun rose and warmed Meya Suerta's streets, newly sanctified by fire, and baked the walls and roof of this high attic room, and heated the air around him, and the only reason he knew it was morning was that he could not breathe.

He made himself rise and walk through the humid dark and open the bottle left on the table—how long ago? The wine had soured. He drank anyway. He coughed and spat, and drank more.

At last he sat down. The chair was a relic of Alejandro's reign, once beautiful. The last of the gilding had flaked off a century ago. The velurro cushion had disintegrated long before that. Five times he had replaced the braided rope seat. He supposed he ought to replace the chair itself, but he was never here long enough to justify the bother.

He lit the candles, one in silver and one in gold. His skull grinned at him, whitely shining out of the shadows, and he flinched back.

In the centuries he had owned this building, he'd spent a total of perhaps two months in this squalid atelierro—only to paint the portraits that gave him his next hosts and the additions to the *Peintraddo Memorrio*. He would have to add Rafeyo's face soon.

Another face in the painting, another life memorialized. He sighed a long, draining sigh. Dioniso's had been a good life, productive and useful—but in the end a disaster, and all because of Rafeyo.

The body was calming down. The panic had never been his. It was only the body that had reacted, spurring instant flight. He was grateful. If Zevierin and Leilias had found him, the way they'd found Tazia. . ..

He poured another swallow of wine down his throat. Yes, he was feeling much better now. A little sleep, and later some food—he'd go downstairs and tell the innkeeper to bring him something to eat. They were faithful to him here; he owned the place, after all, the *Deed* painted long ago and tucked into the trunk over in the corner. Successive generations of this same family of innkeepers inherited their trade just as they thought successive generations of his own unnamed family inherited the premises. Once, in the early days, he'd returned after long absence to find the chair had been moved. Two days and an Aguo sketch later, the innkeeper's sister confessed to having poked around the atelierro. Two weeks and a Sanguo painting later, she was dead of a fall down the stairs. Yes, they were faithful to him here ever since.

So he would ask the son of the house to take a message to Palasso Grijalva, and—

Message to whom?

Remaining Rafeyo was impossible. Damn the boy! If only he'd waited, he could have had it all. *Sario* could have had it all. How long since he'd worn the honored regalia of Lord Limner? Not since Riobaro. Nothing had gone right for him since then.

Suddenly he saw this life as Dioniso and this taking of Rafeyo was representative of all his many lives and takings. It had never *worked*. Never the right time or circumstances or luck. Never everything falling into place with sweet perfection. Never finding exactly the right host to bring him back to his rightful place, the place he had held as Sario for too brief a time.

He leaped to his feet and tore the covering from the *Memorrio*. There they were, all his lives except for Rafeyo's, all the faces he'd worn through the centuries.

Ignaddio, lacking the right bloodlines. Zandor, thwarted by Grijalva politics. Verreio, waiting in vain for the then-Lord Limner to die. Martain, condemned by others' envy to insignificance. Guilbarro, destroyed by the incompetence of a criminally stupid sancta sent to heal him. Matteyo, ruined by accusations of collusion in his brother's "suicide." Timirrin, a welcome respite—but nothing of accomplishment, nothing of glory.

Only Riobaro. Only that one perfect life. He gazed upon the wonderful face he had worn for so many brilliant years, the regret more bitter on his tongue than the sour wine.

And after Riobaro? Domaos, and the disastrous affair with Benecitta. Awkward, ugly Renzio. Oaquino—known to the ages as Il Cofforro, The Hairdresser. Ettoro, crippled at thirty-five, whose mother had foolishly offended her powerful half-sister Tazita, Arrigo II's Uncrowned Grand Duchess and ruined her son's chances thereby.

Dioniso had had a chance. Rising to Premio Frato, he'd had the chance to create perfection in Rafeyo.

Gone.

Only Riobaro. Only that one perfect life.

Why?

What had he ever done but to work to the good of his family, his Dukes, his country? He had served so long and so well, he had done things for all of them that any other Limner would shrink to do, that only he, Sario, *The* Grijalva Limner, could ever do—and he was rewarded with only that one perfect life.

He would make another. He vowed it. But first he must rid himself of Rafeyo. If they found him here before he could find another host, he would be lost.

So would Saavedra. He had saved her last night. One day he would tell her about it, how he had saved her life. Right now he must save them both.

But—*who?*

They would lay out Dioniso's body today. There would be no Paraddio Iluminaddio; his death had been sudden and alone. The mother, Giaberta, would come to Meya Suerta from her husband's home and do her ritual weeping and depart. All would know it had been murder; Zevierin and Leilias would tell them. And Tazia, too—he knew enough of her to know she'd try to save herself by blaming her son. He must remember to do something permanent about Tazia.

Rafeyo's sketches were mushy pulp in a Palasso sink by now. Sario had all the paints in his possession—packed neatly in their case, he'd simply grabbed the handle when he'd fled. He supposed he owed Tazia his thanks for giving him precious time to get away.

They could do nothing to "Rafeyo" unless they used the painting of Corasson. But whatever happened to it would happen *at* Corasson. And they knew that. They would not use it. There was no *Peintraddo Chieva* to stick with pins or set alight with fire, there were no paintings at foreign courts or in Tira Virteian cazas or castellos that could be used against him. As for the inheritance paintings done for those wretched Casteyan orphans—those were plain paintings, needing no magic in them.

Rafeyo was beyond their reach.

But Rafeyo would be hunted until they found him and brought him to trial and executed him for the murder of Premio Frato Dioniso. He must find a way out of Rafeyo's body and into another.

Who—?

He stared at the box of paints. He would strengthen them with his own private formulations. Rafeyo had thought he knew so much—he'd known *nothing* of real power. This body could afford to lose the necessary blood. This strong, handsome, perfect young body—

Damn Rafeyo!

Lord Limner Mequel cast a last tired glance around Rafeyo's tiny atelierro. "I do hope that's all for tonight. It's very much past my bedtime."

"It's enough," Zevierin replied grimly.

"The question remains, however—what do we do with what we know? And it must be answered tonight."

"My Lord, is there any reason we can't go downstairs and be comfortable while you decide? And I could use a drink to take the taste of this from my mouth," Zevierin added forthrightly.

"My brittle bones would appreciate a soft chair and some wine. Perhaps your good lady would see to it?"

Leilias—for once the good Grijalva girl—departed immediately to obey. Zevierin held back from offering Mequel any assistance; the Lord Limner acknowledged his tact with a wry smile as he took the younger man's arm.

"She *is* a good lady, make no mistake in it," Mequel murmured as they slowly descended the stairs. "You are fortunate, both as a Limner and as a man."

"I know," Zevierin said softly.

"A piece of advice, Frato meyo. Never think of the years remaining to you. They do not yet exist. And may never exist—after all, crossing a busy avenida can be fatal. You have this day, and you have her love."

"I—I understand, Lord Limner."

"Eiha, understand this, too—that the children she gives you are indeed her gifts to *you*. Any moronno can sire a child. It requires a true man to be a father."

By the time they reached the ground floor, Leilias was ready for them. She led them to a small antechamber, poured wine, made sure Mequel's chair was well-pillowed, and sat down with every evident intent of staying. Although Limner concerns were the concern of no woman, not even a Grijalva woman, this directly involved Mechella.

"So," Mequel said. "Were I reporting to the Grand Duke, I would summarize as follows. We have a painting of Corasson with more—and more vicious—magic than I have ever seen. We have a new paintbrush on the floor, crushed, the bristles burned. We have the dead body of Premio Frato Dioniso and the living body of the Countess do'Alva. And we have no sign of Rafeyo anywhere."

"Not a pleasant sum, no matter how one adds it," Leilias murmured.

"First," Mequel continued after a sip of wine, "and at once most and least important, the Countess. She is found in a place forbidden to women, on the one night of the year when the Palasso is utterly deserted. Her presence is unimportant to the painting and to the corpse. But she is vital in one respect: she was found by a Limner who followed her here, and in this way we discovered all." He smiled slightly at Leilias. "I think we shall conveniently forget your part in this, if you don't mind too much. I'd like to avoid the tedious inquiries that must follow any breach of our little masculine sanctuary."

"I was never here," she agreed. "After I told Zevierin to follow Tazia, I was separated from him in the crowds."

"'Cordo. So Tazia is observed dragging Dioniso's body. For all we know, she intended shoving him down the nearest middens shaft. This is an ancient part of the Palasso and the primitive plumbing is still accessible. But we can be fairly sure she was taking him to his bed, where he would be discovered tomorrow as if he'd died there. Plausible, at his age." He paused for more wine. "However, we know he did not die in his bed. We know almost certainly *why* he died. He learned what Rafeyo was up to. We also know *how* he died."

"His *Peintraddo Chieva*," Zevierin said, nodding. "It's not in the

Crechetta, it's not in Rafeyo's atelierro, or Dioniso's. It's not anywhere we've thought to look."

"Did Rafeyo take it with him when he fled?"

"Probably." Mequel shrugged. "I don't much care. Possibly we
may find an empty frame somewhere with the canvas rudely sliced
out of it. I don't know. What interests me is why he had it in the
first place."

Zevierin sat forward, elbows on his knees. "It would mean
he knew its uses long before he should have known. It also
means—"

"—that he deliberately lured Dioniso to his atelierro to kill
him!" Leilias exclaimed.

"It appears so," said Mequel. "I'd like to know how Rafeyo got
the *Chieva* out of the Crechetta, for none but senior Fratos would
have the key. But considering all else I'm not surprised he accomplished it. A clever young man, this Rafeyo." He sighed. "Tazia's
son."

"He did it all on purpose," Leilias breathed, awed and horrified
in equal measure. "The same night he burned Corasson with the
painting, he'd kill the Premio who taught him such things—so not
just the evidence of the crime but the only witness to his knowledge would be gone!"

Mequel cocked an eyebrow at Zevierin. "Does Mechella *also*
know everything about us? Eiha, don't answer. I'd rather she knew.
Safer that way. Don't look so worried, Zevierin. There'll be no inquiry. A Lord Limner must be practical, which, on occasion, means
forgetful."

"Thank you, my Lord," was Zevierin's humble reply.

"En verro, our secrets seem not so secret anymore, with Dioniso
revealing so much to Rafeyo. And who knows what Rafeyo told
Tazia?"

Mequel sighed. "The point is that Leilias is right, and the murder was no crime of sudden desperation, but of careful planning."

"He certainly planned what he'd do to Corasson!" Leilias rose
to pour more wine for the men. "But did he know its effect on
him?"

"Perhaps he thought only to start a few small fires at Corasson
and let them progress on their own. Accidents of that kind happen
frequently at Sancterria celebrations, with all those torches everywhere. Grazzo, mennina," he said as she filled his glass.

"But he hates Mechella," she told him. "He wouldn't want just to singe a few trees, he'd want to burn Corasson to the ground with her in it."

"He wants my place," Mequel said flatly. "Would his loathing for Mechella be stronger than his ambition? Perhaps he thought that only a *Peintraddo Chieva* could harm him, and because his is not yet painted, he is safe."

"He *is* safe," Zevierin said gloomily. "His paintbox is gone, and there's a pile of sketches soaking in the sink down the hall from his atelierro."

"So we are helpless to punish him." Mequel rubbed his eyes with thumb and forefinger. "Eiha, whatever he knows or doesn't know, believes or doesn't believe about magic, one thing is certain. Dioniso must have wanted very badly to be hailed as the man who educated the next Lord Limner."

"An ambition that was his death," Zevierin said.

"You could use the painting of Corasson," Leilias suggested. "What's done to it would happen there, but we'd know in advance—"

"—and be ready with buckets?" Mequel shook his head. "The painting is of a particular night—*this* night, with the moon and stars all in specific positions. We'd have to wait another year to use it. But you remind me that I want that painting kept safe so Rafeyo will never get at it again."

"Or Tazia." Leilias grimaced. "She'd burn it to ashes even if the agony killed her own son. Personally, I'd like to put it in Galerria Verrada, where Arrigo will have to look at it every time he walks through. But we'd better take it with us to Corasson."

"Arrigo!" Zevierin almost choked on his wine. "I'd forgotten all about him! Do you think he knows anything about this?"

"Or *everything*," Leilias added darkly.

"I prefer to believe he does not," Mequel said slowly. "And I prefer to discover nothing that would convince me otherwise. He will be the next Grand Duke no matter his guilt or innocence."

Leilias's spine became a ramrod. "But if he knew—"

Her husband shook his head. "As many grudges as he has against Mechella, he would never wish her harmed."

"How do you know?" she countered bitterly. "Have you forgotten what happened at that village near Dregez? It could have been his doing—to make himself out the hero to the people!"

"Something else that will not be investigated," Mequel said firmly. "There's a great deal of wisdom in the saying 'Pluvio en laggo,' you know."

"That water may be in the lake, Lord Limner, but it takes only a few drops to poison the whole!"

"Bassda, Leilias."

"The practicality of the Lord Limner extends not just to forget-fulness but to blindness!" Leilias glared at both men.

"Sometimes it does," Mequel agreed blandly. "The subject of Arrigo leads us back to the Countess do'Alva. Naturally, as a no-blewoman she enjoys certain legal privileges. And there is nothing we can prove, in any case. As a Grijalva, however, there are ways of dealing with her."

All Leilias's resentment vanished in a gleeful smile. "Tell! I can't wait!"

"Leave that to me."

"And Rafeyo?" Zevierin put in quickly before his wife could protest.

"Leave him to me as well." Mequel pushed himself painfully to his feet. "People will be coming back inside soon, and Leilias should not be seen here. Zevierin, help me upstairs. Tomorrow morning, when the tragic news that Premio Dioniso died in his sleep is revealed, try to act surprised."

Leilias caught her breath. "You mean Rafeyo's going to get away with this? That nobody will learn the truth? What about the Grand Duke?"

"Cossimio will know what is suitable for him to know, tailored to fit his understanding. This is a matter for Limners, Leilias. You must see that."

"No, my Lord, I do not!"

Mequel's mild eyes turned to black ice. "And what if it were to come out, and the law courts were involved, and everyone was forced to testify? Three things alone would sink us all: the threat to Corasson by magic, Dioniso's death by magic, and the fathering of Mechella's second son—which has nothing to do with magic and everything to do with the stability of this coun-try!"

Both young Grijalvas gaped at him. He snorted and thwacked the heel of his cane on the floorboards.

"The years have addled my joints, not my wits! Do you think I didn't see through that little comedy Mechella played us at the Fuega Vesperra ball? Do you think Arrigo won't bring that up in court, no matter if it paints him the fool? So what if he has no real proof? The people's love for her might even survive it, but the mere suggestion of scandal would ruin the child—not only here but in

Ghillas, where royal bastards are utterly reviled! Tazia and her son will be punished, I promise you. But I will not have this nation further divided between Mechella's partisans and Arrigo's, and I will not destroy any chance of putting Don Renayo *Grijalva* on the throne of Ghillas!"

He coughed, and waved away Zevierin's proffered wineglass. "No, no, I am only sickened by all this tragic folly, I'm in no danger of joining Dioniso. I will say one last thing, and then nothing more will ever be said about any of this. If it enters your minds to make this known, even with little rumors such as were painted in Granidia—" Mequel smiled grimly as they cast involuntary glances at each other. "—recall that I am Lord Limner and Premio Conselho of Tira Virte. As either, I have the power to ruin you. It is not a threat to regard lightly. I admire and value you both, but I assure you I will do the necessary—just as I have done the necessary for sixteen years to preserve the goodly order of this land. Zevierin, escort your wife back to your chambers. I have no need of you after all, I can find my own way to my bed. Dolcho nocto."

"Arriano! You came!"

The young Limner slid into the dim attic room. "What are you doing here, Rafeyo? What is this place?" He sneezed. "Matra, it's close as a wet wool blanket in here!"

"Are you alone? Did you tell anyone? Did anyone see you?" It was surprisingly easy to produce convincing panic; too easy. As Sario shut the door, he took several slow, steadying breaths. He must stay in control of himself. Everything depended on it.

"What do you take me for?" Arriano sounded hurt. "When a Limner—even if he's still an estudo like you and me—sends a note Nommo Chieva do'Orro, you don't even show anybody the envelope! Did you know that every Limner in Meya Suerta is looking for you? What's all this about your killing Premio Dioniso?"

"I didn't do it. I'm innocent." It was true, in a manner of speaking. Rafeyo had not killed Dioniso. Sario had. "You have to believe me—Cabral and Zevierin did this, because of my mother—"

"Cabral's at Corasson, and anyway he's not a Limner. And do you seriously mean to paint Zevierin as a killer?"

"He'd do anything for Mechella, you know he would—even betray his oaths! *He* painted Corasson, *he* made it seem that I murdered Premio Dioniso—Matra ei Filho, I was Dioniso's student, just like you! I loved him, and now they're saying I murdered him! You have to believe me—you have to help me!"

Arriano sat down on the single chair, folding his hands atop the table. "I do believe you. But why did you run away?"

"Wouldn't you?" he challenged.

"Perhaps," the younger man admitted grudgingly. "I have to tell you, Rafeyo, my advice is to return to the Palasso and let the Viehos Fratos handle this. They'll find out if Zevierin is the guilty one. They always find out everything eventually."

Bizarre to hear his own words quoted back at him. "Return? How do I know what lies Zevierin's been telling about me? And his wife, Leilias—they're Mechella's creatures, I tell you, they—" He braced his fists on the table and hung his head. "Arriano, I have to leave Meya Suerta."

"Are you mad? Here, drink some wine, calm your nerves."

"I had some earlier—and threw up. You know I've no head for liquor."

He could scarcely believe his luck as Arriano of his own volition tilted the open bottle over a dirty glass. "Eiha, *I* need a drink, even if you can't stomach it."

"I can't return," Sario repeated, counting off the seconds in his head. "It won't be just the Fratos, it'll be the Grand Duke looking into this. He worships Mechella, and Zevierin is her creature— Cossimio will never allow the truth to be revealed."

"No Grand Duke has ever . . . interfered with . . . with the Fratos. . . ."

"And the Ecclesia would love a chance to discredit the Grijalvas."

"Eccles . . . no . . . won't go . . . that far. . . ."

Sario paused. "Arriano?"

"Mmm?" he answered dreamily.

"Lift your right foot from the floor."

It was done.

"Set it down again, tapping lightly three times."

It was done.

"Grazzo do'Matra—ei do'Acuyib," Sario whispered. Then, in a voice of gentle command, "Arriano, I mean you only good. I will make you Lord Limner."

"But . . . Mequel. . ." Thick black brows quirked in a frown over a formidable Grijalva nose. None of Rafeyo's handsomeness or charm, or that dazzling smile. *Regretto,* he sighed to himself.

"After Mequel dies, of course. You want to be Lord Limner, don't you?"

"Oh, yes." His face smoothed into an idiot's grin.

"Everything I do will accomplish that. And you'll help me, won't you?"

"Yes."

"Of course you will." Sario brought from under the table the array of paints he'd spent all day preparing. The portrait he would produce with Arriano's saliva and sweat and blood would not be the finest. It didn't matter. No one would ever see it except him. Not even its subject.

As he began the quiet chant that settled his mind, the ancient Tza'ab phrases rolling liquidly from his tongue, he allowed himself a final lamentation. Not for Arriano, but because Arriano was not Rafeyo. Vast talent, good looks, family connections, healthy lineage—none of his requirements was fulfilled in Arriano.

Except for the only requirement that now mattered. Arriano was *here*.

FIFTY-SIX

Rafeyo was never seen again.

His mother believed he still lived. Everyone else believed him dead. Lord Limner Mequel said nothing one way or the other, but allowed the Limners and Grand Duke Cossimio—and Don Arrigo—to assume Rafeyo dead by Mequel's own magic, justice done for the murder of Premio Frato Dioniso. Frankly, Mequel didn't even worry about Rafeyo, for whether he still lived or had truly died, he was ruined, helpless, and mercifully gone.

Of the painting of Corasson, nothing was said. It was taken by Zevierin and Leilias to the estate and presented to Mechella. She placed it in the very spot Rafeyo's old drawing had occupied. If admirers asked the name of the talented Limner, she replied that it had been an anonymous gift. She never knew what it had been meant to accomplish. She never learned that when the roof was retiled that summer, some of the old tiles were found to be singed brittle and black. Cabral, Leilias, and Zevierin considered such knowledge dangerous to her peace. They would protect her, and when Zevierin grew swiftly old, as Limners inevitably did, they would find another young and loyal Limner to take his place. With luck, one of Leilias' sons would have the Grijalva Gift.

During a shattering private hour with his father's Lord Limner, Arrigo learned that the Countess do'Alva had decided, with her husband's consent and indeed his encouragement, to emulate Garlo's middle son and enter a Sanctia. The place she chose was the wealthiest in Casteya, and in it she would devote herself to good works and religion. Her desire to do so was quite genuine, Mequel said amiably. Arrigo, too angry to notice that the expression in the Lord Limner's eyes did not match his tone of voice, made threats. Having anticipated this, Mequel told him as much of the truth as Cossimio knew: Tazia and Rafeyo had conspired to use Grijalva magic against Mechella, and in pursuit of this goal Rafeyo had murdered Premio Dioniso. The Sanctia was Tazia's refuge from punishment; death was Rafeyo's. Arrigo, after a stunned instant in which Mequel read guilt in his eyes (and decided to be blind to it), began to protest: no real evidence, Tazia innocent of the murder, surely she had explained—

"Of course," said Mequel, smooth as silk. "There is always an explanation. There is also—always—truth. Your particular truth, Arrigo, is that you will never see Tazia again. You will be a good and dutiful son to your father, a generous and thoughtful husband to your wife, and a loving and devoted father to your three children. How you populate your bed is your own business, except for two other truths. You will father no child, and you will bed no Grijalva. These are your truths, Arrigo. Always."

Serenissa Grijalva, hearing strange rumors in the women's quarters of the Palasso, proved herself more wise than ambitious by marrying the son of the Niapalese wine merchant who'd courted her in secret these two years. She went home with him that winter, bore five daughters as beautiful as she, and never looked on a do'Verrada male or set foot in Meya Suerta again.

Tazia remained at the Sanctia for a year and a half. She kept mostly to her cell, and had only one visitor: young Arriano Grijalva, who had been her son's friend. He came to the Sanctia shortly before Fuega Vesperra in 1268. She died most unexpectedly in her sleep during Penitenssia that year, aged only forty-four. Her death, attributed to natural causes, went unnoticed by nearly everyone—though it greatly puzzled Mequel, whose painting had rendered her merely compliant.

Lissina, Baroness do'Dregez, died in 1286 at the colossal age of ninety-two, mourned by all. Her *Will* was powerfully binding, for Zevierin survived her, and at a solemn ceremony Grand Duke Alessio III invested his aunt Lizia's daughter Riobira do'Casteya with the titles, styles, dignities, rights, and properties of Dregez. The Viehos Fratos were livid, and hid it badly. Zevierin ended up painting the official portrait.

The day after that ceremony was marked by the first time in history that commoners were admitted to Galerria Verrada—by prior application only, investigated and confirmed by the young man newly assigned to the task, and for only five hours in the afternoon. Still, it was a fine beginning, and from now on there would be monthly public days when anyone granted a ticket could view the most splendid treasures of Tira Virte.

That evening, the widowed Grand Duchess Mechella took a private tour. She was more often seen in Meya Suerta since Grand Duke Arrigo III's death of heart failure two years earlier, in 1284; her son had redecorated her suite and it pleased her to use it on occasion. She stayed out of his political troubles, never having had a taste for such things, and did not in fact come to the capital very often. But she would not have missed the Galerria's first public day for worlds. After all, it had been her idea.

Mechella smiled to see one of her Casteyan orphans at the main desk. He rose and greeted her warmly.

"A tremendous success, Your Grace—though we had a close call with a draper's little boy and one of Grand Duchess Gizella's scent-pillars! Maesso Cabral, a pleasure to see you. May I summon a curatorrio to guide you around?"

"I think we can manage," Mechella assured him, glancing playfully over her shoulder at Cabral. "Are you enjoying your new work, Iverrio?"

"Very much, Your Grace. It was kind of you to think of me."

"Eiha, you've organized Casteya for Count Maldonno these ten years, I felt I ought to have the benefit of your skills and education for a while! Go along home if you like, you needn't wait. I have a key."

"Grazzo millio, Your Grace—my wife didn't expect me until midnight, after all the fuss today! Did I tell you the paintings you lent for this first exhibition collect the largest crowds?"

"That's nice to hear." Taking Cabral's arm, she moved into the Galerria, whispering to him, "If you dare tell me how many years it's been since we first saw these paintings together, I'll refuse to believe you."

He gave her a wink. "If I dare tell you that you're even lovelier now than you were then, will you believe that?"

Laughing, arm-in-arm they strolled the length of the Galerria, commenting now and then on the pictures.

"Do you know," she said, "as often as I've seen all these, I think I still see something new in them each time." With a sidelong glance of blue eyes, she added, "Eiha, I had a very good teacher, after all."

"It's gratifying," Cabral said at last, "that you've forgotten none of what I taught you."

"Amoro meyo, I learned things much more important from you than how to look at a painting. Oh, there's Teressa's *Birth*! Was she ever that little? And I still like your copy better than the original— who painted it? I don't recall."

"Dioniso Grijalva, Your Grace," said a voice down the expanse of tiled floor, and both Mechella and Cabral gave a start. "Forgive me," the man said, coming into the circle of light spilling from the lustrosso high overhead. "I am recently returned from Diettro Mareia, and have not seen the Galerria in some years. I regret interrupting your private tour."

"Not at all, Embajadorro," Mechella said, identifying his rank by the sapphire-blue badge on his sleeve—now that caps and feathers had gone out of fashion, Alessio had gifted his most important Grijalvas with his own personal sigil. "And thank you for reminding me it was Dioniso who painted my daughter's *Birth*. It's been a very long time."

"He had a rather sad end," the Limner went on, fingering the Chieva do'Orro at his breast.

"Sad?" Cabral slanted a look at him that Mechella didn't understand. "He died in his sleep, didn't he?"

"Oh, of course. I've confused him with someone else." He gave a little shrug of apology. "I see that Your Grace has lent the Galerria *The First Mistress*. She's not been seen in here for many long years. It's said she fascinates all who look upon her—much like Your Grace," he added with a smile and the archaic lips-and-heart salute.

"Eiha, the Grijalva charm!" Mechella laughed. "I'm only a woman. *Saavedra* is a masterpiece. We were just about to visit her. Will you join us?"

They progressed to the far end of the Galerria, where Saavedra stood at her table with the huge book open before her, long fingers reaching to adjust the lamp. After a few moments' silent contemplation, Mechella sighed.

"Now, hers *was* a sad end, I should think. Even though nobody knows what really happened to her."

"An odd painting in some ways," Cabral said. "The pose is somewhat awkward, and the things chosen to surround her—especially that book open on the table—are much out of the ordinary. But I don't wonder everyone's fascinated by her. Such poignant beauty, painted so sensitively."

"You know," Mechella mused, "I fancy there's a smile beginning on her lips. It's only a feeling, but—as if she's just read something in that book that pleases her."

The Grijalva nodded. "I understand, Your Grace. Lord Limner Sario's genius was such that anyone he painted seemed alive within the frame."

"Yes, that's it exactly!" Mechella exclaimed. "Every line, every shadow is perfection. He was truly brilliant."

"I am certain such praise from Your Grace would be profoundly gratifying to Sario," Sario said.

GALERRIA 1304

That woman, the bane of his recent existence, had not been content to meddle with the do'Verrada family politics. No, she must go and give birth to a son who had no taste but for the display of his own wealth and who, together with his vulgar bride, felt impelled to remodel Palasso Verrada with the most ill-chosen fashions.

Arriano Grijalva stood in the Galerria foyer and stared in dismay. The once classical lines and clean bright walls of the art gallery had been replaced with the latest Zhinna style, lots of spindly-legged chairs painted black and trimmed with patterns of gold dragons, pedestals burdened with ugly black-lacquered vases, all very eastern and exotic. Worse, riotous gold-leaf wallpaper engulfed the walls, drowning the paintings that hung along the length of the gallery.

The paintings, too, had been rearranged. Instead of the old tradition of giving each magnificent painting, whether *Treaty, Birth, Death,* or *Marriage,* its own place, now they were hung all one atop the other with barely a hand's-breadth between each one. It looked more like a gaudy storeroom than a gallery. How could anyone be so blind? At least Mechella had not suffered from the sin of bad taste. Her son was not so lucky.

He limped forward, leaning on his cane. Arriano's body was fifty-three years old now. He had given it a good run, better than expected, but its time was over. The bone-fever was affecting his hands.

There, in the nook that looked out over the park, sat the Grijalva drawing class, boys and a few girls brought over this early morning from the compound. He had come today for one last look at the boy he had chosen as his successor.

He paused, catching sight of Lord Limner Riobaro's lovely *Marriage of Benetto I and Rosira della Marei.* Matra Dolcha! The fools had stuck it up near the ceiling, surrounded by a series of lesser *Treaties* that utterly destroyed the graceful beauty of line, the linked hands of Benetto and Rosira. Riobaro had drawn attention away from the bride's plain face by lavishing his lush brushstrokes and perfect sense for color onto her gown's emerald green train, which draped in splendid folds down the steps of the sanctuary in the Cathedral.

This insult made him so angry that he began to shake. He tapped his way carefully to a bench and sank down on it. His joints hurt. With difficulty, he unfolded the guidesheet.

The heavy paper was impressed with a border of intertwined roses outlined with gold paint. An appalling affectation! He skimmed over the names of the Dukes, of the Lord Limners. Was there *any* order whatsoever to the changes in the gallery? What had they done with Saavedra's portrait?

A shudder of relief passed through his frame. It still hung in the place of honor accorded it by Mechella after the death of Arrigo—as a constant reminder to her sons, perhaps.

Laboriously he tracked through the tiny calligraphy, seeking Riobaro's work. The exhibit had doubled in size in the last twenty years. Perhaps Grand Duke Renayo wanted to make sure everyone knew he had the greatest art collection of all the crowned rulers.

His eye caught on a title that had been lined out with black ink. *Birth of Cossima.* What had they done with his painting?

Manners be damned. He hammered his cane on the floor. At once the assistant curatorrio came running. They always came running, if a man wore the Chieva do'Orro.

"Embajadorro, are you well? What do you need?" The assistant curatorrio was a well-fed youth with pale skin. Not a fit subject for a painting.

His hands shook as he pointed to the lined-out title. "My—Guilbarro Grijalva's painting, his *Birth of Cossima.* What does this mean?"

"Ah." The curatorrio had the grace to look shame-faced. "The *Birth of Cossima.*"

"Was it removed for cleaning?"

"No, Embajadorro. Last month was the Name Day of one of the young lords. Don Rohario, if you please."

He did not please, nor did he care one jot about Renayo's whelps.

"He asked for it, sir."

"*Asked* for it?"

"He's always in the Galerria, sir. It's a bit of a joke with us. He loves painting. He's even studying painting with Cabral Grijalva. The Grand Duke promised him he could have a painting from the Galerria for his twelfth birthday, to hang in his room."

A spoiled twelve-year-old pup had absconded with one of his masterworks, meant to be admired and lionized, and stuck it in his bedchamber! Matra Dolcha!

He should never have spent so many years abroad, but after the disaster with Rafeyo, he had felt it safest to leave Tira Virte for an extended period. And he had enjoyed his travels, going farther afield than he ever had before, traveling as ambassador—and spy—to the distant north where princedoms and city states like Friesemark and Merse and Vethia were coming into their own. The people were a bit rough around the edges, with their seemingly inexhaustible new wealth from trading ventures, but they had treated him like a king and made much of his talent and his cultured southern background. He had taught them how to appreciate art. And he had sent reports home that had allowed first Arrigo and then Arrigo's sons to make the most of new trading partnerships.

And what had they done with that wealth? He had only to look around the Galerria. He had only to look at the printed page, where his *Cossima* was now part of a boy's private art gallery. What would be next? All the best paintings?

"He wanted *The First Mistress*," said the assistant curatorrio, wrinkling up his face in the most unseemly, pacifying manner. "But His Grace refused. He said his mother, the blessed Grand Duchess Mechella, wouldn't have wanted it moved."

Arriano grunted. It was all he could manage. The nerve of that child! The bone-shattering stupidity of the Grand Duke. He heaved himself up, cursing his infirmities, and limped toward the drawing class. The assistant curatorrio trailed after him, wringing his plump hands.

"You needn't accompany me," snapped Arriano.

The young man bobbed his head and, with a look of relief, turned back to the desk.

According to the guidesheet, the most recent paintings and portraits, additions of the last eighteen years, hung in the nook. Arriano looked forward to seeing them. The work he had seen in the past week, at Palasso Grijalva, had looked stiff and flat, lifelike renderings without any *life* in them. But these would be the best work produced during the years he had been gone.

Even in painting, fashions change, although of course the Viehos Fratos had kept a tight rein on any radical innovations. These could not be allowed. He had adapted over the centuries, but he had never lost the essential touch of Sario's genius: his Luza do'Orro.

He halted behind a row of benches set in a semicircle in the broad nook. Two great windows looked out over parkland. Grijalva children, adolescents mostly, sketched in silence, heads bent over their paper. The Limner in charge greeted him.

"Arriano Grijalva, I presume." This man, too, wore the Chieva do'Orro. "I heard you had returned. I am Nicollo Grijalva."

Arriano barely managed a nod as he surveyed the walls with horror. *This* was the prize of the last generation?

There was a *Treaty,* with all the figures in the right place, all of them realistically done down to the last fingernail and twist of gold braid on the men's coats. It was a *relief* paraded along the canvas. The figures were solid, immobile. That was Renayo II, but he looked like a painted statue, not like a living, breathing man. The painting had no movement.

There was the *Marriage of Renayo II and Mairie de Ghillas.* It was even worse. The painter had talent, clearly, but to waste it on rendering these flat, dead reproductions—for that was all they were, truly. Reproductions.

"That *Marriage* is very fine, isn't it?" said the Limner beside him. "It was Andonio Grijalva's first major work as Lord Limner. You have been out of the country, of course, but Andonio truly changed the way we paint. He took to heart Master Dioniso's famous speech: precision, accuracy, exactitude!" He said the words with a flourish. "So it was fitting that Andonio restored Grijalva painting to its true path." Nicollo curled his fingers over his golden key and kissed the fingertips in a blessing to the dead Andonio. "He was a genius!"

He was a moron! Precision, accuracy, exactitude, of course. But not to the exclusion of *life!*

"There is the *Peintraddo Morta* of the Dowager Duchess Mechella," Nicollo continued. "It was the audition painting done by Andreo Grijalva, who will be invested as Lord Limner at Nov'viva. All the realism of an exact reproduction of the scene."

Without an ounce of spirit. But Arriano said nothing aloud. Nicollo was clearly infatuated with the new style. But the new style was going to have to change.

Arriano nodded stiffly at the other man and limped forward, surveying the students' work. Boys glanced up at him, saw the cane, the sigil, and with wide eyes turned back to their work, some sketching with more concentration, some hiding a smudge with a sleeve, one boy—*his* boy—smiling confidently at him.

His boy. Arriano thought of him that way. He had met the boy already, surveyed his work carefully, looked into his bloodlines. The boy had potential, a good hand, a keen eye, a good sense for color; and he possessed something else that appealed to Arriano's sense of irony. The boy was named *Sario,* in tribute to the long-dead master.

What would it be like to be called by his own name again after all these years?

But now, after seeing what passed for painting—the new "style"!—Arriano wasn't so sure. He paused to watch the boy sketch. At fifteen, he showed good mastery of technique, but he was really only copying. His hand was perfect, but wasn't that precisely the problem with this new "style"? It had no Luza, only lighting that cast precise shadows and figures glossed to the final tiny detail. Even with Sario's mind to direct him, did this boy have enough talent? Did he have an already developing hand of his own, so that when he became Sario, his efforts to reinvent painting, to restore dignity, power, and beauty, would not seem entirely out of place?

There was so much to be done.

His gaze wandered idly over the other students' work and came to rest on two sketches lying askew on a nearby bench.

And there it was. One sketchpad held the usual copy: well-done, lifelike, a rendering that would please an exacting master but with no originality of its own. But beside it! An immature hand, but with a stamp of boldness. This sketch, too, copied the appalling *Marriage,* but the youthful hand had already begun to alter and enlighten. In the *Marriage,* the young bride posed in the formal style, and although every drape of her elaborate gown was correct, she had all the personality of a bolt of cloth topped with a pale head and light ringlets. In the sketch, the bride held her free hand open toward the viewer, her shoulders turned slightly, seeming to entreat her audience to assure her that all would be well. In the *Marriage,* the Dowager Duchess Mechella wore her dignity with a gravity that was simply boring. In the sketch—Eiha! The sly child had altered the pose just enough that it echoed the pose of his very own Saavedra, suggesting a lifetime of waiting.

True, true, it was rough, the work of a talented child, but it had more originality than the portrait it purported to copy.

Arriano beckoned to Nicollo. "Who has done this?" He pointed. Nicollo frowned at the sketchbooks. "It is a shame, isn't it? The grandchildren of Leilias Grijalva have been spoiled shamelessly, say what the others will."

Evidently the relatives of Tazia and the adherents of Mechella's faction were still fighting it out.

"I meant the promising one," said Arriano, willing to concede that the first was left in an uninspiring light compared to the brilliant journeyman sketch of the other student.

"That one!" Nicollo's face lit up. "A bit of a rebel, that boy, but fourteen now—"

"Confirmed?" Matra! It was enough to shake off his disgust at the whole sorry state of Grijalva painting.

"Not officially, but he's Gifted, all right. The little scamp has been having an affair since he was thirteen with a serving wench from the kitchens, and once we found out, we tested her, and she promptly got pregnant. So we think it's likely, quite likely. We have high hopes for the boy."

"His name?"

"Alerrio. He's my nephew. We're hoping to put him forward as Lord Limner."

Alas, my friend, Alerrio will only be Lord Limner if I am in him. But obviously there was still plenty of in-fighting going on within the family. In-fighting he could profit by. "Where is the boy now?"

"He and . . . the other . . . went down to look at *The First Mistress.* There they are now."

Arriano barely saw the other one, the slighter one, a girl, because his gaze was riveted to the boy. A good-looking boy, a bit too handsome, perhaps—as he knew himself, that could cause problems—but well built, strong, with an animated face. He was laughing now at something his companion had said.

"It's a shame about her," Nicollo was saying.

Arriano stopped listening. It was a shame to lose the irony of taking a boy whose name was Sario, but in the face of such potential, it did not—could not—matter.

The two young people sat down on the bench, taking up their sketchpads, oblivious to their elders standing behind them.

"Everyone knows that paints are better now," said the boy in a low voice to the girl.

"Do you really think that makes these *paintings* better?" she demanded in a voice meant to be a whisper but carrying with intensity.

"You just want to paint like the Old Masters," he taunted.

"I do not! But I'd rather paint like them than like this."

She tossed her head, clearly relishing the argument. She was young, twelve perhaps; Arriano could see she would be—not a beauty, perhaps, but a woman worth painting, when she grew up.

Then he realized she was holding the wrong sketchpad.

She held the sketchpad with the altered painting. The boy started drawing, adding lines to the workmanlike reproduction on his paper.

She.

He watched as she began to draw.

"No respect for her elders," commented Nicollo. One of his estudos called to him, and he nodded to Arriano and walked away. Part of Arriano's mind was still in shock. The other part catalogued Nicollo: Gifted, about thirty. Nicollo would be no threat to his plans, not if he thought that Andonio Grijalva was a genius, that Andreo Grijalva, he of the petrified if perfectly detailed *Death,* was a suitable candidate for Lord Limner.

Arriano cast one last glance at the girl and walked slowly down the length of the Galerria. He did not bother to look at the paintings. He either knew them as intimately as he did his own hands, or he had seen them before and did not want to see them again shamefully crowded by the other inmates of this new-made prison.

At the end of the Galerria, in the place of honor, hung *The First Mistress.* At least they had left her space untouched. No other paintings crowded her; she stood alone in all her glory.

Saavedra. It was, truly, a magnificent painting. The memory of the first shock he had received, when he realized that she had moved within the painting, thrilled through him again. In the painting, seen through the arched windows set into the thick walls of the chamber, the light of a spring morning ripened toward the bolder, brighter strokes of midday. The hour candle was cold, its wick curled over, black touched with a hint of grey ash. The lamp no longer burned. And Saavedra no longer stood behind the table.

Amazing. In the two decades since he had last looked upon her she had moved so far within the painting that it was as if his spell no longer held her as tightly. Yet no one had mentioned the change to him. Was it possible the magic blinded them to the truth?

Saavedra now stood almost at the doorway, head in profile. He caught a hint of her face reflected in the mirror that stood on an easel set behind the table. She seemed to be looking *out,* at *him.*

"Do you understand yet that I love you more than any other man can? That you love me?" he asked her, murmuring the words. He felt he heard her answer.

I love Alejandro.

"An infatuation! We are the true soul mates, you and I, 'Vedra. Together we could have done anything, could have saved the Grijalvas from their stupid mistakes, from this parody which they now call art, this *insult* to our name. But I am alone. I am only one man. I cannot do *everything*, control *everyone*."

You tried. Look what you did to me. Her answer fairly sparked off the canvas. *Set me free, Sario. It has been long enough. How long has it been?*

Could she actually see him and hear him? Was that truly her voice he heard in his head? How desperately he wanted her at his side. Alejandro was gone, after all, long melted away into dust. Saavedra had only *him* to love now.

"Someday you will love me as you were meant to."

No answer.

Ah, well. It wasn't time to set her free yet. He must complete the new transfer, build his new host into a force to be reckoned with, become Lord Limner. Then he would be able to paint her out into the world as his consort, as the one woman who truly appreciated his genius and could even share in it.

That thought stopped him.

"You would be laughing at me now, wouldn't you?" he asked her softly. "I have found the perfect host, and yet she is imperfect, because she is a girl and thus not Gifted."

I am Gifted. But said with anger, and fear.

"And I showed you the truth! You will thank me for it. You will see that I am right! And since you are Gifted, why not another woman? How could it be that such talent is not combined with the precious Gift of the Grijalvas?"

It was a small chance, vanishingly small, he knew that. He had never understood what combination of traits or parentage had given Saavedra her Gift. He barely remembered her mother—but then, he barely remembered his own mother, who had had nothing to do with raising him, or perhaps she had died when he was still an infant. It was hard to keep track. Saavedra's father he recalled through the blur of time only because *he* had been a curiosity: A plump, womanish man, he had been confirmed as Gifted and yet never painted a successful spelled painting. Late in life he had sired the one child and then expired some years later, most likely of disappointment.

Many Grijalva women, like the men, had some talent for painting, although it was rarely encouraged. He had looked for it, even surreptitiously tested a few talented girls over the years. No other woman had ever shown any sign of being Gifted.

So. He would take the other Sario and watch the girl. Even if she weren't Gifted, she might make a good, grateful estuda, one who *did* acknowledge his genius, one who had the talent to emulate him. After all, for all these years, his best pupils had always been himself.

He looked up into Saavedra's eyes, reflected in the mirror. Those beautiful eyes.

All is so changed. Tremulous now. *Why do I never see Alejandro but only strangers? What have you done to me, Sario?*

"Be well, carrida meya. Wait for me."

What choice have you given me?

He placed a kiss on his fingers, held out his bunched fingertips as an offering to her. Then he turned and slowly made his way back down the length of the gallery. He would find out the girl's name.

It had been good to travel. But it was also good to be home, to have renewed purpose. Saavedra waited for him. Had she not admitted it herself?

Sario—no, *Arriano*—Grijalva felt pleased with himself.

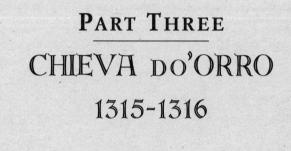

PART THREE
CHIEVA DO'ORRO
1315-1316

FIFTY-SEVEN

Eleyna balanced her drawing board across her thighs and squinted into the morning sunlight as the Iluminarres Procession wound into the Zocalo Grando fronting the Cathedral Imagos Brilliantos. She tested her hands on the drawing paper with a few swift strokes: the tasseled headbands of the banner bearers; the two banners signifying Mother and Son, pure white linen stitched with gold thread; the torches, burned down to stubs, that had illuminated the nightlong prayers for rain; the white lily adorning the man and woman chosen to represent the vineyard worker and his wife, the Exalted.

She began to sketch in the woman, quickly delineating her sharp nose and with three lines suggesting the curl of her black hair, crowned by a wreath of lilies. Her gaze caught on the man. She clenched her hands. How like the Grand Duke to impinge on a people's ceremony in this way, by insinuating his second son into the honored place in the procession. *Must they take every honor away from the common folk?*

She left that space blank, where the vineyard worker strode, eyes caught on the banner of the Son. Instead, she furiously sketched in the sanctos and sanctas who accompanied the procession, the white-robed Premio Sancto at their head. They sang, the monumental hymn "Il Pluvia ei Fuega," while the weight of their ceremonial gold and silver mantles rustled like a stiff breeze across the plaza. Eleyna bit at her lip, trying not to remember the only other time she had seen Don Rohario, the Grand Duke's second son. But the humiliation was too fresh for her not to remember.

She sketched the outlines of the cathedral hastily and then hatched in shadows. By concentrating on the twin bell towers and their fat shadows stretching over the long arcade of the Palasso Justissia, she managed to thrust the unwelcome memory to the back of her mind. The banner bearers climbed the steps that led to the cathedral forecourt and stopped beside the huge doors. The procession continued on inside, the hymn changing to the more somber cadences of the old vineworkers' song, "Give Us Mercy, Mother, Your Brillance Burns Us."

Behind the procession, townspeople flooded into the square,

their hats decorated with gold and silver ribbons or with tasseled headbands in imitation of those worn by the banner bearers. Caught up by their exhuberance, Eleyna turned to a new page in her sketchpad and concentrated on the ribbons fluttering in the breeze, lines that connected one face to the next, drawing the eye through the crowd in all its moods: the teasing laughter of young women; the sincere tears of the devout; the excitement of children seeing their first Iluminarres Procession; the solemn bowed heads of elder folk seeing, perhaps, their last.

It was almost enough to drive away all thoughts of that awful meeting, Don Rohario acting as his elder brother's representative, her parents scheming and lying to her so she would have no choice but to say "Yes." Eiha! She never had been able to control her tongue when she was embarrassed and angry, everyone knew that. But after the Don's ignoble retreat, they had accused her of being ill-tempered and ungrateful.

For a moment she forgot where she was. She no longer saw the crowd or heard their singing and festive shouts. The injustice of it stung. Had she been born a male, she might have been Gifted. Then her skill with pencil, with paints, would have been a cause for celebration instead of an impediment toward liaisons with men.

The crowd continued to swell. Eleyna began sketching again, not really paying attention to the movements of pencil on paper. It was her only release when she got agitated.

"I am meant to paint," she said under her breath, her words drowned by voices rising now in song. "I will not let them stop me."

Of their own accord, her hands sketched in the stiff angles of a black hat and, beneath its brim, the scowling face of a middle-aged man. He had the ample jowls of a prosperous guildsman. Her hands drew in the collar with its small pin, golden scales, before she registered the symbol: He was a goldsmith, then, or a jeweler, the two guilds having recently joined forces, following the fashion that had come to Tira Virte from Ghillas together with the new freedom of dress that had become fashionable in the last five years. Grazzo do'Matra! No more confining stays!

A voice rang out: "Let the Corteis meet!"

From that cry, ten others sprang into being.

"Down with the do' Verradas!"

"Let all classes have a say!"

"No taxes without the vote of the Corteis!"

"Let us have the vote!" shouted the guildsman near Eleyna, shoving forward toward the steps of the cathedral. Other men pushed forward. A shrill ululating scream pierced the air. The hymn from the cathedral was drowned in a chorus of protests.

Perched on the second tier of the great fountain that overlooked the square, Eleyna was not at first caught in the sudden forward surge of the crowd. But she caught their fever, the shift from joyous celebration to angry protest. *I will record it all!* Her pencil flew over the paper, recording a pair of squinting eyes, the blunt set of a mouth, a little girl reaching, frightened, toward her mother.

A pack of young men swarmed up onto the fountain, carrying handpainted signs or banners sewn with three broad stripes: blue, black, and silver. In their excitement they jostled Eleyna. She barely caught her sketchpad, but her drawing board plummeted, falling with a splash into the roiling waters of the fountain. Cursing under her breath, she tucked her sketchpad under her arm, shoved her pencil into the pocket she had sewn into her skirt, and clambered down. But the swelling crowd got in her way. She clung to the stone steps, unable to move.

"Let me get it, Maessa." A man several steps away shoved his way down to the base of the fountain and without minding shoes or trousers waded into the spray and fetched out her drawing board. It dripped water on the stone, painting the granite dark gray, as he climbed back up to her.

Behind him, like an afterthought, came a press of young men, singing a coarse drinking song while waving their signs and banners enthusiastically. They came so quickly that Eleyna had to retreat up another tier and partway around the fountain. She no longer had a clear view of the cathedral. Mist sprayed, winking in the sunlight.

She found a square of stone and held her ground. There he was! As he fought his way toward her, she studied him. In his late twenties, he had a bland, round, ordinary face, a familiar face, but one she could not place. His black hair was cut without flair, unlike most of the young bravos around her, who seemed as vain of their appearance as enthusiastic about their political views. He had no grace to speak of, skinning his knee with a grunted curse as he scrambled up beside her. But his hands. . . .

She always noticed hands, and his had long, tapering fingers and broad, strong palms, the kind of hands it was a pleasure to paint. And—there!—a telltale smear of dried paint.

"You're a Grijalva," he said, without giving her the board.

With the crowd roaring around her, her sketchpad creased and her dress disheveled, Eleyna lost her temper. "You'll get no access to Palasso Grijalva from me!" She grabbed the drawing board and tugged it out of his hand. "There is a painting academy on Avenida Shagarra. You would have better luck applying there."

He only smiled. His preternatural calm in the midst of a swirling protest made her apprehensive. The crowd's murmur began to crescendo, growing agitated and ugly.

"I only wish to escort you home, Maessa." He had to shout to be heard above the noise. "I was watching you sketch. You are talented, are you not? Truly gifted." He meant it not as flattery but as a plain fact which both he and she ought to recognize.

It stopped her dead. She ought to go, but she could not bring herself to move. This man, this stranger, knew something about her that no one else, not since Grandmother Leilias had died, knew, or admitted. Not Gifted—no woman could be Gifted—but gifted with a true talent as fine as that owned by her Gifted male cousins.

More young men leaped up onto the fountain, climbing higher and higher until a trio finally braved the spray to vault themselves to the finial. A compatriot threw a banner up to them, and they draped it over the statue of Duke Alesso to howls of approval from the crowd below.

"Let the Corteis meet!"

"No taxes without our consent!"

More, and more yet, swarmed up onto the fountain for a better view. A woman shrieked and a baby wailed in fear. Eleyna was caught, pressed backward.

"Who are you?" she cried, but a great roar broke loose from the crowd as a second blue, black, and silver banner was unfurled on the roof of the Palasso Justissia. In the crush, she was forced to stumble backward while the stranger was caught by the tide and swept away from her. She lost sight of him. Water misted her hair and neck. A woman in an apron and skirt stained gray with ash stared at her, at her sketchpad and drawing board, then pointed, away, where a line of green appeared, wavering, down one of the boulevards.

"Look there, amica, down the Boulevard Benecitto. The Duke has called out the Shagarra Regiment. Chiros!" The woman spat into the fountain. She held a basket filled with dried crusts of bread. "They say that in Ghillas there is fresh bread for all people, even the poor, taken from the nobles' kitchens."

The hymn "Novva Pluvia," The New Rain, started in one corner of the zocalo, swelling in volume as most of the crowd took up the song. But the words sounded now more like a threat than a plea to the heavens: *"With the new rain we shall be set free!"*

Mist—or were those tears?—stung Eleyna's eyes. Why shouldn't the people of Meya Suerta protest? Weren't they, like her, forced to be ruled without having any say in what they chose to do? She was twenty-one years of age, had been a widow for two years, but her parents thought of her only as a pawn to be used to further their ambitions.

First they had used her in the Confirmattio, and when through two Confirmattios she had failed to conceive, they had married her off to Felippo Grijalva, who had already outlived two wives. It was only after a stillbirth and Felippo's death during the Summer Fever that they had grudgingly allowed her the run of the studio, but only because Grandmother Leilias had insisted upon it. Leilias had power within the family.

Now Leilias was dead. Dowager Duchess Mechella was dead. Mechella's grandson, Edoard, first son and heir to Grand Duke Renayo II, had gotten grudging permission from his father to reinstate the old tradition of a Grijalva Mistress, the Marria do'Fantome.

What better choice than a young widow who had already proven herself as good as barren?

"All I want to do is paint!" she cried, if only to that chance-met stranger who had admired her talent. But he was lost, and the great shout that rose from the crowd as it finished the last verse drowned out her voice.

Fleeing the press of the crowd and the approaching soldiers, yet more people surged up onto the fountain. Too many. It was too crowded. Eleyna fell to one knee, catching herself and skinning a palm on stone, clutching her precious sketchpad, dropping the drawing board, and scrabbling for purchase. She could not stay here. The Grand Duke's soldiers were coming.

Lowering her head, using her elbows, she fought her way down the basins and tiers of the fountain. She almost lost her footing when she reached the ground. People were caged together by others like so many chickens brought home from the market. Their shouts blended into an unintelligible din. She shoved and elbowed her way, stumbling over a crumpled body, was swept first to the right, then to the left, fighting against the current, but at last she managed to get out. As she reached the fringe of the crowd, opposite the cathedral, the going became easier. She had reached the Avenida Oriale when the first shots were fired.

Not bothering to look back, Eleyna ran. And hated herself, for was she not running back to the safety of Palasso Grijalva? That was not safety, but a prison!

Her parents wanted their daughter to be Don Edoard's mistress.

Mistress to the Heir to the throne—that was power! That was influence! By that means they could control the Viehos Fratos, power which had been denied to her mother's branch of the family for two generations—her mother, who was the niece of the fabled Tazia, mistress to Arrigo III . . . the woman who had dared to try to kill Grand Duchess Mechella.

But Eleyna didn't care about that kind of power. She wanted no part of it. That was why they had never understood her.

She ran now, back to them, only because she was afraid. Behind, the dull roar turned into riot as the noon sun beat down on the city of Meya Suerta and a volley of musket fire broke the peace of the Iluminarres Procession.

FIFTY-EIGHT

Roario Alejandro Enricci Clemenzo do' Verrada, second son of Grand Duke Renayo and the late Grand Duchess Mairie, was the last person in the cathedral to realize that a riot had started outside in the zocalo.

The weight of the ceremonial clothing made it hard to move, but since he had no responses to speak, no verses to declaim, he had long since lost track of the ceremony. He stood in front of the altar—his appointed place—and stared at the monumental altarpiece that dominated the Sanctuary. The Mother, Her infant Son sitting on Her knee, gazed down on him. She wore cloth of gold robes in the antique style, draped elegantly along one arm; the other arm was shadowed by Her Son's chubby figure. It was an old masterpiece, the only item saved from the original cathedral when it had burned down in 1155. When the cathedral was rebuilt, the *Birth of the Holy Child* took pride of place.

Matra Dolcha! It was a glorious painting. Roario knew its history well: It was the last masterwork painted by the legendary Sario Grijalva. Although over three hundred years old, its fine golden luster still shone as if it was freshly painted: the calm, embracing gaze of the Mother, the delightful and delighted infant smile of Her Son, the attending angels with wings upswept and both sun and moon casting light over the Throne. The luza itself was so subtly done that it was only from this close that Roario could see how that light played in the robes of the angels and along the form of the Mother, golden sunlight painted ever so slightly distinct from the pale silver beams of the moon.

There was something almost magical about it. Even at great state ceremonies like this one, when he might kneel among a thousand worshipers, Roario still felt Her gaze like the weight of his robes. It wasn't heavy, but reassuring: solid, tangible. Even when his dear mother had died and he had knelt, weeping, at the service given in her honor, even then the serene gaze of the Mother had soothed him. Even when his father had remarried that beautiful but brainless northern princess with her cartloads of gold and a merchant fleet as dower—but no ear for music, no eye for art and the most horrific accent—even then, as he stood through the marriage ceremony, his anger and frustration and disappointment had slowly drained away.

He let that peace pour over him now, as if it were a whisper for his ears alone: *All will be well.*

When a sancto jostled his elbow, Rohario started. A strange roar echoed through the cathedral.

"I beg your pardon, Don Rohario," said the sancto, a white-haired man Rohario knew instantly: Sancto Leo was chaplain for the fourth service each month, a kind old man with a particularly gentle voice. "Please, my lord. We must hurry. You must get those robes off."

"But the ceremony isn't over yet."

"There is a . . . disturbance outside, my lord. Please. We must get you back to the Palasso."

Slowly it dawned on Rohario that, despite the calming presence of the altarpiece, Sancto Leo was terrified.

"What kind of disturbance?" He shrugged off the heavy robes into the waiting arms of a white-faced servitor, then took a few steps toward the great doors. In the vast nave of the cathedral, people milled: sanctos, sanctas, other members of the procession. The high vault made them all appear tiny, insignificant compared to the majesty of the Matra ei Filho. Rohario saw no sign of the Premio Sancto or the frail Premia Sancta.

"I beg your pardon, my lord. This way. We're going out through the chapter house. It isn't—" Leo broke off, waving away the servitor, and grabbed Rohario's arm to tug him toward the door that led into the rooms behind the Sanctuary.

"It isn't what?" protested Rohario.

The old man's grip was amazingly ironlike, reminding Rohario of his old nurse, Otonna, who would come every day at noon to drag him out of the Galerria back to the schoolroom for his lessons. Because he hated scenes, he gave in.

Sancto Leo led Rohario into the warren of small rooms where the Premio Sancto prepared his lessons. Several other men, servitors and sanctos, followed like so many frightened sheep.

"It isn't safe," said the old man. "A riot has broken out. Nommo do'Matra! What has the world come to? This would never have happened when I was a boy. Why, Grand Duchess Mechella, Matra bless her memory, would have ridden out in her carriage and the mob would have prostrated themselves at her feet in shame. It's a terrible thing, a terrible thing."

There were no windows in these back rooms, so Rohario could not look outside. He had never seen a riot, never even suspected one might happen in, of all places, Meya Suerta. But he had heard that in recent months mobs had burned down the king's palace in Taglis and rioted for bread in the city of Niapali. Maybe, like a plague, the restlessness had now infected Tira Virte's populace.

"Eiha!" said Rohario suddenly, dredging up some gossip he had heard in passing at a concert four nights before. "It's something about the Corteis, isn't it?"

"Matra ei Filho!" exclaimed the old man. "What is it you do all day, ninio? Do you know nothing of what goes on in this city?"

"Of course I do! I'm helping my brother Edoard arrange for a Grijalva Mistress."

Sancto Leo stopped in his tracks. It was gloomy back here; a few candelabras leaked light into the air. But there, above a mantle, hung a perfectly charming portrait of Premio Sancto Gregorrio IV at his Ascension. That would have been—what?—one hundred years ago. Rohario recognized it as the work of Oaquino Grijalva. Because of the Premio Sancto's elaborate headdress, Il Cofforro was unable in this painting to show off his famous talent for rendering hair in exquisite lifelike perfection. Instead he had elaborated the jeweled and braided headdress to the finest detail.

"Isn't it beautiful?" breathed Rohario. "A shame to hide it in here."

He looked at the sancto for confirmation, but whatever words he meant to say next died on his lips. The old man was frowning at him with . . . with . . . undoubtedly, with disgusted scorn. On the wall behind Sancto Leo hung a mirror, trimmed with gold flecking. Dimly, Rohario saw himself reflected in it. No wonder Sancto Leo was appalled! Rohario's lace cuffs were askew, and his starched white neckcloth had crumpled under the weight of the robes. Hastily, Rohario attempted to tidy himself, aware of the old man's gaze on him.

"And you," said Leo, "are supposed to be the intelligent one in the family. Matra! It is no wonder the people riot. What has the great do' Verrada bloodline come to?"

Rohario gaped at him, cuffs forgotten.

Into the silence came the muffled reports of musket shots from outside.

"We must get Don Rohario to safety," murmured one of the servitors.

Rohario heard an odd noise. Though he had never truly heard screaming before—except the time when his brother's horse, forced over too high a hedge, had broken its leg—he recognized it at once. The sound sent shivers through him.

"Come," said Sancto Leo. "We must go. We must hope Avenida Shagarra remains clear."

Rohario followed meekly. But when they emerged through a side door of the transept onto the avenida, they were swept at once into the riot. Rohario cowered against the towering cathedral wall. The rush of the crowd was like the unstoppable roar of the Rio Sanguo in flood. There was no way to cross safely. Amazingly, a group of poorly-dressed young men shoved through the panic-ridden mob, against the current, heading *toward* the zocalo. They held knives and broken bottles in their hands. The crowd poured past, oblivious to everything but its own panic.

"Come, my lord." Sancto Leo dragged him forward.

"Is it the poor people who've come out? What is this?" Rohario stared at the pack of young men. Such rags they wore! No wonder they were angry.

Sancto Leo followed his gaze. "*Neosso do'Orro!* Those are not poor boys, Don Rohario. They are respectable apprentices by the look of them."

"But the way they're dressed—!"

"We'd better go!" whispered one of the servitors urgently.

A swaggering tough straggling along at the tail end of the pack of young apprentices turned and looked straight at Rohario. A strange expression passed over the young man's face. It looked rather like the expression that had overcome his old nurse Otonna the time his little sister Timarra had asked for the fairybook love story of their grandparents, Grand Duke Arrigo and the beloved Grand Duchess Mechella, and how they were always devoted to one another.

But this time, the expresson was directed at *him*.

Sancto Leo shoved Rohario behind him. "Go!"

Six apprentices broke free from the others and plunged through the fleeing crowd toward Rohario. Shots cracked out in bursts from the zocalo. Screams rent the air.

Servitors dragged at Rohario's arm. He wanted to run; he knew he ought to. He recognized the looks on their faces. When he was younger, Edoard had beaten him up many times. But he just couldn't believe these *commoners* would hurt him. And anyway, he couldn't leave the old man.

"Merditto alba, no?" shouted the nearest young tough, the swaggering one, as he closed in.

Although the crowd continued to flood down the street, Rohario suddenly felt that he, his scant retinue, and these half-dozen apprentices were alone in the world. Rather than reply to the insult, he stood his ground stiffly.

The young tough shoved Sancto Leo aside and stopped right in front of Rohario, glaring at him. They were about the same height, but the apprentice's shoulders were perhaps twice as broad. "Quello passarro, chi'patro?" he asked insolently.

"You will not speak that way about my blessed mother!" said Rohario, anger sparking. He punched him.

Unfortunately, the years of lessons in fencing and sparring had never paid off. Edoard hated the competition and Rohario had been happy to oblige by either always losing or avoiding practice altogether.

He knew he was in trouble when the apprentice hit him back. A fist slammed into his head, sending him reeling. He staggered back against the wall, was pummeled by another punch and slammed up against unyielding stone. Though ringing ears, he heard Sancto Leo pleading. "That is Don Rohario. You must not hurt him!"

Rohario heard the spat curses of the apprentices in reply. He covered his head with his arms, but they only kicked him in the stomach. Eiha! The pain washed through his gut. Why did they hate him so much? They didn't even know him.

He heard Leo's anguished yelp. With a flurry born from desperation Rohario fought his way free to aid the old man. Two of the servitors were down. The other sancto had fled.

"Stop it!" Rohario cried, flailing out wildly, head down, bulling his way through to the old man. Leo had fallen to his knees on the cobblestones. "He's just an old man!"

Kicked hard from behind, Rohario stumbled and went down to one knee, righted himself, jerking up. To go down under this pack would be fatal.

Shots rang out. Sancto Leo gasped and spasmed. Blood fountained from his neck. Rohario grabbed the old man before he toppled over. He braced himself, expecting more blows, but the apprentices scattered to run with the crowd, yelling, screaming, taunting.

A rock stung Rohario's ear. He looked up. There, advancing like avenging angels, came a line of the Shagarra Regiment.

"My lord! My lord!" cried the last servitor, cowering behind him. "They're shooting everyone. We must run."

"I won't leave the sancto." He sank down, cradling the old man. Blood leaked over his hands.

The soldiers fired. A woman stumbled and fell, mouth open in surprise and terror, and began to crawl after the others, struggling, hands clawing at the cobblestones. The crowd trampled her. Rohario ripped his gaze away and looked up at the line of soldiers. They advanced steadily, without mercy.

He let the old man down onto the stones and rose to face the guard. He lifted a hand. To his surprise, it was not shaking. "Stop! In the name of Matra ei Filho! Help me with this holy sancto."

Of a miracle, it worked. Soldiers broke rank. A captain drove his horse through the mob and reined up beside him. "Matra Dolcha! Don Rohario! What are you doing here? Sarjeant Rivvas, take the Don back to the Palasso. Take ten men as escort. Now!"

Strong arms grabbed Rohario.

"But Sancto Leo—!" cried Rohario, protesting.

"Your father will have my head if you're not brought safely back," the captain said. "Get up! Get *up!*"

Rohario was dragged onto the back of a horse, forced to cling to the sarjeant as if he were a child, not a man who had achieved his twenty-second birthday.

Ranks of mounted soldiers surrounded him. He caught a glimpse of Sancto Leo lying broken on cobblestones, but his escort swept him away. They rode swiftly through the streets. All around Rohario saw the remains of the riot, men and women lying dead, wounded, crying in pain, left to die or care for themselves. Once he saw a child—a child!—lying with arms outstretched, like a shattered Zhinna doll. How could this happen? What was going on in Meya Suerta?

By the time they reached the Palasso he was too numb to do anything more than submit listlessly to the attentions of the Court physician, who agreed that he had a few bruises, nothing more. His steward and body servant led him to his chambers. There he sank down on his bed and stared at the wall. They left him alone, but he could hear them whispering on the other side of the door.

After a few minutes, Rohario could stand it no more. His bedchamber stifled him, as it had never done before. It was a glorious room, fitted to his exact taste. He stared at the moldings that framed the door and the fireplace, gilded with gold leaf, at the marquetry floor, and at the paneled wall boards painted with roundels and wreaths of flowers. He stared at the painting he had commandeered from the Galerria: Guilbarro Grijalva's masterwork, the *Birth of Cossima*. He had wanted the other painting, of course, but because it had been Grandmamma Mechella's favorite, his father refused to remove it from the place of honor to which she had restored it.

Now, staring at the baby girl whose tragically early death cast an aura of inexplicable sorrow over the room, Rohario was reminded of the child he had seen lying dead in the streets. Another thought intruded: the baby Cossima's seat on the knee of her mother was remarkably similar to the pose of the Blessed Baby Child on the knee of the Holy Mother, in the cathedral altarpiece.

What was the use? It was as if a curtain had been ripped away from the wall of his room, revealing the ugly streets outside. Everything had changed. He could no longer get pleasure from the incomparable genius of the long-dead Guilbarro's magnificent painting.

Rohario heaved himself up off the bed and limped out past his servants, brushing them away, and walked the long route through the Palasso toward the one place where he could always find peace: the Galerria. It was closed now, empty except for him and his two trailing servants, who kept their distance out of respect for his anguish.

He hobbled to the end of the Galerria, the place of honor, where the famous portrait of Saavedra Grijalva—*The First Mistress*—hung in all its glory. Exhausted by the walk, he sank down on the bench. He would have gotten on his knees, to do her the obeisance that she deserved, but his servants watched. And anyway, his knees hurt, scraped raw by stone.

Rohario stared up at her. In the portrait, Saavedra stood with one hand on the latch of the door, iron-studded, iron-bound, that led out of her chamber. With her head half turned, she appeared to be looking into a mirror that rested on an easel. Both in profile and—more subtly—captured in the mirror, her face, her expression, her intelligent, expressive eyes, seemed more alive to him than did most of the Courtfolk among whom he walked every day. Rohario liked to believe that she waited for the return of her lover, Duke Alejandro.

Unlike the Holy Mother, whose aspect was serene, Saavedra radiated a passionate strength that fairly crackled from the painting. Rohario had admired her since he was a little boy. His nurse, even his parents, had told him often enough that when little he had been a whirlwind of energy that only the Galerria could calm. Here, in front of this portrait, was the only place his soul was truly at ease.

"All is not well in Meya Suerta," he whispered to her, wishing desperately that *she* could hear him, afraid that his attendants might think him mad for speaking to a painting. "I don't understand the world anymore. An old man whose only fault was in trying to spare me was killed."

She did not, of course, reply. He only imagined she did.

All is so changed. Why has it changed so?

He tried to explain, about riots in neighboring countries like

Ghillas and Taglis and Niapali, about the common people making demands as if *they* should have a say in the governance of the land. But it all sounded so absurd, and in any case he had paid so little attention to the world outside the Palasso that he did not truly understand it.

He gave up. After all, it was only his fancy that she could somehow hear him; she had died over three hundred and fifty years ago. He sighed, straightening his cuffs, and stared at her. The women of the Court seemed like pale reflections of her, lost if a pebble was tossed in their midst, swept away by the merest brush of one hand.

The Court . . . which these days fawned over its newest member. Edoard had made a fool of himself over Johannah. Hers was an insipid beauty, and she had no light, no strength, in her eyes. *Oculazurro corassonerro:* blue eyes, black heart. Not that Rohario thought Johannah of Friesemark, now Grand Duchess Johannah, had enough intelligence to be malicious. She liked her clothes and her jewels and her pet miniature greyhounds and her gossip. Even *she* wasn't stupid enough to risk losing all that by falling in love with her husband's grown son.

But Edoard had nothing better to do than to fancy himself in love with his father's new bride. Rohario had been privileged to witness the argument.

"You would be better off with a Mistress!" their father had shouted.

"Then I will take a Grijalva Mistress!"

"Have you no respect for your Grandmother Mechella's memory? For the anguish she went through?"

But Edoard, like stone, had stood firm against Grand Duke Renayo's rage and gotten what he wanted. He always did.

Despite himself, Rohario had to smile as he remembered the embassy he had himself been *requested* to lead on his brother's behalf. There was a young widow, handsome in the Grijalva way. She was the granddaughter of that Leilias Grijalva who had been the confidante of the blessed Grand Duchess Mechella. Perfect in every way, Lord Limner Andreo had assured Edoard.

And Edoard, having observed the young woman through a secret watchhole during a service at the Sanctia of the Holy Fountains, had decided in his usual impulsive way that she was indeed perfect. He bought horses the same way.

Eiha! In the interview the young widow had kicked up a fuss, to her parents' obvious embarrassment. Rohario studied Saavedra now, wondering if there were more than a passing resemblance between the two women. Or perhaps it was only the young widow's fiery spirit—although at the interview's embarrassing end her own father had called her shrewish. Perhaps it was four hundred years of Grijalva blood showing in raven-dark curls, straight nose, the slant of her eyebrows; some memory in her face of her many-times-great kinswoman, Saavedra.

The woman in the painting waited, so lifelike that Rohario sometimes felt as if, should he extend his hand, she would take hold of it and step out of the portrait. Her gown, done in the style of those times, actually seemed to have weight; the ash-rose velvet of the fabric gleamed softly. Now and again, when the light was right or the Galerria quiet enough, Rohario imagined her head had turned just the tiniest bit, or that her hand had changed position, one ringed finger altered so slightly, or that the bands of light in her suite of rooms were shading from midday toward afternoon.

But of course that was impossible.

He sighed, rested his chin on a hand, studied her face. And was struck by revelation.

She was the model for the Holy Mother in the altarpiece in the Sanctuary of the cathedral. How could he not have seen it before? There were little changes, of course: The shade of hair was different, the robes of the Holy Mother purposefully even more antique than Saavedra's gown, and the Mother wore no earthly adornment except for Her holiness while Saavedra held dangling from one hand a handsome golden key on a golden chain, symbolic of her family's wealth and traditions.

This portrait was a study done from the life, while the Holy Mother was copied from a face recalled through the veil of years. And the great Sario Grijalva had done both paintings, one at the beginning of his distinguished career, the other at the end.

Rohario heard footsteps. He turned, wincing at the pain in his shoulders and ribs, and discovered Ermaldo, Count do'Alva, Minister of State and distant cousin to the do'Verrada family. Ermaldo halted a few paces away, looking more impatient than respectful. "My lord, His Grace wishes to speak with you now. He is deeply distressed over the death of our holy brother, Sancto Leo, who was tutor to His Grace."

Rohario grimaced as he rose, this time not only from pain. This was all it took to make a total ruin of the whole grim day. Again he was responsible for the death of someone his father cared for.

He had spent the last two years staying out of his father's sight. Now he would be reminded of the ugly truth all over again: It was Rohario's fault, and Rohario's fault alone, that his beloved mother, Grand Duchess Mairie, had died of the Summer Fever two years ago. He had only wanted some lilies to put in a vase at her bedside. How could he have known that the flower vendors were contaminated with the Summer Fever? His father had never forgiven him.

"I'm coming," he said to Ermaldo. He cast one last beseeching glance toward Saavedra, again catching sight of her eyes in the mirror.

Where is Alejandro?

Was that whom she thought of? Her lover, Duke Alejandro?

"Long dead," he whispered, feeling a sharp sadness at the mystery and tragedy of this beautiful woman's life. Then he followed Ermaldo to the Grand Duke's study.

FIFTY-NINE

"You were not injured badly, I trust?" The Grand Duke did not look up from the sketch of a *Treaty* that lay on his desk, nor did he glance at his companion, Andreo Grijalva. The Lord Limner stood half in shadow, head turned to look out the window into the private courtyard of Palasso Verrada, where acacias bloomed. In the pause before Rohario spoke, the Lord Limner moved out of the shadows to look at the young man. The painter lifted an expressive eyebrow, no doubt a comment on Rohario's disheveled clothing. A faint aroma of oil and turpentine sifted through the room, emanating from the Grijalva.

"You have not answered me," said the Grand Duke, still without looking up.

"I am not badly injured," said Rohario. "Your Grace."

"I understand you attempted to save the life of Sancto Leo."

"He was protecting me, Your Grace. Anyone would have tried to help him."

"How were you assaulted?"

Rohario suddenly recalled Leo's angry words: *"Do you know nothing of what goes on in this city?"* "The Iluminarres Procession turned into a riot!"

"So my conselhos have reported. The instigators will be captured and punished."

How could the Grand Duke speak so coolly, after the horrors Rohario had witnessed? "But, Patro, shouldn't we first find out what caused them to *start* the riot?"

"How kind of you to show some interest in governance, Rohario." The Grand Duke's tone was so sarcastic that Rohario flinched, clenching his hands. The Grand Duke placed a finger over a face on the sketch—from this angle Rohario could not see who it was—and beckoned with his other hand to the Limner. "Andreo, I do not want Count do'Palenssia standing there. If he is standing as far as possible from the do'Najerra representative then it will suggest his son ought to be as far removed from the do'Najerra fortune as possible. I want the do'Najerra heiress for Benetto. He will need all that gold for his upkeep, because he will never be capable of anything except playing with toy soldiers."

Renayo looked up, eyes shot through with unspoken accusations. Rohario cringed. The fever that killed his mother, brother, and baby sister had also permanently crippled Benetto in mind and body. Dismissively, Renayo looked down at the treaty.

"Of course, Your Grace," said Andreo. "I will do what is necessary." He moved to sit in a winged side chair with a red brocade pillow. The tails of his green silk coat trailed down toward the carpeted floor, and his vest, stitched in green and gold thread, showed in its full sartorial glory.

The Grand Duke was, as usual, dressed more simply. He wore a high, doubled-down shirt collar and a bow-tied cravat, nothing fancy, and a saber-gray dress coat in the new northern style, square cut and double-breasted. Clothing did not concern him as long as it was perfectly cut and made of the finest materials. Wealth concerned him.

He rolled up the *Treaty,* handling the stiff paper with care, and examined two smaller sketches that lay beneath it. Edging closer, Rohario saw that one was a series of pencil studies of half a dozen young women; the other showed a harbor scene, with two ships, four merchants, and offloaded cargo. It looked like a preliminary sketch for a minor *Treaty.* But it also looked old-fashioned, without the clean—and, in Rohario's opinion, boring and stilted—lines of paintings done in the modern style.

"I don't like these," said the Grand Duke. "They look undisciplined."

The Lord Limner sighed in the manner of a man much put upon. "One of our Itinerrarios returned last month. He was posted abroad soon after his eighteenth birthday, but by going abroad at such a young age, he absorbed fashions from these other countries that are not in line with Grijalva standards. Too much emotion."

Rohario sidled up to the side of the great desk. Renayo, still ignoring him, appeared not to notice he was there. The harbor sketch was interesting, but the miniature portraits caught his eye. For five years now, neighboring kings and princes had been sending painted miniatures of their daughters to Tira Virte in expectation of Don Edoard's coming of age and needing a wife. Most of the miniatures were well-executed; few painters gained court favor if they could not flatter their subjects. But these sketches had real life in them. Names were carefully printed beneath each one: Lady Elwith of Merse, Princess Alazais de Ghillas, Judit do'Brazzina, Countess Catarin do'Taglisi. The first two were lovely young women, the other two still girls of twelve or fourteen, but each seemed so individual that Rohario felt he knew them and could predict how they would act on first meeting. Elwith looked robust, Alazais gentle and shy, little Judit appeared to be suppressing a laugh, and the delicate do'Taglisi countess looked like a rabbit trapped by hounds.

"But he's an ambitious young man," added Andreo. "Works very hard. Thinks of nothing but painting. But he's too much in the thrall of the Old Masters, too opinionated. He seems to think that since he was baptized with the name of Sario, he ought to be given the same authority as the first Sario had. Eiha, these young people!" He glanced at Rohario.

Renayo frowned at the portrait studies. He had gained many frown lines, on his forehead and around his mouth, since Mairie's death. "Edoard is not ready for a bride." Then his tone changed utterly. "Rohario. Andreo tells me the young woman did not agree to the liaison. What did you say to her?"

The accusation left Rohario speechless.

"I beg your pardon, Your Grace," interposed the Lord Limner, "but I interviewed Eleyna's parents myself. They had nothing but praise for Don Rohario's performance, and you can be sure they would criticize any obstacle put in the way of such an alliance. They said Don Rohario was courtly, polite, and presented the offer with every grace and flourish. Any girl might have been flattered. Alas, there is some bad blood on her mother's side. Although she is well-connected on her father's side, on her mother's she is related to Tazia Grijalva. I will say no more on that subject!"

"She doesn't *want* to be Edoard's Mistress?" Renayo looked up, startled.

"She is . . . headstrong, Your Grace. Her grandmother spoiled her with an idea that she could devote her life to painting. Be assured she will accept her duty."

The Grand Duke looked genuinely puzzled. "I saw a miniature of her. She's a handsome enough girl. This is a fine opportunity. Edoard seemed quite taken with her, and I want him to have what he wants *now*."

In other words, Renayo wanted him out of the way of the new Grand Duchess.

"I assure you, Your Grace. Her parents will talk sense into her. Don Edoard need have no worries on that score."

Traded off as if she were a fine mare at the mercado! Thinking of the rebellious Eleyna Grijalva made Rohario wonder about the rebellious apprentices. Were they, too, pawns in a game over which they had no power?

"Very well." Renayo pushed the portrait sketches to one side and squinted more closely at the harbor study. "Arrange for Edoard and the young woman to stay at Chasseriallo for a few days. They can consummate the Marria do'Fantome there. Don Rohario can accompany them. Some country air would be good for his injuries and would allow him additional leisure to seek out a new pursuit in life."

The sarcasm dripping from his father's voice was not lost on Rohario, but he was by now almost inured to it. Far worse was the prospect of enduring Edoard's company for that long and having to watch the Mistress resign herself to Edoard's attentions. But women often said *No* first, in order to increase the reward once they did give in. Rohario remembered Eleyna less as a discrete placement of eyes and mouth and chin and more as a whirlwind of furious energy. He would keep out of her way.

The Grand Duke traced over the harbor sketch with a perfectly manicured forefinger. "Until this young Limner can work in a more precise manner, he will not paint any official documents." Renayo unrolled the first *Treaty*—a finished sketch, Andreo's work—and the corners of his mouth played up as he studied it. He smiled so rarely these days. "This will do very well." Without looking up he added, as an afterthought: "You may go, Rohario."

Rohario gave him a stiff bow, nodded at the Lord Limner, and backed out of the room. He knew his father's style. He was being banished. But he paused before he shut the door. This wasn't right! He should go back in and demand to find out what was going on in the city!

Through the crack, Rohario heard his father speak again. "I don't know what to do about the succession, Andreo. Ghillas is finally ours for the taking, if what our spies say is true. But my children are all fools. Edoard can think only about horses, women, and wine. Benetto is a simpleton. Timarra is afraid of her own shadow and plain to boot. And Rohario—eiha! He's a useless fop. He flits from interest to interest like a butterfly, all pretty colors and no substance. I allowed him to study painting only because Zio Cabral insisted, though it's no fit pursuit for a lord. But after four years he gives it up overnight! For no reason! Matra Dolcha, Andreo. How can I trust any of them with the knowledge I must in time pass on to my successor? Not one of them is worthy of the throne of Tira Virte, much less that of Tira Virte and Ghillas together."

"You are young yet, and still healthy, Your Grace," said the Lord Limner calmly. "You will have other children."

Rohario stiffened and turned away. There stood Ermaldo, sur-

veying him with his usual air of disdain. Was it common knowledge that Grand Duke Renayo despised his own children? Aching
in every joint and muscle, Rohario limped back to his suite.
Listlessly, he directed his servant to pack. There was no point in
staying here.

⸺ SIXTY ⸺

Beatriz always told her to come in the back way, through the servants' quarters, but Eleyna hated subterfuge. She pushed her black curls out of her eyes with the back of a hand and marched up the front steps of the Grijalva compound. The two old men sitting side by side on a bench beside the shop door watched her dramatic arrival. One lowered his gaze; the other smiled. Eleyna didn't know whether to be furious or relieved.

"Davo!" She addressed the man with lowered eyes, a servant who had for sixty years ground and mixed paint for the Grijalvas. "You must close and bar the shop for the day!"

"Sit down, mennina," said the other man. He patted the bench. It was so old that the wood was as smooth as polished stone. "Where have you been?"

She had not expected to confront Grandzio Cabral. Expecting her mother, she was already primed for a great argument, and the words poured out. "I went to the hangings. The Shagarra Regiment rounded up twenty men accused as ringleaders of the Iluminarres riots and dragged them before the magistrate. The men weren't allowed to plead their own case! And now—only ten days later!—twelve of those men were hanged. What kind of justice is that?"

"Swift justice, mennina," said Cabral mildly. "Or are you thinking of giving away your bedchamber to a family of beggars now?"

"There will be trouble all through the city. This very afternoon!"

"Be trouble in the hall if you don't pretend you've been here with me all afternoon, Maessa Eleynita," retorted old Davo, coming to life as he always did when he thought Eleyna was threatened. She had won his heart long ago, begging *him*—not her Grijalva uncles—to teach her the mysteries of pigments and paints. He sat with his back to the open shutters. The scent of oils and solvents, the life's blood of the Grijalvas, drifted out from the shop.

"You're my only advocate, Davo." She took his stained, gnarled hands in her own.

"You're a good girl."

"You ought not to be walking to such places unescorted, Eleynita," said Cabral in that same mild voice.

"I'm a respectable widow. I'll do what I want!"

"You want to watch men hanged?"

"Someone must witness! I sketched. Here." She sat on the bench next to Cabral and rested her sketchpad on her dress, careless of the fine green silk. Opening the book, she paged slowly through it. "Look how restless the crowd is." Individual faces, the cut of a coat or gown, tableaus of men watching and glimpses of children darting through the crowd: She had caught them all. "They built the gibbets by the marsh. The shop ought to be closed for the day, as a protest if nothing else. Those men weren't allowed to speak on their own behalf."

"That isn't our decision to make, carrida meya."

"To allow the men to speak? Or to close the shop?" She hesitated, then rushed on. "Don't you ever mind it, Grandzio? Taking their orders, living under their thumbs? And you twice as old as any of them?"

"Of whom are you speaking?" She heard the reserve in his voice. He glanced at Davo, but Davo had served the family for so long it was impossible he not suspect.

It was not the politic thing to say, but Eleyna had never let that stop her. "The Viehos Fratos. The men who wear the sigil of the Golden Key."

Cabral did not reply for a long while, but he gestured with one hand and old Davo got up obediently and retreated into the shop. Here, in the peaceful Grijalva compound, the executions seemed very far away, as indeed they were: They had taken place on the opposite side of town, as far as possible from Palasso Verrada. Here, at Palasso Grijalva, was like another world, one not torn by the press of bodies, by the angry whispers and exhalation of fear and hatred, by the awful jerk and sway of the executed men dangling from the noose. Here was quiet sun and a street slumbering in siesta. A cart piled high with lemons and limes trundled past. Two children rolled hoops at the intersection. From down the arched tunnel that led into the main courtyard, Eleyna heard the faint singing and laughter of the serving girls, washing clothes in the stable trough: *"My beloved awaits me at the fountain."*

"Leilias spoke freely with you," said Cabral at last, folding his hands neatly in his lap.

"You know she did! Grandmother believed in my gift!"

"As do I, mennina."

Eleyna shut her eyes on sudden tears, bowed her head, and laid it on his hands. His skin bore calluses and lesions, the legacy of his years of grinding harsh pigments and tempering them into paints.

"Now that Grandmother is dead, you are the only one who believes in me."

He stroked her hair gently. "The Itinerarrio, Sario, has been looking at your paintings. He is one of the Gifted, and he admires your work."

She looked up, aware her cheeks were warm. "I haven't met him yet. Since the Iluminarres riot, Mother has kept me in the matron's courtyard, painting portraits of those awful lapdogs the court ladies keep. Matra ei Filho, now Grand Duchess Johannah wants a portrait done of her greyhounds. She saw the miniature I did of Countess do'Casteya's pugs, and she wants me to do another of hers, only with the greyhounds in a pastoral scene, by a farmhouse. It makes me sick! Look at these! Look!" She pulled away from him and flipped through the pages of her sketchpad. "Children dressed in rags. Men who could barely walk for hunger, all come to the hanging—but for what? People spoke of Ghillas. There was a terrible rumor going around that seven days after the bread riots the common folk in Aute-Ghillas burned the palace there and put the king to the sword. Is it true?"

The rumor did not appear to surprise him. "How could I hope for such news to be true? Everyone knows that we Grijalvas serve the Grand Duke. If the Grand Duke is attacked by people who believe such rumors, then so will *we* be attacked."

"That's true, I suppose. Like a disease, jumping from one city to the next. It still wasn't right to hang those men like that, though."

"You had a customer in looking at your *Battle of Rio Sanguo*."

"You're trying to distract me. Nicollo told me I ought to burn it. But it isn't a disgrace, though he may think it one." She tilted her head to one side, catching a sudden fusillade of faint gunfire, a harsh melody borne on the breeze. "Matra!"

Cabral got up from the bench and took a few nimble steps down to the avenue, staring along the empty street. His hair was as pale as the zinc white they used in painting the coldest, purest whites, but he walked with the vigor of a man of forty. Almost eighty he might be, but he was stronger than Gifted painters half his age. Had he ever regretted his health, or wished he could trade it for the Gift? She never had the courage to ask.

Now he merely shook his head. "Nothing. Go into the hall, Eleynita. I'll take care of things here." He clucked reprovingly. "These are hard days."

She kissed him on the cheek and hurried inside, her mood entirely changed. Who had come to look at her painting? Would it be bought? Perhaps chosen for display at Galerria Verrada?

"No!" Eleyna recognized Agustin's voice. A moment later the boy came pelting out of the arcaded walkway that led to the gardens. He saw Eleyna and veered toward her. "I won't go through the Confirmattio," he muttered, hiding behind her. "It's so degrading."

"Agustin!"

"There are other ways to know. Why do I have to be tested, except so they can do to me what was done to them? I won't do it!"

She sighed. There *they* came, their voices like the mutter of the crowd at the hangings: an uncle, three male cousins, and her mother. She braced herself.

Dionisa strode forward first, sweeping her old-fashioned bustled skirt past a tight turn where the arcade emptied into the courtyard. She advanced on her daughter and son with the confidence of a woman who has achieved the ultimate authority: mother to a Gifted son. She fixed her glare on Eleyna. "It isn't enough that *you* act in this way, is it? You must infect *him* as well. Go at once to your chamber. I will speak with you later."

"I won't go," said Eleyna softly.

"He's as loyal as a dog to her," muttered her uncle, Giaberto.

Agustin huddled closer behind her. Although he was now taller than she was, although he was now fifteen, he could only sustain short spurts of defiance. His artist's soul was like a fine piece of porcelain: admire it, handle it gently, and it will transform a room with its beauty; drop it and it will shatter. Eleyna was not so delicate. As Dionisa ever reminded her, wishing her son had been born with fiery resolve and her daughter with the more demure sensibility.

"This is Conselho business," objected Nicollo. "You may go, Eleyna."

"Then Agustin will go with me. Come, Agustin." But she trembled as she said it and not just with anger. It was not wise to push Viehos Fratos too far. They had powers that others did not. She had learned that the hard way, five years ago.

"I have had enough of this!" Nicollo was furious.

"Let her go," said Dionisa, "and take the boy, for now. It is only a formality, after all. He has shown his skills already." Always they shrouded the Gift in secrecy, even when speaking among themselves. "We will discuss what to do next."

At moments like these, Eleyna admired her mother for the way Dionisa imposed her will upon her male relatives. Agustin was a rare thing; there had been few boys in this last generation who had passed the Confirmattio—she had heard Leilias comment on it many times. Leilias had borne two Gifted sons herself, but no other Grijalva woman since had given birth to more than one. Dionisa knew the worth of what she had; the Viehos Fratos knew that she knew, and knew also that she would not sit back and let them take the boy without her guiding the hand that wielded the paintbrush.

Eleyna did not trust her mother. But having said she was going, she could hardly object now. She took Agustin by the hand and together they crossed through the great ballroom, into the south courtyard, and from there along an arcade smothered in oleander into the tiled courtyard around which the private suites were clustered.

Though it was cool, Agustin was sweating. He dipped a hand in the fountain, brushed his fingers along the cool tile, and wiped his brow. Their sister Beatriz came into the courtyard through the door that led into the library, and she crossed toward them.

"They don't need to test me," Augustin continued as Beatriz stopped beside him and gently brushed a stray curl out of his eyes, "if they already know that—" He broke off when their cousin Yberra came in from the arcade. Yberra came from that line of the family which had lost the ability to produce Gifted sons. Andreo was the last. Yberra might suspect there were secrets among the Viehos Fratos, but she remained ignorant of the Grijalvas' true power.

"The hem of your gown is dirty," said Agustin to Beatriz, changing the subject quickly. "You've tried to brush the dirt from your gown, where you were kneeling."

"Beatriz!" Yberra pressed a hand to her bosom—and there was a lot of bosom there—and looked horrified. "You haven't been *gardening* with the servants again, have you? I thought you were reading. Eiha! I've heard *news*." This last word spoken dramatically. "I overheard Andreo telling Mama you ought to marry Fransisso."

Eleyna shuddered.

"Of course I will do what my parents ask of me," said Beatriz calmly.

"Of course you will," said Yberra sweetly, shooting a stinging and triumphant glance toward Eleyna.

"I'm so sorry we must go now, Yberra." Eleyna grabbed Agustin's elbow and hauled him away.

Beatriz hurried after them. "Eleyna!" she said in a whisper as they climbed the stairs, first one flight to the corner, then turning to go up again, until they reached the third landing. Here Eleyna opened the door that led into the suite of rooms belonging to their mother and her first cousins—doomed by the fall of their aunt

Tazia, whom none of them had even liked, to be relegated to the least desirable corner of the compound.

But they were handsome enough rooms, Eleyna reflected as they walked along the corridor. Large windows looked down over the courtyard, giving way to a whitewashed wall bordered by *azulejos,* the blue and white rosette tiles trimmed with green that were the symbol of Palasso Grijalva. So handsome that Dionisa had made no effort to throw Yberra's sonless mother out of her better-placed rooms. Instead she had beautified her own, as if announcing her refusal to be stained by Tazia's bad name.

They walked into the safety of the parlor. Eleyna tossed her sketchpad and her shawl onto a couch.

"You needn't antagonize Yberra," said Beatriz.

Eleyna shot her a glance but said nothing. Beatriz was so kind that it was impossible to be angry with her.

"I'm going back to the studio," said Agustin. "Davo says he's got a new batch of dye from the madders, and we're going to blend rose madder for watercolors."

"Don't do anything foolish," said Eleyna.

"Davo won't let him," said Beatriz.

Agustin's fine mouth quivered into a smile. He was a boy made homely by years of delicate health. That he had survived the Summer Fever two years ago was a miracle granted by the Mother. His robust twin siblings had not been so lucky.

"I won't," he promised. He kissed his sisters and walked distractedly away into the hall. Eleyna wandered out to the balcony that overlooked the street. Beatriz followed her. They leaned on the wrought iron railing that was twined into the shapes of keys: ornate door keys, skeleton keys, tiny jewel-lock keys making a lacework at the corners.

Eleyna contemplated the broad avenida. "Look how few people are out. It's too quiet, and not just because it's siesta." She heard no more musketfire.

"Mother will scheme until Agustin is named as the next Lord Limner," said Beatriz gently, a soft reminder. Indeed, she appeared the gentlest of creatures in her lavender morning dress, white lace gloves held in one hand, black lace shawl draped becomingly over her dark hair.

Eleyna's lace shawl was tangled at her shoulders, and now she fussed with it self-consciously, although Beatriz was the last person who would berate her for carelessness. "Agustin isn't strong enough to be Lord Limner. He'll refuse it."

"Can he refuse Mother?"

"He can refuse her once. I can refuse for him, in his name, after that."

"You can't be his strength forever, Eleyna."

Love and desperate anger made her voice shake. "Can't I? I won't marry again, and I'll probably outlive him. He needs to be protected."

A crash came from the parlor, followed by a curse. Beatriz started and hurried back into the parlor.

"Where is she?" demanded a male voice. "Where is that ungrateful daughter of mine?"

"Now, Patro," began Beatriz in her soft voice.

Eleyna swept back through the curtains that screened off the balcony, stopping to close the glass doors behind her, carefully, latching them. "I am here, Patro." She turned to face him.

Revirdin had lost his cane, perhaps on the edge of the carpet, and knocked over a slender side table, breaking a Zhinna vase. Now Beatriz settled him in a chair while he glared at Eleyna as if his mishap with the table was her fault. The carriage accident that had ruined him for painting had not improved his temper, and it had only gotten worse in the last seven years as his daughter's gifts flowered.

"Do I hear that you continue to refuse the young Heir?" he demanded. "Eiha! When I think how long we argued with Andreo and the Viehos Fratos to let *you* be brought forward as the candidate, once it was known the Heir wished for a Grijalva Mistress. No, no, they said, you would prove intractable. But even I thought you would do your duty to your family. And if not that, then be swayed by the many presents he will shower on you. It is even likely he will give you land and a manor house—that's traditional. Many a Grijalva Mistress has married into the nobility after her lover is wed. Have I raised a fool?"

"I don't want presents! I don't want a noble husband!"

"No more of that, filha! Your mother is coming. Give me my walking stick, Beatriz."

She already had it in her hand. Now she gave it to her father, and Revirdin Grijalva rested the ebony cane across his legs, clutching it with his left—now his only—hand. His right arm ended just below the elbow. A black ribbon tied off his jacket sleeve so that it would not flap or get in his way when he moved about. He also had refused a move to rooms on the ground floor, where he would not have the painful climb up three flights of steps. Now he rose in courtesy, as was expected of a man greeting a woman, although the gesture caused him to grimace even when he was expecting the pain.

Dionisa entered alone, having shed her escort of Limner brother and cousins and in-laws. "Sit down, Revirdin." She kissed her husband on the cheek, coolly, and nodded to Beatriz, who promptly helped her father resume his seat. Dionisa turned her steely gaze on Eleyna. There were, as usual, no pleasantries. "You *will* be Don Edoard's Mistress. You are good for nothing else."

"I can paint."

"You are barren."

"I won't do it!"

"Don Edoard has seen you and wants you, though Matra help him when he is subject to your temper."

Revirdin snorted. "My mother always said that Arrigo, bless his departed soul, was in thrall to Tazia's spiteful tongue."

Dionisa spared her husband a glance, but no more than that, before she rapped the table hard with her knuckles for emphasis. "It is decided, Eleyna. We will no longer indulge you. I have already spoken to Giaberto. He wanted Lord Limner Andreo's position; he's as good as Andreo. But of course the Grand Duke would not allow him to become Lord Limner because he is Tazia's nephew. It didn't matter that her sisters repudiated her. Eiha! What's past is past. Now Don Edoard has seen you and wants you. Everyone says the young man is headstrong, spoiled, and a bit stupid. You can have anything, all the power—"

"And be like Grandzia Tazia, whose sisters repudiated her?"

Dionisa's expression turned from imperious anger to a mask of rage. "Beatriz, leave the room."

"Yes, Mama."

Eleyna did not try to call her sister back. She did not want to subject Beatriz to the diatribe she could see was coming.

But Dionisa's voice did not rise. She spoke in a devestatingly normal tone. "We have received a private message from the Grand Duke that you are to be escorted to Chasseriallo in three days' time. Know this: Giaberto and I are determined that if you will not agree to Edoard of your own will, then you will agree *despite* your will."

Eleyna's heart pounded in her ears as the full horror of her mother's calm statement swept over her. Fear and anger choked the words in her throat. It grew so quiet in the parlor that when her father coughed, it sounded as sharp as the crack of a musket.

Eleyna had to bite down on her lower lip to stop herself from trembling. "You would do to me again what you did to me with Felippo?" She almost sobbed aloud. "How could you?"

"We will do what we must. A portrait is already half-finished—
not Giaberto's finest work, by any means, but sufficient to the task.
In three days the Grand Duke will send servants to escort you to
Chasseriallo. In what state of mind you go is your own choice. I
will expect your answer tomorrow. If you agree and give me your
word on your Grandmother Leilias' honor, you are free to go untouched. Adezo. Go to your room. Your father and I have matters to
discuss."

Struck dumb with helpless fury, Eleyna could barely muster
enough composure to walk out of the room. When she came to the
bedchamber she shared with Beatriz, she collapsed on the bed,
burying her face in the coverlet.

How could they? *How could they?*

Five years ago . . . Matra Dolcha! If they were willing to do it
then, why not now? She had been sixteen, defiant, stubborn, determined to make her mark as a Grijalva—by painting, the art that
flowed through her bloodlines. She had endured the Confirmattio—twice!—did not conceive although all of the boys involved later proved to be unGifted. Because of that and because
she refused to obey her mother's strictures about a Grijalva woman's duty, her parents agreed to marry her to Felippo Grijalva.

At sixty, Felippo had already buried two wives, who had between them produced a Gifted son as well as five other children.
Most importantly, he had fulfilled his duty as a competent but unin-
spired copyist for his more illustrious Gifted relatives, painting un-
spelled copies of the spelled *Treaties* that were sent to foreign
courts as binding records of these agreements. Chiefly, he had assisted in the delicate undertaking that led to the betrothal of Mairie
de Ghillas to Renayo II rather than to her Ghillasian cousin, Ivo IV,
who had stolen the Ghillasian throne out from under Renayo's
nose.

So the Conselhos, in their wisdom, had rewarded Felippo with a
handsome and very young bride, one he had chosen himself.

The bride had refused.

The tears came fast now. Eleyna pressed her knuckles into her
eyes, unwilling to relive the humiliation.

But she could not help remembering the day of his funeral, sitting in the widow's chair beside his deathbed, one hand clasped to
her bosom with genuine grief . . . only to find the besotted girl's infatuation with which she regarded her elderly husband fading
away, dissipating, as she stared at his face in the repose of death.
Mourners filed past while she struggled to make sense of her
thoughts.

Matra Dolcha! He repelled her! Old, lecherous, with the scabrous skin that came of handling paints for many years . . . yet she had doted on him, petted him, flattered him. Now the emotion slipped off her like water. She hadn't liked him at all. She had refused him. She had refused her parents, her relatives, utterly refused.

"I will not marry Felippo Grijalva."

She had sat beside his bier that day and finally understood she had been living in a dream for almost three years. Waking, she had stared with blank confusion at her black lace gloves and the old black gown twenty years out of date, cut to her figure, its tight stays constricting her. She had heard the condolences of her relatives as through a wall, muted by stone.

In the end, Leilias told her the truth: The Limners had stolen her blood and tears and used their Gift—their magic—to paint her into acquiescence.

"I was against it!" Leilias had railed. "Eiha, you can be sure I was against it. But Tazia's blood bred true in that line, whatever her sisters claimed. They did it without anyone else knowing, Dionisa and Giaberto. And once it was done, eiha! 'No harm done.' That's what the rest said. 'Won't hurt the girl to learn some humility.' With Zevierin dead, Matra bless his fine soul, and my Justino dead as well, poor child, and Vitorrio still abroad, there was nothing I could do but appeal to their honor. That a son of mine would countenance this! You can be sure I told Revirdin what I thought of allowing them to spell his own daughter! But you are back with me now, mennina. I won't let them touch you again."

But Leilias was dead, killed in the last, belated burst of the Summer Fever that had carried off Felippo in its first flowering. Two months after his death, Eleyna had caught it and miscarried that poor deformed child, her final penance.

"They will not touch me again," she swore into the pillow. The pillow did not, of course, reply, but the soft linen cover absorbed the last of her tears. She heard the door open and close softly and reared up, ready to confront the intruder.

It was Beatriz. She held a basket of oranges and grapes. "I thought you might be hungry."

Eleyna flung herself down on the bed again. "I'm not."

"You might be later. Mama has decided to lock you in the room. I rescued your sketchpad from the parlor."

"Grazzo." She was too exhausted by now to feel angry about this final insult. Locked in her room!

"Grandzio Cabral is outside, waiting to talk to you."

"I don't want to talk to him!"

Eleyna's temper never had the slightest impact on Beatriz's composure. "Of course you don't, but you might as well greet him kindly, since you have no choice."

At that, Eleyna began to chuckle. "Oh, Beatriz, how do you manage it? If I have no choice, I might as well show my true feelings. Don't you have any?"

Beatriz smiled at her and went to the door. Normally no one but their father or brother was allowed into their private suite, but Cabral was not only their great-uncle but a man who could speak his mind to the Grand Duke himself. If he wished to speak to his great-niece in the privacy of her bedchamber, not one soul on the council was likely to argue.

Cabral, looking suitably somber, entered carrying a painting under one arm. Setting it on the easel propped up in one corner of the room, he lifted the protective cloth off to display Eleyna's own painting, the *Battle of Rio Sanguo.*

In the foreground the future Duke Renayo held his dying father, Alesso, while to the left a captured Tza'ab warrior prostrated himself. Beyond the mob of retainers lay the battlefield itself, still littered with the dead, and the plains of Joharra stretched out into a distance made golden by the sun newly unveiled from the clouds.

"Very fine, which you know," said Cabral with fine disregard for Eleyna's tear-stained face and the crumpled bedding, evidence of her distress. "Most painters can't resist copying Bartollin's *Battle,* but you instead chose to echo the old *Morta* of Verro Grijalva done by Piedro Grijalva. An echo, no more, just enough to touch the eyes and set the heart to wondering. But it's not in the modern style. I wonder if you have given too much brightness and detail to the background. It pulls attention away from the little triangle you have drawn—"

"They say I don't use classical forms, Zio, but I do! You see it, don't you? Renayo in the center with the other two figures below him, one on each side."

"It is well composed," said Cabral.

Eleyna forgot, for a moment, all her trials. *Well composed.* Those were words to treasure.

"A steward from the do'Casteya household has expressed interest in buying it for Count Maldonno's Galerria."

Count Maldonno—the Grand Duke's cousin!—wanted to buy her painting! "And what did Andreo have to say to that!" she demanded triumphantly.

Cabral adjusted his sleeves. He still had beautiful hands, dark with age and the legacy of harsh paints, but strong. His mouth twisted into a grimace, an odd expression that Eleyna could not read. "'It is not a style based on the classical form of statues. It is too wild. Too undisciplined.'"

Eleyna sighed. She had heard all this before.

"But," said Cabral, pulling the cloth back over the painting, "it shows a fine use of color and composition, and it has life. You are becoming an excellent painter."

"I am as good as anyone alive today!" Then she flushed. "But I am not Gifted. So I am worth nothing to them, especially because I am not a good copyist."

"It is precisely because you are *not* a good copyist that you show the gifts you do, and they cannot forgive you for that. To them, art only matters if it serves the Gift and thus the family." He sighed and sank down on the feather bed beside her, one hand tracing the Grijalva rosettes embroidered onto the bedspread, Beatriz's work. "Once, I believed as they did. What will you do, Eleynita?"

Eleyna clasped her hands firmly in her lap and refused to look into his eyes. "What have you come to say to me?"

"Be Edoard's Mistress now. Keep him happy for a few years. He has other duties. While he attends to them, you are free to paint, and to paint unobstructed by your parents and old uncle. When he marries, then you will gain an honorable retirement. He may dower you with a country house. You can live there with perfect propriety because you are a widow, and you can paint to your heart's content. It is the easiest road to get where you want to go."

"To be a whore?"

"We all are forced at times to make choices we don't like."

She jumped up, paced to the window, back to the door, and back to the bed again. "It's a terrible choice. I can give myself over to him in return for what I can get from him. Or I can refuse, in which case Zio Giaberto will simply paint me into acquiescence." She stared challengingly at him, willing him to look shocked.

He did not even look surprised. "It is better to choose the path with your eyes open."

"The only way I'll know they haven't *painted* me into liking him is if I continue to dislike him! How can I be his Mistress if I look at his face and want to turn away? It would be better to make them paint me. At least then I wouldn't feel anything."

Cabral smoothed the sleeves of his jacket, the fussy movements of a man who had once, perhaps, been vain of his appearance. Or cared how he appeared to another person. "Women marry to the benefit of their families, not according to the dictates of their own hearts. Your grandmother Leilias, my dear sister, was an exception. She married where her heart led her, and even then she married knowing Zevierin would die before her. Grand Duke Renayo wants Alazais de Ghillas for Edoard, not because of her pretty face but because marriage to her would irrevocably give Edoard the thrones of both countries. Renayo has not forgotten that *he* was Enrei's named heir, not Ivo. Edoard will not be allowed to remain unmarried long. A year or two at most."

Eleyna walked to the window, looked down into the courtyard at the fountain of tiles. Water splashed over the rim of the upper bowl, sliding down yellow and blue patterns to spill at last into the bright yellow basin where the water collected, strewn with bubbles.

"Perhaps it would be easier for Eleyna," said Beatriz quietly, "if Mama and Papa allowed me to attend her at Chasseriallo. Then she would have a companion."

"You are an unmarried girl," said Cabral.

"I have an infant son in the crechetta."

"That is true, and I think it an excellent idea, Beatriz. Don Edoard is not, alas, the most stimulating companion unless one likes horses and hounds to the exclusion of all else. However, you are not a suitable duennia."

"Davo's wife Mara, then," said Beatriz instantly. As if she had already considered the question. "She can act as duennia. I can act as companion."

"Why not?" said Eleyna recklessly, turning back from the window. "I would be glad of your company, Beatriz. I always am. Perhaps it won't be so bad after all." But her voice stumbled over the words.

"Then you agree?" asked Cabral.

She refused to bow her head. If she chose this path, then she would do so with her eyes open. "I do. I give my word. If I may be allowed to paint—"

"Between fittings, mennina meya," said Cabral. "You will have to have gowns and walking dresses and riding clothes, that sort of thing. You will entertain, go to balls—"

Court life! It was too awful to contemplate. But contemplate it she must.

"I can stand in for you, at fittings," said Beatriz quickly, as if to forestall an explosion. For Beatriz's sake, Eleyna held her tongue.

Cabral rose and gave them each a kiss. "May I let the Casteyan steward know you have no objection to Count Maldonno buying the painting?" As a parting shot, it was effective. Her painting to hang in the do'Casteya collection! She could only nod dumbly. Cabral bundled up the painting and left.

Matra Dolcha! It had all happened so quickly. And imagine, Beatriz protecting *her!* Eleyna laughed suddenly. "You can't be fitted in my place, though it's kind of you to offer."

"Do you want to stand for hours for all the fittings?"

"Of course not. You know I hate—"

"Then hush. We're close enough in size that it won't matter. Trust me, Eleyna. Say nothing. All will be well."

With that assurance Eleyna had to be content.

⊷ SIXTY-ONE ⊶

Sario Grijalva stood beside one of the great arched windows that let sunlight pour into the Atelierro. The sun was warm and bright; it was another cloudless day in an uncomfortably dry winter. The other Viehos Fratos stood at the end of the long Atelierro, beside the stove, watching young Agustin Grijalva bite his lower lip just before he took a lancet and pricked his forefinger.

All these changes! Instead of each Limner being granted his own atelierro, as was traditional, they had ten years ago expanded the Atelierro where the unGifted limners worked. How it irritated him to have to profess approval when an old custom was tossed aside like a marred canvas, but too often his solitary voice raised in protest was ignored or—worse—marked as suspicious. Annoyed, Sario watched with his newly-young and gratifyingly sharp Limner eyes as red welled up from Agustin's pale skin and was dripped into a tiny glass vial for storage.

The other men—only seven of them, one stooped with bone-fever though he was only thirty-eight—murmured appreciatively. Giaberto went so far as to pat young Agustin on the shoulder. It was a momentous occurrence when the Viehos Fratos acknowledged a new apprentice—even one who had not gone through the usual Confirmattio. Still, there would be years of apprenticeship before the boy painted his *Peintraddo Chieva*.

Too slight, thought Sario. *He won't live long. He's fragile, too sensitive, too compliant.*

Damn these sour pedants anyway! They had ruined the flower of Grijalva blood. The horrible stiff classicism he had deplored ten years ago as Arriano Grijalva had not, miraculously, vanished in the intervening period. As the new Sario, he had chosen the life of an Itinerrario so his years abroad would act as the excuse for the new more vital style of painting he intended to "bring back" with him—the painting that would revitalize and change what they now called the "Academy" style.

But he had returned to find the "Academy" style draped like an antique robe over everything else, smothering it in the stark detail of its rigid folds.

There were so few Gifted Limners left after the Summer Fever, itself so disastrously reminiscent of the Nerro Lingua that had nearly destroyed the Grijalvas—that was, perhaps, paradoxically, responsible for the Gift. Which was now stretched too thin. Once, admittance to the inner circle—to the rank of Aguo, Semmino, or Sanguo—was an honor reserved for the finest and most influential Grijalva Limners. No longer. They called Giaberto Premio Frato, but now the title meant only that Giaberto was Andreo's likely successor. Already there was talk of allowing Agustin to attend meetings of the Viehos Fratos—*before* he had painted his *Peintraddo Chieva.* And influence was measured purely by relation within the family.

Vieho Frato Sario might be, but the others refused to acknowledge his genius. This Sario's mother had died in the intervening years, Grazzo do'Matra, and his remaining relatives had proven weak. Cabral and Leilias's faction ruled the Conselhos now, though Leilias—and her dangerous knowledge of a long-ago night—was dead.

He had no supporters, no adherents. The only painter for whom he had the slightest respect was a young woman who was now, he had just learned, being carted off to provide bedplay for the young Heir. They actually thought she was more useful to them as a Mistress than as a painter just because as a woman she could not be Gifted!

Chieva do'Orro! What had the Grijalva bloodline come to? Had they forgotten everything about painting; had they forgotten the secrets of the Tza'ab he had worked so hard to procure, of the Golden Key itself, in their pursuit of wealth and power? Had the Gift become more important than the *art?*

I will not let this happen. I cannot let this happen.

Sario was twenty-six now. Yet he would gladly cast off this body and take on a new host, one with more influential relatives, except there were no suitable candidates. At least ten promising boys—one of them known to be Gifted—had died in the great Fever two years ago. Those who survived had proven unGifted, except for this boy, Agustin, who claimed good family connections but poor health. He was of no use. And taking an older man was too dangerous an option.

Sario was tired of waiting.

"Eiha, Sario. The boy has talent, no?" Nicollo Grijalva sidled over to him.

"The sister is the better painter."

Nicollo smiled patronizingly. "You're only twenty-six. You

have the luxury of these new romantic notions. Acceptable for the streets, perhaps, but not for court art."

"The Grand Dukes have always dictated fashion, of course." He allowed himself a sneer. "Do they dictate what is true and beautiful in art, now, as well?"

"It has always been so," said Nicollo with a mocking bow. Eiha! Nicollo had treated Arriano with respect, when he had met him briefly eleven years ago, when Arriano was a respected and powerful Embajadorro and Nicollo merely a young Limner struggling for position. But Nicollo was the sort of man who, once given power, used it as a height from which to look down on the less fortunate.

"It has not always been so!" retorted Sario, then stopped. What was the point of arguing with these imbeciles? They knew nothing. Copyists!

Nicollo raised an eyebrow, a trick he used to cow his students. Sario fumed.

The others of the gathered Limners drifted away, leaving Agustin with his uncle in front of a full-length mirror. Giving Nicollo a curt nod, Sario walked over to watch the boy attempt his first tutored spell.

"I've done this before," said the boy with a stab at bravaddio.

"Is that so?" asked Giaberto calmly. "In your rooms? Privately, I hope."

"No. I did it under Eleyna's supervision. I used colored chalks on a piece of silk, using a bit of my saliva and a touch of pine oil. I drew roses, and we put the silk under Beatriz's pillow, to see what she would dream of."

Shocked, Sario waited for Giaberto's reaction. How had the young *woman* found out such secrets? But Giaberto remained calm. "Did she dream of roses?"

"No. She dreamed about pigs. She always dreams about pigs. But she said they were rose-colored pigs." Agustin giggled. Sario, attuned to the nuances of facial expression after long, long experience, saw that Giaberto was furious but hiding it.

"What really happened?" Sario asked suddenly.

Startled, Agustin played nervously with the pencil in his hand, rolling it over and over again through his fingers. "I did try the dream silk, roses one night, pigs another, Grandmother Leilias the third time, and a bell the fourth. Every morning Beatriz had dreamed of the things I painted on the silk."

"And?" Sario asked.

Agustin fidgeted.

"Is there more?" Giaberto asked abruptly. Agustin began to bite

at his nails. His uncle slapped his hand down. "Never do that, mennino! Your hands are your life!"

"Eleyna doesn't know, but I painted a silk that showed her painting and put it under my mother's pillow. I even took a little of my
blood and mixed it with watercolors. I . . . I heard blood makes a
spell more potent. I drew some things—keys—interlaced along the
border. I thought Mother might dream about Eleyna painting instead of—"

"Matra ei Filho, you imbecile!" swore Giaberto.

Agustin visibly wilted.

"It's a clever idea," interposed Sario, liking the boy's audacity.
"But you must learn the secrets of magic before you employ them.
You do have a great deal to learn."

"I thought it would work. But it didn't."

Giaberto's dour face cracked slightly. "Eiha! It's true. I remember the first time I realized what power I held in my hands. I
thought I could do anything!"

*And you could have, if only you'd the skills and the ambition.
But like the rest of your colleagues, you've grown small-minded.*

"Then you'll still teach me?" Agustin asked in a small voice.

"Of course," said his uncle quickly. "A Gifted son of the
Grijalvas is never abandoned by his fellow Limners, not as long as
he abides by the Golden Key. Adezo! I have given thought to what
you might try this afternoon. Go to the window. Davo always
sweeps at this hour. When he comes to the fourth tier of the side-
walk, farthest from the portico, he stops to sit on the bench, there.
You must draw him, in light charcoal, on the glass, using a bit of
your saliva. Fix in your mind the idea that one of us here upstairs
wants him. Needs him. Make him come to us. This is what is
known as a suggestion spell. This is the most basic spell, and the
safest for you, since saliva can be rubbed out with no effect on you.
It is the spell you must first master before you can move on to others. Go on."

Looking half-dubious and half-thrilled, the boy walked over to
the windows and craned his neck to look out.

"That was well seen of you," said Giaberto, "knowing that to
praise the boy's curiosity would allow you to warn him about the
dangers of our magic."

Well seen! Sario eyed the other Limner with misgiving. Had
Giaberto not had similar thoughts himself as a boy? Had he not experimented? There were always some sorry boys who did only
what they were told. Giaberto had not struck him as that kind.

Giaberto Grijalva was about thirty-eight. He might live under the thumb of his twin sister, the elder by one hour, but it wouldn't do to underestimate him; he and Dionisa clearly shared the same ambitions. No doubt being born twinned with a Gifted brother made Dionisa more likely to give birth in her turn to Gifted sons. With two more boys in the nursery and four living daughters, she was a force to be reckoned with.

"For my part I have seen that you have talent," continued Giaberto unctuously. Sario recognized the tactic: By such means did aspirants for Lord Limner woo possible allies. "You could go far—but not if you antagonize Andreo and Nicollo."

"They no longer understand art!"

"There, you see? I do not myself care for this new, emotional style you are championing. It doesn't have dignity, nor suitable exactitude. But I am not blind to my niece Eleyna's talent, which is considerable, even while the others ignore it. I can see that you, too, have a strong, original style. But your mother is dead and you have been outside the Viehos Fratos for eight years. You didn't endure the Fever that decimated our family. You are still accounted an outsider. Defer to your elders until you have formed more influential ties."

If you only knew, you would never dare speak to me like this! You would be on your knees, begging me to teach you even one tenth of the knowledge I have hoarded away over the centuries—

"Sario!"

The sound of his name—his *real* name—still had the power to startle him. As he turned, he caught sight of himself in the mirror. He froze. Who was that ordinary-looking man who stared back at him? *That* wasn't Sario!

Of course it wasn't. It was merely flesh. He regretted, again, not choosing the other boy—what had his name been? Alerrio, yes, that was it. At least he had been a handsome youth, and Sario was tired of the bland face of his current host; at best it served to make his companions believe he was innocuous. But Alerrio was one of the many Grijalvas who had succumbed to the Summer Fever.

"Sario, I am pleased to have a chance to talk with you at last." Andreo stopped and nodded briskly at Giaberto, who immediately excused himself and went off to supervise Agustin's work. "I will come to the point. Grand Duke Renayo finds your style undisciplined. He does not want you to paint the *Treaty* with Merse. However—"

"But no one can do as well with that *Treaty* as I can. I have visited the court! I have conversed with Queen Agwyn—a difficult woman to paint. The rest of you would have to work from my sketches—"

"Sario! I have not done speaking!"

Once, as Riobaro, he would have spoken in the same way to an overly-eager young Limner. The irony did not escape him.

"The sketches you did of the young noblewomen did please His Grace," Andreo continued. "He wants you to do a new set of them, unadorned, painted. He intends to make a choice within these six months for a bride for Don Edoard and then open negotiations. He favors Princess Alazais de Ghillas, so you may be asked to add a suggestion to her portrait, suggestion that could act subtly on Edoard. If you comport yourself circumspectly and paint as befits a Grijalva, you may be allowed to do work on the *Betrothal* and to do some of the composition for the *Marriage*."

"If I refuse?"

"If you cannot work within the confines of Court life?" Andreo shrugged. "Your work as an Itinerarrio was excellent, your communications invaluable. I am only sorry you left Ghillas before the troubles there erupted. Then we would have had your witness to the events. As it is, the Grand Duke's agents bring home a different story every day. We have had a second report that King Ivo was killed by the mob. What has the world come to?" He made a clucking sound, rather like a hen.

A hen, indeed. More like a bantam cock, in these ridiculous new fashions that could not decide whether they wanted to be as plain as a common bricklayer's working clothes or as tarted up as a whore's, square cuts with cheap bright colors! But Sario forced himself to speak calmly. "I am not permitted to do *Treaties* or any paintings destined for the Galerria, then?"

"Some Itinerarrios are not fit for Court work. It is up to you to prove yourself, Sario, and to please the Grand Duke. There are other men waiting their turn, whose skills are superior to yours and who have labored hard here with the family to increase our fortunes."

Whose skills were superior! It was all Sario could do not to spit in Lord Limner Andreo's smug face. It was clear, abundantly clear, that he had done well to prepare a second line of defense. Oh, he had been sure they would welcome him home, give him the position due him, shower him with praise, accept his superior claims . . . but he had learned to leave a bolt-hole, to hold secrets in reserve.

"Perhaps I would prefer to return to Itinerarrio service. It might be well to gain exact information of the troubles that have racked

Ghillas and Taglis and Niapali. What do the learned doctors call it? A plague of restlessness. What of the rest of the royal family of Ghillas, for instance?"

Andreo shrugged. "Reports are mixed. They only agree on King Ivo's death, and that the palace was stormed."

"That does not speak well for the fate of Queen Iriene and the daughter, Alazais. A pretty girl." Sario watched Andreo's face closely, but the mention of Alazais made no impact.

"You may be assured that Grand Duke Renayo is concerned about the fate of Princess Alazais. You are aware, of course, that the late King Enrei *named* his nephew Renayo as his heir."

Aware of it! As Dioniso he brought it about by making sure Enrei would sire no children. "But the Ghillassian noblemen had other ideas." That was the trouble with noblemen: there were always too many of them and they always wanted their own way. They had thrown their weight behind then-Prince Ivo, whom they rightly judged would be a weak king. But Ivo's weakness had led to his downfall at the hands of the mob.

Andreo gestured dismissively. "Pluvio en laggo. Now, however, the situation has changed. Don Edoard's claim is doubly strong, through Grand Duchess Mairie, blessed be her memory. If Edoard marries Alazais . . . well, should you bring news of the princess, I am sure Grand Duke Renayo would look more favorably upon your painting."

"Let me consider for a day," said Sario. "I might prefer to return to Itinerarrio service. Regretto — If you will excuse me."

He gave Andreo a curt nod and left, walking down the length of the Atelierro. Here, now, all of the Limners congregated and did most of their paintings; it was considered uncivil and indeed rather odd for a Limner to paint in the privacy of his own personal atelierro. At least the space itself was well-lit and comfortable. It was a huge chamber, filled with light from windows ranged along both sides, one set looking out over the street, the other over the courtyard. Oak beams bridged the ceiling, and great timber supports made an aisle down the center of the hall. These supports were so massive they were used as the portrait gallery of the masters. On each of the four sides of the huge pillars of wood hung one of the self-portraits of the Gifted Grijalva painters, a Galerria of the family line. The portraits of the living Limners resided in the Crechetta, of course. But once a painter died, his portrait was either consigned to the storage attic—if he had contributed no greater gift than service to the family—or displayed here, in the Atelierro.

Down the centuries Sario walked, looking up into eyes that were familiar to him, men he had known, liked, hated, battled. Men who had been himself.

He stared back at himself, in almost a dozen fine portraits: Arriano, Dioniso, Ettoro (his brilliant career cut short by acute bone-fever), Oaquino. Thank the Mother that Renzio had been put into the attic. He did not want to look into that homely face again. Even Domaos had been left in the Galerria, as an object lesson for Grijalva boys who grew too attached to women beyond their touch. And there, Riobaro, his great masterpiece of a life, that magnificent candlelit self-portrait surrounded by the gold frame marking him as Lord Limner. Timirrin, generous Matteyo, even Guilbarro who had lived so short a time but painted so brilliantly. Verreio, Martain, Zandor—and the first, Ignaddio.

And there, almost next to the door, he stopped and looked at his own face. He had almost forgotten how brightly he shone, how intense. No wonder Saavedra loved him.

If only that damned Alejandro hadn't gotten in the way. . . . He shook himself free of the old anger. No matter. Saavedra was safe. She would always be safe; she was waiting for him. It just wasn't time yet. He had work to do.

As he went out the door and started down the steps, he passed Davo, who was climbing to the Atelierro with a confused expression on his seamed old face.

Out on the street Sario walked slowly, musing. That was the advantage of age. He understood the necessity of planning, of being prepared, of having options. He had learned better than to think that his influence would be equal in every life. Often he had to start from scratch. Even with careful planning, there were bound to be mistakes. He ought to have chosen Alerrio, for instance, not succumbed to the urge to take his own name back again. Then Alerrio would not have been in Meya Suerta when the Fever struck, would not have died; Alerrio's family had been grooming him for the position of Lord Limner.

He should never, as Domaos, have taken up with Benecitta do'Verrada, heartless creature that she was. He should not have chosen Renzio, that graceless oaf. And Rafeyo! That had been a disaster barely recovered from. That was the risk with every life, that something lay in wait he could not predict. That the bloodlines would not be stable. That an accident might happen, unforeseen. That the Viehos Fratos would not give him his due.

That he would be, again and always, alone.

Sario wasn't in the mood for waiting, not in this life. Arriano had been patient. Now it was time to act.

He barely noticed the city, quiet after the hangings two days ago. His feet took him by remembered ways to the wine shop and up the stairs to his atelierro, hedged in by painted spells. He barely glanced at his *Peintraddo Memorrio*. Instead he went directly to the bed and pulled his traveling chest out from underneath. He unlocked it and lifted the heavy lid.

Inside were clothes, an ancient silk robe packed in paper, his skull wrapped in velvet, and a scrap of cloth from one of Saavedra's gowns. Tucked into one corner was a smaller wooden chest, the length of his forearm and about half that wide. Carefully, he lifted it out and set it on the table.

Standing, he unlocked it and, reverently, lifted the lid.

He had lied to them, of course. It didn't do to be too free with vital information.

Lying on top was a heavy gold seal ring bearing the quartered arms of the Ghilasian royal family. Below it lay a length of pale gold velurro wrapped around a short, stubby object. Beside this rested several small caskets, some of them jeweled because such things were what had been at hand when he had needed them, and tiny glass vases wrapped in rich burgundy velurro, smelling of sweet clover.

If the Grand Duke controlled all, then it would be necessary to control the Grand Duke.

It had been tried—once and only once—to make the Duke a puppet. Had that been the first Clemenzo or the second? He could not recall. Lord Limner Alfonso had conceived of the idea of making the Duke speak, think, indeed act only as the Grijalva Limners willed it. Sario—he had been Zandor then—had told them the experiment would fail, and it had.

After two days the court physicians had proclaimed Clemenzo ill with a sickness of the mind because of his disjointed speech and jerky movements, because he quite suddenly had no knowledge of a horse's fine points or of military tactics and would lapse at intervals into a stupor. The Viehos Fratos had destroyed the painting and arrogant Alfonso along with it. But experiments were always useful because they tested the limits of power.

It was one thing, say, to cause a woman to fall in love with a man; that changed the rest of her not at all. Suggestion spells acted on only one part of a person's mind, usually the part ruled by emotion and impulse. A human being was an infinitely complex creature, full of subtleties that the boldest paint strokes could not duplicate . . . except in the hands of a master. But he was getting ahead of himself.

Sario had manipulated Duke Alejandro perfectly well without the aid of magics and paints. After all, he and Alejandro gave each other mutual benefit and aid. Both families prospered. So had the alliance of do'Verrada and Grijalva continued over the centuries.

And yet all was not well in Meya Suerta. Weakness had crept in: The Grijalvas deteriorated, the do'Verradas were useless, and this plague of restlessness endangered everything they had built. A master's hand was needed to correct things. As Lord Limner he could act swiftly. The Grand Duke named the next Lord Limner. And to control the Grand Duke, one must possess what *he* most wished to gain.

Sario opened up one of the jeweled caskets. Nestled against the ivory silk lining, the rich golden strands of hair had lost none of their luster. In a smaller compartment, shut off by a second lid, the darker, thicker pubic hairs clustered, crooked and short, and next to them the wispier hairs gleaned from arm and leg.

He closed the lid and set this little casket to one side.

It was true that a mob had stormed the palace in Aute-Ghillas. The furious crowd had not even pretended, as they reportedly had in Taglis, to give a mock judicial legitimacy to their rampage. They had gathered up muskets, shovels, pitchforks, and butcher knives and overrun the palace guard, not even noticing their own dead as they fell in swathes or were trampled beneath the surging crowd. Evidently they found it a small price to pay for their revenge.

He had put the eyelashes in a separate jewelbox, because they were so delicate, so easily lost, and so rare. The fingernails and toenails he had put in a cruder box, made of wood; they did not need such careful treatment. Dried blood still adhered to them.

He had had enough warning (one could scarcely fail to hear the mob) to sketch a suggestion spell on himself. "There's no one here." The mob's collective mind had been easy to sway, although the spell itself had been hasty: they never noticed him. They were too intent on their real prey.

There were only five glass vials of blood left. The sixth, alas, had broken in the escape out of the chaos that had gripped Aute-Ghillas. But five would be enough. The blood moved sluggishly when he tipped the vials, one by one, but the essence of sweet clover he had added kept it from coagulating.

So he had stood shielded by the shadows he had cast over their minds, stood half screened by a tapestry in the royal hall, and watched the mob murder the royal family. Rend them to pieces, more like, the royal family and those dog-loyal retainers who had stood with them to the end.

King Ivo had been dragged away, to be displayed on a pike from one of the windows overlooking the gardens and drive. Poor Queen Iriene, an inoffensive woman in all regards, had simply vanished among the corpses.

Sario wasn't sure whether the mob had actually meant to kill Princess Alazais, beloved of the court, the only and lateborn fruit of her parents. But they had killed everyone indiscriminately and she had been tossed just as indiscriminately in among the bodies of her ladies-in-waiting, young women as innocent and stupid and pampered as she was. None had been as beautiful, but beauty is no protector from improvident death.

He unrolled a length of fabric. Within it lay silks torn from finely sewn underrobes, and on those silks he had done rubbings of two palms and the soles of two feet. The journey had not smudged them. He had been careful to set them with chalk. A slight powder still clung to them. He lay them beside the casket filled with golden hair.

Once the mob had poured onward, eager to display King Ivo's body to their assembled brethren on the lawns outside, Sario had ventured forward to dig through the heap of corpses left in the throne room.

After so many years of life, he had learned never to let any opportunity go by—not such a one as this, knowing, as he did, the long and convoluted relationship between Tira Virte and Ghillas, knowing that Grijalvas and do'Verradas had schemed between them to make of Tira Virte a great kingdom, built out of the bodies of many smaller provinces.

What did Renayo want? He wanted Ghillas, a huge new jewel to add to Tira Virte's luster.

Sario was going to give it to him.

He took a gem-studded casket purloined from the music room in the Pallaiso Millia Luminnai and opened it. He had put cloves inside to mask the smell, but a faint scent of putrefaction touched his nostrils nonetheless. Here were scraps from a white linen shift and scrapings of skin, no longer as pale as they had been two months ago, nor as supple. It had been a hasty job.

He unrolled velvet to uncover fingerbones. On the trip south he had managed to boil these, scouring away flesh and skin and blood—he had enough of that elsewhere—so they showed white against the black lushness of the velvet.

For a long while he studied the remains. The clock on the mantelpiece ticked loudly behind him and, at the half hour, chimed.

Moving to the workbench, he retrieved a muller. Then, cupping a delicate fingerbone in his palm, he carried it from table to workbench and laid it on the slab of marble. With infinite care, he began to grind bone into a dust that would be mixed with pigment and media into a new paletto of paints.

⟵ SIXTY-TWO ⟶

Eleyna stared resolutely out the window of the studio, feeling the morning sunlight wash across her body. Her hands clasped the arms of the chair; her left middle finger still hurt where he had taken blood. She did not watch Giaberto paint the finishing touches on the painting that would render her barren. Or at least, she thought bitterly, only seal what was already true.

Except wasn't it true that she could give life through her art? Perhaps all that was generative in her had been poured into the path that led from her eyes to her hands. How unlike her mother she was: Dionisa had given birth to nine children, only two of whom had died, the elder twins. Eight-year-old twin girls and two younger boys still lived in the crechetta. It was not too much of a sacrifice for Dionisa Grijalva to allow one daughter to bear no children in her turn, especially not a daughter who had failed to produce a living child in two rounds of Confirmattio and three years of marriage.

A year or two at most. It would not be so bad.

"It is done," said Giaberto.

She sat, unable to move, astonished and horrified that she had felt nothing. She had passed from one state to the next, but she had no memory of the change. Nothing had warned her. Sunlight bathed her gown, falling in its ripples down to the floor. Surely a cloud should have veiled the sun, altering the light, shadowing her body. She would have painted it so, using light and shadow and the composition of the frame itself to tell this story of loss.

"The carriage comes in one hour," said Giaberto unnecessarily.

Gowns had been sewn and packed. Her pencils, chalk, paints and paper, even two prepared panels of wood, were arrayed in a locked chest together with some of the Grijalva jewels: all the items she and her mother deemed most precious—though they did not agree on which was which.

She rose and, without asking her uncle's permission, came around to look at the painting. At the far end of the room Agustin drew on glass, immersed in his studies. Giaberto hesitated, as if to shield the portrait from her. When he did move, he palmed a vial of oil: tincture of fennel, she thought, from the lingering scent.

She studied herself. Only her body from neck to hips was fully painted, highlighting the curve of her abdomen and breasts under her white muslin gown. The rest of her, head and skirts and hands poised lightly on the chair arms, was unfinished, a shaded brush sketch against the ground.

A strangely giddy feeling took hold of her: Her torso was the only part the family controlled. The rest was hers to finish.

Eleyna nodded coolly at Giaberto. She could not truly be angry at him. Like her, he had his own hidden ambitions. She left the studio, descended the stairs, and made her way to the tile courtyard. There she waited by the fountain, letting the play of the water on the azulejos soothe her.

At midday the servants brought four chests down, three for her and one for Beatriz, brought traveling bags for the duennia, Mara. Beatriz looked sunny and sweet in a white traveling dress of muslin stamped with deep purple patterns so tiny they seemed more suggestion than reality. Mara, a white-haired, spry old woman, was dressed in a sober gray gown in the style of Grand Duchess Mechella's time; one of "Mechella's orphans," she had found service in Palasso Grijalva.

At last the carriage arrived. Her mother hurried down—to make sure she went. Grijalva servants escorted her to the street and a liveried servant helped Eleyna into the carriage. Beatriz and Mara followed. The door shut. The latch clicked into place. With a jerk, the carriage started forward.

The journey to Chasseriallo seemed entirely too short. They drove up into the hill country away from the marshlands. This time of year, the countryside lay bountifully green around them. A few puddles were all that remained of this morning's rain. Vineyards and olive trees covered hillsides. A line of cypress trees marked a nobleman's house.

"That is the lodge belonging to the do'Casteyas," said Mara. "They raise hounds there."

It would have been nice to paint hounds, long-limbed, graceful creatures, rather than those awful fat pugs, beloved by the do'Casteya Countess of this generation. But at least Count Maldonno appreciated her painting!

"You've been here before, Mara?" Beatriz asked.

"I have traveled in the service of the Grijalvas." The old woman kissed bunched fingers and touched them to her heart. "I saw many things, good and ill."

"Such as?" Beatriz loved stories about the old days, the more lurid the better.

"Pluvio en laggo, mennina. It is better not to stir up memories that will do no one any good."

The carriage slowed and turned, lumbering down a lane set between poplars. Pasture spread beyond, and sheep grazed. The carriage trundled up a rise and they saw, below in a hollow, the slate roof and stone tower of the hunting lodge. As they started down, it vanished from view. More trees appeared, an orchard of tangerine, lime, lemon, and fig.

Eleyna shut her eyes. She felt nauseated.

"Look at the gardens!" said Beatriz in an awed undertone. "I shall be happy here!"

It was such an odd thing to say, and infused with such meaning, that Eleyna forgot to be anxious. She opened her eyes to see Beatriz's face shining as she stared out the window.

The carriage wheels crackled over gravel as the horses rounded the drive and were led through a gateway. Once in Chasseriallo's courtyard, the coachman opened the door and a footman helped them out.

The courtyard lay all in sun except for the western wall, whose shadowed rim presaged the coming end of day. White gravel was raked in pinwheels, giving the courtyard a festive look, and at every window flower boxes bloomed with chrysanthemums and bright marigolds. But the courtyard was empty. No servants waited beneath the arcade. No curious maids stared down at them from the balconies. Don Edoard had not come outside to greet his new Mistress.

The doors that led into the lodge flew open. An elderly man hurried out, followed by servants, who took the luggage.

"I beg your pardon, Maessa. I am Bernadin, Don Edoard's steward. If you will come with me, grazzo." As was proper, he addressed his comments to Mara. Eleyna felt slightly ill, realizing that she might have to endure an elaborate fiction designed to mask her real purpose here. "The young Dons arrived yesterday, but then we had news of a fair at the village of Ramo Treio, which lies some twenty miles farther into the hills." They crossed under the arcade and entered the lodge. The entryway was dark and dank, very old-fashioned. "It was all quite unexpected, the possibility of a cock-fight—although I beg your pardon to speak of such things in front of the young ladies—a horse race, some horse trading perhaps. Eiha! Here we are."

Looking relieved of an onerous burden, Bernadin showed them into a parlor made gaudy by the amount of gilt ornamenting the ceiling. He retreated, closing the door behind him. Eleyna, watching him go, could not but be struck by the monumental frame of marble columns, one on each side, that encased the door, which was surmounted by a marble frieze of cavorting nymphs. She might as well be in a mausoleum.

A slight man stood warming himself by a brazier. He stood next to a huge window that looked out over a field of poppies and wild grass. This window was framed by an imposingly ugly window case, columns of gilded wood and a pediment topped by two reclining ladies carved in blond wood.

After a pause, the man turned. An almost comical expression crossed his face: dismay quickly smothered by a noble attempt at polite interest. He was young, with light hair and attractive features. But it was not his face that caught Eleyna's eye: it was the perfection of his clothing. He was so terribly well-dressed that of himself he seemed a commentary on the appalling decor of the room.

"That is not Don Edoard," said Beatriz in a low voice.

Eleyna tore her gaze away from his perfectly tied cravat. She felt herself blush. "That is Don Rohario."

The young man touched his cravat, inspecting it with his fingers. "You are here," he said; unnecessarily, Eleyna thought.

There was an interlude of silence while they all collected their thoughts. Footsteps sounded above, the servants moving through the upper level. The clock on the sidetable clicked over the quarter hour, chiming merrily. Finally, Rohario cleared his throat and ventured forward a few steps. "It appears I am to be your host for a day or two. My brother is, unfortunately, not here." He took three more steps forward. "You are Eleyna Grijalva."

"Yes, I am. We have had the honor of meeting, have we not, Don Rohario? May I present my sister, Beatriz, and Maessa Mara? Where *is* your brother?"

He rubbed his hands together as if they were cold. He coughed. "Eiha. Yes." He went on haltingly, obviously embarrassed. "Edoard heard there was a fair—"

"In Ramo Treio. Your steward mentioned it." Despite everything, Eleyna was beginning to enjoy herself. Let *him* squirm now.

"Yes. My brother is enthusiastic about—" He coughed again. He wasn't just embarrassed; he was mortified. "Horse racing is one of his enthusiasms. I, ah, I—"

"You don't care for horse racing?" Eleyna asked sweetly.

"Eleyna!" scolded Mara in a whisper.

"No, I don't. He intends to buy a horse or two, but he has a terrible eye for horseflesh. If one of the grooms isn't there to advise him, he buys the worst broken-down old hacks—" He stuttered to a halt.

With each passing minute, as the absurdity of the situation mounted, Eleyna's heart lightened. "When will he be back?"

Rohario turned his head and looked mournfully at a panel of men riding to the hunt, painted in an overly-colored style, copying the Old Masters without the least understanding of their genius. "That's just it," he said reluctantly. "I don't know."

"Matra ei Filho," said Beatriz under her breath.

Mara pressed a hand to her bosom. "Neosso do'Orro!"

Eleyna snorted. Unable to stop herself, she began to laugh.

⇥ SIXTY-THREE ⇤

It was an unmitigated disaster. Rohario could only assume that he was doomed to humiliate himself in front of Eleyna Grijalva time and time again. He fiddled with the buttons on the sleeve of his coat, caught himself, stopped, and cleared his throat.

"Dinner will be served in three hours," he said finally.

The two sisters looked much alike, attractive as most Grijalva women were rumored to be. Eleyna was petite, Beatriz more robust and slightly taller. But for all the seeming fragility in Eleyna's build, Rohario did not trust the iron gleam in her eye; she was being pleasant now, but he had heard her explode in temper. Beatriz looked more tractable.

The duennia whispered to Eleyna.

"I'm not tired." The gleam in Eleyna's eye brightened dangerously.

"I would be honored to show you around," said Rohario hastily. In fact, he had been bored.

"Are all the rooms like this?" asked Eleyna. "It reminds me of the Galerria."

Matra Dolcha! Rohario bit down on a grin, since it was unseemly of a man to make a jest of anything related to his mother. "Grand Duchess Mairie was a fine woman, may her memory be blessed, but it is true she and my father believed that gold and ornament are the chief marks of good taste."

"'Solidity, conveniency, and ornament.'"

He laughed. "The three qualities that make a magnificent building. You have read Ottonio della Mariano's monograph?"

"His architectural studies are very good. If there must be so much ornament, however, I would rather it be less solid and more of a piece."

"Eleyna!" This blunt speaking clearly shocked the duennia.

But Rohario was delighted. "You must see the banquet hall! It hasn't changed in three hundred years. Most of the suites upstairs were redone twenty years ago when my mother decided to use Chasseriallo as a retreat. That's when the lower rooms were redecorated as well, and larger windows added."

"All in this style?" Eleyna asked, looking dubious. As well she might.

"Less monument, more ornament," he said, and she responded with a chuckle. At last! He had found someone who detested these styles as much as he did.

"Might we tour the gardens as well?" asked Beatriz in a prettily hesitant voice.

The duennia coughed again, meaningfully, but Robario was not in a mood to placate old-fashioned notions of propriety, not after his father had exiled him to this awful old house that had only two fireplaces and the most execrable wallpaper.

"It would be my pleasure," he said enthusiastically.

Afternoon quickly became evening as he showed them round the apartments. The women finally left him to go upstairs and dress for dinner. In his bedchamber, Roborio whistled as he tied his cravat, adding an extra flourish. Should he leave the lowest button on his cuffs unfastened, as was fashionable these days at Court? Or ought he to be more formal? After much consideration, and examining the effect from every possible angle, he decided in favor of the more conservative style. Grazzo do'Matra his waistcoat did not clash with the wallpaper; that had been chance good fortune. And since he preferred evening coats of the finest subtle gray, a color beyond reproach, he was certainly safe there. At last he was satisfied. Even a woman with as sharp an eye as Eleyna Grijalva would notice nothing amiss.

But soon enough Edoard would return. Roborio grimaced. Edoard had been so keen to take a Grijalva Mistress, but like most of his enthusiasms this one had as much permanence as the wink of frost on a cool morning. As soon as the sun rose, it melted.

But Edoard was not here now.

Over dinner Roborio and Eleyna argued about which of the Old Masters was best. "No, I can't agree," he said over fricando of veal. "Just because Guilbarro Grijalva's life was cut tragically short doesn't mean he can't be counted among the finest masters."

"I will agree that his *Birth of Cossima* is a masterpiece."

"Why not Riobaro? Everyone acknowledges him as one of the finest painters of the Grijalva line."

She considered while a servant offered her curried rabbit. "His work is beautiful, of course, but I can't help thinking it derivative. As if he was trying to let someone else speak through his hands. I can't explain it."

Roborio laughed. "Then who?"

"Sario Grijalva, of course. His altarpiece, his portrait of Saavedra—"

There was an uncomfortable pause. *The First Mistress.* Rohario fidgeted in the silence while the servants brought round puddings and a buttered lobster.

Mara coughed. Eiha! What an annoying habit. But Rohario was grateful to her for breaking the silence. "Any painter would wish to emulate Sario Grijalva," Mara said.

With a flourish made dramatic by the use of a silver fork, Eleyna came back to life. "But too many painters have tried to copy Sario's style rather than creating their own. Aldaberto and Tazioni painted in their own way. There is much we can learn from them. Miquellan Serrano was—"

"Eleyna!" The old duennia looked scandalized. "That any Grijalva would praise the man who painted that insulting *Rescue!*" Then she looked abashed, as if she had not meant to remind Rohario of the Grijalva's chi'patro origins.

"He was a fine painter," insisted Eleyna. "No matter that he feuded with our family. It is ridiculous we only praise Grijalva painters. Others have genius as well. There was a painter in Friesemark named Huesandt who died about fifty years ago. *He* is a true master! He paints his subjects so beautifully that you feel as if you know their inner hearts. And there is another painter from Friesemark, Meyseer. He uses light beautifully. He had a pupil known as 'The Vethian.' She abandoned her family and husband in Vethia in order to study with Meyseer, throwing her old life away only to paint." Her face shone when she spoke so passionately. It startled and disturbed Rohario. In his father's court, enthusiasm was suspect. He pretended to indifference. "Have you seen these reproductions? The work of these painters?" she continued, leaning forward. Her hair, bound up with ivory combs, and the simple necklace of pearls she wore shone in the unsteady light of the candlabra.

Her words made him remember with awful clarity the Iluminarres riot: the young apprentices who had attacked him with such anger; Sancto Leo's senseless death. What had provoked it all? What else was out there in the world that he had ignored, or never known existed?

"No," he said quietly, chastened. "We have seen none of their work in the Palasso. My father wants only the paintings from Tira Virte displayed in the Galerria, and Grand Duchess Johannah is not interested in art." Then, wanting to see her face light up again, he asked: "But perhaps you could tell me more about them."

The next morning Rohario got up at midday as usual, but he found the breakfast room empty. He barely tasted fresh rolls and tea before he ventured outside.

The gardens lay beyond the courtyard wall. Once part of the fortifications for the lodge, the wall was now a picturesque ruin, worn down by time and rain. Through gaps in the wall he saw the winding trails, the topiary, and swathes of white flowers coming into bloom with the rains. The last droplets of morning rain still clung to the blossoms and to the leaves of trees, although by now the sky had cleared, bringing with it the sun.

There, among the flowers, he saw Beatriz. She looked lovely, carefully cutting stems and placing flowers neatly in a long basket. She wore a handsome bonnet and a morning dress cut to reveal her graceful neck.

She greeted him prettily and without the least sign of self-consciousness. "It is a lovely garden, Don Rohario. Your gardener tells me the herb garden has been let run wild." Thus she pleaded, with a nicely understated silence.

He smiled politely. "I am sure he would let you take the garden in hand." As he spoke, he looked around. "I have not seen your sister."

"She is painting," said Beatriz.

Abruptly he saw the corner of an easel protruding from behind a screen of rhododendrons. "Grazzo." Painting! Of course. She was a Grijalva. Matra grant that her work was at least competent. He had never found himself able to lie about art. Never. Not even his own.

Eleyna was so intent on her work that she did not notice him walk up. The duennia did, of course; she acknowledged him with a curt nod and went back to her embroidery. He was not the quarry she was interested in. Rohario stopped a safe distance away and surveyed the work that grew on a cotton canvas covered with a red-brown ground.

Eleyna worked with a paletto of six colors, painting rapidly but with confidence. The garden took shape before his eyes, the fallen wall, the drooping trees, the highlights of bright flowers, and Beatriz in their midst, kneeling in a place she must have knelt an hour or so ago, although she had since moved on. Somehow the clouds, the tower, the sweep of the garden itself, led the eye to Beatriz who, in white with her hair spilling out from her bonnet, seemed herself to embody the spirit of morning. Unlike the current style, in which the painter took pains to remove any trace of brush-stroke from the painting, giving it a smooth glossy coat, Eleyna made her brushwork part of the texture of the painting.

Rohario just watched, afraid to disturb her concentration. When a servant hurried forward, he signed for a chair and, when it was brought, sat. Intent on the painting growing in front of him, he did not notice the time passing. Eleyna worked with remarkable con-centration, as if she were in a trance.

Matra Dolcha! She was *good!* Even in a fa presto piece like this, where she dealt with the design and the form and the colors in the painting all at once, she painted with a quality of brightness and life that staid Lord Limner Andreo never dreamed of. There were flaws, to be sure, but the spontaneity of the landscape was as much a part of its interest as its composition.

A servant brought coffee and plum cakes and set them out on a table. Catching sight of the movement, Eleyna paused and glanced over at Rohario. She smiled, as if sensing his enjoyment, and went back to work. He smiled, unable to help himself. He felt he had never been happier in his life than at this moment.

"It is done," said Eleyna, sitting back.

"It's beautiful!" He jumped up. Then, self-conscious, he ap-proached the easel cautiously.

She looked startled. Her sunhat had come loose and it hung at her back, blue ribbons dangling. "Do you think so? You needn't flatter me just to be polite."

"You must know you're a fine painter! Of course there's some roughness because you painted it in one sitting, without a prelimi-nary sketch, but that's part of its charm."

She smiled again, this time so brilliantly he almost staggered. "You understand!"

He understood.

He thought, for a moment, that a cloud had dimmed the sun, be-cause his sight clouded over. But the sun's light did not waver. It was like being caught in the riot again, thrown this way and then that, unable to get his footing, lost in a tumult.

Rohario understood that he had fallen in love . . . with his brother's Mistress, a Grijalva woman who had—despite her initial reluctance—seen the multitudinous benefits of her new position as Mistress to the Heir.

He smiled wanly in reply and looked out across the garden, struggling to find words that would not give away the terrible emo-tions seething in his heart. In the distance, Beatriz looked up toward something he could not see. She rose, basket of flowers dangling from her arm, altogether a captivating sight.

A horseman rode into view. The gardens were not, of course, an appropriate place to ride a horse and especially not a creature as obviously ill-tempered as this one was. It shied at every shrub and flowerbed.

The rider jerked the horse up hard and dismounted. Giving his reins to a groom, he approached Beatriz. He had the saunter of a man entirely at home in his body and with his position in the world, a thick shock of gorgeous light brown hair, and an expansive laugh which was not, alas, ever forced. Women had been falling over their feet to attract his attention since he was fourteen, and not just because of who he was.

Eleyna rose from her chair. "Who is that?" She lifted paint-stained fingers to touch her black hair. Belatedly, she realized her sunhat had come off. She groped frantically for it.

"That," said Rohario flatly, his pleasure in the day, his heart itself, torn to shreds, "is my brother, Don Edoard."

⊷ SIXTY-FOUR ⊷

Paint stained her fingers and she knew her hair was disheveled; it was too late to pretend her sunhat hadn't been hastily retied. Worst, drops of paint stained her morning dress, but the fine geometric pattern imprinted onto the white muslin almost disguised them. Her painting forgotten, Eleyna stared as Don Edoard tucked Beatriz's hand into his elbow and walked up along the winding path toward her. Their slow progress gave Eleyna the leisure to examine him. Only slightly taller than his brother, he had the grace of an athlete. Where Rohario had inherited his grandmother's delicate features, Edoard was clearly a son of Tira Virte, bold nose and thin face softened by his light Ghillasian hair. An interesting face.

I shall have him sit for a portrait.

Edoard and Beatriz disappeared behind a hedge, then reappeared not ten paces from the easel. Beatriz was smiling, Edoard laughing. He had a marvelous laugh.

"Here is Eleyna," said Beatriz.

He came forward and, taking her hand, bowed low over it. He did not, Grazzo do'Matra, attempt to kiss her hand, although she felt alive to the press of his fingers on hers. "Eleyna. It is a pleasure to make your acquaintance. Your lovely sister tells me you are a painter, which should not surprise me, I suppose, since you are also a Grijalva, but I did not know that women painted or perhaps only that they sketched, as the Court ladies do to while away the time."

"Yes," she said, carefully easing her hand out of his grip. "I have been painting."

He came around the easel to look. "Ah, yes, very fine. Very beautiful. I see your sister here. How appropriate. And who is this charming woman? It is not every day that three beautiful women visit me at my hideaway. Mara? You are a welcome guest, I can assure you." He kissed the duennia's hand. Mara blushed and, almost, simpered.

"Rohario. Eiha! You will want to see the hunter I bought. Now, corasson meya," he continued, turning back to take Eleyna's hand with proprietorial interest and place it in the crook of his elbow, "we will go in to luncheon, which I am informed is quail cooked with some kind of sauce—you know how cooks are, they have

every kind of sauce and several courses none of which I can pronounce, since all the cooks we employ come from Ghillas, and
though dear departed Mama did try to teach me how to pronounce
all those words, I have never managed to. She despaired of me.
'Edoard,' she would say, 'the only language you can speak is
hound, but at least you speak it well.' "

He chattered on in this way, mercifully content with the occasional murmured assent from Eleyna. They went into the lodge and
were served luncheon in the intimacy of the dining room.

Edoard was not precisely a boring speaker. But when he got
launched into one of his monologues, she found her attention wandering. It was like sitting in the tiled courtyard at home during
Sperranssia, sketching while listening to the strolling gittern play-
ers as they serenaded the ladies of each house in the hope of gaining a kiss.

". . . of course no one expected Zio Alesso to die so early, in fact
that is the reason dear Mama never wanted me to take up hunting
because he was thrown while taking a hedge, but Patro always said
he had a terrible seat, so I suppose it was only a matter of time."
Edoard smiled.

Eleyna by this time had absolutely no idea of what he had been
saying. "Only a matter of time before he was thrown?" she asked,
terrified he would realize she hadn't been listening.

"What a clever beauty you are, carrida meya. That is what dear
Mama always said about Teressa—my aunt, that is, who married
that man from Diettro Mareia whose name I can't pronounce—that
it does a woman no good to be beautiful if she remains stupid."

Eleyna smiled, knowing how vapid she must look. *Moronna!*
She felt completely at a loss.

"Our Zio Alesso," broke in Rohario, looking exasperated, "visited this lodge frequently, enjoyed its rooms and gardens very
much, and four years after he became Grand Duke got thrown from
his horse within sight of it."

"Grand Duke Alesso died *here?*" asked Beatriz, intrigued by this
lurid detail.

"I can tell the tale myself, Rohario." Edoard pushed his chair
away from the table. The others hastily rose with him. "I would be
delighted to show you the new hunter I bought," he added, offering
his arm to Eleyna.

"Of course."

They walked out into the courtyard and from there to the stables.
Edoard was uncharacteristically quiet. Rohario, whose own expression betrayed annoyance, trailed behind, escorting Mara and

Beatriz. Obviously Rohario did not want to be here. Only the Grand Duke had the power to force him to remain. But why? This must be what her mother wanted from her: to ferret out all the secrets of the do'Verrada household. Eleyna shuddered. It was all so very chilling and nasty.

"Are you cold?" asked Edoard. "We could return for a wrap."

"No. Thank you."

"Here we are. Do you like horses?"

"I have not yet mastered the drawing of them."

It was dimmer inside the stables and it took a few moments for her eyes to adjust. Ahead, something was thumping loudly against a wall.

"My lord!" A groom hurried up. "The new chevallo is muito fuegosto, very fiery. You can hear him kick. It would be better if you stay away until we calm him down."

"I will return at a better time. This way, carrida meya. We will go see the hounds."

Once they got outside, he brightened considerably. They had managed to lose the others. Edoard placed his other hand over hers where it rested at his elbow. Eleyna smiled tremulously but went numb inside. She remembered Felippo's marital attentions as through a veil, could see them, could feel them, his hands and his body and his lips, but it all seemed to have happened to someone else, someone she no longer knew.

"If you are cold, we could go back to the lodge. There is a fireplace in my suite. I will have it lit."

And they would be alone in his private chambers.

"I would like to see the hounds." She barely choked out the words.

"Eiha! They are fine dogs. We do'Verradas have been breeding these hounds for many generations, and I am sure the original three bitches came as a marriage present from Casteya. I can never remember these details, but if they are of interest to you, there are records the Palasso clerks could easily find, since I am sure they have little enough to do otherwise. Patro is never interested in the old records except as they relate to trade and as for the rest of us . . . we children were never scholarly, which disappointed dear Mama, for she dearly loved a good philosophical discussion and only Rohario ever bothered to read any of the old academics. But he always must say something cutting, and after it happened once too often Mama refused to include him in the discussions any more. Here are the kennels. Framba and Fraga are the two bitches.

Vuonno is named for his size, of course, but Suerto is the finest of the pack, aren't you, mennino?"

Edoard let go of her and gave his full attention to the red-brown hound who loped up to him. Clearly the hound adored his master, and as clearly Edoard loved his dogs. At once, Eleyna saw how he was meant to be painted.

"I will do some preliminary sketches," she said, caught up with the idea. "You shall stand in the field with your musket, the hound beside you."

"Magnifico! You shall do your sketches of all the hounds. We shall make a little galerria of hounds here at Chasseriallo."

Eleyna could not help but laugh at his enthusiasm. He took her hand in his and bowed over it, kissing her fingers. He smiled up at her. His eyes were really very handsome. Perhaps this wouldn't be so impossible after all.

She heard Beatriz's voice. Edoard heard it, too—she saw it by his expression—but he did not release her hand. So it was that Beatriz and Rohario and Mara came into sight in time to see the end of this affectingly intimate scene. For some reason, Eleyna blushed. Matra ei Filho! She was no longer an inexperienced girl, to be caught blushing when a man admired her! Every one of them knew what she had come here for. Yet she pulled her hand gently from Edoard's grasp and turned away, so she might not have to look the others in the face.

"I will begin now," she said, to cover her confusion.

Edoard snapped his fingers and a servant came running, to be sent for easel, parchment, and sketching box.

"I so love dogs," said Beatriz to Edoard.

Rohario stalked off to stare out into the fields.

Servants returned. Eleyna seated herself and arranged her things about her. "I will start with the hounds," she said. "Some sketches so I learn to know them."

"Come, Don Edoard," said Beatriz in her kind way. "You must show me the gardens."

"Are you not going to sketch me?" Edoard asked plaintively.

"Of course." Eleyna sharpened a pencil with a knife. The hounds had such clean, interesting faces, and unlike the pampered, surly dogs owned by the court ladies, they had a lively exhuberance and, like Edoard, a certain amount of simple charm.

"I hope, Don Edoard, that you see that my sister will entertain herself without a thought for us." Beatriz's words slid smoothly past. Eleyna caught her sister's movement out of the corner of her eye as Beatriz led Edoard away. Mara followed them. "Your father deeded Chasseriallo to you five years ago?"

"Yes, as is traditional. I had just turned nineteen. . . ." His voice faded into the distance. Eleyna marked their going with one part of her mind, but Vuonno had been installed for his sitting, and as he was a good-natured but restless creature, she had to work quickly to capture him.

Rohario still stood off to one side, face in profile. His pose was so strikingly theatrical she could almost imagine he had taken the stance deliberately. She sketched him quickly, frowned, and tried again on a different corner of the paper. That was better, but it didn't quite capture the set of his shoulders and the peculiar discontented sweep of crossed arms and jutting chin.

She drew him again, this time giving him the whole page. The handler brought Framba up for her sitting. Hastily, blushing, Eleyna got a new piece of paper out, covering up the sketches. But she remained aware of him standing not close enough to speak to her but not so far away that she could forget he was there. Try as she might to lose herself in the sketches, she felt him watching her—or, when he saw her glance his way, *not* watching her. At last he left and she could work in peace. Much later, Beatriz returned.

"Where did Don Edoard go?" Eleyna asked.

"He went to look at his new horse. It has calmed down." Beatriz busied herself retying her bonnet. Her fingers, damningly, showed stains from digging in the dirt.

"I thank you, Beatriz. I know you are only trying to help, but I must become accustomed to him in the end."

"Of course you must, but there is no need for you to worry yourself about something that must grow in its own time."

Eleyna wondered—not for the first time—how someone so understanding and kind could be, at moments, so irritating.

They all met again at supper, which they took in the dining room under the glowing candles of the chandelier.

"You are remarkably lovely tonight, carrida meya," said Edoard as he led Eleyna to her chair. Then he spoiled the effect by turning to Beatriz and drawing her away from Rohario. "And you as well, Beatriz. If you will sit on either side of me, I would be the happiest man in the world. I have looked over the sketches. I hope you do not mind that I looked at them without asking you first—"

Hands rifling through her sketchbook without her permission! Eleyna strangled a protest and smiled blandly at him.

"—but I could not wait to see my dear creatures, although I noticed that you did a few little drawings of my brother as well. I am terribly jealous you have not sketched *me* yet. . . ."

Eleyna dared not look at Rohario. "I was just warming up my hands, Don Edoard."

"You will sketch me tonight, then?"

She blushed, intensely aware of Edoard's interest in her, of the other meaning behind his innocuous words.

"The flowers from the garden look lovely arranged so in the vases, do they not, Don Edoard?" said Beatriz. "You picked them with such an eye for color."

Distracted, Edoard turned toward her. "I only followed your wishes. I know little enough of flowers."

"You know more than you think, Don Edoard. Our grandmother Leilias was a perfumier, and she taught me the knowledge of flowers and scents and herbs. Here are red chrysanthemums for Love, honeysuckle for Affection, and lilies for Peace. Your cook prepared the chicken tonight with a touch of marjoram."

"What an exceptionally clever woman you are, to have noticed such a thing. Does marjoram have meaning as well?"

Beatriz smiling prettily, her cheeks a little flushed. "Blushes, my lord."

"I did not know flowers and herbs could speak of so much."

"There are many hidden meanings in the things of the world, if we only know where to look."

Something about the way Beatriz said those words made the hair on the back of Eleyna's neck prickle. She glanced toward Rohario, but he was sitting sullenly, fork in one hand, staring at his giblet pie, which lay eviscerated on his plate. Mara watched her charges with misty-eyed approbation.

"Whatever can you mean?" Edoard leaned toward Beatriz, his eyes alight. "You sound positively mysterious."

Mara came alive. "It is time for us to retire to the parlor." She rose briskly and whisked Eleyna and Beatriz out with her. The steward led them to the parlor, where Eleyna found her sketchpad sitting neatly on a sidetable.

Mara sat down on a couch and began embroidery. Eleyna drew Beatriz aside. "What did you mean by saying such a thing to Don Edoard?"

Beatriz was unrepentant. "If what Grandmother said is true, then he will have to know the secrets of the Limners sooner or later."

"But—"

"*But?* He obviously knows and suspects nothing. You can tell it from his face."

"I'm not sure he's intelligent enough to understand—"

"Eleyna! He speaks sensibly enough about gardening and estate management."

"Is *that* what you spent the afternoon discussing?"

The door opened and Edoard entered. "I beg your pardon," he said lightly. "My brother has a headache and had to retire."

"I'm not feeling well either," said Mara, rising. "Beatriz, will you escort me to my room? I need an arm to lean on."

Beatriz touched Eleyna on the hand, fleetingly, but the brush of her fingers comforted. The ploy was so transparent, and yet . . . there was no reason to put off the inevitable. They left. Eleyna stood, one hand resting on her sketchpad, and smiled nervously at Edoard.

"Sit, carrida meya." He prowled the room. She had a sudden idea he also was nervous.

"I'll draw you," she said.

He smiled and sat in a plain oak chair. Its simplicity set off his golden evening coat and silver waistcoat. The pale watercolor wallpaper was a fitting backdrop for his brown hair and dark eyes. But he could no more sit still than could a toddler, or his hounds. Yet while he sat *there,* he could not be close to her *here.* Why had she ever agreed to this? The evening's likely progression unfolded in her mind: conversation, a glass of madiera, intimacy, lovemaking. She burned with embarrassment. He fidgeted.

"I am reminded of the family portrait we had done some years ago, before the fever, for of course that was when poor departed Mama was still alive and little Mechellita and Alessio, and my poor brother Benetto who was quite stricken with fever. He's never been right in the mind since. It's true that Grandmother Mechella would not abide her sons having a Grijalva Mistress. I should not have mentioned it in front of your sister, she is very young and innocent—"

Matra Dolcha! What would Edoard think if he ever learned about the Confirmattio, which Beatriz had, by her own admission, enjoyed immensely, or about Beatriz's infant son who was at this hour asleep in the crechetta in Palasso Grijalva?

"—but now that Grandmama is dead I saw no reason not to ask Patro if I might restore the Marria do'Fantome." Here he paused, waiting for her answer. For her invitation.

"Arrigo's mistress Tazia was my great-aunt." She bent her head over the sketchpad. The far corner of the parlor took on immense interest. Her thoughts in tumult, she concentrated on rendering the corner in exquisite detail, its simple table and vase and single burning oil lamp set against the pale striped wallpaper.

She felt him stand. Her face flushed with heat. If only she could concentrate enough, she could somehow banish him from the room, as if, not existing in her thoughts, he thereby could not exist beside her.

But she was no Gifted Limner.

He stopped beside her and, ever so lightly, rested a hand on her shoulder.

Agustin.

Agustin was a Gifted Limner.

"I thought you were drawing me," he said.

"It is for my brother Agustin," she said wildly. They called her unGifted because she was a woman, and yet she knew in her soul that she had been granted the gift of art and that it was her duty to Matra ei Filho to make the world come to life in her paintings. This moment, now, would never have happened to her had she been, like her brother, a Limner.

"He is just learning to paint," she went on, not knowing what words would come next, not wanting to insult Edoard, "and I promised him I would make sketches so he could see other houses, other places. His health isn't very good, you see, and he almost never leaves our Palasso, so this is my way of giving a gift to him. . . ." She trailed off.

"I will call Bernadin and have this perfect sketch sent immediately to Meya Suerta."

"It isn't necessary—"

"Of course it is not necessary, but since I can do it, why should I not? You must write a note to your brother. I will ring for Bernadin. No, no, you must write. I will keep silence. What is his name?"

She took out paper, uncapped her pen, and blotted the ink. She hardly knew what to write. "Agustin. He is just fifteen."

"Ah, he is the same age as my sister Timarra. She is a sweet girl, very quiet. My father scares her. Not that he means to, but he has strong views and, alas, Timarra has none. She would be perfectly content to sew in the garden and will make a dutiful wife when it comes time for her to marry, although knowing Patro, he will send her to farthest Vethia where she will be perfectly miserable and cold. But forgive me." Bernadin came in. "You will wish to send your letter. You are finished? Bernadin, have this delivered to Palasso Grijalva. Yes, send a messenger along *now*. He may wait for a reply if the boy wishes to send one. Agustin Grijalva, that is right."

When Bernadin had left, Eleyna said, voice caught on a tremor, "Thank you, Don Edoard. You are very kind."

He turned at that instant, and his face wore a mocking expression which vanished as soon as he spoke. "Am I? I think I am rather selfish."

She flushed. He approached her cautiously. She was afraid to look away. Stopping beside her chair, he extended a hand. Obediently she took it, and he lifted her to stand close beside him. With his other hand he brushed a stray curl of hair back from her face. "Are all Grijalva women as lovely as you and your sister?"

She smiled but could think of nothing to say. If she spoke, she would betray her fear. Matra! What had she to be afraid of? This was nothing new for her.

He leaned forward and kissed her lightly on the mouth. She struggled to relax into him, but her free hand clenched tight and her whole body stiffened.

After a moment he pulled away from her and dropped her hand. The barest smile was caught on his lips, lingering there, but she could not interpret it.

He took a step, circling her to look down at her sketchpad. "I can't imagine how it is that you make these lines on the page to create pictures. It is as if I am seeing through your eyes, no? Rohario has told me many times I have no 'eye' for art, whatever that means, and what Patro says . . . eiha! It is not worth boring you with what Patro says. He is not fond of his children—"

"Surely not!"

"We disappoint him."

She forced herself to swallow. It was the only way to get herself to breathe. These confessions made her wildly uncomfortable.

"Benetto is an idiot—I mean it not to castigate the poor boy, it is not his fault—and Timarra cannot bring herself to utter two words together and she is not even a pretty girl, which is a terrible thing for her since Grandmother Mechella and our own dear departed Mama were both beauties. Rohario—eiha!" He flung a hand up in exasperation. "*Rohario.* So Patro has married a new wife and hopes to sire more suitable children."

At her exclamation, he lifted a hand. Edoard was not precisely smart, but he was, she was coming to see, not precisely stupid either. "Do not worry for me, corasson. My claim to the throne of Ghillas is fully as legitimate as King Ivo's, more legitimate, some would say. Patro wishes to marry me off to Ivo's daughter—what is her name? I just saw a fine sketch of her the other day, it was brought back by one of your cousins or at least I assume you are all cousins of one sort or another."

He smiled at her. It was the same smile he offered Mara, or Beatriz. Or his hounds.

Eleyna had a sudden revelation: this endless talking was Edoard's way of putting other people at their ease with him, or himself at his ease, she could not tell which or even if his monologues served both purposes.

"I am not as clever as you, corasson. You can create such beauty and I . . . I can only enjoy my hounds and admire beautiful women."

He rested a hand on her arm, still smiling, and she tried, oh she tried mightily, but she could not help herself. He was too close.

"It is too soon," he said as he released her, turning away. But not before she saw his smile fade.

"It is not you. Forgive me."

"There is nothing to forgive. Bernadin will show you to your chamber."

Flushed, humiliated, she fled the room without gathering up her things.

·—⊸◈ SIXTY-FIVE ◈⊷—·

Sario left Palasso Grijalva one month after arriving, ostensibly to resume his career as an Itinerarrio. He rode north until midday, stopping at a village coach house where he had been deliberately generous with his money one month ago so as to assure himself a cordial reception when he returned. There he stabled his horse and arranged to get passage on a wagon back into Meya Suerta the next day. There he hired a new horse and rode north until evening to Arguena, a town sitting athwart a crossroads.

At the Inn of the Blue Rose he found the Ghillasian servants he had left behind, a girl who had done sewing for Queen Iriene and her cousins, two brothers who had served in the Ghillasian palace guard. He had won them over with favors and tips and won them free of the general massacre of the palace's inhabitants. Now they waited for him.

The innkeeper directed him to the stables, where the brothers paid for their keep by working as stablehands.

"You have news?" asked the elder brother eagerly.

"It is possible." Sario assumed an air of deep gravity. "I must go alone. The agents I spoke with fear for their lives if it is discovered they had anything to do with saving the life of a member of the royal family."

"Why has it taken so long?" demanded the younger brother. "They have no devotion to our king." He spit into the straw. "They only waited for a good ransom offer."

"We shall see. In the meantime, wait for me here. In ten days you will know by the ringing of the bells that the Feast of Imago, the Vision of Life, has come. I shall return after that time. Give these coins to your cousin. Let her purchase good cloth and sew a few gowns. I doubt not that if the lady does live, she has nothing left her. After such an ordeal you must not be surprised to find her much changed in spirit."

The two soldiers knelt a moment, hands over their hearts, then rose and took the money.

In the morning Sario was content as he rode north. After a few miles he veered south in a loop that took him safely around Arguena and back by midday to the village coach house, where he

returned the horse and took the wagon back to Meya Suerta. He arrived in his atelierro above the wine shop at twilight.

Too restless to sleep, he lit lanterns and set them on the table,
hung them from the rafters, and worked long into the night, grinding and mixing paints, making brushes. As he grew tired, his pulse
began to pound in his head like the beat of a distant drum. He grew
too warm and, taking off his jacket and waistcoat, worked only in
his shirtsleeves; after a time he removed his boots as well, and
through the soles of his feet his pulse and the slow creak and settling of the old house merged and became one. Under his breath he
murmured words untangled from the illuminations that decorated
his *Folio,* the pages taken so very long ago from Il-Adib.

His pigments he mixed with poppy oil, blending in a bit of
beeswax and amber that had been dissolved in hot oil. To his white
paints he added the dust of bones and the powder gleaned from
dried skin, to his yellows the gleam of golden hair. Finger- and toenails he ground to powder and blended with his ultramarine and
cerulean blue. With the vestiges of a linen shift, worn down until it
was as fine as sand, he gave texture to his viridian and green earth.
The other parts of body hair he added to his siennas and umbers,
the yellow earth and browns. To vermillion, blood; and blood diluted by lavender oil he used to mix his rose madder. Into his lamp
black he blended all of the remains, just enough to flavor it.

He prepared the board, a panel of oak as tall as he was, and covered it with a gray ground blended with essence of myrtle, for the
Dead, and iris, for Magical Energy.

Perhaps the sun rose outside. Perhaps it set. His shutters remained closed and he could not tell. That time passed at all he
noted only because the man who ran the wine shop brought food
and ale twice a day to the door of the attic and took away anything
that was left there.

By now he was too flushed even for a shirt. He stripped. The
warm air of the atelierro woke his skin, like the touch of a lover, although he had not had a lover since he had taken this Sario's body.
To do so would somehow profane his love for Saavedra.

His fingers sought out a lancet. He held it in a candleflame until
the metal gained a faint nimbus. Holding it up, away from the candle, he watched lines of heat evaporate from the edged metal. He
lowered it to his arm.

The blade lay sharp and hot against his skin. The sensation
aroused him. He cut.

As the blood flowed down his skin his whole body tingled. Long
ago he had felt this way, touching a woman, caressing her, pene-

trating her. Now only the art, only the painting, the exaltation of a spell, the knowledge of what was to follow as he prepared his body, his paints, the very air of the room laden with incense . . . his breathing tightened, and he only just caught his seed in a glass vial. Losing some of his blood onto the floor, but there was more blood; he took what he needed and clamped a hand down over the cut. The stinging faded, as it always did. The pain was nothing against the promise of power.

He laughed, and laughing brought tears. The fragrance of herbs brought with it memory of taste, and so he prepared himself with blood and seed, tears and saliva. With these essences he blended his own self into the paint.

It was time to begin the spell. On the table he set out candles and an incense burner, a shrine for the Matra ei Filho. On either side he laid the many sketches he had done of his subject. He now took the *Folio* out of the locked chest and positioned it carefully in the center of the table. He opened it to the correct spell slowly, letting each page slide through his fingers, feeling the grain of the vellum and the fine curves of the letters, each one a spark against his skin.

As Arriano he had become lazy, drifting from one foreign court to the next, letting the chatter of rich merchants and the blandishments of pale northern beauties caress him into a soporific lull that had lasted years. Perhaps he had needed a rest after the disaster with Rafeyo. Perhaps he was just getting tired.

No! Never that. It was time to wake up. It had been too long since he had painted a masterpiece. And this was truly to be a masterpiece, a spell he had pondered for years but had not attempted.

Thou shalt not, for it is abomination.

So was it written into the *Folio,* blazing letters on a white ground. What did he care about the commandments of a god to whom he did not belong? He was a Master. *The* Master. There was no one else like him, nor would there ever be, ever. For was he not the Chosen One?

He lit candles and incense. In a low voice, he spoke the words taught him so many many years, centuries, ago. "Chieva do'Orro. Open my eyes to your secrets. Blood and hands possess the power of change." He pitched his voice up a key, sharp, piercing the quiet air swamped in the scent of oil and herbs. "Matra ei Filho, grant this power against death and for life."

He opened his case of oils and dabbed a finger in his oil of sorcerer's violet, touching the oil to his tongue, savoring it, touching it to his naked chest, to his belly, to his penis, to his thighs. With a graphite pencil he sketched the figure onto the ground, putting the most detail into palms, lips, and eyes. With his fingers he rubbed a thin priming into place over the drawing.

He began to chant the words written in the *Folio*. The syllables came readily to his lips. As he spoke them, his awareness stretched and altered so that he slipped away from himself, deeper into his limner's mind yet out toward the painting beyond, as if he could pour himself out through his hands, through the brush.

He began to paint.

The figure took shape before him, first shaded on over the drawing, then coming to life in layers of color, light tones at first, followed by richer, deeper glazes and coloring. It was to be all one continuous piece. He must not stop for longer than it took to drink a few swallows of ale, to eat a few bites of bread, to sip at coffee or touch one or another oil to his lips to give himself strength, to light new candles. To stop was to condemn the painting to dry into the stillness of death. Yet he must paint with the perfection of a finished piece which would normally have had time to dry after the underpainting was complete.

None of that now. He painted with the words of foreign sorcerers, the Al-Fansihirro, on his lips. He saw her standing before him in his mind's eye, imagined her youthful body beneath the light, fashionable gowns she wore. This vision passed from his eye to his hands, and she flowered and took form.

Into the shadows and lines of her skin he began the skein of symbols that would bind the painting over into truth. Her hands rested gently against her hips, palms out; her feet stood firmly on oaken floorboards. Her skin took on a rose hue, and her lips shone with caught breath. Her eyes were as fine a blue as he had ever seen—more perfect, perhaps, than her eyes had truly been, but was it not the duty of an artist to recover the heart of his subject, not just the outer seeming?

Far away he heard bells ringing. A crack of light shone through the shutters, sunset or sunrise. Once he had known which direction the window faced, but it was no longer important.

He bound her shadowed places with the tiny script and symbols of the oscurra. With a brush made of a single coarse hair he painted the oscurra into the lines on her palms, wove them into the delicate puckering of her lips, and with their substance patterned the fine blue flecking of the irises of her eyes.

Echoes of bells rang in his ears. He stepped back, almost staggering. A wave of exhaustion swept through him, as it always did; so much blood he used, so much of his potency, to create. He dabbed a finger in oil of myrtle and traced the sign for *heart* on her chest, invisible to the eye. His brush dropped from fingers suddenly nerveless. The chamber whirled once around him, but he caught himself. Groping at the table, he found the bowl of cloves. He chewed on one, steadied himself with deep breaths, touched the *Folio* though he did not need to read its final words.

He moved to stand in front of the painting. Though his sight clouded as his trance lifted from him, he could see that she was perfect, a perfect likeness, the fresh, young, innocent girl standing naked in his atelierro, waiting. . . .

He stepped close, closer still, and breathed the breath of life onto her, his creation.

The painting trembled. It was as if the wet paint stirred of its own accord, pushing out from the panel, expanding, like a flower unfolding at dawn. Startled, he took a step back.

She followed him.

Shadows became solid curves, lines became flesh. Princess Alazais of Ghillas stepped out of the painting onto the cold oak floor. She stood, watching him with a kind of vacant curiosity. She was breathing. Her skin shone, as if sheened with sweat. The light gray ground, outlining her form, and the plain room were all that remained in the portrait.

"You are Princess Alazais," he said in a soft voice, gentled by astonishment, smoothed by the knowledge of his own genius.

"I am Princess Alazais," she said. Her tone mimicked his tone, although her voice was a delicate soprano. Her expression did not change.

"Sit," he said, pointing to the chair.

She sat.

He saw his cot. With what remained of his strength, he staggered over to it. There was much to do. He needed to instruct her. What about food? Did she know to eat? Would she walk blindly out the door? How much did she understand? Of what was she truly made? Poppy and myrtle and iris, his blood and hers, the dust of her other body? There was so much to do.

But he had no strength. The magic had taken it all. He collapsed on the cot and fell into sleep the instant his head touched the pillow.

❦ SIXTY-SIX ❦

The Feast of Imago dawned with clouds hanging heavy over the fields and the vine-swagged hunting lodge. Early in the morning, before anyone except the servants was up, Rohario sat on one of the old trestle tables in the banqueting hall and idly turned the dusty pages of an old book. Outside it rained, a propitious beginning to the day celebrating the Visitation of the Holy Mother and Her Son, who had appeared before a lowly camponesso and his wife while they pruned the vines at dawn in a misting rain. Rohario watched the steady drizzle through the thick windowpanes, the glass throwing waves of distortion onto the steady fall of light rain.

The last eight days had been a misery. Edoard was edgy and short with him, overbearingly polite to the women. Mara walked everywhere with a barely hidden frown. Eleyna rarely appeared except in front of her easel, painting the hounds, sketching intricate studies of the various rooms of Chasseriallo. Only Beatriz Grijalva maintained an air of gentle good humor, and Rohario was beginning to find her endlessly sunny nature annoying, if only because it set off his own sulks.

For, as his dear Mama had been wont to say, sulking was not only unattractive but useless. *"You are too old to sulk, Rohario. It tires me, infuriates your father, and does you no good at all."* Mama was always right.

Still, this wretched situation brought out the worst in him, even while he watched himself act like a sullen adolescent boy as if he were the observer in the Galerria scrutinizing a detailed painting. The Matra had blessed Edoard in that regard: he was oblivious to the effect his behavior had on the people around him.

Rohario sighed and studied the crabbed writing on the page, reading the words out loud:

> *Thus did Duchess Jesminia stand, supported by her handmaidens who did not fear to take the plague from her but would by their devotion risk dying with her. Though her body was frail, her voice was strong. Thus did she speak to the assembled multitudes as was recorded by Sancta Silvestra.*

*"By my faith in Mother and Son, I will not allow these my
faithful servants the Grijalvas to suffer under such un-
warranted suspicion. They are innocent of all they have
been accused of. So come they with my blessing to be reconfirmed by the Ecclesia—"*

He broke off and lifted his head.

She stood in a shadowed corner near the door, as still as a statue,
listening. The sight of her shivered through him like a lightning
bolt. It was not fair that she affect him this way!

"What are you doing here?" he snapped.

She started, almost bolting like a rabbit, then stepped out into the
central hall. "That looks like an old book."

"I found it in the library here."

Over the last few days she had lost her fierce demeanor. She
seemed, indeed, quite unlike herself. "I beg your pardon. I did not
mean to disturb you." She edged along one wall toward the far
corner. "My brother Agustin sent me a letter. I left it here last
night. . . ."

Why should she have left a letter in the banqueting hall? No one
ever came here; that was why it was his favorite retreat, even if the
servants sometimes forgot to dust the tables and benches and
thereby allowed his clothes to get dirty.

Following the line of Eleyna Grijalva's sight, Roharto suddenly
saw a scrap of white parchment lying neatly on one corner of a distant table. It had not been there an hour ago.

"Here it is." She grabbed the parchment. "I beg your pardon. I'll
go now."

"No! I mean—don't feel you must leave."

"I'm working on Edoard's portrait."

She is unhappy. The thought flashed through him with the audacity of a five-year-old child scampering into apartments where
he has no right to be. She *was* unhappy. This notion left him
speechless for a moment, while she retreated to the door.

"I can read to you," he blurted out, then was aghast. He had
grabbed this book at random, intrigued by the faded and cracked
leather binding, but this long-dead scholar's history of the feud between the Ecclesia and the Grijalva family had instead caught his
interest. But surely Eleyna would not want to have her family's
chi'patro origins thrown at her head.

She fingered the parchment nervously. "You read well."

She was humoring him. So had people done all his life. "Yes," he said bitterly. "A pleasant reading voice. A passable talent for art."

"Eiha," she said abruptly, revelation dawning. "Grandzio Cabral tutored you in art—"

That stung.

"Nazho irrado," she said swiftly.

He pushed off the table and brushed dust from the tails of his morning coat. "Cabral Grijalva did his best but failed to find more than that 'passable' talent in me." He attempted a smile but could not manage one. "I do not know who was more disappointed, he or I."

"I'm sorry."

"Do'nado. You wish to go—" He gestured.

"No, I—grazzo— Read to me as I paint. What I heard sounded interesting."

She felt pity for him and his passable talent, she who had such a true gift. But even knowing that, he could not resist her. "As you wish."

As he followed her down the broad staircase that led to the hall adjoining the ducal suite, he could not help but wish himself in another body, in another life. He was mightily tired of being a "useless fop," but young noblemen did not have professions or callings, as his mother had been fond of pointing out. *"It is our Matra-given duty to rule, Rohario, and theirs to work and to serve."*

He ran into Eleyna just as she gasped, stopping short. His heart pounded when she backed up against him. . . .

He knew the feel of a woman against him. Mama had made sure that even this part of his education was not neglected. *"You will not chase the pretty servant girls who work in the Palasso. That is not fitting behavior for a do'Verrada, and I have gone to great trouble to find girls from Meya Suerta who look presentable in livery and who can also perform their duties efficiently. I will not have them interfered with. There are respectable establishments where boys are initiated into these mysteries, and that is where you will indulge your curiosity."*

He had indulged his curiosity quite freely.

Now he noticed that the ornate door leading into the ducal suite stood partly open. Here, in the corner where the stairs gave out onto the corridor, he and Eleyna watched unnoticed as Beatriz Grijalva slipped out through the half-open door, wearing a brocaded morning robe over an elaborate nightdress. She turned back to the man standing in the doorway.

Her face was radiant. She leaned forward—

To kiss! And not a sisterly kiss, either.

"Eiha!" murmured Rohario.

Eleyna pressed him farther back. He stumbled backward up two steps, stood there for a long while, breathing hard, not sure which was the more shocking discovery: that Eleyna Grijalva was leaning against him without the slightest evidence of self-consciousness or that Edoard had, as he intended, taken a Grijalva Mistress.

"What have I done?" murmured Eleyna under her breath. She covered her face with a hand and wilted into his arms. He barely managed to set down the book in time to catch her.

It was a glorious sensation, holding her. He had held women before, but he had never felt like this.

"I have forced her into this." Eleyna was talking into her hand. "Mennina moronna! How could I have expected otherwise?" She pulled away from him. "I beg your pardon," she said stiffly. Tears ran down her face. He reached to brush them away, but she walked forward, leaving him behind as if she had already forgotten him.

He grabbed the book and hurried after her. The corridor was empty now, the door into the ducal suite shut tight. Had that vision been a dream?

Eleyna walked as if in a trance to the salon Edoard had set aside for her use as an atelierro. She sank down onto the stool set in front of her easel and stared at the half-finished painting. The letter from her brother hung, forgotten, in her right hand. Rohario stood under the lintel, not sure whether to enter or leave. He could not bear to leave her alone, not after she had received such a shock. Yet they were hardly on terms of such intimacy that he might dare to offer comfort. Only the rain sounded, heard through the veil of the great paned windows that looked out onto the parklands.

She slipped the unread letter in with her sketches, then studied her painting: Edoard, still in half tones, standing with a musket draped in the crook of his elbow, his four favorite hounds placed round him and the ruined wall with its view into the garden as backdrop. It was so quiet that Rohario heard, from the breakfast room, the muted sounds of servants setting out the silver. He smelled freshly baked bread.

Eleyna shook herself, coming to some resolution.

Examining her paletto of colors, she chose a pale blue as a base and into the faintly sketched-in landscape beyond the wall inserted a tiny female figure, dressed in a white morning dress and a plain bonnet. She was, quite deliberately, drawing her sister into the portrait of Edoard.

It was the kind of thing Grijalva limners did: every peintraddo contained a message. Now, forever, the young Edoard would be memorialized with his Mistress—and, of course, that she stood in the garden was entirely appropriate, for Beatriz was not only a lover of flowers but in her own way a fine flower herself.

A dull sadness settled on Rohario. He could not identify its source, only that it grieved him to see Eleyna pragmatically erase her grief by recording the truth for all to see.

Through a door set in the wall opposite Eleyna and her easel, Rohario could look into the dining room, empty at this hour. Eleyna *still* had not noticed him. He sidled along behind furniture, careful not to touch anything, and escaped into the dining room, leaving the door open behind him. He placed the book on the table and sat down heavily, resting his chin on intertwined fingers.

How could Edoard so humiliate the woman he himself had chosen? How could she possibly return to her family now? One followed certain rules: a Mistress must be barren and preferably a widow. One did not choose a young rose—Beatriz could scarcely be more than eighteen—in the first flush of youth and of obvious value to her parents as a marriageable daughter who would likely bear many children.

Patro was going to be very, very angry.

But since when had Edoard cared about Patro's anger?

"Eiha! There you are, Eleynita. What are you—?"

Eleyna cut Beatriz off. "How could you? Mother will be furious!"

From this angle he could not see into the room, but he could hear clearly enough.

Beatriz laughed softly. "I will protect you from her, I promise."

"I am not afraid of her anger for my own sake! Matra Dolcha! You must despise me. I am sorry, Beatriz. I am so sorry. If only I had behaved as I ought, you would never—"

"This was what I wanted all along."

"What you *wanted!*"

Rohario desperately wanted to see into the room but dared not move. What Beatriz Grijalva, that innocent virgin, had wanted all along! He could not fathom it.

"I watched you fight them, Eleynita. What did it get you? Eiha! Worse than a lock on your door. It took no great intelligence to see the change in you between the day you told Mother you would never wed Felippo and the day you stood simpering beside him at your wedding. I swore that would never happen to me."

"But I thought—"

"That I wanted to be a brood mare for the Grijalvas?"

"You made no protest at the Confirmattio. I hated it!"

Beatriz laughed again, without a trace of malice or self satisfaction. "You had Fransisso and Jonio and the awful chiros brothers. No wonder you hated it. I had better luck." Rohario imagined, in the brief silence that followed, that Beatriz was blushing. "I enjoyed myself, and why shouldn't I have? They were young, and clean, and enthusiastic, and well-looking enough. Why not enjoy, when it is possible to, rather than fight just to make a point?"

"I had good reason to protest!"

"Of course you did. I would have expected nothing else from you. But what I expect for myself is something different."

"I'm beginning to think I don't know you at all."

"I am sorry for that, but you are so transparent I could hardly tell you everything that was in my mind for fear you would one day lose your temper and let everyone know."

"Matra ei Filho, Bellita! Perhaps you will tell me what is in your mind now! I thought you only came here out of the kindness of your heart, but now—" Her voice trembled. "I thought you were content to follow the path laid out for you by Mother and Father and Giaberto."

"Do you think I like living in the Palasso any more than you do? Having the Viehos Fratos rule our lives? I want to attend balls and concerts, dress in the latest fashions, enjoy myself. Not marry Fransisso Grijalva and produce one child after the next, each one scrutinized, each one carried away to the crechetta while I sit dutifully on the bench beside the fountain, planning to rule the Viehos Fratos through my Gifted sons. I want to plant a garden with whatever flowers and herbs I choose, to continue Grandmother Leilias' notebooks and observations on the ways of plants. I want to have children when I wish to have them, and when they are grown, I will dower myself to the Sanctia, where I will tend gardens and pray in peace. *Away* from the family."

This did not sound like the innocent Beatriz with whom Rohario had become acquainted!

"You aren't barren, Bellita. If you should conceive a child—"

"You can be sure Grandmother taught me about essences of plants that prevent conception. I do not need to rely on the Limners for *that!*"

There was a long silence, during which Rohario puzzled over these provocative hints that Beatriz had inadvertently given him about life in Palasso Grijalva. The picture she painted did not match the image he had always cherished in his mind.

"You should have been an actress," said Eleyna finally. Rohario could not tell from her voice whether she was about to laugh, or cry.

"As if that would have been permitted! And if I had protested, as you did, if I had insisted, then they would have painted me into compliance. As they did to you!"

He heard a little sound, a wordless catch of the breath, that was surely Eleyna's reply, all that she could manage.

"Eleynita! Grandmother Leilias wanted us to understand what had been done to you so we could fight against it!"

"How can we fight?" Eleyna murmured. "You know what they're capable of."

"I'm beginning to think *I* don't know *you* at all! It was your example I always held up for myself. You taught me there was a reason to want to escape."

"*You* don't understand. They can still force you to do what they want."

"But there is Edoard now." Rohario heard triumph in Beatriz' usually sweet voice.

"They could—"

"You are not thinking!" cried Beatriz. "Why should they do anything? They have what they want—a Grijalva Mistress for the Heir. I have what I want. When Edoard marries, I will get a manor house and a fine dowry. Perhaps I will marry a count, as our great-aunt Tazia did, although not, I hope, with the same unfortunate outcome! I do not want to rule as Nazha Coronna. I just want to be left alone to live my life *as I please*. To marry whom I please, if I marry at all. Then I can raise my children as Grandmother Leilias and Uncle Cabral were raised—in my manor, all of us together, including my little 'Rico."

"But—"

"This is so unlike you, Eleyna! You are full of objections. I thought you would be pleased! I would never have done this if I thought you wanted to be Mistress, but I thought you did not want Edoard."

Rohario sucked in a breath.

Eleyna's reply took forever, and ever, and yet even longer. The rain misted down outside, a light drone. A gardener walked by the window, face shadowed by a wide-brimmed hat. He wore a curl of grape leaves pinned to his loose shirt, the symbol of the Visitassion, and in his right hand he carried pruning shears. In a hearty voice, audible through the glass, he sang the joyful hymn, "Ila Visitassion."

When Eleyna spoke at last, her words came hesitantly, as if to contrast with the gardener's joyous song. "It is not that I want Edoard, or do not want him, just that I . . . can't bring myself to—"

"I can bring myself to, and I have, and I'm not sorry for it, Eleynita. And you will be sorry when I steal every fine dress in your wardrobe and then order a dozen more besides. But I won't have you thinking I did this for you!"

Rohario could barely think, he was consumed by such delirious happiness. Eleyna did not want Edoard.

But why in heaven should Eleyna then turn around and want him instead? Edoard was by far the more eligible and attractive. "Moronno," he whispered to himself.

"—and they will expect you to produce Gifted sons," Eleyna was saying. "They will not let you marry as you please or live outside the Palasso, even with your manor house and the protection of Don Edoard."

"I had more than one conversation on the subject with Grandmother before she died, while you were thinking of nothing but your art and then your husband." Beatriz sounded unnervingly pragmatic. "Only men are Gifted, but it is the Grijalva *women* who produce Gifted sons, no matter who the father is. The man's seed must not matter. Grandmother had two Gifted sons, neither of them by Grijalva men. So I can have Gifted sons without marrying a Grijalva. It is like the pea plants Grandmother grew. Some were tall, some short. Some had red blossoms, some white. Some had wrinkled peas, some unwrinkled. There must be a way to know what caused each plant to become one or the other. Just as we can trace the lineage of Gifted Grijalva males through their mothers and mother's mothers."

Eleyna laughed, a refreshing sound. "You and Grandmother and those boring pea plants. That's what comes of too much gardening!"

"Ah!" said Beatriz in an altered tone. "Here is Edoard."

Edoard! An instant later, Rohario heard his brother speak.

"Corasson meya."

There was a moment of awkward silence. Rohario stood and edged toward the door.

"Eleyna, I appear before you with some embarrassment. I hope you will forgive me. Your sister assures me—"

"No, grazzo, Don Edoard. I am very happy for you and Beatriz. We will all come to see that it is for the best."

"Most generous. Now, Bellissimia, I have sent a letter to Patro asking him to prepare the Dia Fuega ball for us, at Penitenssia, in

Palasso Verrada. But in the meanwhile, I have sent messengers to my particular friends, only some twelve or fifteen of the young men and women who are my companions at Court, to join us here at Chasseriallo in seven days' time. We will amuse ourselves with dances and games and hunting and strolls in the garden and music, whatever you most wish. If you do not wish, I will send messengers and tell them not to come—"

"Not at all, Edoard! I want nothing more than to amuse myself! You cannot imagine the dreary life I have led up until now. But— eiha, Edoard. Have I the right dresses to appear before your friends?"

"En verro! You must have more dresses. More jewels! I shall send to Meya Suerta and have a dressmaker conveyed here—only the best. I will ask Lizia. She inherited the do'Dregez fortune, as you might know. We are the same age and cousins twice removed, and she can recommend a fine dressmaker, for Lizia is the woman who sets the fashions, and together the two of you can do everything as you wish to make you the most beautiful woman in Tira Virte. You will like Lizia."

But will Lizia like Beatriz? Lizia do'Dregez was the granddaughter of Arrigo III's elder sister Lizia, and every bit as formidable a force in Meya Suerta as her redoubtable grandmother had been. Lizia would see Beatriz as an opportunity, not a threat. Once Lizia made it clear that Beatriz was acceptable, no one would snub the new Grijalva Mistress. Perhaps Edoard was smarter than Rohario gave him credit for.

"We must have a horse for you as well," Edoard continued, "a placid gelding, I think, since you have not ridden very much. Come, we will go this instant and consult the groom."

"Edoard, you promised we would speak with the gardener about planting a new herb garden."

Thus engaged, they left the room. Their chatter receded down the hallway.

In the hush left by their leaving, he heard a soft sound coming from the parlor. Eleyna Grijalva was weeping.

SIXTY-SEVEN

Long dead? Can this be true? Surely only three days have passed. And yet the boy whom I see in the mirror has become a man, and the clothing they wear now, all the people I see passing by when I look in the mirror, all is so strange to me.

Could he truly hear me? Did he know I spoke of Alejandro when he said those words, "long dead?"

It cannot be true. Even Sario could not be so cruel.

Matra Dolcha, let it not be for nothing that I have read Sario's Folio and struggled to find a way out of this prison though he left me nothing, no paints, no brushes. Let Alejandro's child be born and come to know his father. Let it not be for nothing, I beg you with all my heart.

All for nothing.

She had thrown away her chance to have children—however small that chance might have been—for nothing. The suggestion spell painted on her had died with Felippo, but this one would not die until she herself did, and then it would no longer matter. Groping, she found a handkerchief and dried her eyes. She had not minded very much being painted barren when she thought there was a purpose in it. Now, still young, she was like a tree that has been pruned back so far it will never bear fruit.

And yet. It left her free to paint. She was of no use to them now.

She rifled through her sketches and drew out the three letters Agustin had sent her, fingering the fine marbled paper, itself a reminder of the manufactury that had brought the Grijalvas their first fortune. What amazing magic these simple pieces of parchment revealed! Agustin wrote with a graceful, if boyish, hand.

> *Dearest Eleynita,*
> *Uncle Giaberto says we can spy through paintings and carefully rendered studies of chambers and halls into the palassos of other countries. That is why the Itinerarrios and Embajadorros are sent to foreign courts. So when you sent me the drawing of the corner of the parlor in*

Chasseriallo—so precise! so exact in every detail!—I thought, if not only that, spying through paintings, could I not also redraw the scene in the same exact detail, at the same time of day, with the same lighting, only add this letter to you, and have it be there? Please send word by a messenger if you receive this, for then we will know it is true.

Your devoted brother, Agustin.
Please remember to burn this letter.

She had found the letter in the corner of the parlor seven days ago, in the evening, after a dinner made agonizing by her embarrassment and Edoard's puzzled but formal politeness. In fact, Edoard had found the letter, and she—with an instinct for danger—had snatched it out of his hand before he could read it. But perhaps Beatriz was right: perhaps Edoard deserved to know about the Grijalva Limners and their magic. Knowledge hoarded was knowledge that could be terribly misused.

Eleyna opened the second letter, sniffing back the last of her tears.

Dearest Eleynita

It is true! It works! I received your letter and sketch of the dining room by messenger today, and Mother tried to grab it out of my hands, but I thought of what you would say to her and I did say it, and I was amazed she did not scold me, but she did not! Perhaps it will not be so bad being a Limner, even though I must paint all day and there is no time to roll hoops with the little ones and I am always tired. But please don't worry about me. It is so amazing, I only wish you could study here with me. I would give you my Gift if I could, since you deserve it more than I do. I know you don't care so much about having children, but I cry at night thinking I'll never have any of my own. I hope Beatriz and the twins will have many nieces and nephews for me to love. Do not think I am sad about being a Limner, but I sometimes think about what I am losing by having the Gift. I must never tell Mama, for she tells me that I am her One True Hope. I miss you very much.

Your devoted brother, Agustin.
You are wondering what I used. I used ink on parchment and mixed tears and sweat into the ink to give it potency.

To give it potency. Had the other Limners started this way? Regretful of what they had lost? But the Limners she knew had been eager to give up their fertility in order to be granted the power of the Chieva do'Orro. As she would have, in their place.

She closed a hand into a fist. *I will not regret what I can do nothing about.* She opened the third letter.

> *Dearest Eleynita,*
> *Please do not forget to burn my letters. I am afraid Zio Giaberto suspects what I am learning to do, but I won't tell him. I just won't. I don't like the way they want to rule me. They want me to obey them without asking why. When I ask them questions, they cluck like so many fat hens and say unkind things about you, and I won't let them criticize you. You're a better painter than any of them! Even if they are Limners. Well, you are an artist! So there! I have bad news to report. Nicollo's carriage was set upon by ruffians and turned over. He broke his legs and an arm, and the arm is infected so badly the Viehos Fratos have called in a sancta. But the rumor is that it wasn't ruffians who tipped the carriage but protestors, honest apprentices, who want the Corteis to reconvene, who think the Corteis ought to vote on what taxes the Grand Duke can levy. Zio Giaberto says it is the influence of the rabble, a disease from the north. Some people even say the entire royal family of Ghillas was murdered by a mob, but I don't think people would do that kind of awful thing. Mother always comes in to make sure I'm sleeping, so I daren't keep the candle burning long. I hope you are happy. Your letters are very short, but I suppose you must be cautious.*
> *Your devoted brother, Agustin.*

She was not barren.

She was an *artist*.

She chuckled. Spoken by a Limner, the words therefore became truth. Even if that Limner *was* her devoted little brother.

"Please do not forget to burn my letters."

Eiha! It was past time to do so. She went to the side table, where an oil lamp stood. Lighting it, she removed the glass sleeve and stuck the first letter into the flame. It crisped swiftly and with a satisfying aroma.

"Eleyna? I smelled—" Don Rohario stopped, staring, caught

halfway into the room. Behind him, the dining room lay in serene elegance, the long ebony table and twelve matching chairs, two long sideboards inlaid with ivory and faience, and the tall windows looking out over the park. And that horrendous wallpaper. For a long moment, while the parchment flamed, she stared, seeing his beautiful clothes framed by ghastly pale cherubim fluttering through a gilt forest of vines and fanciful leaves.

"Careful!"

She laughed, dropping the scorched corner, and blew on her fingers. "Forgive me. You startled me just as I was engaged in a rather furtive activity."

"I see." He held the book in one hand; the cracked and dusty leather contrasted oddly with his sober morning coat and neatly-buttoned cuffs.

Of course. She had forgotten about his offer to read to her while she painted. "These are my brother's letters. He is just fifteen. He writes everything to me and then begs me to burn his letters so no one else can read them."

To her surprise, Rohario paled. He wandered away to the window. "I wrote poems to a girl once, when I was fifteen," he said, without looking at her.

"Did she burn them?"

His back was to her, so she could not see his expression only the shake of his head. "My mother found them."

"Oh." Something in the way he said those simple words made her want to know what his mother had said and yet fear to ask. She stuck the second letter in the flame and watched it roar to a quick conclusion. Then the third. Agustin's secrets were safe.

The silence became oppressive. Suddenly Eleyna realized how many people would have to be told about Edoard and Beatriz. Humiliation curdled in her gut.

"It must feel awkward," said Rohario abruptly, "now that Edoard has taken your sister for his Mistress instead of you. I hope . . . you are not too distressed."

"I did not truly want to be Edoard's mistress," she said, too quickly. "Not that I don't like Edoard, it was my mother's wish although I agreed—but—I just. . . ." She floundered. "Eiha! I'm making a fool of myself, aren't I?"

"I don't think so."

She dusted the last flakes of black ash from her fingers and walked over to her portrait of Edoard. "I must finish this before the guests arrive."

"Matra Dolcha! I had mercifully forgotten the guests. How I hate Edoard's parties!"

"I don't like parties either. I suppose Beatriz will be happy."

He sighed. "I hope you will forgive me if I say that I wish I did not need to be here."

"Why do we need to be here?" The idea came to her, as startling as it was unbidden. "I need only finish the portrait. I don't wish to endure the ill-placed pity of your brother's noble guests!"

"Perhaps *your* family will welcome you home, but I am not at all sure my father will want to see me."

"Why do we have to go home at all?" It came to her with the reckless beauty of a painting done in one inspired sitting. *She did not need her family anymore, nor they her.* "I have a small inheritance set aside for me by my grandmother. Nothing much, but I could rent a room in Meya Suerta. I could make enough coin to live on, painting *Deeds* and *Wills* and *Marriages*. Many a painter does so." But none of them were women, alone. "Of course it is impossible. It would not be safe or proper."

She examined the portrait of Edoard. Why hadn't she thought of it before? Painters and draughtsmen could always scratch out a living. If she could find wealthier clients . . . but a young woman without father or brother or husband to protect her was fair game in the rough world outside palasso walls.

She spun to face Rohario. *Why not?* It was risky, of course, but there came a time in life when you had to shut your eyes and leap forward on faith. The audacity of the idea dazzled her. She could not live alone and friendless in Meya Suerta—unless she had a companion, someone safe, a *brother.*

⚷ SIXTY-EIGHT ⚷

Agustin Grijalva sat in one of the stuffy attic closets crammed into the storeroom beyond the Atelierro and tried not to breathe. If he took in too deep a gulp of the stale air, he would cough helplessly. That had happened three days ago, when he had tried this for the first time, and he had barely escaped being caught. Now he fortified himself with a pouch of water and an infusion of fennel in honey.

The plank floor was cold and uncomfortable. His skin ached. He had gotten a terrible rash yesterday, but a salve of aloe had soothed the worst of the stinging pain. Despite that pain, Agustin bent his entire will upon the rectangle of parchment, prepared with oil from his fingers, that he had propped up on his bent knees against a thin piece of wood. At this awkward angle, his neck hurt. His skin pulled and burned. Probably he was going to get blisters all over.

But he did not move. He stared at the detailed sketch, bordered with an elaborate skein of symbols that he had drawn onto the parchment using pen and ink mixed with the tincture of his own blood.

He looked at a drawing of the long table that sat at the far end of the Atelierro. The setting sun shone, casting barred shadows along the table, just as he had observed it to do at the seventh hour after midday. At this hour, on the occasion of the Great Feasts of the year, the Grijalva Conselhos met. Once the Conselhos had been only the most senior Limners; now they included any family member, even women, made senior by age or influence.

Agustin intended to spy on them. He prayed to Matra ei Filho that it would work.

He knew he could never sketch every person in correctly, or even guess in what arrangement they might sit at the table, so he had only sketched in the table and the shadows. If he could catch the lighting just right and trigger the spell before the Conselhos assembled, then he could listen in on the whole thing. But was the sketch accurate enough? He had studied Eleyna's drawings—the ones she had sent him from Chasseriallo—with the greatest care, but she had seven years of training beyond him as well as the better eye. Still, he had done his best to place the shafts of light as they would fall over the wood grain, illuminate the highbacked chairs, touch that one square of plush Tza'ab carpet.

"*That is the test of magic,*" Zio Giaberto had said. "*For a spell to be triggered, the rendering must be perfect. Nothing else will do.*"

"*What if a man is Gifted with magic but not with the ability to draw?*" Agustin had asked.

"*Then his Gift is worthless. But while there are greater and lesser talents, I know of only three cases in our long history of Gifted males who simply could not learn to use their Gift. With enough drilling and practice, even a child with little natural aptitude for art will suffice as a copyist and can serve the family by performing certain routine duties which still demand the use of magic but not, perhaps, any great artistic talent. But do not worry, Agustin, you are not one of those sorry few. Your talents are evident.*"

"*Eleyna should have had my Gift,*" he had said recklessly.

"*I am not interested in having this discussion again, mennino. Your devotion to your sister is admirable but misplaced. Continue with the recitation.*"

Recite he had, and did now, words from the *Folio,* to seal the magic, to trigger it. Whispering to himself helped him not to cough. But as he waited, the air grew thicker and thicker by some agency he could not know. Then, as if melded with the air, whispers floated to him.

"*. . . Cabral will vote against us again . . . too much influence . . . isn't Gifted, but always had the favor of the Grand Duke . . . hush, here come the others. . . .*"

A confused jumble of soft noise. Agustin unfroze himself. His shoulders ached. No one was standing outside the closet door, trading secrets. The magic had worked.

"*Greetings, cousins. We are gathered here to toast the Feast of Imago with this very fine Palenssia red. I know there is dispute at the Ecclesia about whether the Exalted were pruning back vines destined to produce a white or a red when they were visited with the Image of Matra ei Filho, but I trust we may give thanks to Their Blessed Visitassion with any fine vintage and leave the quibbling to the scholars.*"

Shared chuckles. Agustin did not get the joke, and in any case, he was annoyed. He could not see anyone. Surely this spell was supposed to allow him to *see* as well as *hear* the Conselhos. *Merditto!* Eleyna would have done it right. She had helped him with the dream spells, relating to him the secrets of Grijalva magic that Grandmother Leilias had told her. It had all made sense to *her.* The only time he ever felt as if he could manage what was going on was when he tried to think as he supposed she would.

Eiha! Hearing would have to serve. Of course that was Lord Limner Andreo giving the first toast. But Agustin desperately wondered who else was there—Grandzio Cabral, according to the whisperers he had first heard. But their voices had been so muffled that he could not identify them.

"*. . . before we adjourn for the service at the Cathedral, I do have a piece of unexpected news to impart. I have just received a courier from Chasseriallo. . . .*"

"*Matra ei Filho! Has there been some disaster?*"

"*Now, now, Nicollo. Let us not look at things in the worst light always. Let us say instead there has been a change of plans.*"

"*I'll kill her.*" That was Agustin's mother, definitely.

"*You needn't worry, Dionisa.*" Even through the muffling effect of magic and parchment, Agustin could tell Andreo was as amused as he was irritated. "*At least one of your daughters knows her duty to the family.*"

"*Beatriz!*"

So many voices, speaking at once, and laughter.

"*Matra Dolcha, Cabral, have you no shame?*" Dionisa again. "*Beatriz has not been protected, she is still so young—and she is fertile!*"

"*Leilias will have taught her everything she needs to know. I see I underestimated those girls.*"

"*Cabral is right.*" This was Andreo once more. "*Eleyna was the better choice for many reasons, but clearly not the choice Edoard made.*"

"*She pushed Beatriz into it, I just know she did! And I will have her whipped when I get my hands on her! Matra! I'll whip her myself!*"

"*I assure you, Dionisa, Beatriz will bear no children by Edoard. Now recall this: The Marria do'Fantome has been restored. That is the important thing.*"

Eleyna was not Don Edoard's mistress. Beatriz was.

Agustin choked. He gulped for air, groped for the cup of water, tipped it over, and dropped the parchment as he broke into racking coughs.

Through the haze of gulping for air he heard their voices continuing, a shift in topic but one he could not follow. He desperately tried to catch his breath. What would they do to Eleyna?

"In here, I think." These words did not come through the parchment.

The closet door opened and he blinked up, still hacking, at Giaberto and, beyond him, at the snow-white hair and bland, seamed face of Cabral.

"Get the boy something to drink," snapped Giaberto as he snatched up the parchment.

Cabral pushed Giaberto aside and pulled Agustin to his feet. "Now, now, mennino. I want you to listen to my voice. Listen to my breathing. When I breathe—like so—"

The sucked-in air sounded a roar in Agustin's ears, which pounded with the beat of his own pulse.

"—then you will breathe as well. Not deep breaths. That will only cause you to cough—there, you see. Just with me. That's right. Now come, take a step. Let's get out of this dusty closet."

By the time they got into the Atelierro, Agustin was still struggling to take deep breaths but the coughing had subsided.

"Here is your son, Dionisa," said Cabral. "I think it would be well to have a sancta in to see him."

"As if a sancta would lower herself to venture into our chi'patro Palasso," said his mother furiously.

"Nevertheless," said Cabral smoothly, "although they may have snubbed you, Dionisa, this is your Gifted son who is having trouble breathing. They will know what to do."

Agustin was hauled off to bed and, later, given over to the attentions of a robed and wimpled sancta whose forbidding gaze was as stony as the statues in the Cathedral. But once Dionisa left the chamber—at the sancta's direct order—and the old woman examined Agustin, her features softened.

"Poor boy," she said. "You remind me of my great-nephew, all bones and big eyes. How old are you? Just hold up your fingers. Don't talk. Fifteen, is it? That is the same age I was when my parents dedicated me to the Ecclesia." Agustin wanted to ask if she, like him, had had no choice in the matter of her profession, but he dared not. "Let me listen to your lungs. What's that I smell on your breath? Fennel? Something you brewed for yourself? You have good sense." She said this approvingly, as Eleyna would. Agustin could not imagine Eleyna this old and wrinkled, but the sancta had an iron strength about her that reminded him of his sister.

Not like Beatriz. But Beatriz was now Don Edoard's mistress . . . the thought triggered another spasm of coughing.

The sancta clapped her hands, loudly, and Dionisa hurried in. "I want a cup of boiled water."

"But—"

"I want it now."

Agustin could not quite laugh through his coughing, but he would have liked to, at the expression on his mother's face.

"Have you always had this sort of coughing?" the sancta asked him. "Do you get colds easily in the wet season? Is it worse at certain times of year? Don't speak. You need only nod or shake your head. Have you always felt a little weaker than the other children? Is it sometimes hard to catch your breath? Yes, yes." The sancta sighed, caught herself, and turned just in time to intercept the cup of hot water. Rummaging in her woven pouch, she brought out a box and, opening it, sorted through little bags. Agustin could tell they were herbs and flowers, but by this time he could smell nothing.

She made a hot tea for him. After a few sips his spasms subsided.

"You have weak lungs, my child. There is little I or any other healer can do about it. You must walk frequently, not sit indoors all the time—as it appears you do with that pallor you have—but not overexert yourself. An infusion of coltsfoot, licorice, and manzanilla will help you through attacks. If you balance yourself between resting and exercise, eat well, drink a little wine but not too much, you can live a normal life. It is up to you. Do not let your mother bully you. There now. I will go tell your mother and father these same things."

She blessed him and left.

Agustin stared bitterly at the ceiling, plain white, appropriate for the room of a boy who was supposed to think of nothing but painting, creating images against that white in his mind's eye. He was a Gifted Limner, after all.

He squeezed his eyes shut to stop tears. What point was there in crying? There was nothing he could do about it. He took another sip of the tea and felt his lungs open a bit more.

He could never have any of the things he really wanted anyway: sons and daughters to dandle on his knee, a house of his own, a life that belonged to *him,* not to his mother and the Grijalva family. What did it matter if his lungs were weak? He would die young in any case.

He was a Gifted Limner.

And he wished desperately that he was not.

Dionisa refused to let him out of bed for two days and did not let him have pencil and drawing paper to while away the time. He was grateful to be allowed out of bed the third morning after the Feast of Imago. He was, in fact, sitting in his mother's parlor taking a light breakfast of rolls and cheese and licorice tea when Cabral came in, unannounced.

"Your color is better," Cabral observed. "What were you think-ing about so pensively, young man?"

"About how to protect Eleyna," Agustin blurted out.

"I trust that Eleyna can protect herself, but I take your meaning. Right now you must think about protecting yourself. You have been spared censure thus far because of your illness, but I am come to warn you that you are to be called before the Viehos Fratos. Which means I cannot be present."

Agustin choked on a piece of bread, coughing, and managed to finish swallowing without having a new attack. "Are they going to do something awful to me?"

"Do not mention to them that I spoke with you. Listen carefully. They will threaten you, since they do not like to be trifled with. I thought it a clever trick myself, but I have always been at a disad-vantage with the Gifted, you understand, and am more likely than they to think it amusing. But many boys died during the Summer Fever. You are a rare commodity now, Agustin, the commodity on which Grijalva wealth is founded. They will threaten you but can-not risk harming you, not unless you show yourself a serious threat to them, which you and I know you are not. Eiha! I hear someone. Be brave."

Cabral vanished through one door just as Giaberto and Dionisa walked in through the other. Agustin would have found the the-atrics amusing had he not been quaking. Giaberto's expression was grave, and Dionisa looked furious and worried at the same time. Maybe he could have been brave if Eleyna had been here. But he was alone.

"Stop cowering!" his mother snapped. "You remind me of a cringing kitchen maid who's just been caught with her hand in the syrup jar." She broke off, hurried over to him as he sat, staring, too terrified to move, and stroked his shoulders. "Now, now, ninio. You know I will protect you. No one will hurt you. Giaberto and I want only the best for you. But you must act like the little man you are and go with your uncle now."

Used to obeying the commands of his elders, Agustin went.

They waited for him in the Crechetta, eleven dour men, the youngest his fifth cousin Damiano, the eldest a distant cousin who at forty-five was curled into the final stages of the bone fever that was killing him.

Agustin found he could examine old Zosio dispassionately. He would never have to suffer the agonies of failing hands and joints: his lungs would kill him first. This bleak thought gave him heart to face them down.

Lord Limner Andreo lifted a hand. "You may sit, Giaberto. Agustin, you will stand, *there.*"

Agustin complied, standing where they all could see him. The Limners glared at him, except young Damiano who, face in profile to the rest, winked at him. Nicollo looked positively surly where he sat twisted in a chair; his complexion had the pasty dullness of a man whose life is draining from him.

"Do you know, Agustin, how the Gifted discipline those of their own kind who disobey the stringent rules we have set for ourselves?"

He shook his head. Terrified, he nevertheless clung to two thoughts: Cabral had told him he was valuable, and he was going to die young anyway, whatever else they might do to him.

Andreo went on sternly. "We have been given a great Gift but also a terrible responsibility, and we owe service to the Grijalva family and to the Grand Dukes of Tira Virte. You know of the sacrifice made by Verro Grijalva. You know of the capture of his sisters by Tza'ab bandits, of their rescue by the first Duke Renayo. You know they are honored above all other women for their mercy and generosity in bringing the chi'patro children into the Grijalva lineage. You know also that our family was not murdered by the mob during Nerro Lingua only because of the intercession of Duchess Jesminia. All these things we Grijalvas remember. We live on the sufferance of the do'Verrada family, just as they prosper because of our aid to them. Thus, together, we increase Tira Virte's fortunes.

"But we are never safe when plagues strike the city and whispers of black magic race through the streets again, when our name is still mentioned with mistrust in the Sanctias—or when any rash boy realizes the power he holds *in his hands* can be used for his own selfish gain.

"You do not yet understand the power that lives in *your* hands, but you must now learn what it is to be disciplined by your peers. Damiano, bring the portrait of Domaos."

By this time, Cabral's bracing words had been washed away by the flood of Andreo's lecture. Andreo's bland, staring eyes, old

Zosio's racking cough (worse than his own), their collective frown, all combined to leave Agustin in a state of near panic.

Damiano returned with the portrait, and a fine portrait it was, too, of a handsome young man with burning, ambitious eyes and the broad shoulders of an athlete.

Andreo looked as grim as if he were about to pronounce a sentence of death. "Domaos Grijalva chose his own fate. He was brash enough to believe he could have an affair with a do' Verrada daughter and not pay the price. The Viehos Fratos were merciful in his case: he was banished and forced to live his life as an itinerant painter—not an Itinerarrio, a chosen ambassador who may be received at every court with the greatest honor, but a mere traveling artist who must take what work he can."

Andreo paused to give Agustin time to envision the awful fate of Domaos Grijalva.

But why would it be so bad? All contracts in Tira Virte were paintings: as the old saying went, one word might have ten meanings or no meaning at all. There was always work for a good artist.

"In time, Agustin, you will paint a portrait of yourself, your *Peintraddo Chieva,* by which you will prove yourself worthy of a place among the Viehos Fratos. It will be painted with your own sweat, your tears, your saliva and urine and seed, with your own blood. It will hang in the Crechetta." Andreo motioned toward the walls of the old chamber, adorned with the portraits of the living Limners.

"What do you think would happen if we burned that painting?"

His tears and sweat, mixed in ink. Burning . . . four days ago a rash had erupted over him, like a sunburn. He shuddered, began coughing.

Giaberto jumped to his feet. "Don't scare the boy, Andreo. He's still weak."

Andreo slapped a hand against the back of his heavy chair. The crack startled Agustin out of coughing, and he struggled to compose himself.

"The boy must understand. We Grijalvas cannot afford to shelter Neosso Irrados. They must be disciplined or removed. *We* obey. *We* serve. Through our work we are rewarded."

Just as Grijalva girls were told they would be rewarded with Gifted sons, and the unGifted limners told they would be rewarded with security and a wife and the wealth of the Palasso. Eleyna had said often enough that she felt trapped. Agustin was beginning to understand what she meant.

"Agustin," Andreo continued, "do you have anything to say?"

I don't want to be a Limner. Agustin opened his mouth, but he could not say the words. He could not face their anger, their consternation, their scolding. He could not stand up against them.

"I will obey," he said meekly. Alone, all he could do was obey. They frightened him. They were stronger than he was. Matra Dolcha! He hated being afraid all the time.

Andreo nodded with satisfaction. "You are a good boy, and you will be a good painter. You will serve the family, and your reward will be that the family prospers. Do you understand?"

"H–how can you call it a gift?" Agustin stammered. "Why do we have to die so young, and so horribly? Why must we remain sterile? Why can't you change all that?"

Andreo smiled gently, but Agustin found the smile frightening. "Power takes its toll on our bodies. Sterility and early death, however awful they might be, are the price we pay for our magic, mennino. Never forget that."

As if I could.

"There are so few of us," Andreo continued, musing. "And so much to do. Fewer than two dozen Gifted Limners alive now."

No wonder the Gifted died young. They bled themselves dry, just as the ancient heathen Tza'ab illuminators, the Al-Fansihirro, were said to have literally killed themselves by using their own blood mixed with ink to pen their holy book, the *Kita'ab*. The heathen Tza'ab . . . whose blood, through his chi'patro ancestors, flowed through his own veins.

"It isn't as easy as it seems on the surface," Agustin said finally and was rewarded by an approving smile from Andreo and a clap on the back from his uncle.

"You are learning," said Andreo. "Viehos Fratos, let us adjourn to our work."

As they began to move, a hard rap at the door stilled them. Young Damiano hurried to the door, opening it just a crack. He jumped back, expression bright with startlement.

"Your Grace!" He backed up swiftly, bowing.

Agustin had not known Andreo could move so fast. The Lord Limner had come forward, and bowed, before Grand Duke Renayo entered the Crechetta. But he could scarcely stop the Grand Duke from entering the most private Grijalva sanctuary. The other Limners rose, all but Zosio and Nicollo.

The Grand Duke looked annoyed and completely unaware of his trespass. "Andreo! I am in a hurry." His gaze touched and dismissed the chamber and its furnishings. He examined the assembled Grijalvas, pausing longest on Agustin, who squirmed and tried to look innocuous. Agustin had never seen the Grand Duke this close before: a good-looking, stocky man, Renayo had the light hair and delicate features of his Ghillasian heritage. Indeed, Agustin could see very little resemblance between Renayo II and any of his illustrious do' Verrada ancestors. "I trust I may speak freely here?"

Andreo proferred a hand, palm up. "Of course, Your Grace. May I offer you a seat?"

"No. I will be blunt. I have just come from Chasseriallo."

The atmosphere in the chamber, already charged, became taut with expectation.

"I have spoken with my son, Edoard. To my vast surprise at least one third of the sentences he uttered made sense, so I must tell you that your daughter is having a magnificently good influence on him. It was not what I would have chosen, you understand. I was given to believe that the elder daughter, the widow, was Edoard's choice and a better choice besides from our point of view, as well as being the more remarkable in looks, but this other girl is very handsome, too, if rather young. An older woman is the traditional choice. Be that as it may. I am at peace with this decision. It is what Mairie always said: 'A strong woman will be the making of Edoard.' This is a good start, despite my misgivings."

"Your Grace," said Andreo. It answered nothing but seemed to be the response expected of him.

Agustin was awed by Renayo's energy and by the ease with which he commanded the attention of everyone in the room. Now Renayo nodded curtly. "The young woman will be introduced officially to society at the Dia Fuega ball."

"As you wish, Your Grace. May I ask—?"

"Matra ei Filho, Andreo! Of course you may ask. You need not abase yourself! What concerns you? Eiha! Perhaps you are as surprised as I was, no? Of course it was your intention that the elder girl—did she refuse to go, after all was said and done?"

Andreo blinked. "No, not at all. You did not speak to her there?"

"At Chasseriallo? No, I only spoke to Edoard and his charming Beatriz. She is a sweet girl. I wish my daughter Timarra had a tenth of her charm. I quite liked her, in fact. The elder girl—what was her name? Momentito. Don't tell me. Of course." Renayo snapped his fingers. "Eleyna. No, she was not there."

"Not there?" The exclamation came from Giaberto.

Not there!

"Nor was Rohario. I sent him off with his older brother to get him out of the Palasso. Eiha!—if only he would think as well as he dresses. So. Eleyna Grijalva *was* there, was she? Edoard made some confused comments. I didn't put it together at the time, but now—"

Three taps came on the door. Damiano cracked it open.

"I beg your pardon, Zio," the young Limner said in a voice meant to be a whisper which instead carried easily to the others, "but you cannot—"

"Is that Cabral?" Renayo clapped his hands together, once, emphatically. "Of course you must let him enter! Zio Cabral!"

Of course you must let him enter! No Limner dared contravene the Grand Duke's direct order, even in their own sanctuary. Their expressions of consternation delighted Agustin.

The Grand Duke hurried forward to draw the old man into the chamber which Cabral had certainly never seen before in his life. Cabral entered hesitantly. But it was Renayo's expression that surprised Agustin: the Grand Duke addressed Andreo forthrightly and with trust; Cabral he approached with genuine fondness.

"Zio," the Grand Duke said, hand resting comfortably on Cabral's arm, "you asked me to come by when the white iris bloomed. So they have, and I have come to fetch you."

"You are kind to remember me, Your Grace," said Cabral, but from his mouth the polite words gained a sudden sweetness. He glanced once around the Crechetta, eyes wide; then he forced his attention back to the Grand Duke. "You also have news of Chasseriallo, I hear. My niece, Eleyna, how is she?"

Renayo burst into guffaws. Agustin could hardly breathe. The Grand Duke and a limner standing in the Crechetta! And, worse, what had happened to Eleyna?

"No one knows how she is! It appears my son Roherio has done the first manful thing of his entire life: run off with a beautiful woman!" Still laughing, he swept Cabral out with him. Their footsteps receded down the hall.

Inside the Crechetta there was stunned silence.

"Curse that woman," said Nicollo at last in a voice scraped raw with pain.

"Giaberto, prepare a canvas." Andreo shook himself to life and strode over to an iron lampstand. He adjusted the wick in the lamp, although Agustin had refilled the basin with oil that morning and it burned brightly enough, then turned to face the others. "We must track Eleyna down, quietly, so as not to attract too much attention. It is vital we find her. She knows too much."

To Agustin's horror, Andreo turned his grim gaze on *him*.

"*You*, mennino. If your sister sends you word, if you hear anything from her at all, you will come to me at once. She knows a very few of the secrets of the Viehos Fratos, but a very few is too many in the hands of those who could use that knowledge against us, who might destroy with one stroke what we have labored so long, so many generations, to build. She must return to Palasso Grijalva. Here she must stay. Do you understand?"

Agustin gulped down his fear. He did understand. He was beginning to understand the power of the Grijalvas very well. "Yes, Lord Limner," he said obediently.

But in his heart, he knew he would never betray Eleyna.

SIXTY-NINE

Alazais was stupid.

No, stupid was the wrong word. She was blank. She was a white canvas, primed but unpainted.

Sario revised his plans. He had a great deal of work to do before he, her rescuer, could present her to a grateful Grand Duke Renayo. There were always unintended consequences to any action: it simply had not occurred to him that while her physical presence might be reproduced with painstaking exactitude, her mind might not follow her form.

Which was, perhaps, just as well. Sario could do his own forming.

"You are the Princess Alazais, daughter of King Ivo and Queen Iriene of Ghillas, who are, alas, dead, murdered by a renegade mob. It is no wonder that your memory is weak, your nerves overset, having witnessed such a horrific scene."

"I am Princess Alazais, daughter of King Ivo and Queen Iriene. They are—" Here her voice caught. "—dead. Alas. I saw, I saw . . . I saw it happen."

Sario regarded her with approval. She was a skilled mimic, and she picked up his every word, every emotional nuance, and incorporated them into her fragile being. Just as wood or cloth, paper or plaster provide a surface onto which paint is applied, she was the support on which he created the masterwork which would assure his elevation to Lord Limner. He need only apply the final layer— of words and thoughts rather than brushstrokes.

He heard the footsteps on the stairs. Going out, he found a tray of food and drink. It was nothing special, but the rich head of foam on the ale, freshly drawn, the savory meat pies, and aroma of freshly baked bread made his mouth water. He was still weak, though he had slept and eaten more than usual these last three days. But he had been ten days painting her, most of that time in a trance so that he did not notice the passage of day and night. He carried in the tray and, placing it on the table, served them both.

"Princess Alazais is always served by others. She waits for their service, never moving to help herself."

So she waited, and handled the knife and fork daintily, sipped at the ale cautiously and with more pleasure at a mug of spiced tea, all as he had taught her in the three days since her creation.

"Who are you?" he asked again. "What is your lineage?"

She had a voice more breath than tone, but like a feather, she might be tossed in storm winds and emerge unscathed. "I am Princess Alazais, daughter of King Ivo of Ghillas. My mother Iriene is the second daughter of Fretherik, Prince of Sar-Kathebarg. My father is the great-grand-nephew of King Pepennar the Second of Ghillas who died without issue in the year 1238. The throne of Ghillas passed in time to Enrei the Second, who sired Mechella, who became Grand Duchess of Tira Virte, and Enrei the Third, who died without legitimate children in the year 1287. After the death of Enrei the Third, the throne passed to my father, Ivo, his distant cousin. Thus it passes to me, as last survivor of the Pepennid family and only child of King Ivo."

"And if a man were to marry you who was himself descended from Mechella de Ghillas and Mairie de Lillone?"

"The Lillone family is a collatoral branch of the Pepennids. Their claim is not as good as mine, since they were only cousins of Enrei the First, his father's youngest brother's children, but there are sons, descended through the male Lillone line. . . ."

Here she hesitated. Was she struggling to remember the many facts he had poured into her or showing maidenly modesty? Even he, her creator, could not guess. Even a blank canvas contains within its substance certain intrinsic, unique qualities.

She went on. "In Ghillas it is preferred that inheritance descend through the male line. That is why the noble houses of Ghillas rejected Renayo's claim, because it passed to him through his mother. But Pepennar himself established and was confirmed in his claim to the throne through his father's mother's kinship to King Enrei the First. She was Enrei's only daughter and her children alone of his many grandchildren survived to adulthood."

It was so odd to listen to that gentle voice—which in Ghillas had never uttered a word of greater import than to ask for praise for her latest piece of embroidery or her mastery of a new dance step or her appearance in a new gown—reel off the complicated lineage of the Ghillasian noble family.

"Furthermore," she continued, each word perfect, "in this terrible time of strife, it is vital that the throne and royal family of Ghillas be restored and that there be no struggle between competing factions lest the rabble that heinously murdered King Ivo and Queen Iriene gain in strength and destroy Ghillas utterly with this plague of restlessness. Where will it end if the common rabble are

allowed to sit whenever and as ever they please on the throne of
Ghillas, if fishwives and panderers may wield the royal scepter, if
innkeepers and street sweepers believe they can govern as well as
the King and his advisers, who have been granted by Matreia e
Filhei the right to rule as their part in life? Order must be restored
or we will all suffer."

"And you," he finished, "are the one person behind whom the
noble families of Ghillas, the neighboring princes, the landed
classes and the wealthy merchants will all stand."

She gazed at him solemnly with those brilliant blue eyes. Eiha!
Perhaps he had overdone it, made her too perfectly beautiful when
she had actually been a pretty girl but not more than that.

"I am the rightful Queen of Ghillas," she said.

He smiled and patted her on the head as he might a pet dog, were
he the type of person who kept pets. She was, indeed, beautiful,
built a bit more voluptuously than she had been in real life, all of
which was blatantly apparent on a young woman clad now only in
a thin chemise. She stirred not one iota of sexual response in him,
but for decades now only painting made him feel fully alive. The
other was merely a brief moment of satiation.

She waited as he mulled over in his mind what he needed to
teach her. He must bring in a woman to teach her to embroider.
Alazais had loved to embroider—little pillows, sleeves, hems,
ribands, hats, reticules, all manner of frilly things necessary to a
pampered lady of the court. A gift of one of the princess' handi-
crafts had been a mark of favor at Ivo's court.

She also must learn a better Ghillasian accent. He spoke to her
in equal measure in Ghillasian and in his own language, but he
could not reproduce her original charming accent. The real
princess had been a quick study in languages, perhaps because she
also had a good ear for music.

That, too. She must hear music so she could recognize concer-
tos, learn to sing a few appropriate songs. She must learn to dance.
She must know wine. No one would credit a Ghillasian princess
who, no matter how traumatized, could not distinguish between her
reds and her whites.

And though she would of necessity arrive dressed humbly, in
order to lend a certain rough verisimilitude to her story, she must
also know cloth and clothing, be attuned to the nuances of fashion.
The real princess had loved to "dress up," as she had in her naive
fashion called it. She had been even more naive than the young
Mechella, if that were possible, but Mechella had possessed a fine
eye for color and a strong natural sense for cut and weave. The real

Alazais had not been so blessed. *This* Alazais would have the best of taste.

This would all take much longer than he had planned.

He let her watch as he penned a note—he must tutor her in her letters as well—which he would have sent to Arguena, to let her servants know there had been an unspecified delay. Then he made a list, which he had her copy, of everything they would need. In this, as in everything else, she was a quick study.

"Work on forming your letters," he said to her, "until I return. Always remember that you must speak of your past to no one until I give you leave. You are always in danger. We must keep your identity secret."

"I will speak of it to no one," she agreed.

He left the tray of empty plates and cups by the door and went down the stairs slowly, examining the mural painted there. The painting moved by elaborate stages up the stairs and down again, following the trail of the steps of the proprietor who ran the wine shop and kept Sario supplied with food, drink, clean linen and clothing, the necessities of life, when he was in residence in his attic hideaway. The painting itself was bordered by wreaths of vines and flowers and plants; within this border, a man serves his master with fidelity and devoted affection; he raises his own family and passes this duty on to a son or nephew, who in his turn climbs and descends the stairs. Into this innocuous if startling stairway storybook Sario had painted—and repainted, when the painting needed to be renewed—his own blood and tears as well as oils and essences from the herbs and flowers represented: violet for Faithfulness, plum for Fidelity, vervain for Enchantment, and belladonna for Silence.

He had painted similar, if better disguised, spells into the trim that surrounded the doors and windows of the wine shop. Thus was the shop sealed. So had he found refuge here for three hundred years, in the old market district of the city, which had not changed much over the centuries. He had renewed the painting as the old Arriano and would renew it again just before he discarded this body. Coming into the back room of the shop he startled the proprietor, a robust man in his forties who was, at this moment, examining a printed tract.

"I beg your pardon, Maesso." The proprietor jumped to his feet and crumpled the stiff paper in his hands.

"Is that a broadside?" asked Sario, curious to know what had caused Oliviano to color such a deep stain of purple. "Something subversive, I trust?"

"Nothing at all, Maesso."

"Let me see it." *It* was indeed a printed broadside, crude letters and poor ink quality, bemoaning the Grand Duke's resistance to convening the Corteis and protesting the recent executions. "Dangerous sentiments." Sario handed the page back to Oliviano. "I trust you will burn this?"

"Yes, Maesso. I will do it now."

Sario detested these new polite honorifics, Maesso and Maessa, which were now the fashion in the merchant and guild quarters of the city; they were a bastardization of the old guild title of Master. But he had learned to change with the times. "I need some things, Maesso Oliviano. As you know, my sister has sent me her niece from Ghillas—" It was a bald-faced lie, and they both knew it, but it served to smooth over awkward questions. "—and I need a woman to come in, for ten or twenty days, to tutor her in the gentler arts. You know the city well. She must be a woman of gentle birth, born in Ghillas or the daughter of Ghillasians, one who can speak the language with a pure accent, one who can embroider, who can play the lute and teach my niece a few songs, a few dance steps."

The proprietor had by this time recovered from Sario's discovery of the broadside. He was a canny merchant; his father had been content to run the wineshop quietly during Dioniso's life. Oliviano had, with Arriano's permission, expanded his business even as Meya Suerta itself had expanded.

"It will take a few days."

"See that it is done quickly, and I will see that your eldest daughter is provided with a good dowry."

"You are too generous!"

"I think not. This woman must, in addition, board with you and your wife while she teaches my niece."

"Eiha." Oliviano mused over this request. His father would have responded without questioning; Oliviano, about forty now, did not defer to the "young" Sario as he had to Arriano. "We can find room." Disconcertingly, he winked at Sario. "You mean to marry the girl to a young man of good family? She is certainly pretty enough."

Sario's hackles went up. He did not like to be spoken to this familiarly. "That is my business, not yours. Do as I ask and you and your family will be rewarded."

"As you wish, Maesso." The proprietor bowed.

Satisfied, Sario climbed the stairs back to the attic, where he found Alazais carefully copying her letters. She had a beautiful hand, and it disturbed him just a little bit to see those fingers, which yesterday had been ignorant of forming letters, copying his precise writing so perfectly.

Maessa Louissa was a woman with diffident manners, a thin face, a perfect Ghillasian accent, and a gown that was as faded as it was finely made, perhaps ten years out of fashion but precise in every detail. She was the only daughter of Isobella, a lady-in-waiting who had come from Lillone with Grand Duchess Mairie and then fallen out of favor for falling in love—without her mistress' permission!—with a handsome captain of the Shagarra Regiment. Dismissed from ducal service, abandoned by her lover, Isobella had raised Louissa in straitened circumstances and educated her so she might teach compordotta and various of the gentle arts to young women of Meya Suerta who wished to better themselves.

Louissa had never seen a portrait of Princess Alazais of Ghillas nor, Sario supposed, was she curious enough to ferret out the secret or even suppose there was one. She was poor, unmarriageable, and desperate to earn a good wage so she might keep herself and her mother, who had a weak heart.

Indeed, after the second day, she poured out her troubles to Alazais, who listened with a sympathetic manner which Sario approved of even while he sketched various studies of Maessa Louissa's face in order to block out the sound of her soft but persistently irritating voice.

So she taught Alazais for the rest of the month of Imago and into the month of Penitenssia, at whose end the year ended. What year was it? Eiha! It was hard to keep track.

Alazais learned to accompany herself on the lute, simple tunes. Her voice was clear and unaffected. She learned a number of the simpler court dances, during which Sario deigned to partner her while Louissa beat out time and hummed the melody in her reedy soprano.

And Alazais embroidered.

"I have never had a pupil take to this art so swiftly!" Louissa exclaimed one morning, displaying a square of linen covered with a delicate green ivy-wreath pattern. She looked as proud as if it had been her own daughter—the daughter she would, of course, never have.

Sario merely nodded, but he, too, was proud. He had painted into Alazais the potential to do these things. She was a magnificent piece of work. When Louissa went back to her pupil, he went back to his sketching, licking a finger and placing a touch of his saliva onto the pencil. He had done several perfect renditions of Louissa. He need only wait until he was through with her to make sure she would never speak of the work she had done here.

⚞⚞ SEVENTY ⚟⚟

Eleyna surveyed the sitting room with dismay. Beyond lay two additional rooms, bedchambers furnished with old beds built of wooden frames and rope supports, flea-ridden cotton ticking, and yellowing sheets.

"It's an outrageous price for rooms such as these!"

"It is?" Rohario asked.

"Did you bargain?"

"Bargain?"

"You didn't bargain with the innkeeper?"

He toured the room, inspecting the table with two chairs, the cracked windowpanes, the sofa upholstered with a brocaded fabric whose original color was bleached to an undistinguished yellow-white from exposure to sunlight, its pattern disguised by a generous helping of old wine stains.

"I've never seen anything like this before," he said, circling back to her. He looked less disgusted than astonished. "Do people live like this?"

"Like you, Don Rohario," she said stiffly, "I grew up in a palasso. But Grandmother made sure we knew something of life outside. Every girl who grows up in Palasso Grijalva learns to act as a steward for the Grijalva clan. Grandmother even took us to the mercado to bargain, and once—" She laughed, remembering the scandal. "—when I was just sixteen and Beatriz thirteen, Grandmother took us to a taverna to watch tilemaking apprentices dance and sing on Madurrassia. It was a scandal mostly because the new journeymen could ask for a kiss from any unmarried girl, and we were asked for quite a few. Even Grandmother was asked for a few kisses, for her husband was dead by then and she always wore her widow's shawl, even after the mourning period was over."

As this comment faded, it led not to a reply but to silence.

Eleyna went to the greasy window and rubbed at it with a corner of her lace shawl, trying to see onto the courtyard below. The innkeeper had expanded his inn to include the residential apartments in the building built up against his own, an old palasso whose exterior boasted clay-red tiles and whose interior was as faded and worn as a servant girl's three-times-handed-down fancy dress.

She gave up on the window and twined the fringed end of her own "widow's shawl" through her fingers. The black lace was bordered with embroidered hyacinths. If she was to lift those embroidered purplish-blue flowers to her face and inhale, would she be able to smell them? Would the scent ease her grief, as it was said to do?

Except she had no grief for her dead husband. She only wore the shawl to protect herself.

"Of course," said Rohario suddenly, as if it had taken him this long to understand her last words. "Each year at Madurrassia a different guild is invited to Palasso Verrada to celebrate the elevation of the apprentices to journeymen. They come to the throne room, where my father recites the blessing and oversees their elevation. They were always dressed rather shabbily, I thought, but they were never dressed as poorly as the people I've seen in Meya Suerta these last two days."

Looking at Rohario's beautiful clothes, only slightly crumpled from their ride, at his perfectly tied neckcloth—a work of art in itself—Eleyna chuckled. He looked so utterly out of place. No wonder the innkeeper had quoted such an outrageous price: if he dressed like a lord, he might as well pay like one.

"Those apprentices and their families were probably wearing their finest clothes to appear before the Grand Duke," she said. "What you see them wearing here are their everyday clothes. Don't the servants dress so at Palasso Verrada?"

"En verro, they all wear livery. My mother could not stand to have anyone she might see look out of place or shabby. Her family, you see, were noble but poor. She told me that once she married my father, she swore she would dress her own servants in better clothes than those she had worn as a girl."

"Even in the kitchens?"

"I've never been in the kitchens."

"Eiha, Rohario! You frighten me!"

"You think I'm a fool!" He stalked out of the room. Once she had recovered from her surprise, Eleyna followed him. She caught up with him in the busy courtyard in time to hear him launch into a harangue that would put a fishwife to shame. A crowd had already gathered.

". . . how many other of your customers are you cheating? Shall I ask these gentlemen right now? You, Maesso? Have you been overcharged as well? Eiha! I am only grateful that my own mother, may her memory be blessed, will not see my sister and I reduced to such a disgraceful suite of rooms! Your own mother, Maesso Innkeeper—would you install her in these lodgings?"

Having cut to the heart of the matter, Rohario paused to let his audience react. At once, the innkeeper grasped his arm. Rohario recoiled but controlled himself and let the by now red-faced man lead him away to his private office.

Eleyna moved to follow but was accosted by several men.

"Carrida. Grazzo. My heart is yours if only you will receive it."

"I'd like to see what grieving heart she wears under that handsome lace shawl."

"How much is he paying you, corasson? I will double it!"

Flushed and angry, Eleyna retreated to the sitting room. Cursing, she paced the limits of the chamber. Trapped again! She could not venture outside without a man to protect her!

A thin layer of grease covered the tabletop, smeared by plates or fingers, and she refused to lay her precious paper down on such a surface. How could she work here?

Was she so much better than Don Rohario, after all? She had never cleaned a room in her life. She supposed one needed a bucket of water and rags, but where to get the rags and the bucket, much less the water?

Escaping to Meya Suerta had been a reckless decision, perhaps even a foolish one. But she would not creep back, defeated, to Palasso Grijalva. She could only imagine what her parents would say to her, running off with a young nobleman!

Except she was not Don Rohario's mistress.

Matra ei Filho, I'm blushing! She strode to the window and, pounding on the lower corner, got it to open. The fresh air cooled her cheeks. When the door opened, she could turn and with some composure greet Rohario . . .

. . . and the innkeeper and two girls armed with buckets and rags and brooms.

"My good friend Maesso Gaspar has invited us to dine at his table tonight, sorella. We will go now, while these menninas clean out our rooms and make them fit to live in."

"Of course, frato." Brother.

He offered an arm. She took it, though she felt terribly awkward. Anyone with a featherweight of sense would know, would see by their postures, their faces, their way of speaking, that they were not related. Yet what did it matter? Men would think what they wished of her, but as long as Rohario agreed to act as her brother, he served as her protector. She remembered the men who had surrounded her in the courtyard and shuddered.

"What is wrong?" asked Rohario softly as they followed the innkeeper down a series of stairs and landings, painted in the most depressing clay red, to the ground floor.

"Nothing. Just cold." She fixed her eyes on his hands, afraid her face might give something away. He had beautiful, well-proportioned hands.

Edoard had been easy to paint because he was, truly, a man who could be captured in simple colors and lines. Rohario would make a more difficult, subtle, less clearly formed portrait. And in ten years, he might be very different than he was now. That was the difference between the two brothers. Edoard was already the man he would always be; Rohario was only beginning to take shape.

"Here we are." Maesso Gaspar showed them into a well-scrubbed dining hall that smelled of pine oil and almond. He introduced them to his other genteel guests. This room shared a great hearth with the common room. By craning her neck Eleyna could catch, through the roaring fire, a glimpse of the other room and its more boisterous, and less well groomed, inhabitants.

As the first course—an onion soup—came round, Rohario leaned close to Eleyna. "In order to get a better rate, I had to pay in advance. He wouldn't put the bill on credit!"

"How can he know what your credit is worth?"

"It is true I did not tell him who I really am. But I have only ten mareias left. According to Maesso Gaspar, when I asked which wine he served with dinner, ten mareias isn't even enough to buy a bottle of Palenssia red!"

He was so indignant that she barely managed not to laugh at him. "No doubt that is all you are accustomed to drinking. We shall have to work for our living."

"Work?" He paled. "How exactly *does* one work?"

Eleyna looked around the room. It was large, undistinguished, and drearily rectangular. One narrow end boasted the great hearth that divided this chamber from the common room. There was also a long wall of windows looking out over the courtyard and, opposite it, a long whitewashed wall along the inner side of the chamber. She stood up, reaching into her skirt pockets for the bits of charcoal and chalk that she—indeed, every Grijalva—always carried with her.

"I beg your pardon, Maesso Gaspar. I see that this room is reserved for your more particular guests. But perhaps you would like to attract more, and more discerning, customers."

Surprised, the innkeeper offered her a polite bow. "Every man of business wishes to attract more customers."

"If every meal was served to me in the company of women as beautiful as yourself, Maessa," said one of the men seated across the table from her, "then I would come here more often." His expression grew suddenly forced, and he smiled placatingly at Rohario. "Begging your pardon, Maesso."

"It is my sister's pardon you need ask," said Rohario softly but with a hint of menace.

Eleyna took out a piece of chalk and with a few swift strokes drew a caricature of the man on the white linen tablecloth. The other customers guffawed.

"Maesso Gaspar, I am a skilled draftsman and painter. But I must work for my living as must all of you. My brother and I have few resources, and I would willingly bargain with you my work in exchange for our keep. For instance." As she spoke, she began to expand her sketch, and Rohario quickly moved platters and dishes and cups so she had room to work. "That entire wall is simply a white backdrop on which you might hang a few paintings. Or better yet, commission me to paint a mural. It will represent the Feast of Providenssia, the harvest of the grapes, whose prosperity you certainly wish to emulate. But in addition I will weave into this mural the faces of your regular customers so those customers will bring their relations and their neighbors to see this mural. And I will hide pictures of places in Meya Suerta, of men and women from days long past whose stories we have all heard a hundred times during our childhoods, so that not just your regular customers but new customers will come to see this fine mural."

By now others of the guests had moved their tableware aside to leave room for her to sketch. She had to lean far, had to move chairs aside, and she no longer had thought to spare for talking. This tablecloth must be the prototype for the cartoon—the model sketch; it must include every face in this dining chamber, must be the piece that sold the innkeeper on her suggestion. For not only would such a commission give them board and room for as long as it took her to execute the mural, but her work on the piece would attract notice, and the finished piece would attract customers for *her.*

It was not until she finished and paused, before signing, that she noticed how still the room had become. They all watched her as keenly as if they were waiting for her to vanish with her last stroke.

Eleyna surveyed her work. There was nothing major to fault in the sketch: her hand was sure. She had drawn in Gaspar as the padron of Providenssia, dispensing wine and bread to an assembly which included every man and both other women seated at this table tonight, as well as the four servants who had been attending them and who strained to get a good look at the sketch from their stations by the kitchen door. The sketch was not quite balanced. The assembly was a bit too static, and Gaspar needed some kind of backdrop, a good view of his inn and boarding house, perhaps, garlanded with vines and with vases filled with sheaves of wheat, denoting riches to come. But overall she was pleased with it.

Maesso Gaspar clapped a hand over his heart in the pose of a man who has just been surprised by the chest pangs that will kill him. "Magniffica! I agree, at once! When can you start?"

She bit down on a smile. "We have not yet agreed to terms, Maesso Gaspar."

"How much for the tablecloth?" asked the man who had been so rude to begin with. Like many such men, he was converted easily.

She shut her eyes, savoring the moment. Then, with a flourish, she signed the name "Riobaro" to the sketch.

"That isn't your name," objected Rohario. "That says—" He broke off, eyes widening.

"I beg your pardon, Maesso," Eleyna said to her new admirer, "but I am afraid that according to a family tradition I must ask Maesso Gaspar to accept this tablecloth as payment for this meal— for all of us seated here—and as surety for our contract, since I am penniless."

"New to the business, eh?" replied the man. He rubbed his hands together. "I'm a guildsman, Zespiarre by name, and I've got a daughter getting betrothed next month. I'll hire you to do the *Betrothal.*"

"I will accept, Maesso Zespiarre, if the fee offered is sufficient."

"Momentita!" The innkeeper held up a hand. "I want my mural done first."

"You must plaster the wall, Maesso Gaspar, and the plaster needs time to dry before I can put on the underdrawing. For the mural itself, I will need a second, thinner layer of plaster, and I can only do an arm's span wide and tall each day since this layer of painting must be accomplished while the plaster itself is wet. So there will be time for a few, select other commissions. If you can set aside a portion of this chamber, or another room, where I might do those portraits, then I would be willing to allow some viewing while I paint." She could see by his expression that the innkeeper was adding all this into his head and seeing vast new hordes of customers.

"No one will believe a pretty young woman like you can do this sort of work!" Gaspar exclaimed. "Eiha! What a fortunate chance has brought you here!" He winked. "Whoever you may truly be. . . ."

From the other room they heard the sound of music starting, a gittern and drummer, then a singer coming in. It was an old tune, a love song called "Astraventa Eventide."

Eleyna sat down, suddenly tired. She was content to wait while the servants took away the old tablecloth, set the table again, and brought the second course. She ate mechanically, not really tasting the food. Instead, she studied the wall, molding her sketch to its new proportions.

"What will I do?" said Rohario.

"What?" she asked, coming to herself at the sound of his voice.

Before Rohario could answer, they heard a swell of agitated voices from the other room, smothered by the low roar of the fire. The door into the kitchens opened, and an aproned man hurried in.

"Gaspar! The Shagarras are here! They have come to arrest the musicians for performing seditious tunes—"

Shouting from the other room drowned out his next words: "We are the Grand Duke's representatives! You must surrender to us."

"Leave them be! They're only singers."

"When will the Grand Duke allow the Corteis to meet?"

"Murderers!"

Uproar. A chair was smashed against stone. A man yelled in pain.

"Matra!" Gaspar leaped up and ran into the kitchens.

His other guests, including guildsman Zespiarre, made haste to leave. But Rohario hurried after Gaspar. Eleyna gulped down a last bit of roll and followed him. In the common room a fight raged, furious apprentices and guildsmen using fists and chairs against the armed soldiers. A hopeless fight, except for weight of numbers. And their anger, so stark that it was like a wash of color in the room.

"Bassda! I beg you!" No one heeded Gaspar.

Where had Rohario gone?

To her horror she saw him standing on the bar, waving a piece of dirty cloth to attract attention.

"Bassda! Stop!" Rohario cried with the voice of a man who is used to his slightest wish being obeyed. But the dirty cloth carried a glint of gray-silver, and Rohario's coat, picked out because it was the soberest in his extensive wardrobe, was dark blue, accentuated by a black waistcoat and black boots. In all, he seemed to represent in his own person the colors of the forbidden banner that the malcontents brandished.

A serjaent lunged through the crush and, with the butt of his ceremonial lance, hit Rohario hard on the side of the head. Like a stone, Rohario dropped. He rolled off the bar and landed hard on the floor.

➤ SEVENTY-ONE ➤

Rohario groaned.

A female voice murmured words. A moment later he felt the cool drape of a wet cloth over his forehead. He opened his eyes.

Panic clawed in his throat. He couldn't see!

Then, settling, pulse pounding, he realized he could not see because it was dark. A candle burned on the sidetable. He sat up.

Nausea overcame him, and he vomited over the side of the bed. Only after he stopped, after he could breathe normally, did he realize that one of Gaspar's maids held a pail beside his bed.

She cleaned his face and collar with a damp rag. "Is that all, Maesso? You must not sit up when you've a bump on the head."

"I'll lie down again," he murmured, and did so. His head reeled but quieted. "What happened?"

"The guards hit you, but your sister dragged you right out of the common room, and we brought you up here after so you wouldn't be arrested. Gaspar is furious, for the guards have broken most of the furniture and wouldn't even speak of paying for the damages. He's going to take his case to the magistrate. But it won't do any good, en verro, for the Grand Duke never listens to the common people."

"He doesn't?"

She snorted. She sounded remarkably hard-hearted for a girl barely of marriageable age. "Begging your pardon, Maesso, but where have you come from?"

"Not from here, I can see. What happened to the others?"

"The guard arrested all the musicians. My aunt says they are arresting musicians and printers from all over the city for speaking and printing seditious material. Only for saying what they think! But that is a crime here in Meya Suerta!"

"Where is Eleyna?"

She gestured. "In the sitting room, with Maesso Azéma. He wishes to speak to you."

Rising, bucket in hand, she left him. He dared not turn his head to follow her movement. He could not bear for Eleyna to come in and find he had been sick. It was too humiliating. Matra Dolcha! In Palasso Verrada a whole host of attendants would have been swarming around him right now and his least movement would have been the subject of intense interest. Here, he was relegated to the care of a mere slip of a servant girl. It was enough to make him feel sorry for himself.

And yet, hadn't he wanted to see what life was like outside the Palasso? Hadn't he asked to be treated with the same fine lack of concern which, evidently, was meted out to the common folk?

When Eleyna came in and sat down beside him, she actually went so far as to take his hand in hers. "You are well?" she asked earnestly.

"I suppose I am." Rohario smiled at her, then shifted his attention to her companion. Silver-haired, the old man was dressed simply, but the cut and weave of his jacket and waistcoat betrayed him: he was either wealthy or nobly-born. No one else could afford such fine, if understated, clothing. Indeed, he looked vaguely familiar.

"This is Maesso Azéma," said Eleyna. "He has been speaking to me about the protests that are sweeping the city."

"The seditionists," said Rohario.

The old man raised an expressive eyebrow. "We call ourselves Libertistas."

"You are not one of the guildsmen."

"I'm disappointed. You don't recognize me."

Rohario flushed, hearing sarcasm in the old man's tone.

Azéma bowed. "My real name is Leono do'Brendizia. I am the younger brother of Sebastiano do'Brendizia. He died many years before you were born, filho meyo. He was murdered in the ducal prison during the reign of Grand Duke Cossimio the Second."

"Surely not! There must be—"

"—some mistake? I think not. He was in excellent health. I had other sources as well, guards in the employ of the Palasso who were not, shall we say, unsympathetic to the cause my brother espoused. He wished to reconvene the Corteis, which was suspended by Arrigo the Second. When I discovered my brother had been murdered, I vowed to continue his work. However—" He held fine leather gloves, and now he slapped them lightly against the arm of his chair. "—I had no intention of losing my life in prison. I worked in secret, waiting until the time was ripe. So you find me here, now, investigating a young man who was found dressed in the blue, black, and silver of Libera, of freedom."

"*You* instigated the protests?"

He chuckled. "Not at all. When I saw what was happening, the sentiments which were boiling up all over Meya Suerta, the discontent, the anger, the call to restore the Corteis and its powers, the news from other kingdoms of revolts against the tyranny of kings and princes, I merely revealed myself and offered my resources to those guildsmen and apprentices, merchants and respectable landlords, and suggested a few ways in which they might organize for greater effectiveness. The guildsmen of Meya Suerta can easily grow rebellious on their own account. They did not trust me at first. Why should they trust the cousin of the Baron do'Brendizia? But they came to see that I was useful, because I could go to and from Court at will. So. Why are you *here*, Rohario do'Verrada, and not at Palasso Verrada? I must add that your lovely 'sorella' revealed no hint of your true identity or your purpose here."

Rohario did not like the way he smiled at Eleyna, what he might be insinuating about Eleyna's companionship or about his own interest in the young woman. Old rich men like that always thought they could buy anything they wanted!

Irritated, he released Eleyna's hand. "I am *not* the son of Grand Duke Renayo."

"You do not expect me to believe that, I hope?"

"I mean to say I do not expect anyone to know who my parents are. I am not here to trade on my father's authority. I will thank you to keep your knowledge to yourself."

"I will gladly do so," said the old man with a deceptively sweet smile, "unless I find that your presence here threatens the safety of those who are working so very hard for reform. Nor would I want to jeopardize the safety of your lovely sorella, whose identity I have not, alas, ascertained, although from gossip I have heard these past two days at Court I might venture to guess."

"I trust you will not do so in any public place!" By now Rohario was thoroughly irritated by Azéma's arrogant manner. Truly, a man born to the castello could not disguise his origins.

Azéma's smile seemed patently false. "I always take pains to safeguard beautiful women. I must go. Gaspar knows how to reach me, my lord." He bowed, slightingly, turned to take Eleyna's hand in his own, and kissed it. "Florha meya, you must never hesitate if you are in any kind of trouble to ask for my protection."

"I thank you," said Eleyna stiffly. She did not look grateful for the old man's offer.

Azéma bowed again and left the room.

Rohario, suddenly tired, rubbed a hand over his eyes. He had a headache.

"Everyone thinks I'm your mistress," Eleyna blurted into the silence.

Would that it were so!

"I will make such a reputation for myself," she added in a low, burning voice, "that in time no man in Meya Suerta or anywhere in Tira Virte will think of me as anything or anyone except *the artist Eleyna Grijalva.*"

Rohario winced. The motion thrust a stab of pain through his right temple. He bit down on his tongue before he gasped from the pain, but a tiny grunt escaped him.

"Eiha! I beg your pardon for letting Masseo Azéma disturb you, but he is not the sort of man it is easy to say 'No' to."

"I am tired," he murmured. She patted his hand gently and went to find the servant girl, leaving him alone.

He sighed, heartsore, disliking himself right now as much as he had often suspected his own mother disliked him, although of course he had never truly known. Always he chose the easy path: to avoid the real conflict. To avoid speaking with Eleyna about what he truly felt for her. Or what she felt for him.

She liked him, of that he was sure. But even if she could love him, what was he or any man except an obstacle thrown in the way of her painting? And although men—Edoard, his father, the Grijalva limners—thought her more important as a woman they might use to their advantage or their pleasure rather than as an artist, Rohario could not make himself believe it would be better for her to love him than for her to paint. Not after seeing her paint. Not after falling in love with her in great measure because of her gift, a gift he did not share. *A passable talent for art.*

At last, with his head still hurting and the squalid little room dark and stinking of pine oil, he drifted off to sleep.

⚷

In the morning, feeling chastened but not ill, Rohario found Eleyna setting up shop in the dining room, which Gaspar had given over to her entirely until she had finished her mural—with the proviso that customers might dine at a small table or drink while watching her. Wet plaster covered half the wall already.

"You look much better," she said, but she was not really paying attention to him after one close look into his face.

He excused himself and walked out into the city to seek employment. The first day he wandered and stared and came back empty-handed. He had no idea how to "look" for work, and his fine clothing caused more than one passerby to mock him.

Embarrassed by his failure, he spent the next nine days wandering the city, returning only at evening. Nine of his ten mareias went piecemeal in exchange for laundry services, cheap wine, two new neckcloths, a shine for his boots, and bread for the filthy child beggars whose wasted faces broke his heart. It pained him to know that his board and room were provided by Eleyna. But what else could he do but be beholden to her now and hope to repay her later? He had no skills—of course! What nobleman's son did? His passable talent for art might, in an isolated village, be enough to get him employment as a draftsman, but not in Meya Suerta. He was good for nothing except to return to the Palasso, beg his father's pardon, and return to his old life. And this he would not do.

Eleyna had drawn, in charcoal, a huge cartoon onto the plastered wall in the dining room of Gaspar's inn, the sketch over which she would lay down the mural. Now, every day when he returned to the inn, he found a new man-sized segment erupted in brilliant paint over the white background. Padron Gaspar appeared, with generous eyes and round red cheeks, the very icon of the provident patron dispensing his bounty to his deserving and grateful flock. Vines swathed the doorway to the inn and wheat flowered in every niche, so bright and lifelike that he wanted to touch the golden sheaves.

Each day, beside her easel, Rohario found new sketches, for contracts, for *Wills* and *Deeds,* for *Births, Deaths, Marriages,* for the *Betrothal* of Maesso Zespiarre's daughter to a clothier's son.

The more she worked, the more beautiful she became in his eyes. She was flowering.

"At first they came just because I'm young and a woman," she told him, "out of curiosity, like going to see a fish that can live out of water or a dog that can walk on its hind legs. Now they come because they know I am good." She looked up, and his heart fell over itself, but he said nothing. "And you?"

He shrugged.

Glancing once around, she drew a sheet of paper out from underneath the pile. "Look at this," she said in a low voice. The subject matter surprised him: he did not recognize the interior, a semicircle of terraced benches rather like a theater, but he knew at once by the assembly gathered there in their antique costumes that this was a representation of a meeting of the Corteis.

"Eleyna!"

"Bassda!" In a whisper. "Do you like it?"

"You could be arrested for this!"

"It won't be traced back to me. I am going to do a few pen and ink drawings for Maesso Azéma, for the broadsides. It's all very well to print up words, but how many men can read? What of women, who might receive only enough education to do their accounts and to read in the Holy Verses? Just as *Wills* and *Deeds* and *Marriages,* all of these contracts, are done in paintings, so also *protest* can be done in painting. A word can have a thousand meanings, or none at all. Yet if these ideas are drawn as pictures, so that every man and woman can see them, then there will be more who understand."

"But why are you doing this?"

Her expression grew troubled. "En verro, in part because I do not trust Azéma. If I aid the Libertistas, then is it not less likely he will tell my family where I am?"

"You said they wouldn't care where you are."

"I hope they do not, but I don't know. Anyway, Rohario, is what the Libertistas ask for so much? That the people who pay the tax levied by the Grand Duke be allowed to grant permission before the Grand Duke asks for any extraordinary tax? That the Grand Duke and the nobles be subject to the same laws everyone else is?" Now her tone became bitter. "It is no different in Palasso Grijalva. *Some* are given greater privilege and honor than others."

"It doesn't seem too much to ask."

She slid the sketch back under the other papers and turned away from him, back toward her easel. She smelled of paint now, oils and turpentine and other, odder, richer scents. "Regretto— I ought not to criticize your father."

"You must know, Eleyna, that you are free to say anything you wish to me!"

She smiled again, but absently, and returned to work.

The next day, loitering in a wine shop and wondering if it was worth spending his last mareia on a tolerably good white to bring as a present to Eleyna, Rohario overheard the proprietor complaining to a customer.

"Bah! Zelio has the bone-fever again and I must have a letter written by tonight's tide for the ship to Niapali."

A letter written. Rohario stepped to the counter. "I can write, Maesso."

The proprietor looked him over suspiciously. "Have you a good hand? The letter is for a Niapalese wine merchant and must be in the best hand, with no mistakes."

"I have a good hand." This, certainly, was true. "I was trained by a man who now works as a clerk in Palasso Verrada." Also true, if misleading.

"Eiha!" Impressed, the proprietor let his gaze linger on the fine cloth of Rohario's waistcoat. "Down on your luck, no? I will engage you, Maesso, but only pay if the work meets my liking."

Rohario thought fast. "You will provide tools?"

"The parchment. That is usual, of course."

But he must have his own pens, ink, and nibs. "I will return as soon as I fetch my things." He practically ran out of the shop.

The proprietor called after him: "Don't be too long or I will hire someone else!"

It took Rohario half an hour to track down a shop that sold writing tools and two questions once there to ascertain that his remaining mareia would not suffice to buy what he needed. Outside the shop, cursing, he realized he had no choice. He made his way to the Avenida Shagarra and headed up the long slope that led to Palasso Verrada. He had never known what a very long walk it was, all the way up the hill.

The Palasso rose in all its elegant glory above him. It looked vast and cold, and the gates were shut. He paused to brush self-consciously at his coat. Though clean, it had lost its satiny luster: the menninas at Gaspar's were not trained laundresses such as the ones employed at the Palasso, and he had brought only one change of clothing from Chasseriallo, only as much as he could easily carry on the horse which had been returned to the hunting lodge with the groom who had attended them—well paid to keep his mouth shut. Matra! He looked like a clerk rather than a duke's son. But was that not what he intended to become?

The guards on duty recognized him immediately. No chance for a furtive journey up to his suite. With an escort of four gold-sashed Shagarra guards, he was hustled in the main entrance and up the monumental stairs that led to the Grand Duke's study.

The Grand Duke did not look up as Rohario entered the room. He signed his name to a paper and shifted it aside to look over the next document. Nor did Renayo's voice betray any emotion. "You may go, Captain. So, Rohario, you have magnanimously chosen to return. Is the Grijalva woman with you?"

"No." His father's reasonable tone made Roharo nervous.

"But you know where she is, I hope?"

"Yes."

"Where is that?"

"I am not at liberty to say."

Renayo deigned now to lift his head and examine Roharo. He looked entirely bland. Then, unexpectedly, he barked out a laugh. "Eiha! I hear she's a taking thing. I hope you have enjoyed yourself, but she must be restored to her family."

"She is her own mistress, Patro, not mine."

A Zhinna vase of royal blue-and-white ceramic filled with a bouquet of white iris sat on Renayo's desk. He fingered it now, expression darkening, and turned it halfway round, so the scene painted on it shifted: a man bearing a burden crossed a bridge; a hill and two spindly trees, also in royal blue, curved off around to the hidden side. "This is not a game, Rohario. The Grijalvas are more important to our family than you can imagine. Edoard and his young Beatriz are by all reports very happy. While I might be amused now by your youthful daring, it will not amuse me for long, I assure you."

"She does not want to return to her family."

"So you have abandoned her?" This said threateningly.

But Rohario discovered, to his amazement, that his father's threats no longer scared him. "No. I merely returned here for my pens and ink."

"Your *pens?*"

"Yes. I am making my way as a clerk."

Renayo slapped a hand down, hard, scattering paper as he rose. "A *clerk?*" he roared.

The door opened. "Your Grace?" A courtier looked in with a startled expression.

"Shut that door! Get out! Sit down, you young pup!"

"No, grazzo. If you will excuse me, I will be going."

"You will not be going! You will explain yourself!"

"There is nothing to explain." As soon as the words popped out, Rohario felt a tremendous sense of relief, followed hard by a wave of excitement so intense he had to forcibly stop his hands from shaking. "I am no longer living in the Palasso."

"You cannot—"

"I am of age."

"You have no money—!"

"I have Marissiallo and Collara Asaddo, two properties you settled on me when I turned twelve. As soon as I—" He faltered. *As soon as I earn enough money to hire a horse to ride out to them, and see about diverting a portion of their rents for my immediate needs so I can establish myself . . . and Eleyna . . . in a decent apartamento, a place large enough for a studio for her, then perhaps, perhaps, it might be appropriate to think of asking her to be . . . to become. . . .* He swallowed, unable to speak past the sudden constriction in his throat.

The Grand Duke's study had once been a somber room with heavy, dark woodwork, fitting a duke's sober and weighty responsibilities. After Renayo's marriage to Johannah it had been redone in the Friesemarkian style: the woodwork removed, new plaster laid on and painted a pale tangerine with delicately-rendered floral patterns added for accent. The only tasteful room in the entire palasso, it suited the Grand Duke not at all.

"I cannot imagine what you think you are doing." Renayo sounded almost bewildered.

I am breaking free. But Rohario could not say it.

"I begin to think I do not know you, Rohario. Imagine what your mother would say to all this!"

Rohario flinched. He could well imagine what his mother would say to all this. But he was determined not to let her stop him. "Did you know," he said slowly, picking his words hesitantly, "that many of the common people in the city are discontented? They are angry with you for arresting singers and printers, just for speaking their minds."

"For speaking out against *me*. I would be a fool to allow such idle talk, to allow agitators—no doubt gathered like vultures from Ghillas and Taglis—to incite the people of Meya Suerta to riot. But perhaps you would approve of them storming the Palasso. Perhaps we ought to throw Timarra out to them as a sop to their *discontentment*."

"I have heard no talk of storming the Palasso! They want to reconvene the Corteis. The Corteis will not even have as much power as your own conselhos—"

"Only the power to interfere with taxation, to present any sort of ridiculous petitions they might then think they can impose as law. Even, Matra Dolcha, the right to sit in judgment on nobles or even on myself if they so see fit! How am I to govern with these restrictions? We do'Verradas have made Tira Virte a rich country, with prosperity and peace enough to enjoy those riches. They will destroy it in a decade with their quibbling and rioting and demands."

"You don't know that would happen. The Corteis will only be an advisory body."

"And then?" Renayo crossed suddenly to a side table and poured himself tea from the silver urn. Everything in this room, except the white irises, came courtesy of his new wife. Renayo took his tea in one gulp and set the cup down so hard that it chipped. His face was flushed with anger. "Then you can be sure rogues and ruffians and men with no concern but their own gain would insinuate themselves into the proceedings. You can be sure every sort of criminal will be setting fire to this Palasso and murdering every man, woman, and child they find within these walls. As they did in Ghillas. Is that what you want?"

"Of course not! But most of these discontented men are honest guildsmen and merchants. They have as much to lose as you do if the worst comes to pass."

"Eiha! I have raised a lunatic!" Renayo crossed back to his desk, shoved aside the table globe, sending a quill pen tumbling to the floor, and leaned across the desk to glare at Rohario. "Now you listen to me, young sir. Young noblemen have gotten involved with these seditionists before, thinking it an exciting diversion while they're not out hunting. They have, each and every one of them, ended badly. I see you are just as light-minded. I wash my hands of you until you are ready to beg my pardon for this folly."

Rohario could not take his eyes off the pen, which leaked black ink onto the pale frost-and-lily Lillone carpet, which had cost, he now knew, as much as a year's lodging at Gaspar's inn. He forced himself to lift his eyes and look directly at his father. "I cannot do that."

The Grand Duke appeared to be on the edge of an apoplectic fit. "Then I banish you from my presence!"

"Do I have your leave to go, Your Grace?"

"Get out! *Out!*"

Rohario bowed stiffly. He turned. He was a string drawn so tightly that a breath of air would set it thrumming. But he walked without faltering, he left the room without wavering, he spoke briefly, without a tremor, to the attendants outside.

"I am going first to my rooms."

Not his rooms any longer. That his father would simply let him walk away stunned him. But perhaps Grand Duchess Johannah was already pregnant; perhaps Renayo thought he had no further use for his troublesome second son. Two stewards and two guards escorted him. His servants arrived, agitated and pale.

"Don Rohario! How have you fared? Are you well? Is it true that His Grace has banished you? Surely, if you beg for his pardon—"

Still half-stunned, Rohario gathered up his writing tools, rifled through his safe box until he found the deeds to his two properties. He unrolled them and considered the fine hand of Cabral Grijalva, which had rendered the scene and the transfer with loving detail. Rolling them up, he tucked them into a small trunk. He could not resist taking more clothes. Finally he gazed long and hard at the *Birth of Cossima* that hung over his mantel. It was a difficult farewell to the laughing baby who had brightened his every morning.

"Regretto," he said to his frantic body servant, to his downcast steward, "but I must go. Be sure to apply to Don Edoard. He will see that you find new positions."

"Eiha! It cannot be, Don Rohario. No one dresses as elegantly as you. All my fine work will be for nothing on some oaf who cannot tie his neckcloth with the least semblance of style or tell a well-cut coat from one which is merely fashionable. Let me come with you!"

"When I am settled such that I can employ a body servant, you can be sure you are the only man I would trust for that job. But now is not the time, I fear."

At last he extricated himself from their clutches. At last he lugged the trunk down to the gates, which closed behind him. Mindful of what little coin he had left, Rohario carried the trunk for perhaps half a long block down the hill. But he was not accustomed to such labor and had to stop.

"Amico!" He waved a hand and a young man driving a pony cart filled with barrels of olive oil pulled up beside him. "Might I pay you to convey me to the Wheat Sheaf and Sickle?"

The young man had a round, laughing face, and a blue and black kerchief tied around his neck, trimmed with silver ribbon. "I know that place. But it's out of my way. How much can you offer?"

"Here it is, all of it," Rohario said recklessly, pulling out his last mareia.

"Eiha! You look to be a fellow after my own heart, though I wish I knew where to find clothes as fine as those. I'll take you as a favor."

Rohario hoisted his trunk into the back and clambered up. "My thanks."

Cast out from his father's house. Severed at last from his mother's remains. It was too terrible to imagine.

Free to make his own way, however clumsily. And not alone. The day looked brighter already.

SEVENTY-TWO

Thirty-five days of Louissa's nattering was enough to drive any man mad. Although her voice was soft, it had the odd and irritating quality of permeating any room she was in. Two days until the Holy Days of Penitenssia began, six until the Dia Fuega ball. The time had come to act. But right now, this last evening, with an icy rain spattering the paned window and Alazais engaged in embroidering a pillow cover while Louissa read aloud to her from the latest Doumas novel, Sario wanted only to escape from the attic.

Louissa was not the curious sort, to go rummaging about the room once he left. In any case, he had trained Alazais to exacting specifications; she would safeguard his secrets as well as her own. He excused himself and left the attic.

A few broadsheets lay tossed on Oliviano's worktable. Sario noted them with a frown, then bent closer, intrigued. Someone had thought of illustrating the tracts.

The printed pen-and-ink drawing depicted the hangings out on the border of the marshlands. Seven men dangled with limbs as lifeless as puppets; the eighth was still struggling. Women wept. Old men clenched their hands. A thin-faced child, cleverly thrust into the foreground, tugged threadbare clothing tightly around itself, face pinched with cold. Beyond, soldiers of the Shagarra Regiment, each one warm in a cape and padded by years of good eating, watched impassively.

He knew this hand. He had studied her paintings and sketches in that brief month he had resided at Palasso Grijalva after returning from Ghillas. He never had managed to speak with her, except that once, in the zocalo, their interview broken by that damned riot that had erupted during the Iluminares Procession.

He set the first broadsheet down and picked up another. This one pictured the Corteis as it might look, meeting in the Palasso Justissia.

Eleyna Grijalva was drawing seditious material for the Libertistas. How had this happened? Her parents and uncle had sent her off to be the next Mistress.

The third broadsheet showed a family begging in the streets while beyond, through a great lighted window, one saw into the dining hall of a nobleman's palasso where a feast was taking place. It was too crudely sentimental for his taste. Did Eleyna suppose that if the Corteis reconvened, the poor would somehow miraculously vanish? For most of his lives, the Corteis had met in some form. It had only been abolished during—*whose body was I in?*—during Ettoro's time, of course, while Arrigo II was Grand Duke. The Corteis had looked after its own, and *its own* had never, in his experience, included the destitute. There had always been poor people, and such people would no doubt remain in their Matra-ordained place. He felt no particular sympathy for them, although the baby's face drawn lax with hunger was quite well executed, enough to stir a tendril of compassion in his breast. Footsteps and the sound of laughter came from the next room.

Sario pushed the three broadsheets under an account book and pushed open the door that led into the main shop. He surveyed the room. Many customers crowded in, no doubt buying an extra share of wine and ale for the upcoming Penitenssia festivities. Once the Holy Days had been celebrated with more solemnity. In recent years it seemed to Sario that it had mostly become an excuse to get drunk for four days. Eiha!

Oliviano's wife and four sons were busy behind the counter; Oliviano himself sat at a small table haggling with a young man who, by his quill pen and ink-stained fingers, was the new clerk. The clerk looked familiar, but Sario could not place him. After all these years, faces blended together; a nose, a lift of the eyebrow, a dimpling chin, might evoke memories of other faces, other times, and the two, mixing, lost their original essence and became just another half remembered vision. Chance meetings, *Treaties,* portraits, lovers, great upheavals, all had begun to blur into one inchoate mural out of which a few moments stood in stark relief. Only his portrait of Saavedra remained for him as clear and perfectly recalled as on the day he had laid down each brushstroke.

The door to the street opened. A woman, hair hooded against the rain by a widow's shawl, came in. She slid the shawl down to reveal a mass of luxuriant black hair. Il Cofforro would have loved to paint that hair. The clerk looked up; the two exchanged what Sario thought of as "a significant glance."

An instant later, he recognized her.

Eleyna Grijalva! Not cozily ensconced with Don Edoard, nor safely confined to Palasso Grijalva. What were her parents thinking? Widow she might be, but she was young, pretty, and—most importantly—possessed of a talent *he* intended to mold. She could absolutely not be allowed to roam the streets of Meya Suerta.

The door opened again, admitting the smell of the marsh and the sound of bell-ringers on their nightly rounds. "Curfew! Curfew!"

The customers filtered away, complaining in muted voices about the curfew instituted ten days ago by the Commandante of the city guard. The clerk received his pay—knowing Oliviano, less than the work was worth—and rose. He and the Grijalva woman left together.

Sario followed them.

He kept to the shadows, as they did. He expected them to cross the Zocalo Grando without incident, but here, in the great square fronting the Cathedral, they stopped. It was cold and deathly quiet; not one soul stirred. The rain had ceased. But it was the curfew, not winter rains, that had brought soberness back to the city as it prepared for Penitenssia.

The clerk lit a lantern. *Moronno!* A light was sure to bring guards down on them.

Then Sario saw what Eleyna Grijalva was doing: she drew on the stone front of the cathedral, sketching, quickly but surely, a huge chalk mural. Grand Duke Renayo with the Shagarra Regiment at his back held a sword poised over a cluster of poor people who knelt on stone; behind them, a young man dressed in apprentice leathers waved the banner of the Libertistas.

To profane the Cathedral! It was blasphemy. Sario admired her effrontery. It was the kind of thing *he* would have done: Qal Venommo. The poisoned pen.

Once, the clerk shuttered the lantern. Secure in the shadow of the portallas, Sario watched a group of guards walk their horses through the zocalo by the light of their own torches. They passed through without incident and vanished down the Avenida Shagarra.

The lantern flared back to life. A solitary bell tolled the midnight watch before Eleyna finished the mural. Lantern extinguished, the Grijalva woman and her companion hurried away down a side street, gray shadows against paler stone.

Sario slipped after them. Once, they hid while another patrol stalked by. Once, they encountered a pair of night lurkers, but whispered words passed between them, a hiss of *Corteis!*—and on they went, unimpeded. At last Sario tracked them to their lair, a nondescript inn marked by the sign of a sheaf of wheat and a sickle. Eleyna and the clerk disappeared together under the entrance arch.

Eleyna Grijalva and her talent belong to me. Mine to nurture and teach, to bring to fruition. I will make her flower, as no other man can.

He did not intend to lose her to a clerk! To the callow, sentimental art of Libertista politics! Matra forbid her gift be squandered in such a way.

Only he could make sure that she gain her rightful place among the great artists of the Grijalva line, even if she had not been blessed with the Luza do'Orro. A light shone in her, even if she did not have the Gift. That was the mistake the moualimos had made all along, thinking that only a Gifted male could be a great painter.

Over the years, Sario had seen otherwise. There had been none to equal himself, of course, but over many lifetimes he had known, nurtured, fought with, and respected painters, Grijalva and otherwise, who had no Gift but only their eyes, their hands, and their ambition. Even foreigners, estranjieros never met but known through their work, might rival, though never surpass, his talent. All must be seen, must be studied, must be consumed, so that in time he could paint the masterwork that would dwarf all other achievements, that would confirm, for all to see, his mastery of the Golden Key.

Sario returned to his atelierro at dawn. Alazais slept peacefully. The night's work brought back old and troubling memories: Qal Venommo, the poisoned pen.

It was Zevierin who had drawn those caricatures of Arrigo. He had never found proof, but he *knew* it had been Zevierin, with Leilias' connivance. What had been the result of all that fighting between Tazia and Mechella? Nothing important—except the destruction of Rafeyo's hopes and life.

Sario opened the chest and carefully unwrapped his skull, setting it on the table. They regarded each other, he and the skull, living eyes met with empty dead ones. Yet not dead, because Sario still lived and would always live. His own eyes stared at him from the *Peintraddo Memorrio, his* eyes in a dozen different faces. He could not always remember what name went with which face, but what did that matter? All were Sario. Sario alone mattered.

And Saavedra, of course. What he did, he did for her and for the greater glory of Grijalva art. Not for himself.

He sat down in the chair—Alejandro's much-repaired chair, he thought idly—wet a brush with his saliva, and began to paint a watercolor portrait of Louissa. Her delicate hands, clutching a garland of wild geraniums, grew gnarled and swollen as he filled in their color. For the next two days, while he and Alazais had need of her services as they made ready to leave, she must only wonder at the aching in her hands. The full assault of the bone-fever—the arthritis, as the physicians named it now—must wait. Louissa's deterioration must in no way be linked to him. Her eyes in the portrait gained the faintest film of white. . . .

But no. He was remembering Tomaz. There was no need to make her blind. He painted tiny cracks in her lips and a slight swelling to her throat. She must become mute. If the Viehos Fratos had made Tomaz mute, Sario would never have learned what he needed to know, but that had been the moualimos' mistake, thinking nothing important would be left Tomaz once his hands and eyes were ruined. Matra! That had been long ago. He glanced at the skull. Long ago, and Tomaz long since turned to dust.

Alazais stirred, coming immediately awake. It was an unnatural habit of hers, not one he had taught her. She was either oblivious or alert.

"What are you doing?" she asked in her childlike way. He could never predict what questions she would ask.

"I am protecting you." He finished the portrait and surveyed it with a frown. Not his best work but sufficient to the task. He left it to dry while he penned a quick note.

> To Familia Grijalva.
> If you are desirous of knowing the whereabouts of one of your own, you will find her at the Sign of the Wheat Sheaf and Sickle. For your own protection you would be well advised to recover her, for she is involved in Libertista agitation. Look to the broadsheets. That she lives in a common inn does not speak well for the reputation of the family.
> For your own good, I sign myself, A Concerned Observer.

"When Maessa Louissa comes, Alazais, you will ask her to pack your things." Once the watercolor was dry, he tucked the paper inside a chest and locked the lid. Then he took the message downstairs and asked Oliviano to pay a boy to deliver it to Palasso Grijalva.

Louissa arrived. She received the news—that they would be leaving in two days—with a downcast face and many abrupt protestations of sorrow, delivered in a newly hoarse voice. But she collected the various gowns she had ordered at different dressmakers, showed Alazais how to carry herself in them, how to hold her hands with half gloves, with a shawl, with a fan. She packed Alazais' things carefully, with little reminders of proper names for fabric and the correct occasion for certain styles. She did not complain of pain in her hands, but Sario watched her carefully and saw that she paused to rub her knuckles frequently. Having suffered the bone-fever himself in more than one life, he recognized the gesture.

On the second evening he paid her a generous sum, and she left, still crying.

"Are you going to kill her?" asked Alazais dispassionately.

"Why would you think such a thing?" he asked, genuinely curious. He had made no such suggestion to her.

"She knows we have been here."

He raised one eyebrow. "You have your father's political instincts, I see. Ought I to kill her?"

"She was kind, but she is no longer useful."

"Not useful to us, true. But she is an exiled Ghillasian like yourself, Alazais. That should provoke some sympathy in you."

"Should it?" she asked without irony.

"Yes, it should. It is your duty to be sympathetic. To be kind. The people will love you for it. Your relative, the Grand Duchess Mechella, was a master at using a kind heart, a gentle manner, and a sympathetic ear to gain the loyalty of the people. You would do well to emulate her."

"Then you should spare Maessa Louissa's life."

"That is what *you* must choose. I must choose to spare her life because to kill her would raise more suspicions than simply to have her decline into ill health. Now it is time to sleep. At dawn, we leave for Arguena, where we will meet up with your loyal retainers."

She slept.

In the morning, he opened his chest one last time before locking the atelierro and his *Peintraddo Memorrio* away. He wrapped his skull in velvet and placed it inside, then removed the heavy gold ring affixed with the seal of the Ghillasian royal house, the Swan, and gave it to Alazais. "This is yours. Your father had this made for you when you turned fourteen and celebrated your first Mirraflores Moon. It is the symbol of your right to bear the name Alazais de Ghillas, heir to the throne held by your father."

She nodded gravely and slipped the ring on her right ring finger. It fit perfectly.

Then Sario locked the room and led her out, swathed in a cloak, her lace shawl draped over her hair and face. The unwieldy portrait—of attic and floor and ghostly ground in the shape of a woman—he wrapped in blankets and carried out to the cart himself. They traveled north all of Dia Sola. It was appropriate, was it not, that they two travel alone on the day of solitude?

They reached Arguena as the midday bell rang on Dia Memorrio, and there found great rejoicing when Princess Alazais was reunited with her Ghillasian maidservant—who flung herself weeping at the Princess' feet—and the two soldiers. So, thought Sario wryly, are the dead reunited with the living.

Sario related to the waiting servants the awful story of Alazais' narrow escape, of her horrific ordeal at the hands of her enemies, an ordeal which had robbed her of her wits. Of how he had discovered that she lived, had bargained with her captors, had rescued her and brought her here, now, and intended to bring her safely to the court of the do'Verradas.

"There is no time to lose," he said solemnly. "Is it not appropriate that Princess Alazais be brought to safety at a time of year when we remember the dead?"

"Can we trust the do'Verradas?" asked the older brother, still suspicious.

"Eiha, amico, you must remember Grand Duke Renayo's own mother was a Ghillasian princess. He and his sons have a claim to the Ghillasian throne. Princess Alazais must have a husband. Is it not better she have a sympathetic one?"

"I do not know what to think," murmured the older brother, glancing at Sario's golden key, but he was wavering.

"Let me be blunt, amico." Not too blunt; to give away the whole of his plan would be premature. "I have much sympathy for the girl, it is true. Any man would. But especially I do not like the chaos, these ruffians, these *barbaricos,* who have destroyed the Pallaiso Millia Luminnai in Aute-Ghillas. They have burned Grijalva paintings. *Mine!*" From previous lives, it was true, so the blood no longer affected him. Still! "You cannot imagine what an insult that is to a man like myself! We Grijalvas cannot flourish where there is anarchy. I wish for a return to peace and order. The crown of Ghillas lies in the gutter. Shall we leave it there? Or shall we aid those who wish to return it to its rightful place?"

They left Arguena the next morning in a hired carriage, heading south for Meya Suerta. It was the day of Herva ei Ferro, when apparitions were paraded through the streets. No one else, en verro, could have planned it so perfectly.

No one but Sario Grijalva.

⚷ SEVENTY-THREE ⚷

At first, returning to Gaspar's inn weary from a day of writing and composing letters, Roharío thought nothing of the clot of guardsmen who stood in the street outside the sign of the Wheat Sheaf and Sickle. The curfew bells had not yet rung, but in this twilit hour after businesses closed and people hurried home, more and more small "incidents" took place. The Grand Duke now sent his regiments out in force to keep the peace.

Roharío smiled, thinking of the furor that had erupted in the zocalo yesterday at dawn when Eleyna's mural was discovered. It had taken a dozen guardsmen half the morning to scrub the stone clean of chalk. And while they worked a crowd had gathered to watch, to sing, to taunt. Some few rash young men had gotten their heads knocked about by equally rash young guardsmen. A skirmish had been averted by the timely appearance of the frail Premia Sancta, at whose appearance every soul there knelt respectfully.

Roharío ducked his head down as he passed the loitering guards and walked down the tunnel that led into the courtyard of the inn. No need to risk them recognizing him. Ahead, he heard raised voices: Gaspar arguing with a customer again.

Roharío blinked as he came into the courtyard. Torches flared everywhere, drenching the quadrangle in smoke. Guardsmen in the green tunics and gold baldrics of the Shagarra Regiment filled half the courtyard. His heart caught in his throat when he saw clearly the tall, lean man who argued with Gaspar. Dressed richly but simply, this man wore a sigil at his throat: a golden key.

Roharío started forward just as the double doors to the inn slammed open and three men—not guardsmen but servants dressed in Grijalva livery—dragged a struggling Eleyna Grijalva out into the courtyard.

She was furious. Her gaze fastened on the man wearing the golden key. "Zio Giaberto! How can you stomach being party to this abduction? I will not go back!" She kicked one of her captors in the shins. Cursing, he let go of her.

"Eleyna!" Her uncle looked no less angry. "If we have to lock

you in a room, you will return to Palasso Grijalva and do as your
elders bid you!"

"I am not your servant! I am of age, and a widow. I am free to do
with my life what I wish."

By this time, inching closer, Rohario had come within a body's
length of Eleyna's uncle, close enough to hear him reply more
softly: "No Grijalva is free to do as he wishes. Not you, not any of
us. Esteban, Gonsalvo, carry her if you must. I will hire a cart if
necessary. I need not remind you what the penalty is if she does not
reach the Palasso safely."

The two Grijalva servants jerked Eleyna backward. Rohario
lunged, pushing forward between two startled guardsmen. He went
not for Giaberto Grijalva's head or chest, but for his hands.
Grabbing Giaberto's right hand, Rohario bent the middle and ring
fingers back until they strained.

Giaberto froze. "Stop!" he said in a hoarse voice to the guardsmen who surrounded them.

"Let her go," said Rohario. "You have no right to take her away
if she does not want to go."

"We have every right. She is a Grijalva." Giaberto's face had
gone white. "These guardsmen are here under your father's authority, Don Rohario. Will you go against his wishes?"

"I will!"

"No, Rohario." Eleyna spoke quickly, out of breath. "We cannot
win against so many. There are other ways. . . ."

The urgency of her words worked on him so powerfully that
his grip slackened. At once Giaberto yanked his hand free.
Guardsmen broke between them, slamming Rohario up against a
wall. Through the pain he thought for an instant he saw the face
of the swaggering apprentice who had attacked him at the
Iluminarres Procession. But no, these were the same Shagarrans
sworn to protect him.

"Eleyna!" They dragged her away. He could not break free. "At
least do not forbid her to paint!" he cried out after them. Her uncle
jerked once at the sound of Rohario's voice and then turned resolutely away.

Across the courtyard he caught a last glimpse of Eleyna's pale
face. She stared toward him. The force of her gaze was so strong he
strained forward. She was trying to tell him something. The guards
shoved him back; his head cracked on stone, and for a few moments he saw nothing but gray.

Then he was free. The guards surged down the tunnel, out to the street. Eleyna was gone.

He slumped down to the ground, rubbing his head, cradling his other hand against his chest. Damp oozed through his fine trousers: he was sitting in a patch of mud churned up by the morning's rain, but he could not care enough to move.

"Maesso Rohario! Are you hurt? Can you stand up?" Gaspar helped him to his feet, although Rohario scarcely cared whether he was sitting or standing. "Chiros! They charge onto my property! Drag away an innocent woman! Who will be next?" People crowded out from the inn to gape. Rohario registered Eleyna's mural through the dining room windows, a brilliant splash of color stained plain white only in one last unfinished corner. "Which of us will they drag away next? Do we not even have the freedom to live in our own houses? To hire a painter to paint a mural on a wall?"

Slowly Gaspar's words penetrated Rohario's aching head and heart. He lifted his head, though it throbbed horribly.

"Is that not what the Corteis is meant to do?" Rohario asked, his voice gaining strength as he spoke. "Is it not a body of citizens who may safeguard the people of Meya Suerta against the Grand Duke's excesses? Any powerful noble family may call on the Grand Duke for assistance. But what of you, Maesso? Can you go to Renayo and ask his assistance if there has been some injustice in your business? If taxes are raised? Who will help us, when the guardsmen come? Who will help you? Eiha!" Pain stabbed through his temples, and he had to hide his tears with a hand.

"Come, amico," said Gaspar. "You must lie down."

But in the dim chamber, on his soft bed, Rohario could not rest. "Send a message to Maesso Azéma," he said to Gaspar. "I must speak to him."

Gaspar hesitated, then spoke. "You are not a commoner, are you, my lord? I heard the chi'patro limner call you *Don* Rohario."

"Does it matter who I am? Matra ei Filho! Let us not suspect our allies lest they become our enemies."

"Of course it matters," said Gaspar softly. "If it is true you are the Grand Duke's son, then *you* can become the leader of the Libertistas."

It was too much to consider. His skull ached horribly. "Figurehead, en verro. That is what they would want of me."

"That would depend, I suppose, on your own strength." Gaspar smiled with genuine sympathy. "Rest now, amico. There will be time to speak later."

That night someone set fire to the Palasso Justissia on the Zocalo Grando. Rohario saw the smear of ugly hot light through the windows every time he woke from his restless sleep. The fire faded toward dawn, but smoke and low clouds shrouded Meya Suerta all day, a sullen mirror to the unease that hung over the inn, the streets, the city itself.

SEVENTY-FOUR

At dawn she paced out her prison, measuring it, noting the couch covered in the finest blue Zhinna silk, the Niapalese chair and table, and the single painting, a remarkable study of the Grand Duchess Mechella as a young woman presiding over the festival of Astraventa, one hand resting on the tousled head of her younger son, Renayo, the other holding a mirror that reflected a star. And yet Cabral's fine portrait was doomed to languish in this side room because of the prohibition made centuries before by the Ecclesia that art should depict no mother and son together except the Matra ei Filho. Yet if Cabral had been Gifted, she thought, the Grijalvas would have championed his beautiful painting, not hidden it away like this.

Without question, he was the best Grijalva painter alive today. She paced. Perhaps not better than the young Itinerarrio, Sario, who had come and gone before she had been able to meet him. She recalled him vaguely from classes in the ducal Galerria, ten years ago: He had shown no particular spark then, but it was not unknown for a boy's Gift to mature late. The sketches Sario had produced during his Itinerrario service had been fascinating. This was someone, she was sure, who understood what she wanted to do.

Alas, Sario Grijalva had left to resume Itinerrario service. Andreo had been too stupid to keep him here. Moronnos! They could not see quality when it sat in front of their noses!

Eiha! Pointless to think about it.

She paced, measuring the room. Fourteen paces by nine paces, a room on the third floor, hidden away in the warren that was the oldest part of the compound. A couch, a chair and table, a bed and washstand; all furniture of the finest workmanship but a prison's furniture nevertheless. At least she had Cabral's painting to study. Grazzo do'Matra that there were windows in this chamber. There would be light enough to paint during the day. If they gave her paper and paints.

What did they mean to do with her?

Felippo.

What if they meant to paint her into submission again? There were other men who needed brides, families grown rich on Tira

Virte's bounty who would count it a fine accomplishment to feather their nests with a Grijalva bride, even a barren one. Especially if that bride's sister was the Heir's Mistress.

Horrified, she searched, hands shaking, in the pocket sewn into her inner skirt. Let out a gasp of relief, finding paper and chalk and a pencil there. When Giaberto had arrived at the inn she had not thought to grab anything. She smoothed the paper out on the table and wrote, hastily, glancing time and again at the door. Every creak and distant footfall startled her. Soon they would come.

> *I am Eleyna Grijalva. I am a painter. I am writing these words down now so I might remind myself, whatever they do to me, who I really am. I am Eleyna Grijalva. I am a painter. I will paint. It is the gift the Matra granted me at my birth. It is my life. Trust Agustin and Beatriz and Grandzio Cabral, but no others. Trust Ro/ Verrada.*

Staring at these last words, she flushed. Unaccountably the room became warm, although the brazier was not lit. Biting her lip, she added another sentence in tiny letters.

I think I love Ro/ Verrada.

She set down the chalk and covered her face with her hands. These feelings were as sudden and unexpected as if they had been painted onto her. All those weeks together at the inn—Matra ei Filho, but she had simply been happy. Yet she had not *felt* this until now. What had triggered it? In her mind's eye she saw his face, half lost in the smoky glare of the torches. She heard his last words: *"At least do not forbid her to paint."*

Footsteps, coming down the hall. A key set into the lock. She folded the paper quickly, thrust it into her pocket just as the door opened to admit Giaberto and her mother.

"What use do you have for me now?" Eleyna demanded.

"You! That my firstborn should turn into a viper striking her own mother's breast!" Dionisa strode energetically to the window and back, unable to be still. She wore a gown of do'Verrada blue today, as befit the mother of the Heir's Mistress. "You have brought disgrace down onto Palasso Grijalva. Living as a common mistress with a man, in a public inn! Have you no shame?"

Eleyna saw no point in replying.

"The Grand Duke is furious. Furious! He blames you for seducing his son away from Chasseriallo. Why could you not have done as you were told and become Edoard's mistress? Moronna! You would have had wealth, anything you wanted, but you must throw it all away only to spite your family! Now your sister is ruined forever—"

"Surely you overstate the case, Mama. As I remember, Grandzia Tazia married very well after Arrigo married."

"You will not mention her name to me again. Venomma ninia!"

"Dionisa!" Giaberto had remained silent throughout this diatribe, his only movement to massage his right hand. "The child is not poisonous, only strong-willed."

"Bassda, 'Berto! The Grand Duke is furious. Andreo thinks Revirdin and I have made the Grijalvas look foolish, and he is sure to take out his petty irritation against us in one way or another. Beatriz is ruined for a good marriage. Agustin has fallen ill—"

Eleyna gasped. "What has happened to Agustin?"

"You can be sure I will not let you corrupt him further, Eleyna. Here in this room you will stay until we have decided what to do about you. Come, 'Berto."

Dionisa swept out. Giaberto followed more slowly, looking as if he wanted to say something but dared not. The door shut firmly, and the key turned in the lock. Eleyna went at once to the window, but through the bars she could only see the servants' garden and a line of old oak barrels set out to catch rainwater. Twisting her hands on the cold iron, she considered, her mind in turmoil.

A perfect rendering. A portrait, painted with the blood or tears or saliva or seed from a Limner's body. Did she have any defense at all against Limner magic? She would shift all the furniture in her room, each day, twice a day, perhaps. Turn the coverlet over. Sleep with her head at the other end of the bed. Sleep on the couch. But from what she had put together of Agustin's hints and Leilias' murmured secrets, it seemed to Eleyna that suggestion magic was less taxing. What if there was no defense against the subtle insinuation of a new thought, a new preference? No defense except the conscience of the Limners? It was not a reassuring thought.

Oh, Agustin would never do such a thing. Leilias' beloved Zevierin would never have done so, nor Leilias' two Gifted sons, both dead now. Nor would Cabral, had he been granted the Gift. But the others—eiha! She already knew what they were willing to countenance.

A pall of smoke hung over the city, dissipating in an evening wind that soughed up from the distant marsh. A servant brought her food at the midday bell and again at evening. She passed the day pacing, thumbing through the Holy Verses that had been left on the table and drawing increasingly elaborate, impossibly tiny portraits of Rohario in and around the letters of the note she had written to herself. The evening bell rang. As its reverberations trembled into silence, she heard the scrape of a shoe and the snick of the key in the lock. Then she caught the scent of manzanilla tea and of freshly baked bread, and she relaxed. It was only a servant bringing the evening supper.

But it was not only a servant.

"Agustin!" She jumped up and took the tray from him. He had, unaccountably, grown noticeably taller in the past weeks, but his complexion looked pallid. The manservant in the hallway shut the door behind them. Agustin made a little grimace as the door was locked from the outside.

"You are ill?" Eleyna set the tray down and hugged her brother, examining him carefully.

He smiled cheerfully. "No, it is nothing. I only have weak lungs. They will kill me, or the Gift will, eventually. What does it matter which one?"

"Agustin!"

His face wore a new maturity. "Pluvio en laggo. I can do nothing about it. What matters more is that I have learned so much these past weeks!" It flooded out: suggestion spells, the Blooded parchment through which he had listened in on the Conselhos meeting, the careful use of blood and tears to create a spelled painting.

"Eiha, young master! I see you are wearing your Gift proudly, en verro. Can you protect me from a suggestion spell!"

He sat down on the couch. "I am talking when you should be eating. There is onion and tomato soup, still cold. Saffron chicken with rice and peas. Bread, as you see. Fruit tart. Everything you like best. I asked the cook to prepare all your favorite things."

Eleyna laughed, but she sat down. The food did smell very good. "You are not hungry?"

"Not at all. I ate all the leftover custard."

The soup was excellent, as always. "You haven't answered my question, Agustin."

"I don't know," he said seriously. "The *Folio* is locked away, but I have been given a key—made of bronze but of the same shape as the Golden Key worn by the Master Limners—because I am recognized as an apprentice. I'll read ahead."

"Don't do anything that might endanger you!"

"Damiano is twenty-four and already a Vieho Frato. *I* am the only apprentice. They *need* me."

"Surely they have ways of controlling you as well as unGifted family like me," she said bitterly.

He frowned, gnawing on a nail.

"Your hands!"

"Eiha." He pulled his finger from his mouth and smiled sheepishly at her. "It's a bad habit. In a few years I will paint my *Peintraddo Chieva*, which will elevate me to Master Limner status. With all the—eiha! This is what you do not know. In oils, with my blood. Oil and blood is the most potent spell. But if that painting is Blooded, they can use that painting to discipline me or as a threat of discipline to make sure I adhere to the decisions made by the Viehos Fratos."

Eleyna pushed the chicken away, suddenly sick with foreboding. "That would mean, if your essence was intertwined with the painting, if it was blooded with your blood, then to harm or destroy the painting would be to harm or destroy you."

"Exactly."

"The Grijalvas have always kept a tight grip on their own, have they not?" No ambitious Gifted Grijalva boy had ever taken the world by storm, done what he pleased for his own gain. All had served the family. "So they control you. If you do not do as they bid, then they destroy you."

Agustin picked up the chalk she had left on the table and spun it, end over end, through his fingers, as if its motion reflected his throughts. "This very morning I read some old documents from the time of Duke Baltran. The Serrano family were still Lord Limners then. They accused the Grijalvas of black magic. And you *know* what happened after the Nerro Lingua. If we do not protect ourselves, we could all be condemned and impoverished. Or killed."

"Eiha, Agustin. No doubt you speak the truth. It is an effective way to rein in the excesses of those men who might abuse the power they have. But it is easier for you, who have the Gift, to think lightly of it. I can only be its victim. And I do not like that."

"Eat your supper. It is rude not to eat what the cook has gone to such pains to prepare for you."

"You are growing up, picco frato." She dutifully finished her supper. She was too practical to let good food go to waste, especially after drawing so many starving faces. And she had a special fondness for the old cook who reigned in the kitchens and who was always willing to slip treats to those Grijalva children who made the slightest attempt to sweeten her up. The fruit tart, garnished with apricots and nutmeg, was delicious.

"Tomorrow," said Agustin after she finished, "I will bring you some new drawings I have done."

From outside, they heard a muffled shriek.

"Matra Dolcha!" Agustin sat up straight on the couch.

The door opened. Dionisa appeared, a clutch of papers crumpled in her left hand. "Agustin, go back to your room!"

He regarded her calmly. "No, Mama, I will not. I will visit Eleyna whenever I please, as is my right as her brother."

"Agustin! How dare you disobey me!"

If he was at all nervous, defying his mother in this fashion, he betrayed it only by his hands, clasped together and thrust between his knees. Eleyna waited for the explosion, but to her astonishment their mother acquiesced to this rebellion. Instead, thwarted of one outlet, she threw all her anger at her daughter.

"Giaberto tells me that you—*you!*—have been party to this Libertista treachery." She waved the papers, which Eleyna now saw were broadsheets. "Is this true?"

"You did not recognize my drawings yourself but had to have Giaberto identify them for you?" Her mother's anger hurt less than the knowledge that Dionisa cared so little for Eleyna's art that she did not know her own daughter's hand.

"Your beloved Libertistas burned down the west wing of the Palasso Justissia last night! And we found *these* . . . these *things,* these spewings of a dog, being distributed on the streets. Where any man might see a Grijalva's handiwork! You would be ashamed of yourself if you had any shame."

"I must do with my gift what I think is right."

Dionisa ripped the broadsheets into tiny pieces and threw them like so much confetti onto the plank floor. "Eiha! You will not defy me for long, mennina! You have a visitor. I would have prevented him from seeing you, if I could, but Andreo and Nicollo overruled me. It is all very well to say that his father has thrown him out of the Palasso, but I do not imagine the Grand Duke will cut him off completely or refuse to come to his aid if he is not treated with the deference due his station. So I gave in. Venomma! You have ruined all my plans!"

Eleyna rose so quickly she knocked over her cup, spilling the dregs of her tea. Rohario walked in, escorted by Giaberto and—Matra!—Lord Limner Andreo himself.

Rohario had gone to great pains with his dress, although she could see the worn patches at his elbows, faded but not yet fraying. Beside his sober elegance, Andreo's jacket and waistcoat looked gaudy, not rich. But in all those tiny portraits she had drawn today, she had not even once gotten Rohario right: the mouth drawn too thin, or the eyes not dark enough, the brows too arched, his hands too lax, without a pen in them.

His gaze fixed on her at once. Eiha! It was so obvious, now her own eyes had been opened. He loved her. How could she not have noticed it before?

"Given all that has passed," said Andreo without preamble, "the Conselhos would have preferred this meeting not take place, but we agreed to a brief interview."

She tried to speak but could not, not even to say his name. Instead, under the censorious gaze of her mother and uncle and of the Lord Limner, she crossed to Rohario and gave him her hands. He grasped them eagerly. His skin was hot, almost feverish.

"You cannot imprison her in this way," said Rohario, wrenching his gaze away from her to look at Andreo.

"She is a Grijalva, and so have the Conselhos decided," replied Andreo stiffly.

"Eleyna is my betrothed." Rohario released one of her hands and tucked the other under his elbow.

She swayed, stunned by this pronouncement. The world had shifted under her feet.

"Impossible!" cried Dionisa.

"Grand Duke Renayo will never allow the match, and his children cannot marry without his consent," said Giaberto.

"The Conselhos will forbid it," said Andreo. "It has long been forbidden for Grijalva women to associate with the do'Verradas, except the one chosen as Mistress."

Agustin stared gape-mouthed, eyes alight.

I can marry no man, Eleyna thought, but one swift, sharp glance from Rohario, perhaps as he felt her take in breath to speak, convinced her that the wiser course would be to say nothing.

"I own two estates," Rohario continued. "They are sufficient to maintain a household. We are both of age, and we have given our free consent."

"You do not understand, my lord!" said Andreo, suddenly grim. "There is much you do not understand about the do'Verradas and the Grijalvas. If your father gave his consent, I would not refuse mine, but *he cannot.* And he will not. Go and ask him why this must be, for I have no right to speak of such matters to you without his permission."

Grand Dukes did not marry painters, whose blood was forever stained by their chi'patro origins. But what would happen to the Grand Dukes if it became known that they had used magic—forbidden magic born out of those chi'patro origins—to gain wealth and power? Both the Grijalvas and the do'Verradas would do what was necessary to make sure such terrible secrets remained hidden.

"*You* do not understand," retorted Rohario, looking suddenly both arrogant and mulish. Eleyna had never seen him look quite so—forceful before. "I may be out of favor with my father now, but I am still his son—and brother to the next Grand Duke. A do'Verrada—descendant of Duchess Jesminia, to whom you Grijalvas owe your lives!" He wrenched his gaze from Andreo and turned it on Eleyna. "I will free you from this house," he promised her.

"Understand what is in my heart," she said, not caring that the others would hear because this might be her last chance to speak to him with her will intact. She kissed him on the cheek, and he blushed furiously. "This is the truth, no matter what I might say when next we meet. Remember that."

"How can you doubt me?" he muttered, looking bewildered but ecstatic. He kissed her forehead, then released her. "I will return," he said to Andreo.

As he turned to go, Andreo spoke. "Travel cautiously, Don Rohario. I hear rumors that the streets are no longer safe for Grand Duke Renayo's loyal subjects."

"For me they are safe." Rohario kissed Eleyna's hand, gave her a speaking look, and left, attended by Giaberto.

Dionisa marched over to Eleyna and slapped her.

"Mother!" Agustin jumped to his feet.

Eleyna merely turned her back on her mother and went to sit down in the chair. "You have no more power to hurt me."

"Eleyna!" This from Andreo, stern and angry. "Must I explain to you why there must be a prohibition against marriage between do'Verradas and Grijalvas?"

She faced his gaze squarely. "I understand why, Lord Limner. But how can you hope to keep such a secret forever? If the complaints of the people are not heard, how can you be sure the Grand Dukes of Tira Virte will not meet the same fate as the Kings of Taglis and Ghillas?"

Dionisa gasped.

Andreo whitened. "Do not seek to overturn the natural order, ninia meya. We have always worked for peace and plenty."

"And for the gain of the Grijalvas."

"Why should we not protect ourselves? Why not aid the do'Verradas, who aided us when we needed their help? Why else would the Blessed Matra bestow this Gift upon us?"

Eleyna rose slowly. A fire was in her, burning so brightly she must speak now or be scorched by the fever of her passion. Though Andreo stood a head taller, she no longer felt she was looking up to him. "Unless it was not a Gift at all, but a curse! How long will Agustin live? My beautiful brother, doomed to die too young? How quickly do you all die, you who are blessed, and how terribly do you suffer at the end? That is why you must hoard your Gift, call it better than others, although not one of you alive today has painted anything as beautiful as this one of Cabral's paintings."

She flung out a hand, gesturing toward the portrait of Mechella and the young Renayo, dressed according to the times in a perfect miniature imitation of adult dress: wide-brimmed felt hat, coat cut of silver cloth, gold-buckled shoes. He and his mother were drawn so lovingly the heart could not help but respond.

"Look at *that,* and tell me I am lying! You have turned in on yourselves, and now you are dying out. Fewer boys are born. The Gift is failing. What will you have then? You have forsaken those of us—Cabral, myself, untold others—who also hold the Luza do'Orro in our hands and in our eyes, because we do not have the other thing, that *blessing* that runs in your blood and not in ours. But we are the ones, when the Gift fails and the do'Verradas lose their power or see no further reason to take Grijalva Mistresses and Grijalva Limners, who will keep intact the family fortunes that your Gift has built. You must nurture all of us, and you have not. *That* will be your downfall."

"I will not hear you," said Andreo, but by the stricken look in his eyes she saw that he had. "Come, Dionisa."

Obedient, Dionisa accompanied him.

There was silence after they left.

"I am sorry, Agustin," said Eleyna finally.

He smiled sweetly. "Don't be sorry, Eleyna. You always had the gift to paint the truth of the world. Don't stop now." He rose and crossed to her, resting a pale hand on her shoulder, leaning to whisper in her ear. "I will come back, but I will bring some vials. To protect you, if I can. You know what we must do. If you can trust me that far."

Give him blood and tears. Give herself into the power he had in his blood and in his hands. Eleyna studied his face: her little Agustin, whom she had nursed through many a childhood cough; the many illnesses had wrought him into a fine instrument but a delicate one. But beneath that fragile exterior was growing a man.

"Of course I trust you. I will give you what you need."

A rap sounded on the door, followed by Andreo's voice. "Agustin!"

She hated to let him go. "What if they do not let you visit me again?" she demanded. They would paint her into acquiescence— but acquiescence to *what?* She shuddered.

He kissed her cheek. "We can do what we did at Chasseriallo. They can't stop us from communicating, I promise you." With that reassurance, he left. The door was shut and locked after him.

The next day they allowed her paper and pen and chalk, but no paints. The Holy Days came, and she waited alone all through Dia Sola. She drew the dead, those she had lost, those she regretted losing, those she did not. Leilias; her friend and cousin Alerrio; Felippo; the stillborn child; her twin siblings; Zevierin; Leilias' sons. All of them gone now but still remembered. That evening— *finally*—Agustin came with the servant who brought her supper. He looked pale and angry.

"They have forbidden you to visit me," she guessed.

"Andreo himself has done so." He nodded at the servant, who left the supper tray and went out into the corridor—to keep watch, although he also locked the door behind him. "I *hate* them! I hate the way they want to control me!"

"We'll do a drawing of this—" She indicated one bare corner of the room. "—and you can send me letters."

"But you can send none back to me, unless you send one with a servant." He shook his head. "That would be too risky."

She paced; it was the only way, confined so, that she could think. "You can cause a letter to appear. You can hear through a drawing. Then why—" She paused to frown at Cabral's beautiful painting: Grand Duchess Mechella stood with white irises, for Love, strewn at her feet. "Then why can't *I* speak to you through a Blooded painting, if we both have one, perfectly rendered, precisely placed, and all else is the same?"

"The *Folio* says nothing about that."

"Perhaps the *Folio* doesn't know everything!" she cried, exasperated. "Eiha! Are all of the Gifted this pig-headed?" She threw up her hands. "You can hear through *one* spelled painting. What if there were two?"

His eyes widened as he considered her words, and he nibbled on the tips of his fingers, caught himself, and lowered his hand. "Two spelled paintings, in two places, each linked to the other. Let me think about this, Eleynita." Then he laughed. "*You* should have been Gifted. You would have become Premio *Sorella* in no time at all."

The servant stuck his head in. "Master Agustin, I dare not wait any longer—"

"Yes," said Agustin impatiently. He kissed Eleyna and left, already enthralled with the prospect of a new experiment.

After he had gone she sat down and drew, in increasingly fine detail, all four corners of the room.

The next day was Herva ei Ferro. Agustin appeared again—this time carrying a half-finished watercolor portrait of her—and again the servant remained outside on watch. "I brought a lancet," Agustin said, "and vials to catch your blood, tears, and spit. Will you trust me?"

"Of course!" She slid her four best sketches of the room out from under her sketchpad. "Here is what I have done."

He bit a finger. He wore today a plain gray jacket and waistcoat trimmed with black ribbon, suitable for Penitenssia. She herself wore the same plain high-waisted gown she had been brought here in, although the servant who attended her had been given leave to sew on the proper black ribbons.

His expression disturbed her. "What are you thinking?"

He hesitated, then stood and crossed to where the portrait stood on an easel. "You are the most gifted of us all, Eleyna, but no one has ever tested *you*."

"I am a woman. I cannot be Gifted."

"How do we know?" He had such an intense expression in his eyes, a window onto a different Agustin, a frightening one. Is this what he would have become, had he not been worn down by ill health? "You must at least try!"

Matra ei Filho. Wasn't it true that the finest Grijalva painters were all Gifted? Why not her? She caught in her breath between clenched teeth. If only it could be true—

"Let me try," he begged.

In answer she wiped a sudden tear from her cheek and nodded silently.

He heated the lancet in a candle's flame. She did not shut her eyes but watched him cut her hand. The blade stung, but the blood welled up like a promise. With a brush he daubed her fresh blood onto the painted shoulder, then drew the lancet down hard, cutting into paint, scraping through it to the paper beneath.

He yelped in pain, clapping a hand to his *own* shoulder. Lowered his hand. A line of blood, sudden and stark, stained his jacket from underneath.

But she felt nothing. She caught herself on the back of the chair and eased herself down. Tears stung. *Not* Gifted.

"Merditto!" Agustin swore.

She looked up and was startled to find him crying. But not from the pain. It was then she realized she no longer expected, or even needed, to be Gifted. She had her own Luza, and she would follow where it led.

In the end, it was *she* who comforted him.

The morning of Dia Fuega dawned sullen and quiet. Eleyna smelled smoke on the air. Her mother arrived with the servant who brought rolls and tea at the early bell.

Dionisa looked, as usual, irritated. "Cabral wants to see you."

"Sit down, mother! Doesn't it tire you to walk back and forth like that?"

"To think I raised such a daughter as this!" She caught herself as Cabral came into the room. "Cabral! *Beatriz!*"

Beatriz, in a perfect morning gown of white lawn ornamented with gold suns, swept into the room like a sudden brilliant wash of sunlight, like the embodiment of warming fire. "Mother! You are looking particularly handsome, as always. If only I had your waist, but alas. . . ." She kissed her mother heartily and turned to Eleyna. "Eiha, Eleyna! You look positively ragged and worn. That will not do. You are to come with me. We are going to Palasso Verrada this very moment. Then we will perhaps have time to make you respectable."

"What is going on?" demanded Dionisa, but half her attention was on smoothing her hands down over her waist, which did indeed appear to advantage since she wore rigid stays under gowns cut in the old-fashioned style.

"Edoard wishes Eleyna to attend the Dia Fuega ball, Mama. I do not care to go against his wishes. Do you?" She said it sweetly, but the sweetness was laid down over a ground of iron.

"My children are all vipers!" exclaimed Dionisa, but her heart was not in it. She had never, Eleyna reflected, been able to remain angry at Beatriz.

Beatriz grabbed Eleyna by one hand and dragged her toward the door. "You need take nothing from here, corasson meya. I have everything you need, a gown, slippers, a hairdresser. Matra Dolcha! You need a hairdresser. You are positively dowdy."

And so down the hall, down through the compound they went, Cabral dogging their path like a sheepdog herding its charges, while Beatriz prattled on and on about the ball and the furnishings and the refreshments and the perfect gold-trimmed slippers she had found to match her ballgown.

Then they were out in the courtyard, Eleyna out of breath, Beatriz barely taking a breath between her flood of chatter. A carriage waited. Cabral handed them in, closed the door, and leaned in through a window.

"Eleynita, you must listen to me, an old man, but one who has survived many years. Stay in Palasso Verrada until all this furor has died down. Then we will see. You can be sure I will speak up for you as much as my voice is worth anything. Do not think it counts for so little in certain places, ninia meya, even though I am not Gifted. For I have one gift our Master Limners, even the best of them, do not have." With that cryptic utterance, he closed the shutter and backed away.

The carriage moved forward, jouncing over the stones. Through slats Eleyna watched as they moved through the tunnel and out onto the avenue. "Is it safe?" she asked. "I have heard so many rumors about unrest in the city."

"Can't you hear them?" Beatriz appeared unnaturally calm. "We have been granted an honor guard of fifty guardsmen."

Indeed, the noise of the guardsmen, of the hooves of their horses, serenaded them as they drove. "When did you come back from Chasseriallo?" Eleyna asked.

"Ten days ago. I have been staying at the Palasso, although I understand that is not the usual arrangement despite that they must have twenty guest suites. But it isn't safe to travel in Meya Suerta now. We keep off the streets."

Listening to their progress as they rumbled down one of the avenidas, Eleyna felt they travelled with an army rather than an escort. "I don't like how it feels out here."

"Do'nado," replied Beatriz. "We will be safe once we are inside Palasso Verrada."

SEVENTY-FIVE

Sario had seen a city on the edge of riot before. He had watched unrest erupt into destruction. Today it had taken him hours to persuade a carter from an outlying village to convey Princess Alazais and her escort into Meya Suerta.

"To the Palasso? Matra Dia, amico, but do you know what you're asking? Troops everywhere, searching everything on the street, beating apprentices, and ruffians wandering in the alleyways where the troops won't go. It's this disease, they say, a plague come to our beloved country from Taglis and Ghillas."

"Have you been there to see it for yourself?" Sario demanded impatiently.

"I'm not such a fool! I heard it all from—" Then the list would begin: a brother, an uncle, a neighbor, the fourth cousin of the blacksmith's wife.

At last, sheer weight of gold hired a cart and a nervous but young, and therefore foolhardy, driver.

The city was quiet on Dia Fuega, the day of fire, the final day of Penitenssia, but it hummed with a muted, nasty energy as twilight settled down over the city. Yes, indeed, Sario had seen it all before. If he did not reach the Palasso and advise Grand Duke Renayo on how to restore order, his chance to become Lord Limner, to restore Grijalva art to its primacy, would be lost. What if a mob did erupt? What if they burned the Palasso?

He shuddered, thinking of Rafeyo. He would not risk losing Saavedra's portrait again!

"Are you ill?" asked Alazais, more curious than alarmed. She wore a cloak to cover her fine gown and a black lace shawl draped over her bright hair, shrouding her face.

"Cold," he said. *As if a man has walked over my grave.*

They made good time through the streets since there was so little traffic, but as they neared the heights and the long avenues that led up toward Palasso Verrada, they encountered a steadily growing stream of people. These folk carried the great effigies—Greed, Anger, Barrenness, and the others—but not to the cathedral, as was traditional. They carried them toward the zocalo that fronted Palasso Verrada. The crowd was quiet but intently so, like a beast stalking its prey. More came all the time from the side streets, from the alleys, from the apartamentos.

Sario took out his sketchpad. Every time the cart rocked to a halt he touched his pencil to his tongue and drew the cart, its driver, himself and Princess Alazais, all the while muttering under his breath the syllables that would trigger a suggestion: *Make room for this cart. Let it go forward. Move away.*

They came out onto the zocalo and saw the gates of the Palasso rising before them beyond a sea of torches and massed figures thrown dark against the evening silhouettes of buildings. Grotesque skeletons, the great effigies that symbolized sins and misfortunes, bobbed up and down in eerie silence. Countless lanterns lit the monumental staircase that formed the main entrance of the Palasso, a scattering of light like stars. From the far distance he heard flashes of music, the strains of gitterns and clapping hands: the Dia Fuega ball had commenced. Closer, he heard the voices of the crowd.

"They dance while we starve."

"What of the Corteis?"

"They're too busy feasting to think of such things!"

"We are nothing but cattle, to be bred and slaughtered at their whim."

"Press forward," said Sario sternly to the frightened driver. "To the gates."

"But, Maesso, the crowd—"

"—will move to let us by." So they did, with startled glances or a flurry of shoving.

When they reached the gates, Sario jumped down and grasped the bars. Guards—at least twenty—stared impassively at him. "I must speak to your captain! Adezo, you fool! I am a Grijalva Limner." He clasped his golden key in his hand, concealing it from the crowd that moved restlessly five paces away.

The captain hurried up. "What is it you want? We cannot open the gates."

Sario leaned toward him, speaking through the wrought iron bars of the great gate. "I have rescued Princess Alazais de Ghillas. She escaped the murder of her father and mother. By bribes I have gotten her out of Ghillas."

"If it is true—eiha! But if not, and I open the gates—"

Behind them, out in the zocalo, a hymn had started up: "The Mother Grants Her Blessings to All." But it rang out with an angry tone and he felt the crowd gathering in strength at his back like a

lowering storm. *Day of fire.* Sario thought of Rafeyo, of the
Blooded painting in the cart behind—*his* blood—and shuddered.

"Take her forward," he said to one of the Ghillasian soldiers.
The man helped Alazais down and led her to the gates, and while
the captain stared at her, Sario grabbed in his pockets for the little
knife he used to sharpen his pencils. He nicked his finger and
smeared blood on the paper, then sketched the captain in quickly
and rubbed the blood into the drawing. "You must let us in *now*,"
he whispered.

"Quickly," said the captain, gesturing to his soldiers. "Get them
through."

One side of the gates swung slowly open. They passed through,
and although a commotion erupted as they hurried down the avenue that led to the stairs, Sario did not bother to look back. The
captain did not—perhaps could not—follow.

"Wait here," Sario said to the driver and the Ghillasian servants
when they halted at the foot of the stairs. "Let no one touch this
cart, the chests, nothing that is here. I will return. Come with me,
Your Highness."

Taking Alazais by the hand, he climbed the stairs. By now it was
full night. As they climbed, lanterns throwing shadows out across
the tiled wall and stairs, he looked out over the zocalo where
torches blazed and effigies loomed in ominous silence, waiting to
be burned. King Ivo of Ghillas had tried to placate the mob. Such a
course had earned him death.

"You must hurry," he said to Alazais, although he was the one
breathing hard, not she.

Soldiers stood everywhere, guarding the great doors that led into
the Palasso, watching the broad portico, the arched passageways,
the lantern-lit aisles and courtyards. Always the guardsmen
stopped the pair, inquiring their business, but his Chieva do'Orro
unlocked each door. The music sounded louder now, the cheerful
clapping of hands, the rustle and slap of feet treading the measures
of the dance. Moronnos! They danced, oblivious, while ruin
crouched outside their gates. So had the nobles of Ghillas danced.

The gilded doors of the throne room stood open. The heat of the
dance swelled out, a wave as tangible as the anger of the mob.
Pausing in the door, Sario surveyed the great chamber. Ribands of
silver and black decorated the hall, stamped with stylized skulls,
symbolizing the remembered dead. Danza morta figures, sewn
with silver thread, danced from wires strung across the vaulted
ceiling. He remembered—vaguely—being a child and kneeling all
evening on a hard stone floor while prayers were sung for the de-

parted and charms burned to release old troubles. Now, these moronnos laughed and drank and danced!

The quadrillo ended. As the dancers left the floor Sario led
Alazais forward to the center. She stared, amazed by the bright colors and rich gowns.

"Remember who you are," he whispered in her ear.

Grand Duke Renayo stood on the dais. With him was a slight,
very young blonde woman dressed in a white gown with a red sash.
She was too pale to be pretty. Next to her stood the Heir, a vigorous, good-looking young man—Arrigo?—no, this was Arrigo's
grandson. He did not look at all like Arrigo. With him stood a
handsome young woman who was certainly his Grijalva Mistress.

Sario strode toward them. "Take off your cloak."

With an uncanny sense of drama, Alazais dropped her cloak
from her shoulders just as the Grand Duke noticed their approach
and turned to face them, looking puzzled. The black cloak fell and,
falling, created a focus; every gaze in the hall shifted to look at her.

"Your Grace." Sario halted and bowed. "I am Sario Grijalva, the
Itinerarrio assigned to Ghillas. The rumors are true. King Ivo and
Queen Iriene are dead." A gasp, first, from the assembled nobles.
Then murmurs, hushed when Renayo—who did not look surprised—raised a hand to quiet them. Sario went quickly on. "But
one thing has been salvaged from the wreckage, and I have brought
her to you for safekeeping."

"Cousin! I beg you, grant me sanctuary!" Alazais fell to her
knees in the perfect suppliant's pose, clutching the tails of
Renayo's evening coat. Sario had not instructed Alazais to perform
this gesture but, like any masterpiece, she had a presence beyond
that intended for her by her creator. The Grand Duke automatically
took her hand—which bore the seal ring of Ghillas—and lifted her
up. He saw the ring; he recognized her face.

They were all of them struck dumb with astonishment. As the
Grand Duke recovered, as Don Edoard stepped forward to take
Princess Alazais' delicate hand in his own, Sario was already plan-
ning.

There were spells to paint. Portraits to prepare. He did not have
the time or energy to persuade them with words. What else had the
Matra given him this great Gift for, if not to use as he knew was
right?

SEVENTY-SIX

Eleyna fled the ball early and found refuge in the quiet of the empty Galerria. Lanterns burned in silent glory beside the doors, white with gold trim, that led into the Galerria. She lifted a lamp down and let herself in to the long wing that housed the painting collection of the do'Verradas. On pedestals at long intervals lamps stood, burning low, their light only enough to delineate walls and windows. The paintings themselves lined the walls like images caught in memory.

How strange to stand here in such stillness. She had only come here before as part of a group escorted from Palasso Grijalva, students brought to copy and learn from the old masters. Always the Galerria had been bright with sunlight, filled with the expectant hush of visitors staring at the great masterworks, of tutors declaiming in muted voices about this *Treaty* or that *Marriage,* this *Birth* or that *Death,* all displayed on walls that were themselves testament to the proud history of the do'Verrada lineage.

Linked for all these years with the Grijalvas, who had aided the ducal family every step of the way. With forbidden magic.

Far away, winding down through distant corridors, she heard like an echo the music from the ball. She walked farther into the gloom. Light shifted around her, a living thing, as she walked, lifting her lamp to illuminate first one, then another painting.

There: Riobaro Grijalva's famous *Treaty of Diettro Mareia,* which cleverly foreshadowed the upcoming marriage of Benetto I to the heiress Rosira della Marei, which marriage marked as well Benetto's assumption of the title Grand Duke, the first of the do'Verradas to so style himself.

Tazioni Grijalva's *Summer Marriage* of a do'Verrada daughter whose name Eleyna did not remember; in any case, Tazioni had clearly been more interested in the breathtakingly lush garden of his setting than in the sour-faced bride and her befuddled bridegroom.

Zevierin Grijalva's beautiful *Mirraflores Moon* in which he had immortalized his beloved wife, Eleyna's grandmother Leilias, as a girl passing into womanhood, her hands cupped to overflowing with red bloodflower petals.

The ghosts of her ancestors, the lineage of the Grijalvas, seemed to stand at her shoulder and whisper in her ear:

See how Bennidito touches his painting with colors so finely blended that they seem as fresh as the day they were ground?

Look! Aldaberto has gathered that shawl so perfectly on the edge of the chair, carelessly thrown there by the girl who has just run to the window to see if that is her beloved, come to serenade her on Sperranssia morning, that you must stretch out your hand in order to catch it before it falls.

Study these, the flowers Dioniso has rendered so carefully, for flowers are one of the languages we Grijalvas speak in our paintings; see how the composition of this Treaty *is enhanced by their placement and made more binding thereby.*

And the *Treaty* made more binding by the blood Dioniso, who had been alive in Grandmother Leilias' time, had painted into it. Which of these Limners had borne the true Gift? Which of these paintings performed merely the spell of great art and which were truly *spells*?

Did the brides won by the do'Verrada heirs have any choice in their marriages? Were all of these marriages—even Andreo's *Marriage of Renayo II and Johannah of Friesemark*—spelled into being, given life and power by the blood and spittle of Grijalva Limners? The paintings crowding the dim Galerria seemed to take on a more ominous cast, so many painted over so many years. So had Tira Virte prospered. So had many a Grijalva boy grown to manhood and died untimely.

And yet, how many children died untimely in any case? How many young women and men of any family married in any wise but to please or enrich their families? Love was all very well for the poor, but it was not practical for the nobility. Too much honor and prestige rested on such matches, the careful disposition of wealth, of heirs, of alliances for the future that could be shaped but never known or guaranteed.

How could Grand Duke Renayo ever have supposed that sedition would creep into his prosperous, peaceful country? All the whispers at the ball had been talk of the Libertistas, of this plague of unrest, of taking a long siesta at a country estate until the riots were quelled.

Where was Rohario? Had his father truly disowned him, as was also whispered? Rohario still had friends at the Palasso. It had not been Edoard who had requested she attend the ball. Rohario had gotten a message to Beatriz, and Beatriz had sent a message to Cabral, and together they had freed Eleyna from Palasso Grijalva.

How Giaberto had found her at the Wheat Sheaf and Sickle not even Cabral knew. Had Azéma betrayed her? Who else had known who she was? Who else would have cared?

By degrees, walking slowly, musing in this way, she came to the end of the Galerria where *The First Mistress* was displayed. Eleyna lifted her lamp. By its light for the longest time she stared at Saavedra Grijalva. It was a huge oak panel, life size, and magnificent in execution, as of course it would be. But it had more than fine execution. It had *life*.

Sario Grijalva had evidently taken more care with the paints he used in Saavedra's figure. The rest of the painting showed its age—tiny cracks, a subtle darkening of pigments—but Saavedra herself showed no such signs of age. Eleyna could believe that she was actually looking at the long-dead Saavedra, the woman who had, according to legend, profoundly influenced the two most powerful men of her time and yet mysteriously vanished.

Who are you, who have come to stare at me? Do I see some kinship in your features, in your eyes? Do you know who I am and why I am here? I am Saavedra Grijalva, and I am here because my cousin Sario imprisoned me here.

Eleyna shook herself free of this musing. All around her the ghosts of her ancestors waited and watched. By this medium her ancestors spoke to her, as if, through their hands, they left a trace of their voices. As if, through their eyes and what their eyes had seen and recorded, the past could speak.

"It is a beautiful painting, is it not?"

She jumped. A drop of hot oil from the lamp spilled on her hand, and she bit off a yelp of pain.

At once the stranger took the lamp out of her hands. She blew on her hand, cooling the little burn just above her thumb.

"I hope you are not badly burned. I beg your pardon."

"Do'nado." Lifting her head, she saw his face clearly in the light of the lamp. "Have we met?"

He had a gentle smile, deceptive, perhaps, because his gaze was intense. "Not formally. I am Sario Grijalva."

She laughed. "Of course I know of you. An appropriate place to meet, is it not? Here before the first Sario's finest masterwork."

"It *is* a masterwork." He held the lamp up so its light illuminated the portrait.

"Indeed. No one now can paint like this."

"You might," he said.

It was an odd comment, thrilling but strangely disturbing. She glanced at him, but he studied only the painting, holding the lamp nearer to Saavedra, who stood with one hand on the door latch. He had a frown on his face.

"I would hope to paint as well as I am able," she said cautiously, "but not in this style."

A sharp glance. "You do not wish to emulate Sario Grijalva?"

"Emulate him? If by that you mean to equal his skill, why yes, then I am so ambitious. If you mean only to imitate him, then no, I have no such desire."

"You think there is nothing for you to learn from his painting?"

This young rebellious Grijalva almost sounded irritated that she was criticizing the man he had been named for! "Eiha! There is much to learn from his painting. Look how beautifully her hands are rendered, where they rest, one on the latch, one ready to push the door open."

"On the latch," he murmured, eyes narrowing as he stared at Saavedra's hands. "Corasson meya, are you trying to escape?"

"Regretto?" He was more than a little strange, this Sario.

He jerked back, becoming aware of her again. "I mean, do you think she is trying to escape?"

"I suppose she is about to open the door to receive her lover, Duke Alejandro. But I can't know what Sario Grijalva intended, or if he intended anything at all, except to capture her here."

"Indeed, I would suppose your guess to be correct."

"I have always wondered," she added hesitantly, "why she holds a golden key."

His intent interest in the painting vanished abruptly and he turned away. She had a choice: to follow him, since he now had the lamp, or to be left alone in the gloom. She chose to follow, wondering if she had offended him with her mention of the golden key. His, burnished with much handling, dangled halfway down his chest. After twenty steps, he stopped and regarded her.

"Yes, Eleyna Grijalva," he said. "You may study with me."

"I . . . I may?" She was by now bewildered. He was not more than six years older than she was; he was already an outcast from the Viehos Fratos. But he *was* a Gifted Limner, and a better painter than she was, en verro, with all the secrets and training granted to Grijalva boys at his fingertips. "You have come back to Meya Suerta to stay? I thought you had gone back to Itinerarrio service."

His expression altered. Eleyna could not guess his thoughts. His peculiar demeanor troubled her, and yet, what he offered . . . if he truly meant it. . . .

"You were to be the Mistress."

"We . . . ah . . . we did not suit."

"Yes. Now it is your sister. Yet you are not at Palasso Grijalva."

"Neither are you, Sario Grijalva. You chose to leave rather than abide by Lord Limner Andreo's rules, I believe. Why should I do otherwise?"

He placed two fingers on his chin and observed her. He had a plain face made interesting by its intensity of expression. How to capture the inner spirit on that unexceptional canvas?

Then she had it. "I know where I've seen you before! In the zocalo at the Iluminarres Procession." She forgot he was Limner and she a mere painter. "I thought you were some brash young artist importuning me for a position in the Grijalva Atelierro!" But he had praised her drawings. That praise still burned warm in her.

"You will study with me," he said curtly. He turned and began to walk. "Come now. I have much to do."

"Much to do?"

"You were not in the ballroom? Of course not. You were in the Galerria, where you belong. I have brought Princess Alazais. I will remain here as her adviser. You will be my assistant."

"Only Lord Limners are granted rooms in Palasso Verrada."

"It is already arranged."

"What has Andreo to say about that?" Eleyna demanded, half amused at Sario's blithe arrogance.

He gave her the ghost of a smile. "You are not convinced, estuda meya. Do not doubt me. Princess Alazais is under my protection. She is heiress to Ghillas. Such a small request as my continued attendance upon her is a trifle. Renayo has already granted it. In any case, a crowd has gathered in the zocalo below. It isn't safe for any of us to leave." They came to the end of the Galerria. Sario opened the door, gesturing her through before him, then bowed and handed her the lamp. "I must leave," he said. "Tomorrow we begin. You will attend me as soon as you have broken your fast."

" 'Cordo," she agreed, dazzled by his assurance, by his swift assumption of prerogative. "You will not need a light, to get back to your rooms?"

"Nazha. I know this Palasso very well. It has not changed so much over the years." He nodded absently at her and left down a side corridor.

Definitely a strange man, for one so young. But in the morning she would begin a true apprenticeship to a Master Limner, a man who wore the Chieva do'Orro. They had denied her this for so long. Now she could truly begin to learn.

⊶•SEVENTY·SEVEN•⊷

Sario approved of the suite assigned to Princess Alazais. It served his purpose. Sunlight flooded her sitting room, and so he had chosen this room as his atelierro. It was quiet here, this the second morning after their arrival at court. Alazais sat by a window, hands folded over her embroidery. Her faithful serving woman stood ten paces from her, ready to act at the slightest sign from her mistress. One of her soldiers waited at attention by the double doors that led into the long Palasso corridors; he and his brother shared this duty.

The windows looked out over the private courtyard reserved for the do'Verradas and their most favored guests. The garden was lush, green with rain but bare of flowers.

Sario watched Eleyna draw.

As requested, she worked on her third study of Princess Alazais. Once the drawing had been done to his satisfaction, she would prepare a canvas and transfer the drawing to a white ground, then layer in the paint. In this way he could watch over her technique every step of the way. He had seen immediately that she was as gifted as those boys he had marked out for himself over the years. She was not Gifted, true, but she would serve his purpose just as well. She was the canvas on which he could prove himself, for a teacher is only as good as his best student.

He had always been his own best student, of course. Certainly, in his first lifetime, he had changed the entire course of the Grijalva family, of Tira Virte itself. As Riobaro, he had left his stamp on the position of Lord Limner, the exemplar every subsequent Lord Limner must compare himself to. But of late he felt more and more that he was struggling against a strong current. More and more it was easier to go abroad—and yet harder, once he had gone abroad, to influence Grijalva painting. As Riobaro he had once commanded the obedience of every Grijalva painter. But now, despite his own great influence as a painter, the latest style had lost everything he had given to Grijalva tradition except that idiotic emphasis on precision, accuracy, and exactitude. He would never have spoken so if he had known they would take his criticism so literally. Eiha! They were not worthy of him!

He needed a student whose skills he could nurture so they

would, in their fullness, illuminate once and for all the truth: Sario Grijalva had no equal.

"Her Highness scarcely moves," said Eleyna. "I've never seen someone who could sit so still for so long."

He took the pencil out of her hand, leaned over her, and added lines to the rendering of Alazais' hands. "Her hands are quiet. You make them look as if they are about to act."

She frowned, studying the change without speaking. Saavedra would have argued with him or scolded him for his presumption. But like Saavedra this one had to admit, in the end, that he was right.

"Yes. I see!" As soon as she saw, her expression flooded with light, the Luza do'Orro; he recognized it at once. She took a fresh sheet of paper and began again, eagerly.

Eiha! It was this quality that had convinced him of her ability. Her desire, manifested in her constant striving. But it was an oddly charged quality, different in tone from that of the boys he had chosen. They had wanted mastery of power as well as art; they had wanted the acknowledgment and the authority as much as they had wanted the secret of the Golden Key. She wanted only the art. She *had* only the art.

Assured now, Eleyna drew quickly.

"Yes," he said, seeing it develop, knowing it would be the correct sketch. "When you are done, you will prepare a panel with a gesso ground, whiting, animal glue, and a third part of titanium white. When it has dried and you have sanded it, you will transfer the drawing—"

"But that's a very old-fashioned technique! A painting done in that way could take months."

"I am not finished."

"I beg your pardon, Master Sario."

"We will practice other techniques, more drawing, in different media, alla prima and so on, while you work on this portrait in the old style."

"Of course, Master Sario." She had the grace to look shamefaced for questioning him. "En verro, I have never painted so closely to the style of the Old Masters."

"Indeed. The moualimos no longer teach oil painting as they once did."

"The moualimos?" She paused, startled, and then chuckled. "Oh, yes, that's what they called the teachers, back—eiha!—fifty years ago."

Impertinent child! "The training given in these days is not nearly as vigorous as what I received when I was a ch—" He barely caught himself. "—as in the days when the Grijalvas were still struggling to establish themselves after the Nerro Lingua. But I have observed that so many years as the accepted masters of art in Tira Virte have made them lazy."

She gave him an odd look, then turned back to survey Princess Alazais. "It has also made the Viehos Fratos complacent, while they yet remain arrogant about their Gifts."

"You know a great deal about the Viehos Fratos."

"My grandmother, Leilias, educated me."

Lelias had certainly been free with the family secrets!

"I am aware she told me much I am not supposed to know," Eleyna added cautiously.

Was that meant as warning? Or invitation? "Then you know that Grijalva secrets must remain secrets."

"And I understand why . . . though it seems these few have enriched themselves, and the family, at the expense of others."

"Eleyna, if you had been born a poor man's child, you would not have such talent as you do. So does the Matra show Her grace."

"But in the Academies there are young men who come from families that have no connection to the artistic crafts. How can you say that only we are so privileged?"

"Let us suppose, estuda, that you were such a child born into such a family." He gestured toward the room they inhabited, its gracious space and high ceiling trimmed with sky blue roundels, lintels dripping with tiny carved cherubs who, frozen forever, held trumpets to plump lips. The wallpaper, of course, would have to go: Sario had grown heartily sick of the cloying scenes of shepardesses, their antique costumes encrusted with gilt, at rest in sentimental pastoral settings. The craftsman's work was adequate, better than the composition. But it must be redecorated in the restrained and more tasteful Friesemarkian style.

Eleyna was staring at the wallpaper with an expression caught between horror and laughter. He plucked the pencil out of her hand. "Would this have been yours?" he asked.

"No." She said it reluctantly. "They do not admit girls to the Academies, not in Meya Suerta. But in Friesemark—!"

"Eiha! We are not in Friesemark! Finish what you are doing, grazzo."

"Yes, Master Sario."

Not an easy student, to be sure. But an easy student would not be as rewarding, nor would a complacent student be able to go as far as he intended her to go. Eleyna Grijalva would, in her own way, be another masterpiece added to his other works. He watched her finish the drawing. Alazais came to life under her hands. Yes, it would do.

A courtier entered to announce the Grand Duke. Renayo, despite his other faults, had no taste for his own personal aggrandizement. He moved through his Palasso with a minimum of retinue, unlike, say, old—what had his name been? Which Duke was it who had not stirred from his bed without at least twelve conselhos, Courtfolk, and servants fawning over his every word and act? Do'nado—nothing mattered but this: Renayo came to pay court to Alazais.

Sario dismissed Eleyna, who took her drawing and retreated out the door. He crossed to stand beside Alazais, who greeted the Grand Duke prettily enough but did not stand, letting him bow over her hand as a lesser prince bows to a greater.

"Your Highness." Renayo sat beside Alazais in a chair brought forward by a servant. He spoke to her in Ghillasian, a tongue Renayo had learned at his mother's knee. "I am pleased to find you alone here, so we may have an intimate little talk." He looked up, pointedly, at Sario, who smiled blandly back at him.

"You may speak freely, Your Grace. It was Master Sario who rescued me from—" A delicate shudder, so perfectly executed. "—those . . . those ruffians who had taken me and . . . my beloved father and mother. . . ." She could not go on.

Renayo patted her hand in a fatherly manner. "There, there, child. What you have suffered! Eiha! You are a young woman of remarkable strength! A credit to your sex. Although we grieve for your parents, you must know they gaze proudly down upon you where they rest safe in the arms of the Matra ei Filho."

"What is to become of me?" asked Alazais faintly.

"We will keep you safely here, ninia meya."

Alazais wore her hair in the new style, half up, blonde ringlets framing her pretty face. No man could suspect this delicate creature to be anything but what she appeared to be: a girl torn from all she knew, struggling to make sense of her new circumstances. Even when her words, uttered in that soft voice, belied her looks. "What of Ghillas? I am the rightful queen, as you know, but how am I to recover what the Matreia e Filei have granted to my family these many years? It would be going against their dictates, surely, to let these ruffians upset the natural order."

"Let us wait a few days before we make plans. There is no need to hurry. You must rest and recover your strength."

Sario frowned. Renayo was not taking the bait as quickly as he ought to. Alazais, as if sensing Sario's frustration, glanced up questioningly at him.

"Your Grace, if I may," said Sario. "You must realize as well as I do that a delicate young woman such as Princess Alazais needs a protector."

"It will not do to rush these things," said Renayo sternly, letting go of Alazais' hands and getting to his feet. "You are young and do not understand matters of state. I must consult my conselhos. I must consult Lord Limner Andreo, *your* superior. But alas, we are confined here for the time being until the mobs have dispersed. I have called in the Premio Sancto and the Premia Sancta to remind those goodfolk among the crowd of the Matra's will in these matters. If the Ecclesia cannot reason with the rebellion's leaders, then I must use force. But I will not act rashly."

"You do not mean to marry Alazais to Edoard?" demanded Sario. *Moronno!* "You would be a fool to lose this chance to increase Tira Virte's fortunes!"

"I would be a fool to divide my Heir's attention in such a fashion! Eiha! You forget to whom you speak, young man!"

Why couldn't this idiot just do what Sario knew was right? "You do not mean to take this advantage to further bind Tira Virte's fortunes with Ghillas?"

"I have other sons," said Renayo icily, but his anger did not deter Sario.

"One who is a half-wit and another, if rumor is true, who runs out on the streets with the Libertistas."

But now Renayo regained self-control. Now he looked amused. "Some young men feel it necessary to rebel before they can return to the fold. And you, my impertinent young friend, understand that I have other resources, should I need them. You may go," Renayo added, his voice dripping condescension.

Sario had no choice but to retreat. But as he walked the length of the sitting room, he looked back to see Renayo settling down for a cozy chat with Alazais. The Grand Duke might deny his ambitions, but they existed nonetheless.

The suite assigned to Alazais was large enough to accommodate a score more servants. Beyond the sitting room Sario had set aside a chamber for himself. It had windows, a single door, and mercifully drab decor: wood-paneled walls unchanged for a hundred years.

Entering and locking the door behind him, he surveyed the room and then shifted a table a hand's width to the right, moved the couch out away from the wall, turned the covers back on his bed.

Placed a branch of candles, unlit, in a different position on the side table.

Finally he eased the cover off his newest canvas. He regarded the portrait of Renayo, still in half-tones, deadcolor and under-painting visible. Renayo stood in a parkland, his booted feet resting on grass, which represented Submission, his hands grasping a bou-quet of blue-flowered flax—the only spot of bright color in the half-finished painting—whose blossoms signified Fate. He needed a tincture of valerian, to increase Renayo's Accommodating Disposition. He should add a peach tree in bloom, a few of the blossoms settling on Renayo's coat, and blend a fine powder of peach blossom into the paint as well. "I Am Your Captive."

Long ago Alfonso Grijalva had attempted to control a Duke and failed. He had not been subtle enough. *He* had not been Sario. But Renayo was not the real problem, not right now.

Sario set the canvas of the Grand Duke against one wall, then placed a new canvas, already primed with a honey-colored ground mixed with his tears, his seed, and a spicing of nutmeg oil. Cutting himself, he bled red blood into poppy oil and used that oil to lighten his pigments. Then, lighting the candles on the sidetable, he rummaged in his chest for his incense burner. The strong perfume of the incense went straight to his head. He gulped in great breaths of it until he was dizzy.

Not dizzy but grown aware of the feel of the air against his fin-gertips, of the muffled noises that marked life within the Palasso, far away from him.

"Chieva do'Orro," he murmured. "Grant this power against life and for death."

He touched oil to his tongue and began to paint. The old Tza'ab words came readily to his tongue, an uncanny echo of the old man's voice, he who had first taught him. So many voices, faces, names lost in the veil of years, but never that of Il-Adib. He shook off the distraction. He must concentrate on what was before him.

The cypress trees, whose shadow is Death.

First a brush sketch, then the underpainting, gaining life with tone and detail. Then, into the interstices and the dark corners of the painting, the shading and the shadows, he traced the chain of signs that linked illness and poison and death, insinuating them into the underpainting so no outward face would ever show of this spell. He murmured, under his breath, each syllable as he painted the oscurra.

Bound them into a chain of oleander that wrapped each slender wrist. Bound them into the eyes, and the fingers, and hid them in black hair.

The candles burned low as the light outside faded to twilight.

There. He was finished with the oscurra. Now the final touch. He took up a new brush, one made of his own hair, and wet it with his saliva. He raised his brush.

A rap sounded on the door.

"Master Sario? Regretto." It was one of the Ghillasian soldiers. The voice wrenched him back to earth. The impact was jarring. "Princess Alazais is asking for you, Master Sario."

Alazais. Who was Alazais?

Yes, yes, of course. He must go. Never mind it. The underpainting would dry and he would finish it later.

Now that he was about to take his rightful place, there was no hurry.

⟡ SEVENTY-EIGHT ⟡

Agustin before his easel dabbed halfheartedly at a watercolor study of the front of Palasso Grijalva while he focused all his attention on the council going on at the other end of the room. The Viehos Fratos were meeting, and they were not pleased.

"—cannot even send our servants out safely to the markets!" How Agustin had come to hate Nicollo's whining complaints. "When is the Grand Duke going to take action and clear these thieves and highwaymen from the streets? Or must we take action ourselves? This is intolerable!"

The Lord Limner's cough hurt to hear. Andreo spoke with laborious slowness. "Nicollo, you understand I am still trying to reestablish communication with Grand Duke Renayo. I have tried sending notes to his study, but something has been shifted in the room. The spell does not work."

There was a long pause while the Lord Limner fought to catch his breath. Andreo Grijalva leaned on his chair back, face gray with pain. This illness had come on suddenly yesterday, and he grew weaker with each passing hour.

"We have heard rumors," said Giaberto, "about the arrival of the Ghillasian Princess. It may be Sario is at the Palasso. Surely you could establish contact with him."

"I have tried."

"Sit down!" snapped old Zosio. "Rest, Andreo. Let others do this work today."

"I cannot—I must get through—the barricades on all the avenidas, the Palasso itself blockaded. . . ."

Andreo broke off. Several voices shouted at once and then came the sickening thud of a body falling heavily to the floor. Agustin dropped his brush and ran across the room.

Andreo lay on the floor. All the others had risen, even Zosio, except for Nicollo who could not. They stared in horror.

They're helpless, thought Agustin with surprise. He turned, ran for the door, and hurried down the stairs, looking for Cabral. He found his Grandzio in the yellow-tiled courtyard, sitting on the bench in the sun, eyes closed. Perhaps Cabral was listening to the fountain, the constant, soothing sound of water. Perhaps, as old people sometimes did, he was reminiscing; his expression mingled sorrow and joy.

"Zio! Zio! Come quickly. Something terrible has happened!"

Despite his great age, Cabral was remarkably fit. Agustin, with his weak lungs, was breathing hard by the time they reached the Atelierro. By some magic Agustin did not understand, his mother had reached the Atelierro before him. She stood beside Giaberto, calmly surveying the situation while two servants brought a litter.

"What has happened?" demanded Cabral, pushing forward.

"He collapsed." Giaberto looked stunned. "He is scarcely breathing. May the Matra grant him mercy."

Cabral frowned down at Andreo, whose breathing, even in sleep, was labored. Andreo's fine hands were curled like claws, like a man in the throes of the bone-fever, and yet his joints were not swollen. His chest rose and fell in an irregular rhythm, painful to watch.

"Has anyone checked his *Peintraddo?*" Cabral asked quietly.

Shocked, Agustin saw the same reaction rise on the faces of the other Limners.

"Andreo has had excellent health," continued Cabral. "There is no reason for him to collapse in this sudden way, even if he were taken with an illness. Which has not, I note, struck anyone else here."

"*I* am not well," protested Nicollo. No one spared him a glance.

"Poison, you mean?" asked Dionisa breathlessly.

The assembled Viehos Fratos looked at her, then at Giaberto.

"Dionisa," said Giaberto quickly, "you must go and prepare a room for Andreo. He must rest in complete quiet. We must send for a sancta."

"I will go," said Cabral.

Andreo was taken away, still unconscious and with Dionisa as his attendant, and old Davo helped Nicollo to his rooms. The others walked in a herd down to the Crechetta where they stood—staring, speechless, and lost.

Agustin went to examine Andreo's *Peintraddo*. Twenty years ago Andreo had been a handsome young man; he had not weathered the years well, having the kind of looks that fade after the bloom of youth. Agustin had heard that Dionisa and Andreo had gone through a Confirmattio together but if they had once shared an old attachment, then it had lapsed in the intervening years under the weight of Dionisa's fecundity, ambition, and the outrageous behavior of her eldest daughter.

The self-portrait looked no different than it had yesterday or last week . . . except, perhaps. . . .

"Zio Giaberto," Agustin said. "Look there." He waited, impatient now, while his uncle detached himself from the others and came over to him. "If you look closely, where you can see glimpses of the underpainting, doesn't it almost look as if it's beginning to age and crack, as oil paintings do when they get very very old?"

At first, as Agustin spoke, Giaberto's expression remained flat and uninterested, as if he was humoring the boy. But slowly he leaned forward and his eyes narrowed.

"Yes. Yes!" His voice caught on the word. "These aren't ordinary cracks. The portrait is barely twenty years old, and Andreo painted it in every way correctly. It should not be deteriorating so soon." Clasping his hands behind his back, he walked back to the others and they all began to speak in low, intent voices as they returned to the Atelierro.

Agustin moved right up to the portrait, squinting. Almost it seemed as if these were not cracks at all, visible here and there, at the lips and the side of the nose, at the lid of the eyes and the collar of Andreo's jacket, but brushstrokes or pencil marks, curving and looping . . . he shook his head and hurried after the others, catching up with them in the Atelierro.

The Viehos Fratos were arguing.

"As senior among you—"

"You can no longer paint, Zosio. If Andreo does not recover—"

"Matra Dolcha, Giaberto! You only say that because your sister has wanted you all along to take the position of Lord Limner!"

"Eiha!" Agustin turned in time to see Giaberto take hold of Andreo's chair and bang it once, loudly, on the floorboards. "What point is there in arguing? The mobs could burn down our Palasso tomorrow! Moronnos! Until Andreo recovers, *if* he recovers, which we must devoutly hope he will, we must have a plan of action. We must communicate with the Palasso, so that we can be forewarned if the Grand Duke takes any drastic measures against the mob. We Grijalvas are irrevocably linked with the fortunes of the do'Verradas. We rise or fall with them."

Agustin had never heard his uncle speak so forcefully, so pragmatically. Always, before, he had seemed the reluctant mouthpiece of Dionisa.

"Surely you can't believe these mobs intend so much destruction?" asked young Damiano, looking frightened.

"Nicollo is crippled because of the mobs," said old Zosio, arthritic hands stroking his cane nervously. "Matra ei Filho! I am glad I am an old man. All these new ideas, this talk of the Corteis and the apprentices having a say . . . eiha! Nothing good will come of it. Nothing good. See what happened in Ghillas and Taglis when the kings did not slap these rebels down in one stroke?"

"Hush, Zosio." Giaberto lifted a hand imperatively. "For good or ill, we are here now. Since the streets are not safe, we need to find a way to communicate—"

"—with Eleyna," said Agustin. They all turned to look at him. Gulping down his fears, he walked up to the table. Its great dark bulk, like the weight of all those centuries of councils held round its black expanse, reassured him. "When she was at Chasseriallo, she sent me detailed drawings of the lodge, and I sent her messages—"

Uproar.

He wrung his hands and was sorry he had said anything.

Finally Giaberto shouted them down to silence. "You did *what?*"

Agustin smiled tremulously. "I read ahead in the *Folio*. It's nothing Grijalvas haven't done for years. I didn't see why I should wait for you to teach me. And—" Quickly, because they glared at him. "Eleyna is in the Palasso."

"But she is not Gifted. If we could only be sure Sario is in the Palasso, if we could only communicate with him. . . ."

They began to talk again, to argue, all wasting their breath. Agustin inched backward, then left. No one marked his going. He was too young, not important enough. But Cabral had spoken with Don Rohario, and Don Rohario was linked with the Libertistas. Surely Don Rohario could, by one means or another, communicate with those trapped by the barricades in the Palasso. Surely Rohario could become the conduit through which Agustin could send that first letter to Eleyna—because he had been *thinking* about her suggestion for talking through two Blooded sketches. It might be possible. As he reached the courtyard, a scream rent the quiet.

"Ai! Ai! Matra ei Filho! Come quickly!" One of the serving women.

He ran, puffing, lungs burning, to the chamber off the great hall from which the shrieks came. He was the first to arrive, and there he stood as others, first his mother and then old Davo and then the servants and finally the other Limners, formed a crowd in the doorway behind him.

Andreo was in seizures. It was so sudden, so violent . . . he jerked, eyes wide but lifeless. Foam frothed at his mouth. Blood ran from his nose. His arms and legs spasmed, flailing, hitting the wall, until he rolled right off the bed and landed hard on the floor.

Agustin ran forward. The serving woman crouched, terrified, in the other corner.

Agustin grasped Andreo's shoulder and, with a heave, rolled the man over. Blood stained the Lord Limner's chin and a last gush of red poured from his mouth and washed down into the curve of his neck. His eyes showed only white.

"Matra!" swore Agustin, staring.

"Get back from him!" cried his mother. Through a fog, he felt her grab his shoulders and wrench him to his feet, drag him back, away from the horrible wreck that was all that was left of Andreo Grijalva.

"Matra ei Filho protect us," murmured Giaberto. "He is dead."

SEVENTY-NINE

Rohario had never seen a council that conducted itself in such an unruly manner. The conselhos at his father's council table spoke only when spoken to and rarely said anything with which his father might disagree. It was one reason Rohario found the Council of Ministers so boring.

This, the second official meeting of the Libertistas, was not boring.

"I say we call ourselves the Corteis and to the hells with those who feel we need the Grand Duke's permission!" That from a brash young journeyman who wore the sigil of the Masons Guild, the most senior of the building trades.

"Sit down, young man! Maesso Torrejon has not finished speaking. We speak each in our turn. Or must I remind you again of the rules we have agreed to for this assembly?"

The journeyman threw himself onto a bench not five paces in front of Rohario, looking sulky but not displeased with his outburst. An equally young friend, wearing the fringed cap typically worn by young men newly come to the practice of architecture, whispered into the journeyman's ear. This surprised Rohario, since architects were received at Court and craftsmen most certainly were not except for formal audiences on certain Holy Days. Somehow these two young men had formed a common bond. Others now commented on the journeyman's furious declaration.

Maesso Velasco pounded a fist on the table he was using as a podium. He had a big, booming voice and a jovial manner underscored by a steely authority. "My friends, my colleagues, let us pray have silence so Maesso Torrejon can continue."

Slowly the crowd of men crammed into Gaspar's dining room quieted down. They might, and did, disagree vehemently over some issues, yet the rules they had agreed to allowed every man there the right to speak.

And speak they did. Maesso Torrejon, representing the cloth merchants. Maesso Araujo, an ostentatious man who headed one of Meya Suerta's prominent banking families. A goldsmith. A notary attached to the civic wing of the Palasso Justissia. Maesso Lienas, a landlord so wealthy he had managed to marry his handsomest

daughter to an impoverished Count. Two sanctos, who had sacril5-
gious views about the Ecclesia's support of the Grand Duke. Even
a man Rohario recognized from Court, a perennial malcontent,
younger son of one of Renayo's ministers. Rohario remained in his
corner and hoped no one would recognize him.

As for Maesso Velasco, his great-grandfathers had parlayed
their shipbuilding business founded in the province of Shagarra
into a trading venture that spanned all of Tira Virte and far beyond.
Rohario knew the Velasco name well from *Treaties* hung on the
wall of the Galerria. Now this scion of that house presided over the
proceedings with solemn forbearance for the most outrageous
speeches and a strict adherence to the time limit given to each man
to present his views.

What they wanted did not sound to Rohario like the demands of
thieves and ruffians.

A greater say in taxation; the right to grant imprimature to any
unusual revenue demands by the Grand Duke. The right to judge
themselves through their own courts and to pass laws that would
affect their own proceedings and the lives of the many craftsmen
and property-holding families who were—they insisted—the back-
bone of Tira Virte. The right to establish the Corteis as an assembly
equal in stature to the Grand Duke's appointed conselhos, whose
ranks were only filled with men of noble family.

One of the sanctos suggested that the right of suffrage, of the
vote to fill the assembly, be granted to all men because all men
were equal in the eyes of the Matra ei Filho. "*Fraternite;* as they
claim in Ghillas!" he cried. He was hissed down.

Rohario frowned as a new speaker stood up.

"Gentlemen, you know me as Maesso Azéma." His silver hair
stood out starkly against the fine cut of his black coat.

"Bloody aristocrat!" shouted the mason's journeyman, not without pride at his own audacity.

Azéma smiled softly. Rohario did not trust a man who moved
through the world so smoothly. "It is true, my young friend, that I
am a relative of Baron do'Brendizia. For those of you who do not
know why I am here today—"

"I don't! Go back to the Palasso, if you can get through the barricades!"

"Quiet!" said Velasco sternly. "Let our friend speak. He has
much of interest to say."

Azéma continued. "I am here because my beloved brother,
Sebastiano, died in the prisons of Grand Duke Cossimio, third of

that name. Sebastiano supported the very cause we meet for today: to reconvene the Corteis. I vowed to carry on his work."

This confession brought a wondering buzz to the chamber. Rohario sighed and hunched farther down in his chair. Gaspar's dining room was overcrowded, and with so many men lining the walls Rohario could see only the upper part of Eleyna's beautiful mural. One white patch, the faint outline of the cartoon still stippled on its surface, was all that remained unfinished. It seemed forlorn, that bit of white caught halfway between starting and completion.

Had she truly said *those* words: *"Understand now what is in my heart."* Matra Dolcha! She had kissed him. *Here.* He lifted a hand to brush his cheek. He could still feel the touch of her lips on his skin, even after so many days.

"To be successful," Azéma was saying in that same oily voice, "you must unite all the discontented factions in Tira Virte, not just the guildsmen. If that means extending your hand to those of us who grew up in the Court, then so be it. No!" He gestured toward the journeyman, who had jumped up again. "My young friend, you look so fierce, but if you want your children to prosper, you will see that united by our common purpose we are stronger than we are divided by our birth.

"To that end, we have a potent weapon to hand which we must use wisely. Sitting in this room is the second son of Grand Duke Renayo, whose sympathies to our cause I have known about for some time."

Matra ei Filho! But it was too late. First one, then another, then all at once the rest: they followed the line of Azéma's gaze and stared. For once, there was complete silence.

"Don Rohario, perhaps you have something to say to these, our comrades?" asked Azéma.

Merditto! Those chiros Brendizias had never been trustworthy. His mother had said so. Despite a flash of real fury, Rohario knew he had to play along. He rose. The men stirred, like an anticipatory beast deciding whether to pounce or let alone. Innkeeper Gaspar, by the door, wore an expression of comical dismay—the secret he had been keeping was, at last, revealed.

"Amicos meyos," began Rohario, although it grated to address these men with such familiarity. "I stand before you . . . at a loss for words. I did not expect to be asked to speak."

A low chuckle from the assembly. He waited it out, struggling to think. Azéma still smiled, but his expression struck Rohario as more malicious than encouraging.

Rohario reached for his cravat, thought better of straightening it here where everyone was watching. "I am not accustomed to politics. Nor did I truly know anything at all about what went on in Meya Suerta outside of the Palasso until just after the Feast of Imago, when I came for the first time to this inn."

"What brought you here?" demanded the journeyman defiantly. The lack of title resonated as clearly as a spoken insult in the chamber.

Filho do'canna! Rohario fought to hide his anger. What could he say that they would believe?

To his astonishment, Gaspar pushed forward. The innkeeper waved expansively toward the mural on the opposite wall. "He fell in love with the lovely young woman I hired to paint this mural!"

That brought guffaws. Rohario blushed, but he felt the tide shift. It was time to forge forward.

"That is not what kept me here!" He stood on firmer ground now. "I have been working—" He had to wait a moment while the buzz died down. "—as a clerk. But I have been listening, also, listening to the voices of the people of Meya Suerta. When I asked my father what he was doing about these grievances—these justified grievances—*he threw me out!*" He waited for that to sink in and finished in a quieter voice. "So I am here."

They regarded him with considering silence, no longer suspicious but not yet convinced.

"What do you mean to do to help us?" demanded the journeyman, jumping to his feet.

Velasco slapped a hand down on the table. "Young Ruis, if you speak out of turn one more time, I will happily throw you out of here. Bassda! Let Don Rohario speak."

But Don Rohario was staring helplessly at his audience, at a loss for words. Azéma's smirk broadened; he seemed positively gleeful.

Perhaps it was only coincidence. Perhaps the Matra truly watched over Her faithful sons. At that moment a rap sounded on the door which then opened to reveal a burly young man holding a cudgel.

"Maesso Velasco," said the young thug, whose coat bore the sigil of the respectable Silk Manufacturers Guild, "regretto, but there is a man here. . .."

"Regretto," said his charge, who belied his polite expression by pushing past the young thug and into the room. He was a vigorous, elderly man with a full head of white hair. He wore a silver key on a chain around his neck.

As soon as he entered the room, a number of the assembled men hissed softly.

"—lackey for the Grand Dukes—"

"—chi'patro—"

"—cursed Limners—"

"Silence!" roared Velasco, losing his bluff joviality. "*All* are welcome to speak."

"I beg your pardon," said the old man, whom Rohario knew well. "I am Cabral Grijalva. I have come here to speak with—" He turned. "—Don Rohario. I did not mean to disrupt your proceedings."

"Do you mean to betray us to the Grand Duke?" demanded young Ruis.

Cabral eyed him mildly, nonplussed by the antagonism directed against him, a man widely known to be the personal favorite of Grand Duke Renayo. "Young man, as long as you bring your petition forward without disturbing the peace, I can assure you the Grand Duke will take your grievances under advisement."

A number of men shouted at once. "Throw him out! Sit down! Sit down! Outrageous! Chiros!"

Velasco seized a knife and with its hilt pounded furiously on the table. "Bassda! *There is to be silence!*" When the assembly subsided, he turned to Cabral Grijalva. "What is it you want, Master Cabral?"

"Maesso Velasco, quommo viva? How is your lovely wife? I remember vividly what a beautiful bride she made."

"The wedding portrait you painted still hangs in our entrance hall, Master. Indeed, I have a daughter betrothed now, and we have only begun to think about her *Peintraddo Marria.* We had spoken of hiring you again."

Cabral bowed, acknowledging the compliment. "I hope you will vouch for my good name, Maesso, before this hostile audience. My presence here at this time is entirely accidental. I received information that I might find Don Rohario at this inn. I must consult him on a personal matter."

"Forgive me, but I must ask you to be more particular."

Cabral carefully adjusted his lace cuffs, as if weighing his words. "It has to do with a young woman, whose good name I do not care to bandy about in circumstances as public as these. I hope you understand."

Rohario walked forward before he realized he had set his feet one in front of the other. "A few minutes alone, I beg of you," he said to Velasco, to the room at large. "Then I will return." He was flushed, he knew it, but the thought that Cabral had brought news of Eleyna set him on edge.

They relented but only so far as to let the two men confer in the kitchens. Here, by the hearth, it was hot, but private if they kept their voices down.

"Eleyna—" Rohario blurted out before Cabral could even sit down on the stool where the cook's girl usually sat to turn the roasting spit.

"—is safely at Palasso Verrada. I think you unwise to allow yourself to become mixed up with these malcontents, Rohario."

"I will do what I think is necessary and right. Most of what they ask for is not unreasonable. It is my father who is unreasonable. If I lend my support—"

"Then you simply lend legitimacy to a pack of ruffians."

"These are not ruffians, Zio! You can see that for yourself. Most of them are respectable men who wish to share in the governance of this duchy—"

"And where will that lead?" A log shifted in the hearth and the fire spit sparks. Cabral chuckled. "Eiha! I did not come here to argue politics, ninio meyo." He adjusted his cuffs again, Casteyan lace, Rohario noted idly, of the best quality. Then the old man went on. "I need this message carried to Eleyna." He drew a folded piece of paper from inside his jacket. "She will give you, in return, a message to carry back to Palasso Grijalva, to me or to Agustin. No one else must know of it."

"Of course I will find a way!" But beyond the kitchen door he heard the muttering of the assembly. He paced, five steps away, five steps back. He had not yet won the trust of the men in there. Going to the Palasso would without question seem suspicious to them. But what did their suspicions matter, compared to Eleyna's need? He took the letter and slipped it inside his coat.

"You should know," added Cabral gravely, "one other thing. Lord Limner Andreo died suddenly yesterday."

"Your sorrow is mine, Zio. I am grieved to hear it. Who will become Lord Limner now?"

Cabral frowned. It was a mark of his intimacy with Renayo and of his own forthright nature that he could be counted upon to be blunt. For four years, starting at age twelve, Rohario had studied painting with his "Zio"—as they affectionately called Cabral although of course he was no relation—until that fateful day he had asked the old man for a truthful assessment of his talent. *Passable,* Cabral had said, *good enough for most, but you will never be a great artist.*

Better not to paint than to be merely passable. Rohario had never touched a brush again.

Cabral smiled softly and squeezed Rohario's shoulder, as a favorite uncle might. "I do not know who will be Lord Limner. I must go, ninio."

"Will you be safe, walking back? One of the young journeymen could accompany you."

Cabral's smile was faint, almost mocking. "Are they yours to command? No, Don Rohario. I am an old man. I have seen too much in my lifetime to be afraid of anything that walks abroad in daylight in Meya Suerta." And he left.

Rohario returned to the assembly. The three dozen men waiting for him looked restless, suspicious, and not easily swayed. It suddenly did not look so easy to break the news to them: Don Rohario, having sat in on their meetings, was now about to return to Palasso Verrada. He thought fast.

"The Grijalva family has sustained a tragic loss. Lord Limner Andreo is dead. But they have no way to carry this news to Grand Duke Renayo."

"Hang the cursed Limner's body up in front of the barricades!"

"Young pup! That is enough! Take him out!" Velasco had truly lost his temper this time. Four men converged on Ruis and dragged him, swearing, from the room. It took several minutes for order to be restored.

"I am not yet through!" cried Rohario. That quieted the rest of them. "If this assembly, this very evening, produces an official set of demands, I will act as your representative to carry the paper of grievances to Palasso Verrada. I will return to you with Grand Duke Renayo's answer."

The outcry that followed his words took Velasco ten minutes of vigorous table-pounding to subdue. Azéma watched with a lack of expression that made Rohario nervous.

But in the end they voted. What an odd concept, that each man might vote on a question put before an assembly. By a scant majority, the Libertista assembly agreed to let Rohario carry the first official statement of grievance to Grand Duke Renayo. There was no going back now.

⟜ ⬥ EIGHTY ⬥ ⟜

Eleyna watched Sario at work. She was supposed to be sketching the fountain, but she could not help but watch a man whose technique, whose complete assurance, was everything she longed herself to possess. She could not help watching him because when he painted he burned with an intensity as strong as a blast furnace, white heat, blinding her to everything else.

He painted Beatriz. Portraits made her nervous after what they had done to her to make her marry Felippo, but she had assisted him in preparing the paletto that would work best to bring Beatriz to life. His paints, this time at least, were as innocent as hers.

Matra Dolcha! How could no one else have noticed? Sario Grijalva was a brilliant, assured, mature painter, so much better than any Grijalva alive today that she could only compare his work to the greatest of the Old Masters. Was it sacrilegious to suggest he was better even than Riobaro, that his genius touched on that of the first Sario? How could the Viehos Fratos have ignored him? They were blind, all of them!

Disturbed by the fierce passion of these thoughts, Eleyna set down her chalk and walked to the great windows that looked over the courtyard. Afternoon sunlight bathed the green lawn and raked garden in a golden glow. The fountain, a replica of the famous hundred-belled fountain found in the old Tza'ab palasso at Castello do'Joharra, flowed ceaselessly, light and water winking in bursts on the moving bells. A faint melody rang underneath the splash of the water.

Beatriz, released from her pose by the entrance of Ermaldo, Count do'Alva, crossed to stand beside Eleyna. "It's very flattering, is it not?" Beatriz asked.

"What?"

"The portrait. I will appear muita bela, no?"

"You are already very beautiful, Beatriz. Look how Edoard watches you."

Beatriz turned slightly. Alazais sat on a couch covered in pale blue Zhinna silk brought by sea—by merchants under the protection of Tira Virte—from that distant land of clouds and hidden emperors. Don Edoard was regaling her with an anecdote, evidently about hunting, but mostly he was watching Beatriz with a kind of doglike befuddlement on his face. Beatriz nodded at Edoard, a smile caught on her lips. He paused in mid-sentence, floundered, then found the thread of his story again. Alazais embroidered without faltering. She looked up once but only to see where Sario had gone. He was conferring with the Count do'Alva.

"How soon will they marry, do you think?" Eleyna asked.

Beatriz shrugged and leaned toward the warmth of the windowpane. "I don't know. Edoard says his father has said nothing of the matter to him, although surely it is the obvious course."

"And you?"

"And I?" asked Beatriz with evident surprise. "When the betrothal is announced, I will get my estate and my freedom."

"Don't you care at all?"

"Edoard is a pleasant, attractive man who is a trifle boring, I admit to you alone. He will marry as his father wishes and after that will consult me from time to time as befits our relationship. And I will have what I want."

"How perfectly cold-blooded! You must feel something!"

Beatriz rearranged her lace shawl, which had slipped. She wore her hair in the newly fashionable style, *Ila Revvolucion,* up in back with a few curls falling so artlessly to frame her face that Eleyna knew the effect had taken hours to achieve. Eleyna could not imagine spending so many hours sitting still doing nothing. But Beatriz had long ago mastered the art of quietness. She spoke calmly now. "Keep your voice down, Eleyna. I am less devoted to Don Edoard, kind though he may be, than you are to your Master Sario."

"I—!"

"Hush, dolcha Eleynita. I know it is not every day that a Gifted Limner agrees to teach a woman. He is very good."

"He is not *good,* Bellitta," she said indignantly. "He is *brilliant.*"

"Eiha! He has a champion in you, I see."

"You don't like him?" demanded Eleyna, fierce in his defense.

"I find his behavior a little odd. I do not think you or I are fated to love any man as Grandmother did her Zevierin."

Like a belated greeting, tossed over a shoulder just as its bearer departed, Eleyna remembered Rohario. His name struck her like a bolt of cold light in a warm, dark room. She had been thinking of nothing but painting.

"That isn't true!" she protested and suddenly had Rohario whole before her, his diffidence that covered a stubbornly rebellious spirit, the line of his jaw, the cut of his jacket. "That isn't true for me!" Or *was* it true? Would she ever love any man as much as she loved to paint?

Beatriz glanced toward Sario, who bowed to Ermaldo and walked back to his easel. Matra! Beatriz had misunderstood her. She thought that she, Eleyna, was in love with Sario Grijalva!

"Beatriz," Sario said. "If you will resume your position, I will soon be done with you. Eleyna. If you will."

Beatriz patted her sympathetically on the hand and left. Eleyna hesitated.

"Eleyna?" Sario asked sharply. He glanced at her, his gaze a flash of dark shadow. Drawn, she took two steps toward him without thinking.

Matra Dolcha! And wasn't she in love with him? Not with him, with Sario the man, but with what he was and what he offered her? It was a sobering revelation. Obedient, she crossed to his side. Beatriz watched her knowingly.

Eleyna sketched, but she was by now too distracted to do more than a cursory study of the fountain. The door into the studio opened and closed; opened and closed. These days, Alazais' sitting room—Sario's atelierro—was the center of Court.

"You are not concentrating," said Sario without looking up from his painting. He had captured Beatriz to the heart. Eleyna saw the stubborn jut of her pretty jaw, the shrouded fire in her eyes, the compliant smile that promised much but gave away nothing important. How much his eye knew of her that she, Beatriz's sister, had not suspected until recently.

Eleyna bit her lower lip and frowned at her drawing. She took a stick of white and tried to give glints to the bells.

"Merditto," she muttered under her breath. It just wasn't working.

He made a noise in his throat, turned, took four steps to her side, pulled the chalk out of her hand, and made three marks on the paper. "There. There. And so."

Eiha! It was perfect. Sunlight glittered off bells shrouded in a mist of flowing water.

"You are distracted," he said. "There is no point in you working now. You may resume in the morning."

Stung, she stood passively while he returned the chalk to her hand and returned to his portrait. Behind her, a man cleared his throat. She spun, startled, to see a middle-aged man dressed in the do'Verrada livery.

"Maessa Eleyna." He bowed, one hand tucked into his jacket lapel. A folded slip of paper peeked from underneath the cloth. "I beg pardon for disturbing you. I have a message. . . ." He cocked one eyebrow up.

"I am finished." Wiping chalk off her hands, she gave her sketch one last angry glance, as if to make it alter by magic, then made her excuses and left the room. The servant followed her out. In the corridor, he handed her the folded paper. She opened it.

> *Dearest Eleynita*
>
> *Terrible news. Lord Limner Andreo died three days ago, we still don't know if it was some kind of plague, but no one else has sickened at all except Nicollo took a turn for the worse yesterday and we fear for his life as well. No one knows what to do. They pretend they do, but I can tell they are all frightened. No one dares go out on the streets. Follow carefully these directions, and perhaps we can talk to each other. First send me a sketch of your bedchamber drawn at dawn. Change nothing in your room, only place the little painting I drew here on a table, somewhere you can sit in perfect stillness and observe it, and mark on your drawing where it is to be placed. Then at dawn, when all the shadows are the same, you must sit there. Only be patient. If I redraw your sketch with my own blood and place it where my sketch was drawn from, it should be possible for us to speak to one another. On no account burn this letter or the little painting. Perhaps you wonder how we have gotten this in to you? Eiha! Your admirer assists us. He has agreed to go to Palasso Verrada to deliver it. Do as I ask.*
>
> *Your devoted brother, Agustin. Please remember you must NOT burn this letter! You will know why.*

She pressed the paper against her breast. Agustin must have put his own *blood* into the tiny oil painting—which was a perfect rendition of a corner of the Atelierro. The shadows were pale, suggesting dawn.

Finally, recovering herself, she looked up to see the servant waiting patiently for her.

"Don Rohario wishes to see you," he said quietly. "He went in to see the Grand Duke—

So little time! She could not know how long Rohario would be inside the Palasso. "I must go by my chambers. Come with me."

She ran. The servant waited discreetly outside while she went through her drawings, searching for one made at dawn. Picking one, she studied it, then quickly and deftly sketched in the paper as it would look laid flat on her sidetable. She memorized the exact position of everything there. Looked it all over once again. Yes, that was perfect. As perfect as the glints on the bells Sario had drawn on her sketch. She rolled the sketch up into a tube, rolled a sheet of paper around it, and tied it with a string.

The servant's face remained blandly imperturbable. "This way, Maessa." She might never have known there was need for haste.

He led her by indirect, narrow passageways—the private halls for the servants, she realized—to the great winding stairs leading up to the Grand Duke's study. At the top of the stairs the landing opened into an anteroom, neatly appointed with a latticework sidetable inlaid with ivory carvings and four Sevris chairs built of pale wood, seatcovers embroidered with sapphire starbursts. Two doors, one ajar, opened off the anteroom.

"In here, grazzo." The servant led her to the door that stood ajar. She paused under the threshold. Inside was a long black table with many chairs. This was a council room, although it was empty now. Two small windows let in light.

At that moment, the door that led into the Grand Duke's study was thrown open.

"—and never come back! You are no son of mine!"

A slender young man backed out into the anteroom. The door was slammed shut in his face. There was only silence as the hard sound shuddered like a living thing in the air and then faded. A soldier shuffled nervously down the steps.

"My lord." The servant spoke softly, but the young man started as at an explosion and jerked around.

The servant pressed Eleyna into the council room. An instant later Rohario entered. The door was closed softly behind him. He gaped at her. He looked stunned. A low noise she had not noticed before penetrated her awareness: The sound of the city beyond. It had a muttering, restless quality. It was also getting dark.

"Rohario," she said, and was amazed to hear his name emerge clearly from her lips.

"He wants me to marry Princess Alazais," he blurted out. "He took the list of grievances from my hand and burned it in the fireplace. Said he didn't need to read the rantings of the mob. But there were men at the assembly he has received here at Court. Men who have appeared in *Treaties* they helped negotiate. Then he told me that I will marry Princess Alazais and become King of Ghillas."

Eleyna felt as if she had been groping in a cloud, only to find a sharp stone.

"Of course I said I would not." He gave a hoarse laugh. "I don't want to be a king. A year ago perhaps I would have agreed to it but—Matra Dolcha, Eleyna. Is that truly you?"

"Yes. I am truly here."

He grasped one of her hands, then lifted her fingers to his lips. Kissed them, while searching her eyes with his own.

"You will marry me, won't you? I don't have anything to offer you by way of title, not now. I'm cast in forever with the Corteis." His grim smile covered a tension as brittle as an old Limner's bones. "But I have two estates. No one, not even my father, can take them from me. Say you will marry me and none of the rest will matter."

Sario will never allow it.

Eiha! She struggled free of her obligation to Sario Grijalva, of her duty to the Grijalvas. She struggled to see Rohario without any veil in front of her eyes, as a painter might.

Hazel eyes, from his mother. His father's light brown hair. A narrow, delicate face made strong by the stubborn line of his jaw and the subtle shading of iron resolve in his eyes. Slight of build, he had gained in these last months a vitality that lent him stature. And of course the absolute perfection of his clothing. Let no one ever say that Rohario do'Verrada was not the best-dressed man of his time.

She laughed, and yet there were tears in the laughter. Leaning forward into his embrace, she stood holding him close, feeling his lips on her hair. She was aware of him, of his physical body, the light pressure of his breath, his arms tight around her back, in an almost painfully immediate way, solid, textural, and very much *here.* She wanted to be close to him. She wanted to be closer still. Old, unwanted memories made her flush, for the shame of what had happened between her and Felippo.

And yet . . . that old shame could not come between them. It could not tarnish the bright warmth of what they had now.

"Regretto. My lord. I must escort you out. If the Grand Duke finds you still here. . . ."

Rohario sighed hard against her, then wrenched himself away, pausing to kiss her on the forehead. His hand tightened on hers until her fingers hurt.

"Corasson meya," he murmured and let her go.

She handed him the rolled up sketch without a word. He took it, and left.

"If I marry any man, Rohario do'Verrada," she said under her breath, "it will be you."

It took her a long time to regain her composure and longer still to get up enough nerve to venture out of the council room. The old chanticleer clock on the table chimed the hour, and the chanticleer flapped its wings. It was almost too dark to see in the unlit room. She slipped out of the room, crept down the stairs by the light of torches newly posted along the walls. No one remarked on her presence. In a daze, she returned to the atelierro.

The chamber was empty except for Princess Alazais, her three faithful attendants, and Sario. By candlelight he added the final glazes and frotties to a fine portrait of Grand Duke Renayo. It was beautifully composed: Renayo stood on a trimmed lawn, under a peach tree, holding flax in his hands. How odd. Grandmother Leilias's teaching leaped unbidden into her thoughts. Flax for Fate. Grass for Submission.

Submission.

She went cold all at once.

Of course it was a ridiculous thought. The Grijalvas worked in concert with the do'Verradas. The Grand Duke kept the portrait of the Lord Limner in his study, so that he might—eiha! Eleyna did not know the details of what exactly he might do. But she could guess. She was just imagining things. Letting her mother's betrayal poison her opinion of everyone else. Sario was giving her everything she most desperately wanted.

Everything except Roharrio, of course. But if she returned to Palasso Grijalva, she would be a prisoner again. She shook her head, trying to throw off all these terrible thoughts. It was only the shock of Andreo's death. That was all. Alazais sat with her usual uncanny stillness, embroidering by lamplight.

At last Eleyna made her feet move, one at a time, and walked over to the Limner.

"Master Sario." She swallowed. Forced the words out. "I have just had word from Palasso Grijalva. Lord Limner Andreo is dead."

"Yes," he said. "Tomorrow I wish you to find the inventory for the Galerria. I want you to record which paintings survive and still remain in the Galerria by Riobaro Grijalva, by Dioniso, Arriano, Ettoro, Domaos—no, not Domaos—Oaquino, Guilbarro, Martain, Zandor, Ignaddio, Verreio, Matteyo, Timirrin, Renzio . . . Eiha! Renzio! What an oaf! Those which are in storage you will have brought out again."

He dismissed this earth-shattering news so blithely that she floundered. "Only those? There are so many others, Sario—"

"Sario! Of course Sario! I will admit Tazioni and Aldaberto as well. And Benedetto. A fine eye for colors had Benedetto. Begin with those. You will study them with particular care. Did I mention how much I admired your *Battle of Rio Sanguo?* A worthy masterwork. I prefer it to Bartollin's."

Masterwork! The praise shocked her into speech. "You do?"

That pulled him away from his painting. "Matra ei Filho! I would not say so if I did not mean it! You see—look here!—how the final touches you put on a painting can give it its entire effect."

She admired his portrait of Renayo. To learn to paint like that! Surely there was another explanation for the symbology he had painted there, an innocuous one. He meant no harm.

"You will paint this well, one day, if you work. Will you work?" He bent his gaze on her. He was so alive. His talent was a fire, the Luza do'Orro, illuminating everything around him. All was bright where he stood.

"What choice do I have?"

He nodded, satisfied. "In the morning, then."

In the morning, then.

She rose early and went to the Galerria, but the assistant curatorrio in charge that day had only the laughable gold-leaf guidesheet. She dutifully marked off each of the paintings belonging to the Limners Sario had mentioned, then painstakingly identified them on the walls. It took all morning.

"But there must be a storeroom."

"Of course there is a storeroom," said the assistant curatorrio, who found her annoying.

He took her there, opening doors into a long attic crowded with shrouded paintings, crates, and dust. She knelt and uncovered a painting. A somber eyed girl-child in an antique costume stared back at her.

"Matra ei Filho! It will take me weeks to go through this, even if I could identify each one . . . surely, Maesso, there is an inventory? I cannot believe these would all be crated and put away here without being recorded first."

"Not done in my time," said the man. "I have my duties. If you'll forgive me." He left her without further ceremony.

She stood, shaking out her skirt, and opened the shutters. Light streamed into the long attic, roiling with motes of dust. Methodically she began to unshroud and uncrate paintings.

In an odd way, the slow repetitious work became obsessive. Long-dead faces stared at her, some with joy, some with sadness, some without the least flicker of interest, as if they were sorry to be standing for a portrait and wished only to be somewhere else. Eiha! They were all somewhere else now, of course: in their graves. She saw, here and there, a glimpse of her ancestors, men in ruffed collars, women in daringly low-cut gowns, with the distinctive Grijalva noses, the dusky skin and gray eyes, that still lived in their descendants: Lord Limners, famous painters, beloved Mistresses.

Old *Treaties*. *Betrothals*. *Deeds* and *Deaths* and the occasional *Divorce* framed with a black border. Matra! Who was this bold beauty who clenched a whip in one hand and a bouquet of white poppies—*My Bane*—in the other? She searched the base of the painting for a clue. Benecitta do'Verrada? Another name that meant nothing to her. She put it aside and went on.

By now her skirt was streaked with dust and no doubt her hair was as well. Never mind. After a while she realized it was getting dark. A massive upright chest with shallow, wide drawers blocked her way. She pulled on a knob and a flat board wheezed out on dry wheels.

Sketches! She sneezed. Here were studies for *Treaties* and, in another drawer, studies for portraits. Alone in one drawer she found a partial study of what appeared to be a painting to commemorate the first Renayo's acclamation as Duke and founder of Tira Virte. It was signed with the florid "S" of an anonymous Serrano limner.

She opened a new drawer. Eiha! Here was an entire series of caricaturos of courtiers, some of them very rude! She giggled, choked on a cloud of dust, and coughed.

She found it lodged along the side of the chest where it had, evidently, fallen many years before. She eased out a sheaf of papers creased diagonally. They crackled as she unfolded them. In this light the writing was too small to read.

Her candle had burned down low. She picked it up and went outside. Glass-walled lanterns flickered in the corridor. She held in her hands an old inventory, its date enscribed at the end: *Completed by order of Tazita Grijalva in the year 1216*. Exactly one hundred years ago.

Imagine! Clutching the precious document, she hurried down to the Galerria. It was closed, dark, and empty, though not locked. Her stomach rumbled. Matra! She had not eaten all day. But her curiosity was more compelling than her hunger.

She lit a lamp and set it on the curatorrio's table. The inventory was divided into two sections: For display in the Galerria. For storage.

At the top of the list for storage, was *The First Mistress, a por-*

trait of Saavedra Grijalva by Sario Grijalva. A short description accompanied the title. A life-sized portrait. Saavedra Grijalva stands behind a table. It is night in her chamber. She is dressed in a gown of ash-rose velurro. She wears a heavy necklace of pearls, and pearls swag her gown. A book lies open on the table. One hand rests on the table, the other points at a line of illumination within the text.

Eleyna rose, hands curled tight on the inventory. Numbly she lifted the lamp by its painted ceramic base and walked—slowly, not truly wanting to get there quickly—to the other end of the Galerria. It was as quiet as a graveyard.

The First Mistress hung in her appointed place. She had a beauty that haunted the eye, for it was so immediately and compellingly sad. Lost forever, as all things are lost. Except Saavedra Grijalva would never be forgotten because of Sario Grijalva's genius.

But Saavedra's face and eyes did not compel Eleyna's attention for more than an instant. With a kind of sick horror, Eleyna examined the rest of the painting as if for the first time.

Saavedra did not stand *behind* the table. It was not *night* in the chamber. It was, by the lack of shadow in the room and the quality of the light beyond the arched windows, about midday. The lamp was snuffed. The candle, fat and honeycombed, sat cold on the sill. A book rested on the table, but it was closed, its spine facing away from her, as if the last page had just been read and the book shut.

And Saavedra stood by the iron-studded, iron-bound door, her left hand resting on the latch, her head turned to look into the mirror. Either there was a mistake in the description in the old inventory or someone had made an inaccurate copy of the painting.

Far away, a door opened. She jumped. Without thinking she blew out the lantern and hid in the drapes that blanketed the farthest darkest corner. The darkness, the measured tread of several pairs of feet approaching her hiding place, the hush of fresh nightfall, all combined to rub her nerves raw. Even the twisted light given off by the few shuttered lanterns seemed ominous.

"You must act, Your Grace," said Sario, his voice heard softly but clearly down the echoing long hall. So smooth. So assured. So full of power. "You know the do'Verradas are crippled without a Lord Limner at their side."

The footsteps came closer. Her heart pounded. They must know she was here. But they stopped before the portrait of Saavedra Grijalva, positioned so she could see by the light of the lamp Sario held their shadows thrown by that light up against the wall and the painting, his shadow looming large over Saavedra's painted figure.

"This news of Andreo . . . so shocking! You are sure it is true?"

"Alas, it is true."

"But you are so young. You say your election will be confirmed by the others?"

"You are the one to make the decision, Your Grace. If you present me to the Viehos Fratos as your new Lord Limner—"

Eleyna bit off a gasp. She dared not stir.

"I do not know you—" This was not the man who had thrown out Rohario. He sounded so unsure. But Grand Duke Renayo *never* doubted himself.

"Of course you can trust me, Your Grace. If I break our code of honor, my brothers have the means to remove me."

"Eiha! Of course. A little gruesome to think on. . . ."

"But necessary, when the power the Matra ei Filho blessed us with could be abused by a man with neither honor nor conscience."

"Of course. It is as you say. You will attend me in the morning, then, Lord Limner Sario?"

"I am honored, Your Grace. I will serve you as faithfully as my namesake served Alejandro do'Verrada." His shadow bowed toward his Duke, dipping over Saavedra's body.

Renayo's shadow made an odd gesture with one hand, but she could not interpret it. Then he left. His footsteps retreated down the Galerria.

Her nose tickled horribly and she wanted very badly to sneeze. Sario did not move. She could not stand this much longer.

He shifted forward into her line of sight, lifting the lamp and walking right up to the painting of Saavedra. He placed a kiss on his fingers and, reaching up, touched his hand to her lips. It was a long stretch.

"Carrida meya. Soon you will be restored to the life you deserve. But you must not be impatient, 'Vedra. You must remember that I know best." He stood there for the longest time, looking at her face, quiescent in oil.

Eleyna hardly dared swallow. The inventory burned in her hand. If she made the slightest movement, the paper's rustle would give her away.

He shook his head as if in reply to an unspoken question. "It is not yet time to free you, corasson," he said to the painting. Then— Grazzo do'Matra!—he left, walking softly down the long Galerria carpet. She did not move until she heard the distant click of the door.

Sario Grijalva was insane.

And Grand Duke Renayo had just appointed him Lord Limner.

Eleyna slipped out from behind the drapes and stared at *The First Mistress:* Saavedra Grijalva, so lifelike, so perfectly caught that it seemed she could step out of the portrait as alive as she had been the day she had posed for it, three hundred years ago.

"How much power do the Grijalva Limners have?" Eleyna whispered, catching sight of Saavedra's gaze in the mirror. How finely Sario had captured that face, its subtleties, its anger, its passion.

Enough power to do this to me. Who are you, my sister? I have seen you before. Can you not help me? Do you not understand what has been done to me and my child?

It was impossible. It *had* to be impossible.

But what if it were true? What if Saavedra Grijalva had not died or fled? What if she had been imprisoned in her own portrait by her cousin Sario? But why would he have done such a terrible thing?

And how could Sario Grijalva—*this* Sario—know?

~•❖ EIGHTY-ONE ❖•~

It had not been necessary to tell the Grand Duke that the Viehos Fratos, those simpering idiots, had no control over Sario Grijalva! Not any more.

No more worrying about affairs with do'Verrada daughters. Ridiculous to have sacrificed Domaos' talent for two years of passion with Benecitta. No more ugly Renzios. No longer would he let a boy with as much raw talent as Rafeyo burn wild with unbridled ambition and twisted hate. There had been so many disasters. Nothing, no life except Riobaro's, had gone as he had planned.

Matra ei Filho! The entire Grijalva line was weakening. How could he welcome back Saavedra when he lived in this undistinguished body? But he had no likely successors. Weak, old, or dead. That summed up the Grijalva Limners quite neatly.

Except for his estuda. If only she had been Gifted, like Saavedra. But the Viehos Fratos would never listen to a woman, so perhaps it was better this way. He would not be tempted. He would not be trapped by the bright fire of her talent in a body whose every word, spoken by his mind through her lips, would be ignored or belittled. He would make her into the greatest artist of her time—barring himself, of course—and through her—with his guidance as Lord Limner, of course—start a new Grijalva tradition, one that would eclipse the stale brushwork of the Andonios and Andreos. When the latest crop of boys in Palasso Grijalva came of age, he would honor the likeliest candidate among them with his presence. Then he could think about releasing Saavedra. When all was just as it should be.

Who must he paint next? Who would stand in his way? Edoard had been spending a great deal of time with Alazais. Would it serve his cause better to have Edoard marry the girl, or to give her to the brother? What was his name? Cossimio? Alessio? Matteyo? No, those were other brothers, other times.

Eiha! How could he do a portrait of the rebellious brother, whom he had never seen? With all of them trapped in the Palasso by the rabble outside, he might as well concentrate his efforts on Edoard. It didn't matter which boy went to Ghillas: Edoard could unite both countries under his rule for all he cared.

Sario realized all at once that it was dark outside. How long had he been standing here in front of his portrait of Renayo? He had completely lost track of time.

A rap sounded on the door. "Master Sario?"

"Come in, Eleyna." So much to do, but he would have years now to perform his most important task: to teach Eleyna Grijalva, to renew art in Tira Virte, and to prepare a new boy for himself. Political considerations were minor compared to his duty to art. He glanced once around the room: his *Death* painting of Andreo and the painting of Alazais were shrouded, safe from prying eyes. Then, remembering that he had locked the door, he let her in.

"Master Sario, I beg pardon for disturbing you."

"Do'nado. Come in, estuda."

She saw the portrait of Renayo at once. He read her horror in her face.

"You know the language we paint into our portraits, I see," he said quietly.

Her color changed as she struggled to control herself.

"Tell me," he demanded. "If you know, then tell me what it says."

She paled, but she obeyed. "Grass for Submission, flax for Fate. Peach blossoms, which say 'I Am Your Captive.'"

How easily the symbology rolled off her tongue. "Leilias taught you well. I am not surprised. I never liked her, but I learned to respect her."

"You knew Grandmother? She never mentioned you."

"Of course she knew me!" He stopped himself, almost reeling from the sudden wrench. He was no longer Dioniso. This Sario had only known Leilias Grijalva as an old woman who, with her brother Cabral, exercised an unseemly amount of influence as Conselhos. Just because *they* had backed Mechella, whose adherents had won the day away from the shamed and reviled Tazia. "She knew us all."

He stalked to the window and glared down into the courtyard. Alazais walked there by torchlight, escorted by some of the ladies of the court. By Arrigo's sister, Lizia. No, no, that was Lizia's granddaughter down there, a handsome young woman with the same forthright manner as her grandmother. How fortunate for him that they bore the same name. He turned back to her from the window. "There is so much to do. Surely you can understand that."

"Why not just paint yourself Grand Duke, then?" she demanded.

He laughed, as much at her indignant expression as at the absurdity of the suggestion. Why did they all accuse him of the one thing he had never wanted? "Why should I want to be Grand Duke? The do'Verradas have their place, and we Grijalvas have ours. Do you truly think the nobility of Tira Virte would accept a chi'patro Grijalva as their Duke? They would rebel in a moment, and even *I* cannot paint every single man in this country into submission. I don't have enough blood. Matra ei Filho, mennina! Just think! What would any painter want in being Grand Duke? I am a painter, not a ruler. No Grand Duke would ever have time enough away from his duties to be anything but a gifted amateur, painting pretty pictures for the ladies. I mean to restore the art of the Grijalvas to its former eminence, to the stature it once had, and if I must be Lord Limner to do so, then so it will be."

For a long time, as if she had not heard him, she stared at Renayo's portrait. Suddenly she spoke softly. "How could you have known Andreo would die—?" She clipped the last word short, aghast, and shot a glance at him, her cheeks pale.

She suspected, that much was obvious.

"I, too, am distressed by the untimely death of Andreo." Lying came easily to him after all these years. "But one cannot hesitate out of a misplaced pity brought on by the misfortune of others." After all these years, he had learned to read other people very well. He saw she now doubted her own conclusion. That she *wanted* to doubt. "Sit down, Eleyna. I must do some studies of you."

She did not sit down. Her eyes flashed. Really, they were her finest feature. "Never! How can you believe I will submit to be painted into your willing slave? It was done to me before, and I swore then—"

"Done to you before!"

"Surely you know I refused to marry Felippo Grijalva, but Giaberto, with my mother's connivance, painted me into accepting him." Tears stood in her eyes, glittering in the lantern light.

Few things had the ability to disgust him anymore. This did. "Eiha! Felippo Grijalva! He had the self-control of a dog!"

Tears rolled down her face as she struggled to contain herself. He admired her strength.

"I was abroad, I hope you will recall," he said quietly. "I would never have countenanced such a thing. *Never.* Eleyna." Now she was vulnerable. He had what she wanted—the knowledge of painting—and she would do what he asked in order to get it. "You know the Viehos Fratos are dying! Stagnant! Eiha! It gives me some sympathy for these idiot Libertistas." She stared at him, searching—but for what? He could see the questions in her eyes, in her stance; he just could not read her mind. "Do you wish to learn what I have to teach?" He knew what she would answer.

"Of course!"

"Then obey me!" Why must the talented ones always be the most difficult? "Sit for a portrait."

"To become your captive?" she retorted. "If I am to be your estuda, I will only be your mirror if you rob me of my will."

Impossible creature. "Moronna! It is my *duty* to protect you from the others. That is why I *must* paint a portrait of you, one that will leave you untouched by mine or any hand." That struck her to silence. It should not have. Surely she should have understood all along that he intended to protect her, just as he had Saavedra. "Do not be pig-headed! Have you not yourself criticized the Viehos Fratos?"

"I have," she said in a small voice.

"Do you not agree the Academy style is worthless? That the Grijalvas have become pointlessly self-absorbed? That the course they have taken will lead to ruin?"

"I do agree."

"Then let me protect you so you can learn from me without their interference! Eiha! *I am right.* You know it. So let us have done with this argument and do what needs to be done. So many things! An inventory of Grijalva paintings in the Palasso. A complete restructuring of the tutorials for the young Grijalva estudos. A new style of painting that will reinvigorate our line; indeed, art in Tira Virte altogether." He let out a great sigh and waited for her acquiescence.

"The inventory," she said hesitantly. "I found an inventory made in the time of Arrigo the Second."

So many lives ago. He could only recall now that he had taken advantage of Arrigo II's coronation to rid himself of Renzio. He extended a hand. "May I see it?"

Her hesitation annoyed him. "I . . . didn't bring it."

This was not about the inventory. Like Alejandro, she needed him. He did not need magic to persuade her, only the rights words uttered with the right emotion. "Eleyna, you must trust me. I want—I need—a student who will bring credit to my name, one whose brilliance will shine because of what I teach him. Teach *her.* If I wanted a copyist, I would not be rebelling against what the Viehos Fratos have become, would I?" He spoke gently now, because she was still skittish. And no wonder, after what had been done to her. Forcing her to marry Felippo, that disgusting chiros. What a repulsive thing to do to a girl! What an appalling thing to do to a child with the Luza do'Orro! He *must* convince her, so it could never happen again. "Let me paint this portrait. I will use white chrysanthemums for Truth, white oak for Independence, water willow for Freedom, and juniper for Protection and Purification. You will help me prepare the paints. You will watch each brushstroke I lay down. You will take the painting with you when I am not working on it. Let me protect you in this way. It is a selfish wish, I know, to have you as my pupil. To want you always to be free to paint, as you are meant to, with me or without me. Grant me this wish, Eleyna."

She struggled against her fears, but he knew what she would do. She had no choice, just as he had no choice. She was, as he had always been, in thrall to the Luza do'Orro, the Golden Light. Of all of them, she was the one most like him.

"I will trust you," she said in a low voice, but as if the admission hurt her. She sat down.

Satisfied, he got out a fresh piece of paper.

⊷ EIGHTY-TWO ⊷

Eleyna rose before dawn and adjusted herself precisely in the chair that faced her writing table. She shifted Agustin's drawing a final time, then waited.

In what madness had she agreed last night to allow Sario to do a portrait of her? She wanted to turn and look at the two sketches Sario had done by candlelight, but she dared not move. Why had she followed Sario back to his chamber? What if he *had* killed Andreo?

Eiha! What if he truly could paint her a *Peintraddo* that would protect her forever from Grijalva magic?

The fire crackled behind her. The servant girl came in before dawn to rake the coals and add new wood. This morning Eleyna had risen and locked the door as soon as the girl left. Now she stared at the parchment that lay flat, squared off, on the table's surface. Suddenly she heard the whisper of distant words.

"Eleyna, it's Agustin. Do you think she can hear me, Zio?"

Though it had not changed, the drawing of one corner of the Grijalva studio now looked uncannily lifelike. She expected Agustin to walk into her line of sight at any moment. But of course he did not. Yet that was his voice, like a voice heard through a keyhole. *Miraculo!*

"Agustin. I can hear you." Her voice trembled.

"Matra Dolcha!" swore Giaberto, sounding more appalled than pleased.

"I told you it would work!" Agustin sounded smug. "Giaberto and Cabral are here with me, Eleyna. Cabral wants you to get the Grand Duke to stand with you, tomorrow, out of the line of sight of the drawing, so that he can listen—"

"Impossible!" Giaberto again. "Can you imagine the scandal if the Grand Duke was found in her bedchamber at dawn?"

"But we must consult with him on the matter of a new Lord Limner," said Cabral.

"Let me speak, grazzo," said Eleyna, desperate to break in. "The Grand Duke named a new Lord Limner. Sario."

"Sario—!"

"That chi'patro chiros—!"

"Forgive me, Zio." She had to find out the truth, yet still she hesitated. She felt she was betraying him. "How . . . how did Andreo die?"

Cabral's voice was cool, cataloging the symptoms. "A sudden illness. Hemmoraging."

"Is it possible—" She forced out the words. "—for one Limner to kill another?"

"You are suggesting that Sario murdered Andreo?" How could Cabral be so calm?

"Eleyna." Giaberto was not calm, yet he spoke with authority. "Tell no one of these suspicions. If you can, go today and see if Andreo's Lord Limner portrait still hangs in the Grand Duke's study, and if it remains untouched. There are powerful protections painted into that portrait, and it *ought* to be impossible for a Limner to harm another unless through that portrait."

"I will do as you ask, Zio." She found that her hands were trembling and that her back hurt horribly, but she could not shift her position lest she break the spell that linked her to Agustin. "Is it possible for a Limner to paint a person into a painting?"

Agustin's gasp she recognized. The other two made incomprehensible sounds.

"That I should be talking about such matters in front of an unGifted limner and a woman!" exclaimed Giaberto. "I have read nothing in the *Folio* that suggests Grijalvas have ever known of or attempted such a horrific deed."

"Then is it possible there was once a copy made of *The First Mistress*?"

"The portrait of Saavedra Grijalva?" asked Cabral. "I never heard of any copy being made, but I suppose such a copy might have been done before my birth. But I can assure you that the portrait hanging in the Galerria is the original."

It was wild stab in the dark, but she had to ask. He was almost eighty years old. "Wasn't that portrait in storage?"

She almost heard Cabral's smile. "Yes. Grand Duchess Mechella and I found it. That's why I know it is the same one."

"Do you remember where Saavedra stood?"

His reply took so long she thought she heard dust settling on the table. "Behind the table, I think. She was reading a book. Mennina, I haven't thought of that day in so many years." He gave a sharp laugh, bittersweet. "Women notice such peculiar things. The Grand Duchess thought Saavedra was pregnant. Isn't that an odd thing to recall after all these years?"

Behind the table. "Zio," she whispered. At last she found her voice. "If a person could not be captured within a painting, explain to me then how Saavedra now stands before the door? Why, if there is no other copy, does an inventory I found dating from 1216 describe her, as you say, standing behind the table, at night?"

"At night!" So eerie, to hear Cabral's shock in only his voice and never to see his face. "It was dawn. I remember *that* clearly enough. The candle had just been snuffed. Mechella commented on the artistry. . ." His voice trailed off only to return with a kind of horrified astonishment. *"I had forgotten this."*

"Sario believes Saavedra is *alive* in that painting."

"Matra Dolcha!" swore Giaberto again.

"I have not been in the Galerria since 'Chella became too ill to walk with me there," whispered Cabral. *'Chella?* Since when did a common limner speak so familiarly of a Grand Duchess?

"Merditto!" swore Giaberto. "Eleyna, we must get that painting to the Atelierro so the Viehos Fratos can examine it."

"How can she get a painting of that size through the barricades?" asked Agustin.

"We must see what Don Rohario can accomplish," said Cabral. "Giaberto is right. We must have that painting here."

Their blithe words alarmed her. "Sario would notice at once! You don't understand, he controls everyone here now."

Giaberto snorted. "We can take care of Sario Grijalva. Just get the painting to us, however it must be arranged. That is an order, Eleyna. Do you understand?"

"Yes." *They* were the ones who did not understand. They were blind to Sario's power and skill.

"That is enough for today, Agustin. You may talk with Eleyna tomorrow."

"Yes, but—" Agustin wanted reassurance.

She gave it. "Beatriz is well. As am I. You are well?"

"Yes, but—"

"Come," said Giaberto curtly. "We must now discuss how you came to devise this, without consulting any of the Viehos Fratos."

"Agustin? Agustin?" Silence met her words. The spell had been broken.

We can take care of Sario Grijalva.

Eleyna no longer believed they could. The Viehos Fratos had *no idea* how powerful Sario was. She was the only one who truly *saw* him, the master at work, who understood his brilliance. She did not want them to destroy him, he who was everything she hoped to be as an artist. Yet what if Saavedra lived inside the portrait? What if that voice she had heard was Saavedra's voice: *"Who are you, my sister? Can you not help me?"* Only a Gifted Limner could free her, if it was true, and she had heard Sario declare to Saavedra's figure that he had no intention of freeing her . . . yet.

Eiha! It was impossible. It could not be true.

But for the sake of the woman in the painting, she could not take the chance. Somehow, she had to get *The First Mistress* to Palasso Grijalva without Sario knowing.

EIGHTY-THREE

The First Provisional Assembly of the Corteis had gone on for fifteen days now. Rohario had made one speech, recorded in the minutes as "Do Not Act Rashly." But he had helped to convince the assembly that it was better to negotiate than to attack.

"We are not barbarians. We do not murder children in the name of liberty." Or some such words. "The Grand Duke will answer violence with violence. There will be death on both sides—"

"A small price to pay for freedom!" shouted Ruis, who had made himself spokesman for a set of unruly young men.

Rohario no longer had trouble speaking to crowds. Indeed, he had a talent for it. "Do you have a young sister, as I do, Maesso?" he had responded. "Perhaps you would like to put her in the front lines? If there must be fighting, then I believe it is better to have a written set of principles on which the Corteis agrees to govern itself before the fighting begins, rather than after, so that every man here has agreed to those principles before we begin squabbling over the gains. In this way you can win over those men who might otherwise fear they would lose everything their families have worked so many generations for to the anger of the mob."

His speech had been only one in a long string of speeches made by various men. But it was naive to think he had not influenced the wealthier scions of Meya Suerta society, for a number of them began at once to agitate for a truce.

Twenty days after Penitenssia, they had a truce. Now they argued over the principles to be included in the document by which they meant to legitimize the Corteis—with or without the Grand Duke's imprimature.

Sperranssia had come and gone. No young men had wandered the streets singing for kisses. Barricades stood in the avenidas. The mercado remained open, but traffic into and out of the city was restricted. Wagons were allowed onto the Palasso grounds, but they were searched for contraband. Grand Duke Renayo did not act. He had not even spoken publicly since Rohario's disastrous interview with him the day after Nov'viva. Some said he had put his trust in the Ecclesia and, indeed, representatives of the Premia Sancta and

Premio Sancto attended faithfully each day of meetings in the guild hall commandeered by the Provisional Corteis.

Rohario did not understand why his father did not take drastic action. Renayo was not a patient man, although he was always pragmatic. But certainly with Meya Suerta in such uproar he could not send the bulk of his army to restore both order and Princess Alazais—and one of his sons—to the throne of Ghillas. Yet neither would he want to expend his substance here in the city when there was so much at stake abroad.

In ten days it would be Mirraflores Moon. Rohario listened to each tedious hour of debate. As long as they were talking, they were not fighting. More than anything he did not want beautiful Meya Suerta to be ruined in the kind of violent brawl that had wracked Aute-Ghillas. He did not want his beloved Galerria looted and burned.

If the world must change, let it change through the pen, not with the sword.

And yet, as the proceedings—and the document that would embody the principles agreed upon in the proceedings—were recorded, he noted that the bulk of the recording was done in words. Not in paintings. The *Contracts* and *Deeds* and *Marriages* that were the staple of Meya Suerta's commerce had a fixed language, long agreed upon, one every merchant and educated man and woman could understand. But this was new. There was no language in pictures that covered it. Eiha! What did this forebode for families such as the Grijalvas, whose fortune had been made in painting?

"We, the elected representatives of the Corteis, will meet as a body equal in authority to the conselhos."

This passed by acclamation.

"The members of the Corteis will be elected without regard to orders or privileges or inherited rights."

"The Corteis shall have the right to investigate wrongs done by the Grand Duke or his officers to individuals or groups of individuals, of whatever rank, in defiance of the law, and to demand that justice be done."

"No taxes can be imposed without the consent of the Corteis."

Rohario penned a quick note and sent it forward to Maesso Velasco, who still acted as unofficial Premio Oratorrio. *I am leaving the assembly for the afternoon in order to join those of our comrades engaged in a thorough search of the records in the Palasso Justissia.*

His movements were watched, of course. Interest in him was intense. He had a constant escort of young journeymen, cronies of Ruis. They were men of about the same age as he, and although they disliked his title and privilege, they now treated him with grudging respect. Accustomed to the language of paintings, they did not have the patience to read through the volumes of tiny crabbed writing that were the records of the earlier Corteis. Four hundred years ago the Corteis had met on a regular basis in Tira Virte. At the time, Duke Renayo I had needed them to help govern the new-made country of Tira Virte. Their power had subsequently waned; one hundred years ago Arrigo II had banned it outright. The old Corteis had not been very powerful. But Rohario had discovered that it was not new, for instance, for the Corteis to abrogate to itself the right to control taxation and to accord its members privileges reserved for the nobility. These archives had been locked away, unavailable to anyone except the Grand Duke's conselhos. Until now.

Rohario led his escort into the basement of the Palasso Justissia. The smell of smoke still pervaded the gloomy basement, a reminder of the fire that had gutted one wing of the Palasso a month ago. Here worked the gleaners, sanctos and notaries, gathering bit by bit knowledge of the words and duties and rights held by the old Corteis. They worked by the light of glass-shuttered lanterns set in rows along plank tables hauled down to this room. Rohario joined them. He pulled an old volume from the top of a stack of old volumes, leather cracked and aging, and opened it. Sneezed at once as a cloud of dust rose off the pages. A polite young sancto handed him a handkerchief. Rohario thanked him and dusted off the book. At Palasso Verrada he would have had servants to do this for him. He sighed and began to read.

> *Due to the illness of Lord Limner Zaragosa Serrano, Duke Alejandro hereby appoints the aforesaid Sario Grijalva as Lord Limner, by the grace of il Matra ei Filho, by the power invested in him by the Ecclesia, and by the acclamation of the people of Tira Virte.*

The date read 951. Sario Grijalva, the master who had painted the altarpiece and *The First Mistress.* Interested, Rohario read on through months of tedious economic business recorded on now-yellowed pages. He yawned. Turning a page, he found a loose piece of parchment stuck into the book. He pulled it out carefully.

It seemed to be a recipe, but the words read like nonsense and the sides of the page were covered with tiny signs, unknown letters, wound together like the endless cracks and seams that riddle a parched stretch of earth. He turned the parchment over.

Here the same hand had written hastily, with many words crossed out or scrawled over, a decree. The writing was distinctive but curiously unpracticed, as if the hand was unused to forming sentences. Here and there the ink had blotched, but Roharío puzzled out the sense of it, and as he did so a rush of foreboding ran up his spine.

> *Let it be agreed that Palasso Grijalva and only Palasso Grijalva will supply the Heir with his Mistress, the one to whom he offers Marria do' Fantome. So shall it be established, by the decree of Duke Alejandro, by the* Peintraddo *painted by the brush of Sario Grijalva, for all time.*

Matra Dolcha! Amazing to have stumbled across this, the foundation of that long and strange relationship between the do'Verradas and the Grijalvas. Yet who had concocted it, Lord Limner or Duke? Or both of them, together, the alliance of Duke and Limner? Oddly enough, he remembered Beatriz's words to Eleyna at Chasseriallo.

"It took no great intelligence to see the change in you between the day you told Mother you would never wed Felippo and the day you stood simpering beside him at your wedding . . . if I had insisted, then they would have painted me into compliance, as they did to you! Only men are Gifted, but it is the Grijalva women who produce Gifted sons, no matter who the father is."

He folded the parchment in half and tucked it inside his coat, then flipped back through the volume, seeking references to the Grijalvas before Sario Grijalva had been appointed Lord Limner by Duke Alejandro. The accusation sprang out at him from ten pages earlier, in crabbed writing added between the perfect scribal hand that had recorded the proceedings of a private session called by Duke Baltran, Alejandro's father.

> *Lord Limner Zaragosa has called for the Duke to revoke the Edict of Protection granted to the Grijalva familia on the basis of rumors of dark magics used by these aforesaid Grijalvas to elevate their position at court.*

Matra Dolcha!
Footsteps echoed hollowly from the stairs outside. It was a wel-

come relief to look up from these dire warnings—until he saw the man who entered the chamber.

Maesso Azéma walked the length of the room to stand beside Rohario's chair. "I am surprised to find you here, Don Rohario, engaged in such industrious activity. You are a scholar? I had not known the do'Verradas indulged in philosophical pursuits."

Because this slur offered no opportunity for a polite rejoinder, Rohario merely nodded curtly at Azéma. He carefully closed the book and stuck it back into the pile, as if it no longer interested him.

"But since I have encountered you here, Don Rohario, perhaps we might speak privately. Grazzo."

Not wanting to cause a scene, Rohario acquiesced. They walked out into the passageway and stood on the drafty stairs, alone.

"You wonder why I come here, perhaps?" asked Azéma. "I, too, am looking for records, Don Rohario. Pieces of a puzzle that may at last be put together to form a coherent picture."

Azéma had a wild, triumphant gleam in his eye that made Rohario nervous, especially after what he had just read about Grijalva magic. Mennino moronno! To give credence to tales told by credulous men three hundred years dead! A cold draft rose up the stairwell. Rohario shifted to keep warm and waited for the old man to go on.

"I have no reason to love the do'Verradas. En verro, no reason to wish them well at all."

Was this meant to be a threat? "It is in your own interest, and the interest of all men of our station, to wish for prosperity, peace, and order in Tira Virte."

"Certainly, Don Rohario. But I remind you that I am an old man now and, as the saying goes, a dying man knows he will never have to pay his tailor's bill."

"I am sorry that your brother died, but it has nothing to do with me."

"It has everything to do with you, because you are a do'Verrada. But that is the point, is it not? Are you truly a do'Verrada?"

This was too much! "You will be careful," said Rohario in a low, taut voice, "how you speak of my blessed mother."

"It is not your mother I am concerned with. It is your grandmother."

Rohario laughed outright. "Grand Duchess Mechella? Everyone knows she was a saint. I cannot imagine what you mean by these ravings."

Azéma smiled. "It was a great scandal, greater than you can

imagine, ninio meyo, what went on between Arrigo and Mechella
and that Grijalva woman. Arrigo and Mechella had two children—
Teressa and Alessio—before they separated permanently and lived
after that time in separate households."

"*Three* children," Rohario straightened his cuffs, fingering the
buttons. Better that than punching the old man. "I suppose you
mean these insinuations to make me lose my temper and embarrass
myself. I think not."

So calm Azéma was. So sure of himself. "I do not forget your father. Let me tell you a story, and I suggest you listen well. The
Countess do'Alva had become Arrigo's mistress again. Arrigo and
Mechella had each their own picca aldeya, their own little village,
as we used to say then. They no longer spoke to or saw each other.
Grand Duke Cossimio was distraught, but despite his wishes they
did not reconcile. So you see, your father's siring can only have occurred in a single meeting of less than an hour, a supposed assig-
nation that took place in a back room at a ball! Even were Arrigo
not so much a prude that I doubt me if he would unburden himself
in such a situation no matter how beautiful the woman, I know
from my experience on my estates that a bull must cover a cow
more than once to ensure offspring."

"You are offensive, Maesso." Deliberately, Rohario used the
common honorific, not the man's title.

Azéma seemed impervious. Perhaps he truly was too old to care.
"Renayo looks nothing like the do'Verradas. He resembles his
mother, they all say. But none of his children resemble the
do'Verradas either. A strange coincidence."

"My mother and grandmother were Ghillasian!"

"So I investigated Mechella's picca aldeya, and whom did I
find? Grijalvas. They were everywhere, these Grijalvas."

"What are you suggesting?" Amazingly, his anger transformed
into coldness, not into heat.

"I am suggesting, Don Rohario, that your father is not the son of
Arrigo but rather the chi'patro child of a Grijalva limner."

Edoard would have struck him, at this point. But Rohario had a
sick feeling that striking this old man would only—in some twisted
fashion—fuel his fire. To imagine the name of his beloved grandmother Mechella—everyone had loved her!—being dragged
through the mud when she was not even alive to speak on her own
behalf!

Eiha! It made his stomach turn! It was all he could do not to spit
at the old man. But he must stay calm. "The Grijalvas have lived
under an Edict of Protection for hundreds of years. We have helped

them as they have helped us. I see nothing suspicious in this."
Others had, three hundred years ago. Some of the great baronial
families had died out in the intervening years. Others no longer enjoyed intimacy with the Grand Dukes. What did the Grijalvas possess that they had stayed for so many generations the favorites of
their do'Verrada rulers?

"Any woman," continued Azéma, as if he had not heard
Rohario's reply, "scorned by her husband and publically ridiculed
by his Mistress, might find solace in the arms of a handsome young
man who is constantly at her side. And there was such a young man
in her household. His name was Cabral Grijalva."

Zio Cabral?

"You have no proof," said Rohario quietly, all the while wishing
he had a sword and could run the merditto do'chiros through the
heart. But what if Azéma had already spread these vile accusations
elsewhere?

"I have no proof," agreed Azéma with that same repulsive smile.
"But I don't need proof. I need only cast doubt, Don Rohario. I
need only make people wonder, and you can be sure I have already
begun to ask questions where others may hear me. Soon these
questions will come to the notice of the Premio Sancto and the
Premia Sancta. Once the Ecclesia is involved, proof will be in the
hands of the Matra ei Filho. I suppose they will ask Renayo to
swear the truth of his parentage on their rings. A small thing to ask,
don't you agree?"

A small thing to ask, indeed. If the accusations that Azéma was
making were false. Rohario felt his heart like a cold stone. Why
else bother to make such accusations, knowing that a simple pledge
on the steps of the Cathedral Imagos Brilliantos could put any
doubts to rest, if he did not have good reason to believe that the accusations were true?

━━◆ EIGHTY-FOUR ◆━━

What is in plain sight is best hidden. Or so Eleyna discovered
when she realized the only way to copy the portrait of Saavedra
Grijalva was to do it openly as an exercise supervised by the Lord
Limner.

Lord Limner Sario. Strange to be supervised by a man who was
named after the master who had painted this great masterwork.
Finding an oak panel had been the hardest part, because of its great
size. Providential, indeed, that Sario had already prepared such a
panel with boiled linseed oil, for what purpose she dared not ask.
But he gave it to her cheerfully enough. The panel took a thin layer
of lean oil paint perfectly.

She sketched *The First Mistress* many times, and each time
Sario corrected her drawing with a line, a shadow, a subtle change.
His copied sketch of the portrait was perfect, so perfect she could
almost believe it was the same hand. At last, when she felt confident, she took an unused soft rag and wiped the surface of the panel
entirely clean.

Now she was ready to paint. For thirty-two days she did nothing
but paint, eat, sleep. At times Beatriz attended her, for Eleyna had
told Beatriz the whole story, but Beatriz had other duties—and
Eleyna did not want Sario to grow suspicious. Once every third or
fourth day she spoke to Agustin at dawn through his tiny painting.

It was impossible, of course, to copy the portrait perfectly. She
could study it minutely but never know exactly what combination
of colors, of underpainting, of tone and glaze, shadow and highlight, he had used to create *exactly* the effect of Saavedra's face
caught in the mirror. Or the subtle depredations flame had wrought
onto the honeycombed candle, cold now, burned down to the last
hour. Or the rich ash-rose velvet of her gown, each swagged pearl
highlighted with a glint.

Who are you? Saavedra asked, or so Eleyna imagined she would
ask, if she were truly alive in the painting and able to see out into
the living world through the reflection in the mirror.

"I am Eleyna Grijalva," she whispered, embarrassed to speak
out loud, yet there was no one to hear. The long hall was forlorn in
its emptiness. Trapped, terrified, alone, and forgotten, Saavedra

would surely be grateful for any least reassurance. Even if this was only in her mind, Eleyna felt compelled to speak.

Are you painting me free?

"No, alas, I cannot do so for I am a woman and not Gifted. But be assured I would if I could. Be assured I am doing this to help you."

I, too, am a painter.

Sisters, then, Eleyna thought. Of the same blood, though separated by centuries. "Why did Sario imprison you?"

Because he loves me, such as he can love anything beyond the vision that drives him.

So Eleyna's mind wandered, painting imagined conversations with a woman in a portrait. Was Sario the only one who was a little insane? Sometimes she doubted herself and her own mind. Still, she worked.

What is in plain sight is best hidden.

"Magnifico. I could almost believe I had painted it myself."

"Master Sario! You startled me." Eleyna touched her lips, as if afraid he had caught incriminating words on them.

But Sario noticed only the two paintings. "I am pleased with your progress, Eleyna. This would indeed fool all but a superbly trained eye. You have amply repaid my belief in your talent."

"Grazzo. It is an honor to work with you."

"Yes," he agreed. He no longer made any pretense about being a humble younger member of the Viehos Fratos. He reminded her of Andonio Grijalva, who had been Lord Limner before Andreo. A man of austere habits and an iron hand, Andonio had ruled Palasso Grijalva, his brothers, and all the young students with utter confidence in his own superiority. Or so at least he had seemed to the ten-year-old Eleyna who had been brought to his attention and then made the mistake of disagreeing with him.

But Sario was different. A monster, truly, for she no longer doubted that he had murdered Andreo or that he ruthlessly controlled Renayo through the portrait. But she could not begrudge him his arrogance. Not about art.

"Why does she hold a golden key?" she asked.

"Because she is Gifted, though she would never admit it." His lips were set in a grim line. So astonished was she by this answer that she gaped at him. Women were not Gifted! Preoccupied, he went on. "Tomorrow, when you are finished, you will come to my atelierro. We must finish your portrait."

Finish her portrait? Made slave or free—

He looked suddenly annoyed, reading her expression. "If you

are not my partisan, Eleyna, then you are my enemy." He spun and
walked away down the Galerria, his footsteps echoing on the marble floor.

She watched him go, then wrenched her gaze away. She must
not think of him so often. Eiha! Where was Rohario now? Was he
well? Was he thriving? To have his bright energy invest the
Galerria would be a mercy. Everyone had become as quiet as
Alazais. It was like living in a palasso of ghosts.

She looked down the Galerria. Was this not a palasso of ghosts,
of dead do'Verradas, their brides and barons, their favorites and enemies, their Mistresses and favored Limners, all displayed so their
influence, their haunting, could never be forgotten or ignored? If
Saavedra were alive and could be rescued, what stories would she
tell?

Almost finished, Sario had said, and indeed that was true. There
remained a few details: the golden key, the particular shine on
Saavedra's fingernails . . .

And there, suddenly, she saw it. The oscurra. Tiny letters and
symbols cunningly woven into the highlights that gave shine to her
nails. Once seen there she saw them everywhere, a pattern spreading out. In light, in shadow, in flame, in darkness, in the folds of her
skirts, in the coils of her hair, in the border of the table, in the
woodgrain of the door. Oscurra, everywhere, framed by a border
that was no obvious border but rather the limits of the chamber.
Even the door was spelled, bound with carven symbols she could
not read, that she wished desperately she *could* read.

"I've seen that door before," she whispered, but it was a faint
memory from when she was a child, exploring forgotten corridors.
Behind the door he imprisoned me. Can you open the door?

Oscurra, patterns marking the magic of the Grijalva Limners. A
door, waiting to be opened. She finally truly believed.

With a new sense of urgency, she put the final details onto the
painting. It was almost dark when she finished, and she was too
tired, far too tired, to do anything but go back to her room and
sleep.

⚜ EIGHTY-FIVE ⚜

The Viehos Fratos gathered in the ancient chamber known as the Crechetta, buried in the oldest section of Palasso Grijalva. Its whitewashed walls gleamed in the light of candles held in old-fashioned iron stands at each corner of the room. It was cool and damp. The Limners stood—what few of them were left—and waited. A single easel rested in the center of the room, a shrouded painting upon it.

Giaberto blew out all the candles until only one remained lit. Shadows twisted in eerie patterns across the room. Young Damiano, looking grim, brought out a lancet and heated it in the candle flame. He walked to each of the assembled Limners—nine now, besides Agustin, only nine—and took blood from them. The warm blade bit into Agustin's arm and he stifled a yelp of pain. He was frightened, but he dared not show it.

Damiano brought the vial of fresh blood to old Zosio, who with his arthritic hands could no longer paint but could still mix colors. As Zosio prepared the paletto with tincture of blood, Giaberto unveiled the painting. Agustin gasped, although he had known what it must be: Sario's *Peintraddo Chieva.*

"Chieva do'Sangua," said Giaberto. "We will all feel pain, for we have blended our power in order to discipline one of our own who has violated the faith of the Chieva do'Orro. No man may wear the Golden Key who uses it for his own sake—" Here he bent his harsh gaze on Agustin, reminding the boy how angry the Viehos Fratos had been when they found out about Agustin's experiment. And yet that experiment had borne fruit, had it not? "What we do, we do for the sake of the Grijalvas and Tira Virte."

Giaberto picked up a brush and began to paint. So is a traitor— the murderer of Andreo Grijalva—punished: milk-blindness clouds the eye; the hands are consumed by a virulent attack of bone-fever. Agustin's hands curled in on themselves involuntarily. His fingers smarted and ached by turns. His vision hazed over, as if a white veil were being drawn across it.

The pain slid off, like water down roof tiles. He blinked, staring. In the portrait, once-proud Sario now stared at the world with a film of white over his dark eyes; his young, strong hands wore the knitted agony of acute bone-fever.

And yet . . . something was wrong. Agustin didn't *feel* anything, and he knew he ought to.

"It didn't work," he blurted out. "It's painted there, but that's all." *That's all.*

The Viehos Fratos had disciplined one of their own—*and it had not worked.*

"What has gone wrong?" rasped old Zosio.

Giaberto wrung his hands as if they hurt. "The fault lies not in my brushstrokes or our blood," he said in a hoarse voice. "The Chieva do'Sangua worked. This portrait must not be Blooded. But I watched him paint it! As did you, Zosio. Matra ei Filho, all of us here supervised this portrait's painting except Damiano and Agustin. It *was* Blooded. It *was* tested. Here." He touched with the tip of his brush a red pinprick on the back of the painted Sario's left hand. "Here, the pin. It is the same painting."

"Could he have painted another portrait?" asked Agustin. Because he had been thinking a great deal about the Gift he now possessed, he went on rashly. "Could a second portrait protect him from this one?"

Zosio snorted, began to speak, and fell silent. With a gesture bred of impatience and anger, Giaberto threw the canvas shroud back over the painting. Little hollows formed in the heavy cloth where it stuck to wet paint.

"I have never heard or read of such a thing being done," said Giaberto harshly. "Where would he have learned to do it? If he has done a second portrait, then where is it?"

"But it could be done, couldn't it?" demanded Agustin. They never answered his questions, not directly!

"No," said Zosio. "It could *not* be done, else we would have been taught how to guard ourselves against such a trick."

"But what else could have happened?" Their lack of imagination was infuriating. "Could he have painted an unBlooded copy and left it here, and hidden the original elsewhere?"

Giaberto shook his head emphatically. "My nephew is right. This painting must be a copy. There is no other possible explanation." He paused, in all ways now the leader of the Viehos Fratos. "Sario Grijalva has gone rogue. He can never again be trusted. We must destroy him at our first opportunity, or he will destroy us first. If he murdered Andreo, then there is no horrible deed he will not stoop to. We are no longer safe."

"But what can we *do?*" asked Agustin when the others, evidently stupified, did not speak.

Giaberto unlocked the door that led out of the Crechetta and opened it. A flood of light illuminated the room, the pale candle, and the canvas shroud. "I don't know," he admitted.

"What do you think, Grandzio?" Agustin asked later that day as he and Cabral sat by the yellow-tiled fountain in the back courtyard, taking some sun. Cabral spent more and more time on this bench, listening and watching the flow of the water as if it were telling him stories or painting him faces in the mist.

"I remember a story Zevierin told me once," Cabral said, fussing with his lace cuffs, a habitual gesture. "When he and Leilias first decided to marry, she suggested in jest that he paint her a man who could come out of the painting only long enough to get her with child and then vanish into the painting again."

"What does that have to do with Sario's *Peintraddo?*"

Cabral smiled. "Patience. I was thinking of Saavedra Grijalva. Her figure *has* moved within the painting. That we have established. Does this mean she is alive within the painting?"

"How could that be?"

"Long ago, in the time of Duke Alejandro, a Tza'ab army threatened to invade Joharra. So Sario Grijalva painted an army."

Agustin snorted. Not even *he* was this credulous. "Brought them to life?"

Cabral responded to his disbelief with a chuckle.

"Did he do it? Did it work?" Agustin almost bounced up and down on the bench.

"How eager you are to hear, ninio." Cabral's gaze fixed on the flowing water of the fountain, as if seeing another scene there. "How unlike dearest 'Chella—" He broke off and shook his head. "But that was a long time ago, alas. This is the story: Sario Grijalva painted an army. Thousands of soldiers appeared miraculously at sunrise across the distant dunes. The Tza'ab fled in terror. But the guerierros do'fantome? They were hollow, hands and faces, nothing else."

"What happened?"

"Ninio meyo, you look positively rapt. I hope you are not enjoying this!" Cabral smiled, but there was a grim undertone to his voice. "Sario painted the dunes bare, and the army vanished, never to be seen again."

Agustin let out a satisfied sigh; that had certainly been a good story. But then, considering it, he turned serious. "What has this to do with Sario's *Peintraddo*? Or the portrait of Saavedra?"

Cabral arranged his hands in his lap, fussily, as a woman arranges flowers. The seams and calluses and lesions on his old hands seemed themselves to tell a story, to reveal secrets, if only Agustin knew their language. "Do any of you truly know what the Gifted are capable of? What if Saavedra Grijalva didn't disappear at all but was captured in a painting?"

Imagine! Then Agustin shook his head. "It couldn't be done. But—" He reconsidered. "What if it *could* be done?"

"How could Sario escape the Chieva do'Sangua, although it was painted onto his Blooded *Peintraddo*? Impossible, too, I think, and yet it happened. I think the Viehos Fratos would be better off discovering what Sario can and cannot do with his Gift, now that they know he is capable of anything. And perhaps they had better start thinking about *why*."

"Why?"

"Why Sario? As a boy he had no special ambition or talent. Has he been harboring ambition all these years and hiding it from us? If so, then perhaps he is more dangerous than anyone here imagines. If so, if he can evade the Chieva do'Sangua, I hope Giaberto and the others are working very hard right now to find out where Sario learned such knowledge."

Water slid down the sides of the fountain, an endless, restless flow, like Agustin's own curiosity, never coming to a halt. He worried at a fingernail with his teeth, caught himself, and wound the offending hand through his thick black hair. "Giaberto says that if a spell was used to murder Andreo, then it is not any spell written of in the *Folio*."

"Of course I have not read the *Folio*. I am sorry to hear such things are written down."

Agustin waited, but Cabral said nothing more. He was not Gifted, after all, and could not be expected to know the deepest secrets contained in the *Folio* and the knowledge passed by word and hand. Cabral could not be expected to truly understand the great burdens laid on the Gifted. . . . Agustin shook himself, disliking his own argument, mouthed from words he had heard the Viehos Fratos speak so many times. If he believed them, then he might as well believe that Eleyna could not ever be a great painter. And he knew that wasn't true.

Matra ei Filho! And where was Eleyna now? Eleyna was alone in Palasso Verrada with a murderer! There must be *some* way to protect her. There had been rash talk in the Atelierro of hiring an assassin! He felt so helpless, thinking of Sario who could, evidently, do whatever he pleased. Eiha. Poor Cabral, who must always sit and wait because he did not have the Gift.

"Do you miss your old friends, Grandzio?" the boy asked, seeing Cabral as impossibly old suddenly. *I'll never reach that age. I'll never outlive all my friends and family, as Cabral has.*

Cabral's smile was as sweet as it was sad. "I miss my old friends, indeed, ninio meyo. You are very kind to sit here with me and give me comfort. But, in fact, I am waiting for a visitor."

"A visitor?" The Grijalvas rarely went out these days and more rarely received visitors. The Picca, normally flooded with buyers in the days before Mirraflores Moon, was empty, and the streets were quiet, under a curfew mandated by the Provisional Corteis.

Old Davo appeared, escorting a man. Agustin stood up, he was so surprised. "Don Rohario!"

"Master Agustin. Dolcha mattena. Do not stand, Zio, grazzo." But although the young do'Verrada's words were polite, his tone, indeed his entire posture, betrayed agitation. "I came as soon as I could," he continued. Then he began to pace, first to the back stairs, then to the arcade that led on into the other portions of the compound, then to the fountain, once around it, pausing to watch the fall of water down the azulejos, then circling again.

"Eleyna is well," said Cabral.

Rohario did not respond. He was, Agustin saw, not pacing as much as peering into every corner and nook as if to make sure no one else was within earshot. The courtyard remained empty; no servants swept the pavement or watered the plants. At a nod from Cabral, Davo left.

"We are here alone, Rohario," Cabral said, "and Agustin is trustworthy. What is it, ninio meyo?"

Rohario jerked to a stop. *"Ninio meyo,"* he muttered. He stared at Cabral in an odd, searching manner. Agustin had a sudden urgent idea that Rohario was about to say something reckless. "Are you my grandfather?"

Agustin tapped an ear. Surely his hearing had failed.

"Matra Dolcha," murmured Cabral so softly that Agustin barely heard the words leave his lips. "So it has come. Where did you hear this?"

Out spilled a confused account: Brendizias and bastards. Agustin was too shocked to make sense of the explanation.

Cabral patted the stone bench. "Sit beside me, Rohario."

Rohario sat heavily, limply, more like a puppet than the whirlwind of energy he had been moments before. There was a short silence. The sun's light spread like water over the paved brick of the courtyard. The fountain ran on. Cabral cleared his throat.

Roharrio shifted abruptly to look at the old man. "It's true. I can see it in your face."

"It is true. But it is a very long story."

Roharrio nodded, acknowledging this fact, not crying out against it. Agustin, stunned, admired his self-possession. And his courage. Roharrio do'Verrada was chi'patro—not a true do'Verrada at all. Matra Dolcha! And if he were, then so was Grand Duke Renayo. Cabral was Renayo's father? It did not bear thinking of!

"I would like to hear the story," said Roharrio quietly.

In the tranquil courtyard with the low rush of the fountain serenading him, Cabral told his grandson the truth.

"It was nothing we intended," he said at the end of his story. "Nothing we sought, 'Chella and I. But I loved her from the moment I saw her—eiha, Roharrio, 'Chella had that quality, that Luza, that goes beyond beauty: she had a true and trusting heart. She gave it willingly and wholely to Arrigo and he threw it back in her face." He seemed about to utter a curse but restrained himself. "You should not blame her for seeking at last—when Arrigo made it obvious he would have nothing more to do with her, when her pain became too great for her to bear alone—the simple but devoted love of a man like myself." He sighed and wiped a single tear from one cheek. "That we made a child together—dear little Renayo—is the greatest *gift* the Mother could ever have given me."

Agustin could not look at Cabral and imagine this mild old man as the *father* of Grand Duke Renayo. The Grand Duke was the bastard son of a chi'patro Grijalva! Roharrio looked dumbfounded but not, oddly enough, appalled. At last he reached into his coat and drew out an old piece of paper. Without a word he handed it to Cabral.

Cabral opened it and examined both sides. "It's very old," he said. "Strange. This resembles the handwriting of Dioniso Grijalva. He was one of my teachers, known for having an eccentric hand. He died under . . . odd . . . circumstances."

"Circumstances having to do with magic, Zio?" asked Roharrio. His voice wavered only slightly.

"Most Grijalva secrets are linked to their magic." Cabral turned the old document over, studying the words. "This side is clear enough, about the Marria do'Fantome, but the other looks like a recipe of nonsense words." He handed it to Agustin.

The boy shook his head. "These are Tza'ab letters, such as I've seen in the *Folio*. The words here mean nothing to me."

"Where did you find this?" Cabral asked Rohario.

"I found it in the basement vaults of the Palasso Justissa, stuck in an old book dated to 950, the reigns of Baltran the First and Alejandro." Rohario cocked his head to one side and stared for a long time at the spray of water lifting from the fountain. "You are truly my grandfather?"

At first Cabral did not answer. They sat, all of them, so still that two butterflies settled on the ironwork back of the bench, then fluttered away, bright yellow wings a fleeting reminder of summer approaching. What would it be like, Agustin wondered, to reach such a great age that the endless daily concerns of life, the joys and tragedies, might finally be assimilated into serenity? He would never know.

Finally Cabral spoke with that serenity, crafted of age and acceptance. "I am truly the father of Renayo. I am your grandfather. I loved Mechella very much, Rohario. She would have remained true to Arrigo had he given her the slightest encouragement. Eiha. I will not complain now, although I know I should not have let my heart lead me onto such dangerous paths. But I cannot regret the happiness we shared."

Rohario hid his face in his hands. His shoulders shook so that Agustin could not tell if he was laughing or weeping. Cabral laid a comforting hand on the young man's arm. In this way, the fountain oblivious to the drama enacted before it, they sat for a long while in silence.

⚷— EIGHTY-SIX —⚷

The girl came in at dawn to stoke up the fire and open the drapes. Eleyna, half-awake, listened to her movements, heard the door open and close with a soft click. She rose and dressed in the same gown and lace shawl—her hyacinth-embroidered widow's shawl—that she wore every time she spoke with Agustin. Filled the lantern with oil, lit the wick, placed it in the precise spot a hand's width from the corner of the table. Then she brought out the parchment and centered it, sides neatly aligned with the table's edge. Sitting, she squared her shoulders and tucked one stray corner of shawl into the ribbon tied around the high waist of her gown so it wouldn't slip and spoil the spell.

Shadows lengthened. Light changed.

"Eleyna." The whisper, a disembodied voice sounding so close that each time she had to stop herself from reaching out across the table to try and touch him.

"Agustin. I am here."

"Beware. Yesterday the Viehos Fratos met to discipline Sario, but it didn't work!"

She heard the urgency in his voice, the fear. "It didn't work?"

"The Chieva do'Sangua did not work. Sario has protected himself—"

That suddenly, Sario burst out of her closet. She stared at him, astonished, then shook free of her amazement, began to stand.

Too late. Even that instant of shocked surprise was too much. He grabbed the lantern, wrenched open the glass shutter, and with palpable fury drenched the parchment with hot oil.

She grabbed for his wrist, got oil on her arm, but it was futile. The parchment shriveled and blackened, not quite catching flame. She ripped off her shawl and smothered the paper, but it did not matter. The damage was already done.

Surely it was only in her imagination that she heard Agustin scream.

Sario yanked her away from the table. "How could you betray me like this! I am teaching *you!* I chose *you!* Not even a Gifted boy. I saw your talent and chose to nurture it when no one else would. How could you!"

"*Murderer!* That was my Agustin!"

He slapped her. Furious, she slapped him back, hard enough that a red stain stood out on his skin.

"Canna!" he swore at her, spitting in his fury. He grabbed her by the wrist and dragged her after him, out into the corridor, down the long halls to Alazais' suite. Only a few servants walked quietly through the halls at this early morning hour. They looked, but they said nothing. No one questioned Lord Limner Sario. Not anymore.

In shock she let herself be pulled along. Hot oil scorching a blooded painting. *Matra Dolcha, have mercy on him. He is only a child, a delicate filho like Your own.*

Alazais was awake, sitting on her silk couch. She looked up as they entered, did not respond to Eleyna's terrified yelp but went serenely back to her embroidery. Sario dragged Eleyna farther back, into a chamber with only one door.

He shoved her inside, closed the door behind him, locked it and pocketed the key, and then stood, staring at her, eyes bright with angry recriminations. "Where did they learn to talk through paintings? Why was I not told?"

Truly a monster, because he did not care. "That was Agustin!" A sob was torn out of her. "Is he dead?"

"Burned, certainly. Dead, perhaps." He shrugged. "You used me, Eleyna." His tone was plaintive. "I have offered you everything I know and you repay me like this! And they—! That they would keep such a secret from *me* but tell an unGifted woman—!"

She could not help herself. She would not give the Viehos Fratos credit for what she and Agustin had devised. "It is not their secret," she cried triumphantly, and by his startled expression saw she had stricken him. "Agustin and I discovered it. No one else. We did not need your *Folio*—"

"Bassda!" His expression, enraged, scared her into silence. "You? *You!* UnGifted and untrained. . . ." He touched his key, almost caressed it, and a strange distant look settled on his features. "That I should find the one, and he a woman." Abruptly he controlled himself. He gestured to the small chamber. A cot stood in one corner. There was a chair and table, two easels, paints, a locked chest, and a number of canvasses stacked along the walls. "Here you will stay."

"What do you mean to do to me?" She caught her breath, an eerie calm descending on her now, replacing rage and fear.

He moved to one of the easels and pulled off the cloth: her *Peintraddo*. The truth of her revealed: the Luza do'Orro in her eyes and face and a brush in her hand. Such beauty: it rested like the ashes of burned paper in her mouth. He touched tongue to finger, and that finger to her painted lips. "It is finished. I can do nothing *to* you, estuda meya. You are safe from the Grijalvas, but you are also safe from me, if that is what you feared. I kept *my* part of the bargain, though you have betrayed *me.*" This spoken querelously, like a boy whining over a childish injustice. "If I burn this painting to punish you, then I kill myself."

"You killed Agustin," she whispered. But perhaps Agustin was only burned. The parchment had not truly caught fire. *Matra Dolcha, make it be true.*

Sario was oblivious to her, caught in his own monstrous concerns. "Yesterday I felt a burning on my hands, a fever, but as if it were happening to another body, not my own. My vision clouded for a moment, then cleared. So I knew they were attempting the Chieva do'Sangua. And I knew then I was harboring a traitor. Which could only be you. But I did not expect—to speak to each other through the painting! *I* should have thought of it!" He stopped suddenly, cocked his head as if listening, then hurried out the door. She heard the key turn in the lock, then silence.

Matra ei Filho! What had happened to Agustin? Retreating, she collapsed onto the cot and lost herself to weeping. And, later, to a kind of blank staring.

Nothing. No one. Too heavy to move. Perhaps he had imprisoned her within a painting. Perhaps this weight of air was what it felt like, dragging her down. Not grief at all, but paint and oscurra, the spelled boundaries confining her, forever and ever.

⚡→ EIGHTY-SEVEN →⚡

It was dark. How had it come to be twilight so soon? Where was she? Eleyna sat up. The canvas cot creaked under her weight. The chamber looked unfamiliar, dark shapes bulking against the wall, easels like ungainly human figures, stick legs and enormous bellies, the angular shadows of the table and chair.

It all came back to her. She had to shut her eyes, the force of memory was so like a sudden blinding light turned full on her, who had been lost in darkness. She had slept while Agustin died, if he was not already dead. Matra ei Filho. Beloved Agustin. She caught a sob in her throat. Heard the key turn in the lock.

She stood as the door opened and Sario entered the room, holding a lamp. He carried a tray in his other hand: a dinner of lamb, bread, vegetables, and fish smothered in a garlic sauce so strong she smelled it from across the room. He brought a fine white wine to drown her sorrow.

She ate, because it would be stupid not to. The silence smothered her, like a thick layer of paint, applied to a canvas in order to hide the image beneath. When he left, taking lamp and tray with him, it was too dark to see, to do anything except grope back to the cot and lie down. Clearly he did not mean to leave her fire, in case she chose to revenge herself by burning one of his spelled paintings, or glass or fork or knife with which to cut into the paint and cause him pain. That night she would have done so, had she the means.

In the morning he returned with rolls and goat cheese and tea. Again he watched her. His scrutiny made her uneasy.

"I give you a choice," he said finally, as if he could not keep silence against his better judgment. "I cannot bear to see your gift go to waste, *you,* who should have been Gifted. I will continue to teach you, if you wish still to learn from me."

"Never! Not from you, not from the monster who murdered my brother!"

He sighed, so mild, so reasonable in the light of day. "I *believe* in your talent, Eleyna. Who else does? Who can teach you what you want to know?"

No one else, truly.

Sario brought out pencils and paper and went to the window. In the courtyard below the bloodflowers were in bud, a few already blooming. Six days until Mirraflores Eve. He began to sketch. Her feet worked of their own to move closer to him, so that her eyes might watch him draw.

This man had shattered her life and murdered her beloved brother.

She turned away and sat on the cot, hands thrust between her knees so they would not betray her. After a while, uttering no word of excuse, no word of reproach, he left, locking everything behind him.

But he came back in the afternoon. "I am the only one who will teach you, Eleyna," he said. "*All* the secrets of the Limners."

"You murdered Agustin," she whispered. *All the secrets.* Matra Dolcha, protect her from this temptation.

He went back to the window and began to sketch again. She turned just enough to watch his back, the assured movements of his hands, the set of his posture as he drew. She rose, but not to look at *him*. He was a monster.

He knew so much.

She crept two steps closer. He worked on, pretending not to notice her. How did he shade the flower petals *just so,* to suggest their rich crimson color?

Matra ei Filho, was she not also a monster? For she knew at that instant she could not resist him, and she hated herself for it. But she asked for pencil and paper.

He spent the rest of that day with her. Evidently he had Renayo so deeply in his control that he no longer needed to monitor his activities every hour of the day. A servant brought luncheon. Sario left at dusk. He locked away all the tools and paint and left her without a lamp. But it was not quite dark.

She explored the room. On one easel her portrait still stood, oscurra twined into the brush her image held, twined into her black hair and the iris of her eyes. The simple beauty of the painting brought tears to her eyes, and more yet when she saw that he had woven cunningly into the border framing the *Peintraddo* a pattern of golden keys, each wrapped into the next. Monsters, both of them. She must not forget what he was! She forced herself to look away.

On the other easel rested the portrait of Renayo. Sketches of nobles and servants littered the floor in one corner, tossed there like refuse, and yet each was a testament to Sario's genius. She listened at the keyhole but heard nothing. Then she examined the canvasses that leaned against the wall. Here, a half-finished portrait of Edoard. There, the portrait of Beatriz, mostly done but evidently abandoned. Some landscapes, a study of an old country house which Eleyna did not recognize, and one delicate and touching study in pale watercolors of the fountain of bells in a rain-washed courtyard.

In the most shadowed corner stood three larger canvasses, their faces hidden against the wall. Carefully she tipped them out.

Matra Dolcha! The first was a fine study of Andreo Grijalva. She recognized the oscurra hidden in every part of the portrait, though she could not read it. Sario had not yet taught her. But she could guess the intent.

Cypresses, for Death.

Behind Andreo was a portrait of Nicollo Grijalva. His was not as elaborately detailed with the scratchings of the hidden language, but there was a strange blood-red spot on his chest, as a pinprick, stuck in skin, would leave blood.

The last panel was the largest. Eleyna set the others to one side and moved this one away from the wall. It was almost dark. At first she could not quite decipher the shapes, because there was an odd blotch in the center of the painting.

It was a room, stark and poor, perhaps an attic since it had a steep ceiling and a bare plank floor. A few nondescript pieces of furniture, including a cot much like the one here, furnished it. The blotch was not a blotch at all but bare gray ground, shaped in a human form.

She leaned closer. The panel smelled oddly of myrtle. *Speak With the Dead.* Shaped in a woman's form.

Heart racing, she stepped back hastily. Was this how he captured people and imprisoned them in paintings? By painting a room and leaving space to paint the body into the room? Is this where he intended to imprison her?

Moronna. The painting of Saavedra was over three hundred years old. This Sario could not have painted it. Like blue roses, it was impossible. And yet . . . two Sario Grijalvas had become Lord Limner, *that one* and this one. She had seen the self-portrait of the first Sario—handsome, dark-eyed, with Tza'ab brown skin. He looked nothing like *this* Sario, who was a typical if rather plain Grijalva, the chi'patro blood worn thin.

And yet . . . if *this* Sario had discovered that such a spell could be accomplished, why not try it for himself?

If only she had a lamp! She peered closer, and closer still. Was that a strand of gold caught along the hairline? Here was another. A woman with blonde hair. There were only two women with blonde hair in this entire palasso: Princess Alazais and her Ghillasian servant.

Ridiculous.

But she carefully replaced the paintings so Sario would not know for certain if she had moved them.

The next day, when he came for her lesson, she said nothing to him, asked him no questions except the expected ones. "How do you know so much, Master Sario?"

He smiled gently. "I have lived a long time."

The soft words made her shiver, although the rainy season had all but ended and the courtyard outside was flooded with sunlight. Princesses brought to life from paintings. Young men who had lived for centuries. These fantasies seemed absurd in the fine light of a brilliant day.

But not even the sun could erase the chill in her heart.

Like Saavedra, she was a prisoner. The days passed uneventfully. Sario spent hours of every day with her. Matra Dolcha, but he was a fine painter. He knew so much.

He is a murderer, and I, because I did not turn him away, I am no better. Agustin, forgive me.

As Agustin would. So did she weep for him, and pray that he lived.

Mirraflores Eve dawned bright and with a sudden outpouring of flowers. Shrubs bloomed in splashes of foam and wine and sky. The bloodflower beds broke into a breathtaking array of crimson. Servant girls in perfectly groomed livery tossed petals onto the walkways, and Timarra do'Verrada spent the morning with Princess Alazais picking up the petals and mixing them with spices and ground-up leaves to make scented sachets.

Sario arrived just after the midday bell rang.

"Interesting news," he said cheerfully, as if he were a gentleman calling to bring the latest gossip. "This provisional assembly of the Corteis has approved a *Constitussion,* which they will present to Grand Duke Renayo in two or three days as a kind of flowering of their assembly, I presume, together with a notice that they intend to call elections for the Corteis."

He had sketch paper tucked under one arm.

She pulled it free and smoothed it out on the table. "What is this?"

"Roharia do'Verrada. I finally got a look at him. He is now an influential member of the Corteis. If they indeed call elections to be held next month, he is likely to run for and win a seat." He laughed. "A do'Verrada sitting in council with commoners!"

"What do you mean to do with him?" she demanded. Then, unable to help herself, she grabbed the pencil out of his hand and added a line to the sketch. "This isn't right. This way, you see? He has a strength in him that you haven't captured."

There was a sudden silence. She looked up and was abruptly aware that *she* had corrected *him*.

He jerked the pencil out of her hand, leaned over the drawing . . . and did nothing. He studied the sketch.

Finally, he straightened. "I see." His expression was unreadable. "Matra Dolcha," he swore, speaking as if to himself, as if he had forgotten she was there, "that I should find the one and he be a woman, and unGifted! You would find this amusing, I think, corasson."

She flushed to hear the endearment, realized an instant later that it was not addressed to her. To whom, then? Where had she heard that tone of his before?

"It is not yet time to free you, corasson." Corasson . . . Saavedra. Of course.

Sario glanced up, listened, then abruptly left the room but not so quickly that he forgot to lock the door behind him. Eleyna spent the rest of the day alone, a long day, troubled as she was by these thoughts of a woman trapped, alive, in a painting.

As twilight spread over the courtyard below, painting the chamber with shadows, she heard the faint sound of singing, the sweet light voices of sanctas raised in the Hymn of Flowering, sung for girls celebrating their first blood.

Like the blood of the Limners. *Matra Dolcha, have mercy on Agustin. As every girl comes into her womanhood, so grant him a man's life. . . .* Such as it was, for a Limner who could never sire children and whose Gift would be cut short by early death.

The key turned in the lock. The door cracked open.

"No!" shouted Sario. "No! I forbid it!"

Fainter, Grand Duke Renayo's voice. "I . . . I think you ought to listen to Lord Limner Sario. Really I do. But in truth, Sario, you must admit . . . tradition . . . it's normal for young women to go out . . . how can we refuse the pleadings of these venerable sanctas?"

A determined push sent the door flying open. Of course! Grijalvas had no power over the Ecclesia. There stood Beatriz, armed with three wimpled sanctas who smelled of rosewater. Behind them stood Sario, livid, and the Grand Duke, confused and weak and pale. Guards accompanied them, but no one dared raise a hand against the three old sanctas, whose hands and faces were as wrinkled as their white robes were starched and clean.

"Come, ninia," said one. Another took her by the arm and led her out as if she were a half-wit. Eleyna, too stunned to react, barely managed to set one foot in front of the other. Sario was swearing. Beatriz was smiling prettily. So they led her through the suite, singing the hymn "The Mother's Blood Gives Us Life" in voices still strong and true. A cart and horse and driver waited in the kitchen's courtyard. Beatriz helped the sanctas up into the back.

"The portrait—" cried Eleyna, coming to life as she realized she might actually escape.

"It is here."

"Not the *copy*—"

"What you want is here. Eleyna! *Get in!* We must go *now.*"

Eleyna got in, but she could not get her bearings. They rattled out through an arched tunnel that led to a back gate. The Sanctas' presence gave them passage through the Palasso gate, gave them safety running the gauntlet of barricades that had turned Meya Suerta's streets into a maze of obstacles. Yet the mood tonight was wild and sweet, celebratory.

"A new flowering for you, blessed sancta!" called a cluster of girls to the women in the cart as it passed. The sanctas signed a benediction. The cart trundled on. From every inn and most houses came the sound of singing and laughter.

"Why are they all so happy?" asked Eleyna. Her freedom made her dizzy. She could only remember the whitewashed walls of Sario's chamber, the endless portraits hung in the Galerria.

"The Corteis will meet again," said the eldest sancta. "They are happy for this sign of the Matra's blessing upon them."

"Do you think it a blessing?" asked Beatriz curiously. "It is a great change."

"So says the Matra: that every thing Her hand touches flowers with Her grace."

"Even Sario Grijalva?" Eleyna murmured under her breath.

Beatriz leaned close against her, whispering into her ear. "Were you lovers?"

She shuddered. Were they not bound in a way more intimate than that of mere flesh? But she could not speak of this even to Beatriz. It was too shameful. "How came these sanctas to help us?" she asked instead. "They have always disliked the

Grijalvas, and you—the Mistress!—are everything they speak against."

"I simply asked. Whatever they may think of me, Eleyna, they are compassionate."

They came at last to the torch-lit doors that opened into Palasso Grijalva. Servants ran out and at Beatriz's direction took the huge portrait, bundled in cloth, and carried it inside. Beatriz thanked the sanctas sweetly and with evident sincerity. They blessed her and, still in the cart, rolled off into the night.

Eleyna and Beatriz hurried down the tunnel and emerged into the central courtyard. Torches flowered here, a haze of light and smoke driving away darkness. A woman stood in the entrance of the great hall. She started and walked quickly forward.

"Beatriz! Thank the Matra that you have come!" It was their mother. Eleyna braced herself. "Eleyna! Matra ei Filho, our prayers are answered. My poor darling has been asking after you." Dionisa took Eleyna by the hand and led her forward. Dionisa looked wan and exhausted. Eleyna went meekly, shocked by the change in her mother's disposition. Beatriz followed.

Dionisa took them to a side room off the great hall. The ghastly smell of infected flesh permeated the little chamber. Without a word Dionisa handed handkerchiefs to her daughters. Eleyna covered her nose with the cloth. Beatriz did not bother to use hers; instead, she hurried forward to the bed.

To Agustin.

A sancta knelt at the bedside, praying. Eleyna needed only one look at him, at his blistered face and hands, his burned eyes closed in a fitful sleep, needed only one deep breath of the air of this sickroom, to hope that Agustin would die soon. Her handkerchief was already damp with tears.

The sancta looked up as Beatriz knelt beside her. She nodded, then looked toward Eleyna. "You are the elder sister? He has asked for you, but I have just given him a sleeping draught. He will not wake for many hours, I pray."

"Is there any hope?" asked Eleyna in a hoarse voice.

"Nazha. I am sorry."

"I will stay," said Beatriz. "You know where you must go, Eleynita."

"Yes." Numb, Eleyna left the room.

Her mother followed her. "Is it true Sario murdered Andreo?" Dionisa asked the question tentatively, as if afraid to know.

"Yes. I must go to the Viehos Fratos now."

To her horror, her mother acquiesced without a fight. She just let Eleyna go and returned to Agustin's bedside.

Eleyna climbed the stairs to the Atelierro. *Monster. Monster. Monster.* Each word echoed with the fall of a foot on a stair. *I no less than him for letting him teach me even after I knew what he had done.*

At her uncle's order, Damiano reluctantly let her in. The Limners stood around the portrait of Saavedra, staring, pointing, arguing. There were so few of them. They looked so weak, especially compared to Sario's strength and his great skill. No wonder he despised them. No wonder he wanted only to restore the Grijalva family to its former glory.

Eiha, moronna! Soon you will be murdering them at his behest!

"You have seen the oscurra," she said. They grumbled but did not stop her from approaching. "Here, the pattern begins. . . . Where is Cabral?"

"He is not Gifted," said Giaberto gravely.

"*I* am not Gifted. He is eldest here. It was *his* memory of this portrait that made us all admit the truth, was it not?"

So demoralized were they that Damiano was sent to fetch Cabral at once, with no further argument. When he left, the arguments broke out again. None of them wanted to admit to the horrible truth.

"But you cannot move people into or out of paintings!" protested Zosio. "It is not possible. I would suppose he painted this in order to force her to leave Tira Virte."

"No." Giaberto shook his head. "Eleyna is correct. If we read these oscurra, we see binding spells, not suggestion spells. Damiano searched for ten days through our old storerooms and found an inventory done in the time of Cossimio I. Unless we have multiple copies of this portrait displayed in the Galerria, she has certainly changed position within the painting." Only Zosio grumbled. The others, with their stricken faces, had obviously already admitted the truth. Giaberto spoke plaintively. "But if she is truly alive in there, how to get her out?"

"I have now studied this painting thoroughly," said Eleyna. "The door looks familiar to me."

Damiano returned with Cabral as she spoke. The old man stared at the portrait for a long time, with evident feeling, one he did not share with the others. After a long while Cabral shook his head as a servant girl shakes down cobwebs with a broom. "Familiar, but distantly so. Like Eleyna I feel the door rests somewhere in this Palasso."

"We three will go look," said Giaberto.

They made their way into the oldest part of the house, ancient corridors whose plank floors were warped by time, whose corners no longer fit at proper angles. Some of these were servant quarters, some storerooms. But there was also a flight of stairs, dimly seen in the gloom, that led to a whitewashed corridor grayed now with dust and years.

"Strange," muttered Giaberto. "I thought I knew every part of this Palasso. I don't recall this."

They missed it the first time they walked down the corridor, although how they could have missed it when it stood right there in the wall—only magic could cause such blindness. It was a door, an ordinary door and yet not ordinary at all: old polished mahoghany with a wrought-iron latch, painted with a border of faded sigils. Iron-studded and iron-bound.

Cabral opened it, for it was not locked by any mechanical means. It was simply *not there,* unless one knew it must be and therefore saw it. Eleyna shivered to think that no one had known in over three hundred years—no, *one* man had known. Sario had known.

In the chamber behind the door dust lay in swathes so thick her footsteps left a visible trail. Slowly they entered. More slowly Eleyna turned once round, gaping. Through the dust and grime she marked traces of old grandeur and all else the same as it was in the portrait: windows, a table, a candle and a lamp, a mirror set on an easel, its face so smothered in dust she could see no reflection at all. The setting lacked only the jewel-encrusted book and the woman.

"Here she was painted," said Giaberto in a low, awed voice. "Was this *her* room once? Must we clean this in order to free her?"

Cabral ran a finger over the table and dust rose into the light.

Eleyna sneezed. "Couldn't you . . . paint the other side of the door and . . . spell it free of binding oscurra, so Saavedra could open it? Isn't she already trying to?"

"Matra Dolcha," murmured Giaberto, turning to look at her. "Of course! It needs nothing more complicated than that, perhaps. You should have been Gifted, ninia meya."

She flinched away from him.

"I beg your pardon," he said quickly. "Forgive me, Eleyna."

"You meant no harm, Zio." The harm had already been done, all those years he and the others had denied her.

"Come, Eleynita." Cabral took her arm. Together they returned to the Atelierro.

As Premio Frato, Giaberto took command of the others. "I will take the risk onto myself," he said, "for the rest of you must remain strong if I should fail."

Eleyna stared as he began his preparations. Never had she thought to witness this! He took a lancet, warmed it to a blue heat in a flame, and pierced his skin. He mixed paints with his own blood, and although she half expected it, no misty supernatural haze rose from the blooded paints, nor did they sizzle or burn or show any sign of their new state. Tears he took, and his own saliva, and a cloudy substance from a vial already prepared.

There were many panels in the Atelierro. They chose an oak panel, set it against one wall, for it was too large to rest on an easel. From memory Giaberto sketched the door onto the ground, Eleyna and Cabral correcting him there, and there, and *there*. Then he painted—at the first attempt—an old mahogany door, iron-studded, iron-bound, with a border of sigils, set against a plain whitewashed wall. Twined into the border he painted the symbology she knew: hazelnut oil for Knowledge, leaf of the waterwillow for Freedom, rosemary for Remembrance.

The middle night bells rang across the city, a long peal announcing Mirraflores, the month of flowering, of restoration, of fertility. Into the wet paint he set oscurra, lines as delicate as the tracings on a palm, as a bird's feet tracking through damp marsh sand, as the striations on a petal: *There is no binding here. There is freedom.*

The first hint of dawn stained the rooftops when he finished and stepped back.

"Matra ei Filho!" swore Cabral.

It was not precisely movement. It was a shifting, a flowing, a sudden sense of urgency.

The door is open!

The chamber in the great portrait was complete to every last detail. But it was empty, as if no person had ever resided there. Giaberto collapsed into a chair just as the latch turned in his painting.

The door opened. A woman stepped carefully down an unseen step and walked into the room. She stared, blinking her eyes against unaccustomed light. Like an unspoken exclamation, she laid an open hand against her own bare throat, a breath caught, held, and at last released. She walked, gingerly, to the wall and ran unwrinkled fingers down the smooth grain of wood. She spun, slowly, ash-rose skirts belling out, and surveyed the entire chamber. At last she walked up to Eleyna and touched her, first her arm, then the fabric of her gown and the ribbon at the gown's high waist. The woman's skin was cool to the touch, but she was manifestly alive.

"You are Eleyna," she said. She had an odd, rich accent unlike anything Eleyna had ever heard. "I saw you painting, and you spoke to me. I am Saavedra. How long has it been?"

◆═══◆ EIGHTY-EIGHT ◆═══◆

Three *hundred and sixty-three years.*

She sat in a chair in the Grijalva Atelierro—*so changed! so much larger!*—and regarded her audience: nine Gifted Limners; an old man; a young woman the same age as herself.

No. *Not* the same age. Impossibility. Sario had made it so.

The other was young, the other Grijalva woman. *She* was not. She had added it up, once told: *Three hundred and eighty-three years old.*

Matra ei Filho. What had he done, what had he wrought with Gift, with Luza do'Orro, with unflagging ambition, ruthless execution of such undertakings as he believed were necessary?

With Raimon's approval.

She closed her eyes. Sanguo Raimon was dead twice over: once, by plunging his Chieva into his *Peintraddo;* and again, killed by years, by decades, by centuries.

Three hundred and eighty-three years old.

By far the oldest Grijalva.

Irony. And anger. That he could, that he *would,* do such to her.

So much time. So little reflection of it, save in the mirror he had painted into the portrait. And even less reflected in her face, her body. The child was but three days older, despite its father's death centuries before.

Alejandro. Dead.

They sent for food, and she ate ravenously, unable to deny the needs of her body newly freed from imprisonment, from the bindings of oscurra. And yet her thoughts, profligate in their haste, rebelled against such truths as were new to her: she was but three days older; the child was but three months within her womb.

She ate, ignoring their fascination. They watched and whispered, all save the young woman, Eleyna, who sat at her side. Waiting.

Alejandro. Dead.

Saavedra set down her fork with a muted clatter of metal on metal. Her hands shook; she could not hold them still. Was it some rebellion of her body? Some decaying of flesh now freed from painted preservation?

Pain engulfed. *Matra Dolcha*—

No. Not decay. Grief.

"Dead," she said, and heard the tremor in her voice. "Alive yesterday. Dead today."

Eleyna's voice was quiet. "Who?"

"Alejandro." She had loved to speak it. Now it hurt, knowing he could not hear it. "Alejandro Baltran Edoard Alessio do'Verrada, Duke of Tira Virte."

"Regretto," Eleyna murmured.

Grief might be mitigated by anger. She used it so. "But Sario is alive. And I will have my revenge."

"Sario?" It was the old man, Cabral. "Sario Grijalva? But of course he is dead. Ignaddio Grijalva painted a touching *Morta* of him. It hangs in the Picca."

She flinched. " 'Naddi—?" But he too was dead. All of them, dead. "What is the Picca?"

"It is a small galerria we Grijalvas use to exhibit paintings to the public."

"To the *public?* But—no one save Grijalvas are permitted into our home!"

"Now," the old man said kindly, "they are."

Eiha, but it hurt; they knew far more of her than she of them, and the world they inhabited was centuries beyond hers.

"That isn't important," Eleyna said crisply, offering no offense despite her tone. Saavedra liked her at once and hoped to know her better. Indeed, the world *had* changed; Eleyna Grijalva, an unGifted woman, stood among the Viehos Fratos. "How can you believe that Sario Grijalva is still alive?" Eleyna asked.

Despite the question, Saavedra sensed that the young woman already knew the answer. Knew more than she had yet admitted—perhaps even to herself. She rose from the table, pressing hands against actual wood instead of *painted* wood, and walked—*Sweet Mother, to walk again!*—to the huge panel set against the wall, and studied it. Examined the remains of her imprisonment.

Genius, of course. She could see it in each line, every shadow. How could no one look upon the work and not know the hand that painted it?

"Sario," she said. "My Sario." Even without her body in the portrait, the composition remained superb. "Here is the mirror," she said, indicating it. "Here, set upon the easel. A conceit of his, I am certain, as it was a conceit to paint in the *Folio*. Such things are of arrogance, of certainty of self, and very like him." She turned slightly, looked at the Limners, and saw they did not as yet understand. "Here," she said clearly, indicating it again. "Because of the mirror I came to understand what had been done to me, and that the world beyond my frame continued, even if Saavedra Grijalva did not." Grief tugged at her. "Not the Saavedra any of *them* knew."

Cabral's aged face was frozen into a complex transformation from incomprehension into bitter, and horrified, understanding.

"When I found I could move, I studied first the book—and then discovered the mirror. And in it I saw people. So many people, so many years . . . an ever-changing galerria of people, with faces and clothing far different from any I knew." She found it easier now to speak of it; she was free, and her past was no one's present. "There were times I could see nothing, trapped by darkness as if a cloth had been draped over the panel—but once I found the mirror I could see. Sometimes I even believed I could hear their voices speaking to me, though their accents were strange—as strange as yours are now to my ears." She turned to Eleyna. "You I saw most recently, because you worked before the painting."

Eleyna nodded. "I copied you."

"And there was Sario. Always Sario. His clothing changed, his companions . . . but he was always there. To visit. Perhaps to gloat." Tears threatened; not of grief, not as they were for Alejandro, but for what had become of a boy who had promised so very much—and delivered far more. "I last saw him standing beside you."

Eleyna looked away, looked guilty—now that what she had guessed was confirmed. "Yes, his name is Sario also."

Cabral objected. "It's the fashion to name Limners after those who preceded them."

"No." Grief was extinguished. Certainty took its place. "It was he. *My* Sario. Matra Dolcha, do you think I don't know the man who betrayed and imprisoned me?"

"But it can't be," Cabral protested. "This Sario looks nothing like the Sario of your time. I've seen the peintraddos. I remember when Sario was born. *Our* Sario."

Giaberto spoke now. He was Eleyna's uncle, and clearly Premio Frato. As Arturro had been, as Ferico, as Davo. But they were men from her time, not from this time; this time was Giaberto's. "I myself recall when he was confirmed as one of our number, and when he painted his *Peintraddo Chieva*." He gestured sharply; he did not believe her. "You see, here is his portrait. We brought it up from the Crechetta, to study in better light."

She moved to look at it. A man, not so different from a man of her time: hands racked by bone-fever, eyes whitened by milk-blindness. Infirmity at odds with the youth of the face.

Saavedra shook her head. "This is not the man I saw standing beside you, Eleyna. That man wore the face of *my* Sario." She turned. "You have already undertaken Chieva do'Sangua, have you not?"

Giaberto was startled. "How can you know that? Or *of* that?"

Saavedra smiled, walked slowly back to the table. She took up a piece of bread, examined its crust, its weight—*bread-baking has not changed, at least!*—and then turned to face them all. "I know because I, too, am Gifted." For the first time she opened her hand to display the key. She knew its weight well after so many centuries. "This key, this Chieva do'Orro, is mine. I underwent my own form of Confirmattio, do you see, when Sario himself forced it upon me. Thus I have earned this, and the rights with which it endows a Grijalva."

A torrent of protest, of conversation, from the men. Nothing from Eleyna. Saavedra let the protestations, the objections, wash over her, immune to their sting, their immediacy. She had heard them before. Had *made* them before, to Sario: *"A woman may not be Gifted."*

Giaberto was definitive. "Only men may be Gifted—it is a woman's duty to bear Gifted sons. That key is no more than a symbol of the sacred bond and service between the do'Verradas and the Viehos Fratos."

Meanwhile, the only other woman in the room waited them out in silence, watching the First Mistress who had also, by her admission, confessed herself the first Gifted woman as well.

Saavedra met Eleyna's steady eyes. "Do you envy me?"

The young woman's face colored. "Matra Dolcha!—I confess it. I do envy you." And then, quietly, "Regretto."

"No regrets," Saavedra said. "Not now. Nor should you regret it. The Mother grants us such things as she chooses."

"But if you are Gifted—" Cabral stepped forward hesitantly. "I beg your pardon. Excuse me for asking, but . . . was Mechella right? Are you with child?"

"En verro," Saavedra answered evenly. "The child who would have been born more than three hundred years ago is still to come."

Cabral sighed deeply.

Oddly, unexpectedly, tears sprang into Eleyna's eyes. She turned away abruptly.

Saavedra reached out at once, without thought. "No, I beg you—grazzo, don't turn away from me! Matra ei Filho, you of them all

may have the vision to understand. Would you deny me that?"
Tears now threatened her own eyes. "Matra Dolcha, but I am alone
here, out of my time, robbed of what and who I know—save for
this child, *Alejandro's* child, who will know nothing at all of his father, of his mother's time, save what he is taught of ancient history." Her throat threatened to close. "You see it, don't you? You
feel it? In your heart, in your head?"

Eleyna stood with her back to Saavedra. After a long moment
she turned with infinite slowness. Extended a trembling hand.
"Forgive me . . . I don't begrudge you your Gift." Their hands
clasped. "It is true you have no one . . . and if you wish, you will be
as a sister to me. As much as Beatriz, who *is* my sister. And
Agustin—" Her voice failed abruptly; she released Saavedra's
hand. "Zio, regretto. I must go down to see if Agustin is awake."

"Go, then, ninia meya."

With regret, Saavedra watched her go. Then turned to Giaberto.
"Who is Agustin?"

It was Cabral who answered, with anger as much as grief.
"Agustin is her younger brother, newly Confirmed. He is dying because Sario burned one of the boy's Blooded paintings with lamp
oil."

Saavedra flinched. Then kissed her fingertips, pressed them to
her heart. "Matra Dolcha . . . *which* Sario?"

"This one." Giaberto indicated the painted face she did not
know. "But our Chieva do'Sangua failed."

She did not reply at once. She knew how Sario protected himself.

"We have not yet answered how he did it," continued Giaberto,
taking her silence for astonishment. He glanced at the portrait.
"Unless this man is not truly Sario. Not *our* Sario." He looked now
at Saavedra. "You are certain it was Sario you saw in the mirror?"

For the first time in her life—her magic-perverted life—
Saavedra Grijalva used the vow that even they could not deny.
"Nommo Chieva do'Orro." She saw it register. Saw their shock.
"His clothing changed, but his face remained the same. As did the
Chieva he wore." She felt cold suddenly, and shivered. "Perhaps he
put the mirror there to be cruel—or merciful, in his own way, for
his own reasons. But I think this mirror showed me the truth—the
true world, his true face. And that world *always* contained Sario."

"Then if you saw him with Eleyna—if you saw *your* Sario with
our Eleyna. . . ." Cabral's face was gray. "Forgive my doubts,
grazzo, but it is difficult to believe."

She spread her hands. "As difficult to believe in *me.*"

Giaberto's voice shook. "How can this be?"

It was painful to speak; all was yesterday to her, and centuries to them. "Neosso Irrado," she said. "You don't know him as I do, as I *came* to know him—and still do not know him even though he had lived among you. I came to understand—too late!—there is nothing Sario will not attempt. There is no power, no magic, granted by our Gift that he cannot master and employ." She drew a breath. "There was no one in my time, and no one in *your* time, who was—and is—like him."

Giaberto accused now. "You sound as if you love him!"

She did not shirk it. "I loved him as much as I could love him. As I loved no one else. But there is love, and there is love—and what I gave *him* was entirely different from what I shared with Alejandro."

"Ninia meya." Cabral spoke the words with compassion and gentleness as he took her hands into a comforting grasp. "It would please me if you considered me your uncle, as you are to consider Eleyna your sister. You are a Grijalva, one of us, a part of me—" And he laughed. "Old enough to be my grandmother many times over, I fear, though far younger than I!"

An old man, older than the other Limners, broke the moment by pounding his cane on the floor. "Bassda!" His voice was reedy, cracked; clearly he was in the final stages of the decay that consumed Limners. "All this talk of Sario—*this* Sario, *that* Sario!—when I want to know something truly important." He stared at her harshly. "Niapali yellow—how was it made? We can only imitate it, but it lacks the quality of the old paintings. How was it made?"

Too many shocks. Saavedra laughed. "You can no longer make Niapali yellow? Matra Dolcha—then it is most fortunate I am here, is it not?"

Cabral released her hands to raise one of his own in a sharp gesture. "Momentito!"

Odd, to see an unGifted limner granted authority within the Viehos Fratos. But already she trusted him, craved his kindness, his wisdom—and she needed friends so badly.

He had their attention now. "Sario is a danger not just to us, but to all of Tira Virte. If what Eleyna says is true, and Sario *has* painted a portrait compelling the Grand Duke's obedience to him alone. . . ." He shook his head; implication was plain. "Let us say it is true, that the first Sario Grijalva yet lives. How could such a thing be done? Only by a Gifted Limner, no? And there are none save Grijalvas."

Giaberto objected yet again. "But how can this be?"

Wearied of their quarreling, Saavedra left them. She went instead to the *Peintraddo Chieva* of Sario Grijalva; of *her* Sario. And stared.

Only days ago . . . days, not centuries. Days ago that she had spoken with him, argued with him, knew him for what he was, what he had made himself; that she had lain in Alejandro's embrace, taken joy in their union, knowing they were meant to be together for as long as one of them lived.

She yet lived. He had died three hundred years before.

Pain welled. To escape it, to transmute it, Saavedra turned sharply to the knot of Viehos Fratos. To Cabral.

"You," she said, and beckoned. When he came, she took his hand into hers. "Of you, he would have been jealous. I understand it now, far more than I could at the time; this much his insanity has taught me." She gestured to the painting. "This man would have envied you, envied your power—"

"I have none," Cabral said stiffly. "I am not Gifted."

"En verro, your power lies in another direction. In lifespan. In fertility." She sighed. "He told me once he wanted nothing to do with children, but I believe he lied. And he told me also how he believed a Limner lived on only through his paintings—and how he would find a way to change that." She looked at Cabral. "You have studied the history of Tira Virte. How long *did* the first Sario live?"

"I believe he died at thirty-five."

And Alejandro—did he live a long life, or a short one? And was there another woman to share his bed, to bear his children?

Of course there was. The do'Verrada line continued to this day, three hundred and sixty-three years later. But she could not bring herself to ask. It hurt too much.

"You have asked," she said to Giaberto, "how Sario could yet live. I believe I know. I read every word in that book—" She indicated the book that lay, closed, on the table in the painting. "—that book, which is his copy of the *Kita'ab*. You know it in its incomplete form as the Grijalva *Folio*. In it I read of a spell to transfer one man's mind, his spirit, to another man's body—"

The door to the stairwell clicked. Everyone started and spun around.

But it was only Eleyna. "Agustin is still asleep." Her face was drawn. "Perhaps it is more merciful that he never wakes, if he must only wake to pain." Her stricken gaze settled on Saavedra. "I heard what you said." She drew breath, released it. "A day or two ago I asked Sario how he knew so very much—and he said: 'because I have lived a long time.' It seemed such an odd thing to say, for a man only six years older than I." She glanced now at the others, then to Saavedra again. "I can find out if this is true. I must return to the Palasso."

"Matra ei Filho—you would do that? Risk that?"

"Impossible," said Giaberto. "It is too dangerous."

Cabral was less definitive, but his protest echoed Giaberto's. "Eleyna, bela meya, you must know that if Sario is able to compel Renayo's actions, he will certainly do the same to you."

She shook her head, infinitely certain of her course. Saavedra could not help but admire her calm courage. "He can neither harm me nor compel me." She stared defiantly at her uncle. "He has already painted a portrait of me that will leave me forever free of Grijalva influence."

Saavedra examined the young woman, reassessing her. Handsome without question, if not beautiful; young, vital; but more importantly there was a fierceness about her that stirred response in Saavedra, a familiar desire to share a part of it.

And in that instant she recognized it in Eleyna, as she had always recognized and acknowledged it in Sario. Luza do'Orro, the Golden Light.

A painter. *That* was what she had been doing with Sario, to know him so well: painting. Learning. Kindling her own Light.

And yet. . . . "Does he love you?" Saavedra asked. He had always loved her as much as it was possible for him to love something other than his own vision, but if he had lived so long, surely there were others. Or, perhaps, *one* other.

Eleyna flushed but held her voice steady. "He is not my lover. But. . . ." The hesitation betrayed deep feeling. "I am his estuda."

Uproar. The Viehos Fratos had truly decayed; Saavedra could not recall such petty argument so constantly diverting the men of her day. *They will not permit her to go.*

As she would have gone; as she *had* gone—and into such danger as had brought her here, to this day, when she should have been dead, together with Alejandro.

"But only I *can* go back!" Eleyna cried. "He trusts me, and believes I trust him. Tell me what I must do, and I will do it."

Giaberto began to pace. "Mennina moronna," he muttered.

"Yes," Eleyna agreed. "But it must be done, Zio."

He swung on her. "If it is as you say—if he has painted a Blooded portrait of you, then you are truly safe from him as no other can be. Eiha—then you *must* go." He swabbed perspiration from his upper lip. "First you must free Renayo from his influence. Find the portrait, place it in a vat of turpentine diluted by water, let it soak. When it is well and truly ruined, add more water, pitchers of it, then pour all down the drain. So his power over the Grand Duke will end, without destroying him."

"Why don't I just *burn* it, or any other he has done?" Eleyna asked harshly. "What he did to my Agustin, let me do to *him*!"

Saavedra stopped the argument before it continued unabated. "I must see him," she said simply. "I must see this man to judge him for myself."

Eleyna, standing so close that only Saavedra heard, murmured: "If it *is* he, imagine how much of painting he knows!"

Indeed, the Luza do'Orro. Woman or no, Eleyna was as much a Limner as any.

Crisply, Saavedra said, "I suggest Eleyna go to him, but she must carry a note. From me, in my handwriting, which he—*my* Sario—knows. And if it is indeed that Sario, he will come to me." She looked at the young woman, his estuda, knowing how painful her next command would be. "When he is gone, Eleyna must destroy all of his paintings in the manner Giaberto has described. All. And once Sario comes to me, here in this Atelierro, we all of us must deal with him. Viehos Fratos. I. As perhaps only I can." No pain in it, now. Only ruthless necessity. *As he taught me.* "I will require paints. I will require this floor scrubbed clean."

Giaberto stirred uneasily. "What do you mean to do?"

Saavedra smoothed both slim hands down the heavy folds of her skirt. "Sario is brilliant, but he made two disastrous mistakes born of his certainty that no one could see what lay before him—or her." She drew breath to tell them. "First, he proved to me that I, too, am Gifted . . . and he painted the *Folio* that was also *Kita'ab* into the room. There I read secrets—*recipes*—of powerful Tza'ab magic." She nodded once. "I promise you, Nommo Chieva do'Orro, that I will trap my cousin so he can harm no one again."

They no longer questioned, she saw; acknowledgement, acceptance, was begun. A young Limner brought paper and chalk, set both upon the table.

Cabral's voice, quiet and calm. "There is one more thing before we act so precipitously. A thing that you, the Viehos Fratos, must know, and that all the Grijalvas will come to know." He glanced briefly at Eleyna. "As you have no doubt heard, the Provisional Assembly has finished drafting its Constitussion. In two days they will meet in the Cathedral Imagos Brilliantos, at the feet of the Premio Sancto and the Premia Sancta, and the assembly will present this document to the Grand Duke." He looked at each of them, including Saavedra. "And on that day I believe an eloquent man of good birth will stand and proclaim in the Blessed Names of Matra ei Filho that Grand Duke Renayo is a bastard. A chi'patro Grijalva, in fact. Not a do'Verrada at all."

It shook her profoundly, even as it shook them, though the reasons were different. For them, their Duke was threatened; for her, the taint of Tza'ab blood running in the flesh of a man believed to be do'Verrada was all too immediate. Once again her hands closed over skirt folds to clasp the slight swelling that betokened her own chi'patro do'Verrada.

"Surely," she said, "your Duke Renayo may have this man exiled or imprisoned for such insolence."

Cabral smiled sadly. "And what if such insolence is true?"

Giaberto snorted. "Lies! These Libertistas have no shame. There is no more contemptible slur they may find, en verro—they will stoop as low as they must. Cabral, how can you believe anyone could accept this?"

"If the accuser, this eloquent man of good birth, is the cousin of Baron do'Brendizia? If he demands that Grand Duke Renayo swear on the sacred rings of the Premio Sancto and Premia Sancta that he and his heirs are truly do'Verrada?" Cabral shook his head slightly. "What if he cannot swear it, for fear of his soul? Who dares lie before the Matra ei Filho?"

Giaberto's face flushed an unbecoming deep red. "Do you mean to suggest, Cabral, that you *believe* Renayo do'Verrada is not Arrigo's son?"

It was beyond Saavedra, until Eleyna leaned close and whispered explanation: Arrigo was the current Grand Duke's father.

Giaberto's laughter was wild. "Even if it were true, for some impossible reason, can you imagine what it would do to Tira Virte? To reveal that the man who is Grand Duke is *not* a do'Verrada?" He shook his head. "Arrigo's first son died without issue. His daughter married that nobleman from Diettro Mareia, and her children are foreigners."

In her head, Saavedra used the old term so familiar to her: *estranjiero.*

Giaberto went on. "Arrigo's sister, Lizia, has only two surviving grandchildren, both of her son Maldonno: the young Countess do'Dregez, who is named after Lizia, and her brother, the future Count do'Casteya."

"En verro," Cabral agreed quietly.

"We are already perilously close to riot with these Libertista agitators, Cabral. What would happen to the Grijalvas? Without the Ducal Protection issued and upheld by the do'Verradas, where would *we* be?" Giaberto shook his head angrily, clearly frustrated. "I think you are a revolutionary, Cabral. And agitator. Why else would you take up the case of a discontented madman?"

Cabral's calm disintegrated. "Cabessa bisila, 'Berto! So that we may be prepared with a reply! Precisely so we may protect Tira Virte, the do'Verradas, and ourselves. We must warn Renayo."

Giaberto flung up his hands in disgust. "Grand Duke Renayo a bastard? Impossible! And if it *were* true, what filho do'canna is supposed to be his father?"

Cabral shut his hand over his silver Chieva and gripped it tightly. "I will thank you, 'Berto, not to speak of my mother in such a fashion."

Silence. Even Saavedra understood the implication. *It is truth: a do'Verrada does not rule Tira Virte.*

Eleyna went pale and murmured a man's name. Saavedra did not know it, any more than she had known Arrigo's name. *So much now I neither know nor understand.* The world had shifted under her feet, robbing her of foundation. And yet from the ruins of her life something new must be built. Not merely for her own sake.

Into the thunderous silence left by the cessation of the shock, she spoke of something infinitely personal. "What became of Alejandro?" she asked. "He, too, was a Duke—a do'Verrada Duke, with no hint of bastardy or chi'patro in his flesh. What became of him?"

Eiha, but it hurt: the knowledge, the acceptance. Never to see him again, save for portraits; never to touch, to embrace. Never to speak to him, only *of* him, and to strangers.

Estranjieros.

Cabral's voice was gentle. He understood her grief. "He reigned many years. He married—"

"The Pracanzan." She knew it. She and Alejandro had spoken of the woman, and she had cried into his fine velurro doublet.

"En verro. Though he married later than his conselhos desired. Because, the tale goes, of the great grief he suffered when his beloved left him." Silenced then by the living embodiment of that loss, and the truth of its departure, Cabral halted awkwardly.

They came at last, the tears, nurtured as much by the compassion in his voice as by her own pain. But he knew, did Cabral; by his own confession, he knew as well as she the sorrow in loving one forbidden.

He went on gently as she wiped tears away. "With Sario Grijalva as Lord Limner, Alejandro ruled Tira Virte with a generous and even hand for many years. He is beloved as one of our great Dukes."

She smiled. "He became, then, what he feared he could never be." And recalled so clearly how she had assuaged that fear.

Silence still. They waited for her, stunned by her. *Fearing* her. She saw it in their faces, in their postures. She had seen that regard before, those postures, in men and women who looked at Sario.

Save for Cabral, and Eleyna. Who understood for utterly different reasons why they need not fear her at all.

I will have them all respect me. I am as they are: Gifted. But I am not Sario. Again she cradled the swelling deep beneath velurro folds. *Alejandro, amoro meyo, I swear to you by the love we swore to one another that this child will have what is due by right of birth and blood.*

She gazed upon them all, recalling their shock when Cabral confessed the truth: Tira Virte's Duke was of bastard blood. Drew a breath. It was time. Far past time, because of Sario.

"I do carry a child," she said. "Alejandro's child. Grijalva. Chi'patro. But also do'Verrada. What will become of *him?*"

━━◆ EIGHTY-NINE ◆━━

Of course she returned to him. She came humbly and begged his forgiveness.

The Courtfolk in the Palasso had celebrated Mirraflores Eve with a ball. He had not attended. He was furious. Furious! Let them dance while the mob crouched waiting outside the gates, with their hulking beast's patience born of long days of boredom and the knowledge that their trap—their Constitussion—was soon to be sprung. Let them dance while his heart raged within.

It galled. *She* and the boy, one unGifted, one untrained. How had they discovered this means to speak through Blooded paintings? How much more could he have done had *he* thought of it! Had he killed Il-Adib too soon? Had there been more the old Tza'ab man meant to teach him?

He had sat the entire night, long after the lamps and torches were extinguished, in his private chamber, and stared sightlessly at his canvasses. Surely he had done enough—and yet it was *never* enough.

He was Lord Limner now—again!—as he had intended all along. Grand Duke Renayo was his to command. Through Princess Alazais, Renayo would rule Ghillas or even annex Ghillas as a new province as Alejandro—with Sario's aid—had annexed Joharra. If these Libertistas proved too dangerous, he would simply murder some as he had murdered the last male heir to Casteya, allowing Tira Virte's first Clemenzo to wed the last daughter of the house of Casteya and thus bring it into Tira Virte's orbit as well. The title of Duke had not been worthy enough for the first Benetto, so he—as Riobaro—had through a series of Blooded *Treaties* arranged the marriage to the della Marei heiress, whose political ties and colossal wealth had enabled Benetto to declare himself Grand Duke. If he—as Sario—wished, Renayo could now style himself with a grander title. Prince. King. For all these years and years he had served the do'Verradas and Tira Virte. Just as he had been taught to do.

But why? What did it matter, any of it? What was the point of being Lord Limner? What did he care who ruled, or if these Libertistas had their Constitusion?

His estuda had left him! What was the point in life if not to pass on his great knowledge? If not to be acknowledged as the greatest Grijalva painter who had ever lived?

It had been so fine a joke for so long, his own private jeer at all the moronnos who thought themselves such experts about art and never recognized that all those pictures had been painted by one hand. But amusement had long since palled. He felt an intense compulsion to unlock the Galerria this very night, to change all those false attributions. *Sario Grijalva* on this painting, *Sario Grijalva* on that, *Sario Grijalva* on all the finest pieces.

And he could do it. He could steal inside the Galerria and sign the truth on each and every one of *his* compositions. The truth, at long last.

To stand before them all, to acknowledge that all these works were his and more besides, to watch their eyes as they realized how much they owed to him and him alone. Where would the do'Verradas be without his skills? How many thousand Tira Virteian youths would be dead in battle if not for his cunning that had kept war at bay? Which of the great merchant houses would still be struggling in anonymous squalor in tiny villages had he not made their country an economic power? Who among the scented bravos swaggering their titled wealth through the Court would be sweating in their own barley fields, no better than peasants, if Sario Grijalva had not done what he had done?

But no one would understand. All the beauty, all the achievement, all the benefits of his long, long life. . . .

No one *could* understand. Except an estuda, properly trained. *She* must remain faithful to him, just as Saavedra always had.

Nothing else mattered. Nothing.

The night passed with agonizing slowness.

But in the end, in the morning, at the midday bells on Mirraflores Day, she returned. Of course she returned. "Master Sario," she said, head bowed modestly. "I beg your pardon. I have come back."

"Of course. Adezo! You have finished, I presume, the copy of the portrait of Saavedra? We will go at once to the Galerria and examine it. Then we shall decide which painting you are to begin next."

"Yes." She hesitated, then handed him a folded piece of paper.

"What is this? Can't it wait?"

She dared look him straight in the eye. The true Luza do'Orro, this one! *She,* who had discovered a new spell, she who was not even Gifted. "You must read it now."

He rolled his eyes. Eiha! As well to humor her for a moment. Women took strange notions into their heads on Mirraflores. It was expected of them. He took the paper and unfolded it hastily, impatient to continue their work.

And staggered.

It is the only way, Sario.

Her writing. *Her* voice, echoing down through the years: *"Burn it. Burn it down, all of it. Everything in the Crechetta."*

Here, on this paper, in fresh ink, those simple words that had bound them irrevocably.

It is the only way, Sario.

In *her* handwriting.

His hand shook as if with a palsy. He looked up, caught an expression on Eleyna's face, the face of a child who has opened a door and seen a monster. But it passed. It all passed, sooner or later, one life into the next.

"Where did you get this?" he demanded, shaking the paper almost against her skin.

"At Palasso Grijalva."

He crumpled the paper into a ball. "You betrayed me, to *them!* How could you? You are my estuda!"

She did not answer, just stared at him.

Saavedra's handwriting. He knew it as intimately as he did his own. Everything about her, for she was so much a part of him that it was almost as if she were his own creation. He pushed past Eleyna and walked out the door. Walked out through the suite, through the sitting room where Alazais sat passively on the silk couch, embroidering. Her head moved, to look at him as a sunflower turns with the sun, but he did not have time for her inane comments. She was nothing, a trifle.

He ignored the stares as he strode through the Palasso to the Galerria. It was impossible, of course. He flung the doors open and almost ran down the long hall.

Stopped. There she was, in her place. Moronno! To think that Saavedra could have gotten free without him! No one knew. How could they know? How could they alter the great spell he had wrought?

And yet . . . This *was* her handwriting. He walked closer. Closer still. Came to the brink, until he could practically step into the portrait.

He smelled the tang of drying paint. *Eleyna's* copy!

What had they done with Saavedra?

Still clutching the note, he ran to the stables. "I need a carriage, a horse, a conveyence! Adezo!"

"Lord Limner Sario, it is inadvisable to travel outside the Palasso grounds—"

"Now! Moronno! If I must ride in a butcher's cart, I will do so!"

In the end, it was a vegetable cart. Perhaps he looked an odd sight, a well-dressed man sitting next to the grizzled old driver, but none of that mattered. People stared and pointed, but they let them through, for the riot had died down days ago and today was Mirraflores, the day girls celebrated their passage into womanhood.

He smoothed out the crumpled paper, hearing old echoes in his head.

"I carry a child!" she had cried, when he cut her, when he proved to her she was Gifted. Alejandro's child, growing beneath her heart even as Sario painted her. Alejandro's fertile seed, that had taken root. Never would he countenance this. Saavedra was his! His alone!

Or had there been other reasons? It was so long ago. He could not remember them clearly, not anymore.

"Here we are, Maesso," said the old driver. "Begging your pardon, my lord, but we've been sitting here and you haven't moved. I'd be grateful if you'd get down. My granddaughter has a feast tonight, and I'm not willing to be late so that you can stare at nothings in the air. Matra Dolcha, these Limners. I've heard it said before they're all half-mad, but I never believed it until now."

Sario shook himself and looked around. They had indeed come to Palasso Grijalva, which lay quiet, as dark as if it had been abandoned, emptied, given to the passing years. Shaking now, he sprang down and ran through the tunnel that led to the courtyard.

He wrenched open the doors that led up to the Atelierro and took the steps two at a time. Threw open the doors at the top.

Matra ei Filho! There they stood in the light that flooded the great chamber, nine buffoons and old Cabral, looking as if the cat had come in and caught the mice at the cream. There was, of course, no sign of Saavedra. They had tricked him.

But there, behind them, he saw the back of a huge panel. He knew it instantly, although he could not see the image. He could *feel* it, his work, his sigils, his blood and tears and seed and spittle melded with oak and oils and pigments, sealed with the oscurra he had learned from the old Tza'ab, the secrets of the Al-Fansihirro.

He walked across the plank floor. And was stopped.

Stopped dead. His feet could not move.

An instant later he knew it for what it was: a spell painted onto the floor. Moronno that he was, he had walked straight into their trap, right across the floor into the circle of oscurra that now ringed, and weighted, his feet. He had not believed them cunning enough to do it. Or perhaps this, too, had been Eleyna's idea.

Enraged, he lifted the paper and displayed it to them. "Who has done this?" he shouted. "Which of you? Why did you steal my painting?"

"I have done this." She stepped out from behind them: masses of coiled ringlets, clear gray eyes. "'I will do as they tell me,'" she said, echoing words he had long since forgotten, words that now accused him, in *her* voice.

Blessed Matra, her long-silenced voice.

She quoted him again. "'I will give them a *Peintraddo Chieva,* but it will not be the real one. That, I will keep. That, I will lock away. And only you, and only I, shall know the truth of it.'" Her face was the same, but her manner was harder, angrier. "*I know you,* Sario. I know it is you."

"'Vedra." Her name, on his lips. Like strokes made by a hand long barred from painting, the form came with difficulty. But it was her. Glorious Saavedra. "I was only waiting for you until the time was right. Then I meant to release you." He did not move to touch her, not yet. "It is too early. Who has done this? It was for *me* to do!"

"Not too *early.* Too *late.* By many years too late, Sario." He did not comprehend her anger. Saavedra was never angry with *him.* "By what right did you tear me away from Alejandro? By what right did you paint me into a prison from which you had no intention of releasing me?"

"That isn't true!"

"I have lost my life!" she cried.

"Lost your *life?* I saved you from death! From becoming a gaping, empty-eyed skull, from becoming dust like all the others. Like *Alejandro!*"

"You did not save me," she said fiercely. "You *robbed* me. Robbed me of years, of those I knew and loved, of all the things in the world—*in my time*—that I treasured. All I have left of them is you—and the child."

He flinched. *The child.* The one thing he could never give her—

he, who was no man in the eyes of the world, only and eternally a boy who painted. Was that why she had turned to Alejandro? "'Vedra," he pleaded. "You don't understand—"

"I understand this, Sario: that you will pay the price for what you have done. I have prayed before the altar, I have asked the Matra's forgiveness, asked Alejandro's forgiveness, for what I must now do. But I will give my child—Alejandro's child—what is due him, and if that means I must sacrifice you, be certain I shall do it."

What had happened to his faithful, pliant Saavedra? She who had always known and accepted his Gift and his destiny? She had always loved him best. Except she had *dared* love Alejandro, who had nothing to recommend him except a handsome face—with its crooked, imperfect tooth!—and that restless animal energy that drew the eye—and his people—to him. Alejandro was *nothing*. Alejandro was only what Sario had made him. Once he made her understand that—

"Tie his hands behind his back," Saavedra said to Cabral. She looked long at the assembled Limners, all but Sario. "You Viehos Fratos were always so enamored of your own power that you forgot—forget!—how fragile a thing it is."

"We have never forgotten," Giaberto protested.

Never forgotten. The words hung in the air. Never forgotten, just as the first Sario, as Riobaro, as Oaquino and Guilbarro and all the others he had been, were never forgotten because their genius lived on in their paintings.

Blessed Matra! *They meant to bind his hands.*

Cabral advanced on him with a length of stout rope. Sario was strong, but Cabral with the aid of young Damiano was stronger. It was not just physical strength that overwhelmed him; it was the sight of Saavedra, *alive,* staring at him, her great beauty incandescent once more in her face. But her face was turned against him, her gray eyes as hard as granite and her lips set and unforgiving.

It was Saavedra who bound his hands, though she set no hand on him. It was she who imprisoned him, though she moved no step from her place among the Viehos Fratos. From her place at their head, for any moronno could see at once that they deferred to her.

To the First Mistress! How Riobaro would have laughed at the irony. Perhaps all the Mistresses would have laughed: sweet Benissia; poor doomed Saalendra; exquisite Corasson; Rafeya; the incomparable Diega; Lina; confident Tazita; practical Lissina; that canna Tazia. They knew that a Mistress might have secrets that a Lord Limner could never know.

By whose power had the Grijalvas truly won their place? Through the Limners, or through their sisters and female cousins?

So he, the greatest Lord Limner, faced Saavedra, the first and most famous of the Grijalva Mistresses. How had they come to be at odds?

" 'Vedra," he began. He must only convince her. Once she understood what they could accomplish together—

"Take him from my sight," she said coldly. "My Sario is dead to me. Dead; as is Alejandro, and Raimon and Ignaddio and all the others I knew. What stands here is only the remains of Sario."

Dead. Not that. Never that, spiritless meat and bone.

"I *am* Sario," he cried. "You know is it I, Saavedra. You know I am here, though I wear another man's body. The body is nothing, only flesh so that I might live another life, so that I may perfect—" He broke off.

They looked, oddly enough, horrified, as if something he had said had caused them all revulsion. They looked as Eleyna had looked, at the Palasso, staring at him as if he were a monster.

But tears glittered in Saavedra's eyes. She *did* understand, then.

"Is there no chamber where you may confine him safely?" she asked of the others. "There is much to do if we are to be prepared for the assembly two days hence."

" 'Vedra, don't abandon me now. I *need* you."

"En verro," she said. "As you always needed me."

At that instant he felt a burning along his skin, in his eyes and on his tongue. He had lived far too many years not to know his body's reactions intimately, not to know what each presaged.

"My paintings!" he cried, horrified. "Someone is destroying *my paintings*." Soaking them. Ruining them! "You must stop this, 'Vedra!"

She came forward, but only to bend and brush water on the patterns painted onto the floor at his feet, to dissolve the oscurra. *Her* oscurra—the Gifted woman. So she had finally admitted it, accepted it—and used it against *him!*

She stood, stared at him, seemed to study him, seeking *what* he could not know. Only that she, of them all, would surely understand him. And forgive him. She always had.

" 'Vedra—" he whispered.

She turned her back on him.

The others led him away. There were too many, and he had never learned how to fight in any obvious brute physical fashion. Not in any of his lives. His hands were too important.

But none of that mattered. What mattered was that Saavedra had returned to him. She had returned, only to forsake him once and for all time.

When they shoved him into a small whitewashed chamber, empty of furniture or any adornment, and locked the door, he stood in the center of the room and wept.

← NINETY ←

Roario entered the Cathedral Imagos Brilliantos by the side door through which he had left it in such haste six months before. That day, when Sancto Leo died in his arms, had changed his life forever. It had set him, and perhaps all of Tira Virte, on a new course whose direction could not now be altered.

He found his father waiting in the Premio Sancto's private rooms beyond the side chapel of the great cathedral nave. Renayo sat in a gilt chair, clearly tired. Il Cofforro's portrait of Premio Sancto Gregorrio IV gazed with vague fondness down on the Grand Duke. Roario eyed the portrait with a new misgiving. He had learned so much from Cabral Grijalva. *My grandfather.*

Had Oaquino Grijalva spent his own blood and saliva in that painting? Had he spelled it so that the gentle solicitude that Roario imagined beaming from Gregorrio's seamed face was not a true reflection of the man's kindly personality but only a magic set there by the painter's hand?

He dreaded looking on the great altarpiece, on the serene aspect of the Matra, for surely She, too, was a magicked rendering whose serenity enveloped Her worshipers not through their devotion but through a spell created by a mortal man's bloody hands.

And yet, if the altarpiece granted peace for a measure of time to those who gazed on it, where was the harm?

"Don Roario." Renayo addressed him abruptly, and Roario started and, bowing, came forward. "I have agreed to meet with you, as you requested."

"You look tired, Your Grace."

"Your concern is charming, I'm sure. What do you want?"

Grand Duke Renayo *did* look tired, almost worn away, although surely these last two months trapped in Palasso Verrada with the imminent threat of riot hanging over the city would have been enough to exhaust the strongest man.

"I thank you for agreeing to meet with me, Your Grace. I know we did not part on good terms—"

"I said I never wanted to see you again and I am not sure I have changed my mind," snapped Renayo. "Get on with it!"

This flash of spirit encouraged Roario, who had begun to wonder if his father, so subdued, was under some kind of spell. "I have said so many unlikely things to you, Your Grace, that I am hesitant to speak now, for fear you will not believe the strange and awkward tidings I bring." He had rehearsed this speech a hundred times. It sounded stiff.

Renayo sighed ostentatiously. "You are to be Premio Oratorrio of the Corteis, I suppose? It is the only position due your consequence."

"No." The suggestion threw him off his planned speech. A few of the wealthier landlords and merchants had indeed proposed electing Roario as Premio Oratorrio, First Speaker of the Corteis; Roario counted himself lucky that the proposal had been shouted down before he could himself refuse, in case the Provisional Assembly actually approved such a course and then interpreted his refusal as arrogance. "I will stand for election from Collara Asaddo and if elected will serve in the same capacity as any other representative."

"If you believe that, then you are a moronno. But I suppose you do not believe it and only say such things because they are expected of you. The farmers and artisans of your own estate will not refuse to elect you, I assume."

"I assume the same thing, Your Grace. All of the men standing for election have rank or property. You do not suppose we are allowing any sort of unpropertied ruffian to enter the Corteis? Respectable men have the wisdom to govern."

Renayo snorted, shifting impatiently in his chair. "Surely this is not all you have to say? To try once again to convince me to embrace this new enthusiasm? If I must accept it, I must, but only to spare Meya Suerta and our beautiful green earth the horrible conflicts that have wracked Ghillas and Taglis. And because I yet have hopes for Ghillas."

Roario paced to the portrait, frowned at it, the beadwork of the headdress so cunningly portrayed that each bright bead reflected an unseen light, and walked back to stand before his father. "We are alone, Your Grace?"

"The Premio Sancto has assured me there is no one to overhear us. I must trust him, as we must all trust the Ecclesia and its representatives."

"Then what I say now I must assure you I say most reluctantly, and only because events force me to it." His father's wan face scared him. "You *are* tired, Your Grace. Might I get you wine?"

"I have been ill," said Renayo softly.

And so he looked, thin and wasted. Nevertheless, it was time to forge ahead. "Forgive me for speaking plainly, Patro. Leono do'Brendizia, who is cousin to the current Baron, intends to stand up in the assembly and accuse you of being a bastard who has not one drop of do'Verrada blood in him."

"I see."

"You *see?* Is that all you have to say? Matra Dolcha, Patro, you do not even look surprised. Do you mean to tell me you have known all along?"

Now Renayo rose. "Perhaps I always suspected. We rarely saw Arrigo when I was a child, although we were sent to stay with him for part of the year." He poured himself wine from a crystal pitcher set on a side table. "Certainly Cabral treated all of us as if we were his own children. Matra Dolcha, but we were all very happy at Corasson. The servants did not *quite* speak of it openly, for they were the most loyal staff I have ever encountered. As we all did, they, too, could not fail but to love my mother. But when I became old enough and went out into the world, I saw other households and drew my own conclusions."

"And you said nothing of these conclusions?"

Renayo laughed harshly. "What was I to say? That I thought I was a bastard? I had no reason to believe I would ever sit on the throne of Tira Virte. And when the crown of Ghillas passed to Ivo and not to me, and then Alessio died unexpectedly, what was I to do? Arrigo had acknowledged me as his son. Was I to shame my mother publicly by refusing to take the throne because of ill-timed scruples? I think not. I did my duty to Tira Virte, and I continue to do so to this day."

Rohario swayed and, groping for a chair, sat down. "You never told me."

"Why should I have told you? You were vain and useless, your brother has as much common sense as a loon, and as for Benetto and Timarra—eiha! That was my bitterest disappointment, to see none of the great do'Verrada virtues reflected in my children."

"Certainly I have always been aware that we disappointed you and Mother," said Rohario peevishly, unable to help himself. "Did she know?"

Renayo took a draught of water. "She knew nothing but what it pleased her to know, blessed woman. Her single-mindedness was her greatest virtue. Mairie knew what she wanted and how to get it. I was not about to tell her that her handsome and rich do'Verrada husband was more likely a Grijalva bastard!"

"What do you mean to do?"

Renayo took his time, replacing the glass next to the pitcher, adjusting the black-lacquered tray so that its sides squared off against the table's edge, before he sat down again. "It is a dangerous thing, to accuse the Grand Duke of being chi'patro. Edoard must marry quickly and to our advantage. You I would have married to the Ghillasian girl, but . . . eiha, there is something strange about her. She wanders back and forth in her suite looking for Sario Grijalva. Eleyna says she fears there is a Limner spell—" Here he stopped short.

Eleyna! But this was not the moment to broach the subject of marriage.

Renayo sighed. "I have not revealed to you yet the secrets of the—"

"—Grijalva Limners? Zio Cabral has told me that and more, Patro. That is why I am here now."

"Cabral admitted he is my father? Matra Dolcha!" Color glowed in his cheeks and his brusque resolve came back to him; he jumped up and paced, back and forth, in the small chamber. "It *is* true, then! Eiha! Just as well Mairie died before she could hear such bitter tidings. She would have hated knowing that her husband was one of *their* bastards!"

"You do not hate knowing it?" This man, *this* Renayo, was a stranger to him.

"Cabral is the kindest man I know. Arrigo did his duty by me, but he never showed me a moment's affection. Matra ei Filho, ninio, you must know that the Grand Dukes of Tira Virte are what we are today because of Grijalvas and their magic."

The words came out unbidden and unplanned. "I mean to marry Eleyna, Patro. What do you think of *that?*"

Renayo laughed sharply. "You are certainly *my* son, although I don't know where you got this bull-headed streak. I can't even fault you for loving a Grijalva, since it seems to run in the blood. Eiha! Throw yourself away on her, although a prince born of the Ghillasian bloodline could do better! She's a taking thing, and brave enough, and a fine painter. Do you know that she copied the portrait of *The First Mistress* and hung it in place of the original, and *no one noticed?* Poor Andreo. Gift he may have had, but I don't think he was half the painter she is."

"These are changed words for you, Patro."

"Changed words for changed times, as you yourself have said to me many times in the past months. Eleyna also told me that Sario Grijalva held me in his thrall for two months. I do not at this moment look kindly on the Gifted Limners who have served and enriched my predecessors by performing such spells on other unsus-

pecting souls. Decisions have already been made, and plans laid.
Drastic measures for drastic times. We agreed it is the only way."

"*We?*" Rohario demanded. "What do you mean to do?"

"What must be done. What perhaps should have been done
many generations ago, before we and they painted ourselves into
such a corner." Then he laughed, almost wildly. "Painted into a corner! An apposite saying, don't you think? Bassda! Who is it? Who
are you there?"

For an instant Rohario thought his father had gone quite mad,
but then he heard the plaintive voice.

"Your Grace, where are you?"

Renayo grimaced. "Eiha! The heifer has wandered out of her
handler's keeping. Why did I ever marry her? All that tempting
gold and those trade assurances. Though she's pleasing enough in
bed, I suppose, and relieves me of the necessity of taking a mistress."

Shocked, Rohario gaped at his father, but a moment later a door
opened and Grand Duchess Johannah, a vision of white softness,
entered the chamber with several of her ladies-in-waiting at her
heels. "I'm so frightened, Your Grace," she said in her tiny voice,
"all those rough men waiting out in the Cathedral. Might I wait
here with you? I feel so much safer here." Her gaze fluttered over
Rohario; she blinked, staring, then fastened herself onto her husband, clinging to his arm.

"Come, amora meya." With a sigh, he led her from the room.

Drastic measures for drastic times. Rohario did not follow his
father but went out the way he had come and circled around to enter the Cathedral by the great front doors. There were indeed a
great many rough men waiting, if one defined rough men as any
man who was not born into the nobility. But they waited, to
Rohario's eyes, with remarkable patience and restraint. These men
were respectable in their own circles, guilds and merchant houses,
banks and landlord's associations. They had as much to lose as did
the Grand Duke if Tira Virte dissolved into the chaos that had torn
apart Ghillas. Yet they choose to risk their lives and families and
property in the name of *Libera.* Freedom. They chose to risk it for
the sake of this Constitussion.

Like Eleyna, who had thrown away her chance at wealth and influence as the Heir's Mistress because she wanted, because she
needed, to paint.

Certainly there were restless young men aplenty, huddled in
groups but overseen by elders who kept a strict eye on these potential rabblerousers. Rohario admired the calmness with which the

assembly waited. After two months of spirited and often angry meetings they had agreed on a Constitussion, and now they meant to present it to their Grand Duke and institute a new method of governance in Tira Virte, one that acknowledged the position of the Grand Duke, that acknowledged his importance and his time-honored privilege, but that granted privilege and power to the men of substance in the land as well.

Rohario walked forward quickly. The mason's journeyman, Ruis, called out a cheerful greeting; he had, in the end, become protective toward *His Lordship,* as he liked to call Rohario, and had defended him against the slurs of newcomers.

In one of the side boxes toward the front, near the altar, the shipbuilder Velasco gestured toward a free seat. Rohario slid in beside him. Velasco was seated here with other dignitaries, wealthy merchants, and a few noble landowners who had joined the Libertista cause.

"You see," said Velasco proudly, gesturing expansively to the crowd, "that we are civilized men here, who can bring about change without resorting to riot and mayhem. This will be our finest accomplishment."

"Do you think the Grand Duke means to sign the agreement?"

Velasco looked surprised. "Indeed, Don Rohario! You did not know? I was summoned last night to the Palasso, where I met with His Grace. He has already assured me that he will sign the document and agree to all of our terms."

Too amazed to reply, Rohario was grateful for the entrance of the Premio Sancto and the Premia Sancta. The assembly, buzzing before, quieted swiftly. As soon as the church elders had taken their seats on either side of lamp and altar, a captain of the Shagarra Regiment entered, leading the Grand Duke's retinue. Trumpets and banners were noticeably absent.

But Velasco stood, calling out in a loud voice: "All rise for the Grand Duke, Renayo, and for Grand Duchess Johannah and Don Edoard do'Verrada."

Rohario rose, as did every other soul in the vast nave of the Cathedral. The effect was stunning. Every man there rose to grant respect to the man whose authority they meant to erode. In an odd way, it was reassuring.

Renayo entered, looking stern and dignified. Edoard looked bewildered, but then, he never truly felt at home anywhere except in the out of doors. The Grand Duke paid his respects to the Premio Sancto and the Premia Sancta and then took his seat in the ducal box to the left of the altar, his chair placed to the forefront.

Velasco, as presiding Premio Oratorrio of the Provisional Assembly, rose and walked forward with deliberate slowness, holding the precious parchment in his hands. He knelt before the Grand Duke—Rohario admired the careful way in which Velasco and the other senior men went out of their way to show their respect for the dignity of the ducal office—and handed the parchment not to Renayo but to one of his conselhos. The conselho cleared his throat and read the entire document aloud.

The men assembled in the pews listened with intent silence. Renayo's expression remained grave. To Rohario's relief, they got through the entire document without anyone disturbing the peace. The bench on which he sat grew harder and harder, and despite himself he realized he was growing restless. Waiting. Anticipating.

It came as soon as the conselho, finishing, handed the document to Renayo.

"I will be heard!" There, on the opposite side of the nave in another aisle box, stood Azéma. "By the right given by the Ecclesia to any man to challenge falsehood, I challenge the right of Renayo Mirisso Edoard Verro do'Verrada to sign this Constitussion. He is *not* the son of Arrigo. He has no right to the ducal throne. His signature does not constitute a legal binding mark."

So much for peace.

Rohario hunched down, covered his ears with his hands to shut out the roar of many voices shouting all at once, then thought better of the gesture. Better to face the trouble square on. In the great sanctuary the noise echoed doubly loud, so loud that he wondered if it could shatter the huge glass windows or the fine glass vessels that held the holy wine blessed by Matra ei Filho.

Strangely, if he could indeed discern any order in the madness, at least half of the shouting and cursing and wild uproar was directed *against* Azéma. There was hope, then. Renayo had adherents, even among those who sought to limit his power.

The Premio Sancto struggled up out of his holy seat and lifted a hand, but no one took any mind. The tremendous uproar showed no sign of abating. Even when the frail Premia Sancta rose, even when Rohario could see her mouth move, her words drowned by the tumult of louder voices, the shouting and hubbub did not quiet. Renayo sat stone-faced and watched the assembly. How could he ever come to trust in this assembly if this was how they behaved? Rohario bit his lip and then, at last, made up his mind to act. He stood up.

But at that moment the great doors of the Cathedral opened, light flooding in to sculpt new and darker shadows along the aisles.

A procession entered, a short line of men dressed in dark formal coats and trousers, gray caps tucked under their arms. Each man wore, around his neck, a golden key on a heavy gold chain. Each man carried, in his right hand, a copy of the Holy Verses. Behind them walked servants dressed in plain livery, bearing two huge shrouded shapes that could only be. . . .

Paintings! They were so big that Rohario could not imagine what images they might be. Behind the paintings, escorted by Cabral Grijalva, walked a man whose arms were chained behind him. Rohario did not recognize him, but he also wore the sigil of the golden key. Directly behind him walked a woman veiled in black lace that hung to her waist; her ash-rose gown belled out beneath the veil, by its color and style a relic of ancient days. Behind her clustered other Grijalva adults and children, a mass of them, coming forward like postulants. *There!*

"Eleyna!" He called her name, leaning forward, but she either did not hear him or chose not to hear. Her expression was grim. Her sister Beatriz, looking preternaturally calm, held her hand.

He could not look away from Eleyna. He could not bear to let her stand alone. He, too, had Grijalva blood in him. Why should he not join their number? He grasped hold of the half wall, ready to leap over it; a hand on his arm stayed him.

"Your place is here, Don Rohario," said the man beside him, misunderstanding the intent of his movement, "not with your father. You have chosen your place, and that is to stand with us."

Just as Eleyna had chosen, in the end, to stand with the Grijalvas.

Rohario bowed his head. Remembered his father's words short hours ago: *We agreed it is the only way.* He sat down. Now the voices that had moments before been shouting against the Grand Duke or against Azéma shouted new words: "Grijalvas! Limners!"

The Grijalva Limners knelt, not before the Grand Duke but before the Premio Sancto and the Premia Sancta, who sat down again in their chairs. The servants holding the great paintings unveiled them and slowly turned them so that all could see: *two* paintings of *The First Mistress,* the most famous painting in Tira Virte . . . except that one of the paintings lacked the figure of Saavedra Grijalva. The room was a perfect reproduction, but it contained no woman.

The veiled woman strode up to the dais. She stood there while slowly the assembly quieted until only whispers disturbed the great hush that now fell in the cathedral.

"If I may beg your indulgence," said Cabral Grijalva. His voice carried sound and true in the vast gulf of the cathedral. His age of itself made him worthy of attention. "If you would examine these, Your Holinesses, you will see that the paints of this one are old and cracked and faded in color, yet it is perfect in execution, as befits a portrait done by one of the Old Masters. And here, a copy done recently: can you smell the faint odor of paint? Can you see that it is not dry yet but only beginning to dry down through the layers?"

The Premio Sancto touched his heart as though astonished. He pointed at the painting that displayed only an empty chamber.

Cabral went on. "For many years, Your Holinesses, you and your predecessors have heard but ignored rumors of magic born into the Grijalva line. Of Grijalva Limners working together with the do'Verradas to increase our country's fortunes. And so, together, they have. For I am come today as senior Grijalva alive to tell you that it is true. That there is magic in the Grijalva blood, though it touches only a few of us."

Rohario leaped to his feet. But he was alone. No breath stirred the air, no shout, not even a whisper. Every man in the Cathedral strained forward to hear what Cabral Grijalva would say next and how the Premio Sancto and the Premia Sancta would reply. He sat.

"I am not one of those Limners, Your Holinesses, for they are doomed by that same Gift to die young, but I swear to you now on this holy ground that there are such men in the Grijalva bloodline. And that for these many years they have faithfully served the do'Verradas and Tira Virte, offering up their lives. But in the end, perhaps, it was our own fear that has punished us most. Though we have struggled all these years to serve only the Dukes who protected us, there are always those few among us who choose to serve themselves. That is why we must throw ourselves upon your mercy and the mercy of the Ecclesia, which has scorned us as chi'patro for so long."

He paused, as if seeking permission to continue. So long Their Holinesses hesitated. Rohario wanted to jump up and shout: *You cannot deny them now!* But he held his tongue. And at last the Premia Sancta signed for Cabral to go on.

His voice remained even. "For the greatest of the Limners, Sario Grijalva, out of hatred and envy imprisoned his living cousin Saavedra, the beloved of Duke Alejandro, in this portrait, so that she might never love another man but himself. This same Sario, by unspeakable means which no other Grijalva has learned or dreamed of, extended his own life over the endless years. This Sario murdered Lord Limner Andreo out of blind ambition and sought to control Grand Duke Renayo for his own ends."

Shocked mutters rose from the benches, but Cabral waved them to silence impatiently. "This is *not* how we Grijalvas serve Tira Virte. We bring Sario Grijalva forward now, still wearing the same name although he wears a different body than the one he was born into almost four hundred years ago."

The Premia Sancta rose laboriously and tottered forward. She examined the two paintings with her fingers. Rohario saw that she shook her head. The assembly was so quiet that the loudest noise was the rustle of cloth moving as people shifted in their seats, the squeak of leather shoes on the floor.

When the old woman spoke, her voice was as robust as her body was frail. "These paintings are as you say, Master Cabral. Yet what proof can you give me? Here I see Saavedra Grijalva, and here—" She gestured toward the painting that displayed only an empty chamber.

The veiled woman slipped the black lace from her head.

There was a moment of stunned absolute silence. Then everyone spoke at once.

But they quieted immediately when Saavedra Grijalva raised a hand.

Saavedra Grijalva! Could it be? How could it possibly be she? And yet, the painted chamber in which she had stood was empty. Where else could she have gone?

Rohario stared. This woman he had admired for years from afar, and yet, standing there, she looked so different, not in face but in substance: a beautiful woman, truly, but one he did not know. And when he sought and found Eleyna, her face was infinitely sweeter to him and far more familiar, though he had gazed on Saavedra Grijalva's face in the portrait for the whole of his life.

"I am Saavedra Grijalva," she said in a rich voice that carried easily to every nook and distant corner in the Cathedral. A rich voice, one marked by a curious accent. "I am truly she, and I was captured and imprisoned in this painting by the magic of my cousin, Sario, who stands accused before you now, guilty by his own admission."

Sario Grijalva stood with head bowed. He did not move or make any sign that he heard. Rohario could not see his expression.

"I have come to you, here," Saavedra continued, "to beg protection for myself and for my family from the hand of Grand Duke Renayo and at the feet of the Premio Sancto and the Premia Sancta. If my family has sinned, it has only been because of their desire to serve. They have held their duty to the do'Verradas above all else. This I know, for I watched the Grijalvas regain the position of Lord

Limner and I see now how changed is Tira Virte, how much stronger, how much richer, how much more populous, since that day when I was cast into this imprisonment.

"How did you come to be free?" asked the Premia Sancta.

From the floor, from—of course!—Ruis, another question: "How can we believe this is true?"

She smiled gently and answered the Sancta first, as was fitting. "Once it was discovered I was alive within the portrait, it was simple enough to paint a door—the other side of that door, do you see?—without binding spells, so that I might open the latch and walk free. And as for you, young man! Come forward!"

Eiha! Rohario admired her audacity.

"You I do not know, but I ask you to examine that painting closely. Have you ever known a mirror in a painting to reflect a face? Have you? Look."

Ruis looked. He jumped back, astounded. "I see my own face!"

"Now. Let Sario Grijalva look in the mirror. You, young man, look and see what face is reflected."

Sario was led over, unresisting. Ruis gasped out loud. "It isn't his face! It is another man's face, *there!*"

Eiha! Again the assembly dissolved into confusion. Men stood on the pews for a better view, while others banged their hands against wood, crying for silence. At last, while Saavedra Grijalva waited with complete composure, they quieted.

Throughout, Renayo sat without changing expression. Rohario looked from him toward the gathered Grijalva family, and there he saw Eleyna, looking into the crowd, searching . . . searching . . . he refrained from waving his hands, but there! She had seen him. As if it were enough to mark him, she returned her attention to the dais.

"Two days ago I emerged from my prison," continued Saavedra. "Five days ago I was alive in my proper time. Five days ago I spoke. . . ." She stumbled over the word. Grief harrowed her face. "I spoke to Duke Alejandro. But I never had the chance to tell him that I was pregnant with his child."

By now, at least one of the men sitting near Rohario was wiping tears from his eyes.

Her voice rang out more strongly than ever, as clear as the great bells that rang from the tower. "I admit, to my shame and his, that this child was chi'patro! That word has been used often enough against my family. But it is all I have left of him, and I will not be ashamed. I beg you, Your Holinesses, to forgive this sin." She threw herself on her knees before the Premio Sancto and the Premio Sancta.

"Matra Dolcha, ninia," said the Premia Sancta, giving her hand to Saavedra. "What is past is long past. You have suffered enough."

"What of my family? Must they be punished as well, for the Gift given them by Matra ei Filho, which they have nurtured in secrecy for these many years?"

The two Holinesses bowed their heads.

At long last, Grand Duke Renayo rose. He looked as dignified and noble as Rohario had ever seen him, his dark blue coat perfectly cut—if ten years out of date, for Renayo refused to give in to the new styles. Matra! And why should he if he did not wish to? The old style suited him. For the first time in his life, Rohario truly admired his father.

"I must interrupt," Renayo said, "for there is a piece of business we have not concluded. I have not yet signed this document." While the assembly gaped, still caught in the drama of Saavedra's confession and absolution, Renayo took a pen from Velasco and signed the Constitussion with a flourish.

A great cheer rose, shaking the high windows and the gold-plated chandeliers.

Renayo waited until the cheering died down, then walked over to stand beside the Grijalva Limners. There were only nine of them, one so bent with arthritis he could barely stand, another as young as an apprentice. They did not *look* dangerous.

"It is true that the do'Verradas have benefitted from the service of the Grijalva Limners," said Renayo. "And yet, secrecy is abhorrent to the Ecclesia. So in the spirit of this Constitussion which I have signed tonight, I make this pronouncement: That all Limners and all painters of any lineage may compete for the honor of painting the official documents of the court. I abolish the position of Lord Limner and instead appoint a Council for Documents, which will award commissions for the execution of portraits to document official proceedings as they are needed."

More wild cheers. Bemused, Rohario wondered if his father might end up more popular after the institution of the Corteis than before. Truly it was a miracle that the Matra ei Filho had blessed Tira Virte with the wisdom to change without resorting to the violence that had destroyed other kingdoms.

"As for these Grijalvas who stand before you now, I am honorbound by the Edict of Protection bestowed by Alessio the First and renewed by the first Benetto. It is time for that edict to pass out of my hands and into those of the Ecclesia."

Renayo bowed his head humbly. So did many of the men in the gathering, clasping hats to breasts. The Grijalvas, slowly and perhaps with some reluctance, knelt before the Premio Sancto and the Premia Sancta. All of them bowed their heads, even the great Limners, whose arrogance was legend—*all,* except for the accused man. Rohario sought out Eleyna's dark head, saw Cabral—*grandfather!*—kneeling with his white head bowed and his dignity intact.

At last Saavedra Grijalva raised her head and stared straight at Their Holinesses. She was proud yet also humbled by tragic experience, and she was as majestic as a queen in an elegant gown three hundred years out of date and yet as new-looking as if made last week.

"Matra Dolcha, ninia, we cannot forsake those who come to us for mercy," said the Premia Sancta, taking her hand and lifting her up. "Rise. For you have sinned grievously, but it is the mercy of the Matra which gives us life and hope. So come you under Her gentle hands and be forgiven."

Under the gentle hands, Rohario thought, of the great altarpiece painted by Sario Grijalva with his own blood. The altarpiece in which the Matra was a portrait of Saavedra herself. How could they *not* forgive her?

Renayo came forward and took Saavedra's hand. "What you have suffered, bela meya, is beyond description. I will not allow you to suffer more." He turned to the assembly. His voice penetrated into the depths of the cathedral. "Is it just that Duke Alejandro's child be stained and cast out?"

"No!" they cried, a thousand voices in agreement. All but Azéma, who stood alone, a fragile reed fighting hopelessly against the rising tide.

"Can you swear, Saavedra Grijalva, on the book of Holy Verses that this is the true child of Alejandro do'Verrada?" The Premio Sancto held out an old leather-bound, gilt-encrusted volume of the Holy Verses.

Saavedra laid first her palms, then her forehead, on it. The great dark mass of her unbound hair hid the book from view, yet no one needed to see it clearly. It was enough that they felt, with her, that it was there. "I swear it." She lifted her head so all might hear her words. "This child I bear within me is the child of Alejandro Baltran Edoard Alessio do'Verrada, he with whom I pledged love. This I swear on the Holy Verses of Matra ei Filho, may their blessings be upon me."

"This child she bears would have been Duke of Tira Virte, had he been a boy." Renayo extended an arm toward the Grand Duchess. No, indeed, Roario realized abruptly. He was extending it toward poor bewildered Edoard, who stared at Saavedra as though at a vision which portended good fortune or, perhaps, ill. "So in the spirit of this new Constitussion which you have presented to me as your Grand Duke, I hereby as is within my rights and powers betroth Saavedra Grijalva to my son, Edoard, and I grant legitimacy to the child born of this issue. If it is a boy, I name that child *Heir* after my son Edoard."

By this time the assembly was too worn out by revelation to do more than raise a murmur that soon passed. Renayo clasped Saavedra's hand in Edoard's. Roario saw, now, what the plan had been all along, concocted, as always, by the Duke and his Grijalva allies. *We agreed it is the only way.*

Grand Duke Renayo had never been a man to let others control his destiny. The Grijalvas did whatever they needed to do, in order to survive.

Renayo surveyed the assembly and drew himself up, for he remained, lest they forget, their Duke. "As for the other accusation," he said scornfully, "I will not dishonor my mother's memory by answering it, but I swear—" He knelt before the Premio Sancto and the Premia Sancta and kissed their rings. "I swear on these rings," he continued, rising to his feet and gesturing toward his son and his son's betrothed, "that my Heir is the true child of the bloodline of the do'Verradas."

NINETY-ONE

Eleyna was holding Agustin's linen-swathed hand when he died. He had awakened only twice in the last two days, once in agony and the second time so weak that the pain no longer seemed to bother him. So at last, and mercifully, he breathed his last the evening after the great meeting at the Cathedral.

"A shard of the Mirror returns to the Great Soul." The sancta in attendance closed his blistered eyes.

Dionisa wept uncontrollably, though Beatriz attempted to comfort her. They interred him the next morning in the family tomb. By midday Beatriz had packed her few possessions, including two fat notebooks, and made her farewells.

"I must go," she said to Eleyna. "If a Grijalva dedicates herself to the Sanctia, then the Ecclesia will see we are worthy of their protection and their forgiveness."

"But your balls and your manor house and your fine gowns, Beatriz! What about them?"

Beatriz smiled sadly. "I will study plants, Eleynita, and find a better way to treat burns, so that some poor child will not have to suffer as Agustin did. At the Sanctia I will be allowed to garden. I will grow pea plants, and study the notes Grandmother made, and someday I will understand the Grijalva Gift."

"Understand it?"

"Surely you don't think it truly is a blessing drifted down from on high?"

"What do you mean?"

"There must be an explanation, Eleyna! Why it passes to some men and not others, and not to women at all, except in one case. Why it makes male Limners sterile but left Saavedra fertile. I intend to find out the answers to all these questions! We Grijalvas have only *used* the Gift. We have never tried to comprehend what it is and where it comes from. And why *we,* of all people, chi'patro descendents of Tza'ab bandits, developed it."

In the end, Eleyna had to laugh sadly. "You always get your way, Beatriz. I can't imagine how you manage it."

Beatriz kissed her and left with the sanctas.

Eleyna stood in the courtyard and let the sun's light stream down

over her. The rains had gone, leaving in their wake long days of sun
and warmth. In another few months the great heat would settle over
the land, but for now there was only the glory of perfect weather.
The light was bright and clear. Painter's Luza, by which light a limner might draw her subject with perfect clarity.

Inside Palasso Grijalva the mood was subdued. On the Feast of
Astraventa, in thirty days, Saavedra would marry Edoard.
do'Verrada. Renayo had insisted on a proper wedding, with full
state honors. He did not intend to slight Edoard's new bride or,
more importantly, the child she carried. Already Saavedra spent
most of her time in the Palasso. She and Renayo got on very well
together, or so everyone said. Pragmatists, both of them.

"Come, ninia, sit out here in the sun." Giaberto emerged from
the shadowed arcade, leading Alazais. The girl looked dazed, but
she sank down onto a bench passively, her hands clutching a piece
of unfinished embroidery. She was dressed plainly, in a simple
high-waisted white gown worn over a white shift. She had evidently forgotten to put on her shoes; barefoot, she sat and smiled
vaguely at Giaberto.

"Where is Sario?" she asked in her level voice. "I am the
Princess Alazais. My father and mother were . . . killed by the
mob." She shuddered delicately, and Eleyna, in her turn, shuddered
to see this creature.

For creature she was. That much Sario had admitted. Alazais
was not a woman; she had been painted into life.

And yet she was in some peculiar fashion a woman, living,
breathing, talking, asking again and again after her creator. No one
understood how Sario could have managed a spell of this magnitude.

"It is abomination," Saavedra had declared, and the others
agreed. Sario Grijalva was an abomination. He must be punished,
and in such a way that he could never again threaten the fragile
peace the Grijalvas had painted among themselves, the
do'Verradas, and the Ecclesia.

But Eleyna had not been permitted to attend that meeting of the
Viehos Fratos. She was, again, excluded.

From out of a distant corridor she heard her mother weeping,
ragged sobs that went on and on and on.

For Agustin.

Eleyna wiped tears from her cheek and went to confront the man
who had painted a woman to life and killed an innocent boy. They
held him in a plain-featured room deep in the warren of the
Palasso. It was furnished with a cot and barred with a lock of iron.

"Maestra," said the servant guarding the door. He bowed to her. They all treated her with respect, now that her role in freeing Renayo and in painting an almost perfect copy of *The First Mistress* had become known.

Maestra. The female form of *Master.* She liked the sound of it.

"I must see Sario," she said, and he let her in at once. The door was locked behind her.

Sario Grijalva stood in the center of the room, staring at blank wall. After a long pause, he turned. Seeing *her,* he started forward. "They won't even give me chalk, a pencil. It is an agony, not to be able to draw!"

Agustin's murderer. The greatest Limner the Grijalvas had ever known. It horrified her to see him beg like this.

"You know I can bring no such thing. Even chalk on wall might be used—"

"Eiha!" He jerked away from her and sank down onto the cot. "I cannot bear to live if I cannot paint."

Matra Dolcha! This was not the man she remembered. This was not her arrogant moualimo. Since Saavedra's arrival he had been like this, despondent and pathetic by turns. Something in him had broken. Eleyna stood there, not knowing what to say. She should hate him for killing Agustin, but, by the Blessed Matra, she could not. She could hate what he had done—hate the arrogance and cruelty that had fueled the action—but she could not hate *him.*

He looked up suddenly. His face was scored with grief. He looked immeasurably old, eyes scarred with memory. "You are the only one who visits me. Does 'Vedra ever speak of me?"

"We see little of her here. She is to marry Don Edoard."

"No one told me." He retreated into his own agony. His hands, still tied behind him, twitched like creatures that had a life of their own. "I have seen no one. No one! They all have forsaken me."

"I have not." She said it before she knew she meant to.

He jumped up and crossed to her. He looked crazed by that inner voice that drove him. "Yes. Yes, you have not, because you are like me."

She recoiled from the words.

"Free me, estuda," he murmured, glancing toward the locked door. "We will go away, you and I, and paint. We will do nothing but paint."

Tears stung in her eyes, but perhaps only because she was ashamed that even now his words tempted her. To do nothing but paint. To think only of art. To be taught by, to aspire to become the equal of, the greatest Grijalva painter who had ever lived.

"You are like me. You know it is true."

"I know it is true." She wept not only for the shame but because it was impossible. "But I cannot do what you ask."

For a long uncanny while he stared hard at her, and she met his gaze without flinching. She knew what he was. Then, with a twitch of his shoulder, he sank down onto the cot. All the intense passion drained out of him. He knew he was beaten and that she could not help him, though a part of her desperately wanted to.

Without looking up, he spoke. "You alone I can trust. You alone. Estuda meya, you must do exactly as I say. Will you?"

"What do you want me to do?" she asked cautiously, but he had already gone on, sure of her acquiescence or not caring, so desperate to unburden himself.

"There is a wine shop, and over that wine shop, an attic. The proprietor's name is Oliviano. The deed is hidden behind a false panel of wall marked by a painted ivy wreath. My heir is named as the one who will speak these words to him: Al-Fansihirro." He waited. She repeated them. Satisfied, he continued. "With this the shop becomes yours. Go up the stairs to the atelierro. You must resist the wards. Dilute the paintings with water and soap, only enough so that you can enter the atelierro. And there, you must find the book. You must burn the book. Do you understand? Burn it. It is all in my head, all the knowledge. I no longer need it, but no one else must know it."

"What book?"

"The *Kita'ab.* You must burn it."

She swallowed. "A copy of the *Kita'ab?* How can that be?"

"I was given it, many years ago, by an old Tza'ab man. The *Folio* the Viehos Fratos have is an incomplete copy, lacking so much . . . so much. Say you will do as I ask."

"Yes. Yes, I will. I can." On this matter, at least, she knew what was right. "That way no one else can do what you have done."

"Moronna! What do I care if others follow after me, if they seek as I sought? I do not want them to find what I possessed! Only I, Sario, will have mastered the *Kita'ab* and the hidden magic. Only I! I am the true master of the Gift, and there will be no other to follow me. Do you understand, estuda?" He was shouting now. "You alone I grant the right to paint as well as I have painted, to be the master after me, but to no one else will I give my knowledge of the Gift. No one else can have that!"

He *was* mad. But he was also right.

"I will go," she said at last. "I will do as you ask."

"Burn it," he said fiercely. "Burn everything you find there. Will you not set me free, Eleyna?"

She looked at the door, barred and locked from the outside, then back at him. "I cannot set you free. You know I cannot. Matra Dolcha, you murdered my dear brother. How can you expect me to forget that? To let you free to perhaps do it again to some other woman's brother?"

But he thought only of himself. She should have understood that about him all along. "I cannot live this way, in prison, forbidden forever from my art. Do as I ask, I beg you."

She went. His directions were easily followed, and to her great surprise she recognized the wine shop. Rohario had found employment here in his brief life as a clerk.

Rohario. She had last seen him in the crowd at the Cathedral. Then there had been a note, written in his beautiful handwriting, informing her that he had to visit his estates and would be back soon. Assuring her of his love.

Love was a strange word, speaking of what binds one soul to another. By that measure, she loved Sario Grijalva, monster though he was. *"You are like me."* Forever bound to him, she must work his will in this matter at least.

Eleyna introduced herself to the proprietor, Oliviano. She surprised him with her knowledge of the deed's hiding place; she spoke the word that marked her as heir. She commandeered soap and water from his good wife. Odd, to go to the stairs and feel so sharply that she *ought not* to be going there. But she got down on her hands and knees and scrubbed away the oscurra painted into the wood. Imagined Sario shivering in his cell, as his blood and saliva dissolved in plain soap and cold water. How she wanted to study the spiraling mural of leaves and vines and flowers, but she dared not. She dared not let its magic take hold of her mind before she could erase it forever.

She finished and opened the door with the small bronze key sealed into an envelope with the deed.

"Up here I left the food for him," said Oliviano, treading almost on her heels, curious and yet afraid. "At the door. Farther I never went."

"I will go in alone," she said.

She opened the door and walked in. The chamber was long and dark. She opened shutters and looked out over rooftops and the tiled facades of apartment houses and shops. She measured the chamber with her feet, blew dust off the tabletop. This was the atelierro in which he had created Alazais; she recognized it from the

painting. There was a chest under the bed. She pulled it out and unlocked it with the key.

A few stoppered clay pots. A tiny silver jewel-box. Three glass
vials filled with old dried red pigment. A skull.

She shuddered and set the skull on the table, then reached in and
pulled out a book so ancient that it crackled with age when she
opened it. The flowing script was alien to her, but the borders!
Eiha! She had never seen such sinuous lines, weaving in and
around the calligraphed words. The parchment itself was heavy,
thick, and when she ran her finger across the page, feeling the thin
line of ink that was the body of each letter, she felt as if the page itself was warm and somehow alive.

She turned the pages, but all of it was nonsense to her. She could
not even recognize letters. But its great age and the flowing, beautiful border drawings attracted her. Words were not as familiar to
her as the language of image, yet even words could eventually be
deciphered. And in the words rested the knowledge Sario had
hoarded for so long. She closed the book hastily.

In the room there was also an easel, broken down, and behind it
a huge panel shrouded by a yellowed linen cloth. Of the rest of
Sario there was no sign, no paints, no brushes, no paraphernalia of
his life and work. After all, his life went into his paintings, not into
the detritus of daily living.

Carefully she folded the linen shroud away from the panel.
Stared, hands caught in linen folds.

It was a portrait of many men, each face stark against the background and all of it decorated with an almost invisible border
whose flowing oscurra and twined intricacies threaded through the
painting like a living creature, an unbroken link. Some of the men
wore the clothing of centuries past, one the fashions of ten years
ago. She recognized Sario—her Sario—at once. Matra Dolcha!
There was *Riobaro* Grijalva, the great Lord Limner! She had
scrawled his signature on a tablecloth at Gaspar's inn, as tribute to
the dead master's famous gesture. Wasn't that Dioniso Grijalva?
First among them was the first Sario, his image clear but marked
with age.

One man's mind, his spirit, transferred to another man's body.
And this, his *Peintraddo Memorrio,* his true self-portrait, recorded
those lives. She recognized the herbal border: water willow for
Freedom, vervain for Enchantment, juniper for Protection, white
oak for Independence, golden roses, twined through the portraits,
for Perfection.

He had murdered sixteen men and inhabited their bodies, lived their lives. Whose skull out of all of them had he kept, which rested now on the attic table?

A lamp stood on the table. Eleyna lit it. For a long while she watched it burn. Then she sought and found a jar of oil to replenish the flame.

Tearing off the first parchment leaf, she held it up next to the fire. Sario, in each of his lives, watched her. She could believe that somehow, in his cell, he could see her through his Blooded, painted eyes. *"To no one else will I give my knowledge of the Gift."*

Only to her. Had he not promised to teach her *all* the secrets of the Limners? And more besides, the secrets only he knew, that he had puzzled out over three hundred years of unnatural life? All of this he had given into her hands, no one else's. Because she was like him.

Her hands shook as she held the page closer to the lamp's flame. Fragile with age, its buttery grain and flowing script beckoned her, whispered like *his* voice. In time, she could puzzle out the words, as he had done. Given enough time, she could know everything he knew and, although she had no Gift to paint spells herself, she could take on students of her own, teach them—

Matra Dolcha. *This* was where such thoughts led: to pride; to arrogance; to ruin. To death. With this knowledge he had murdered Agustin, Andreo, all the men in the *Peintraddo,* and countless unknown others: their memories, their lives, lost forever.

Cursing him, she set a corner of the ancient parchment into the fire. The borders flamed and shriveled. The letters flared with silver light and sparked and died. Their ancient beauty turned brown, then black, then exploded into white flame, scorching her fingers. She yelped and dropped the page.

So would *she* be burned, if she followed Sario's path. Weeping, she watching the page flame and die. When only ashes remained she turned to stare at his *Peintraddo Memorrio.*

Walking over to it, she brushed her fingers lightly over the painting as if to read what traces of him might remain there. So cracked in some sections, ancient and yellowing; new, almost fresh, in others, the style altered by the passage of time and fashion but yet demonstrably the same hand. It was a masterwork, these men who regarded her from the canvas. Each one an individual and yet each one bearing the eyes of the original: desert-bred brown. It should have been an awkward composition, and indeed one section of the painting remained unfinished, white ground unsullied by sketch or underpainting or the glazes and frotties of a finished portrait. Yet the *Peintraddo* was of a piece. Even had she not known some of the men, recognized some of the faces, she could have traced Sario's life through each of the men he had inhabited. His skill drew the eye from life to life, a natural progression. Hidden deep within the colors she distinguished oscurra, delicate tracings like the hidden story of his life traced across years and faces.

"Burn everything you find there." But she could not. She could not destroy it.

She sniffed hard and wiped tears off her cheeks, then crossed back to the table. Skull sat next to *Kita'ab,* in their juxtaposition telling the essential story of his life: the knowledge that had killed the first Sario—though Sario still lived—killed what was best in him, he who had succumbed to the worst that hides in ambition. What else had the Tza'ab written in this holy book? Not only bad things, surely; might there not be *good* written here as well, things Sario had ignored? She could not judge.

She fingered the pages and knew then she could not burn it. Yet neither could she keep it. That much she had learned from Sario Grijalva.

Closing the heavy book, she set it gently inside the chest together with the skull and locked the chest with the bronze key. She covered his *Peintraddo* with the shroud, locked the attic door behind her, and walked back through quiet streets to Palasso Grijalva. Grand Duke Renayo's carriage stood in the courtyard. Lights burned in the Atelierro. She hurried upstairs, knocked, waited, wondering what reception she would receive.

They let her in.

"I am glad you have come," said Cabral, moving to greet her. "Sit here, mennina. Witness."

She was shocked to see not only the Grand Duke but also the Premio Sancto and the frail figure of the Premia Sancta. They were seated on the other side of the chamber. On an easel in the middle of the great chamber stood a painting of a plain whitewashed room, no windows, no doors, no furniture except for a mirror, propped on an easel, that reflected candle and lamp flame from the unseen end of the tiny room. Iron stands stood in the corners holding hour candles. Two lamps hung from the ceiling, and Saavedra's artistry was such that their flame suggested the first flare of light in a newly-lit lantern. Otherwise the room was featureless. Not even the plank floor had any distinguishing marks.

Saavedra stood beside the easel, preparing her paletto. She was now dressed in a high-waisted white gown stamped with small lavender sigils; Eleyna recognized it a moment later as one of Beatriz's gowns, let down at the hem to accommodate Saavedra's greater height. The Viehos Fratos sat to one side, and poor Edoard sat behind his father, gazing at his bride-to-be with a look compounded of equal parts worship and terror.

Eleyna winced when the Limner woman stuck herself calmly with a lancet, drawing blood and mixing it in with the paints. The Premia Sancta murmured an audible prayer. But no one objected.

"Bring him up," said Saavedra.

And when they brought him up, she asked: "Is there anything more you wish to tell us?"

"There is nothing I wish to tell you," Sario said, "but I wait for you to thank me for forcing you to acknowledge your Gift."

She ignored this. "The secret of your long life? How you come to be here now? Whose bodies and lives you stole? I know what you did, for I have knowledge of my own, gleaned from the book you painted into the room with me. It is that book, Sario, which taught me all that I need to know now, this night. For what I mean to accomplish here."

He set his lips and would not speak.

"Place him there," she ordered. They shoved him forward until he stood within a circle painted on the floor. Only then did they unbind his hands. They turned him so his back was to Saavedra.

Facing this way, he saw Eleyna at once. His eyes lit.

Saavedra lit a candle and set it under a painting of Matra ei Filho. She began to speak words under her breath, a melodious chant that filled the room with its soft humming noise.

"Don't forget, Eleyna," said Sario in a low, intent voice, staring at her so fixedly she dared not look away from him. "There is no golden key you can hold in your hand that will effortlessly give you the mastery of painting. What we Limners wear is only a symbol of what we strive for."

Out of the corner of her eye Eleyna saw Saavedra painting, the bold, confident strokes of a master intending to paint alla prima, a finished portrait in one sitting.

"Don't forget that your ultramarine is excellent for glazes." He went on in that same rushed manner. "But it will soften if it is stored when already made with oil, so you must add a little wax."

Beside her, Cabral shuffled his feet nervously back and forth as Saavedra painted and the light waned.

"Whiting is excellent to cut pigments for sketching colors, but Ghillas chalk has greater brilliance. . . . For your drying oils, linseed dries most thoroughly but poppy yellows less with age."

Damiano stood and lit lamps, and their combined glow cast a

strange brilliance over the chamber, as if locking them all within a single frame.

"When you use a linen canvas, which must be of the best quality, prepare it in this fashion. . . . In tempera, use only eggs from city chickens for your light complexions, but eggs from country chickens for your dark complexions."

Renayo coughed. The Premio Sancto murmured the evening prayer in his sonorous voice, a counterpoint to Saavedra's soft chanting.

"For the thinnest covering of color use your fingers. . . . If a passage of work is not quite right, you must be prepared to discard it and begin again."

Eleyna smelled wax and turpentine, resins and oils and the sweat of many bodies in a confined room; other scents, multiplied, herbs and earth and wood, the years worn into the plank flooring by the steady tread of feet and settled into the walls by the weight of every word spoken and gesture made. Urine. Tears. Sweat. Saliva. Seed. *Blood*. With their own bodies the Grijalva Limners engendered their Gift.

"Above all, Eleyna," he said urgently, "remember *patience*."

With a flare, the lamps flamed and then in the next instant all went out, as if a gust of wind had cleansed the room of their presence.

All was silent.

A single candle illuminated the dim chamber with long streaked shadows. Sario was gone. The Premia Sancta spoke, in a low voice, the blessing for the dead.

Cabral stood and with Giaberto and Damiano relit the lanterns until the chamber blazed with light. Saavedra, head bowed, did not move.

But in the painting a man stood, his back to the viewer. Eleyna gasped and rose quickly. It was Sario's back; she recognized it, as well the clothing he had been wearing, as well as the hint of his profile, the cut of his hair.

But it was not Sario's face that showed in the mirror. It was a different face, the face of the first Sario, he who had been dead over three hundred years. Caught at last in a place where he would never age, never wither, never die. Looking, at the last, at his greatest masterpiece: *himself*.

Eleyna burst into tears and ran from the room.

─ ✦ ─ NINETY-TWO ─ ✦ ─

"Eleyna! Eleynita! Aren't you ready yet?" Beatriz swept into the room and surveyed it critically. "This looks less luxurious than my Noviciata's cell, bela. And your atelierro downstairs hasn't been swept yet!"

"Those shapeless white robes and that stiff wimple look very fetching on you, Bellita."

Beatriz laughed. "My garden is sprouting very nicely, I'll have you know. The sanctas have given me a tidy plot for my little experiments. I've added some herbs to their herb garden as well, and ordered it much better than it was before."

"And I have fifty students signed up," Eleyna retorted, "although classes do not begin for a month! If this room appears spare to your eye, that is only because you think I ought to fill it up with embroidered wall hangings and black-lacquered Zhinna vases and all of that awful fashionable furniture. I finished painting the *Deed* to this apartamento only five days ago. You cannot expect I have had time to furnish it decently."

Beatriz helped her button up the back of her gown. "If you are going to act in society as an important woman, sorella, you must have a ladies' maid and all kinds of servants. There is only Davo, downstairs, and you can hardly expect him to dress you!"

"Be patient, Bellita. Once Rohario and I are married, he assures me his steward will secure the very best servants. I will let Rohario arrange all those things. He likes doing them."

"He is back? You have the Ecclesia's dispensation?"

Eleyna could not help but flush, so she busied herself folding her lace shawl. "The Premio Sancto himself gave his approval, although I thought I detected a twinkle in his eye when he declared that we must marry on Sancterria."

Beatriz snorted. "As if Sancterria's fires will cleanse your blood of all its stains."

"Rohario returned to town for Saavedra's wedding."

"Of course! It seems all of Meya Suerta is in the streets, waiting for the festivities to begin. Astraventa is a propitious holiday, is it not, on which to hold a wedding? Especially when the bride has already *caught* a star in her mirror."

"Beatriz!"

But she only laughed and made Eleyna stand in front of the mirror while she arranged her hair. "I never imagined that a Grijalva bearing the bastard child of a do'Verrada would be this popular. Eiha! That is the best I can do with your hair." Distracted, Beatriz wandered over toward the window, and her eye caught on the shrouded canvas frame which Eleyna had only this morning carried to this room from its attic hideaway. "What is this? A new painting of yours?"

Eleyna spun around. "Don't uncover that, if you please."

"As you wish," said Beatriz, one eyebrow raised. "A mystery, I see." She brushed the yellowed linen shroud that draped the painting with her fingers, frowned at the dust, and then leaned to look out the open window. "Eiha! There is Sancta Louissa and her poor mother, taking a bit of air while they wait for me. Theirs is a heartbreaking story, I assure you, but I will tell it to you later because I see Sancta Juania, whom I affectionately call the Snake, peering up here with her beady eye. She is getting restless. I must go!" She kissed Eleyna on the cheek and crossed to the door.

"Wait!"

Beatriz stopped, turned, and her eyes widened. "What is this, Eleyna? You look so serious on such a festive day."

For weeks this burden had laid heavily on her shoulders. How easy it would be to let Beatriz walk out the door and keep it for herself. So much knowledge, waiting only for her, for someone, to unravel it. She took in a deep breath, unlocked the chest that sat in a shadowed corner, and took out the book. Lifting it, she offered it to Beatriz.

"This once belonged to Sario Grijalva," she said. The heavy book seemed to burn on her hands, but she did not waver. "It is an ancient copy of the *Kita'ab*—the Tza'ab book that became the *Folio*."

Beatriz just gaped at her.

"I could not burn it, although I should have! I could not be the one to judge." Impatiently she thrust it forward. "Take it! I entrust it to you, Beatriz, who are the best of us. I can trust you to choose what is right."

Suddenly Beatriz's eyes filled with tears. "You do not trust yourself with the knowledge it might contain?" she asked softly, compassionately. "Dolcha Eleynita, you are not truly like him, even if you loved him."

"I have looked into my heart, Bellita. I am not so different than he was, not truly. I will paint as no one has painted before me, I will make a name for myself: the artist Eleyna Grijalva. But what if a part of me craves more, even more, if I begin to use others, care only for myself and nothing for anyone else? No, I will not give in to it. Not as he did." And once more she held out the book.

A shadow crossed Beatriz's face, quickly replaced by that heart's calm that so soothed all who knew her. She simply nodded and took the ancient book out of Eleyna's hands.

Without another word they walked together through the sitting room and into the parlor, where they parted. The silence weighed on her, now that Beatriz was gone—and the *Kita'ab* with her. Slowly Eleyna felt her heart lightening, the shadow lifting.

Yes, she was like Sario; that she could not regret. But she also had the wisdom to turn away from the worst that was in her, as he had not in himself.

Behind her, a door was thrown open. A moment later, Roharic spun her around and kissed her.

"I went to Palasso Grijalva first," he said. "I had forgotten, I confess, that you would no longer be there. This is all so new." He surveyed the parlor with the same critical eye with which Beatriz had surveyed the bedroom. Freshly painted, it still reeked of paint, but the windows were thrown open to ventilate the chamber. "The rooms are spacious enough, and elegant, and I approve of the Friesemarkian style. Grazzo do'Matra the artisans here know how to reproduce it! The parlor downstairs will be sufficient for meetings, and I hope my comrades' arguments will not disturb your classes overmuch. But I will *insist* that we retire to Collara Asaddo in the summer heat. It is a charming place, very rustic. Land management is a peculiarly interesting profession. Almost as interesting as politics. I can't imagine why I didn't discover these things before."

"Because you were vain and useless, corasson meya."

He laughed. "Eiha! True enough. Your mother was furious when she saw me. You did not leave in your family's good graces, Eleynita."

"I did not. You know they did not want me to leave. But I no longer fear my family."

He preened a bit, of course. He thought that *his* protection had freed her from them. She saw no reason to disillusion him.

He spun slowly, examining the room. He had come up with a new way of tying his cravat. Soon, no doubt, the youngest members of the Corteis would all have adopted it. Eiha! At least the assembly would not suffer from poor taste in clothing!

Roharic stopped short when his eye fell on the portrait hanging above the mantel. "This is new! Who has painted such a fine portait of you, corasson? It is magniffico!"

"It was done by Sario Grijalva." She braced herself for his reaction, but he showed no repulsion, only curiosity.

"I thought you destroyed all of his paintings."

"I did. All but the one of poor Alazais."

He cocked his head to one side and regarded her, smiling. His smile had improved immeasurably since the first time she had met him. There was nothing spoiled or facile about him now. "All but that one. And *this* one. Do they know you have it?"

"No." She held her breath.

"It is a lovely picture of you, Eleynita. We will keep it always." Let the breath out. "Of course."

"But. You must agree to paint a portrait of me, which we will hang beside it."

Two portraits. But that was all there could ever be.

"What is this down-hearted look, guivaerra meya?"

"There will be no portraits of children to hang beside them."

"We have spoken of this before, Eleyna. And we will not speak of it again." He took her firmly by the arm and led her to the bank of windows that looked down over a private courtyard. Acacias bloomed, and lime trees stood in a tidy row bordered by a brick walkway. Masons worked on a fountain, a smaller replica of the fountain of bells. She and Rohario stood together in companionable silence until the chimes announcing the wedding began to ring.

She kissed him. "We will do very well together, Rohario."

"I should hope so! Come. Patro will be furious if we are late. He says I am always late these days, but it is only because of the endless meetings. I didn't realize that ten men could have twenty opinions, and all expressed so forcefully!"

But she could tell by his tone and his expression that he loved his new life. Imagine, a do'Verrada as a member of the Corteis! Truly, times had changed.

"Which reminds me," he added, attempting to sound diffident but betraying pride. "The Corteis intends to commission you to paint the official Document of Assembly. The elections will be held next month and the first assembly will convene at Providenssia."

"*I* to paint it! Rohario!" *The official Document of Assembly!* "I could not have expected such an honor so soon. Did *you* make them offer it to me?"

"You overestimate my influence. I think it was the mural at

Gaspar's inn, if you want to know the truth. They all want to be flattered as kindly as you did for him. Eiha! We really *had* better go."

As she waited for him to check his cravat in the mirror—he was still a little vain, after all, and had all those young men to influence in the matter of fashion—she surveyed the parlor with great satisfaction.

A spacious room, open and airy, with lofty windows that let in light along two walls. Room enough for a couch, easels, workbench. Room enough to paint. Here she would take lessons from Cabral, as long as he was alive to teach her. And from Giaberto and the older Grijalva Limners, if they deigned to come here. Here the best of her students would come to take lessons from *her.* Here she would pass on the Luza do'Orro to those who desired to know.

Technique and understanding and that unnamable, unquenchable *need.* The secret of the Golden Key.

"I hate this color." Rohario frowned at his waistcoat. "*Why* must tangerine be fashionable? It is time to make it unfashionable. Eleyna." He caught her gaze in the mirror, and for an instant it was like looking into that other mirror, the one in the portrait that had once held Saavedra. And the one that now held Sario. "There is one thing I've been wondering. If it's true—which I half doubt because it sounds so incredible—that Sario Grijalva lived so long by living other men's lives, then who was he in those other lives? Always Sario, or someone else?"

There were some truths not meant to be shared. For in the end, he had given this last secret into her hands alone. "He never confessed," she said calmly. "He never told anyone, not even Saavedra."

In time, perhaps, she could bring Sario's *Peintraddo Memorrio* out of storage and display it, as it deserved to be displayed. As his last and greatest monument.

The bells rang, a new beginning. She smiled and took Rohario's arm, and together they left the room.

"—this way, Baltran . . . through here. Do you see? No, no, ninio! We're not going back outside. This way. Grazzo."

The curatorrio was halfway down the Galerria, attending to a group of bankers' wives, their black lace shawls draped becomingly over their hair and disguising the low necklines of their fashionable gowns.

"If we are very quiet, Baltran, we might slip by without—"

"Patro!" The child grabbed his wrist and tugged him to the window. "Do you see the new cannons, Patro? Look how fine they are!"

Alejandro sighed and gave way to the inevitable. He had to endure the courtesies and graces and interminable small talk of the bankers' wives, respectable women of good society, each one. He knew their husbands and had met them at dinners or presided over their daughter's presentations at court. Blessed Matra, at least Teressa enjoyed such duties—human foibles never failed to amuse her.

When they had gone he waited for their voices to fade (*"Such a handsome young man!"*), for their figures to vanish through the Galerria doors. Baltran was now standing in front of a *Marriage,* hands stuck in pockets, looking monumentally bored.

"Why must we, Patro? There are nothing here but pictures!"

The child was never content. He was restless, always thinking, but what he thought about bore no resemblance to the thoughts that wore at Alejandro. This boy always thought about new things, new creations, new ideas, and he had questions, questions, questions. None of which there were answers for.

Alejandro thought about the past. "Just think, ninio, you are related to every do'Verrada hanging here on these walls."

Baltran sighed expansively. "Patro, I don't like painting. I want to go to the theater. There are explosions on stage for the battle scene! And fireworks afterward. Grandmama 'Vedra says she will take me. Do let me go!"

"You will walk with me. You will be Grand Duke, in time—"

"When I am Grand Duke, I am going to have all these paintings carted off somewhere else!"

Alejandro smiled. A ten-year-old might have grandiose plans. Certainly he had had such when he was ten. But there was no need to shatter the child's illusions. Time and life would do that easily enough. Baltran would come to understand why this Galerria was important, to the do'Verradas *and* to Tira Virte.

"For now, you are only Heir to the Grand Duke. Since I am Grand Duke, I may order you to come with me."

"You must have the permission of the Corteis first!"

"Not for the governance of my own son."

Baltran laughed and ran ahead, although he knew he should not run in the Galerria. Alejandro did not have the heart to call him back.

My own son.

Bitter, that blow. Worse still the endless secret councils about what to do. Grazzo do'Matra that his father had been dead by then, killed in the succession wars in Ghillas. Only that was the greatest irony of all, wasn't it? Edoard was not his father. His true father had lived four hundred years ago. But Edoard had never minded that. Edoard had raised him as if he were truly son of his own seed. Just as Alejandro now raised Baltran.

No one must know. That was what they had all told him. No one must ever know.

"Patro! Patro! Here is your *Birth!* Here is the *Marriage* of Grandmama and poor Grandpapa. Tell me again about the battle! Is it true he was leading a charge?"

In fact Edoard had stopped during a retreat to help one of his young lieutenants, who had been wounded in the stomach, and gotten his head blown off for his pains. It still hurt, remembering the day the message had come. It hurt because he had realized then, at ten years old, that his mother did not love his father as much as he did.

"He died because he was a good, kind, honorable man, Baltran. Remember that."

Baltran did not reply. For once, he seemed to be examining the painting. "Is it true Grandmama is magic, Patro?"

Alejandro smiled wryly. "No more than I am. Where did you hear such a thing?"

"Most people say it. They say that the Grijalvas are all magic, but that they threw themselves on the mercy of the Ecclesia before you were born and the Premia Sancta lifted all terrible stain from them."

"They confessed it openly, it is true. In front of every person in the Cathedral. You know Grandmama's story well enough, do you not? How she was captured in a painting and held prisoner for three hundred years?"

Baltran made a face, unimpressed by this tale, and began walking down toward the end of the Galerria, having evidently decided to do his duty as quickly as possible so he could be free. "But you know what else they say, Patro." Here he bit his lip, recalling words overheard, probably from somewhere he ought not to have been listening.

"What is that?"

"They say, 'Ha! Ha ha!' " He imitated a big man's belly laugh, enjoying the exaggerated sound and the way it flattened in the air. "'Do you call that magic, that they painted flattering portraits of Dukes and beguiled do'Verrada Heirs with their beautiful women?' What does 'beguile' mean, Patro? What did the beautiful women do? Beautiful women like Grandmama?"

"Certainly beautiful women like Grandmama."

Luckily the boy's mind was already racing ahead. "Why does Grandmama not live at the Palasso? Why must she go live with her old family? She must love them better than me." He stuck his lower lip out, pouting, then grinned, knowing full well that his Grandmama 'Vedra doted on him and his little sister Mechellita.

As she doted on me. But Alejandro had to smile. Saavedra was not an easy woman to live with, or to have as a mother. She was the flame to which all moths fluttered and he but one frail boy among the rest. Dote she might, but she also expected nothing but the best from him. "Her family needed her, ninio. Once I married your mother, she left us in peace."

That she now ruled the Grijalvas as she had ruled Edoard before them, with an iron hand, he did not doubt. That she loved him fiercely he doubted less. Still, he wondered sometimes what it would have been like to have an ordinary mother.

They skirted a few other clots of visitors gathered around this *Treaty* or that *Marriage,* wealthy travelers from out of town who did not, with a casual glance, recognize him or Baltran, Grazzo do'Matra. Alejandro surveyed the collection with approval. Over half the paintings had been moved to a new building that adjoined the recently-built Corteis, the chambers that housed the assembly, and now the Galerria received fewer visitors, which pleased

Alejandro greatly. The most monumental and famous paintings had been moved to the new Galerria Nacionalla, but he preferred the collection that was left here, a more intimate and subtle portrait of the Grijalva legacy.

Of which he was the crowning achievement. The child bearing half do'Verrada and half Grijalva blood on the throne of Tira Virte. Yet the crowning irony was that he would be first.

And last.

"Wait, Baltran!" But Baltran was far ahead of him. Teressa's child, certainly, with that quick wit and all those damned questions. Alejandro did not know who Baltran's real father was. He had never asked, trusting to his wife's good sense to pick a man with suitable bloodlines and an ability to keep his mouth shut.

He had agreed to the marriage and counted it good fortune that he liked his bride and that she liked him. Teressa, named after her grandmother, the eldest child of Arrigo and Mechella, had been brought up in a revolutionary household. She had received an intense education in the classics and her father, a bit of a cracked pot (as they said in the lingua merditta) as well as the Principio della Diettro Mareia, brought scientists in to his Palasso to perform their peculiar experiments.

When Saavedra had bluntly outlined Alejandro's problem to his new bride, Teressa had accepted it calmly. He fancied she considered him a peculiar experiment, the nature of which had not yet been solved. Indeed, Teressa loved nothing more than entertaining his Zia Beatriz—now Premia Sancta—who always arrived with her white sancta robes stained with dirt and grass and a ridiculous beatific smile on her face, babbling about her cursed pea plants and the secret language of the ancient Tza'ab mystics.

"Patro! Patro!" From the very end of the Galerria, Baltran's piping voice pierced the quiet. "They've taken Grandmama's portrait!"

Alejandro sighed. He hurried forward, passing one of the large alcoves that thrust out into the park without looking closely at the small group of people seated before the paintings displayed there.

"Ninio, you must learn to temper your voice," he said, coming up beside his son.

"Grandzio Rohario doesn't temper his voice. He roars with the best of them."

"When you are fifty-three years old and a thirty-year member of the Corteis, then you may roar with the best of them, too. What is wrong?"

"Grandmama's portrait is missing."

"Yes. We agreed it would be exhibited in the Nacionalla."

"But why, Patro? Why not the other one? All we see of *him* is his back and the room is so ugly. I like to see Grandmama's beautiful face much better."

Alejandro gazèd up at the painting known as *The Mirror of Truth*. He had been told the story many times. But to see the face in the mirror, a different face from that of the man who stood with his back to the viewer, still gave him a shiver. So much was revealed in this painting, about his heritage, about the nature of the Grijalva Gift, about the truth of his, Alejandro's, own parentage. About the truth of *what* he was.

"Why *is* his face different in the mirror, Patro?"

"Because the face he wears on his body is not the face he wears in his heart."

Baltran eyed the painting with deep misgiving. "Eiha. I hate paintings. Grandzia Eleyna says that you can read what they tell you, all these *Treaties* and documents, by knowing the language in which they are painted. But why can't we just write it all down? Wouldn't that be easier? Patro!" His mind jumped again. "Will we get a semaphore installed in the Palasso? Maesso Oswaldo says that news can travel from Aute-Ghillas to Meya Suerta in twelve hours with semaphore!"

News can travel as fast as a voice can speak, when Grijalva Limners speak through their Blooded paintings. But Alejandro did not say it aloud. Oh yes, the do'Verradas knew, the Ecclesia knew, the Grijalvas knew; even the Corteis knew. But no one *believed* anymore. They wanted their semaphores. So much more reliable. So much more *scientific*.

"Come, Baltran. We have seen enough for today, I think."

The boy was gone like a shot. Alejandro did not bother to slow him down. He took a long look at the portrait of Sario Grijalva. Not a portrait at all, of course. It *was* Sario Grijalva, greatest of the Grijalva Limners, punished for his crimes by being imprisoned in the portrait, painted there by his cousin Saavedra's Gifted hand.

She had made a good life for herself, had Saavedra. Of the other children granted to her and Edoard in their brief and not unhappy marriage, only one had been a boy, and he had died in infancy. The other three had been girls, grown now, all married. Alejandro could not help but wonder sometimes what would have happened to him had Saavedra never been trapped in that painting. He would have been born, Alejandro I's chi'patro child, and raised in Palasso Grijalva. He would have eaten, breathed, and lived painting from the day he was old enough to hold a piece of chalk. Perhaps some of *his* paintings would have hung here, in the Galerria Verrada.

The curtains in the corner stirred. He started, stepped back, then relaxed and extended a hand. "Come, bela, it is only I, 'Sandro. Don't be afraid of me."

She crept forward. She was dressed quite indecently, of course, in a yellowing white shift and tattered lace shawl, but as the years went by she became more and more like a wild cat, shy of humans and quick to bolt. The servants called her Ila Luna, the crazy woman.

"Sit beside me, bela," he said, hoping to coax her out, but she would only come as far as the first square of sunlight on the marble floor. She was indeed beautiful, and so young. Forever young, except for the fine cracks beginning to show on her skin and the odd yellowish tone she was acquiring, the result, his Zia Eleyna had once told him, of Sario Grijalva using inferior paints to create her.

Loud laughter sounded from down the hall, a new group of visitors, and Ila Luna darted back to the safety of the curtains. He waited, but she did not peek out, although he could see where she hid by the lump in the heavy fabric. Poor mindless creature. He wondered, suddenly, if a Grijalva Limner might learn secrets that could somehow cure her of her affliction or if she was doomed to wait beside her imprisoned creator until, like an ancient painting, she finally crumbled away.

He walked slowly after his son, stopped when he saw which party inhabited the alcove. Baltran had stopped, too, held there by that irresistible force which attracts an isolated child to any group of animated children.

Eleyna Grijalva had brought a class of youngsters to the Galerria. They sat in front of Guilbarro Grijalva's famous *Birth of Cossima,* each with a sketchpad and pencil, copying the master's work. Baltran barreled over to his "Grandzia," bowed shyly, and was rewarded with a stately kiss. Then he sidled over to two girls seated demurely on a bench, their sketchpads resting on their knees, and promptly began to interrogate them.

Eleyna swept back her silver hair and turned. She caught sight of Alejandro. Smiling, she walked over to him.

"Your Grace," she said in her lovely voice. She had a magnificent self-confidence, but of course, how could she not? She was the acknowledged master of painting in all of Tira Virte. Acolytes came from foreign lands for the privilege of studying with her. Kings and queens begged her to paint their portraits. "It is always good to see you, ninio. You haven't been to a drawing lesson for two months."

"The cares of state," he said, but he could not smile, though he meant it to be a jest.

"Alas," she said, and nodded, understanding.

"Is it too late?" he asked suddenly. "Is it too late for me to ever learn properly?"

"To learn to use your Gift to its fullest? It likely *is* too late, Alejandro, though I'm sorry to say it if it pains you to hear it." He bowed his head, and she went on. "But it is never to late to study painting, not if you truly wish to learn. It is never too late to use the time left you to its fullest. Many have come late to painting and yet flourished because of their desire to learn and their willingness to work. You are talented, and you love to paint, only—" She gestured toward the walls, indeed, to the entire Palasso. *His* Palasso, now.

"Eiha. That is the great irony, is it not, Zia? The Grand Duke has many duties, and painting is not among them. In ten years Baltran will be twenty and I could retire without too much fuss, but I will be forty and at the end of my life, no?"

"How long your life will be compared to Limners who used their own blood and tears every day we cannot know. And can any one of us truly know how long we will live? You must not think of that, ninio. You have your duties, and you have discharged them well. You are a good man and a fine Grand Duke, Alejandro."

"Even if my heart lies elsewhere?" He gestured toward the *Birth of Cossima.*

"That is up to you. You may not go as far as you wish. You may not have the talent you hope for. Even in Palasso Grijalva only one in each generation became Lord Limner."

He reached and took hold of the chain that hung round her neck, lifting the Golden Key. "You are not Gifted, yet you wear this."

She smiled softly, sadly. "I have earned it."

Alejandro looked at Baltran, who was chattering excitedly in his high voice about steam locomotives.

So many mysteries to be solved. So many secrets to be learned. Eiha! There was no use in bemoaning what had gone before. "I will come next week. I promise you."

"I will look for you, mennino." She gave him a kiss on the cheek and went back to her students.

All those do'Verrada faces, painted by all those Grijalva hands. And here he stood, Grand Duke Alejandro do'Verrada, the second of that name. He who was also a Grijalva Limner, half trained but

without question Gifted. It was a strange ending, indeed, to the
story that had started with his mother four hundred years ago.

Nothing in the least remarkable about Sario Grijalva. Not outside,
where men could see.

She halted before the portrait, a vigorous woman still though her
once-glorious hair was now white except for a few streaks of black,
the last reminders of her youth so very long ago. She was still beautiful, for age and dignity grant a new kind of beauty to women, to
those who have endured.

The Mirror of Truth, they called it, and perhaps they were
right to call it by that name. But to her it was now and had always been a reminder of her own prison, though thirty years had
passed since she had walked into freedom, through a door bound
with iron and the painted oscurra of a Lord Limner, into a
changed world.

Out of necessity she had made a life. She was not unhappy. Like
a new pigment handed to an eager limner, there were ideas abroad
in this world, colorful, bold, and exciting, that she was glad to have
seen. Would never have seen, in the Meya Suerta of her birth, stul-
tified by the drab and rigid rules of compordotta. Here, they accepted her as Gifted Limner. Indeed, for thirty years she had led
them, Premia Sorella, as they called her now. Not once had they
questioned her right to stand among them. Never again, after the
acrimonious departure and undisputed success of Eleyna Grijalva,
had they questioned the right of the unGifted Grijalva limners to
forge out on their own, to make their own reputations, free of their
service as Grijalva copyists.

It was a good time to be alive, en verro.

For every gift there is a price to pay.

She studied the painting. He stood, dressed in a dark coat with
long tails extending midway down his thighs, with cuffs fastened
by ivory buttons, barely visible, for she could see only his back.
His back—and a hint of his face in profile, an undistinguished face,
dark eyes, black hair.

But that was not the face she saw in the mirror. The mirror
caught the light of candles and lamps at angles and within its confines showed her the other face, his true face: brown hair, brown
eyes, desert-dark skin. Nothing in the least remarkable about Sario
Grijalva. Nothing, except for his Luza do'Orro, that shone more
brightly than any other's. Perhaps it was an illusion given by the af-

ternoon sunlight, but she thought she could see it, his Luza; actually *see* it, a tremor in the depths of the mirror, a ghost of light trembling around him.

She found his gaze and held it, he who looked out at her from the mirror. He saw her; she *knew* that he saw her. Who better to know, who had once endured this captivity?

'Vedra.

His voice. Was it only her imagining, or did he, too, as she had, hear voices, see the parade of faces and fashions that passed in that same mirror, his view onto the world outside his prison? Her prison, once.

So must he wait now, as she had done for so many many years while all that she knew died and passed into dust and distant memory. Eventually the candles and lamps that illuminated his prison would burn low and then, finally, their light would fail altogether, leaving him in endless night.

They had all agreed it was a fitting punishment.

Again, more insistent now: *'Vedra!*

He loved her still. He would always love her. This burden she bore in silence. And a greater burden yet, that she still loved the Sario she had once known, the boy she had grown up with. What he had done could never be forgiven and must not be forgotten, so that the boys—few now—still born with the Gift might understand the dangers of power gone unchecked.

But neither could she forget nor dismiss his Light.

"You are the best," she said, for it was true. It was in her to tell him the truth. He was the greatest Limner born into the Grijalva line. "And yet you were also least among us, for in the end you gave in to the worst in yourself, because you only cared about yourself, no matter what you said about your duty to art."

I know what I am.

"Was that not also your downfall?" she asked him. "Could you not have acknowledged your great Gift, served the Grijalvas, and accepted your fate, as the rest of us do?"

Never.

En verro, she believed him. It burned in him so brightly.

But she was older now. She had lived, and she had endured. She had lost her beloved. Had lost a kind-natured and solicitous husband. Lost an infant child but borne four others who yet lived and had themselves produced grandchildren for her. She was a Gifted Limner, acknowledged as a fine painter, and was foremost among the Viehos Fratos. And her son—first-born and most beloved, for

he was the fruit of the passion of her youth—reigned as Grand
Duke of Tira Virte.

It was in her, this gracious spring morning, to be generous. She
folded her Golden Key within her hand, kissed her fingers, and
signed him a benediction.

PEINTRADDOS DEI TIRA VIRTE

(from La Guide Michallin, *by Enrei Michallin;*
Librairie dei Arteio; Aute-Ghillas, 1419)

*First Assembly
of the Corteis,*
by Eleyna Grijalva,
1316.
Oil on canvas.
Galerria Nacionalla
do'Tira Virte.

This huge canvas, depicting the opening of the newly elected Corteis, is the most famous Tira Virteian painting of the last century. Its sheer technical brilliance and subtleties of characterization, demonstrate why the artist was the most sought-after painter of her time. In a triumph of movement, lighting, and composition, the legislators are shown taking their seats, greeting friends, chatting with the Premio Oratorrio, sorting through papers—all in morning sunlight streaming through the high windows. Note particularly the illumination of the arched palm branches carved in relief above the Oratorrio's podium, representing the Victory of the People.

Certain famous personages are brought into prominence by their placement in pockets of warm golden light. The artist's husband, Rohario do'Verrada, is flanked by Ruis Albanil, the mason's apprentice who had just begun his tempestuous rise to power; several men who would make their mark on the law are similarly set off. The artist herself is seen in the shadows, identifiable by the paintbrush half-tucked in her pocket and the Chieva do'Orro around her neck.

The Abdication,
artist unknown,
1358(?).
Oil on canvas.
Picca Grijalva.

A family portrait in the style fashionable throughout the mid 1300s, this painting of Grand Duke Alejandro II, Grand Duchess Teressa, and their two children is remarkable not only for its charm but also for the informality and curious humor with which it treats its serious subject.

Alejandro, seated, offers the do'Verrada signet ring to his son Baltran, who kneels at his father's right. The youth is primly dressed in a black suit relieved only by the singular corsage pinned to his lapel: red clover for Industry, a fig leaf for Argument, and daisies for Innocence. The young Mechella leans affectionately against her father's left leg; a circlet of oak leaves, for Independence and Bravery, crowns her head. Scholars who argue for a later date than 1358 cite this circlet as evidence, for at that time no one could have predicted the affairs (she refused to marry her long-time lover, the composer Friedrich Shopan, claiming that marriage was a prison devised by men for women), scandalous essays, and impassioned public debates that would mark her notorious career as a campaigner for the rights of women.

Grand Duchess Teressa stands behind her husband's right shoulder, one hand on the back of his chair; she regards the painter—and the viewer—with an ironic eye. At her waist, half-concealed by the chair, she holds a small wicker basket of walnuts, signifying Intellect and Strategem and, no doubt, the Grijalva propensity for smothering their paintings in often nonsensical floral symbolism, especially since Teressa was the most self-effacing of Grand Duchesses, conscientious about her children and her charities but certainly uninvolved in the cares of government.

Most debate on this portrait centers on the figure of Alejandro. He does not look ill or even particularly old—perhaps a flattery by the artist—though his seated pose is evidently meant to mask the unidentified illness that forced him to abdicate at the age of forty. In his lap rests a bouquet of blue roses, which in Grijalva symbology represent Impossibility. From his left hand dangles a golden key, a reference possibly to his mother's Grijalva ancestry. More curiously, scattered under and around his boots are pea plants, some still in flower; research has revealed no iconographical meaning for the humble pea, but the sweet pea appropriately symbolizes Departure. That the sweet pea was intended is further borne out by Alejandro's chair; it is everywhere minutely inscribed with tiny writing—lately identified as that of an ancient Tza'ab mystic cult—recently translated as a single phrase repeated over and over: "Here it ends, I am free."

Alejandro officially abdicated in 1358 due to ill health and retired to Palasso Grijalva. No death date has ever been firmly established for him. The claims of certain art historians that this painting is by Grand Duke Alejandro himself, done many years after the abdication it records, are completely unsubstantiated and entirely ridiculous.

The Mirror of Truth,
by Saavedra Grijalva,
1316.
Oil on wood.
Galerria Verrada.

The prize of this small but exquisite collection—not as well known as the impressive collection at the Galerria Nacionalla but in its own way of great interest to the art lover—is Saavedra Grijalva's acknowledged masterpiece. This intimate, detailed, and keenly perceptive character study is all the more remarkable for the fact that the subject stands in profile with his back to the viewer.

Usually identified as Sario Grijalva, a painter of minor talent, the man wears clothing in the style known as *Ila Revvolucion* in honor of the great revolution which, after many years of tribulation and war, freed Ghillas from the tyranny of kings and nobles. His profile reveals the rather bland face of a typical Tira Virteian native, black hair, dark eyes, with a bold Grijalva nose. But a different face is seen in the mirror—sharper of feature, darker of eye, complexion as brown as a Tza'ab tribesman's.

Many scholars have argued over the meaning of this painting. Does it represent the chi'patro origins of the Grijalvas? Does it allude to a dark tale of captivity and loss, as set down in lurid detail in the novel by Branwell Brontis and later adapted into an operetta by the Strassi brothers? Does the centuries' difference in clothing suggest the modern man looking back to the unknowable past? Or does this painting, as some claim, express as allegory the Matra's ability to distinguish the true heart of that man brave enough to look into the mirror of his soul?

What makes the painting most affecting, and indeed its triumph as a work of art, is its surpassingly delicate use of light. The two candles in the windowless room have long since guttered out, the wicks cold and the melted wax solid in their iron stands. One of the two lamps is no longer burning, leaving Sario to contemplate the mirror by the light of a single lamp. Soon, the painter seems to suggest, this light, too, will fail, leaving him in utter darkness. What the man so captured thinks of this fate as he stares at his reflection we cannot, of course, ever know.

SELECTIVE LEXICON

i   "ee"

j   "h" (as in *junta*); thus Grijalva is Gree-*hal*-vah

ll   "y" (as in *mantilla*); thus castello is kass-*tay*-oh; exception is Mechella (Meh-*chel*-ah)

qu   "kw" (as in *quick*); thus Mequel is Meh-*kwel*

z   "dz"; thus Tazia is *Tahd*-zee-uh

When in doubt, use Spanish rules.

adezo	"now"—ah-*dayz*-oh
Al-Fansihirro	"Art and Magic"; Tzaab term—Ahl-Fahn-see-*hee*-roh
alla prima	rapid painting completed in one session—ah-lah *pree*-mah
amaniaja	"tomorrow"—ah-mah-nee-*ah*-hah
arborro	greenhouse, conservatory—ahr-*bohr*-oh
arcana	magic—ahr-*cahn*-ah
arrtio	"artist"—*ahr*-tee-oh
atelierro	"studio"—ah-tell-ee-*air*-oh
azulejo	rosette tiles; Grijalva symbol—ah-zoo-*lay*-ho
bassda	enough, silence, shut up—*bahz*-dah
borrazca	"storm"—bohr-*azh*-kah
camponesso, camponessa	"country person," peasant—kam-po-*nes*-oh/ah
chassarro	"chase," the hunt—shah-*sahr*-oh
chi'patro	"Who is the father?", bastard—chee-*pah*-troh

chiaroscuro	the play of light and shadow in art— kee-are-oh-*skoor*-oh
chiros, chiras	"pig," "sow"—*chee*-rohz/rahz
Confirmattio	"confirmation," Proving—Kohn-feer-*mah*-tee-oh
'cordo	"accord," I agree, okay—*kor*-doh
curatorrio	"curator"—koor-ah-*tohr*-ee-oh
do'nado	"of nothing," no problem—doh-*nah*-doh
dolcho, dolcha	"sweet"—*dohl*-choh/chah
duennia	chaperone—doo-*en*-ee-ah
eiha	"and so," well, anyway—*ay*-ha
en verro	"in truth," really—on *vay*-roh
estudo, estuda	"student"—ehs-*too*-doh/dah
filho do'canna	"son of a bitch"—*feel*-ho doh-*kan*-ah
grazzo	thanks, you're welcome, and please— *grahd*-zoh
guivaerra	"jewel"—gwih-*vay*-rah
Il Aguo	"The Water"; Grijalva Master; counter-parts are Il Seminno (Semen) and Il Sanguo (Blood)—Eel *Ah*-gwoh, Seh-*mee*-noh, *Sahn*-gwoh
Kita'ab	Tzaab holy book—Kih-*tahb*
lingua merditta	common vulgarisms, gutter language— *leen*-hwah mayr-*dee*-tah
lingua oscurra	"hidden language" of painting— oss-*koor*-uh
lustrosso	chandelier; lus-*troh*-so
Luza do'Orro	"Golden Light"; rare vision, genius— *Loo*-dzah doh'*Ohr*-roh
mallica lingua	"wicked tongue," sarcasm—*mahl*-lee-kah
mareia	unit of money—mah-*ray*-uh
marrido	"husband"—mah-*ree*-doh
Menninos do'Confirmattio	"Children born of Confirmattio"

moualimo	"teacher"—moo-ah-*lee*-moh
nazha coloare	"no color," pencil drawing—*nah*-zhah koh-loh-*are*-ay
Neosso do´Orro	"Gilded Youth"—Nee-*oh*-so doh-*Or*-ro
Neosso Irrado	"Angry Youth"—Ee-*rahd*-o
Nommo Chieva do´Orro	"In the Name of the Golden Key"—*Nom*-mo Chee-*ay*-vuh do-*Or*-ro
Nommo Matra ei Filho	"In the Name of the Mother and Son"—*Mah*-trah ay *Feel*-ho
Paraddio	"lighted walk"—Pah-*rahd*-ee-oh
Iluminadio	Ee-loo-mee-*nah*-dee-oh
Paraddio Luminosso	"torch walk"—Loo-mee-*noh*-soh
Peintraddo Chieva	"Key Painting," discipline painting—Payn-*trah*-doh Chee-*ay*-vuh
Peintraddo Memorrio	"Memorial Painting"—Meh-*mohr*-ee-oh
Peintraddo Morta	"Death Painting"—*Mohr*-tuh
Peintraddo Natalia	"Birthday Painting"—Nah-*tahl*-ee-uh
Peintraddo Sonho	"Dream Painting"—*Sohn*-ho
Qal Venommo	"Poison Pen," graffiti—Kahl Ven-*nohm*-oh
reccolto	"harvest"—reh-*kohl*-toh
Saluto ei Suerta	"Health and Luck"—Sah-*loo*-toh ay *Swear*-tuh
Sihirro ei Sangua	"Magic and Blood"—Sih-*heer*-oh ay *Sang*-gwah
Tza´ab Rih	*Tzah*-ahb *Ree*
velurro	"velvet"—veh-*loor*-oh
Viehos Fratos	"Old Brothers," Limner Council—Vee-*ay*-hohs *Frah*-tohs
zhi	"yes"—zhee
zia, zio	"aunt," "uncle"—*zhee*-ah/oh
zocalo	square, plaza—zoh-*kahl*-oh

ACKNOWLEDGEMENTS

Russell (Agent Provocateur) Galen
Danny (Mr. International) Baror
Michael (Magic Fingers) Whelan

and
the fax machine at the Athens Gate Hotel, Athens, Greece
—MR

various overnight mail services
—JR

Howard Kerr, for artistic advice
—KE